BEYOND THE WALL OF TIME

The wail that came from her throat felt as if it had been ripped from the depths of her heart.

She raised her eyes from the bodies of her enemies. On the platform beside her stood her friends and acquaintances – and her brother – staring at her with wide eyes and white faces.

'Kill me,' she begged them, signing shakily. As her hands moved, flesh flicked from her fingers and fell to the ground. 'Please. Kill me now.'

No one moved.

She took a step backwards at the expressions of horror on their faces. Her foot caught on something and she stumbled, her heel grinding, then sliding, in wetness. Another step, then another.

'Arathé, don't.' This from her brother.

Another step. Her heel balanced on the edge of the platform.

'I must,' she signalled, then closed her eyes and took another step.

By Russell Kirkpatrick

The Fire of Heaven Trilogy
Across the Face of the World
In the Earth Abides the Flame
The Right Hand of God

The Broken Man Trilogy
Path of Revenge
Dark Heart
Beyond the Wall of Time

RUSSELL KIRKPATRICK

BEYOND THE WALL OF TIME

THE BROKEN MAN
BOOK THREE

www.orbitbooks.net

ORBIT

First published in Great Britain in 2009 by Orbit

A CIP catalogue record for this book
is available from the British Library.

ISBN: 978-1-84149-671-9

Typeset in Goudy by Palimpsest Book Production Limited,
Grangemouth, Stirlingshire
Printed and bound in Great Britain by
CPI Mackays, Chatham, ME5 8TD

Papers used by Orbit are natural, renewable and recyclable
products sourced from well-managed forests and certified
in accordance with the rules of the Forest Stewardship Council.

Mixed Sources
Product group from well-managed
forests and other controlled sources
www.fsc.org Cert no. SGS-COC-004081
© 1996 Forest Stewardship Council

FSC

Orbit
An imprint of
Little, Brown Book Group
100 Victoria Embankment
London EC4Y 0DY

An Hachette UK Company
www.hachette.co.uk

www.orbitbooks.net

To Dorinda,
with love

CONTENTS

Maps   viii

Prologue   1

FISHERMAN   5

1. Blood on the Sand   7
2. The Canopy   37
3. Swordmaster   58

COSMOGRAPHER   81

4. Loss   83
5. The Volunteer   104
6. Corata Pit   129

QUEEN   159

7. The Reluctant God   161
8. Shipwreck   185

Interlude   215

FISHERMAN   223
9. Cylene   225
10. Shaky Ground   244

COSMOGRAPHER   265
11. Mensaya   267
12. The Snare   290
13. The Limits of Love   306

QUEEN   327
14. Death of a Captain   329
15. The Wagon   353
16. Life Without End   372
17. Godhouse   391

Interlude   417

THE BROKEN MAN   423
18. The Bronze Map   425
19. Andratan   454
20. The Broken Man   480
21. Son and Daughter   505

Epilogue   523

Acknowledgements   535

Extras   537

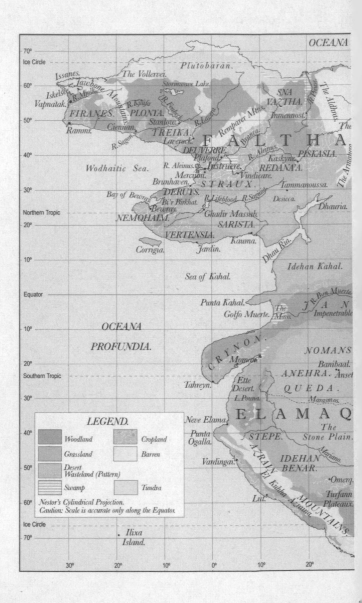

OCEANA

70°
Ice Circle

Plutobarán.

60°
Issanes. Iaiebone The Vollervei. Stormwave Lake.
Iskelsee. The Mulle
Vapnatak. Mountains. R. Kjluja SNA
50° FIRANES. PLONIA. R. Frodnax VAZTHA.
Stanlove. R. Leane. Immennost.
Rammi. Ciennan. TREIKA.
R. Sagon. Laverack. DEUVERRE. F A L T H A
40° Plafond. R. Aleinus. Byance. The
Wodhaitic Sea. Instruere. Kaskyne. PISKASIA.
R. Aleinus. Mercion. REDANAA.
30° Brunhaven. Vindicare. Tammanoussa.
DERUTS. STRAUX.
Bi'r Birkhat. Lifeblood. R. Sagunia. Desicca. Dhauria.
Northern Tropic Bevran. Ghadir Massah.
20° NEMQHAIM. SARISTA.
VERTENSIA. Kauma.
Corrigia. Jardin. Dhau Ria.
10° Idehan Kahal.

Equator Sea of Kahal.
Punta Kahal. I A N
10° OCEANA Golfo Muerte. The R. Bon Muerte.
Mara Impenetrable.
PROFUNDIA. C R I N O N NOMANS
20° Momen. Banibaal.
Southern Tropic ANEHRA. Anset
Tahreyn. Ette QUEDA.
30° Desert. Marasmos.
L. Pouna.
Neve Elama. E L A M A Q
40° Punta STEPE. The Stone Plain.
Ogalla.
IDEHAN
50° Vardingai. BENAR.
Omerq.
Lut. Turfann
60° MOUNTAINS Plateaux.

Ice Circle
70° Ilixa
Island.

LEGEND.

Woodland		Cropland	
Grassland		Barren	
Desert			
Wasteland (Pattern)			
Swamp		Tundra	

Nestor's Cylindrical Projection.
Caution: Scale is accurate only along the Equator.

30° 20° 10° 0° 10° 20°

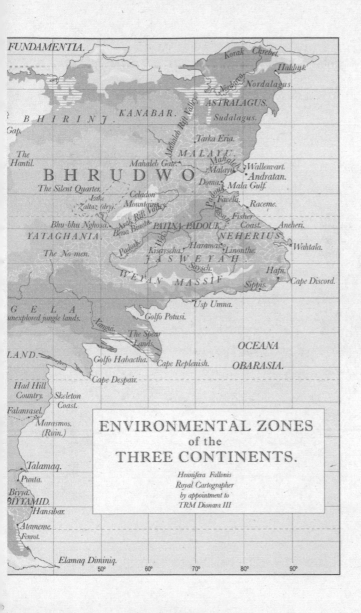

BRONZE MAP

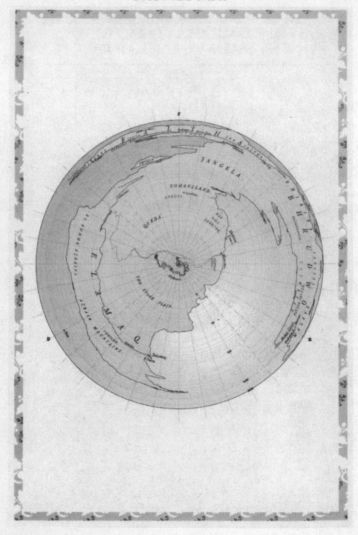

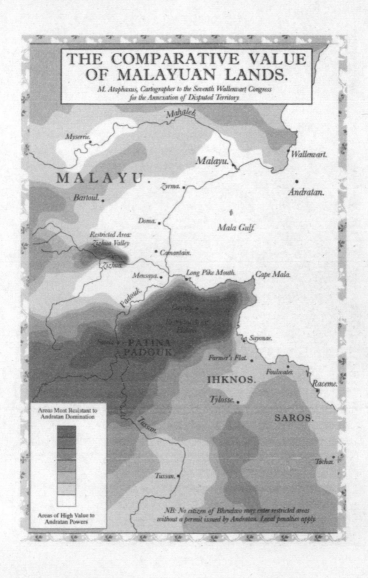

THE COMPARATIVE VALUE OF MALAYUAN LANDS.

M. Ataphaxus, Cartographer to the Seventh Wallenwart Congress for the Annexation of Disputed Territory

Mahalea

Myserrie.

Malayu.

Wallenwart.

MALAYU.

Zyrma.

Andratan.

Bartoul.

Doma.

Mala Gulf.

Restricted Area: Zizhua Valley

Camantain.

Zizhua.

Mensaya.

Long Pike Mouth.

Cape Mala.

Padouk.

Senta

PATINA PADOUK.

Sayonar.

Farmer's Flat.

Foulwater.

IHKNOS.

Raceme.

Tylosse.

SAROS.

Tussan.

Tochar.

Tussan.

Areas Most Resistant to Andratan Domination

Areas of High Value to Andratan Powers

NB: No citizen of Bhrulavo may enter restricted areas without a permit issued by Andratan. Legal penalties apply.

PROLOGUE

HUSK STRUGGLES TO REMEMBER WHAT it is like to think with clarity. Seven decades of unrelenting pain have created a permanent cloud in his mind, as though looking through smeared glass. He constantly has to fight off a desire to go to sleep and never wake up, has to keep resisting the creeping lassitude that threatens to engulf him. Cannot remember what it used to be like living as a normal human being, agony not the most important part of his life. Even now, despite his link to the unlimited power from the void beyond the world, and the freedom from pain it brings, he finds it difficult to focus on the important things happening in a remote valley a few hundred leagues away.

Part of Husk's trouble is he does not know the location of the House of the Gods. Normally this would not matter. His magical contact with his three spikes does not depend on his knowing where they are. But designing a strategy does. The place on which his attention is focused, the place where his hosts now contend with the gods, is to be found at perhaps a half-dozen locations in the world at once, and yet fully in none of them: a paradox of the kind of which the gods are distressingly fond. He has spent a deal of time trying, in mounting desperation, to comprehend how the Godhouse works, but he is still no nearer a useful understanding.

So he preoccupies himself with questions. Will the travellers – his spikes and his enemies – emerge into Patina Padouk, the land from which they entered this version of the House of the Gods?

1

Or, as happened in Nomansland, will they appear somewhere else? Husk cannot lay his plans until he knows. Trouble is, with all the fog in his head he fears he may have missed some essential clue.

Husk hates not knowing things.

He needs to know where everyone is because he must decide whether to confront his enemies here, in the Undying Man's fortress of Andratan, or there, wherever *there* might be. He wishes to destroy his enemies in a way that pays them back for his years of suffering, while, of course, risking himself as little as possible. Best of all would be a public triumph here at Andratan. Himself in the Tower of Farsight, at the head of a vast crowd of people, all watching the Destroyer and his cursed consort writhing out their agony in ways that reduce the memories of his own pain to pleasant inconsequentiality. It is no longer enough for him merely to remain alive. Not even enough to be immortal, the rich prize now almost in his grasp. To truly live he must destroy them both. No; more accurately, they must be destroyed again and again. He must be able to return whenever the mood takes him to watch them suffer. A public gallery in which the continual destruction of Stella and Kannwar is the main installation, that is what he needs.

He wonders just how many centuries it will take to cancel out his own hurt. If his hurting will ever end.

Events in the House of the Gods are seriously limiting his supply of power from beyond the wall around the world. The three gods are all drawing deeply from the hole in the world – that blessed opening first made when the Son and Daughter drove their Father out – and their combined power is squeezing his tiny, unnoticed conduit until it is almost shut off. Nevertheless, his small link continues to restore him. Husk has grown new limbs to replace those seared away by the Destroyer's magic, but their fragility means he cannot yet walk on them. He now breathes air unmixed with his own blood. But his great plans, his plans for his transformation to godhood, the elimination of all who might possibly hurt him and the subjugation of everyone else, await a respite in the hostilities between the gods.

He is patient. He can wait.

In the meantime, Lenares is the great danger. She seeks to close the hole in the world, despite having taken advantage of it. Ironic, this. She had managed to ensnare the Daughter by tying something – Husk is not exactly sure what it is she tied – to someone beyond the wall. Husk does not know who, though Lenares herself is convinced it is her dead foster mother. Her use of mathematics was flawed, but it worked nonetheless. Lenares has tapped into her own source of power, drawing on it unwittingly to help her to capture the Daughter for a time; and, worryingly, may draw on it again, perhaps accidentally interfering with his plans. It is unlikely she will learn how to harness her power, especially given the logical, mathematical cast to her mind and its associated limits. However unlikely, Husk cannot risk her interference. He must find some way to eliminate her. No elaborate revenge, no desire to inflict pain; he just wants an end to her.

Another question nags at him. Has he any further need for his spikes? Arathé, Conal and Duon have served him well but, unless his new-found power is totally severed, he no longer needs them. In fact, he continues to expend energy to keep hold of them that he could better use to strengthen himself. And it is not as though his spikes are of much use to him. Conal is blinded in one eye and in all his opinions, and his recent possession by the Father has rendered him untrustworthy. Imagine if the Father seized the lad's mind while Husk was in possession of it! Arathé is becoming increasingly wary of the voice in her head, and is devising ever-cleverer ways of keeping him out. And Duon is trying to deceive him. A futile attempt – Husk can read the outer layers of the minds of those he has spiked – but it makes the Amaqi captain, of whom he had high hopes, less dependable.

Husk had supposed the huanu stone would aid him in defeating the Destroyer, but now wonders even at this. The stone is now as much a risk to himself as it is to the Destroyer. It could undo the magic keeping him alive, could sever the supply of power from beyond the wall. And it is now beyond his reach, sewn into the lining of a pack left behind on the *Conch*, which is probably a good thing. Too dangerous to allow his enemies access to something that could do him so much damage.

The same logic can be applied to the immortal blood he had

planned to drain from Stella. Not yet in his possession, and just as likely could be used to promote someone else to the ranks of the deathless. With his own conduit to the raw power of the void, Husk need not risk the problematic – and painful – immortality offered by the blood. Maybe he needs to keep the blood and the stone away from Andratan. The only difficulty with this line of thought is his inability to prevent them being brought north regardless. With bravery and intelligence he has set all this in motion, and now it appears he is powerless to stop it.

Husk frowns with newly restored facial muscles. Now there are two ways to become immortal his options have increased, so he ought not to be feeling the anxiety as strongly as he does. Thump, thump, thump goes his heart. His blood hisses through his veins and threatens to erupt from the tips of his fingers. The bubble and fizz of fearful thoughts must be resisted or they will – unman him. But it is so hard, despite the fact he is familiar with despair. Desperation has shaped him over the foggy decades of pain, yet despair is so much sharper now he has real hope.

But he will resist the temptation to give up, to crawl away to some dark corner of the Destroyer's dungeon and die. He reminds himself that, due to his new power, he is Husk no longer. He will put his self-imposed name aside and take his old name back. Deorc of Jasweyah. No; he reconsiders: Deorc the Great. Far more suitable.

Husk laughs at himself, at the caricature of evil he seems about to become. All he needs is the cackle and he'd be the legendary Jasweyan Witch-Hag reborn. No matter: whatever his name, the common people will make fireside tales about him, and he will be around to hear them. He'll make them forget about their folk villains, the Witch-Hag and the Undying Man both. The commoners will have no need to fear anything but him. And, oh, he will work hard to ensure they fear him.

He licks his lips, tasting the victory about to be his; and, though he knows it to be a cliché, cannot resist the laughter bubbling up from within him. The thick walls of Andratan ring with the sound, and the denizens of the fortress pause in sudden fright.

Their fear is balm to Husk's scarred soul.

FISHERMAN

CHAPTER 1

BLOOD ON THE SAND

THERE IS A SILENCE FAR deeper than the mere absence of sound. It can settle on a scene despite, say, the thin wail of a woman weeping. Even the laboured breathing of someone in severe pain does little to disturb such stillness. This silence is a calm, black pool of quiet. It is the sound of shock.

Noetos remembered all too well what such silence sounded like. He had experienced it in the Summer Palace, in the aftermath of the slaughter of the Neherian gentry. It was a stunned disbelief at what had happened coupled with an expectation that he would soon wake up to find nothing of the sort had occurred. But, of course, it had.

No waking from this nightmare.

He watched from a distance as his travelling companions stared at each other, eyes wide, saying nothing. When finally they began to move, it was in slow motion, hands fluttering with the need to do something but not knowing what. The fisherman had been nothing but an observer of the events leading to a man's castration and the violent death of the one who had wielded the knife, but he could help now with restoring calm. Guidance, order and leadership were what were needed. He made his way towards the tight knot of people, ready to assist.

'He is gone.' The one-eyed priest's voice was a ripple of sound breaking the deep silence as though a pebble had been dropped in a pool.

'Yes,' said Duon, looking up, his hand on Dryman's unmoving chest. 'He's gone, all praise to the gods.' This was followed by a grimace, no doubt as he realised anew just whom he was praising.

Noetos strode across the sandy floor of the enclosure, and his two children followed him. Three piles made up of enormous slabs of rock were the only interruption to the smooth floor, apart from the figures gathered around the dead, the injured and the maimed. And a smaller rock soaked in blood.

The thought came to him that of the three groups drawn together in the contention of the gods, his had fared the worst. Gawl and Dagla were dead. Of the miners, only Tumar and Seren remained. The Fossan fishermen Sautea and Mustar were still with him, but they had come north because of Arathé, not him, and might well leave at any moment. Omiy the alchemist had betrayed him, Bregor had left him and Noetos had not succeeded in getting Cylene to join him. True, the Amaqi had just been reduced from four to three with the death of Dryman, but that had been their only loss. *If you don't count the loss of thirty thousand soldiers*, he reminded himself. *Even I haven't failed that spectacularly.*

The Falthans had done best. All eight remained alive, though Stella had apparently lost an arm – she used some form of magic to disguise this, but it was only intermittently effective – and the priest an eye. *They haven't had whirlwinds and Neherians to cope with.* He frowned. *But now we all have to deal with angry gods and mysterious voices in people's heads, as well as blood and death delivered by human hands.*

'I didn't mean the mercenary,' Conal snapped. 'The Most High, the Father, he is gone. I have my own voice back again. And I won't be using it to praise any gods, that's for certain.'

'What is it like, priest?' Heredrew asked him, his voice deceptively gentle. 'What does it feel like being forced to do the bidding of the Most High? Do I detect anger, friend? Unhappiness at being made the mouthpiece of a god?'

Conal scowled and turned away. No doubt the continuation of some irrelevant debate, Noetos thought. Some people would argue at a graveside. More important than any argument were the three figures at the centre of the gathering: the dead mercenary, who had been some sort of avatar for one of the gods; the maimed servant, who lay on his back, his breath rasping; and the grieving cosmographer.

It was this last person Noetos made towards. Lenares always made him uncomfortable with her uncanny way of seeing things, her facility with numbers, and her lack of the simple social graces that kept people from hurting each other unintentionally. *And in that last, hypocrite, how is she different from you?* She was unpredictable, and Noetos was not the only one who found her difficult, he was sure. He was able to overcome his reluctance and approach her not because of some kindness of heart, but because of his regard for Cylene, her twin. The sister Lenares hadn't yet met.

'Are you all right, Lenares?' he asked her.

She looked up at him from where she knelt. 'Am I all right?'

Those wide eyes, their shape so familiar to him – no, not hers, her sister's – blinked slowly once, twice, thrice. Noetos wondered whether he ought to repeat the question. Had it not been simple enough?

'Of course she's not all right, Father,' Anomer said from beside him, then turned to the girl. 'Here, come with us, Lenares. You need food and drink. We'll talk of what we should do about all this after you've eaten.'

He stretched down an arm. Hesitantly she took it, although her white face and hurt eyes remained totally focused on Torve.

'I don't want to leave him,' she said.

'Let those skilled in healing tend him. You should let us tend you.'

Clearly reluctant, Lenares allowed herself to be led away a short distance from Torve, but kept her head turned so the Omeran would not be out of her sight for a moment. Despite her oft-expressed dislike of being touched, she made no motion to prevent Anomer rearranging her dishevelled clothing. She seemed not to notice it.

That's the other reason she unnerves me, Noetos thought. He had never seen anyone able to devote themselves so completely to one thing at the expense of everything else.

The Omeran servant was in poor condition. His wound had been cauterised but, however well the procedure had been done, the red mess between his legs was clearly giving him intense pain. Noetos was not certain what had happened to precipitate this, but it seemed the mercenary had discovered Torve and Lenares engaged in an intimate act – *the* intimate act, apparently – and had decided to castrate the fellow.

'Who was this Dryman, that he could do this to you?' Noetos asked.

Torve offered no reply.

Captain Duon lowered himself to his haunches with a groan. 'Aye, that's the question. I may have some answers for you. It is time to lay everything out for all to hear, I think. Then we can judge what must be done.'

'Here?' Arathé asked, her hands flashing. 'Are we safe here? Won't the gods hear our conversation?'

'Who knows?' the southerner replied. 'I doubt we're safe anywhere. But I think we may have a short time to ourselves before the gods return to resume their meddling. The Father has achieved his purpose, and the Son and Daughter are disembodied for now. We must take this time to decide what we are to do next, and for that you need to hear what I have to say.'

Stella raised her head from bending over another prone figure. 'I do not mean to offend,' she said, 'but whatever answers you provide may be somewhat suspect. Before we hear from you, we need to discuss the matter of the voice in your head. I am wary of our plans being overheard.'

'But I can assure you—'

Stella shut him up with a wave of her left arm. 'Later. First we attend to the injured. There is a man over here bleeding from the head. His brother does not seem capable of dealing with him.'

'You know who those two are, don't you?' her guardsman growled. 'Two of the Umerta boys. Lenares' brothers. The southerners apparently hired them as porters.'

There was the briefest quiver in the woman's arm, the smallest suggestion that she wanted to withdraw, but she said, 'And now they are hurt. We must care for them nonetheless.'

'Like they cared for you?' Noetos said, pointing at her missing forearm and hand.

'That . . . wasn't the Umertas.'

Beside her, the guardsman stared at his feet.

'More to talk about,' said Noetos. 'Or perhaps more secrets. Well, if we are to cleanse and bind these wounds, we need water and cloth.'

'In hand,' the guardsman said. 'Kilfor and his father have gone back to one of the other rooms in this place. There was a pool of cold water there. There's plenty of cloth in our packs, spare clothes and the like. We have all we need.'

So there was nothing for Noetos to do but sit and wait. Others attended those who needed help, others made decisions, others did the things necessary for human survival and comfort. He sat on the sand and ate food handed to him, then lay down and tried to rest, while all around him people busied themselves.

He found the experience of not being needed profoundly unsettling.

An indeterminate time later – it seemed like an hour, but time felt greasy here and it could have been a few minutes or a day or more – Stella asked Duon to explain the voice in his head. Noetos pricked up his ears at this. He'd been expecting, and dreading, this confrontation and the likely outcome.

'We'll speak Bhrudwan,' Stella said as the others trooped over to where she sat. 'We've all picked up enough of it over these last few months to understand each other.'

Noetos acknowledged the point as he raised himself to his elbows, then his feet, and followed the others. Most of the Falthans spoke the Bhrudwan common tongue with something approaching fluency, and even the southerners seemed able to understand it, though occasionally they struggled to make themselves understood. Some common language root, no doubt, made it easier to learn.

11

More evidence to support the story of the three gods originating from the same place, he supposed.

Arathé sat to one side of Duon, Conal to the other. Torve lay quietly nearby, only the bunching of his facial muscles betraying his pain. The remainder of the travellers gathered in a group facing the three of them. *As though they are to be judged*, Noetos thought.

Perhaps Duon felt that too. 'There's no conspiracy here,' he said. 'We kept nothing from you. It's taken us a long time to realise what is going on in our heads, and even longer to work out that each of us shared the phenomenon with two others.'

'So what is it?' the old scholar Phemanderac asked in his reedy voice. 'Whose voice speaks in your mind?'

Duon sighed and scratched at his unshaven chin, making a rasping sound. 'More than two years ago now all three of us were in the Undying Man's fortress of Andratan at the same time. I was visiting as an emissary of the Amaqi Emperor, while Arathé had gone there to learn magic. Conal—'

'I'll tell it myself,' the priest snapped. 'I was there as an emissary of sorts, part of a delegation from the Koinobia, the religious movement based in Instruere that some know as the Halites.'

'A spy,' Phemanderac said.

Conal denied it, but no one was fooled. With a voice cloaked in anger at all the injustices visited upon him, the priest described his heroism and courage in playing his part to undermine the Undying Man. The gist of it, at least as it seemed to Noetos, was that the Father – referred to as the Most High – had used the priest as a mouthpiece. Then, some time after that, months perhaps, he began to have thoughts that were not his own.

'Thoughts about women?' Sauxa asked neutrally. 'Perfectly natural, son. We all have them.' His son spluttered a laugh.

'Not about women,' Conal said, though he coloured. 'I began to harbour rebellious thoughts about the Koinobia and my master, the Archpriest.'

'Also perfectly natural,' muttered Stella. Noetos doubted the priest heard the woman's words.

'The point is,' Duon said, 'all three of us spent time in Andratan concurrently, and all three of us have since experienced remarkably similar symptoms. A cynical voice in our heads, goading us to do things to its advantage. A supply of superhuman strength, though not under our control. I experienced it in the fisherman's company.' He nodded to Noetos, who sensed what was coming. 'We wiped out more than a hundred enemies between us, many of them heavily armed.'

The words were out before Noetos could bend the conversation away from the subject. He'd rather it was forgotten; he was trying to forget it himself.

Arathé waved her hands and spoke in her distorted voice. 'I survived a knife in the back,' she told them while Anomer translated. 'The voice exercised magic to keep me alive and heal me quickly.'

She then had to explain the context of her statement to those not familiar with the story of what had happened to her first in Andratan and then months later in Fossa. Questions followed, one or two of them vehemently expressed, particularly from Heredrew the Falthan. Noetos could think of no reason why the man should be so particularly concerned.

Robal then described how Conal had rescued Stella from the rogue Lord of Fear. 'Never seen such strength and speed,' the guardsman told them. 'And afterwards the priest seemed unaware of what he had done.'

More questions followed, another story painstakingly told, more time wasted. This was followed by an account of Conal's attempt to kill Stella and Heredrew in some Falthan city. This story actually begged a few questions, but Noetos forbore. He was becoming increasingly uneasy about the amount of time they were spending in the House of the Gods. Though he knew it was irrational, though he acknowledged the gods would be able to find them anywhere they went, he still felt vulnerable here. And all the while a dead body lay on the sand a short distance away.

'So,' he summarised, before anyone else could launch off into yet another tale, 'you all hear the voice of someone you do not know. He's a magician, able to lend you powers you don't normally have. And, by all accounts, he does not necessarily have our best interests at heart.'

Three nods.

'You think someone in Andratan put something in your heads.'

Again, three nods.

'Then there's only one solution,' he said, the words forming before he could question them. Pre-empting the obvious conclusion. 'You three need to leave the rest of us. It is too dangerous for you to remain.'

There was a general indrawing of breath.

'Father!' his son cried out. 'How can you even suggest such a thing?'

Noetos found himself asking the same question. His own daughter, whom he'd thought lost! Yet he had a responsibility to everyone here.

'Having a presence amongst us capable of slaying anyone without a moment's warning is simply intolerable,' he said.

'There are many among us with such power,' growled Heredrew from somewhere behind him, in a voice that made the hairs on the back of his neck stand up.

'You have that power yourself!' Duon shouted at the fisherman. 'Must I tell everyone here all the details of what happened in the Summer Palace at Raceme? You drew power from a voice in your head!'

This was not where he wanted the conversation to go. 'That magic came from the sacrifice of my daughter, who acted as a conduit for hundreds of refugees from the city,' he said angrily. 'A perfectly legitimate exercise of her magical powers. Nothing at all like yours.'

He decided not to mention that the voice in her head might well be able to reach him through her. Might even have assisted him in the Summer Palace. If the others couldn't figure that out, he'd not help them.

'You'd drive your own daughter away?' This from Stella, in the gentlest of voices.

'I do not see it as driving anyone away,' Noetos replied wearily,

aware – and secretly grateful – that he was going to lose this argument. 'Rather, we are simply depriving our enemy of information.
How can we help our three friends if our every plan is overheard
by the voice in their heads?'

'Spoken like a soldier,' said Stella. 'Perhaps I'd feel more
comfortable were you to speak like a father.' She stared at him
with something akin to loathing on her face.

Why do people always follow sentiment rather than common sense?
He gave it one more try. 'As her father, I want Arathé to have
the best chance of getting free of this curse that has her in its grip.
If that means sending her away – in the company of a priest and
a very capable soldier, I remind you – so we can work out in secret
how to save her, then that is what, as a father, I ought to do. If I
give in to sentiment and keep her here beside me, we all might
lose our lives.'

Incredibly, as he scanned his fellow travellers, he found himself
facing a dozen hardened expressions. *They don't understand.* None
of them, it seemed, could take the tough decisions. His son's atti-
tude he could comprehend, but the others were leaders. This ought
to be the sort of equation they dealt with on a daily basis. He
wondered at the scrupulousness that forced him to argue for what
was right and against what he wanted. Was it some failure in him;
or was their rejection of his argument their failing?

They hate me, he realised. *They think me unfeeling. They will never
follow me.*

'You should not send them away,' said Lenares. 'If you send them
away they will be hurt. The hole in the world will swallow them
up. We need to protect them.'

Murmurs of agreement rippled across the group.

'Very well,' Noetos said, trying to contain his anger and hide
his relief. 'But this decision should be reviewed often. And those
three' – his finger punched the air in their direction – 'must report
to us every word this voice speaks in their minds. No more secrets.'

Without waiting for a reply, he rose from his position at the
side of the gathering and strode rapidly away across the sand,
scuffing at the dirt. Walking off his frustration and confusion, just

as he had done in Fossa after every argument with Opuntia. Just as unsuccessfully.

He returned a few minutes later – it felt like a few minutes later – to find a fire lit and people eating food that would surely have taken far longer than a few minutes to prepare. Time itself was playing tricks here; but then it was the House of the Gods, in which the rooms moved about and the entrances could seemingly be anywhere. He squatted down near the fire.

'Now, to the question you asked earlier,' Captain Duon said, drawing his gaze across those gathered around the fire and nodding to Noetos. Duon's features were pinched, his lips pursed, as though about to deliver unwelcome news. 'Who was Dryman?'

'He was a liar,' Lenares said. 'An evil and cruel man. Look what he did to my Torve!'

Duon was clearly familiar with interruptions from the young cosmographer. 'Yes, he was a liar, but even more, he was a deceiver. Lenares, you have a great gift, but you did not penetrate Dryman's disguise.' His voice was gentle. 'That is because Dryman had help from a god. You saw how he died. The Father, through Heredrew and Stella, confronted Dryman and spoke to him as the Son. The Father tricked his Son and killed the body he inhabited, Dryman's body, but the god escaped before Dryman died and so continues to live.'

'The Father called him Keppia,' Lenares said. 'Keppia spoke to the Daughter through Dryman's lips, and she called him her brother. Yes, he was the Son, Torve told me that.' Her brow crinkled in concentration. 'But I don't know how he managed to hide it from me for so long.'

'There's more, Lenares.' Duon sighed. 'Dryman was the Emperor of Elamaq.'

Her eyes opened wide; Noetos could not remember seeing her surprised. 'I know, Torve told me that too. He tried to tell me for weeks, though I didn't understand. But how did you work it out?'

'I overheard him talking with Torve,' Duon said. 'Only a few days ago, or I would have warned everyone. I'm sorry I didn't reason this through sooner. In fact, I now have reason to believe the Emperor planned all this well in advance of us leaving Talamaq.'

Lenares stood and started to pace. 'The . . . No, I would have . . . But I *saw* the Emperor on the balcony as the expedition left.' She paused a moment. 'No. I saw *someone* on the balcony. Not the Emperor. Someone pretending to be the Emperor.' She pulled at her lip. 'Therefore the Emperor must have been somewhere else. Someone took his place because . . . because the Emperor wanted to leave Talamaq without people knowing. He left with us. Disguised himself as Dryman the mercenary, and I could not tell because I've never seen the Emperor's true face. He always had it hidden behind a golden mask. I knew something was wrong though. I just didn't know what.'

She rubbed at her reddened eyes, then turned away. Everyone watched quietly as she walked the few steps to where the body of the mercenary lay wrapped in cloth. No one spoke.

They all know this is hers to reason out, Noetos realised. *She's the one who prides herself on knowing secret truths about people from their numbers. The others are giving her the opportunity to deal with the blow to her pride.*

'Look,' she said as she pulled aside the cloth covering the corpse's bloody face. 'There's the callus where his mask rested on the bridge of his nose. Why didn't I see? I can see now! All the clues were there. Torve tried to tell me, but for so long he could not. I wondered why, I thought Torve was keeping secrets.' She pulled the cloth over the face. 'But you weren't,' she said, turning to the Omeran. 'You weren't. I am sorry, Torve. You had to obey him. You wanted to tell me. But I couldn't work it out! And because I couldn't work it out, he cut you.'

'I tried,' Torve said, his voice little more than a croak. 'I tried to tell you.'

The man needs water, Noetos thought, but before the thought was fully formed Stella reached out with a skin.

The Omeran handed back the water skin, cleared his throat and continued. 'I didn't know who he was either, until he revealed

himself the night we stayed with the Children of the Desert.'
Noetos had no idea what Torve referred to. 'That child – I'm so
sorry, Lenares, but the Emperor commanded me and I could not
disobey him.'

'I understand,' Lenares whispered. 'You are Omeran.'

'Torve, you should not have to tell this,' said Duon. 'But it must
be told, so allow me to continue. The Emperor seems to have
conceived a desire to torture innocent people, and he forced his
servant Torve to accompany him on their expeditions. I overheard
him commanding Torve to obey him in this, which was when I
began to piece this together. Too late to be of any use, regrettably.'

'We tortured hundreds of people,' Torve said, his eyes closed,
his voice like stone grating on stone. 'The innocent and the guilty.
Anyone unfortunate enough to find themselves in the dungeons
of Talamaq Palace. My master kept notes. He . . . he wanted to
discover the secrets of death.'

'Because he wanted to live forever,' Lenares said triumphantly.
'I saw that when I first met him.'

'Yes. I did not want to help him, but he was my lord. Despite
appearances, he was a good master. He treated me like a human,
a real person, and even loved me in his own way. He loved me
more than he loved anyone else.' The man's voice broke. 'I loved
him in return. He made me into more than any Omeran has been
for a thousand years. He taught me how to read, gave me books,
and granted me access to the Great Library. He dressed me in
finery and took me to his court, despite the murmurs from the
Alliances. He relied on my counsel. I would have done almost
anything for him, even without the need to obey him. But not
torture people; I didn't ever want to do that, even though—' He
swallowed, lowered his face, then looked up again a moment later,
his eyes clouded. 'I enjoyed the science of death, the thoughts it
generated, the speculations we shared as we took people through
the gates of death.' He lowered his head and hissed, whether in
pain or heartache, Noetos could not tell.

'When he sent me north with his army I was saddened and
gladdened both. I was sent from his side for the first time since I

was gifted to him as a child, and felt abandoned. Yet I was relieved also, because now, I believed, the torture would stop. But when Dryman revealed himself to me I was forced once again to help him. We researched dozens of people on our way north. I am so sorry. His death – it has lifted a great burden from me, but . . .' His face crumpled.

'I don't understand this,' Phemanderac said, wriggling uncomfortably and grunting as he resettled his bony backside on the sand. 'Everyone has a choice to disobey, even if it costs their life. You seem a good man, Torve. How could you do such things?'

'Omerans are bred to obey,' Lenares said. 'Everyone knows that. Mahudia said that just as an olive tree cannot produce grapes, so an Omeran cannot go against his master's commands. Three thousand years of careful breeding has produced animals that cannot disobey their masters.'

'Animals?' Phemanderac looked puzzled. 'Torve is a man, not an animal.'

Duon snorted. 'Not to the Amaqi. They – we – destroyed every race of men who opposed us, save the Omerans who, in return for their continued existence as a race, pledged to serve us. I am embarrassed to say it, but our religion declared them less than human many centuries ago, which gave us the right to do with them what we desired. Most of them live brutalised lives of unquestioning service. Torve here is a well-known exception, and at the court was often referred to as the Emperor's pet.'

'So it's impossible for you to disobey your master?' Arathé signalled, Anomer stepping forward to translate. At Torve's nod, she frowned. 'How terrible. But you tried?' Another nod, more emphatic this time.

Noetos did not have to open his mind to her to be able to read her thoughts.

'Why?' said Lenares suddenly, breaking a short silence.

'Why what?' Noetos responded, more gruffly than he intended.

'Why did the Emperor leave Talamaq and travel north with his army? And why in disguise?'

'I seek answers to the same questions,' Duon said. 'And I have a third: given he was both Emperor and god, why did he allow his army to be destroyed in the Valley of the Damned?'

'He wanted it to be destroyed,' Torve said. 'He encouraged the most powerful Alliances to supply their best soldiers and their strongest sons for this expedition, but my master never intended them to get past the Marasmos. He told me later that he recruited mercenaries from all parts of the empire, save Talamaq itself, and salted the Marasmian army with them. He supplied gold and weapons to the Marasmians. Thus, by ridding himself of the major Talamaq houses, he strengthened his hold on the empire.'

'So he never intended his expedition to succeed?' Duon's face had gone white.

Torve grimaced with pain; the conversation was clearly claiming what strength he'd regained. 'His supposed expedition, no. But his *true* expedition, yes. We went north, Captain, because you reported what you had learned of the Bhrudwan tales of the Undying Man, though I am sure you merely confirmed what he already knew. My master greatly desires – desired – immortality and planned to wrest the secret from the Bhrudwans. He did not believe he needed an army to do this. In fact, the fewer people involved in his true purpose, the better.'

'He wanted to be immortal, did he?' asked Heredrew, leaning forward, a look of strange intensity on his face. 'Maybe he ought to have done his research more thoroughly before settling on such a desire.'

'Perhaps speaking to an immortal or two might have cured him of the craving.' Stella sounded angry. 'They might have told him how very poor a bargain he would likely make.'

Heredrew spoke again. 'So this man, with the aid of a god, planned to become immortal by – doing what exactly? How did he think he would achieve it?'

'By drinking the blood of the Undying Man,' Torve said to the tall Falthan.

Heredrew chuckled. 'From what I hear of the Undying Man, I suspect your Emperor underestimated the strength needed to complete his task. How, after all, do you obtain the blood of an immortal? Especially one as powerful as the Lord of Bhrudwo?'

'My master was a very patient man, and he had the assistance of a god. I believe that without the intervention of another god he would have achieved his goal.'

'Good thing he didn't then,' old Sauxa said, sucking at his teeth. 'Better one insane tyrant than two.'

'Better none at all,' said Robal, making to rise.

'You gave me your *word*!' Stella hissed at the guardsman, grabbing his arm.

Robal growled, but went no further. People turned their heads to them, but neither Stella nor Robal offered any explanation. The guardsman settled back on his haunches.

Secrets, secrets. 'Still not telling us everything?' Noetos said. 'How can we make decisions unless all the truth is exposed? I, for one, would have appreciated knowing I was travelling north with a god-possessed emperor. I presume there are no more hidden emperors or the like among us?'

The silence at this question stretched on a little too long. Noetos found himself growing faintly suspicious and more than a little angry. Lenares sat there pulling at her lip as though she wanted to say something, but even she kept quiet. It smacked of a conspiracy.

'No?' he said eventually. 'Then we are all who we seem? Excellent. We had one bad man among us, but now he's dead. So we can carry on to do what we intended to do. Except – what was that exactly?'

'Different things for different people, as you well know,' said Kilfor.

The plainsman's father spread out his hands. 'Then that's the next step. Deciding what we intend to do from this point. Me, I make decisions best on a full belly and with a wench by my side.'

'Your belly always looks full, old man,' said his son. 'And you'll get no volunteers for the other.'

Sauxa barked a laugh. 'Nevertheless, it's time to eat. Then I hope we quickly finish with all this talk so I can leave this uncanny place. Men of Chardzou like their walls open to the breeze so they can see their enemies coming. These cliffs make me nervous.'

Kilfor grunted. 'Aye, old man, I'm with you on that.'

The talking occupied most of the remaining light and was still not done when the sky started to dim.

'We'll need to be gone from this place before dark,' Noetos advised them. 'I do not want to be trapped here overnight.'

'Safest place we'll find, I would have thought,' his son responded. 'Better than camping out in the trees with those archers and their poison arrows.'

'I would rather face poison arrows than vengeful gods. They could return at any time.'

'But that's just it, Father. We have to face up to the gods, or abandon the world to them. It might as well be now as some later time.'

Anomer parroted the argument Phemanderac had offered earlier in the afternoon. The Dhaurian scholar had made an impassioned speech on the heels of prevarication from Captain Duon. The captain had been uncertain, not knowing what their next move ought to be, and Noetos had decided that for all the man's courage he would have made a poor leader. By contrast, Phemanderac had argued with passion, pointing out how they had been drawn together and outlining what he thought their responsibility to be. 'We have to face the gods,' he had said, 'and help get the world back in order.' If that meant helping to destroy the Son and Daughter, so be it. His sentiments had received widespread support from members of each of the three groups.

Anomer had spoken of sacrifice in the cause of saving the world and, embarrassingly, used Noetos as an example, telling everyone how his father had risked his life to save Raceme from the whirlwinds. As one, the travellers had shifted their attention to him.

'I still have my one purpose,' Noetos had told them. 'I intend to continue north to Andratan, there to make the Lord of Bhrudwo answer for the crimes of his servants, the Neherians and the

Recruiters, including those perpetrated on Arathé's body. More than that I will not say, given who might be listening to us.'

He swung his gaze to the three infected by the voice in their heads to underline his comment. What was the point in discussing plans if they could be overheard?

His two children were talking together, Arathé flapping her hands, Anomer's head bent next to hers. More secrets, no doubt. *Tell me what you're saying!* he had demanded, firing the thought at his daughter. She had started, given him a sidelong glance, but said nothing.

Noetos's comments had claimed the attention of the Falthans. 'Tell us more of these crimes,' Heredrew had asked, his request supported by Stella and her guardsman. So Noetos had related the story of the recruitment of his child to Andratan two years previously, emphasising it had initially been in line with her will – knowing the oversensitive Falthans were likely to misunderstand him – and telling them how she had been treated while training in that dark place. Stella had obviously been shocked when Noetos had revealed how Arathé had lost her tongue and the other things that had been done to her in the service of the Recruiters. More interesting, however, was Heredrew's reaction. The man's face clouded with anger, and his hands clasped and unclasped, as though reliving some dreadful experience. Perhaps someone he loved, or even he himself, had suffered at the hands of the Undying Man.

'Stands to reason,' Robal had said when Noetos was finished. 'You have a dungeon under your castle, you expect things like this to happen. You authorise them, you take part in them. I don't know why anyone would be surprised at this.'

A strange thing to say, and Heredrew's reaction was even stranger. 'I doubt even the Lord of Bhrudwo knows everything that goes on in his dungeons,' he'd said. 'Immortal he may be, but I have never heard it claimed he was omniscient.' Why the man defended someone who had obviously done him wrong, Noetos could not say.

After discussing Arathé's plight, the Falthans had gone on to argue that they had already made common cause with the Father, whom they called the Most High. Here they called on Lenares' knowledge to supplement their own. The girl explained that her numbers had shown her how the Father had been cast down from the House of the Gods by the Son and the Daughter, and that the fall had cracked the wall surrounding the world.

'Each day that passes, the hole in the world gets bigger,' she had told them. 'Every thread that is snapped weakens the fabric separating the world from the gods and whatever else lies outside the wall. Every node burned out is the death of someone who ought not to have died. The hole is now large enough for the Son and Daughter to reach through and act directly upon us, as you have seen. In the past, the gods had to content themselves with manipulating others to achieve what they wanted. Now they can bend the natural world to their will. They rocked Talamaq with earthquakes, they killed my foster mother Mahudia with a lion, they attacked Raceme with whirlwinds, and we were all there at Lake Woe when they sought to kill us with the fireball. Since then they have destroyed the tea house in Ikhnos with a flood, eaten my travelling companion, and burned a village by fire. There is even evidence that they are messing with time; that the linear flow of time is threatened. What is may be irretrievably mixed together with what was and what is yet to come. The Son and the Daughter have harnessed the power of fire, water, earth and wind, and perhaps time itself. All the magics are in their hands. Either we find a way to close the hole in the world or the world itself will become a wasteland, a battleground between the two gods to see who is the stronger.'

She had faced many questions after that. Not everyone there had heard all the stories of the gods, and their history was picked over with much debate. Heredrew, who seemed to be as much a scholar as the old Dhaurian, confirmed Lenares' account of the creation of the Son and Daughter and their subsequent rebellion against their Father. Falthan legend, apparently, tallied with this account in that the Father had arrived in the north, with a small band of refugees in tow, three thousand years previously. The telling took an hour or more, but at the end of it the group had assembled a history that dovetailed the various folklores of Faltha, Bhrudwo and Elamaq. The tall Falthan, Heredrew, downplayed the role of Kannwar, the Undying Man, as betrayer of the Father and source of the enmity between Bhrudwo and Faltha. He received little support in this view from the others.

'You mentioned a travelling companion, Lenares,' Noetos had said. 'You said he was eaten. Can you tell us what happened? I don't remember hearing this story.'

Her response was the most fascinating part of the afternoon's discussion, at least to Noetos. After she had been claimed by the flood at Yacoppica Tea House, Lenares explained, she had taken up with a boatman – Olifa of Eisarn, she named him. Noetos had sat up at that, and his son reacted similarly. His miners, who had been talking quietly amongst themselves, seemingly uninterested in the debate, were struck silent. The sordid tale of how Omiy the miner had sought to force himself on the young cosmographer did not surprise Noetos, and her god-assisted escape made him grin fiercely.

'A fitting end for one so false,' he had said. 'Omiy deserved everything he got. He pretended to be my friend so he could get his hands on the huanu stone.' Noetos laughed bleakly. 'No-one will get their hands on it now, not unless I can find the *Conch* and recover my pack. I want that stone. More valuable than Old Roudhos, he named it, because it absorbs magic, rendering magicians powerless. With it I will neutralise the power of the Undying Man should he refuse to give me a satisfactory explanation of the activities in his dungeons.' There was no explanation he would consider satisfactory, of course, and he knew everyone took his meaning. 'The thought of that traitor Omiy ending up in a shark's belly pleases me,' Noetos had concluded. 'I take it as a sign we will all be granted vengeance against those who have done us wrong.'

He had directed a sympathetic glance towards Heredrew, who looked more embarrassed than encouraged at his words. Noetos had decided then that he must seek Heredrew out and talk with him in an attempt to draw out the story of the man's suffering at the hands of the Lord of Bhrudwo.

At the end of the talking it was clear that the Falthans wanted to travel north, though their reasons for doing so varied depending on which of them spoke. They apparently wanted to make common cause with the Undying Man against the gods.

Stella spoke last, and directed her speech to Noetos. 'If you please, after the gods are brought low and the hole mended, you may have your time with the Undying Man and receive satisfaction one way or another.'

Noetos muttered something they could take for agreement if they wished.

'You don't intend to wait, do you, Father?' Anomer said, squatting on his haunches beside him. Around them the conversation moved on. 'You'll move against the Undying Man before you know all the facts.'

'How can I wait?' he answered, stung by his son's knowing voice. 'In order to get an unguarded answer I must take him by surprise. Otherwise he will dissemble and I will be no nearer an answer as to why he rules this land with such a heavy fist. And why his servants take the tongues of innocents.'

And I do not want him forewarned of the fact I intend to drain his magic and kill him for what he did to your sister, he thought after Anomer withdrew, apparently satisfied.

Satisfied? Not likely, not Anomer. His son was building up to something. Unsettled ever since his mother died, Anomer had come to a truce of sorts with his father aboard the *Conch*. But Noetos had no doubt his son would have more to say, and soon.

Arathé sat alone as the others cleaned up their camp. Because it seemed somehow sacrilegious to leave anything behind in what was once the Throne Room of the gods, the travellers picked up every scrap of food and every bloodied cloth. The largest task would be carrying out Dryman's body; predictably, her father wanted to burn or bury it, but no one else would have this. Noetos sat near the entrance to the room, glowering at proceedings as though he were a particularly dyspeptic overseer. *If only you could see your-*

26

self, Father, she thought, but did not send the thought to him. She had her own distress to deal with.

It had been clear to her for weeks that the voice in her mind was not there to serve her interests. Although she could point to times when it had warned her of approaching trouble, it seemed there were many more times when it had drawn trouble to her. Comparing her experiences with those of Duon and Conal had revealed similar occurrences. The gods seemed to be able to sense the connection between them and the voice, and it drew their power, as did any use of her magic. More, she now had a name for this connection: a spike. At least, that's what the voice had called it.

The voice had manifested earlier when Torve had been describing his participation in the tortures ordered by his master. As always, it began with a warming at the back of her head, just above her neck. Then a torrent of derisive laughter cut through her horrified thoughts.

So, you object to using other people to further your own ends, little swan? He had taken to calling her this in mockery of the story of the beautiful swan maiden, which he must have pulled from her memories. *I would have thought someone who has been given so much suffering herself would be pleased to hear that she is not alone in the world.*

Then you don't know me as well as you claim, she had responded with heat of her own. *I was under the impression your magic allowed you to read my thoughts. Clearly I was wrong if you really think I would be happy to hear of anyone suffering.*

Not even the one responsible for what happened to you? The voice seemed to stroke her mind like a fretboard, plucking at memories of anger and resentment. *Yes, you know who he is. And I do know you. Deny you've thought of revenge, little swan, and I'll prove you a liar.*

Of course I've thought of revenge. But thinking it and acting on those thoughts are entirely different things. I'll never do to anyone what the Emperor and his servant did, nor what the Recruiters did to me.

He snorted. *Have you learned nothing through my spike? Revenge*

27

is a necessary emotion. It motivates you to rid the world of something evil. You act as though there is something intrinsically poisonous about the notion.

You might rid the world of one evil, but the cost will be the raising of another. If I had the power to bring down the Undying Man, and acted on that power because I wished to avenge the wrong done me, I would simply ascend in his place. Much as you intend to do, I'd guess. I'm right, am I not?

The voice affected nonchalance, but Arathé was sure she could hear agitation in the words. *You know nothing of what I intend to do.*

No? She aimed her thoughts recklessly at him. *I know that you put spikes in three people when they visited Andratan about two years ago. To do this you must have been in Andratan yourself. And because you hate the Undying Man and plot his downfall, I would guess you are locked in his dungeon. You want us to do what you yourself cannot –*

Partway through her explanation, the warm place at the back of her head began to grow hot. By the time she'd reached the last thought, the pain was nigh unbearable.

I have a problem with your thinking, the voice said, its poise recovered, as waves of pain pulsed through her head. *If I continue to have this problem, I will snuff your thinking out. I could do it easily, little swan. I could take control of your own hands and force you to wrap them around your lovely neck.*

Her hands and arms tingled and began to rise without her volition, frightening her even more than the pain. She fought him, but her limbs were his. Nothing in the dungeons of Andratan had scared her half as much.

Or I could have you cast yourself from a cliff. If you anger me, I might make you kill your friends first. The voice was laden with mock sorrow. *I have no idea how effective you would be as an automaton, but I'd find a way to deceive your friends into thinking you remained in control. So keep your thoughts to yourself and I'll let you live. Do we have an understanding?*

We do, she told him, ashamed at her cowardice. *Please . . .*

The voice vanished in an instant, but the pain and the horror took a great deal longer to fade.

I harbour a monster, she had said to herself, and wept quietly.

'You're not happy, sister.'

'You have eyes at least,' she said to Anomer, her hands busy shaping the words her tongue could not. 'More than our father. He's noticed nothing.'

His eyes narrowed. 'Something really is amiss. Normally you defend him past reason.'

'I am sorry, I have run out of energy to defend anyone.' *I'm going to lie to my brother about something important for the first time.*

'This is not like you, sister.'

'I feel so weary. So much has happened, we have come so far, and I am near the end of my endurance. My legs feel as though they cannot walk another step, and I do not want to see any more suffering and death.'

'Is this why you will not speak mind to mind? It would be so much easier for you.'

Anomer sat beside her on the cooling sand and put an arm on her shoulder. She rested her head against his hand.

'I am tired, Anomer,' she whispered, her hands flickering desultorily. 'The effort of mind-speaking has left me exhausted. I have had enough of gods and voices and earthquakes and whirlwinds and fire. I do not want revenge. Let Father confront the man, if he must. I just want to go home.'

He will believe this, she thought, sorrow bubbling up in her chest.

She allowed her tears to roll down onto her brother's hand, her misery compounded by the necessary but cruel deception.

The perversity of life brought Mustar to her on the very evening she had decided she must remain alone.

He limped across the sand and sat with a groan in the same place Anomer had left only a few minutes before. Arathé dashed away her tears, but could do nothing about her undoubted redness of eye. She smiled at him.

'You look tired,' he said.

'And your leg still gives you pain, I see.'

She had to sign slowly: Mustar had not yet fully mastered her language. At least he didn't need Anomer to interpret for him. He frowned. Arathé noted with dismay that even his frown crumpled his attractive face pleasingly, lending his chiselled features a mock-serious air.

'My leg?' he said. 'Only when I'm inactive for any length of time. Arathé, what do you think of this place? Does it make you feel' – he cast about for the word – 'uncomfortable?'

There was something irresistible about the young fisherman. Unlike the cliff-girls of Fossa, Arathé had never been impressed by his broad shoulders and rippling muscles. Instead, it was his sly sense of humour, a cheekiness that immediately took her side, engaging her, that she found most endearing. There was something carefree about him. He listened no better than any male, to be sure, and was certainly not a person to whom she would ever confide her closest secrets. But talking with him made her feel lighter somehow. She'd missed his banter on board the *Conch*, where he'd been absorbed in the rowdy single men's section of the steerage cabin. He was certainly a welcome change from the intensity of her father and brother. So if Mustar found the House of the Gods uncomfortable, and troubled to say so, the feeling must be strong.

'Dead bodies make me uneasy,' she replied. 'I haven't noticed anything else.'

'No, it's the place itself. There's a sadness here. Do you remember Old Man Cadere's family?'

'The Cadere Row mob?'

Arathé had heard about them from her father but, given their rather unsavoury reputation, had not mixed with them. Old Man Cadere had gone through four wives, one after the other, and they had given him over twenty children – twenty-four by some counts, twenty-five by others. They had all lived in a ramshackle house built of little more than driftwood and brushsticks. Then the old man had died and the family immediately scattered throughout

Fossa. Some eventually came back to Cadere Row and built new houses there, giving the street its name, but the old house was never again occupied.

'I went to see the family house once, when I was little,' Mustar said. 'Thought it would be a good place to play. But the roof had fallen in, and the walls had turned white and splintered. All the life had gone out of it. It was only an old abandoned house but it frightened me. Later I learned the old man's sons had argued over who was to inherit it, and in the end decided that since no one could agree on who should have it, it was to be left uninhabited. This place feels like that. There was so much life here once, Arathé. Can't you feel it? I can imagine the Father's two special children playing in the room with the large objects. Or all three sitting together, Father, Son and Daughter, watching the mist from the pool making wonderful patterns. I imagine I can hear faint laughter at the edges of my ears. And when the children were grown, I see them in this room with their Father, sitting on their three chairs, making decisions together, guiding, influencing the world of men.' He closed his eyes. 'Then arguments. Disagreements over what should be done and who should do it. Two children trying to grow up, to become independent of a proud and powerful father.'

Now Mustar was talking of his own childhood, Arathé knew. His father, Halieutes, had been the Fisher of Fossa before Noetos and had won widespread renown. Of course, he might just as well have been describing her own formative years.

'It must have been difficult growing up in the shadow of such a great man,' she signed, and he nodded, unconscious of how she had read his meaning.

'It was, I think. And the Son and Daughter would have contended with their Father, wanting to prove themselves to him, until they could no longer stand it. I feel their anger and frustration, Arathé. I feel the cliffs crowding in on me. The House of the Gods would have become a prison. I hear the arguing, the reasoned voice of the Father, the words that make perfect logical sense even as they stifle the life out of you. Then one day things went too far and the children left in anger, only to return in strength to drive their hated Father from this place.'

'You sound like you sympathise with them,' she said.

'Of course I do. No matter how bad they've become, there must have been a point when the Father might have done something to make things turn out differently.'

'So how did you turn out so well?'

He opened his eyes, his dark brown eyes, and turned to her. 'You think I've turned out well?'

'I—'

'Arathé, you never saw what I did with the cliff-girls. Nothing they didn't want, to be sure, but I did it anyway, knowing it was wrong. Women, they . . .' He struggled for words, and waved his hands desperately at himself, obviously thinking he was not communicating his meaning. She nodded to him to continue.

'There was a woman in cabin class on the *Conch*. An older woman, travelling alone. She made a suggestion to me.' His face coloured, and suddenly Arathé didn't want to hear any more. 'I moved in with her for the best part of a week. She . . . I . . . Arathé, I'm sorry. I'm not a good person.'

Her heart plummeted. There was no reason why this should matter, but it did.

'Why do you apologise to me?' she signed. 'I am not your father or your sister. And you are not Keppia. You haven't killed people for fun or possessed others. You're not trying to break apart the world so you can prolong your hateful life. So you slept with a woman who desired you. Where is the harm?'

His look was full of helplessness and something else. 'It would be harmful,' he said quietly, 'if it hurt someone I hoped might desire me.' Then he turned away.

Her chest flooded with renewed hurt. 'Oh,' she said, a grunt more than a word. To be desired and not pitied . . . *Oh, Alkuon, not today. Not when someone truly dreadful holds my life in his hands.*

He waited for her to speak, this young man who thought himself reprehensible merely for taking and giving pleasure, betraying no one in the process. While she harboured a secret that ought to be screamed to everyone in this place, a warning of how cruelly she was enslaved, of what the voice might make her do; a secret so shameful she could never share it with Mustar, with anyone, for fear of losing everything.

She had no choice. She so wanted to take him in her arms and love him, to let his openness wash away all her sordid memories and fears, but she could not do it. She could not open to him and still keep her secret, so she must remain closed. And the sadness of this was how he would inevitably interpret her actions.

'Mustar,' she said, her hands weaving the words as though constructing the bars of her own prison, 'I do not desire you. I cannot. I am too broken. Please, give me time.'

He smiled wanly. 'I thought this was so. You want time? You have it. And hopefully one day you might forgive me for the woman in cabin class, and the many other terrible things I have done.'

'Truly, Mustar, it—' she began. But he had stood up and was already walking away from her.

Arathé sighed. Best, perhaps, if he thought her angry with him. If the voice in her mind thought Mustar was a threat, it would not hesitate to use her to remove him. She could not stand that. As much as she desired his comfort and closeness, she had to put beautiful, dangerous Mustar out of her mind. From now on she would have to keep well away from those she valued most.

'Father, we must talk.'

'Son, I have matters to discuss with Captain Duon. And, as you can see, I am helping him bear an unpleasant burden.'

'You are by no means the only one with an unpleasant burden. But if you don't listen to me now, you'll be continuing north on your own.'

Ahead, Duon stumbled on a slope of slippery, worn rock reduced to the consistency of glass. They were in a room of rippled blue stone with a steaming pool set in the rocky floor.

'Steady, there,' Noetos called, and the southern soldier grunted some answer he failed to catch.

There was no doubt the House of the Gods was beguilingly

beautiful. Each room had its own hidden or obscure function, and every room contained a numinous feel: the sense that someone immense had just left or was about to step in. Noetos prided himself on his practical bent, but even he found himself distracted by the shapes, the colours, the way the light pooled or rippled or reflected. Others of the party ran from one side of the room to the other, exclaiming over this strange relic or that incomprehensible artefact.

'I thought we had worked our way through this,' Noetos said with a sigh. 'I agree with you: I have acted selfishly and did not consider my family's needs during this affair. Cylene helped me see the truth in your words. What more, son?'

Noetos could see that for some reason his words had angered the boy, but Anomer kept his temper in check. *I had such hopes for him. But unless he matures, and swiftly, he will not be able to assume leadership of the family, let alone Old Roudhos. As he is at present, I could not even mention the possibility to him.*

'What more? Has Arathé mind-spoken you of late?'

Noetos had to think for a moment. 'I've overheard one or two of her thoughts, but nothing directly. I thought it a result of her increasing ability to communicate with her hands and voice. People are working hard to understand her, you know.'

Anomer ought to be pleased at that, but it appeared he wasn't.

'You didn't think to question why she has been silent? She's at the end of herself, Father, can't you see that? Two years of abuse at the hands of the Recruiters, then home to Fossa and safety for a matter of hours, followed by the loss of her family. Did you think how that might have affected her? The journey north, battered by supernatural storms. Hearing about the death of her mother and not even being able to travel to the grave. The events in Raceme, when it seemed we were to be snuffed out by the fingers of a god at any moment. How much did her magical rescue of you and her part in the defeat of the Neherians take out of her? And then the walking, the weeks and weeks of it, followed by a month or more of starvation on board ship. All the time she's been plagued by voices and battling to come to terms with what's been done to her. Father, she's worn out. She needs a rest.'

Noetos heard the implied condemnation in his son's voice. Anomer might as well be shouting it in his ear.

'I saw you and her talking earlier, before we left the Throne Room. Is that when she told you all this?'

'She . . . yes.'

'So, before you spoke to her, you didn't know how seriously she has been affected by events? If so, why are you angry at me for not knowing until I was told?'

'When I learned this is not at issue. Father, we must do something for her sake. Leave off this path of revenge. Let's find somewhere to make a home.'

The party entered a room none of them had seen before. According to Lenares, the rooms were not fixed, changing order at random. This room had something resembling blood trickling from pocked walls, and it pooled in small depressions on the sand. It felt far more sinister than any of the other rooms. One of the crimson rivulets seemed more recent than the others: it had not yet worn a channel in the wall, and its pool was less than a handspan across.

The red pools exercised a strange fascination on Noetos. What did they represent? Why was one of them so recent? A fanciful thought struck him: he imagined they were the blood of those who had died as avatars of the gods. What properties would such blood have? Would it leave a mark on the skin? What would it taste like? He wrestled his mind away from the thought.

'I will speak to her, find out what she needs. Malayu is a large city. Perhaps a physic there can help her.'

Anomer punched the fist of one hand into the palm of the other. 'Will you never listen? She needs assistance now, not later, and especially not in Malayu. Unless she receives the help she needs now, there will be no Malayu.'

'No, son, it is you who refuses to listen. I have cast my net and I am obliged to wait until the time is right to haul it in. I will not abandon it now, not when the shark I seek to catch is still swimming in the open sea, savaging anyone who swims too close to his jaws. We are going north because I agreed to this with the other leaders. There are larger issues at stake than my desire for revenge or Arathé's health. Arathé has a voice in her head that is somehow linked to all this, and she has a power we need. I can't allow her to abandon this task or hinder others in their execution of it.'

'Can't allow her? By Alkuon, Father, what are you going to do? Order her to feel better? Carry her north like you're carrying Dryman's body? This is not your decision. Either she regains her health and vigour or she and I leave you. We will not follow you mindlessly just because you ask it of us. Do we have an understanding?'

After the boy had taken his leave, Noetos reflected that he'd been wrong in his assessment of his son. Worse luck. Anomer was ready to take command. Too ready.

It was only as they left the blood room that Noetos noticed the corpse's wounds had begun to bleed anew.

CHAPTER 2

THE CANOPY

THEY EMERGED FROM THE HOUSE of the Gods into a thunderstorm of breathless fury. One after another the travellers left the dry, sandy floor of the last room and passed between the two portal trees to be assaulted by slashing rain and continuous flashes and booms. Nothing made it clearer that the House of the Gods was truly in another place than passing from blue sky to dark clouds and driving rain.

Noetos blinked as he stood on the waterlogged plateau with the others and waited for the last of their party, Tumar and Kilfor, to appear. He was soaked in moments, his hair plastered to his head.

'Is this natural?' Seren yelled in his ear between cracks of thunder.

'Don't know!' Noetos replied, then looked around for Arathé. *That this might be of the gods is something I should have considered,* he chastised himself. He could see no more than ten paces in any direction, so thick was the rain; the air was milky with it. That shadow there was likely his daughter – no, it was too tall. It hurried away from the portal, shoulders hunched.

'Here, have you seen Arathé?' Noetos called to it, and took it by the shoulder. The figure swung its other arm around and delivered the fisherman a solid blow on the shoulder, then snarled and shook him off.

'There's no call for that!' Noetos cried, and he automatically went for his sword, but remembered he was weaponless; he looked up as the figure disappeared into the murk. Noetos hadn't recognised what he'd seen of the face. One of the porters perhaps. He glanced at the hand he'd used to grab the figure's shoulder. His fingers were smeared with blood. As he stared at it, the rain washed it off save the faintest residue.

What's the fool doing running off when he's clearly still injured?

He stumbled across his daughter a moment later. She was helping rewind one of the porter boy's bandages, while the other looked on. Noetos looked from one to the other, confused. *Neither of the porters then.*

'The storm, Arathé,' he said. 'Is it of the gods?'

'I don't think so,' she said, leaving off her work to sign the words. 'I get no sense of power from this. Just a sense of being far too wet.'

'Did you see someone hurry past a moment ago?'

'I've been busy with Gennel's loose bandages since we left the House of the Gods.' She tsked. 'Whoever bound these wounds wasn't paying attention to their task.' Talking done, she returned to her work.

Noetos found himself studying the fading marks on his hand in the pouring rain. What had he seen? He had just about convinced himself it had been wet sand, not blood, when Tumar approached him.

'Heredrew says we need to talk.'

'What about?'

The miner's answer was drowned out by a crack of thunder that shook the earth. The fisherman's shoulders hunched involuntarily. It reminded him of the moments he had spent with Mustar fleeing the gods in Raceme.

'Why don't we return to the House of the Gods and wait out the storm?' he suggested.

Tumar shook his head vehemently and a look as close to fear as Noetos had seen materialised on the miner's face. 'Not goin' back there,' he said, his eyes darting back and forth.

'Why? What happened?'

'Come 'n' speak to Heredrew.'

He led Noetos, Alkuon knew how, unerringly through the battering storm to the portal trees. Heredrew had seated himself under the tree to the right of the entrance. Most of the others were gathered there, though the tree itself provided little shelter from the rain.

'I saw what I saw,' Kilfor was shouting as Noetos approached. 'You've seen all manner of miracles on this journey, even been involved in a few of your own, so the story goes, expecting all the while for us to believe you, yet you quibble at this?' He glanced in Noetos's direction, at Tumar, and said, 'Ask the miner!'

'I am not questioning your truthfulness,' Heredrew began.

'He is telling the truth,' Lenares said.

The tall Falthan stared at her. 'That means nothing. I have no doubt he has described truthfully what he saw, which is little enough. What we need to decide is the relevance of his speculation as to what it means, and where the body has gone.'

Sauxa leaned forward and shook a finger at Heredrew. 'My son is a drunkard, a lecher, a coward and has a feeble mind,' he said, 'but he's no liar.'

Kilfor's mouth twitched in what looked like exasperation.

The Falthan turned his attention to Noetos. 'Did you see anything unusual as we emerged from the gods' house?'

Who decided you should run this court? Too late now: the man was in control.

'A man rushed past me,' he said, loud enough for them all to hear. 'I did not recognise him. I grasped at him, but he struck my hand away, leaving blood on my fingers.'

Multiple pairs of eyes looked down at his hands.

'The rain has washed the blood away,' he finished.

Heredrew wrinkled his long nose. 'Did you not get a clear look at his face?'

'No, but I can guess whom it might have been.' *See how you like this, Falthan.* 'Just as we left the Room of Blood – you remember that strange room with what looked like blood flowing from the walls – Dryman's corpse began to bleed.'

This occasioned mutters from the party.

'Did anyone else see this?' the Falthan asked. When no one responded, he added, 'How is it you saw it?'

Why so sceptical? Noetos wondered. 'I was helping carry the body at the time,' he said. 'Later, when Tumar and Kilfor took the body from Captain Duon and me, the bleeding appeared to have stopped again. It was strange,' he admitted, forestalling Heredrew's likely next question, 'but I didn't mention it because, frankly, I'm not totally sure how dead bodies behave. I haven't carried many before.'

'They don't up 'n' walk off,' Tumar said.

'No,' said Noetos. 'But this one has. I gather the corpse came alive as you carried it through the portal?'

Kilfor nodded. 'Someone believes me, at least,' he said. 'Except we weren't carrying it. We'd put it down to change places. Heavy thing, a corpse. Almost as heavy carrying as lugging my father to bed after one of his drunken debaucheries. Soon as it hit the ground, the thing shook itself, got to its feet and ran off, faster than thought.'

Lightning flashed, illuminating the entire party. Lenares groaned, at what Noetos could not say.

'Dead bodies shamble,' Stella's guardsman said.

'Seen many, have you?' Kilfor replied to his friend. 'Or are you going by the night-stories the old man used to tell us? Remember "The Shuffling Dead"? Well, this wasn't like that. The body seemed more alive than when it was alive, if you get my meaning.'

'I don't feel well,' said Lenares.

A young woman stood. For the moment Noetos could not remember her name; she was one of the Falthan party, a quietly spoken lass who spent most of her time close to Phemanderac. A scholar like the old Dhaurian, that was as much as Noetos could recall. Pretty, though, in a bookish kind of way.

'So Dryman's corpse is missing,' she said in a precise voice, 'and two men claim to have seen the body come to life. Another touched it and blood came off on his hands. Given where we were and what has been happening to us, I see no reason not to suspect that Dryman is now alive again.'

Murmurs from around the gathering. Noetos waited for a

lightning flash, just like the story of the seaman's ghost, but the dark sky did not cooperate.

'What we do not know,' she went on, 'is what this means. Is the god back in charge of the body? Or is there some power in the House of the Gods that undoes death?'

Now the sky flashed and the air roared. Around them the rain eased off somewhat. Lenares moaned and put her hands to her head.

Kilfor smiled gratefully at the woman. 'Thank you, Moralye,' he said. *Ah, Moralye*, Noetos thought. He didn't remember ever hearing her name. 'At least someone believes us – uh.'

The man's hand dropped to his stomach, where an arrow shaft protruded.

'Down!' Noetos cried, but people were already moving. Even as the plainsman cried out and slumped to the ground, the others dived for whatever cover was available.

'It's the hole in the world!' Lenares cried out, then screamed as an arrow took her in the leg.

They are shooting at sound, Noetos realised, as Duon called out: 'Poisoned arrows! Everyone quiet!'

Flat on the ground, Noetos heard two shafts whistle over his head, but no thunks. The captain had hopefully been lucky. His turn to chance to luck.

'Into the House of the Gods!' he cried, and dragged the nearest person to her feet. Arathé.

Lightning flashed, illuminating the entire party. Lenares moaned. Dizziness tickled Noetos's mind. *Something . . . is wrong.*

'Dead bodies shamble,' said Robal irrelevantly.

Come on, man, move, there are poison arrows! Noetos wanted to shout at the guardsman, but he couldn't form the words. Time itself felt greasy, stretched out. Broken.

'Seen many, have you?' Kilfor said. 'Or are you going by the night-stories the old man used to tell us? Remember "The Shuffling Dead"? Well, this wasn't like that. The body seemed more alive than when it was alive, if you get my meaning.'

What? This is the strangest feeling. He knew they were in danger . . . something about arrows . . . but he could not quite remember . . .

A young woman, Moralye, stood. 'So Dryman's corpse is missing, and two men claim to have seen the body come to life. Another touched it and blood came off on his hands. Given where we were and what has been happening to us, I see no reason not to suspect that Dryman is now alive again.'

For some reason Noetos was reminded of the story of the seaman's ghost. He hadn't thought of that story for years – or was it moments? Why did he feel as though he had experienced this before? And what did arrows have to do with the story?

Moralye continued. 'What we do not know is what this means. Is the god back in charge of the body? Or is there some power in the House of the Gods that undoes death?'

Lightning flashed, followed immediately by the crack of thunder. *Lenares*, Noetos thought wildly. *She will moan and put her hands to her head. She'll cry a warning about the hole in the world – arrows – Kilfor – oh, Alkuon!*

Lenares moaned and her hands went to her head.

'Thank you, Moralye,' Kilfor said.

Fighting with everything he had, Noetos struggled against something – against the flow of time itself – and bunched himself.

Kilfor was still talking. 'At least someone believes us – uh!'

Noetos launched himself at the plainsman and took him in the stomach, knocking him to the ground. He felt the arrow streak past his right ear and *thock* into the portal tree.

'Down!' he cried, as he knew he would.

Kilfor cried out, but it was a cry of surprise and anger, not pain. *Things are changing. Are you aware, Lenares? You're dead if not.*

'It's the hole in the world,' she said, but it was little more than a whisper, not a shout. With no sound to shoot at, the arrows never came.

Duon is supposed to warn us about the arrows. Noetos waited, breathing hard in the wet grass, Kilfor lying inert beside him. Only silence.

No one dared move. They could hear movement in the grass around them. Noetos could sense the approach of a group of people, but sound attracted arrows, that was the lesson here. Keep still and stay alive.

A bare foot kicked him in the shoulder. 'Get up.'

He rose slowly to his feet, arms extended, hands raised in what he hoped would be taken as a conciliatory gesture. None of the others moved.

A man stood before him. Behind the man were at least fifty of his fellows. All were dressed in little more than loincloths and jerkins, and most held bows in their hands. At least half had arrows at the ready, some nocked. All poisoned, if the stories about the natives of Patina Padouk could be believed.

These natives, Noetos recalled, were an unpredictable lot. The official history of Roudhos, written by Bryant of Tochar, suggested that the Padouki had once had this part of Bhrudwo to themselves, covering it as far as their forests extended. How did the famous line go? 'The whole of southern Bhrudwo was once a green city, with the Padouki its only inhabitants.' Locals told a different story, one of Padouki invasions of their farmland, of crops burned, of children taken, of villages feathered. Noetos had been inclined towards the official version, but the look of these people made him wonder.

They loosed poisoned arrows at us. They don't care if we live or die.

'Where is Keppia?' the man asked. 'Has he remained in the Godhouse?'

A reasonable Fisher Coast accent, Noetos observed. Just one more oddity in a hatful of them. 'No,' he answered. 'He has left us.'

'We offered your people safety out of respect for Keppia. Why now should we grant you leave to be in our heartland?'

'We are leaving,' Noetos assured him.

Around him, members of the party had only now raised their heads. 'Leave the talking to me,' he said to them.

'You may be leaving, but you are still here,' the leader said. 'It is death to be found in the heartland uninvited, even for one of the Padouki. How much more so for one of the tree-eaters?'

'As I said, we are leaving. The sooner this conversation is finished, the sooner we will be on our way.'

The man signalled and ten of his fellows stepped forward, arrows at the ready.

'You're going to tell us it's not that easy, aren't you?' Noetos said. *Time to put this man off balance.* 'Where did you study? Tochar?'

'You have an ear,' the man replied grudgingly.

'And you have bows and arrows. Had you wanted to kill us, we would be dead. So what is it you want?'

'We have no love for you, tree-eater, so do not presume to cow us with your arrogance. Your lives are spared only because we do not know if killing you will offend Keppia. And since he is not here, we cannot ask him.'

Just as well for us then, Noetos acknowledged silently. 'What was a Padouki warrior doing in the Tochar academy?' he asked.

To his left Heredrew signalled vigorously, but Noetos paid him no attention. While others kept their heads down, it was his time to lead.

'Or are you a Fisher Coaster gone native?'

The man's face darkened, but none of the men either side of him stirred at this insult. *None but him speaks Bhrudwan. I have learned something, at least.*

'This is not about me,' the man ground out between clenched teeth. 'You have asked your last question. Keppia would understand if you end up dying in agony, andali coursing through your veins.'

'Very well then. What would you have of us?'

The man ignored Noetos's impudence. 'You are to be taken to the Canopy. There our elders will decide what must be done with you.'

The Padouki did not, apparently, bind their captives, but nor did they allow them to keep their weapons. Swords, knives and even Phemanderac's staff were bundled up in linen ropes and carried on the backs of three of their captors. *We have a few weapons they cannot take from us*, Arathé reminded herself. *Even if they are double-edged.*

The rain ceased as they tramped across the plateau, and by the time they reached the cliff-edge the sun had come out. There, a thousand paces above the steaming forest, they stopped for food and to take in the vista. Even the most frightened of captives surely could not help but be impressed by the view. Arathé shaded her eyes and gazed down at the dark forest stretching to the horizon in every direction save for the plateau at their back and a faint blue line on the eastern horizon, no doubt marking the sea. The trees smoked in the heat of the sun, giving back to the sky much of the moisture that had recently rained down on them. Above, glorious white clouds formed as the captives sat and ate the fruit doled out to them.

'Beautiful. Unique. Beyond the grasp of mortal men.' Their chief captor stood beside her father, his arm outstretched. 'Every tree a sacred pillar of our temple, some of them three thousand years old and more.' Her father was about to imperil them again, she knew. Like the old Red Duke of Roudhos, who had been burned at the stake by the Undying Man, Noetos, his grandson, never knew when to leave well enough alone. Couldn't help himself. Yet it was just as well someone in their party had his persistence. Whatever had happened back there in front of the Godhouse door had nearly killed them all. Arathé had felt her father fight against the relentless stream of time as it seemed to double back on itself; perhaps others had tried, but he was the only one to succeed.

'You're about to tell me how outsiders have cut down the trees and put the spirit of the forest in jeopardy, aren't you?' Noetos said. 'How we evil tree-eaters are always destroying the sacred grove of something-or-other. Do not bother, friend. Our journey is more important than a few trees. The whole of Patina Padouk is as nothing beside it.'

'You *want* me to feather your friends?' the man asked, incredulous, and raised his bow.

'For Alkuon's sake, Father, be silent!' Anomer hissed.

'None of you understand, do you!' Noetos said. 'Something happened to us back at the portal that just might make everything we've done, or might do, completely irrelevant. Did you all sleep through it, or am I the only one with courage enough to talk about it?'

Arathé listened intently. Even the Padouki leader took a step closer, holding up his hands to keep his bowmen from loosing their arrows.

'Are you talking of the double-time?' he said.

'You have a name for it?'

'No, but one of my warriors called it *datinala*, which means "two-time." A good name, I thought. It's happened once in living memory, coincidentally when last Keppia visited the Godhouse. Perhaps not a coincidence. This time was much longer in duration according to some of the older warriors.' He swept an arm out, indicating those behind him.

'Did you see it as we did? You found three of us with your arrows the first time, but none the second?'

'We did,' the man acknowledged. 'It made many of our warriors nervous.'

'Not as nervous as it made me, I'm sure.' Her father sighed. 'Look, we've begun this all wrong. *I've* begun this wrong. Whatever happens in the next few days and weeks will affect Patina Padouk as much as the rest of the world. Believe me, we are at the heart of it. Why otherwise would we be travelling with a god?'

The man grunted. 'As I said, that is all that has kept you alive. But where is he now?'

Lenares came forward. 'Do you have cosmographers in your culture?'

Noetos took her hand and began to pull her away.

'Leave me alone!' she said. 'Don't touch me!'

'Let the woman go,' the Padouki leader commanded, then addressed Lenares. 'What are cosmographers?'

'Special people who can see the meaning of what the gods do,' she announced. 'Did you know the gods are trying to break into the world so they can live here all the time? Would you like them living in your heartland if they succeed?'

The man grunted at that, and turned to his warriors. A rapid exchange followed, in which the warriors became more and more animated.

'We must take you to see the elders,' their leader said eventually. 'They have spoken of something like this, but we warriors do not pay heed to such talk. The elders will, however, want to hear what you have to say. Come, no more discussion. Save it for the

46

elders. Before them you must measure every word and apportion it like the purest rice. You will need more courage than I,' he finished darkly.

The winding trail down from the plateau took an entire after-noon, the slow pace clearly frustrating the Padouki. The captives began to droop with fatigue. None knew exactly how long they had been within the House of the Gods, but it had certainly been at least one sleepless night. Phemanderac seemed to be faring worst. Moralye and then Stella kept him upright and walking, but even the effort of staying awake appeared to be draining him.

During one rest break Arathé drifted closer, watching with concern as Moralye tended to the old scholar. The woman dabbed at his mouth with a cloth, whether to wipe away fluid or to try to make him take water, Arathé could not tell. She did, however, hear the old man say distinctly: 'You should have left me up there, dear. The House of the Gods would have been a pleasant place to sleep.' Then he noticed Arathé standing there and nothing else was said.

Dusk had begun to reduce vistas to silhouettes by the time they reached their destination. In a grove of trees indistinguishable from hundreds and thousands they had passed during the long day – except perhaps for an extra patina of age, an extra breadth of trunk – the Padouki leader called a halt. He jerked at a liana that looked exactly like all the others, and then waited.

'We should have been here hours ago,' he said. 'The elders will not be happy.'

'Some of us are old and infirm,' Heredrew said. 'We have injured and maimed among us. How could we keep to your schedule?'

The man did not answer him, instead indicating that he should stand aside. 'Clear a space. The ladders are extremely heavy.'

At his word a pile of hempen rope thudded to the ground. The man tugged the liana again, and a rope ladder arose from the pile and stretched upwards into the trees.

'Your infirm will wait here,' the man said. 'They will be guarded. If they give any offence they will be cut down with no more concern than a Malayuan woodsman has for a blackwood tree.'

Phemanderac remained behind, with Moralye as his guardian,

as did Torve, of course, and the two injured porters: the others who Arathé had thought might struggle to make the climb – Mustar with his leg, Sauxa and his age, Conal with his lost eye, and, most disadvantaged, Stella and her missing arm – all elected to make the ascent.

'Be certain,' said their captor. 'There is no going back. We will neither wait for you nor render any assistance.'

'How do your own old and sick make the journey?' Noetos asked as he set his foot to the lowest rung.

'They do not. At some point in the life of every Padouki he or she elects to remain in the Canopy, never to return to the ground.'

Arathé struggled to make the ascent. The trees were enormous, and there was no indication of how far she had to travel, just a barely perceptible lessening of the tree's girth as they rose, hand over hand, into the green world. She could think of nothing further removed from the bleak sterility of Fossa's cliffs, the black and grey fences that had once been her too-close limits; then again, she wondered how long a Padouki child could live in a tree before conceiving a desire to escape, just as she had.

She was amazed – shocked – at how quickly she tired. She could still see the ground rocking back and forth beneath her feet, hadn't even reached the first great branch before she began to shake, her muscles cramping. Above her, Noetos slowly drew away; beneath her, Anomer began to make worried comments. Arathé was worried herself. How far had she walked in the past months? Halfway across a continent? So why did one rope ladder exhaust her?

You've not used these muscles in earnest for years, said the voice in her head in a tone of bored instruction. *You should have stayed below with the old man. Except, of course, I would not have let you.*

She tried to ignore him. Offer him nothing, perhaps he would discard her. Up and up, her knees struggling to lock so she could raise herself to the next rung.

In the increasingly long pauses between rungs she caught swirling glimpses of the forest around her. Oddly, its closeness obscured her view, making it difficult to get any real sense of what the forest looked like. Extravagant was the word that seemed to suit. A profusion of broad leaves was visible in every direction, on the trees themselves, on the parasitic plants growing on the trees, and on the plants that grew on them. As she climbed higher the occasional shaft of sunlight picked out a ridiculously colourful plant or a flitting bird – the outrageous spike-crested bird, the spear-billed bird and the blurwing bird, or so she thought of them. A tiny blurwing darted between a crimson pitcher-shaped plant and a bush as large as a tree – though it grew from the trunk of the tree they climbed – covered in yellow flowers that looked like bells. It was a magical place, or it would have been a magical place if people weren't forcing her to climb ever higher.

At least a hundred feet above the ground, the rope ladder steadied. She glanced upwards and saw the underside of a broad platform. At last. From somewhere she found a surge of strength and, panting heavily, hauled herself onto the platform.

From somewhere? She knew where.

See how we need each other?

She refused to reply. He would think she was too tired to think straight. Unless, of course, he could read these quiet under-thoughts. Desperately she hoped not.

Look around you, little swan. Look up.

With a sinking feeling, she realised this platform was not their destination. Already many warriors, tired of waiting, were ascending another ladder, their captives interspersed between them. More came up behind her.

I can't. She collapsed on the platform and began to sob. *I can't.*

With a rush of heat the back of her head seemed to burst into flame. Her hands went to her head – at least she thought they did, but in reality they jerked out and clasped the platform. Her legs splayed wide and she found herself on her feet.

'Aaaaa!' she screamed.

'Arathé!' her father and brother both cried.

She could do nothing, not even acknowledge them. She had become a prisoner in her own body.

Now you learn, said the voice, the sound wreathed in the crackle of flame.

One hand grasped the ladder, one foot found a rung. The other foot swung up, struck for and missed the next rung – she slipped forward, a rung catching her under the chin. That, and her foothold, kept her from falling.

Stupid bitch, stop fighting me!

The ladder spun left and right and Arathé felt she would spit up everything she had ever eaten. But even then, in danger of falling and with fire in her head and stomach, she had enough spirit to reply: *What happened to "little swan"? You need some help overcoming a girl?*

His answer was to seize her again and send her scurrying up the ladder. Within moments she had caught the rearmost of the warriors; heedless, the voice sent her climbing right over him. The Padouki cried a warning and his fellows began to duck out of her way by clinging to the underside of the ladder. It jerked and twirled crazily as she passed man after man and even members of her own party. She saw Kilfor's pale face with eyes wide open, and Stella gamely clinging on with her one hand. Mustar called out to her, but she could not hear him for the sound of burning in her head.

In this fashion Arathé was driven up another two hundred feet or more to the Canopy, where the people of Patina Padouk made their homes. She collapsed on the high platform, body shaking, limbs jerking like the legs of a frog. The burning sound faded and her head cooled. Tentatively she raised a hand to her head, expecting fried skin, scorching at the least, but found her scalp and hair intact.

I never want to experience that again.

She lay on her stomach, head hanging over the edge of the platform. Her eyes came into focus: she was staring into darkness, which resolved into forest twilight. She thought she could see the ground far, far below.

This time she could not control her stomach.

The captives were given a few minutes to recover. These Noetos spent with Arathé, trying to find out why she had behaved so strangely. His daughter would not even look at him, let alone engage in conversation.

'Please,' he begged. 'Tell me what is wrong.'

She turned away, obviously distressed.

'The madwoman is to go first,' their chief captor said. 'We nearly lost a man when she rushed up the ladder like a sow in heat.'

He'll pay for that remark. 'She will need my help to climb,' Noetos answered, careful to keep his voice respectful. 'Is this permitted?'

'You may assist her,' said the man grudgingly. 'However, if she knocks anyone from any of the walks, you will both pay with your lives.'

As they set off along a swinging bridge suspended between trees, Noetos began to notice signs of a city in the Canopy. Everywhere he looked trees sprouted huts of various descriptions: large, small, squat, tall, peak-roofed, slope-roofed, open-walled or closed-walled. Roofs and floors were made of wood, while hides generally served for walls. Each hut was aligned the same way and open at both ends, presumably to allow for better airflow. Given the sticky heat of the forest, he'd certainly want it that way.

The dwellings were by no means marvels of engineering: this was not the fabled City of the Clouds, subject of nursery tales. Ramshackle and lightweight, they looked as though they would be blown away in any sort of wind. There was no beauty to them. No carving above the doors, no added colours or patterns on the hide. Perfunctory. The same could be said for the swaying bridges between platforms. Certainly there were far too many signs of recent mending for the fisherman's peace of mind.

What peace of mind? He had a daughter who had begun acting as though touched by madness, and she would not speak to him about it. His son, as usual, blamed him for all their problems. And there was the matter of their capture and imminent interrogation – though, given the calibre of the magicians in their party, he rated this one of his lesser worries. Of more concern was a dead emperor wandering around somewhere. It would doubtless be a very long time before Noetos again experienced any peace of mind. He would not waste time worrying about creaking and dilapidated walkways a few hundred feet above the ground.

Within minutes he was lost. Were they to escape their captors, he doubted he could find the ladder. Unless they were lucky and found it by chance, or there was more than one ladder, the guards assigned them were superfluous. *At least for me: how I miss my sword! Perhaps one or two of my magic-kissed fellows could do something.* He wondered what Heredrew might be planning; the tall Falthan magician was surely not a man to be held against his will. He would be going along with this for his own purposes.

The hut they were taken to was possibly in the poorest condition of all the buildings Noetos had seen. Strangely, it was by no means the largest: the fisherman had expected a gathering like this to be held in some temple or civic building. If they had such things. Patina Padouk was the northern neighbour of Old Roudhos, but very little was known about its inhabitants. Did they worship gods apart from Keppia? How was their society organised? He tried to remember if any of his tutors had spoken of the forest lands as part of his education. Surely this small hovel could not be a temple or gathering place.

Across the open end of the hut had been placed a rough criss-cross grid of sticks, with a door-sized opening allowing entrance. Noetos had wondered how inhabitants prevented themselves falling from the huts during a high wind, and the sticks offered an explanation. Inside, all was smoke, gloom and sweat. Every available space had been taken by a near-naked body. Dozens of eyes peered at him as he walked across the rough timber floor and found a place to stand against the wall to the left, close to a recessed place in the floor filled with dirt, on which was set a small fire. *In this heat? What for?* The bitter smoke curled lazily in the close air; more than one of the captives succumbed to coughing fits.

The muttering petered out into silence. Now the sounds included the crackle of the fire, a steady, rhythmical creaking as the hut moved back and forth, much coughing and snuffling, and repeated sniffling coming from a gap-toothed old woman with a vacant look in her eyes.

Noetos looked about him, but could not tell which of these people would turn out to be their inquisitors. No-one wore clothes distinguishing them from the rest, and there was no one group of faces more keenly focused on them than any other. The warrior captain stood nearest the door, but even watching his eyes gave no indication of what was to happen or who was in charge.

It soon became clear the silence was a test — perhaps the heart of the interrogation. As a technique it had served his father well, often drawing the guilty to speak more openly than they might while defending themselves against specific questions. Few of the others would know what was happening here. Noetos wished he could alert them somehow, but he was certain it would count against him. *Please be patient*, he thought, wishing he could communicate with his eyes.

Inevitably it was Conal the Falthan priest who broke the silence.

'What's going on here? Why have you captured us? What right do you have to hold me? I am a priest of the Koinobia, a representative of the Most High. You ought not hinder His plans. I've already seen Him strike a man dead.'

There's a guilty man, Noetos judged, even as the priest opened his mouth. *And a fool.*

The silence seemed even emptier after the priest finished speaking. There had been no noticeable reaction to his outburst. Nothing gained, plenty lost. Though it might be that Noetos simply failed to see the clues these Padouki provided; their ways seemed so different as to be impenetrable.

Seren nodded off first. This did not alarm the fisherman. The miner had borne more than his share during the journey. The man wanted answers as much as anybody, but day after day of hoisting a heavy pack had taken it out of his broad shoulders. However, when other captives struggled to keep their eyes open, Noetos began to grow nervous. His eyes swung to the fire.

'Put it out,' he said thickly. When no one moved, he screamed: 'PUT IT OUT!'

He lurched forward and snatched up a gourd, upending it over the flames. An acrid stench filled the hut.

'Now that wasn't the cleverest thing I've ever seen,' Heredrew observed, seemingly unaffected by the smoke. 'Let us hope the patient can provide another specimen without too much trouble.'

'We are in a physic's room?' Noetos asked, confused.

'I have no doubt. The wood used on the fire is coated with a mild narcotic, designed to calm nervous patients. Our people are tired, and those with no magical insight or experience at regulating their bodily responses have been taken into sleep.'

'So why am I awake?'

'I would have thought,' Heredrew said, 'the answer to that was obvious.'

He's wrong, the fool Falthan is wrong. I could not touch the huanu stone if I had magical ability.

The warrior leader moved a pace towards them. 'The elders will see you now,' he said. 'Leave the sleeping ones here. They would not have survived the questioning.'

'I will not leave my friends unless you guarantee their safety,' Noetos said gruffly.

The man raised an eyebrow. 'Many hosts would construe such fear as an insult. But since you are completely in our power, I understand your concern. Your friends will be well looked after.'

Noetos wanted to give this man nothing, but what could he do?

Eight of the captives were taken to another hut: Heredrew, Stella and Conal were the three Falthans though Noetos was certain Phemanderac and Moralye, born and raised in legendary Dhauria – so intimately bound in the story of the Undying Man – would also have remained awake had they been here. Captain Duon led a bewildered Lenares. The cosmographer seemed half-asleep and responded feebly as Duon explained to her what was happening. Anomer and Arathé had remained awake and followed their father. It worried Noetos to leave Seren, Tumar and his two fishermen, Sautea and Mustar, back in the physic hut, but the warrior leader was right. They were completely in the power of the Padouki.

The Hut of the Elders was some distance away across the Canopy. A rising wind set the bridges swaying and Noetos found his attention taken by keeping his balance. A man of open spaces, of sea and shore, he could not make sense of direction and distance in the tops of the great trees. This was further compounded when they were forced up narrow ladders consisting of nothing more than notched branches. Their guards climbed with nonchalance, some with bows in hand or bags of weapons and stores, while the captives wrapped themselves around the ladders and inched their way upwards.

Finally the captives stood before the door of a hut almost identical to the one they had left.

'Come in,' said a woman's pleasant contralto.

Lost, confused and almost completely off balance, Noetos ducked to enter the building, a hand on his daughter's shoulder. He was made to line up with the others along the side wall of the hut.

This time there was no doubt as to whom they would be speaking.

'Siy tell me you taken on the plateau at door of Godhouse,' said a broad-faced woman of middle years. Her voice was like golden syrup poured into his ears and he found it easing his troubled mind. A *trick, of course*, he told himself. Four older women flanked her, two on each side.

He nodded to the woman, as did Heredrew. *How will these elders cope with two spokesmen?* At least he and the tall Falthan seemed to be of similar mind. *They refused to speak to us, so we should be slow to answer their questions.*

'That plateau our heartland. Outsiders not allowed in our heartland. Unless you supply best reason for this, you will be ended in traditional manner.' Such a beautiful voice.

Heredrew laughed. 'I haven't heard the Wordweave used so clumsily in some time,' he said. To the others he added: 'It's a form of basic magic. The speaker weaves a surreptitious meaning between her words. I believe we are supposed to feel safe, among friends, and therefore willing to answer their enquiries. You realise she just promised to kill us all?'

Yes. Noetos had heard the words, had even known what they implied, but it simply had not disturbed him, so sweet had been her voice. Magic. How he hated it.

'The Bhrudwan Recruiters use it,' he said, remembering that

night in Fossa. He was about to explain about the Recruiters, but Heredrew nodded.

'They are trained in all the arts of the Voice.'

How does he know?

Now he understood what the woman was doing, her voice didn't sound quite so compelling.

'Do I explain traditional way enemies of Padouk are ended? They are taken to tallest tree in Canopy and cast to ground. Is noble death for Padouki. Not so noble for guests. So unless you wish to descend more quicker than you came up, please tell. Tell now.'

'Here are our reasons,' Noetos snapped, tired of the manipulation. 'First, your man Siy gave us leave. This was after he filled our companion, the god Keppia, with arrows.'

'He kill Keppia?' the woman said, her mouth stretching wide, whether in surprise or in a smile, Noetos could not tell. 'Keppia dead?'

'No, even the andali did not hurt him,' the man Siy said. 'This man is correct. I granted them leave because there was no other choice; they were in the company of the god. We have not seen him for many years, and all Padouk remembers what happened when last we resisted him.'

'Ai, he slaughter Fumi Canopy,' the woman said, and the women on either side of her pulled their lips back, exposing their teeth in an expression of grief. 'All who live there die when mother tell Keppia not to take daughter. He kill Canopy and take daughter anyway.'

'You are angry at Keppia,' Heredrew said. 'So are we.'

'You his friends. You still-awake ones maybe gods too, little gods. Now he not here to protect, we likely end you quick.'

Noetos took a step forward. 'You told us we were to be judged because we went into your heartland. You lie. You want to kill us because you think we are Keppia's friends. But we are no friends of Keppia. We want him dead, him and his sister Umu both. In the House of the Gods we slew his body, but he has escaped us. The body may have come back to life. Please give us leave to pursue the body and end it forever. If you have any ability to sense the truth, believe me when I say we have devoted ourselves to destroy the gods.'

One of the old women eased herself to her feet and began shouting in a language full of consonants.

The spokeswoman nodded. 'Ai, Ashana is right. We not want Keppia dead. He die, we lose our gift. We want him to leave us alone. Go away, not come back.'

'What gift?' Heredrew asked.

'Too many question,' said the woman. 'We end you.'

'NO!' Lenares strode forward. 'You are afraid Keppia's death will mean you die too. I can see your numbers: you are very old, and these, your aunts, are even older. Many hundreds of years old. You are afraid that the gods will take your long lives from you. But if you listen to your selfish fear, the gods will win.' Another pace towards the elders and now she was shouting. 'You must not kill us! We are the only ones who know what is happening in the world! Do you know about the hole in the Wall of Time? Have you sensed the forest behaving strangely? Are the trees falling without explanation? Are the rivers overflowing out of season?

'I have held Umu captive. There are powerful magicians among us. We are trying to prevent the gods breaking into the world from beyond the Wall of Time. We have to keep them out. If we can close the hole, we can stop the gods destroying the world and you can keep your long lives.'

The five elders stared at her, mouths open. Two of them rocked back and forth, hands on their heads.

'You are dangerous as gods,' said the woman. 'We end you and Keppia will be grateful. Padouk become great once again, Bhrudwo die, we are content. Siy, take them to place of ending.'

She waved an arm and the warriors moved in over the captives' protests.

'Make end of them,' said the beautiful voice as Noetos and the others were dragged from the hut.

CHAPTER 3

SWORDMASTER

ARATHÉ! ARATHÉ! NOETOS DIRECTED HIS mind-cry outwards. *Please, speak to me!*

No reply came: whether because his daughter could not hear him or chose not to respond, he could not say.

The big fisherman despised feeling helpless. His family sword remained on Captain Kidson's ship, along with the huanu stone, but even that powerful artefact would not have been able to protect him here. It was effective only against magic, and it did not, after all, take magic to throw someone from the top of a tree. The death that followed would be an entirely natural one.

Why had the Padouki split him from the rest of the captives? He tried to ask, but none would – or could – answer him. Were he with his children he was sure he could have devised some way to escape. Perhaps the warriors had sensed that, and this was the reason they had separated him from the others.

He allowed himself to be led across one of the swing bridges. Such a dangerous method of moving from one place to another; each fragile, wind-tossed bridge less than a pace in width, making it difficult for people to pass if travelling in opposite directions. Perhaps there was some well-understood collection of routes around this tree-city that kept people from getting in each other's way. However it was done, Noetos and his three captors met no one coming the other way.

All the while Noetos looked left and right to see where they had taken his children. He could not see them. They might be anywhere. *Arathé has magic*, he reassured himself. *So does her brother. They will take care of themselves.* For now it was himself he needed to think about; himself and the others left in the physic hut, vulnerable without magic to protect themselves.

He hated feeling vulnerable. But if Arathé refused to mind-speak with him, then vulnerable he was. He would have to rely on natural means.

The natural means left to him were few, but they might be sufficient. Could he do this? His old weapons tutor had spent time instructing him in unarmed combat, but he had not practised it in years. And this was his enemies' natural environment.

There are three rules to combat without weapons, Cyclamere had said. *Get in close. When you are there, fight without honour. And use your weight.*

Simple enough.

He feigned a stumble and grabbed at a warrior's arm. Beneath him the narrow bridge swung in the opposite direction to his movement, as he had anticipated and allowed for. The man managed a cry of alarm, but did not react quickly enough to save himself. Noetos lowered his shoulder, got under the man's chest and stood. Momentum did the rest.

'Sorry, I'm sorry,' Noetos said feebly as the man tumbled down into the shadows. There would be a moment when the other two guards would not believe their fellow had fallen, and a moment longer when they would not realise it had been deliberate. His apology would make them uncertain of what they had seen, slowing them further. He moved before realisation hit them.

The first he disabled with a short punch to the ribs. He threw himself at the doubled-over figure and pushed him into the third man, who had finally drawn a knife. *That's the problem with bows and arrows, boys*, Noetos thought as he used his opponent to block the man's attempt at a thrust. The knife-wielder hissed, then swept his weapon in a wide arc at throat height – just as his partner stood, having recovered from the blow to his chest. The tip of the blade took the man under the chin, etching a red line across his throat. His scream faded to a gurgle and he fell heavily on the slats of the bridge, his blood spraying across Noetos's feet.

The remaining guard stood for a moment, staring wide-eyed at the knife in his hand, then dropped it and ran. 'Khlamir! Khlamir!' he shouted as he disappeared. In moments he had vanished in the trees, though the fisherman could still hear him calling.

Noetos had not expected that. He would be lost if the Padouki brought numbers to bear against him, but he would not be able to keep pace with the warrior in his own environment. So he let the man go. Instead, he picked up the knife. A poor weapon, but better than none at all. Within moments there was shouting in the distance. A response to the warrior's shouts? Or something else entirely?

Something else, it seemed. A thin column of smoke rose above the trees some distance away. Noetos considered making for it: the smoke could be coming from the physic hut. He hoped it was his children causing the trouble, but there were other magicians amongst them. *Could be Heredrew*, he thought as he stepped over the dead warrior and moved as quickly as he could to the end of the bridge. *Whoever, at least we're fighting back*.

He ran towards the smoke, making no attempt to conceal himself. *Speed, speed*. The first few bridges were empty. A group of small children blocked the fourth. So much for his theory of the well-understood routes.

'Get out of the way!' he shouted.

The children laughed and pointed at him. In the distance a woman shrieked, the chilling sound followed by a detonation that shook the forest. The laughter stopped.

A shout from behind him. He turned to see the warrior leader two bridges away, sprinting towards him, sword in hand. Noetos could not believe how fast the man moved.

'Move! Please, move aside!'

The children, oblivious to the concerns of adults, ignored him, mouths wide open, eyes riveted on another rising column of smoke. 'Khlamir! Khlamir!' one called, pointing to the oncoming warrior and then the distant smoke.

The fisherman charged at the children. Cries of exuberance changed to shouts of fear. He fended one little girl away, pushing her to the ground, and strode through a pair of boys. He stumbled over a fourth child, so young it was most likely barely weaned, and grabbed at the rope rail. The bridge swung alarmingly, pitching back and forth, and the children shrieked. Noetos turned; the small girl had been thrown over the rail and clung to it with one hand, her body dangling over three hundred feet of emptiness.

The other children fled towards the advancing warrior.

Cyclamere, what would you advise now?

He knew, damn his old tutor. He thrust out a hand and snatched the child by her upper arm. She squealed as he dragged her back onto the bridge, then kicked and clawed at him, spitting ferociously, her little face screwed up with hatred.

Noetos dragged himself to the far end of the bridge, the girl clinging to his leg. He kicked her in the face. She cried out and let go, then scurried away to join her friends, blood running from her nose.

The warrior leader – Siy, he remembered the man's name – arrived at the far end of the bridge. Noetos raised the knife.

'No further!' he cried. 'Or I take this knife to the children.'

The warrior laughed. 'If you had it in you to slay children, you would not have rescued the girl.'

Noetos grunted. Disconcerting to hear such insight expressed in perfect Fisher Coast Bhrudwan. 'I'll cut the bridge down then.'

Another laugh. 'Now you are not thinking. Again, you will do nothing that will result in the death of the children.'

'Whereas your people will happily sacrifice strangers to appease the Son.' Noetos decided to gamble. 'Not you, though, Siy. You have Tocharan training. Your tutors would not have advocated such a thing. Even the Neherians would not do this.' He slipped the knife into his belt.

'The Neherians would do anything,' said the warrior. 'You know nothing if you do not know that. I could tell you stories about those folk fit to freeze your blood. But you are right: this is folly, and unworthy of the Padouki.'

'Then let us go.'

'No. Surrender and I guarantee your deaths will be clean. I vow that I will personally travel to your home town and tell your relatives how bravely you died.'

'My home town is destroyed.'

Noetos found, as he said the words, a deep regret rising within him. Why he should care for a place he had hated, he could not understand. He would have sworn he could not have cared whether Fossa sat smugly in the sun or was burned to the ground, but apparently he had been wrong.

'I will ensure you are buried with honour,' the warrior persisted.

'You must let us go. The cosmographer was right, warrior. We are the only hope of defeating the gods.'

The man called something and the children made their way to his end of the bridge. 'You do not understand,' he told Noetos. 'The Padouki owe Keppia a great debt. In exchange for allowing him to make an entrance to the Godhouse in our sacred heartland, Keppia gifted us with the life of trees.'

'What do you mean?'

'The Padouki live very long lives,' said the warrior. 'As long as the trees they tend. I told you I spent time at the Tochar academy, yes, but this was in the time before the Red Duke of Roudhos. I served the Red Duke, and was already high in his service when I saw him burn in the war against the Falthans. I marched to Instruere and watched the Undying Man's victory and his defeat. Afterwards I assumed another name and served the Red Duke's son. Yet this is only a short part of my life, do you understand? Would you give up such a gift to save a few people who have made enemies of your god?'

'What? You served the Red Duke's son? Demios? But Demios—'

A noise behind him made him spin around. Three warriors stood there, bows drawn.

'You tricked me,' Noetos said with heartfelt bitterness.

'Aye. The most effective traps are baited by the prey. Shame you never went to the Tochar academy.'

No, but Cyclamere constantly told me that, using exactly those words. He was right: I never listened, and now I will pay for it, as he warned.

Another explosion rocked the treetops. Arathé ducked as splinters showered over the Canopy. Heredrew was doing something to the huts; expanding the air inside them so quickly that they blew apart. She had seen dozens of Padouki plummet to their deaths as a result. She had also seen Stella walk away in disgust.

We don't have the luxury of cherishing our enemies, she thought.

No, you do not. It does not serve me to see you die here.

The hated voice. Arathé was minded to change her opinion simply because it agreed with her.

Then get us out, she thought at him.

The Falthan seems to be doing a creditable job, said the voice, half-admiringly. *But I must look after my interests. Very well. Prepare yourself.*

The familiar burning took hold of her. *Curse you, curse you,* she drove at him. *I didn't mean like this!* Then everything went white.

The Padouki had magic, it seemed, but their power was sorely limited. When Noetos finally found the source of the smoke, it was to discover a large group of Padouki women standing together on a platform, arrayed against Heredrew, alone on a bridge. They were doing something to the air between themselves and the Falthan sorcerer: it swirled like smoke, one moment hardening as though frozen and then softening in the next. Their stance was purely defensive, trying to keep the man out. Losing the battle, and they knew it. Noetos had seen a similar look of horror and resignation on other faces he had fought. He had probably worn that look himself a time or two.

As he watched, one of them sighed and collapsed onto the platform. Their swirling mist jerked, then shrank a little. Heredrew advanced a step across the bridge. Noetos regretted he did not have the power to lend the brave Falthan assistance. Though he probably didn't need it.

Another woman faltered. Her hands went to her head and it

burst open like a rotten fruit dropped on the ground, spattering those either side of her. What remained slumped to the platform.

Oh, woman, you made us do it. Noetos felt no better at the thought.

'Have you seen Arathé and Anomer?' he called.

Without turning, the tall Falthan inclined his head towards a swing bridge to his left. 'Some time ago,' came his voice.

Noetos wished he had language sufficient to stop this butchery, but tongues had never been his gift. He ran towards the bridge the Falthan had indicated, and tried to ignore another shriek from behind him as he reached the far side.

No control. Prisoner in her own mind. She – her hands, her body – *she* was doing these terrible things. Hands rending, feet smashing, stamping. Mouth . . . He ensured what she did was far worse than it needed to be, trying to soak her in blood and guilt.

She would have vomited if she could. Oh, Alkuon, she would have died, would have ended her own life in a moment, had she been given the choice.

Anything but this.

Noetos had bidden her farewell the day the Recruiters took her north. 'Don't surrender to anyone,' he'd said. 'Many people will want to use you for their own purposes. Even if your desires coincide with theirs, promise me you'll not let them own you. Promise me, my girl.' He'd made her promise. Her mother had given her different, more practical advice, but her father had been proven right.

Father! Noetos! she screamed, but she knew her voice went no further than the confines of her head.

The Canopy was aflame, the treetops filled with acrid smoke. The haze and the many cast-down bridges defeated Noetos time and again. Occasionally he saw one of the other captives; once he caught sight of Anomer leading Robal, Kilfor and Lenares across a bridge perhaps fifty arm-spans distant. They could shout to each other but, even after spending many long minutes trying, could not find a common path to connect their bridge to his. In the end they made off just before a dozen Padouki warriors ran onto the bridge. Noetos had a few moments of danger as they loosed at least four arrows in his direction, but the billowing smoke that had previously frustrated him now served to keep him safe.

By chance – though by this time he must surely have traversed every bridge in the whole of Patina Padouk – he discovered the Padouki armoury, or what passed for it. One of the single-branch ladders led him to the highest of the platforms, on which a small hut stood, guarded by two frightened young men nowhere near old enough to shave. Neither appeared to have a weapon.

'Non, non,' the larger of the two boys cried when Noetos emerged on the platform. 'Khlamir!'

'Your Khlamir isn't going to help you,' Noetos said, knowing he would not be understood, but hoping his tone of voice would soothe them. 'Just step aside and you'll be safe.'

'Khlamir! Khlamir!' they both cried. 'Khlamir!' And they rushed him.

He should have used the knife, but he couldn't, not on children. *What is this? From the butcher of Raceme, the man who went through the Neherian ballroom with a sword?* With mingled disgust and regret he cast the knife aside and braced himself.

With a whoosh the elder boy hit him, head and shoulder, in his stomach. The other lad took him around the knees. In moments he was on the ground, both of them working with fists and elbows, pummelling at him. He took a few painful blows before he was able to retaliate. Freeing his arms, he took them both in a bear hug. Their arms beat ineffectually at his back as he rose slowly to his feet. He could crush the youngsters to death if he chose.

He would not choose.

'Put them down, please,' came a voice from behind him.

The killing strength went out of Noetos. He turned to face the warrior leader.

'What's to stop me dropping these young ones over the edge of the platform?' Noetos asked, breathing heavily. The youngsters squirmed in his grasp. He thought perhaps he might have broken one of the lads' ribs.

The man took a pace onto the platform. 'We both know you will not,' he said. 'It is your grace and failing, this foolish tender heart you have. Otherwise you would be an effective killer.' The man assumed a stance and quoted: 'When the killing starts, all sentiment must be thrust aside.'

'I presume you left these two boys in charge of the armoury,' Noetos said. 'That is not the action of a war leader. You quote from Cyclamere as though you have read his books, yet your own tactics fall some way short of the great man.'

To his astonishment, the war leader sheathed his sword, put his hands on his hips and laughed raucously.

'Put the children down,' said the man, still spluttering. 'I will not strike at you, I give you my word, this time for the compliment. Again, life for life. Let the boys go, and I will let you leave, this platform.'

Noetos released the boys. One of them had indeed been hurt: the younger boy crabbed across the platform to the war leader, holding his chest, his eyes filled with tears. The other stood beside the man and spoke rapidly, head downcast, no doubt apologising. The incessant 'Khlamir' was the only word Noetos recognised.

'Why do they call you that?' he asked, edging his way towards the low entrance to the armoury.

'If you enter that building, I will ensure you do not come out,' said the man, and drew his sword. 'They call me Khlamir, friend, because that is what I am. Their swordmaster. The one who is training them to supplement their bow-skill with the power of steel.'

And then it hit him. A hundred small clues rearranged themselves in his head.

No.

Yes.

Siy the Khlamir. A swordmaster who had served successive generations of the Roudhos, including his own father. A man who might fondly remember tutoring a young boy, or decide to avenge the deaths of his fellow warriors.

Oh, the danger.

'You will let me leave the platform?' Noetos said carefully.

'I will also allow you a weapon,' the man decided, 'not that it will avail you much. You have earned this, at least, for your compassion. You will find your people's weapons in a sack just inside the armoury.'

Noetos hesitated, though he now had good reason to trust the man's word.

'Go on! I will wait here, on the far side of the platform. But be quick. The battle is no doubt drawing to a close. I wish you well, but fear you will try to rescue your companions. You will lose your life if you make the attempt, but perhaps it is the most honourable course open to you. I am sorry for this, but you ought not to have entered the lands of the Padouki.'

Noetos walked to the opening, bent down and scrabbled in the darkness until he felt the coarse weave of the sack. It clanked with the sound of steel. He found a blade, Duon's by the feel of it, fastened the scabbard around his waist, then stood and faced the war leader.

The man's dark eyes narrowed, switching their gaze from the sword on the fisherman's hip to his face, but he stood aside to allow Noetos access to the ladder.

'Troubled by memories, old man?' Noetos asked as he descended the ladder. 'So am I, if it is any consolation. My thanks for my life.'

Sliding the last few rungs, he saluted the downturned face, turned on his heel and ran, the sweat turning cold on his back.

The voice released Arathé with a sudden snap of withdrawal. She searched her mind for any sign of him, then – oh so reluctantly – looked around her. Hoping it had been a nightmare.

Flesh, not her own, hanging from her fingers. A bloodied stick on the ground beside her. Her only weapon, save tooth and claw. The red-white shapes of bodies on all sides, smeared viscera, shattered bones, blood and pulp. The taste – she spat, then bent over and vomited. The smell.

The memories. Crystal clear.

The wail that came from her throat felt as if it had been ripped from the depths of her heart.

She raised her eyes from the bodies of her enemies. On the platform beside her stood her friends and acquaintances – and her brother – staring at her with wide eyes and white faces.

'Kill me,' she begged them, signing shakily. As her hands moved, flesh flicked from her fingers and fell to the ground. 'Please. Kill me now.'

No one moved.

She took a step backwards at the expressions of horror on their faces. Her foot caught on something and she stumbled, her heel grinding, then sliding, in wetness. Another step, then another.

'Arathé, don't.' This from her brother.

Another step. Her heel balanced on the edge of the platform.

'I must,' she signalled; then closed her eyes and took another step.

He saw them standing together, his children vulnerable, exposed and unmoving. Three bridges away, and for once he could trace a route that would take him there. Drawing Duon's well-balanced sword he strode forward, then broke into a run as he saw what was unfolding.

He pounded over the first bridge as she took a step back. *Arathé!* Across the second, heedless of how he set it swaying. *Anomer, do something!* He punched a hole in a slat with his foot as he leaped onto the third bridge, but barely noticed. Her heel hovered over a hundred vertical paces of nothingness.

This bridge was longer, with a small platform in the centre. He was not going to make it.

He flung himself onwards. A few more paces. She moved her hands and stepped backwards off the platform.

He reached out, too late, as she—

—as she hovered there for a perceptible moment, before his and Anomer's hands closed over hers, pulling her back to the platform.

Did you think I would let you go so easily? said the voice. *You and I, Arathé, have only just begun.*

A shout. Here came the war leader, followed by a dozen or more warriors armed with bows. As the man stepped onto the bridge, Noetos released his daughter's hand, and turned and faced him.

'I thought you were a man of honour,' he said.

'I thought you would run faster,' the man replied. 'Besides, I have questions for you. I am sorry about your friends, but our orders are specific.'

His men lifted their bows.

Noetos gestured around him at the gruesome remains. 'And I am sorry about yours. I will stay to answer your questions.'

He watched the swordmaster's face carefully and saw the exact moment when the carnage registered with the man. The tanned face paled, his thin lips parted, his eyes widened.

'They attacked my daughter,' Noetos said.

How could he not have recognised the man before now? Yes, he was garbed as a savage, not as the urbane tutor and faithful retainer Noetos remembered, but surely something about the voice, the man's bearing, his perfect Tocharan accent, ought to have alerted him. What would the war leader do now he was confronted by the violent deaths of his countrymen and women?

'Your *daughter* did this?'

'Aye. We were travelling with a mad god, friend. How could we have survived in such company without skills of our own?'

He raised the tip of his sword. To the others he said, 'Find a way down to the ground. I will ensure you are not followed.' Then he dismissed them from his mind, preparing for the conflict ahead.

'We have brought serpents into our house,' said the war leader.

The bowmen were at least fifty paces distant, with leaf and bough between, but at a signal from the swordmaster they nocked arrows and loosed in one fluid action. Noetos had not thought they were in range. Despite having seen the power of the Falthan magicians, the fisherman flinched as the flight whistled past.

The air in front of the captives shimmered, then turned opaque, like tree sap or glue. None of the missiles reached their targets.

'I am tired of being shot at with arrows,' Heredrew said. Beside him, Stella grinned.

'Go!' Noetos growled at them, and gave his attention to his adversary.

The bowmen retreated at another signal from the war leader. He came a few steps across the bridge. 'Questions, then,' he said, his level voice masking his anger. 'Here is my first question. You look familiar with a sword on your hip. Why is that?'

Noetos strode to meet him, putting as much confidence in his stride as he could, and took a stance on the small central platform. 'Recognise me, do you?'

'No, but I recognise the stance. I taught it to my more able pupils.' The man drew a sword, a full two hands, and settled into his all-too-familiar stance. 'Where did you learn to stand like that?'

An assertion of his identity would not be enough: Noetos would have to prove himself. 'Guess!' he said, and made his attack.

A downward blow, turned mid-strike into an upward thrust. A standard Cyclamere sequence. *I know nothing this man has not taught me*, he conceded, but he did not allow the knowledge to consume him.

The blow was parried, of course; the man opposite him had, after all, taught it to him. Supremely confident, the Khlamir did not assay a response, though he could have. Noetos had been counting on that. *His given word holds him.*

'Are they teaching the Khlamir method at Tochar now?' the war leader asked. Noetos essayed a couple of stabbing flicks, leaning in with his upper body. His opponent danced away, untroubled.

'I have no idea,' Noetos answered. 'I learned to fight like this in the grounds of the Summer Palace at Raceme, under the tutelage of a remarkable old man.' Another downward cut, begun slowly but with a disconcerting acceleration: a Cyclamere specialty, and hard to master. The war leader defended the blow, though with a little difficulty. 'I wasn't much of a pupil though.'

'I tutored a few noblemen in Raceme,' said the Khlamir. 'They were all as old then as you are now, and none had your skill. Who are you? I will have answers!'

'You'll kill me for them?'

A feint to the left, then a short downward cut from the shoulder. His blade rang on the swordmaster's, skittering across the steel with a rasping sound.

'No. But I have no doubt I will wound you. You are surprisingly proficient, too skilled to be disarmed unhurt. Better to hand over your sword.'

Another blow from Noetos, another block from his opponent.

'A further question occurs to me,' the man said. 'You are large, if a little slow, and have obviously been well trained. Why are you not trying to use your weight against me?'

'Because,' Noetos replied, shaping a two-handed blow from his left shoulder, 'my swordmaster taught me better.'

A blow from the right, then another, both parried with ease. Time to speed things. Time to gamble.

Arathé! See my need!

The effect was much as it had been that day in Raceme's Summer Palace. All motion around him slowed as though time had been carved into discrete moments and then spread apart. He could act in and between the moments, while the swordmaster was confined to normal time.

A third blow from the right, taking the man's blade near the hilt as he drew it back. Then a smart slap to his exposed right shoulder with the flat of Duon's blade. A step back and pause, allowing the man to catch up.

'Not possible,' the war leader hissed, his eyes wide.

'No, it is not,' Noetos agreed, and readied himself.

'I will not be toyed with,' the man said, and launched a furious attack. Blows from high, then low, one continuous movement; a spin, then two further strikes from left and right, one from the shoulder, the other from the hip. All delivered with main strength, designed to drive Noetos back from the platform and onto the unstable bridge.

Even in this strange magical state, Noetos had some difficulty meeting the swordmaster's attack. The man disguised the direction of each stroke, giving Noetos no time to respond. Fortunately the fisherman had something other than normal time in which to frame his response. Taking each blow on his sword, he allowed himself to smile, catching and holding his opponent's gaze.

'You are too slow, friend,' he said. 'Past your best.'

'I have been past my best for a century,' the man said, panting heavily. 'Still there has been no one in Old Roudhos to match me.'

'And still there is not,' Noetos said, lowering his sword. 'I have a secret, Cyclamere.' The man blinked at his use of the name. 'You once told me I'd never make a swordsman, but I practised after you left our service. I even took your advice about leading with my left shoulder.'

Cyclamere brought the point of his sword up, then lowered it as his eyes narrowed. 'Noetos?' he said, his voice rough, as though he had just woken from a deep sleep. 'But you died along with your family.'

'So everyone was told.'

The man licked ashen lips. 'You have been in hiding ever since?'

'Aye,' Noetos said.

'I looked for you,' Cyclamere told him after a pause. The man's eyes had begun to water. 'A year I searched, and found no evidence you were alive.'

'I hid well.'

His old arms tutor puffed out his cheeks. 'As I live, it is you. You have Noetos's lip as well as his build. Or the build he would likely have grown into.'

'I learned to like vegetables,' Noetos said.

'Aye, I can see. I am . . . glad you live. And angry that your family died.'

'I am pleased to hear you searched for me,' Noetos offered in exchange.

An awkward silence fell between two men unused to unmasking their emotions.

'I will tell you this, Cyclamere,' Noetos said eventually. 'I am travelling north to make the Lord of Bhrudwo account for his crimes.' He was aware of how vainglorious this must sound. 'I have been joined by others. We are opposed by the gods themselves, or, at least, two of the three. We have been drawn into the conflict of the age, and it seems the Neherian destruction of Old Roudhos is only a part of it.'

'Do you intend to make the Neherians answer for what they did to your family?'

Just as Noetos had hoped, the venerable swordmaster had been drawn in despite himself.

'I already have,' he said. 'I long to tell you how the nobles of Neherius were struck down. How this sword avenged the cruel deaths of my family. Come with me and I will explain everything.'

Cyclamere sighed, a sound of genuine regret. 'Unfortunately, young Noetos, I cannot. As much as I loved your family, my loyalty is to the Canopy of Patina Padouk. I do not blame you for what has happened here today,' he swept his hand across the grisly scene, 'but I can hardly leave Patina Padouk in this condition.'

'And my loyalty is to my companions, who have chosen to stand in the path of gods determined to break the world.'

'I will not stand against the gods.'

'Against Keppia, you mean.'

'That is exactly what I mean. And would you sacrifice a life hundreds, if not thousands, of years long, leaving your friends and family behind, to serve a man you believed dead?'

'If it would lead to saving Roudhos, then yes, I would,' Noetos answered fiercely. 'And who said anything about serving? Or sacrificing? You'd lend your sword arm and your knowledge when and where you chose, and I doubt there would be anyone who could seriously threaten your life.'

'You're forgetting magicians. A good sword is no proof against a magician.'

'If a good sword is no use, why are you so revered among the Padouki?'

'Because our magicians are not strong,' Cyclamere answered, rather frankly in Noetos's opinion. 'The little power at our disposal comes from the gift that Keppia gave us. We think of it as a small side-stream, only a fraction of the raging flood Keppia used to keep us alive.'

'You're afraid to offend him.' Noetos did not ask this as a question.

'For myself, no. He is ignorant, rude and without honour or depth of spirit. Why would I bow to the likes of him? However, I am fearful of what would happen to my people if he withdraws his patronage.'

'They would die?'

'Aye. I am ready to die, though I would miss this world. Who would not want to wake up for one more morning and breathe in the forest scent? Or listen to his grandchildren at play? But my children and grandchildren are not ready for death. You fight for your family and your country, Lord of Roudhos. Would you not give me leave to fight for mine?'

Another explosion shook the trees, sending leaves quaking and branches rattling. Over Cyclamere's shoulder black smoke began to billow. The warrior did not turn his head at the sound, not even a fraction.

'We can't stay here,' Noetos said. 'We must fight each other, or combine to rescue those in trouble, or agree to separate. If we fight, you will die, as I have a source of magic you cannot counter. If we separate, I believe the best we can hope for is that one of us will successfully protect his family. One, or probably both, of us will lose everything. But if we combine our efforts against the gods, we can prevent them breaking the world.'

The warrior frowned. 'To prevent the world breaking, Padouk must pass away?'

'Perhaps not,' Noetos said, but inwardly he acknowledged the truth of Cyclamere's words.

'Then let the world break. My people and I will watch it together.'

After Cyclamere had left him, gone to search for those who needed his help, Noetos struggled along depressingly familiar bridges and platforms towards the smoke. As he drew closer, flames became visible, their hungry tips rising above the foliage. Not even the beginnings of a light drizzle could quench them.

He had never been any good at puzzles. Didn't have the patience for them. His father had insisted problem-solving be part of his education, and had imported all sorts of intricate devices to test his son's abilities. He solved them, all right, with the aid of hammers and saws. He'd always been fond of the direct route. Trouble was, there was no direct route to solving this puzzle. The harder he tried to approach the fire, the further he seemed to get from it. No hammer or saw was going to realign the bridges to allow him direct passage, and he found himself doubling back time and again.

Arathé. Can you tell me where you are?

No answer. Of course there would be no answer: he'd probably exhausted the girl earlier, and that after whatever she'd done to the people who had tried to take her.

Arathé?

Still no answer.

He told himself not to worry; there were many reasons why she might not wish to mind-speak him. Perhaps she was speaking to someone else, or the damned voice in her head had her attention. *Or*, his mind whispered, *she's unconscious, or dead.*

Sighing, he carried on.

Her body sapped beyond easy recovery, Arathé groaned as she made it to another platform with pursuit close behind. Running across the bridges hadn't been so bad, but climbing down the rope ladders had taxed her sorely. Her knees and ankles seemed unable to lock in position and time and again she had slipped from the rungs. She had been prevented from falling only by her own desperate grasping and, latterly, by the captain's strength. But now, as they took a moment to gasp in much-needed air, she could see even his strength was coming to an end.

She and Captain Duon had become separated from the rest of the travellers at some point in the last few hectic minutes. The others had responded to a call from what sounded like Anomer, but Duon had held her back, unsure if the shout had come from friend or foe. He had apologised for his caution, but as a result they had lost contact with the others, and there was no chance of retracing their steps.

Frustratingly, she could not communicate with the man. Her speech depended on the fine muscle movements of her fingers and hands; movements severely compromised by her exhaustion. She doubted he could read her words anyway.

Time to risk it.

Duon? she sent. *Captain Duon? Can you hear me?*

A faint buzzing tickled the back of her head. At the same time Duon grabbed her arm.

'Was that you?'

Yes. You can hear me.

'I can. But so can he.'

She didn't need to ask who 'he' was. *He can hear us anyway if we talk out loud.*

'Come on,' Duon said, taking hold of her arm. 'We have to find our way down before the Padouki catch us.'

Arathé groaned again. More than anything she wanted somewhere to lie down and close her eyes, to wake up in some different time and place with one fewer person in her head. She didn't have to have a long life or a happy one, just one in which she could rest peacefully and call the inside of her head her own. The chances of either happening seemed remote.

They hurried across the only available bridge, then made two random choices of direction; only to find themselves on a platform with an upwards ladder and nothing else. Though she'd always thought of herself as a capable girl, Arathé found herself sobbing at the thought of the climb. But she dared not think of . . .

Out of strength, little swan? All you had to do was ask.

'I hear him,' Duon said. 'He's spilling over into my mind.'

Once again the power of the voice seized her and she found herself a prisoner in her own mind, her body set to climbing the ladder without her willing it.

I'll watch over you, Duon said in her mind. *I'll stop him using you to do evil things.*

No reaction from the voice. Had he heard Duon's mind-voice? Could he hear when he was in possession of her? Could this somehow be used against him?

Ah, little swan, I hear everything. But struggle away, and as you do, realise that in so doing you provide me with rich entertainment.

She reached the top of the ladder and the power drained from her limbs. There, on the platform, huddled into a ball, lay Conal the priest.

Just as he despaired of ever reaching the physic hut, and despite being absolutely convinced he'd taken a wrong turning, Noetos suddenly found himself there. As he'd feared, the hut was the source of the fire and was little more than a burnt-out shell. The flames had moved on to the tree to which the hut was anchored and the Canopy was in some danger of catching alight. The tree burned with a green flame and gave off acrid black smoke, fortunately blowing away from where he stood.

There was no one about.

The Padouki had fled, that much was clear, but the burning shell of the hut gave no clue to the fate of the non-magical travellers. He'd left his friends asleep – should have been asleep himself, given the drug had worked on all those without magic – and already, as he looked about wildly, guilt had begun its work on him. Could he have found his way here earlier? Ought he to have tried harder to enlist Cyclamere's help? Would the time spent sparring with and talking to his old mentor – to be honest, time that had given him deep satisfaction – turn out to be self-indulgent?

'Noetos!' called a voice from somewhere in the smoke. 'Your daughter wants to bid you farewell.'

The three of them were together, the victims of the nameless voice's spikes, shackled to each other with invisible, unbreakable chains. The voice had manipulated them from the start, had separated them like sheep from the rest of the flock, and was using its power to keep them alive. Or shepherding them to their deaths. The voice was silent on the matter.

Arathé tried to read the faces of the two men for any evidence they had suffered an experience similar to hers. Conal's face was ravaged: in the last few weeks fat had melted away from around his jowls and under his chin, and the hollow where his eye had been glistened with suppurating fluid. The normally immaculate priest was rough-shaven and lank-haired. He had been devastated, no doubt, but not by the voice. He had achieved his demise all on his own.

Captain Duon, on the other hand, seemed unchanged. Unless one looked closely. She could make out the hollowness around his eyes, and noticed his hands shaking slightly.

Has he hurt you? she asked them.

Conal turned away with a snort, which served as an answer of sorts. Duon simply nodded, then added, 'But not in the way he hurt you.'

They both knew then. She felt she would die of horror and shame.

Come, my children, said the voice. *Just a little further.*

Please, she begged the voice, as they stumbled along yet another bridge. *Please let us go. What are we to you?*

Not very much, not now. The question is, what are you to him?

Arathé coughed as they stepped onto a platform shrouded in smoke, and stumbled on the uneven boards.

Careful now, you don't want to fall, not in front of your father.

Across a gap of fewer than ten paces stood Noetos, shoulders slumped, his outline shimmering in the superheated air. Before Arathé could think of a way of attracting his attention, Captain Duon called out.

He looked up. Despite the heat shimmer and smoke haze, she saw the emotions flicker across his face: surprise, delight, disgust and frustration. She could be sure she hadn't imagined his disgust, and knew it to be justified, but it hurt her all the same. She dissolved into tears.

'Arathé, wait there! I'll find a way to get to you.'

'Stay where you are,' Duon commanded him, not in his own voice. 'I am taking your advice, fisherman, and removing these three from harm. They will be returned when I have finished with them.'

'You bastard. I know what you did to Arathé. What makes you think I believe you'll keep her safe?'

'Nothing.' This time it was the priest who spoke. The struggle on his face was terrible to watch; she knew just how helpless he felt. 'But I can guarantee her death should you seek to rescue her. You must realise I have the power of life or death over them.'

A sudden burning smote Arathé in the back of her head. She screamed and fell to her knees. Her father shouted something, but she could not make it out over the roaring in her brain. Then silence as the pain ceased. She raised a hand to her nose; it came away bloodied.

'When I learn who you are, I will find you and kill you,' her father said.

Conal laughed wheezily. 'Come, then. Find me and kill me if you can. As long as you stay away from your daughter.'

Noetos watched them go, three shambling figures energised by an unholy power. He put his head in his hands and wept.

'She is your daughter?'

The voice did not register for a moment; then his hand jerked automatically for his sword, but another hand rested there, preventing him from reaching it. He relaxed, took a deep breath and nodded to Cyclamere. He was unguarded; the man had his measure. Even were it available, his magical speed could not save him should his former tutor wish him dead.

'Aye. My elder child.'

The Padouki warrior grunted and stepped back from Noetos. 'You have another? Safe, far from here, able to carry on the Red Duke's line?'

Despite all he'd said it mattered to him, clearly. Cyclamere was still in his heart a servant of Roudhos.

'No. Anomer is here also, hopefully alive, his magic helping protect the rest of our company.'

'Their mother?'

'Dead, as much as killed by my hand.'

He couldn't keep the bitterness, the self-recrimination, from his voice. Cyclamere would hear it.

'You have many stories to tell.'

'Aye.'

The man grunted again. 'It seems I need to hear them. You are right, young Roudhos: I have unfinished business with your family. I have done what I can here. You and I, we must work out how to rescue your daughter and protect your son, then it seems I must aid you in defeating the gods. The elders will have to protect the Padouki as best they can.'

COSMOGRAPHER

CHAPTER 4

LOSS

SOMEWHERE IN THE THICK GREY mists of her childhood, Lenares could remember being told a story. It went something like this. Shell was a beautiful girl who met and fell in love with Gord, a boy who worked on her father's farm. He wasn't at all the sort of boy her father would have approved of for his daughter: his cheeks were wind-chapped and ruddy, his hands calloused and his pockets empty. But they loved each other regardless, and settled to run away together.

Shell spent her last night on the farm packing her treasured possessions into a shoulder bag, and a sweet smile played on her lips as she thought of Gord and the road they would walk together on the morrow. Her father noticed the smile and asked her why she was so happy. She told him she was looking forward to the harvest, and thought no more of it.

Her father was not convinced and, following his instincts, paid a visit to the single men's quarters. There he observed Gord, a quiet, dependable chap, gathering together his worldly goods with the same sweet smile on his face the farmer had seen his daughter wearing earlier. Immediately the truth of his daughter's perfidy became clear, and he spent the night sharpening his favourite axe.

The next morning Shell slipped out early from her house and met with Gord on the southern road. They hugged and kissed as they celebrated their boldness and cunning. At that moment, however, Shell's father stepped out from behind a tree, his axe in his hand. Shell and Gord stood there helpless as he –

Lenares knew how the story ended. She could remember giggling with misplaced delight at the description of what happened to the foolish lovers. And she now knew the terrible reason why her father – her real father – had told his daughters that story. But what she knew most of all was how Shell must have felt standing over the broken body of her beloved. What it felt like to have a broken heart.

The ladders and bridges and platforms weren't a problem to Lenares. The only problem was getting the others to listen to her words. It took them a long time to believe her when she said that this was a number problem and they ought to follow her. People were stupid, really, thinking that numbers were abstract things, of no use in the real world. 'That's all very well in theory,' they said, as though reality and theory were opposites. Well, this was the real world, and her numbers and patterns could tell her how to solve the problem of navigating the Canopy.

Palaman had taught all the young cosmographers about the problem of the Seven Pasture Gates. The Third of Pasture was the largest but least populated of Tal-amaq's suburbs, and residents often farmed the spaces between buildings. A man had a series of fields connected by gates, and on one particularly busy day he'd got to thinking about whether it was possible to visit all his fields without going through any gate twice. According to Palaman, who had been Chief Cosmographer even before Mahudia, it was not possible, and he demonstrated the problem on the board for them all. He explained what topology was, how the angles and distances of the paths between the gates were irrelevant. The relationship of the gates to each other was the thing.

So Lenares searched her memory and thought about the relationships between the bridges and platforms she'd travelled across since being hauled up into this three-dimensional city. It was a lot harder than the Seven Pasture Gates: she could remember forty-one platforms, thirty-four bridges and sixty ladders. How many combinations were there that would lead her from where they were now to the ladder they initially ascended?

It was a strange thing. Despite her broken heart, despite the horror of what she had seen, of what had been done to her beloved Torve, she could not help herself. She simply had to solve the problem; could no more have refused than water could have stopped flowing downhill. This was what she was.

'I have seventeen solutions,' she said calmly as the others crowded around her. 'I will use the solution that keeps us furthest away from where we are likely to meet people. If we come across anyone I will try another solution.'

'Good, good, Lenares,' Heredrew said. 'Let us make a start before the Padouki locate us. I don't want any more killing.'

'You seemed to enjoy it enough,' Robal growled. 'Why stop now?'

He was jealous, that Robal. He wanted Queen Stella for himself. He especially didn't want Heredrew to have her. His jealousy was a bad thing; Stella knew about it and it made her angry. A younger Lenares would have said something publicly, but this Lenares had learned discretion. Sometimes it was better for people to discover the truth themselves, Torve had said.

Oh, Torve.

Six hundred and twelve, went the counter in her mind. Six hundred and twelve times she had said his name to herself since it had happened. But there was nothing her wishing could do to undo the past. He was maimed now, and they could no longer love each other, not in that way.

Not that they had, not fully. The Emperor had been mistaken. Perhaps if he had arrived in the House of the Gods a few minutes later he might not have been, but that was a perhaps and therefore not true.

So, what did she feel for Torve now? She still loved him, she knew that for certain, but it was a different kind of love – it had lost that delicious pink edge of excitement. It was now more reserved, a little frightened even. Scariest of all, she didn't know if he still loved her. Did he? The old Lenares would have asked, would have searched his numbers for the truth, would have confronted him. But the new, grown-up Lenares knew that truth sometimes took time to form. How could he know yet how he felt, so soon after his manhood had been cut away from him? How could he know anything but pain and humiliation? Like a flower, their love would die if she pulled it up by the roots to see if it still lived. She would wait patiently until he knew what he felt for her. Oh, but it was so hard to wait.

A very scary thought struck her, the scariest she'd had yet. Perhaps he blamed her for what had happened. And if he did, wouldn't that kill his love? Would he show her a pretend flower, so as not to hurt her feelings, or would he be angry? Oh, she so much wanted to peep, to look at him with her number-sense.

The others followed her as she led them across empty bridges and up and down ladders.

'We must be getting close,' one of the men said, more in hope than certainty.

'I'm sure we passed that tree not ten minutes ago,' another man said. 'Bark looks just like my first wife's face.'

'Probably a mirror then,' said the first man.

'Be quiet,' Lenares told them. 'I need silence so I can hold all the possible solutions in my head.'

'Consider yourself told off,' the second voice whispered to the first.

'I can hear whispers too,' she said.

After that there was nothing but their feet scraping across timber and rope hissing through their hands, along with the muted noises of the forest canopy. Occasionally they heard the sounds of pursuit, and once they looked up to see a band of Padouki men stamping across a bridge above them; but either the warriors were searching for someone else or they were lazy, because they didn't look down. Lenares chose a different solution anyway, to be safe.

Oh, Torve.

There were so many other things to think about that Torve had fallen asleep by the time she was able to check on him. For a while she thought about the hole in the world, which had grown much larger since they had entered the land of the Padouki; and every death in the Canopy above them ripped the hole still wider. Lenares had set herself the task of driving the gods away and closing the hole behind them, but she had no idea how she was going to do it. Even when she had controlled the Daughter she had doubted her ability to repair the damage the gods had made; now she had nothing except her clever mind and a connection – a *possible* connection – to her dead foster mother on the other side of the hole. How that might be exploited was a mystery.

Others would surely take care of mundane things like food and water, their destination and choice of route. The warriors and wizards among them would protect them from anyone who sought to attack them, like these foolish tree-dwellers. But only Lenares could save them from the gods. It was a heady responsibility, one she intended to take seriously.

They had found Moralye hiding behind a tree some distance from the base of the ladder that finally brought them down from the Canopy. She immediately sought their aid for both her charges, Torve and Phemanderac. The philosopher's cough was back, rattling his chest, and Torve was hot and feverish.

'Infection was almost a certainty,' Stella remarked, her voice low.

'Will it kill him?' Lenares asked her.

'Don't know. Phemanderac is our best physic, but he's in no condition to help Torve. We'll get no assistance from anyone in Padouk. We need to find someone soon though.'

Her numbers told her that the queen was more worried than she was saying. So Lenares had taken one handle of the improvised stretcher they had prepared and told them to hurry.

She tugged back the blanket and took stock of the Omeran. His face was hot and running with sweat, his eyes glassy. The inflamed red mess around his groin – oh, *Torve!* – seemed almost to glow with a malicious light, and red lines were creeping up towards his stomach and down his thighs.

'You are getting sick,' she whispered in his ear. She didn't want the others to hear what she said to Torve; already she felt mortified knowing what they knew about. Those things ought to be private! It was as though they had been watching, and although they had all been polite, keeping an eye on Torve's worsening condition as they made their way through the jungle, she could sense some of them had questions they would never ask her.

None of her fellow travellers were Amaqi, though, and that made everything much easier to bear. These people didn't know that Omerans were considered animals. Well, they knew, because Lenares had told them, but they didn't believe it. Nor would they believe Lenares herself was considered a half-wit by many Amaqi. Had Captain Duon still been with them, she would have found things far more difficult.

So many pressures.

It took an hour for anyone to remember the porters. Kilfor asked where they had gone, and Moralye was forced to admit they'd sneaked away during the night. Good, Lenares thought. They were her brothers, but she'd felt nothing but anger towards them.

They reached the forest floor at dusk, though it was difficult to tell due to the persistent rain and low cloud cover. There had been no night in the House of the Gods – which was odd, Lenares told herself, given she and Torve had spent a night in the House back at Marasmos – and everyone was very tired. Kilfor had hurt himself, stumbling on a ladder and ricking his knee, and hobbled with Stella's guard, Robal, supporting him under one shoulder. Robal himself wore a rough rag bandage on his right arm, having caught the tip of a blade, but had taken no serious harm. Heredrew and Stella walked wearily together at the rear of the group, just behind Sauxa, Mustar and the miners who were now carrying Torve's litter. Moralye and Phemanderac completed the party stumbling along just behind Lenares, he mumbling feverish words to the woman in a language the cosmographer could not understand.

They were in trouble, she knew. No one could tell what direction to take to get them out of the forest. They had no plans to find shelter for the night, and were quite soaked by the rain. It was not cold, but night would likely bring sickness. Noetos, their leader, was gone in search of his daughter and the other two voice-possessed, or at least that had been his son Anomer's guess. And Anomer had himself left the group near the base of the Canopy, remaining there to wait for his father.

That left Heredrew. A number of the others, primarily his Falthan companions, were somewhat unwilling to accept his guidance. Not surprising, she thought, considering his numbers: the man was nearly a god himself. He had been alive for centuries and had many magical powers, though apparently healing others was not one of his strongest. Nor was trustworthiness. What she could clearly see – that deception and falsehood were his defining characteristics – the others no doubt intuited, or had learned from experience.

So the leadership had fallen to her. Tired, wet, injured, sick and apathetic, none of the others had the energy. But, for all her self-confidence, Lenares knew she was a fraud. What did she know about leadership? She was a cosmographer, the only cosmographer left in the world, but her leadership was spiritual, not practical. Now that she had no centre, she had no way of leading the travellers in the right direction. Worse, the travellers did not even have a common direction in mind, so which way was correct?

So on they stumbled, led by a fraud, one eye open for pursuit, the other closed in exhaustion.

By the time full night arrived, Lenares was sobbing with pain. Her clothes were wet through, chafing her skin until it was raw and, in some places, bleeding. Her limbs were leaden, her whole body shaking with weariness beyond belief. Worse, she had failed those she led. A while ago Anomer had emerged from the side of the path they had taken and, after greeting the others, had drawn her aside and told her they were only a few hundred paces from the Canopy. She must have led them in a circle, yet she had tried so hard, been so careful to keep behind her the place where she thought the sun had set. At least the boy hadn't told everyone of her failure, but the smarter ones would be able to work it out.

At his words she had nearly collapsed where she stood.

'Lead us,' she said to him. Pleaded with him. 'I have no idea where we are.'

'I'm not familiar with getting about in a jungle,' Anomer said, shaking his head.

'I only know the desert,' Lenares replied. 'Big spaces and wide-open skies. It's a place of truth where everything can be seen. I cannot find myself properly in a land where the horizon is only a few paces away. So much is hidden.'

'I think I understand.'

Lenares smiled wanly. 'I'm not sure I do.'

'My father is still out there somewhere, searching for my sister and the two others missing. He has led the Padouki warriors away after him, I think, so we should be safe for a time. Nevertheless, we must find somewhere to rest well away from the Canopy.'

'Should we try to help your father?'

Lenares didn't much like the grumpy Noetos, but he was the nearest the group had to a leader. She would put up with him if it meant she didn't have to find a way out of this jungle.

Anomer laughed, a bitter sound. 'He wouldn't thank you for getting in his way. You'd probably end up under a pile of rubble or with a sword in your belly. He's a dangerous man.' He cleared his throat. 'Now come, we have to move.'

As the group trailed after her – still believing she led, not knowing how poorly she served them – Lenares thought for a moment about how sensitive this young man was, and how bitter. And she wondered how long it would be before she became like him.

Later that night, under a stifling blanket of darkness, without any of the stars that signified open heavens, Lenares finally asked herself the question that had been hiding nervously in her mind the whole miserable day.

Am I really the only cosmographer left?

She felt guilty for asking it. What was anything compared to Torve's loss? Yet she could do nothing more for her beloved: she checked him regularly, ensuring he was as comfortable as his wound allowed, trying to get him to take water, and whispering encouragingly to him when no one else was listening.

'Mahudia,' she whispered, and gave her invisible line a little tug. 'Mahudia, are you there?'

The line went somewhere. Not exactly 'up': the hole in the world wasn't a real, physical hole, just as the wall in which it occurred was not a physical wall, even though it manifested itself in the real world from time to time. Not up, but out from herself into the world of people, events and the relationships between them, all bound together inside the wall, something Phemanderac called the Wall of Time.

Tug, tug.

For a while nothing happened; she felt no resistance to her tentative pulling. The fear that the line might snap, or come falling out of the hole to lie uselessly at her feet, kept her from applying any real pressure. She whispered her foster mother's name, half-afraid that Keppia or Umu would overhear her and come roaring down the line, mouth open wide to engulf her.

'Mahudia?'

It began as a faint ripple in the line, a slight tensioning, as though the connection had snagged on something.

'Is that you?'

Yes, came a reply, not in words or anything else Lenares could describe objectively. A sort of vibration coupled with the barest sense of a personality. But where was she feeling the vibration? Not in her real hands. And her eyes did not see Mahudia's face, but it was there nonetheless, as wispy and ephemeral as smoke.

This could be a trap. Perhaps Umu had hold of her string and was trying to ensnare her. But there was no way she could prove who was at the other end, and she so wanted her mother . . .

I saw what they did to Torve, said Mahudia.

Lenares began to cry, huge heaving sobs that seemed to tear her rib cage on the way out. She ran further into the pitch-black forest so as not to wake the others. So as not to be seen crying. She cried for what seemed like hours, wishing she could feel Mahudia's arms around her. Listening to the cosmographer's words of comfort.

'What's happening?' she asked her mentor eventually, when the hiccoughs had subsided. 'What am I doing wrong?'

I don't see very much from here, Lenares, said the voice at the other end of the string. *I'm not a god. Just a lost soul out here beyond time, drawn close to your warmth and now bound in your trap.*

'Am I holding you? Should I set you free?'

No, dear, you misunderstand me. I am bound because I choose to be. This is the place I can help you most.

'Does it hurt, Mahudia? Is it a terrible thing to be dead?'

Yes, sweetheart, it hurts. But it hurt even more to be alive, and those who choose to be content out here in the void can forget about the pain of life and just learn to be. I'm sorry, Lenares, I have no words for this. But it does hurt to be near the breach in the Wall of Time, to see someone I love in distress. The closer I get to you, the more life pulls at me, draining me of the serenity I feel here.

'I don't want to hurt you.'

And I don't want you to be hurt. I left you exposed, my dear foster daughter, because I insisted on occupying myself with that dreadful man Chasico. This is my way of making it up to you. We don't feel guilt here, but then there usually isn't anything we can do to put right what we've done.

Something occurred to Lenares as Mahudia whispered to her, and her drawn face became animated. 'Could I pull you back into the world? Could I make you alive again? I could, couldn't I? Let me do it, Mahudia, please.'

No, little one. The breach isn't yet wide enough. You would destroy the barrier between you and the timeless void. Countless numbers would die, exposed to the cold austerity of eternity.

'I don't understand.'

Keppia and Umu seek to come back into the world, body and soul. To do this they have to destroy time. This means undoing enough of the relationships between people – the things people do, say and think; the events that separate one moment in time from another – that time begins to lose its meaning. You will notice the effects before long.

'Like time repeating itself? People saying and doing the same things?'

92

Ah, that has happened already, has it? Unless the gods are stopped, it will happen again and again, more and more often, until all times recur at once.

'Can you help me stop them, Mahudia?'

A long pause. The rain, now diminished to a light drizzle, pattered down on the trees overhead.

No. The answer came as little more than a breath.

'What can you do?' The girl's voice came out as a timid squeak. 'Can you do anything to help me?'

I can give you advice, Lenares, but I must be careful. If Umu finds me anywhere near the hole she will destroy me utterly. She knows someone up here aided you in her capture. It wasn't your numbers, you know. You were wrong, my dear: that dividing by zero method just served to focus your mind. It was me. I used your link to the hole in the world to trap her.

'Can we do it again?'

She will destroy me. No doubting the fear in Mahudia's voice.

'But you're already dead,' Lenares said, knowing how selfish she sounded. How could she know what Mahudia endured in that cold place beyond time, or how much it pained her to draw close to the world?

I am dead, Mahudia said, a faint hint of steel in her words. *Eaten by a lion. Eaten by Umu herself, hence my link to her and the source of my ability to help you trap her. If she sees me here she will know what I did, and she will absorb what's left of me into herself. It is what they do, these terrible gods: prey on the souls in repose beyond the sky. If she finds me I will become her food. That has already happened once, child. If it happens again I will cease to exist.*

'I understand,' Lenares said, her voice low.

I see you do. Genuine warmth infused her mentor's words. *I never would have believed it, my Lenares, but you are developing empathy. My child, growing up.*

'I'm not your child, not really. I met my real family, you know. They were not very nice.'

I wondered if you would. Dear one, don't be distressed at what you found, nor surprised your feet led you there. You are exposed to the

93

pattern of time, and the gods are pulling the threads. It is no wonder you ended up back where your thread began. Be happy you escaped your family when you were young. And now at least you have met your other half, and you can combine your strength against the gods.

Lenares held her breath a moment, trying to work out what Mahudia meant by that, especially the last. It was almost taking shape in her mind.

'My other half?' she asked. 'What do you mean?'

The faintest of hisses came from the thread binding her and Mahudia. *Have you not – but that was the whole purpose!* A silence, then, in a calmer voice: *Ignore me, child, I do not see too well from where I stand. I must go now. Already I have been here too long. I must not be discovered.*

'Please, don't go! Explain to me what you meant by my other half. Do you mean Torve? Is he my other half?'

She waited, but there was no reply. The thread hung motionless before her. But despite her desire to learn more she would not tug on it again, not now at least. Not if her Mahudia was in danger from Umu. If only she had not let the treacherous god go!

The pain had subsided to a dull discomfort, but Torve knew the amount of pain associated with the cut itself was irrelevant. He was ill with corruption. His wound had become infected and without medicine he would die. No one said this openly to him; his new companions spoke encouraging words, but they would abandon him when he became too inconvenient. It was what people always did with Omerans, after all. Even Lenares would leave, driven by her obsessive compulsion to search for and destroy the gods.

He wished they would abandon him. He liked the forest, its blanket of leaves, its thick silences and warm, moist breath. So much better than the stark, sterile desert where one was exposed to the world's mocking gaze. Nothing but heartache came from the sands and rocks of Elamaq. Let the others go on to do whatever it was they felt they had to do, while he remained here, lying still as the leaves filtered down to smother his face, as he decayed into the rich soil of the forest floor.

'Feeling sorry for yourself, lad?'

Torve still struggled a little with the Bhrudwan language, but Heredrew spoke with such clarity he was easy to follow. 'You read minds,' he replied.

'No, but yours is a face with few secrets.' The tall Falthan hunched down beside him. 'You're gravely ill, my friend. You ought to feel sorry for yourself.'

Torve smiled. It hurt to smile, he discovered; his cheeks and his forehead ached for a few moments after he carefully relaxed his muscles. 'They have not told me, but I know. I will not leave the forest alive, it seems. Please tell the others to go on without me.'

'I will do something better, but only if you keep my secret.'

'Secret? What use is a secret to me?'

'This one could rip our little group apart.' The man's elongated, bony hand shot out and grabbed Torve's arm. 'You kept secret an emperor's identity, they tell me. I command you to keep my identity just as secret.'

Torve hadn't known it was possible, hadn't thought it through, but as the compulsion took him he realised he had been a fool. Omerans would always be susceptible to commands. He had not overcome three thousand years of breeding after all. His surprise deepened into shock. It wasn't just the realisation that shook him. Heredrew was doing something to his body. The strangest, most unsettling mixture of warmth and cold had begun to flow into his arm, and from there, it seemed, directly into his blood. He began to fizz as though someone had exchanged his blood for fire. His muscles spasmed and shook and his spine began to arch.

'Bite on this,' the Falthan instructed him, and forced a stick into his mouth.

The pain intensified, the darkness around him seemed to flee and he could suddenly see everything – trees, rain, people – in shades of white. The pain moved down his limbs to his torso, and from there centred on his groin, a mounting conflagration of agony. He found himself grinding his teeth on the stick. His head jerked back and he looked up into Heredrew's eyes – and saw a monster. A face cracked like a dry lake bed, eyes mere pits in the skull, skin raw and ancient, a nose eroded to little more than a scarred nub.

Heredrew's secret.

'Thus I am exposed to you,' the Falthan – or perhaps not Falthan – man said, his normal rich voice replaced by a dry rasp. 'Keep this secret if you want to keep your healing.'

The pain began to subside. Torve lifted a hand to his mouth and brushed away the remnants of the stick.

'I can offer you nothing but my thanks,' he said.

'I don't deserve them. I have not healed you fully, lad, and for that I apologise, but there are reasons. First, I don't want this to look too suspicious, and I am reluctant for our companions to recall my previous healing. Second, I have someone else to heal tonight, and I must husband my remaining strength after the events of the last few days.'

'But I don't—'

'Say nothing of this. Remain where you are and allow the others to minister to you without comment. Do not question me about this now or at any time in the future. And above all, keep my secret. Do you understand?'

Torve nodded, but he understood nothing. As the magician walked stiffly away, he whispered: 'But I don't know what your secret means.'

The man did not hear him, or, if he did, chose not to acknowledge his words.

Later that night Lenares came to see him. She would know, he could not keep his healing from her; but he tried, pretending he was asleep. It seemed, however, she was not aware of the change in his numbers. Something had blinded her.

'Torve, Torve, I'm so sorry,' she whispered as she ran her fingers gently through his hair. 'I did this to you, I was so selfish, I wanted you so much, I liked how you felt when you pressed close to me. I knew Dryman didn't want us to . . . to whatever.'

She couldn't say the word even now; perhaps she didn't know any words for it. Warm, salty drops began to patter onto his forehead.

'I should have figured out who Dryman was, but I didn't think like Mahudia taught me.' Her voice had thickened and she spoke louder, loud enough, perhaps, to have woken him had he in truth been asleep. 'I was proud. I didn't think anyone could keep secrets from me, even though I understood you couldn't tell me what you knew. I was proud and I was stupid.'

She began to sob.

'I even let Umu go. If I had held onto her I could have made her heal you. And then I had to watch as Dryman took his knife to you.'

Nothing more for a while, just more tears on his face and her thick breathing. His healing was hidden from her by her own grief.

He felt so deceitful. What he ought to do was to open his eyes and offer whatever comfort remained for him to give. He ought to tell her he was healed. But he couldn't. Trapped by who he was, by who he'd been bred to be, Torve lay there helpless as his Lenares sobbed out her heart, apologising to him again and again, until her words and her tears faded into cold silence.

She finally sighed one last time and left him. He lay there the remainder of the long night, thoroughly desolate.

Across the sheltered campsite from where Torve lay, Lenares hunched in on herself and tried to gather her thoughts. Mahudia was dead and hidden from her; Torve was dying – he hadn't even stirred when she'd blubbed all over him; and Mahudia had said that Lenares had made a mistake with her calculations. She was dizzy with confusion and loss: not only was the love she had barely discovered about to be taken from her, she had clearly lost her mathematical infallibility. One mistake, that was all it took, and she could no longer trust herself. What other mistakes might she be making? Who might suffer as a result?

The nearest she could come to her possible error was in the application of Qarismi of Kutrubul's dividing by zero. Mahudia had hinted at it. Qarismi's theorem had been how she ensnared the Daughter: dividing the hole in the world by nothing and creating a web to catch her. It had worked too, or so she'd thought.

Ought she to have divided the hole in the world by zero, or divided zero by the hole in the world? There was a clear mathematical difference: one made no sense. She could not remember which one she had attempted. The thought cheered her a little; she could accept a mistake in her understanding or application of a principle, but not one of computation.

Her ragged breathing slowed. She had not truly realised just how much she relied on her ability with numbers to define who she was. If she should lose that . . . would it honestly be more of a loss than losing Mahudia or Torve?

Yes, she whispered to herself, deeply ashamed.

'Your thoughts must be important ones,' said a voice beside her, so close she could feel the speaker's breath tickle her ear.

'Don't—' *touch me*, she was going to say, but she held her tongue as she tried to work out who it was. His face was barely visible in the darkness.

'Anomer?'

'Sorry to frighten you,' the boy said. He crouched down on his haunches and turned his face slightly away from her, allowing a little light from the cloud-shrouded moon to illuminate his features. 'I could hear you talking to yourself and wondered if you wanted company.'

The words formed themselves in a line on her tongue, ready to be delivered: *No, go away and leave me alone, tend to your own business*. It was what she wanted to say, what she would have said before coming on this journey. But she knew it would be rude to say those words, and Anomer had been kind to her earlier, not telling the others how badly she had led them.

'Thank you, I would like that,' she forced herself to say.

Was it telling lies like this that had undermined her ability with numbers and caused her to miscalculate? She wondered if her numbers required literal honesty, and if her attempts at being like others would eventually make her like everyone else: innumerate and lost.

'Sorry to blunder in on you with no warning,' he said, smiling. He really did have nice teeth.

'It was my fault,' she replied. 'I thought I was leading everyone sonwards, but I must have brought them around in a huge circle.'

'I meant now, Lenares, not yesterday afternoon. Though I hope I didn't frighten you then either.'

She could feel herself turning red. 'You didn't frighten me. But I was scared when I found out we had gone in a circle. Can you find your way through jungle like this?'

'I found you, didn't I?' Not the answer he had given her earlier.

'Then you could lead us,' Lenares said, unable to keep the hope from surging through her voice. 'Without your father here, no one seems to know where we should be going.'

'Ah, there it is. As to that, my father is searching for my sister and the two others still missing. I must pursue them and offer any assistance I can. But I will find them and bring them back. We will all gather together again and decide then what to do: whether to continue following my father's fixation with the Undying Man or strike out in some different direction. But if you are looking for a leader, why not follow Heredrew? He seems a knowledgeable and trustworthy man.'

Lenares was about to reply when a shriek ripped the night in two.

Dulled by her lack of sleep, Lenares trailed Anomer by seconds, but despite catching an ankle on a hidden obstacle of some kind – possibly a root – she arrived at the source of the noise before anyone else. The screaming sounds came from the normally quiet woman Moralye, who was shaking as she made the unearthly noise. She stood over a prone body as though preparing to defend it. A dead body.

'What's wrong, Moralye, what's wrong?' Stella asked, rushing towards them, then looked down and gasped.

Lenares could have told them. Would have, but she had learned they didn't like her displaying her facility with numbers. She'd only taken a glimpse at the woman's half-obscured face, but that had been enough.

'He's dead!' Moralye said, her voice starting to crack. 'He won't wake up!'

Lenares found herself frightened by the intensity of the woman's emotion. While she herself had managed to grieve after a time, it had been in private; she would have been mortified had anyone witnessed her distress. But Moralye didn't seem to mind who knew she suffered.

Isn't this a kind of truth you cannot emulate? a sly thought said. *By hiding your feelings, aren't you lying to the world? By expressing hers, isn't Moralye telling the truth?*

Lenares wanted to ignore the idea, but she sensed an important truth in the words, waiting to be unpacked. She put it aside for the moment, to be examined later.

Stella's face underwent a series of changes so swift none but Lenares would have noted them. Shock, denial, even momentary relief as her mind rejected what she saw; then horror tinged with acceptance and the beginnings of anger.

'Who did this to him?' the Falthan queen asked as she bent over the unmoving figure and began to remove the thin blankets he'd been wrapped in.

'I don't know,' Moralye answered, her voice spiralling down towards normality. 'He was . . . he was like this when I made to wake him for a dose of his medicine.'

'Medicine?' Stella turned her face, hardened by anger, to the young woman. 'What medicine? Why does he need it?'

'I have been administering it twice daily: once at midday and again in the early hours of the morning. He needs it for his chest. You knew he was ill. Surely you have heard his laboured breathing? Have you not seen me crushing the roots?'

'I knew he was sick, yes, but not that he was close to death. Why did you not say?'

Moralye wilted under the hardness of the woman's face. 'I did say. At least, I said he was unwell. Remember, I stayed behind with him when the rest of you went up to the Canopy. He instructed me as to what root to seek out and the correct dosage to administer. I did not realise he was in serious danger of dying. I did nothing wrong.' Her face crumpled and she began to sob. 'I forgot that every sickness in someone so old brings them near to death.'

'But you did do something wrong,' Lenares said, and the pale faces of those awoken by the noise swung towards her. 'At least, you think you did.'

This was both right and wrong, Lenares realised, as she found herself caught between two conflicting thoughts. Right, because the woman was desperate to hide something, and deception should always be uncovered. Wrong, because Anomer had helped Lenares hide something only a few hours ago.

The woman put her hands to her face, obscuring any view Lenares might get of her numbers.

'I . . . I don't know,' she said eventually. 'I think I may have given him his medicine twice yesterday. I was tired, so tired, and I became confused.' Moralye cleared her throat, then raised her voice a little. 'As well as being one of the greatest scholars in this age of the world, he had become my friend. I would not willingly do anything to hurt him. But I . . . I couldn't remember if I had dosed him at midday, so I gave him a dose mid-afternoon. He was coughing so, and there was blood in his sputum. I couldn't remember!'

Stella reached up and pulled the woman down beside her. Both faces were streaked with tears. Lenares realised the light was growing: dawn was coming belatedly to the Padouk forest.

'I doubt your actions killed him,' the queen said to the young scholar, her own voice rasping with hurt. 'But you should have told us he was so badly ill. There is at least one among us who has demonstrated a past facility with healing. Heredrew might have been able to save him. He has on at least one occasion previously.'

'I'm so sorry,' Moralye said, her voice relapsing into a wail. 'I thought he knew his own condition. I trusted him to tell me if . . . He said nothing, made no complaint, so I thought . . . I'm sorry!'

So Heredrew is a healer! Lenares had not seen that in the man's numbers; but then, he wore his face like a mask. What might a healer be able to do with Torve? Ease his passing? Keep him alive? Make him whole again?

'Phemanderac was the most beautiful person I ever met,' Stella said simply, standing and wiping her eyes. 'But for his intervention,

Faltha would have been lost to the Destroyer a generation ago. He is a hero whose true tale has never been told.'

Moralye groaned like a woman in pain as she got to her feet. 'He was the most important man in Dhauria. The young scholars worshipped him.'

'I wish Leith was here to say something,' said the queen, 'but as he is not, I will say it for him. Phemanderac loved Leith like a brother, and more; but never once behaved in anything other than an appropriate manner. For that, and for many other things, he earned our undying respect.'

A deep voice came from somewhere in the shadows. 'The man had a sharp mind. He taught me a great deal about how to think.'

Sometimes Lenares could decipher a lot from what someone said, even if she couldn't see them. *Heredrew knows something about this death.*

This time she would keep quiet; this time she would not embarrass someone who, in all likelihood, had an innocent explanation for the way his numbers added up. Instead, she would seek him out later and ask him to explain himself.

The prospect made her instantly nervous, even a little frightened, though she could see no reason for her fear. She had faced the Emperor himself, a much more ruthless man than this kind if somewhat austere Falthan, and had bested him with nothing more than the truth.

'To come so far,' Stella said, 'only to fall in an unfamiliar land. It is an injustice.' She choked back tears. 'I'm sorry, old friend, that we dragged you into this.'

Those gathered around the cold body of the Dhaurian scholar continued to share their observations on his life; sombre words interspersed with lengthy silences as a watery sun rose to send slivers of light shining through the trees. The morning dawned cloudy but dry, with the promise of real heat later: already the bushes and trees had begun steaming. Around them the forest lay quiet save for the muted chatter of birds; the animals no doubt keeping their distance. It seemed, though, that the trees held their breath in honour of the dead man. Fanciful – no doubt the cessation of the storm led to the feeling of peace – but even Lenares felt it.

She remained some distance apart, listening to the expressions of grief with one ear while worrying at how she would approach Heredrew, this man who frightened her; how she would convince him to help Torve, and what, if anything, she should say about his involvement in the death of the scholar.

Torve eased himself to his feet. For the first time since the events in the House of the Gods he experienced no pain, just a general tiredness little different from the soreness one feels after a long day's walk. He spent a moment stretching his muscles, then picked his way over to where the travellers stood in a circle. His Lenares stood a little way from the others and so she saw him first.

She shrieked out his name. Every head turned in her direction, then to him as she raised her arm, pointed and ran towards him, her face open and hungry.

Torve held his breath. Perhaps twenty paces separated them. Twenty paces and the loss of his manhood. Not a distance that could ever be spanned. Yet Lenares seemed to have forgotten his loss; her naked hunger burned itself on his mind, frightening in its intensity. Lips parted, nostrils flared, eyes wide open. A pace short of him she froze, her face suddenly stricken, and reached out a hand hesitantly; it was as though the life had gone out of her. Everything he had feared.

'Torve, are you . . . I don't want to – please, Torve, don't go!'

But he turned away anyway, unable to face her intensity, and he strode off towards the forest, head down as though flinching from a blow.

CHAPTER 5

THE VOLUNTEER

'HE'S STILL TRACKING US.' THERE was anger and not a little admiration in Duon's voice.

'Just our luck,' Conal growled. 'That *canone* will never give up.'

'Foul language for a priest,' Duon said, and felt a little hypocritical, having taught him the word in the first place. Duon had used it frequently in the last two days.

'Not a priest, not any longer. Just a hunk of meat. I can't do anything he doesn't want me to.'

For the third time that afternoon the man took the sharpened stick and thrust it towards his own stomach; as with the first two attempts, his hand stopped abruptly just short of piercing the skin. Duon was sure it was no act.

Arathé mouthed her words and waved her hands desultorily, saying something like, 'He won't let us die.' It was hard to tell exactly; she was so tired her hands didn't form the words properly.

Captain Duon would never have believed he would be wishing for his own death. Even after the horror of the Valley of the Damned, when as leader of the Emperor's army he'd lost thirty thousand men, he had not sought to end his life. He'd thought then that he'd known despair, but what he had felt then was akin to joy compared to this. This complete loss of self. Slavehood without a moment's respite. Of course he wanted to live, but he'd take death over a continued existence as the puppet of a cruel magician.

'Your father will keep tracking us,' the priest said. '*Canone.*'

He seemed to enjoy the flavour of the word, the smuttiness of it. Small rebellions, all they were capable of.

Duon sighed. 'Noetos wanted us to go our own way, but now he comes after us. The faster he comes, the harder the voice drives us.' *I just want to lie down.*

Never. You're mine until you burn out.

Physically sick at the sound of the voice, Duon responded with anger. *May the hour come soon, especially if it inconveniences you.*

His words had as much effect as a gnat biting a horse, he had to acknowledge. Certainly not worth the voice answering him.

Noetos had trailed them ever since the voice had led them down from the Canopy. They hadn't been difficult to track, Duon surmised: one by one each of them had tested themselves against the hold on them. The resultant struggles gave the fisherman noise, broken foliage and, in Arathé's case, blood to follow. All the efforts proved futile, as Duon guessed they would, but each of them would keep trying, he was sure.

To escape the hold the voice had on him was now the sole desire in Duon's heart. Arathé had told them of the indignities the voice had forced her to commit, and he had seen for himself the way her body had been possessed. The voice had done similar things to him, he knew, though at the time they had seemed praiseworthy. The inhuman speed and strength in the Summer Palace; the ability to swim even with a broken leg; surely they had been sign enough. But because their effect had been laudable, he'd not questioned the voice closely.

Not that it would have mattered. The voice had demonstrated his absolute mastery of his charges, and their fate was clear. He would continue to reside in their minds, his presence making Duon sick to his stomach, and whisper his mocking words while scheming new atrocities for them to commit. Then he would take possession of their bodies, compelling them to do his will. And so it would go until they died, discarded, hands and hearts blackened by all they had been forced to do.

There must be some way out of this dilemma, he thought – knowing he was likely overheard, but safe in the knowledge that the voice would expect such thoughts. And this was their first and greatest problem: they needed to find some way of communicating with each other without being overheard by the voice. Duon never knew when he was under observation. Lately it seemed the voice hovered constantly in his mind. So there was no way even of telling the others to think of ways to outwit the voice. He assumed Arathé might have an idea or two, but held little hope that Conal would add anything. The man had been pitifully self-absorbed since the three of them had been thrown together.

Duon had a few ideas of his own, so tenuous he had barely thought about them – which was exactly how they had to stay, given his enemy could pluck the thoughts from his mind. Maybe he already had, and even now sat back laughing at Duon's futile efforts. This was his greatest fear.

Arathé's method of communication, part vocal, part physical, was a code of sorts. There was a good possibility the voice hadn't learned her code; why should he, given he could discern the thoughts behind it? Perhaps Duon could slip a few oblique coded phrases into their conversation, sideways as it were, so as not to attract the voice's attention. Worryingly, it might be that Arathé was already trying to pass him messages in her hand signals, which could explain why they appeared different. Not exhaustion at all.

Only one way to find out.

The voice drove them through another copse, uncaring of the prickles and barbs plucking and cutting at them, seemingly un-interested as to whether Noetos could use the disturbance to track them. Duon held Arathé's gaze for a moment longer than usual, then made a tiny gesture with one hand. One. First the numbers from one to nine, then progress to simple words. Surely she would catch on.

By late that day Arathé had more than caught on. The trick, Duon realised, was to consider neither what he was doing nor why he did it; that way the voice was less likely to tumble to their plan. He would form a 'natural' thought – how *tall* those *six* trees were;

how *quickly* the *sky* grew *dark* – and make Arathé's word-gesture as he thought the word. Before the middle of the day the young woman had taken the lead; now he echoed her gestures, learning them, but being careful not to repeat them until sufficient time had passed. *Progress* was frustratingly *slow* – he fumbled the complex gestures for frustration – but within a *day* or two they would be able to *hold* a *conversation* in private.

You are up to something, the voice said, cutting across his thoughts. Pain speared through Duon's temples as though his head had been placed in a vice. *Conspiring against me?*

Hardly. Icy fear materialised in his stomach, spreading quickly to his limbs. *Just bored.*

You're not talking to each other. A sigh of mock exasperation. *Given up already? That would be disappointing.*

What remains to be talked about? You have us, heart and soul. We breathe only because you allow it. Each of us has tried to commit suicide and you have prevented us. At least you have separated us from our companions, so their lives are not endangered by our presence. You heard our speculation as to what your plan for us might be.

All the time he signalled, tiny gestures with his hands, hoping Arathé could interpret them. Learning, learning all the time.

I do have a task for you, the voice said in tones infused with unholy satisfaction. *In fact,* it continued, amplified now so it rang throughout his head, obliterating all extraneous thought and sensation – Duon knew this meant all three of them were hearing the words – *I want you to take cover behind those limestone bluffs to your left.*

A pause, and a sigh, and the pressure relented for a moment. Duon glanced ahead: the trees thinned out, exposing an old man's ragged mouthful of rotten teeth-like rock jutting up from green gums. Perfect cover, backlit by the sun, making it impossible for one coming upon them to tell if an ambush had been laid. A dreadful suspicion began to form in Duon's mind.

Fool priest, those pale stones that look like columns. Listen carefully, all of you. Hide from the path and make yourselves comfortable. No noise at all – no talking, no whispering. You think you know how

107

bad I can make things for you? You don't know a fraction of what I am capable.

Arathé must have guessed the voice's intention also, for she began struggling with a desperate intensity. Duon felt the response as pain in his mind, and could only wonder how terribly the girl suffered. She threw herself to the ground – or was thrown – snatched at a rock and tried to dash it against her own temple, but instead threw it away with a despairing cry. After a few moments' juddering and shaking she rose stiffly to her feet and continued forward as though nothing had happened, the only evidence of the battle of wills an almost inaudible wail issuing from between her bloodless lips.

Under instructions to leave as little evidence of their passing as possible, the three captives scrambled up a short slope of broken rock and passed between two tall pillars into a shadowed recess.

Sleep, the voice commanded.

Disheartened, Duon realised the voice's power over them was increasing over time. He now had the power to—

Judging by the lengthening shadows, Duon regained consciousness perhaps two hours later. The girl and the priest slept on, weariness drawn roughly on their young faces. Duon kept his mind at rest, his thoughts slow, to defeat any trigger the voice might have set to alert him to his captives' wakefulness. *He can't be observing us all the time*, Duon reasoned, *or he in turn would be little more than our captive. He must have other things to do; surely he must relax his control at some point.*

What he intended to do was a risk. He moved slowly, wriggling his body and extending his arm so his left hand lay in the sunlight between the two tall limestone pillars. The lowering sun cast his shadow down towards the path; he tested it by moving his fingers. Barely visible, but if the man was as good as Duon thought he was, it might well be enough.

Soon he heard the rattle and rustle of someone coming up the path. Beside him Arathé and Conal stirred, then sat up.

Think of other things. How to give Arathé a warning not *to speak, not to warn her* father *of the* danger *he is in, perhaps by* shouting *the word* ambush.

The voice came alive, crushing his thought. *You'll not warn her of anything. You think she doesn't know? I told her myself. She deserves to know it will be by her hand her father will die.*

Up! the voice shouted, and his power impelled them to their feet. One after the other the three emerged from the crevice and together they rushed down the slope. Partway Arathé stumbled on a boulder and fell on her face.

Clever girl, Duon acknowledged. Her bravery – or desperation – was undeniable.

Noetos awaited them at the base of the slope. Duon's warning had worked – to a point.

Fool fisherman! You ought to have fled!

Conal and Duon were on him in a moment, knocking him to the ground. Duon had no idea what the man had been expecting, but clearly it had not been an attack from his companions. It seemed he still did not truly appreciate the nature of their possession. In those first few moments of scratching, biting and rending, the two men taught him better.

With astonishing strength Noetos threw them off and staggered to his feet, bleeding from half a dozen places on calf, thigh, arm and face. 'What are you doing?' he had time to cry before Arathé, screaming in terror and revulsion, was thrown into the battle.

You have a sword, fisherman. Use it! We beg you! But Duon could not shout the words: the voice still had hold of his throat.

He snatched up a lump of wood and began slamming it into the man's back and side, each blow drawing a grunt. *Fight back!* he begged the fisherman. But the man merely countered their attack, slithering out of their grasp again and again.

A thought insinuated itself into Duon's mind as his teeth found purchase in the soft area above the fisherman's knee. *Arathé has magic: why doesn't the voice attack Noetos through his daughter's magical ability? Could it be he cannot control it?*

Examine it later, he decided.

Something thumped him a heavy blow on the forehead, sending

him spinning away onto the rocks. Against his will he stood up, then spat something out. Flesh. He would have thrown up if he could.

As his vision cleared, Duon realised a second person had joined Noetos in the affray. The man's face was familiar, but for a moment he couldn't place it.

The swordmaster.

The Padouki warrior stood alongside Noetos. His sword remained sheathed, the man doubtless under instruction not to harm his assailants. Clearly some agreement had been struck, though who could know what Noetos might have been able to offer the Padouki to abandon his people. Duon's muscles tensed, ready to resist his captor.

Stop fighting me, the voice commanded. Duon heard the compulsion in the words, though not their full force; they had not been meant for him. Clearly Arathé was giving him trouble. Duon would have cheered.

Because you'll ruin everything, the voice responded in anger to an unheard thought. An answer to Arathé perhaps. *Your struggles might reduce me, but you'll never defeat me. Even when you came closest to death I survived. And I am stronger now than I was then, far stronger.*

The voice is vulnerable, Duon realised.

No more time to speculate as they were thrown back into the wrestling match. A shriek from Arathé as the Padouki's booted foot took her in the mouth. She tumbled away, blood streaming across her face. Duon found himself circling the fisherman, who stood favouring one leg, partly because of the bite Duon had taken from it. Conal lay a few paces away, moaning feebly.

'You should not be able to resist me,' the voice said through Duon's mouth.

'Unless, of course, I have assistance from another such as you,' came Noetos's reply, delivered through swollen lips.

'Another? One of the gods perhaps?'

'Implying that you are not,' Noetos said, and smiled. 'Every contact we have with you makes you weaker. You reveal yourself without gaining anything in return. Soon we will discover who and where you are. You are not safe from us. When we find you we will kill you.'

Duon's mouth hissed at the man.

'I know you are not doing this, Duon. We will take our leave now and trust you to work out a way to defeat your captor. Please try, for the sake of my daughter.' The fisherman glanced at where Arathé even now scrambled to her feet. 'I undertake to stay away from you, Arathé, so you need not concern yourself with killing me. Between us we will work out a way to see your captor driven out. I am not abandoning you.'

Her reply was to throw herself at her father, hands outstretched, fingers spread like claws. He darted backwards, moving with astonishing speed for such a big man, and avoided her lunge. Within moments the pair of them had sprinted back down the path towards the forest and disappeared into the shadows.

The voice in Duon's mind cried out in wordless rage, but behind the roar Duon fancied he could hear two thoughts joining his own in delight.

The travellers came to the end of the forest late on the third day down from the Canopy. There had been no serious pursuit; twice they had encountered lone forest-dwellers, but news of events must have circulated, as in both cases the men fled.

They emerged from the forest at the crest of a minor escarpment and into the teeth of a stiff breeze. Near the edge of sight, perhaps a morning's journey distant, lay the ocean; above, horsetail clouds reared high into the sky. Between the forest and the sea lay a strip of farmland, already blanketed with twilight. Here and there the lights of houses twinkled amid the rumpled hills.

'Thank you, Lenares, on behalf of us all,' Stella said, as they breathed deeply of the crisp evening air. 'We would likely have walked around in circles forever without your guidance.'

It wasn't me, she wanted to say. *Anomer led us and made it look like I was in charge*. But she held her tongue as Anomer had counselled.

'They want to believe in you as a leader,' he had said earlier in the day, as they scrambled across a limestone ridge. 'The more they trust you, the more likely they will listen to your advice. And, whether you think it or not, you are our hope. Only you seem to understand the hole in the world. We have found ourselves in trouble before after ignoring you. I do not want us to die because we wouldn't listen.'

His words made sense, she wasn't stupid, but the deception still went against everything in her nature. Lying to achieve a greater good. Well, not lying exactly, just failing to tell the whole truth. It all sounded like excuses, and this when a part of her so much wanted to be in charge, loved and adored by those following her. Better not to indulge that feeling, especially when the love and regard had not been earned.

She tried and failed to keep her glance from straying behind her to where Torve stumbled along at the rear of the group. What had she earned there? She'd not had the courage to find out; again, a new experience for her. Once nothing would have stopped her from asking the most awkward of questions of anyone at any time, but now . . . now she understood why some questions were awkward, and why someone might reply evasively if such questions were asked. How her quest for truth had sometimes kept truth from her.

Torve had spent much of the day in conversation with Heredrew. She'd burned with curiosity, but could not bring herself to ask what they discussed so earnestly. Afraid. Such a paralysing emotion, fear. There was no doubt she was becoming more human and less Lenares, and the change frightened her.

It frightened her, but not as much as the red-rimmed smear now edging its way into her consciousness. The hole in the world had returned – so soon, too soon after the Daughter had escaped and the Son had been banished from his earthly body. Lenares had hoped they would have weeks to think of ways to counter the depredations of the gods. But here was the hole, coming closer as though borne on the east wind . . .

She fell to her knees and vomited.

'Lenares, what is wrong?'

For a moment she thought the voice was Torve's, but the hand on her shaking shoulder was pale like hers, not dark. She looked up into Anomer's beautiful, concerned eyes.

'Get everyone together,' she whispered.

An hour later the sun had set and the remains of their meal were being buried, the better to dissuade scavengers from scouting their camp, and by then Lenares had no doubt.

She raised a weary arm and pointed to the east, to the inky darkness. 'The hole in the world is coming,' she told them, and received groans and curses in reply. 'It's in the wind, somehow. One or both of the gods approach us, bringing some calamity with them.'

'Could be a plague,' Kilfor said. 'We get plenty of plagues back home in the Central Plains. Sickness in the air.' Surprisingly, his father nodded his assent.

'Not a plague,' Heredrew said. 'Not coming from the sea. Plagues come from the land.'

'A storm then,' Moralye said. 'Dhauria once suffered a storm so severe the lightning set fires in the lower city. Over twenty people were killed.'

'It's much larger than a storm,' Lenares said. 'The gods want to break open the Wall of Time, and to do that they have to kill thousands and thousands of people. A storm wouldn't do that.'

Another dishonesty: she had no real idea what a storm could do.

She sighed. 'Actually, I don't know how many people a storm could kill. It is hard to imagine wind and rain killing thousands of people.'

There: she felt much better for speaking the truth as she saw it. Even though it reduced her standing in the eyes of the others; at least as Anomer had explained it.

'The east coast sometimes suffers tremendous storms and the flooding can do great damage,' Heredrew said, his eyes narrowing. 'I remember a savage storm sweeping up the Panulo River during the reign of the Red Duke and near destroying the city of Tochar. I was forced—'

His mouth snapped shut.

'Near everyone knows, Kannwar,' said Robal the guard, a strange smile playing on his face. 'Those who don't will soon work it out. How long ago did the Red Duke reign?'

'He died seventy years ago,' said Heredrew, his eyebrows beetling at the guard. 'I've explained that my sorcery has given me a long life.'

'It has,' said Anomer. 'But it doesn't explain why a sorcerer from Faltha remembers a storm that, according to the history I was taught, occurred over a century ago in Bhrudwo – and afterwards, says Abraxi the scholar, was hushed up by the Undying Man. If he were here today I'd ask him why.'

Lenares looked from Robal to Anomer, then took in the expression on Stella's face. What her numbers had not told her, logic began to put together.

'You were never going to keep it secret forever,' Stella said on an exhaled breath.

'You all know?' Heredrew said resignedly.

'What do you care, great man?' Robal's face had turned red with anger. 'Nothing any of us can do about it.'

'What do I care? You fool, I care a great deal! Don't you under-stand, you brainless bull, how much I need the help of everyone here to defeat the gods?' He leaned forward, intimidating without meaning to. 'If any of you walk away, our chances of preventing the world's end diminish to almost nothing. Because so many of you would be . . . threatened by what I am, I have dissembled. Not for my benefit, but for yours!' He sighed. 'More of you apparently know than I believed.'

'Know what?' Moralye asked. 'What is being said? Who are . . . you?' From the look of horror on her face, the revelation hit her between words. 'Oh, oh no, it was you all the time – you allowed us to find Kannwar's old scroll justifying his actions, you have manipulated us ever since.' Her face had turned deathly white. 'Did Phemanderac know?'

'Yes,' Heredrew said simply. 'He knew before we left Dhauria. And no, he didn't approve, but he realised he had no choice. Matters had moved well past his understanding, as I will explain.'

Lenares felt as though she was about to expire. 'Are you the Undying Man? Kannwar of the North? The man my Emperor sought to defeat?' But she knew the answer. The numbers poured through her mind.

The tall man nodded. 'At your service,' he said, and held out his hand.

She slapped it away. 'You lied to me. I can't be of any use to people if they keep *lying* to me! I need truth!'

Red mist swirled in her brain. A small part of her mind spoke. *Don't lose control, they'll think you're a lackwit.*

'Why can't people tell the truth!' she screamed.

Her numbers began appearing in her mind, rising into her consciousness, obliterating her sight. She no longer saw nor cared how the others reacted. She was ready to abandon herself to her sea of numbers, to the way the world really was, when someone whispered in her ear.

'Lenares, I love you. Please don't leave us.'

At his words she fell in a swoon.

'—was all the things you say, and more,' a voice was saying. 'You have every right to be horrified. But as I explained, my goodness or evil is not the issue. I've been asked to do something important that is also in my own interest, and I have agreed.'

Someone said something Lenares did not catch.

'Proud? Of course I am proud! Knowing that, you should ask why I would tolerate being questioned by people like yourself, having to put up with your suspicion and hatred, when I could wipe you out with a gesture. The Lord of Bhrudwo, suffering the scorn of the ignorant! I am here, hazarding so much, including my empire and even my life, to save you and your world.'

Lenares opened her eyes to darkness and a howling wind. The air on her skin was warm, bringing her out in a sweat.

'Why is there a fire?' she asked, her words coming out as a croak. 'It's too hot for a fire.'

'There is no fire,' said a voice in her ear. His voice. 'The wind is warm.'

At his words she relaxed, sank back to the ground and closed her eyes. Let her numbers learn as her ears listened.

'That may be so,' said a Falthan voice. Sauxa. 'But I lost an uncle and three older brothers in the Falthan War. My father told me what it was like having to grovel on the road as you and your army rode by. He told me what you did to those who stood up to you. My father himself lost a hand to one of your generals for refusing to draw water like a woman. Destroyed him, it did.' The man's voice was taut, nothing like the laconic, teasing tone he normally used. 'Even if you offered us eternal life,' he finished, 'I can see no reason to insult his memory by cooperating with you now.'

'You have it all wrong. Well, actually you have it mostly right. But you are not cooperating with me; I am cooperating with you. Isn't it your desire to bring down the gods and heal the hole in the world?'

'Aye, but not at the cost—'

'Then I can help you. In fact, I am commanded to assist you by none less than the Most High himself.'

'Makes no odds,' Kilfor said, his voice prickly like the hiss of a cat. 'We're not staying with you. If I thought it would do any good, I'd bury this knife between your shoulders and consider my life well spent.'

'Already been tried.' The voice was weary. 'Ask your friend Robal how successful he was at killing me. Ask Stella what the consequences were – ask her whether she misses her arm. Please listen: I'm not defending my actions. You already know as much of my story as anyone alive, and more than I'd care to tell you. By your lights I'm evil, and I'll not waste your time denying it. But consider this. You're a farmer, well used to pragmatic decisions: if your hated neighbour died, wouldn't you use his bullock if he left it to you in his will? Wouldn't you count every day on the plough behind that animal as a victory? Don't you see that every day I remain in your service, pulling your plough, is a victory for you? The Most High has had his way with me after all, two thousand years after I first resisted him, and I have had a bare few months

116

to come to terms with the futility of all I have done throughout those long years. It will take time, but you'll come to terms with me, I'm sure.'

'Never,' Sauxa said. 'My sons and I, we're leaving. Come, Robal, be my son in this. Don't submit to this monster.'

Somewhere a woman drew a deep breath but did not speak, and Lenares' numbers filled in the gaps. *Robal will not leave because Stella remains with Heredrew.* Connections between the travellers were more complicated than she'd realised.

'I'm staying,' the soldier said. 'I ignored your advice when you bade me remain in Chardzou and marry your daughter, and well I did, sharp-tongued and loose-moralled as she was. No offence, old man, but I'm telling you the truth and you know it. I'm ignoring your advice again now, even though I know that, against all odds, it's actually good advice. I am a guard, and I'm guarding Stella. I will guard her until she releases me from service.'

The old plainsman struck his leathery palms together in ironic applause. 'Fine speech, son, but your woman don't need guarding. If anything, you need guarding from her. Cards on the table, since we're discussing our business for all to hear: you're staying because you're thinking about what's between her legs. You still think you have a chance with her, while anyone with eyes can see she'll take up with Mister Magicman when all this is over. No, don't interrupt me, boy, nor you, my queen; you owe me at least a few moments' courtesy for all I've done. Robal, you're here to do the dying, while these fine folk play games with the world. What do they care about anything but themselves? When have the nobles and the rich ever cared? And after you and the miners and even young Miss Scholar are dead, all stare-eyed and cold, they'll find solace in each other amid the ruins of the earth. "Oh, if only we could have saved them all," the queen will say. "Let's build a temple here to remember them by," the Destroyer will reply, smiling his most sincere smile. That's how it will go, don't doubt me, son. And the few people left alive will worship the immortals, just as they wish, and we'll be no better off than if the gods had wiped us all out.'

Robal coloured, but took a step towards the belligerent old man.

'So your advice is to do my duty only when there's no danger in it. But as soon as circumstances turn against us, let's bugger off and leave them to it. No, Sauxa, I will stay. You would think less of me if I left with you.'

'You're a fool,' the old man said flatly.

'You'd be the best judge of that,' Kilfor snapped. 'If we're leaving we'd best go now, before my friend persuades me to stay. I'm not sure we wouldn't be safer here with these people, hateful as at least one of them is.'

Lenares opened her eyes. 'Please do not leave us,' she said, and heard the rustle and scrape of people turning towards her. 'Danger draws near, and you will have no protection against it. Remember that Umu and Keppia want your deaths to help break open the Wall of Time. What magic do you have to keep yourselves safe?'

'We might indeed die,' the old man said proudly, 'but at least we'll die free of this man's evil.' He waved a hand towards Heredrew.

'Then go,' the tall sorcerer said. 'But when trouble comes, try to find us. We won't turn you away.'

Within minutes the plainsman and his son collected their gear and strode away. Robal hung his head as they trudged into the forest, intent on retracing their steps all the way back to Faltha.

'Nothing good will come of this,' he muttered, then turned to Heredrew. 'Even when you try to be good, evil comes of it. I heartily wish the Most High's plans did not include you.'

For another full day Duon and Arathé practised their code, debating whether they could trust Conal with their secret.

'We have no choice,' Duon argued, moving his fingers seemingly at random while suiting his thoughts to the signals' meanings. 'I have a plan that must involve him.'

'A plan?' Arathé eventually replied. This code took so long, it was difficult to remember what had been said.

'The voice is vulnerable,' Duon signalled carefully, taking many minutes to frame thoughts capable of carrying the words he wanted. 'He explained this to you. Your struggles weakened him. He had to put forth much strength to keep you alive, making it harder to retain his grip on all three of us. We must damage him more severely still.'

'What are you suggesting?' she gestured slowly. 'That one of us should die?'

'Yes.'

Her fingers stilled for a long time after that.

They continued to walk daughterwards into the lowering sun, talking desultorily as they went, spirits seemingly broken. It was so difficult thinking of innocent thoughts with the code embedded within, while at the same time trying to talk of other things and even on occasion rail at each other and their fate. Duon felt as though his mind had fragmented, one part listening for the voice, another trying to work out what was intended for them – nothing good, he could be sure of that – and still another engaging in the wordplay of their code. He would not have believed he was capable of such mental acrobatics.

'Why does this concern him?' Arathé signalled, flicking a finger towards Conal. 'He won't volunteer. He is more likely to give us away.'

'Because we need all the strength we can get,' Duon replied. 'And Conal is strong.'

'Stubborn.'

'Yes.'

'I volunteer,' Arathé signalled firmly.

'Of course you do. So do I. So this must be decided by chance. Once we have explained things to Conal we will draw lots.'

Duon subsided into silence while Arathé worked at establishing contact with the priest. For the better part of an hour he seemed unresponsive. Duon gritted his teeth and hoped the young woman would not press too hard. It would take only one mistake and the voice would – would what? There was nothing he could do, short of burning out their minds, save pinning their hands to their sides. Even if he realised they had employed a code, he would not be able to understand it, at least not in time.

Understand what? The voice turned up just when least wanted.

Understand what you want with us, Duon extemporised. A chill ran down his back. Had the voice seen through their ruse? *If you are so powerful, why do you need us?*

Warm bodies, Captain. There are things I need to do, people I need to kill or at least delay, and you three are my weapons. Get used to thinking of your body as a killing device. I'm considering making you sharpen your nails and file your teeth. And we need to find blades for you and the little swan. Don't dissemble: I know you're both adept. A shame the fisherman got away. His sword would have been perfect in her hands.

Who are you? He'd asked that question so many times.

The knowledge can do me no harm now, the voice said. *I am halfway to becoming a god. You may call me Husk, the broken man, one who has endured a lifetime of pain and is now emerging to bring justice and recompense to the world. And you, my brave captain, are to be my hands – for now, until my elevation is complete. Then I will find some end for you as inglorious and bitter as I can conceive, to repay you for the way you've struggled against me.*

He would not beg, would not show any emotion at the threatened fate awaiting him. *You have been drawing lots of power from the three of us,* Duon thought, making careful signals as he shaped the words in his mind. *How far short are you of making the godhood stick?*

The clever Bhrudwan girl understood him, as he knew she would. She brushed past a bush and snapped off a few sticks, ostensibly using them to clean her nails, but in doing so discarded all but three and shortened one of them. Around them the light began to fade; soon the three of them would effectively be struck dumb by the darkness.

I do not rely on you for my power, the voice – Husk – said with contempt. *My strength comes from elsewhere. In a matter of only a few weeks the world will bow before me.*

A few weeks? Duon could not wait one more night. Even now Conal could be blurting their plans to Husk, earning them a burned mind. He was prepared to die – would welcome death – but he wanted a chance to take their enemy down with him. He was sure Arathé felt the same way.

Beyond the Wall of Time

You need to strike now then, before the world goes dark with the reign of the Son and the Daughter. Fingers shaped the relevant words. *You may only get this one chance.*

You are right, Husk replied, *and I'm touched at your concern for my wellbeing, but why would you wish to promote my cause after what I've done to you?*

There are others I care about. I want them safe now, and if that means I have to volunteer to die, I embrace death. One earthly ruler is surely better than two evil gods bent on breaking the world apart.

There, that was as much as he could risk. Now to think of something else, anything other than – no, he must not think about it.

You've promised alliance with me in the past, only to work against me. I know how badly you wish my death. And now you profess some sympathy with what I intend to do. Why should I not be suspicious of this?

Because I have friends whom I wish to live, Duon replied, frantically keeping his thoughts calm. *If you can kill the gods, you offer the best hope for us all.*

Except for you.

Duon nodded a mental assent.

And any of your friends I decide to take captive. If you are uncooperative, of course, or if you decide to try any more tricks.

No more tricks, Duon promised, projecting as much sincerity as he could muster.

This was the most dangerous part. A three-way conversation where surface thoughts had to match what was spoken, all to disguise the real discussion taking place. Duon had real doubts about his own ability to sustain this two-level mode of thought, let alone what mistakes might be made by Conal the priest.

Surprisingly, the youngster proved adept. They had been granted an evening's respite by their captor, who had allowed Duon to choose the level summit of a tall rocky outcrop as their resting place. As they made the necessary preparations for sleep, the signing began.

'Arathé, do you have the sticks?'

'Yes.' She placed them beside the fire Conal had lit.

'This is foolishness.' The priest made little effort to hide his anger; Duon could only hope he'd disciplined his mind. 'We ought to wait for the voice to make a mistake. He can't keep us all under control all of the time.'

'He's managed so far.'

'We're wasting time,' Arathé signed, and picked up the sticks. She held out her arm, her hand masking the true length of the stick. Though one was far shorter than the other two, all appeared to be the same length. 'Time to choose.'

'I choose not to participate.'

'Then, priest, you are the volunteer.'

No need for a comment; his face made his response clear.

Arathé pulled out one of the sticks, about the length of her longest finger, then cast it into the fire. 'Cold tonight,' she said aloud, though Duon had just been thinking how warm the night was.

'Long,' she added.

'One chance in two then,' Conal said. He took a stick, groaned, and hurled it into the flames.

'Short,' Arathé said unnecessarily.

'I'm not doing this!' Conal cried aloud.

'You have to,' Duon signalled urgently, not able to mask his thoughts. 'Jump or we'll push you!'

What is this?

The dirty little Falthan is insulting us, Duon said, aiming a reckless swing at the whey-faced Conal. *After all we've been through. I'm going to knock his head off.*

He charged at the priest, taking him in the midriff. The man gave a tiny squeak of fear, then bellowed as they hit the ground. Their momentum took them a few paces further.

A pace too far.

Looks like I drew the short straw too, Duon thought as blackness opened up below him. The two men went over the bluff together.

The back of Duon's head seemed to explode with light and heat. Magic snatched roughly at his falling body. His limbs stiffened, relaxed, then stiffened again. The voice in his mind screamed in pain and fury. Just before he hit the ground, Duon heard a dull thud. Then the world flashed white and he vanished into it.

Lenares had no idea what time of the night it was. The wind howled around them like a vengeful mother trying to destroy the killer of her children. At least that's what it felt like to Lenares, who wondered at one point whether the Padouki had conjured up the storm. For storm it was; the gods were bringing something catastrophic towards them, a greatly enlarged hole in the world wrapped in cloud, wind and rain.

While the night was blacker than the insides of her eyelids, she didn't need sight to be able to see the hole drawing nearer. The slowly rotating circle, still many leagues out to sea, had ripped a hole clear through her comforting pattern of numbers. The red tinge of wrongness impressed itself straight onto her brain, bringing with it nausea, constant shaking and a fear such as she'd never known.

'This will be very bad,' she told Stella, who, along with the rest of the travellers, had given up trying to sleep. They stood or sat in small groups in various places around the campsite, mostly near the remains of the fire, which the wind had extinguished some time ago.

'Are we in serious danger?'

'Yes. It's coming directly towards us.'

'Is there anything we can do?' Stella asked Heredrew.

You should be asking me, Lenares thought but didn't say.

'Not much against such a storm,' he answered. 'Deflect the wind a little, strengthen any shelter we construct or take refuge in, fend off any debris the wind blows at us and keep ourselves dry, that's all.'

'It might be enough.'

'What would be better'n any 'mount of magical protection would be t' move further inland,' said Seren the miner, having to raise his voice against the wind. 'These storms aren't common this far south, but we've seen them burst against the coast and arrive at

Eisarn as little more'n heavy rain. A big storm'll take plenty o' lives on the coast. Further away we are, the better.'

'Surely it would not be safe back in the forest,' Moralye said. 'The wind would break branches and throw them down upon us.'

'Break branches and uproot trees,' Robal said. 'A dangerous place to be. But better the forest than the coast. I feel sorry for those trapped in the path of the storm.'

Lenares wondered if Robal was thinking of his friends Kilfor and Sauxa.

Kannwar – Lenares supposed she ought to think of him as the Emperor of Bhrudwo and not as the make-believe Falthan sorcerer – was plainly unhappy. 'Have any of you experienced a Mala Gulf typhoon?' he asked, beckoning them all close.

The travellers shook their heads and shrugged their shoulders.

'We're not safe here,' he said. 'Especially if the typhoon is un-natural and aimed at us. But I have a million people to worry about, all living on the shore of the Mala Gulf. If we remain here we will lure the typhoon across a heavily populated part of the Gulf. These are my subjects: I cannot ignore them. I suggest we head south as swiftly as we can, dragging the storm away from the cities of Malayu and Doma.'

'There is no "if,"' Lenares said. 'You must not doubt me. The hole in the world is coming to eat us up.'

'We cannot neglect the people in the storm's path,' said Stella. What little of her face Lenares could see appeared careworn. 'The cosmographer tells us that every unnatural death enlarges the hole. How large will the hole be after a million deaths? We ought to do as Here – as Kannwar asks us, not only for the sake of the people who might otherwise die, but for our sakes and everyone's.'

'Aye,' Seren said. 'And bring it down instead on Raceme an' the countries of Old Roudhos. Haven't they suffered enough?'

Kannwar growled deep in his throat. 'There are no easy choices. But whatever we do we ought to do swiftly.'

'Are you our self-appointed leader, Destroyer?' Robal asked, bristling.

'If anyone leads us, it is Stella,' came the impatient reply.

'Because I won't follow you. You say you're following the orders of the Most High. Fair enough, I can't prove you wrong, and if you and Stella are to be believed he did turn up and help kill the Elamaq Emperor. But where is the Most High now? Surely he could use his power to deflect the storm? Why should we follow you when we could be following him?'

'We can have this debate on the journey south,' Kannwar said. 'Every step we take away from the Mala Gulf will save lives. Should we not be on our way?'

Lenares wished people would ask the most important questions rather than always getting themselves diverted. 'Where are we going? I know you said "south," but we should confront the gods. We had a chance in the House of the Gods but didn't take it.'

'Oh? Who was it let the Daughter escape?'

Cruel Kannwar, not knowing she'd had no choice. Her face reddened, and she thanked the darkness that prevented the others seeing her discomfort.

'I thought she would help me. I made a bad mistake. But the Father should have done more. He should have killed the Son and the Daughter. Or is he not strong enough?'

'I don't know how strong he is,' Kannwar said. 'But he is reluctant. Please, this is another issue best kept for discussion after we leave this place. As for where we should go, we need to find somewhere as far away from other people as we can, accessible within as short a time as possible. The key is to keep the gods from killing people and enlarging the breach in the Wall of Time. The House of the Gods would be ideal, but I doubt we can lure the gods back there. So south to start with, at least.'

Seren spoke. 'You want somewhere both isolated an' reasonably close? I think I know just the place.'

Duon opened his eyes to darkness, noise and pain. Groaning, shrieking, cursing and sobbing filled his ears as he struggled to see anything in the blackness around him. The void beyond the world? Surely he was dead and in the realm of lost souls, just reward for his mistakes and his cowardice. But no, his nose told him he was still in the land of the Padouki, unless lost souls smelled of sap and leaf mould.

As for the sounds, Duon realised the groaning was coming from himself.

Still alive then.

He wasn't sure how he felt about that.

He closed his eyes and concentrated on the back of his head. He could sense something . . . it was different from the spike through which Husk had tormented him . . . Now he focused on it, the sound of shrieking grew louder. It sounded like wind in the trees – it was wind in the trees – but it was also Husk, screaming in agony. Sweet, sweet music.

Gradually the music faded away into silence and darkness.

When next Duon came to, someone was speaking. *He couldn't hold us all*, came the voice, a beautiful voice that brought tears to his eyes, the voice of an angel. *He spread himself too thin trying to keep us alive. He believes he should have let us all fall to our deaths. He regrets it now.*

Arathé? Is that your voice?

Yes, Duon. The connections Husk made seem to work still, even though he no longer sustains them.

It worked then?

Perfectly, it seems. The joy sparkled in her voice.

You sound beautiful, like a god. Did you die? Are you a god?

She laughed, and tears rolled down his cheeks at the sound. *No, I'm just Arathé. You sound magnificent yourself. I think it is just how everyone sounds when we bypass the body and communicate directly, mind to mind.*

Husk didn't.

No, he didn't, she agreed. *Nor did Anomer or my father – but perhaps Husk had distorted their voices too.*

Duon knew there were more important matters to discuss, but right now he felt reborn, overwhelmed by sensation. There was something of the eager child in him.

I felt that way too when I awoke, Arathé said.

126

You can read my thoughts?

Just as Husk could. Any thought you shape into words is clear to me, while the images and colours and memory fragments underneath are just blurs. I'm sure you can read my thoughts in just the same way.

No, no, I don't think I ought – can Conal read our thoughts? He was suddenly shy, uncomfortably aware of how unpleasant a place his mind must be to a visitor.

No, he can't. Sadness communicated itself along their link.

Oh, Duon thought, reading her mind without meaning to. *I see. He cannot read our thoughts because he is dead.*

Yes. When you went over the bluff with Conal, I threw myself over the other side. I decided that was our best chance of overtaxing Husk's strength. It wasn't bravery, she added in response to his sudden admiration. *I didn't care to live on if we'd failed, his lone slave. He ought to have let us all fall, but he couldn't let go of his plans quickly enough. I felt him try to strengthen my body against the impact, then attempt to do something with the air around me to cushion my fall. Whatever he did worked in my case, but you and Conal had fallen a few seconds earlier and he didn't have as much time. I'm sorry.*

Why are you sorry? he asked, and read her answer.

Oh.

The beauty of her voice and the wonder of her mind had all but blinded him to the pain, but now she recalled him to it, he could feel his leg pulsing with a slow, grinding ache.

You've broken it, she said, *in the same place you broke it before.*

How did you know – he'd have to stop asking her that. Of course she knew.

I don't think you will be able to walk. I'm not sure whether to wait here with you or get help.

How do you know Conal is dead?

I've checked his body. It's broken.

The poor man.

Yes. He died swiftly, hopefully without pain. She held out her memories.

He died only a little while ago?

I tried to help him, but it was too late.

Duon chose not to examine her memories, even though she made them available to him.

Don't wait for me to get better. You need to find your family. Send someone back for me when you rejoin the others. Someone with magic enough to heal. That Heredrew, perhaps; he healed me the last time.

Ah, she thought. *I have a little magic. Perhaps I could heal you.*

Her thoughts sounded doubtful and Duon could see her annoyance and confusion. She'd never been taught to heal people. It would be like working in darkness; she might do more harm than good.

As to that, I have an idea. More of a hope really. He opened his mind to her.

It might work, she said. *But what if he's waiting for us to make the attempt? Might he not ensnare us again?*

Perhaps. But can we afford to ignore such a possibility? We can both hear him: he's obviously in agony. We've done him serious harm, as was our intention. Why not see if the connection can be exploited?

I need to rest before I try anything, she admitted. *And then there's Conal. I'm not leaving his body lying here to attract whatever animals live in these parts.* An image of Duon fighting off wolves came into her mind, associated with anxiety and a sense of loss.

We'll decide in the morning, he said, not so much ending the discussion as echoing her thoughts.

The decision made, Duon relaxed, allowing the comforting darkness to roll over him.

CHAPTER 6

CORATA PIT

'IT'S CALLED CORATA,' SEREN SAID, breathing heavily. His bandy
legs struggled to keep pace with Kannwar's long strides. 'One of
the Factor of Malayu's dirty little secrets. Can't believe y'don't
know about it, pardon my forwardness, yer 'onour.'

'No pardon necessary,' Kannwar said, but Lenares could tell he
had been angered by the man's familiarity. 'You don't associate
with outsiders much, do you?'

'No, m'lord, it's bin either down the pit or workin' on the Altima
Road e'er since I was old enough to hold a pickaxe. Plain speakers,
us miners. No point in wasting words when any of 'em might be
your last, eh?'

Lenares found herself fascinated by the exchange. Kannwar was
succeeding in keeping his temper in check, but the miner was
definitely provoking him, and Lenares felt certain the provoca-
tion was deliberate. Did Seren know the risk he was taking?
Kannwar was a murderer, a man steeped in blood, whose idea of
truth was to say whatever he thought would advance his own
interests. Seren ought not to be placing himself in the path of
such a man.

'Then tell me about Corata and the Factor of Malayu,' said
Kannwar, 'and speak plainly.'

The miner cleared his throat. 'Corata's the biggest mine in
Bhrudwo, far bigger'n Eisarn Pit where I come from. It's a mountain
o' granite that sits on the land like a stone in a bowl o' porridge.

Three leagues wide, it is, or so young Dagla told me; his family came from there, he said. They cut the stone out an' use it for all manner o' buildings. Not round here; the peasants can't afford it, seemingly. In Malayu City and other big places. Seems that it was t' be kept a secret from the bigwigs in Andratan – that's yourself, sir – because of the hope they'd find huanu stone there. The Factor wanted it for himself, Dagla said.'

'How did your friend Dagla know what the Factor intended?'

'Dunno, sir. It's widely known, that's all.'

'Hearsay then,' Kannwar said. 'Evidence enough, however, to ensure I will ask my Factor of Malayu a few questions.'

The look on his face frightened Lenares: all the animation had drained from it, leaving a blank mask.

The travellers now numbered eleven. Phemanderac they had buried with tears and many regrets, but rather than returning to Dhauria, Moralye had elected to stay a while longer with Stella and Robal, the only Falthans left in the party. Conal was lost, along with Arathé and Duon, and Sauxa and Kilfor had abandoned them. Kannwar now led the Bhrudwans. At least, none of that young or ill-educated lot had yet challenged his authority. Anomer was the liveliest of them, while the two miners, Seren and Tumar, said little even when spoken to. Sautea and Mustar, the fishermen, said nothing at all, awed, perhaps, by the Undying Man. They awaited their master Noetos's return from the search for his daughter.

Lenares and Torve were the only people remaining from the Amaqi expedition. She wondered what the Alliance leaders would think now, seeing a half-wit and an Omeran animal acting as their empire's representatives in the most important endeavour in thousands of years. Likely they would seek Torve's death, and Lenares they would bundle off home.

The travellers traversed a land almost completely foreign to one brought up in the desert, as Lenares had been. Every hour she had to remind herself that Elamaq, not this abundant land, was the unusual place; apparently, most of the known world was covered in smothering vegetation, this creeping greenery. It was hard to bear, the shrouding of clean rock; hard, also, not to feel it as some kind of metaphor. Her distaste did not come from the land's lack of beauty. Rather, the land was profligate: water cascading from the escarpment they'd climbed down that morning, gathering in unremarked pools; trees and bushes growing in every possible niche short of sheer cliff-faces; and rain tumbling from the sky at an ever-increasing rate. It was all so wasteful that it made Lenares feel guilty, as though she was again in the Garden of Angels observing the Emperor's private extravagance.

The Padouki lands ended with the escarpment, but the lower land, though sprinkled with cattle and sheep, still looked wild. Mounds of hard rock jutted out from the soft green pasture grass, standing in the fields like giant, unmoving sheep. Swift streams sliced the fields in two, their waters running close to flood levels because of the tumbling rain of the last week. An occasional farmhouse and rare village punctuated the flatter areas. The travellers were working slightly north of east through this lowland, despite Kannwar's original intention to lead the storm south. Seren's idea had thoroughly persuaded him.

The Undying Man had approached Lenares to ascertain whether the miner was telling the truth about Corata Pit. It felt good to know even this demigod needed her wisdom, and she noted Anomer nodding at her during the exchange. She had replied with care. 'He believes what he is saying. That may not be the same as the truth.'

'I understand the nuances at play here,' the magician had shot back. 'His information is second-hand. However, it still seems the best hope we have.' He looked at her with his keen eyes. 'How close is the storm now?'

'It nears the coast,' she replied. The hole in the world burned the edges of her mind, and she could work out to a reasonable degree of precision how fast it progressed. 'Perhaps a day from lying overhead were we to remain where we are.'

'It is speeding up then. Intensifying, no doubt. I can feel its enormous power.'

131

She nodded, one hand pressed against her temple. The red pain was there all the time now.

'Point to it,' he commanded.

She stretched out an arm behind herself, moving it until it bisected the storm's approach.

The Undying Man grunted. 'It will come ashore right over Pouk Peninsula. I will try to retard its momentum a little. I can do no more, not against such power.'

Not entirely the truth, she knew, but she did not pursue the matter.

The land tended gently downhill the rest of the day. A fortunate thing, Lenares considered later that afternoon, as the wind had risen to such an extent that its strongest gusts threatened to blow them off their feet. Certainly it impeded their attempts to move forward. Branches were already breaking off trees either side of their path, a narrow, rutted road of shingle and mud. The sheer intensity of the storm frightened her. Elamaq held no natural terrors like this, save perhaps the fire mountains far to the south. Its weather was slower-acting, if no less deadly in the long run. The sun took longer to kill its victims, but they died nonetheless.

The sky became an unrelenting sea of bruised grey cloud, whipping diagonally across their path from the north. Stella did most of the work of keeping branches and other airborne objects from doing them harm, her illusory hand constantly flicking back and forth. With the roaring of the wind and the crashing of branches, conversation became next to impossible.

Torve walked beside Lenares now, his gait rather narrower, as though he was still in pain. He had assured her that he no longer suffered, but said nothing about his amazing recovery. He did not need to; Lenares could tell his healing was not natural, that one of the party had healed him. She knew who it had been, and was aware of the healer's dark secret. She nursed the knowledge, wondering when best to use it.

Healed he was, but Torve was by no means restored. She wanted to talk to him about that, to find out how much his loss mattered to him. Though the cosmographers had been taught about the ways of men, she had not paid much attention to the lessons. It had not sounded very interesting, to tell the truth: a plumbing puzzle at best, something quite unpleasant at worst. *Don't touch me!* Fortunately, cosmographers were allowed to remain unattached. In fact, the Emperor had encouraged it. Fewer mouths dependent on the public purse, Nehane had said. Lenares had not cared about the reason back then, not able to imagine sharing such awkward intimacy with any man. Now, however, she wished she had listened more carefully rather than playing with her numbers at the back of the room.

Mahudia had encouraged her inattention, of course. No chance the half-wit would attract a mate. Except she had.

She could not ask Torve. Love would compel him to say something other than the honest truth. She would think of someone else to ask.

Light leached slowly from the sky, though there were hours remaining until sunset. What replaced it wasn't darkness exactly, rather a grey blurriness that took the sharp edges from everything, a water-borne haze that left the travellers wading as much as walking. They were drenched, of course, but the air was strangely warm, and apart from the constant chafing they were not uncomfortable.

They met the first refugees from the storm soon after. An old man, his possessions on his back, head down, shoulders hunched, and unwilling to answer their hail, heading away from the approaching weather. He was followed by others: younger men at first, moving swiftly, then families with few possessions. Kannwar tried to get them to turn around, but they were having none of it.

'Rain's falling like the sky's turned to water,' one man said. 'I remember the storm of 1202, and this one's already worse.' They spoke of widespread damage and injuries, and warned of devastation to come.

'They're not safe inland,' Lenares said. 'This storm wants to eat everyone up. If it can't smash them it will drown them.'

'What do you want me to do, girl?' Kannwar asked, anger giving his voice a sinister edge. 'Force them to join us?'

'Yes, exactly that,' she shouted at him. 'Make them come to the pit. Keep them alive and slow the gods down.'

He reflected on this a moment. 'You are a sentimental fool,' he said – which she was not; his words made her angry – but nodded to her anyway. Raising his voice effortlessly, his words boomed over the shriek of the wind: 'Anyone we meet coming down this path is to be detained and compelled to accompany us to the assembly point at Corata Pit. This is by order of Andratan.'

'Your orders don't apply to us, Destroyer!' Robal shouted.

Kannwar stopped in his tracks. 'Whose land are you in?'

'Don't know who owns this patch of dirt.' The guardsman lifted steely eyes to the tall man. 'Maybe the Padouki, maybe Old Roudhos, maybe someone else. I'll do as they ask.'

Stella put a hand on his arm. 'Robal, this is a waste of our time.'

He shook her hand off, not noticing that his arm went right through her illusory forearm, nor her wince at the sight. 'The only one wasting time is this snake, ordering us around.'

'Then do it because I ask you,' she said.

The man stood irresolute for a moment. Lenares could almost read his mind as his numbers flickered across his face: *I should have gone with Sauxa and Kilfor. I want to kill the Destroyer. Why does Stella side with him?* The thoughts were so clear she had no doubt the others could see them too.

The flaming red circle flared strongly in her mind, sparking dizziness and nausea. She clamped her lips together, trying not to vomit.

'Hurry,' she said hoarsely. 'The hole is close now. Terrible things are coming.'

Robal glanced at her, his lip curling with disdain.

'Very well, my queen,' he said and, splattering mud everywhere, strode off to the front of the bedraggled group.

'The man is trouble,' Kannwar said. 'Fortunately he has no power to do us harm.'

'If you think that, you don't understand anything,' Stella snapped at him, and marched after her guard.

The world shrank to a grey nightmare. Conversation was impossible as the wind roared its anger at them. All around them young trees bent and old trees broke, their fall completely soundless in the maelstrom of noise. The few houses they could see close to the road had lost their roofs, and many had been levelled. The injured they gathered up into their swollen band of refugees; the dead they were forced to ignore.

And the dead became more common as the travellers pushed on, bent forward from the waist, into the storm's heart. A young man lay splayed out on the path, his head split by a fallen branch, his once-fine clothes brown with mud. A tiny girl face down in a puddle complete with its own little wavelets, her body rocking in time with the wind gusts. A family ran towards the path, then were lost to view as the roof of a house slammed down on top of them.

Kannwar's magic protected the travellers, keeping out the worst of the wind and debris, but even he could not shelter the hundreds of people following them. Lenares saw the rising anger in his eyes, the almost uncontrollable raging of his numbers. He was insulted, she saw, that there were powers stalking his land more potent than he.

A black column emerged from the grey swirl. Seren beckoned the others and stumbled towards it. The local who had been guiding them – much against his will – nodded, then turned and ran back down the path, pushing through the crowds following them. Kannwar did nothing to prevent him leaving.

The black column was an enormous tower of stone. Perhaps twenty paces across, it was hundreds of paces high, its apex lost in the cloud. Lenares could not discern its function, but there was a formed road beside it, leading down into darkness.

As she reached the road, a strange and frightening vista opened ahead of her. A vast pit stretched into the distance, its sides stepped like a giant staircase or circular arena – an enormous version of Talamaq's Great Circus. The road, it seemed, wound around and around the pit, and Lenares set her weary feet to its rocky surface.

As she dropped below the lip of the pit the storm lost much of its potency, and within minutes they could converse in relative comfort.

Seren, it seemed, had saved them all.

The storm is enormous, he said.

But heading south. The worst of it will miss us, she said.

An image of a vast, rotating pinwheel of cloud with a hole like an eye in the centre filled his mind. *These storms are not predictable*, he warned. *It could turn our way. Even the outer reaches could make life very unpleasant for us.*

Not as unpleasant as it was, she said, her mind-smile irrepressible. *Other people will be suffering.*

How do you know so much about such storms?

He showed her his memories. *You forget I am an explorer. I have seen storms like this in Crynon, where the inhabitants have learned how to survive, and in the Spear Lands, where because of the storms' frequency no one makes their home. The wind comes from one direction, building in intensity until it destroys much in its path, then there is a lull as the central eye passes overhead. After that comes the worst as the wind reverses direction, breaking many structures that had merely bent before.*

I have heard of these storms, but did not appreciate their power. How cruel of nature!

Such storms last for a day at the most before they move on, he said. *Though some places can be unlucky: if the storm changes direction, it might reverse over an area it has previously visited.*

Her mind filled with horror. *Do these storms roam the world constantly? How many are there?*

No, they are born and die, like all natural things. He tried not to think of his Emperor, dead now, who had sought to live forever, but she saw his thought and the pain it caused him. *For some reason they are strongest over water, and die quickly when making landfall. They always come from the ocean: the Sea of Kahal and Oceana Obarasia are their breeding grounds.*

Why have I never seen one?

Your mind is like a sponge, he said, laughing. *There is never an end to what you want to know.*

A good thing, she said, but her deeper thoughts turned to her years in Andratan. There were some things, it seemed, that were better left unknown. He saw her thought but did not comment on it.

You've not seen one because they seldom come this far north.

This one has.

Yes, he said. *But you and I know this storm is not natural. It was bred out of season, and with it the hole in the world comes to destroy.*

They stood together, the two remaining of Husk's three spikes, and stared out over the forests and farmlands of southern Malayu. It had begun to rain, and though the wind was not strong, the air it blew was dank, somehow rotten, as though it had been trapped for centuries beneath the forest floor. High overhead, cloud had given way to dark scudding mist, while off to the east – their right – a blank curtain obscured the lower Padouk River and the Mala Gulf into which it drained. Behind that curtain lay a world open and vulnerable to the gods, one about to be damaged, perhaps destroyed.

What can we do? he asked.

She gave the question some thought. Like him, what she really wanted was to leave all this fear and conflict behind and go somewhere safe and quiet. But she knew that if the gods remained unchecked, soon few safe places would remain; islands of sanctuary surrounded by a storm surge of destruction.

Storm surge? That's your idea. I'm not even sure what it means.

Our thoughts seem to be mixing together. I will withdraw.

No, she said carefully, something pulsing under her surface thoughts. *We are far stronger together than apart. And now we have a potential, if unwilling, ally in Husk, we might well be able to do something to prevent the annihilation of the world.*

Now it comes to it, he said. *Are we willing to do to him that which we despised so much when he did it to us?*

Yes, she said, without hesitation. *Yes.*

'This will be much easier,' Kannwar explained to the travellers. 'Out in the storm we had to shape our shield around obstructions like trees and houses. Not only that, the area where the shield met the ground was vulnerable to the wind. Here, the sides of the pit will protect us. All we have to do is raise a streamlined bubble like a roof. The wind will slide across it, unable to gain purchase. As long as Stella and I have strength, we are safe.'

Lenares watched, fascinated, as Kannwar and Stella held hands and closed their eyes. Something invisible to normal sight pushed out from them. Lenares could sense a faint disturbance in the numbers swirling around her: a slight change in atmospheric pressure, followed by a reduction in the buffeting winds licking and cutting at them as the travellers wound their way down into the pit. The invisible something slipped over her like hot oil, and was lost to her senses.

Then began a battle unlike anything she had seen.

The grey clouds above them seemed to slow, then hover, and let loose a fusillade of hail. Those who had not yet passed through the invisible barrier were battered, forced to their knees by the power of the ice. Kannwar shouted a warning, and some of those struck by the ice staggered to their feet and stumbled forward; others crawled. But a few did not move.

The hail redoubled its intensity, crashing and clattering against the granite walls of the pit and sending chips of stone flying in all directions. As many people were maimed by the granite as by the hail, which now seemed to be the size of fists.

Kannwar and Stella's canopy faltered under the assault. Lenares could see it now: a thin film spreading wider as the magicians attempted to encompass the width of Corata Pit, punctuated by countless indentations from the driving ice. A shriek from a woman not ten paces from Lenares sent people scurrying first towards, then away from a prone body. Lenares returned her glance skywards to see a hole in the canopy. Then another. This time the ice missed hitting anyone below, exploding on the path, sending people in all directions and raising a cry of dismay. A glance at the two magicians told her they were near the limits of their strength.

Despite the danger, Lenares could not contain her excitement. This was the stuff she had read about in the textbooks the young cosmographers were taught from, and in dusty old scrolls she'd found hidden in back rooms. Even Mahudia had not known some of the stories she'd found. The adventures of the wizards of Crynon were her favourites, though she also enjoyed the search for the floating island of Ilixa. Bolts of magic hurled in battle, acts of bravery celebrated, and the forces of evil always vanquished. Mahudia had laughed and said that the good people always won because they got to write the stories.

Lenares wondered whether she would end up as an evil witch in someone else's story.

Stella cried out, and a hundred holes appeared in the canopy. A second later dozens of dull thuds were accompanied by grunts, cries and screams. One continued for a few moments, fading, to be suddenly cut off. Someone had been knocked from the path and had fallen into the pit.

'Why did you bring us here to die?' a woman wailed.

Lenares' eye was drawn to Kannwar. The once-tall magician seemed to shrink, almost as though – no, exactly as though – he had become someone else. The flesh melted from his face, leaving a cracked and broken visage that made those near him cry out in fear. For a moment she feared the battle had damaged him or that his magic had eviscerated him, but then she looked more closely. *I am seeing him as he really is.*

He had abandoned his magical disguise, the mask that enabled him to move in the world of mortals, the better to focus all his energy on maintaining the barrier. He looked a thousand years dead.

Above her the canopy rippled and stretched tight, erasing the dents and holes. The sound of ice beating at the barrier filled her ears. Stella cried out again, this time in exaltation. The roar of ice carried on a moment longer, then ceased.

Hundreds of chests breathed out simultaneously.

The canopy had now stretched to cover the entire pit perhaps a quarter of the way below the rim. A few dozen stragglers remained outside the protective covering, but Lenares could see the effort required to maintain the barrier and realised the people outside were trapped with no hope of rescue. Its thin surface was about a hundred paces above them, though exact distances were hard to tell; the pit was so large that there was little apart from their own small figures to impart a sense of scale.

The hole in the world renewed its assault. Rain again began to fall, steadily but not the downpour of before. There was something different about this rain: each drop seemed to smoke as it struck the canopy. Stella and Kannwar grunted in pain. Lenares could not read what was happening, but a nameless dread began to steal over her.

This would be bad.

Tendrils of the storm formed themselves into vast gnarled hands and reached slowly down into the pit. Lenares had seen those hands before, on a beach south of here, as the gods had grappled with each other in an attempt to control her. Dozens of hooked claws began scrabbling at the canopy, scoring long grooves in the pale surface. The screeching drew dismayed gasps from those below. Films of liquid formed on the underside of the scratch marks, and drops of what to Lenares looked like blood began to patter down among the refugees.

Fearful shouts told her what she had already realised. This was not blood. Near her a little boy screamed thinly, a hand to his ruined face. As she watched, horrified, a second drop landed on his head. Bubbling and sighing, the boy slumped to the ground.

Drops began to hiss and splatter all around them. Lenares felt a burning sensation on her bare left arm; not a direct hit, a splash only, but the intense pain shocked her. When she pulled her arm up to see the damage, there was no mark. No evidence there had been any pain. Yet around her people lay cursing, screaming, writhing, begging, bleeding from dreadful burns.

What?

As the acidic water ate its way into the stone on which they stood, the granite path began to crumble.

'Stella!' Kannwar cried. 'Give me more!'

The Falthan woman groaned, her already pale face shedding its

140

remaining colour. Above them the dripping grooves began to close up. The pattering death slowed.

There was a howl of fury from beyond the canopy and the talons redoubled their efforts, scraping and punching at the barrier, searching, scouring.

Stella sank to one knee.

The howl of fury rose in volume and in pitch until it was a shriek. Lenares knew that voice well, knew exactly who uttered it. Umu.

The talons battered at the barrier a moment longer, then jerked away, turning their frustration on the rocks around the rim of the pit. The air above the canopy filled with percussive booms and flying shards.

Movement caught Lenares' eye: the few remaining people trapped above the barrier, desperate to escape. Two of them tried to prise the canopy open, but could get no purchase on the smooth surface. Another hammered on the barrier. Her faint shouts could be heard in the silences between the crack and smack of rocks.

'No,' Lenares whispered. 'Don't make any noise. She'll see you, and she's angry.'

The talons paused, twitched a little as though searching for the source of the noise, then descended on the small group.

'Open the barrier!' The cry came from many voices, one of which was Stella's.

'No. There is nothing we can do for them.'

The woman glanced up and stopped hammering on the canopy. A moment later she was seized and hoisted into the air. Other taloned hands scooped up the remaining trapped refugees.

Umu wants us to watch.

Each person was held up for display between the fingers of a clawed hand, then, one at a time, deliberately pierced by the sharp thumb-claw as though they were worms on hooks. Those as yet unharmed screamed and wriggled, trying to escape, but none avoided their fate.

I should never have let her go, Lenares thought as she wept.

I am coming for you, Lenares. The god's voice crashed into her mind. *You will not die with the others. I have a special plan for you.*

141

Lenares thought of the terrible last moments of Rouza and Palain. She did not want to give the Daughter ideas, but the images stubbornly refused to leave her head.

Your death will be worse, Umu promised.

The talons withdrew, their victims discarded to tumble to the canopy with a series of thumps. The cloud swirled, rose and melted away. Above the pit the sky turned blue. Below, the remaining refugees cheered. Stella sagged in relief.

Lenares did not. She knew it wasn't over.

'Wait!' Kannwar cried. 'This is the eye in the centre of the storm. Be strong now, for the storm's worst moments still lie ahead of us.'

Groans and shouts of anger and derision followed this statement. But Lenares was not surprised. The gods had not finished with them yet, not by a long stretch.

'Hold,' said a voice.

Arathé turned to where a hulking figure stood, dripping wet, a slightly smaller figure beside him. 'Father!'

'No,' the voice said, and though it was Noetos's voice, to Duon it sounded subtly altered.

Careful, Arathé, a god speaks through him.

She gave mental assent to Duon's warning, but ran over to her father nonetheless. 'It is you! Where have you been? I'm sorry for attacking you, but—'

'But it was not you. I know. Just as I am not your father Noetos.'

Duon worked his way forward until he stood beside Arathé. 'Which one are you then? Do you come to threaten or to bargain?'

'Neither. I come to warn you. Do not attempt to do what you plan.'

Beside him, the Padouki warrior stared impassively, a coiled spring.

Duon fought to keep his place. Everything about the fisherman seemed to intimidate: his voice, his demeanour, his eyes. Something about him had changed. It hurt just to be near him, as though he was some sort of heavy weight. The explorer licked his lips, then spoke. 'Why? Are you frightened that we'll succeed? Is that it?'

'Yes, that is it,' agreed the voice. 'Your actions will succeed, but at great cost.'

'We're prepared to pay that cost,' Arathé said fiercely.

'The cost will not be borne solely by you. Yes, you can tap into Husk's power, but what you do not know is that his power comes from beyond the Wall of Time. Drawing significant amounts of power through him will aid in breaking the wall.'

'But if we can destroy the gods, it might be worth the risk.'

'You will not destroy them, for they are linked to Husk. Should you widen the channel between yourselves and Husk, you will become vulnerable to the gods. They will have yet more bodies to command, from which they can destroy even more of the world. You saw what became of the Emperor of Elamaq, and you have your own experiences to consider. I am sure you do not want them to possess you.'

'I don't believe you,' Duon said.

Arathé took a step back from her father. 'Are you the Son or the Daughter?'

'Neither. I am the giant of the desert, the Most High, the Father.'

Arathé hissed on an indrawn breath.

'You say you are,' said Duon, unconvinced.

'Were I either of my troublesome children, I could have seized you by now and squeezed the life out of you.' The figure blurred and a moment later Duon was taken in a crushing grip by an invisible hand. 'You could not break free, even if you were animated by one of the gods yourself.'

The explorer tried to prise the arm from his throat, but could not move it even a hair: it was as though carved from stone. Already he felt light-headed and, strangely, his cares began to fall away.

'Let him go!' Arathé pleaded.

Duon felt quite pleased at that, particularly at the feelings behind her words. He wanted a chance to ask Arathé to expand on her thoughts.

The pressure vanished and Noetos once again stood before them. 'There was a time for caution,' he said, 'but it is past. Now you must act – but not as you had planned. Go and find the others. With application, you may in time develop the mental subtlety to exploit your connection with Husk, but be careful. He, as much as the gods, still threatens the world.'

Noetos's face began to change, losing some of its fierceness. The god was leaving him.

'Wait!' Arathé cried. 'You have enormous power, far more than any of us. More than your Son and Daughter, surely. Why are you not acting to put an end to all this?'

'Because I cannot,' said the voice, fainter now.

'Cannot, or will not?' Duon asked.

'You are right to correct me,' said the god after a long pause. The voice strengthened a little. 'I will not intervene. The act of creation forbids it. Making something that was not myself, as this world and all within it had to be, meant I had to exclude myself from it. Should I interfere in any substantial fashion, the boundary between creation and myself will break down and all will be subsumed into me once again. That I do not wish.'

'Doesn't sound much different from what the gods are trying to do,' Duon noted.

'It is exactly the same, though they do not know it,' the voice agreed. 'The Wall of Time is the boundary between myself and creation. When something in the world dies, I gather it back to myself, yet it still retains something of itself, though without true independence. To break down that barrier will be to end the independence of the world itself and everything in it.'

'Yet you interfere now,' Arathé observed.

'Yes, but only by invitation, and only as minimally as possible. I am not an agency here. You are the agents. If I am to do anything to assist in healing the breach my children have opened, it will be through people like you.'

Arathé shook her head and her hands flashed. 'I was possessed for near three years. I don't care to repeat the experience.'

'Nor should you,' agreed the voice. 'Sadly, I doubt whether

anything you do will make a difference. It will likely be all you can do to choose which way you die. Yet I do not wish the world's destruction to be hurried by a foolish use of Husk's power.'

Duon's eyes narrowed in puzzlement. 'Aren't you the Most High? According to Phemanderac, the Falthans and Dhaurians say you are all-powerful and can see the future. How can you not know what is going to happen? And why can't you stop it?'

'Because I am not my creation,' the voice said. 'I could know if I wished, but in observing I would change that which I observed. Do you wish to live wondering which actions are your own and which are imposed upon you by a god?'

'I'm not sure most people would notice the difference,' Duon said sourly. 'Actually, I'm not sure I much like the arrangement you've come up with. Couldn't you have thought of something better?'

The voice ceased for a moment and Noetos stood unmoving, as though he was a machine without motive power.

'Your own creation legends tell my story more accurately than you know,' the voice said eventually. 'I was reluctant to accept creation's worship, and wanted my worshippers to go their own way. But time and again they have begged for my intervention, and in my folly perhaps – or whatever other name you care to give to love – I have on occasion granted their wish. I do not believe it has been to creation's betterment. But I am tired, so tired of it all. I am a reluctant god. Like you, I wish for nothing more than to walk away and find somewhere quiet, while others enjoy the produce I have laboured to make.'

'You are . . . not what we expected,' Arathé said.

'A disappointment?' the voice said. 'Would you prefer this?'

The world flashed white and Noetos was suddenly a thousand paces high, towering above them, storm-borne and lightning-eyed. The Padouki beside him drew away, obvious wonder on his face.

'Do I not fulfil your sense of majesty? Is this form something you could worship?'

The sense of weight redoubled, forcing them both to their knees.

145

'Lenares would tell you to stop telling lies,' Duon said. 'The way you appear, and everything you've said, shaves the truth.'

'Of course it does,' said the voice, and in an eyeblink Noetos stood there as he had before. 'It is the curse of language. You do not have words for the concepts you are trying to debate. What words would you use were you to find yourself beyond the Wall of Time? Every thought you have is predicated on time. Is, then, when, would, will, had, have, if: all are dependent on one's temporal perspective. Those outside of time have no need of them. In my need to communicate, the concepts become less than they are in reality.'

'We're ignorant then, mere worms graced by your presence.' For some reason the Most High's words angered Duon, though there was something oddly comforting in the idea of a being far superior to himself.

'No, it's simply a matter of perspective. Beyond the wall you receive a new language, tense-less and not predicated on time. Hard to comprehend, but entirely natural.'

'Do we really have time for such philosophies?' Arathé asked, glancing towards the storm curtain.

Duon laughed. 'That is ironic in so many ways,' he said.

A moment later she saw it herself and began laughing.

'You two are in a unique position to think about such things,' the voice said. 'Do so most carefully, and take counsel from this man, whom you will find much chastened. He likely has dark times ahead; be patient with him, and do not withhold your love from him, or it may go badly for you all. Whatever happens, I look forward – you see, I cannot help but use such phrases when talking with you – I *look forward* to meeting you again and continuing this discussion. Farewell.'

Notwithstanding the god's manifestation as a giant, Duon couldn't help but be reminded of his grandfather. He remembered talking with the old man as a child, his grandfather's slight frame bent over in his chair, his voice frail and his eyes dull. Wise but ineffectual. He'd once been a leader of a minor Alliance and apparently had been accounted a man of substance. The young Duon had despised the old drooler.

Noetos collapsed as Duon was finishing the thought. One moment his body stood between them, the next it lay twitching on the ground. As they bent over him the fisherman began to groan.

'Father?' Arathé signed, and put a hand on his forehead.

Noetos sat up, then bent forward and retched two or three times. Arathé barely withdrew her hand in time. 'Oh, that was terrible,' he said weakly.

Duon and Arathé helped the Padouki warrior lift the fisherman to his feet. They sought shelter from the strengthening rain, finding a small copse of trees growing from a crevice between two large boulders and squeezing in, shoulder to shoulder.

'We came across the priest's body,' Noetos said. 'You did a fair job at burying it, but an animal had been at it. Not really what the lad deserved.'

Neither Duon nor Arathé replied, but the explorer noted his unvoiced thoughts matched hers. *He nearly killed us.*

'So,' the fisherman said, staring intently at his daughter. 'Any gods still in your head?'

'No,' she signed. 'Any still in yours?'

They both laughed, gestures of relief that ended up in an embrace. The burly red-headed man had tears in his eyes as he hugged his daughter.

'I finally feel as though I have you back,' he said, 'for the first time since I sold you to Andratan. Arathé, will you forgive me?'

'Father,' she signed, pulling away from him. Her gestures were emphatic. 'Please, listen to me. You did not "sell" me. I chose to go. I was the one heart-set on the wide world. You tried to keep me at home.'

The big man's eyebrows crinkled as he thought about this. It already seemed strange to Duon that he could not read the man's thoughts, given how open Arathé's mind was to him.

'Did I? I remember differently. Mustar panted all over you all summer like a flop-eared puppy, and I preferred the thought of you learning magic in Andratan to you hauling in the nets with two brats at your feet and you pregnant with the third. You were brighter than us, daughter. You deserved to shine out there in the world, not to be kept in that dreadful, dark, cliff-hedged place I hid in because I was frightened of Neherian assassins.'

'Oh,' she signed with small, tentative movements. 'That's not how Mother explained your views.'

He snorted. 'Arathé, late in our marriage we both painted the other in the worst light possible. She did it, I did it; I don't remember who started it. Opuntia, probably, given her gift with words. But I usually finished it. You and Anomer ended up being the fields upon which your mother and father did battle.'

His words were working on something hard and bitter in Arathé. Duon watched as she prodded at long-held thoughts of anger and resentment.

'So it wasn't us you were angry at? We hadn't failed you?'

'Alkuon, girl, of course not!'

She burst into tears and fell to her knees. Her limbs trembled, making signing difficult. 'You'll have to tell Anomer. He's the one really hurt by all this.'

'I'm so sorry,' he said, his hand ruffling her hair. 'I didn't realise. I was thinking only of my feud with Opuntia.'

He looked up and caught Duon's eye. Suddenly the explorer felt uncomfortable: one moment he had been conversing with a god; the next, listening in on a private family discussion. He turned to go.

'Good idea,' Noetos said, but there was no real heat in it.

Duon noted the Padouki warrior made no move to leave, seemingly having no issue with hearing family secrets.

'Father, you'll have to know some time. Duon can hear everything I think. I have no secrets from him. You can ask him to walk away, but he can't stop hearing.'

Noetos straightened and looked Duon in the eye. It was like eyeing a he-bear protective of his cub. 'You have a link with her? How did this happen?' This time the words carried real heat.

'The voice – Husk, he has a name – the voice forged links to all of us,' Duon explained carefully. Even without the majesty of the Most High illuminating it, the man's gaze intimidated him in much the way Dryman's had; perhaps the look of the god hadn't entirely left him. 'When Conal died, the link burned out, but the connection remained. It's like . . . like a window through which I can see your daughter's mind. She can see mine the same way.'

'Can you close it?'

'Close it?'

'Close the window,' the big man said patiently.

'No!' Arathé said, and Duon shied away from reading the thoughts behind her cry. 'Why should we? Something good has come out of our suffering. It is a blessing, this connectedness, and we might well be able to make something of it.'

'*He* might make something of it,' Noetos said, but the look on his face suggested he realised his words were ridiculous.

'On my honour, I will not,' Duon said. 'I am twice your daughter's age and have half her wit: I am not a match for her. Besides,' he added slyly, 'the young man Mustar still has eyes for her. I have no doubt he'd be much the better match.'

Arathé giggled wickedly and Duon enjoyed the joke. Noetos, however, growled, no doubt knowing they chaffed him; but he let the matter drop.

'I remember hearing the priest describing the sensation of the god in his mind,' he said. 'I thought he was dramatising the experience but, if anything, he underplayed it.'

'What was it like?' his daughter signed.

'Like having my brain torn apart, filament by filament. I didn't think I would survive it, even though I sensed he was trying not to damage me.'

'It felt much the same when Husk took control of us,' Duon said.

'You call him Husk. Is that what he called himself? Did you kill him?'

Arathé told her father what had happened, while Duon resisted breaking in on the conversation. It was so hard to watch such a brilliant woman struggling to speak at a fraction of the pace of her sparkling thoughts. But it would not be right to speak for her.

Why ever not? What virtue is there in allowing me to struggle?
I thought you might be offended.
I'd be offended if you left me to flounder.

Duon gave his assent and joined in the tale, all the time wondering just how difficult it would prove to be inextricably linked to such a brightly burning light as Arathé.

'How long do we have?' Stella asked.

'Could be an hour, could be longer.'

Kannwar didn't really know, Lenares could tell, but leaders were always forced to say something. She frowned. Leaders and lies went together.

'Not enough time to get to safety.' Stella failed to keep the anxiety out of her voice, prompting worried discussion from those around her.

'This is safety. We've seen what happens to anyone outside our protection. '

'I have a father and sister back in Long Pike Mouth,' a woman said anxiously. 'Now the storm's over, I want to find them.'

'Let us out!' someone shouted.

Others picked up the cry. 'Let us out! Let us out!'

Kannwar turned on them. 'You dare command me? You think to order the Undying Man?'

They pulled back from his anger. He had remade his face, but still frightened them. The stories about him were legion, and each one had a cruel twist.

'Anyone we let out will die,' Stella said, trying to sound reasonable.

'But the storm is over,' a man called out.

'No,' she said. 'In the centre of this storm is a small area of calm. It is overhead now. When it passes, the second part of the storm will come. It is likely to be worse than the first part.'

'It's only bad because of you,' said another man, an old fellow with a hunched back. 'What storm ever had claws and acid? There is magic in the air, and I want no part of it.'

'He makes his point well,' Sautea said. The fisherman had been

150

hurt by one of the balls of ice; his arm was damaged, sprained perhaps, or broken. 'This is the same as the storm that followed Arathé. If we get out of its way, the worst that will happen is we'll get a little wet.'

Kannwar growled his disapproval. Lenares took stock of him. His temper had risen, and only the presence of Stella kept him from exercising it.

'How many of you wish to leave?' he asked.

About a third of the few hundred refugees put up their hands.

'We worked hard to save you,' he snarled. 'Take a look at these fools, you with your hands by your sides. This is the last you'll ever see of them.

'Very well. Those with their hands up, get out of the pit. And when your death comes roaring at you, think of the mercy of the Undying Man.'

Not a few of those so addressed lowered their hands, but still fully a quarter of those in Corata Pit lined up to squeeze through a narrow opening Kannwar made in the barrier. Above them blue sky winked at their efforts.

'Are we wrong?' Stella wondered aloud.

'We are not wrong,' Kannwar assured her as the last of the line vanished over the lip of the pit. 'They are wrong, and it will cost them everything. No doubt this will be remade into a story in which I forced them out into the storm while all the while they begged to remain under my protection.' He sighed. 'Now I need your attention. We may have little time and there is something we must do.'

'What?'

'We need to modify the barrier.'

Stella groaned. 'I don't know how much strength I have left.'

'This doesn't require strength. At least, I will supply the strength we need. I want you to focus that strength. You must concentrate on this. Do you see this shape?'

Lenares frowned. Kannwar had shown Stella something without moving his hands: they must be communicating mind to mind. How Lenares wished she had such ability!

'What do I do with it?'

'I am going to spread a multitude of those shapes over the barrier, and you must do the same, keeping the shape just as I showed you. Can you do this?'

She nodded.

A shadow began to grow at the far end of Corata Pit. Lenares looked up: an enormous sheer wall of cloud advanced over the pit's lip. In it vast energies seethed; flashes of light illuminated various parts of the cloud wall.

'Our time has run out,' Kannwar said.

'We need to keep walking,' Noetos urged.

Exhausted, Duon could do no more than plod, feet splashing along the track of sucking mud. Husk's control had sapped his energy; he needed to rest, to eat, to sleep.

'We need to do more than walk,' Arathé signalled, her hands frantic. 'We need to run!'

The first bolt of lightning nearly made Lenares wet herself. Little more than a blinding blue flash, it cracked and skittered against the canopy. Stella shrieked, Kannwar grunted; both sounds were drowned out by a terrifying roar that shook the pit.

The first bolt was followed by another, and another, and then a sequence of them: white-blue daggers thrust at the canopy. The accumulated energy sizzled over the barrier as though searching for weak points, trying to find a way through.

'Exactly what I would have done,' Kannwar remarked between strikes. The rest of his comment was lost in a further series of flashes and roars.

'Will it hold?' Stella asked.

'That depends on us. Now, concentrate!'

Lightning rained on the canopy like hammer blows. Lenares clapped her hands over her ears, but each thump shook her chest so vigorously she found it difficult to breathe. The air smelled burnt, as though it had caught fire.

The barrier held.

The man with the hunch approached her. 'Miss, come and sit with us. One of the magicians wants to try something.' He clutched at her arm.

Most of the refugees sat huddled together a short distance away. Anomer stood before them, addressing them between strikes.

'Hold hands,' he instructed. 'I will try to draw strength from your essenza.' A series of booms echoed across the pit and he waited patiently until the sound had died away. 'I have done this before. You will all feel a little discomfort, but no one will be seriously harmed.'

At this one or two let go of their neighbour's hand, then took it again, embarrassed. Lenares sat at the end of a row and took the chubby hand of a young boy. The woman at the end of the row in front reached back and grabbed Lenares' other hand.

Don't touch me, her inner voice said, a rote reaction with little power. She ignored it. The boy's hand was clammy while the woman's felt scaly. Not at all like Torve's.

Above them a dozen bolts slammed simultaneously into the canopy, which buckled, then snapped back into place. Stella sank to her knees.

'Now,' Anomer said, and closed his eyes. A moment later they popped open. 'Nothing,' he said, disappointed.

Lenares had felt nothing, no surge of power. She had hoped to feel it, to learn more about magic in all its forms.

'I felt something,' someone in front of her cried.

'So did I!'

Others confirmed that something had happened.

Another bright flash lit up the pit, turning the landscape into a searing monochrome. This time the canopy buckled further, and a small area near the centre did not repair itself.

Umu will know, Lenares thought as the thunder cracked and rumbled.

'We didn't feel a thing,' came dozens of voices from behind Lenares.

Anomer waved his arms to get everyone's attention. 'Those who felt the pull of magic, wave your arms.'

Everyone in the rows in front of Lenares waved. She turned to see no raised hands behind her. The woman had let go of her hand to raise her own, but the boy beside her still held her hand in a fierce grip.

It's me. I'm the one blocking the magic.

'Lenares,' Anomer called, 'why don't you come up here and help me?'

She nodded, retrieved her other hand from the boy's grasp and stood up.

This time the flash was unbearable and Lenares squeezed her eyes closed. She counted five, ten, twenty, thirty-two flashes in a matter of seconds, accompanied by roars fit to burst her ears asunder. When the flashes stopped and the thunder cleared, Stella lay unmoving on the ground.

'Are we close enough?' Duon asked.

'We have to be!' Arathé was beside herself. 'There is no more time!'

Duon could see the pictures in her head. She had forced a channel through to her brother by main strength, one that had been open in the past but had been seared closed by Husk. Her mind bled from the roughness of her surgery to reopen it. The resulting images presumably originating from Anomer's eyes – revealed the remaining travellers under siege. As Duon watched, more explosions of light tore across his inner vision, and when they ceased he saw the Falthan woman dead on the path.

Arathé took her father's hand, then dropped it. 'I don't need your hand,' she said. 'I can pull power from you anyway.' She snatched at Duon's hand and began drawing from him.

Duon trusted her, would always trust her. He could see her intentions, but knew also just how little practical experience she'd had at this. As the cavity behind his nose warmed and his chest began to hollow, he hoped she wouldn't draw too much. His small trickle of power flowed into her own river, then on towards her brother.

154

At a nod from Noetos, the Padouki warrior lent his hand. *Anomer*, she said. *This is all we have. I hope it is enough.*

Lenares' cheeks burned with shame. She had prevented the magic from working. Something in her had resisted Anomer's drawing, and everyone knew it. No one would speak to her now, she was sure; the friendships tentatively begun would end. She hadn't meant to ruin things, but who would believe her?

More flashes, this time brighter still as lightning lanced through the growing rent in the canopy. Around her people screamed in fright.

Her mind backtracked. Something in her had resisted – or something on her. Cursing herself for a fool, she drew out the fragment of huanu stone she'd taken from Olifa the miner and strode towards Kannwar. She held it up before his shocked eyes.

'Will this be of any help?'

Duon felt the connection between himself, Anomer and hundreds of other minds. Felt Anomer take the stream of magic, shape it, and aim it at the ragged hole in the canopy wrought by the lightning. Watched as the boy tried and failed to seal the hole shut.

'Most High! Just a little help!' Noetos implored.

The Most High whispered his answer through the fisherman's own lips. 'I will not interfere. So have I sworn.'

'You interfered in the House of the Gods!'

'That place is beyond the Wall of Time. My interference did no harm there.'

'But they are about to die!'

'Yet they may not,' said the Most High, and left Noetos.

Stella lay as still as stone. Kannwar seemed torn: he continued to maintain the increasingly fragile canopy, but also sought a response from the Falthan queen. 'She cannot die, she cannot die,' he chanted over and over, his ravaged eyes sunken like raisins in his head.

'Ma sor Kannwar?' Lenares called, but his eyes were dim and did not see her. She turned away.

Her numbers offered no help: they were unable to keep up with the enormous amount of magical energy coruscating through the pit. She had an idea, but could not tell whether it was sensible or foolish – though she feared the latter. Before she could think, before her mind could persuade her otherwise, her feet took her along the path up towards the lip of Corata Pit.

I am going to die, she realised. *I will be with Mahudia in the void.*

She hoped the others would defeat the gods without her. She hoped the void was not too cold. She hated the cold. At least she would be with Mahudia.

She came to the place where the canopy was anchored to the path. Holding the huanu stone high, she brought it close to the barrier. *Carefully, carefully.* As the stone came within a finger-width of the barrier, the insubstantial membrane began to melt. The huanu stone absorbed magic. Noetos had told her, Olifa had confirmed it, and now she had proof. Quickly she clambered through the barrier, then pulled the stone away. With a ripple and a snap the canopy flowed back into place.

Now the hard part, the part that made her afraid. She inched out over the canopy, her legs shaking like saplings in a storm, making her way slowly under Umu's gaze. She could almost feel the god's eye on her, and knew she would make an irresistible target.

When it came, the flash and boom were far worse than Lenares could have imagined. Her heart seemed to stop in her chest, fluttered for a moment and then began a tentative rhythm. She found herself lying face down on the canopy, her limbs shaking, looking at the upturned faces below. Drawing a deep breath, she levered herself onto her hands and knees, then looked up into the storm.

'You've had a shot at me, Umu,' she called out, her voice small and quavery. 'Is that the best you can do?'

The Daughter's furious voice smote her ears. *What are you doing, little Lenares? Do not interfere in what you do not understand.*

Beyond the Wall of Time

The smell of burning air was very strong out here under the storm. It made her want to throw up. But she had to be brave or this would not work.

'I understand you well, Umu,' she said, 'and one day I will kill you. Maybe today.'

Please, please, repair the canopy while I'm distracting her, she begged silently, hoping someone down there was still thinking.

Put down the rock and we will talk, Umu said, her voice like thunder.

'No.' Lenares knew how to be stubborn. *You won't tell me what to do.*

Out of the corner of her eye she saw the canopy begin to heal. *Hurry, please hurry.* It was taking too long; she knew she had to keep Umu angry.

'I might talk to your brother,' she said.

You will do no such thing! I will kill you first!

'Not while I have the stone, you won't.'

I may not be able to kill you, the Daughter admitted, *but neither can I reward you. Do you know it is within my power to give you magic?*

'I don't believe you,' Lenares said, but she did. She knew Umu could do this. More, she wanted it: the desire leaped from her breast and seized her mind.

Keppia has done it before, you know. He gifted mortals with long life and magical insight. The cosmographer knew Umu spoke of the Padouki. *I'm as powerful as him. Don't you want magical power?*

'Yes,' Lenares whispered despite herself. 'Yes.'

Then put down the stone. I can't perform magic on you if you hold the stone.

Oh, so persuasive. Lenares knew it was a trap, an obvious trap; that she would die under a barrage of lightning should she relinquish the stone. But it was what she wanted. She thought again of the bronze map she had seen in the House of the Gods, of the countries and kingdoms of the world spread before her, of the knowledge that could be hers. It had felt so right to sit on one of the gods' chairs. All the questions she could have answered!

She knew she would make a far better god than selfish, cruel Umu.

Under the hole in the world, in thrall to the voice of a god – but really in thrall to her own desire – Lenares dropped the stone.

QUEEN

CHAPTER 7

THE RELUCTANT GOD

FLASH, CRASH, FLICKER, CRASH, FLASH. So much was happening all at once, Robal found it difficult to focus on one thing – until he saw Stella fall.

At that moment he was looking directly at her, wondering how long she could sustain the energy-draining magic she performed. By *his* side, at *his* bidding. Robal could never forget that. Certainly it dominated his bitter thoughts up until the moment the canopy failed and the fateful lightning bolt struck her. He didn't close his eyes, didn't flinch as the crooked light-sword stabbed down, searing its image on his brain. A second later he ran, ran heedlessly, despite the lurching rock under him, his temporary all-but-blindness and the danger above. Didn't care about that. Knew only one thing. She had fallen.

Robal was at her side even before he noticed she'd been hit, calling her name, shaking her, slapping her slack cheeks, shouting for help. Her hand and feet were charred black, smoking gently. All the hair on her head – her beautiful hair – had been burned away. Eyebrows, eyelashes gone. Skin red-raw. Eyes rolled up in her head. Not breathing. Not breathing.

Dead.

He bellowed the Destroyer's name, but the man was absorbed in the battle. He still hadn't turned to see what had happened. Or maybe he knew and simply didn't care.

He dragged her a few paces, moving her from the vulnerable

161

spot directly below the gaping hole in the canopy. Her skin rubbed off on the rock, came off in his hands.

'She's not breathing,' someone said. The scholar. He'd forgotten her name.

'Get help,' he said, his voice barely able to escape his tight throat.

'Stella?' The Destroyer had finally noticed. 'Stella!'

'She's not breathing.' Robal repeated the scholar's words, not caring how it sounded.

'She cannot die.' The Destroyer's ravaged face could have been wearing any expression: glee, shock, sorrow, exaltation. 'She cannot die.' He reached a hand down to her. Above, the canopy quivered.

Robal stared up into his enemy's eyes. 'If the Water of Life is in her blood,' he asked, 'what happens if her heart no longer beats?'

'I'm going to release the canopy,' the Destroyer said. 'Let everyone know.'

'You can't do that,' said the young fisherman, Mustar. 'Lenares is up there.'

The next few moments were utter confusion. Stella lying on the cold granite, lightning stabbing at the tiny figure seemingly floating on air high above them, Anomer shouting at the refugees, and a sudden weakness that caused Robal to stumble and fall to his knees.

The Destroyer stood over him. 'You want her to live? Then lie still. I'm going to draw heavily from you.' He cast his voice wide. 'Any other volunteers?'

What was the man doing? A paralysing greyness descended upon Robal just when he wanted to do something. Drawing? What was being drawn from him? He tried to shout at the Destroyer, to tell him to stop whatever he was doing, but the world had gone dark.

A few moments later the guardsman resurfaced, floating on a sea of grey. His first thought was of Stella. He tried to rise, tried to move, but nothing happened. Not a muscle would respond. He lay transfixed on the wide stone pathway, staring up at the shimmering barrier. Where was Stella? He tried to remember which way he'd fallen. No memory: he'd closed his eyes on the way down.

Kannwar's muffled voice came from somewhere close, just left of his feet. Stella would be there. All he had to do was raise his head a few inches.

He couldn't do it. The Destroyer had taken strength from him, stolen it, and though Robal knew it had been for Stella's benefit, the simmering anger he'd been resisting finally exploded into a brilliant, perfect rage. He wanted to release everything he was in one howling conflagration aimed at the Destroyer. His fury seared almost everything left within him. Memories, love, virtues: all began to melt, to change shape in the fire.

The Destroyer gave a shout. Was Stella alive? Had she moved? More likely he was reacting to the healing of the breach in the canopy. *Let the thing go. Let fire and death rain down. If she is dead, let no one else live. Especially not him.*

With an audible snap, the canopy vanished.

Robal exulted, and prepared for a fiery death.

A shriek issued from the figure high above as she fell. Another snap and the canopy reappeared, this time lower – but too late to save the cosmographer girl. Directly above him her body continued to fall, twisting and tumbling. A myriad lightning spears were thrown down from the storm, every one absorbed by the new barrier. The crashes of thunder were drowned out by a howl of anger. Robal tried to move his drained muscles, to roll away from where the girl was about to land, but could not raise even a twitch. He closed his eyes.

And opened them again to see the petrified face of the cosmographer suspended a few feet above his own. Her scream had stopped, replaced by frantic panting. He had never seen eyes so large, or a mouth describe such a perfect circle.

Without warning she fell the rest of the way, landing squarely on him. Her knee caught him a blow square in his privates, but he felt nothing. She sprang up, her lower lip bleeding, and looked at him with something approaching horror.

'Don't touch me,' she said, then bent down and picked up a small stone that had clattered to the ground with her.

Is this condition permanent? Robal wondered. *Has the Destroyer done to me what he did to Ma Umerta?* He decided it didn't matter. Perhaps he and Stella could be left lying here together. It seemed the only way he'd get to be alone with her.

No, not permanent, he realised as his legs began to ache, then twitch. The returning feeling grew into an agony of hot pins thrust into his muscles and joints. His voice returned and he bellowed with pain. His mouth filled with phlegm. He managed to raise his head enough to spit, and saw Stella's body lying prone about five paces distant. Willing his leaden limbs to move, he crawled to her side, to touch her ruined skin, her cold hands, her pale face.

'She can't be dead,' he rasped.

'She is.' The Destroyer's voice.

'I thought she was immortal.'

'No one knows the limits of what the Water of Life gives a human body. Clearly we have discovered that immortality requires a beating heart.'

Robal grated a derisive laugh. 'All life requires that, fool. If it were in my power, I would take it from you and give it to her.'

'As would I,' the Destroyer said, and it sounded so very sincere.

'I am willing to give it a try,' Robal said, levering himself to his feet. 'Come now, Destroyer, cut open a vein and give her a drink.'

The man looked taken aback. 'It does not work that way,' he said.

'No? I have seen her killed once, throat slashed by one of your Lords of Fear, and she came back to life. First thing she did was to drink her own blood.'

The Destroyer frowned.

'You didn't expect to be taken at your word, did you?' Robal laughed. 'Gather around, everyone!' he called, his voice cracking. 'Witness your beloved Undying Man, your heroic saviour, refuse to save his most faithful companion!'

He stepped back a pace to the upper edge of the path, next to a collection of digging implements.

The Destroyer took a step forward. 'Be silent, you fool, about things of which you are ignorant.'

'All I am ignorant of,' Robal said as people came closer, drawn by the shouting, 'is why you would refuse to renew the blood of immortality you have already bestowed on her. You captured and abused her seventy years ago, then stood back as she became a pariah in her own land, never denying the rumour that she had been your paramour. You knew they called her the Destroyer's Consort, but did nothing about it. You even knew the curse of immortality could not be passed sexually but let her suffer an un-fulfilled marriage.' He took a deep breath and wiped spittle from his lips. 'That's always been your motto, hasn't it, you paragon: "Use and discard." Now you've used her up you're ready to discard her. Not while I have breath and can wield a weapon!'

Robal snatched up a pickaxe and took a stance, trying not to wobble on his unsteady legs. It took everything he had to lift the weapon from the ground, and cold sweat sprang up on his brow as he struggled to hold it steady.

A few of those watching laughed.

A stone sword sprang from the Destroyer's open hand. At the same time the granite beneath Robal's left foot disappeared. He staggered and almost fell.

More laughter.

'You believe Stella needs blood?' the Destroyer asked, raising the sword.

'That . . . won't be necessary.'

The crowd gasped and pulled back. The Destroyer gave an exclamation of surprise. Robal turned as swiftly as he could – which was not very swiftly at all – and Stella stood there, her skin healing as he watched.

'Stella,' the Destroyer said, springing to her side.

Robal tried to stagger in her direction, but fell to one knee. The pickaxe cracked him a nasty blow on the ankle and he let out a yelp.

'Back again,' she said heavily. 'Thought I'd made it through this time, but no, I've been dragged back.'

'No, my queen,' Robal protested. 'There are those who value your return.'

His heart beat wildly, out of control, and he feared he might collapse or throw up or burst into tears at the sight of her.

'So I heard,' she said, a touch of something – bitterness? laughter? – in her voice.

'You sound different,' said the Destroyer.

'I am different,' she said, but did not elaborate.

'I thought you had died.'

'So did I,' Robal added lamely.

Stella's lips twisted in disgust. 'I did die,' she said. 'Just not enough. I will not speak about it, not now, not here. Besides, we are neglecting the real heroes.'

Hero? Who has been heroic? Robal had not really been paying attention, so focused had he been on Stella and the Destroyer. But the canopy still held, though he could hear a faint background roaring beyond it, and see occasional shudders as the gods worked their magic against it in vain. The injured were receiving assistance, and the remainder of the refugees milled around, sat together talking or stood close by, listening with puzzlement to the exchange.

The Destroyer nodded. 'We are speaking, I presume, of Anomer and his team of brave locals who allowed him to draw from their essenza. They were instrumental in healing the breach in our barrier, at significant cost to themselves.'

He waved a hand to where a few people lay prostrate, though they all seemed to be alive. Anomer looked up from where he bent over a woman and gave them a wave.

Stella spoke. 'And of Lenares the cosmographer, who climbed above the canopy on her own to face the god and draw her fire. Lenares, it took great courage to do what you did, and your act distracted Umu long enough for us to make good the damage she did. We are very grateful.'

The cosmographer girl smiled and blushed, clearly unused to compliments of any kind. A few of the onlookers clapped.

'We were also rendered a great service by two magicians some distance away,' said the Destroyer. 'Captain Duon of Elamaq and Arathé of Fossa gave liberally of themselves, sending their magic to assist Anomer in tapping into the Malayuan locals. We hope they will rejoin us soon, at which time we will thank them in person.'

'And one other,' Stella said. 'Robal, my guardsman, put aside his quarrel with the Undying Man and poured his energy out in a great flood for him to use. I felt it even as I wandered beyond the void. I have no doubt it made the difference. Without the actions of brave men like Robal, the god-breathed storm would have broken through and killed us all.'

Robal wanted to strike the smirking Destroyer down where he stood. He'd put her up to this, nothing was more certain. Poured his energy out? It had been taken without his permission.

'So, miss, when can we leave?' asked an elderly man. 'Some of us want to get back to our homes and families, like, to see what remains.'

'Nothing remains,' said the Destroyer. 'Any houses you had will be debris scattered to the four corners of Malayu. Your families will not have survived unless they took shelter in holes somewhere, as we did. It is a bitter pill, but I will not deal in false hope.' A number of those listening began to weep. 'Andratan will aid in repair of your homes and in the restoration of government. I will ask the Factor of Malayu to make a personal inspection. This land will be rebuilt.'

'Doesn't bring back our families,' someone said.

'No, it does not. There is nothing Andratan can do about that. But we did what we could and kept you alive. We hope you are grateful for that, at least.'

There had been deaths, Robal discovered as he stumbled around after Stella and her shadowy companion. Dozens of them. A handful struck down by lightning, many more by the acidic rain. A few bodies lay further down the stepped slope of the pit: fallen, no doubt, when the canopy was removed for a few moments as Lenares was rescued. They had been dead already, Stella said, victims of the storm-talons, and she pointed to the gruesome stab marks through their bodies.

'How many people lived in the path of the storm?' Lenares asked the Destroyer.

'We don't have an accurate census. Had the storm struck further north, it might have claimed a million lives. Perhaps a hundred thousand people live on the Mala Peninsula and in the towns of Camantain, Long Pike Mouth and Doma, but citizens down this way sometimes . . . ah . . . actively resist enumeration.'

'Tax avoiders,' Stella said. 'We have them too.' She stared at Robal.

'I never avoided any taxes!' he said, angered at her gaze.

'Your friend and his father do. You know that is the reason why their settlement is always on the move.'

'So you don't approve of them? This after they treated you as an honoured guest?'

'I'm not asking about tax,' Lenares said, as abruptly as ever. 'I don't care about money. I want to know how many people the storm killed so I can estimate how much larger the hole in the world has grown. It feeds on unnatural death.'

'A hundred thousand people slaughtered by one storm?' Stella said.

'They may not all have died,' the Destroyer responded.

'But you said before that nothing remains.'

'I said that to keep expectations low. I am hoping people will have some pleasant surprises ahead of them.'

'And suffer in the meantime,' Stella said disapprovingly. 'Perhaps making rash decisions based on your "low expectations." You are a cruel man.'

'I will ask you in ten years' time whether you still think I am cruel. Conditions are different over here. Cultures are more complex. As I have explained to you previously, I must work within the boundaries the people have set.'

'So how many dead?' Lenares persisted.

'Perhaps twenty, thirty thousand,' said the Destroyer. 'Maybe fewer, maybe more.'

The cosmographer shook her head. 'The hole in the world will soon be big enough for Keppia and Umu to do whatever they want.'

'So what are the implications?' Moralye asked in her soft voice.

'The next thing they send against us will be far worse,' Lenares said. 'We have reached a tipping point. From now on, there is little we can do to keep the hole small save killing the gods themselves.'

It took the best part of the night for the storm to blow itself out. For hours the wind shrieked, thumping against the barrier and the walls of the pit. Around the middle of the night a huge crash woke everyone in the camp: the wind had succeeded in bringing down the top half of the thin granite column that had, according to Seren, marked the height of the original granite rock. People shook their heads at the strength of wind required to do such a thing, and after that there was no more talk of leaving the pit. Indeed, many people came up to Stella and Kannwar to thank them both for the protection they had provided.

Stella's head nodded. Her mouth said all the right things, with more graciousness than she herself could have mustered, and in a slightly lower voice. Stella herself was a tiny ball of awareness in the back of her own head, a badly hurt and frightened presence lost in her own mind, not in possession of her own body. A body that now belonged to the Most High.

It is the only way I can save you, he had said as she lay on the ground, the terrible flame scouring her life away. *Don't struggle against me.*

I don't want to be saved, she had replied. *I'm tired. Let me go.*

The Most High had sighed then, a sound encapsulating the weariness of the world. *Ah, if only the world would let go. But you must learn, Stella Pellwen, that the world does not let go, not when you play such a large part in it.*

Save someone else, she persisted. *Others are dead or dying and want to live. Save them.*

If I let you die, many others will follow. Do you want that?

She had responded with anger. *Then don't arrange the world in such a way that it depends on me! Change the story! Write me out of it!*

You know it does not work that way. Your friend Leith knew this, and eventually accepted his role. It's not like you to be selfish.

But I'm so tired! she had cried.

So am I, said the Most High. *I make you a promise, Stella Pellwen. When the world lets me go, I will ensure it lets you go also.*

Reluctantly she had allowed him to fill the empty spaces she had been driven from. Immortal by virtue of her Water of Life-touched blood, she had been vulnerable to anything that stopped her heart, preventing the tainted blood from renewing her skin, muscles and bones. The lightning strike had convulsed her heart, and the blood had ceased flowing. It had taken direct and continued intervention from the Most High to restart her circulation.

Will it always be like this? she asked as another family came to pay their respects.

No. Soon your body will begin to renew your heart. When that happens I can leave you alone.

Why am I so important?

I truly do not know, answered the Most High.

What sort of answer is that? Of course you know.

I do not. I am aware of possibilities, that is all. Every choice you make subtly alters the balance of those possibilities. Because you are one of the travellers you act as a – forgive me the pun – lightning rod to the gods, attracting their attention. Were you to leave, they would have less reason to focus on this group. And in many possible futures you have important tasks to complete.

Always important tasks. I've had seventy years of important tasks. When do I get to rest?

Seventy years? the voice said, and for a moment the Most High sounded ancient. *Seventy whole years? That is a very long time.*

You don't have much of a talent for sarcasm, Stella replied. She knew this was no way to talk to a god, especially not one who had in anger split Dona Mihst asunder and cursed the First Men, but she spoke with the carelessness of one with nothing left to lose.

No, I do not. When people converse with me they are generally seeking answers, not humour.

It was a fair point, and Stella chewed on it for a while.

Around them the refugees from the storm settled down,

organising whatever comforts they could and preparing for sleep. Children cried, old men chattered and quite a few snored; sounds infinitely preferable to the screaming that had filled Corata Pit a few hours previously. There was little to eat, but hunger was a small inconvenience.

I have questions for you, Stella said.

The Most High smiled, lighting up her mind. *I'm sure you do*, he said. *Please ask them, but be patient with my replies.*

She'd intended to ask him about his children, the Son and the Daughter, but her thoughts turned to her own family. Bitter thoughts.

Why did my brother die?

He drank himself to death, said the Most High. *But you know this, so it is another question you wish to ask.*

Why did he have to die while I was away serving you? The question was more accurate, nearer to what she really wanted to say, but the asking carried mixed feelings, anger and guilt among them.

Ah. He didn't have to die. Death attended upon the lifestyle he chose.

That is only part of the reason, Stella snapped. *Why didn't you prevent it? Why couldn't his death have waited until I returned? We rendered you a great service and suffered for it.*

Near the heart of it, this.

Child, you left Loulea with Leith and the others because you wanted to escape the village. You saw your destiny in the wider world. But you did not consider the effect your feigned death had on your brother, who had already been driven half-mad by the drink. It was because you left that he took to it more fiercely than ever. Your leaving precipitated his death.

No, she whispered. But the truth of it encircled her damaged heart.

You have a complaint against me. I hear it and take it seriously. You rendered me a great service, you say, and suffered for it. You wish to know why that should be so.

Stella wanted the conversation to end, but where could she flee to avoid the god?

Yes.

171

You came into my service as little more than a dumb animal, unaware you were serving me, said the Most High. *I yoked you to my service like an ox put to the plough, so that your suffering would not be in vain. At no time during the Falthan War did you choose to serve me: I made service out of your actions.*

So it wasn't your plan that I ended up enslaved by the Destroyer? That my part in the salvation of Faltha was as his unwilling consort, while Leith got to play the hero?

Such petty, bitter words, but they were at her core. How could she keep them hidden from him?

I do not have a plan. Why would I create things separate from myself, entities with conditional freedom, only to prescribe their actions? You acted foolishly and paid a heavy price as you walked on the path you chose. Leith acted bravely and suffered far less as a result – though you have always underestimated the extent of his suffering and guilt. He always believed, for example, he was responsible for his brother's death. Yet despite your different paths, you ended up in the same place. That is because, in the end, you put yourself aside and acted with courage. If I have a plan, it is to encourage people to find the least difficult path possible.

Time to hazard her question. *Is that why you have had so much trouble with your own son and daughter? Because you don't have a plan? Isn't this all your fault?*

A brief silence. She'd shocked him perhaps. But he must have thought about this many times during the thousands of years since his children had rebelled against him. It might be he'd never been called on to explain it before.

Perhaps you see me as a benevolent uncle, someone unfailingly pleasant and indulgent, he said. *If so, you need to dismiss the thought. Love is not always pleasant and indulgent. It can be severe. Sometimes it must be severe.*

Is that a threat? Have I threatened you? How could a mere human be a threat to the Most High god? Oh, I forgot. Kannwar of Dona Mihst has already shown how it is possible.

A wave of anger washed across her emotions. His anger. Before he could speak, she added: *You're about to tell me I'm speaking about* things I don't understand. You will say you cannot explain your inscrutable purposes to such a limited mind as mine. But the problem is this: you tried explaining your purposes to Kannwar two thousand years ago, when he was a child, because you wanted to raise him up in opposition to your own rebellious children. You tried and failed. Don't you see you need to get better at explaining things? Don't you think you ought to become a little less inscrutable?

She waited for his anger to consume her, but his voice remained mild. The problem with Kannwar was not in the explanation or in his understanding, said the Most High with brittle patience. It was his refusal to accede to my plan.

You do have a plan then. She loosed the words at him like an arrow.

I have many plans. Plans for this, plans for that. But I do not have one overall plan within which everyone must fit. Instead I have an infinite number of plans, each one abandoned whenever anyone makes a choice. Kannwar made his choice; I abandoned my plan.

You had a plan for your children too, didn't you? What was it? What went wrong with it?

Very well, he said, and Stella felt a sigh blow across her soul.

Yes, I created the world and all within it. I loved it and made a special place in which I could watch it grow without ruining it. Remember, I need to keep separate from it in order for it to remain itself. You have been to that special place and call it the House of the Gods.

Yet this was not enough for the people of the earth. They came searching for me, besieging me in my own house, demanding I provide for them, that I do the work I had created them to do. This they called "worship."

I thought worship was the reverent paying of respect, she said.

So did I. But the children of the earth have always seen worship as the exchanging of a feather-weight of devotion for a ton-weight of assistance. I gave them mouths, it is true, so they could know desire and satisfaction. But I gave them arms and legs so they could be instrumental in satisfying their desires. What they call worship is the voluntary amputation of their limbs, the substitution of my limbs for theirs. Some of them even wanted their mouths removed so they no longer had either wants or satisfaction.

So I hid from them. Not out of fear or timidity, but because I could not grant them their desire without destroying the essence of what they were. However, the knowledge that I existed in the world, and was approachable, led many of them to cast away their independence, to abandon their responsibilities in endless acts of so-called worship, all designed to draw me out. The children of the earth put themselves in situations where, in my name, they would die without my intervention. They planted no seed, they harvested no crops, relying on me to provide.

They began to die.

I was enraged by the first doubters. 'See,' they cried, 'the Giant of the Desert' – for so they called me – 'does not exist, for he does not rescue those who love him the most. Those who trust only themselves live happy, fulfilled lives, while those who trust him die of starvation and disease.'

So, against my own wishes, I intervened, weakening the Wall of Time. I sent wind to spread the wild seed and rain to help it grow. I let it be known that this was miraculous, a sign that the giant still cared for them. Many of my worshippers left their temples and harvested the grain, but others remained as professional clergy and stole much of the food under the guise of a tithe.

Should I have intervened, Stella? I could have. But then the Wall of Time would have been breached, and I would have swallowed them all.

Then came the Time of Quarrels. Those who had worked hard all their lives, planting and harvesting in season, were jealous of those who had been miraculously provided for. The temple-dwellers tried to extend their demands for a tithe to all who harvested grain, irrespective of who had planted it. The earth became a battlefield, a place of pain and suffering, as each faction fought the other. Even the temple-dwellers rediscovered how effective their own limbs could be. Having neglected them in my service, they used them to deal death to their enemies.

Should I have made them stop, Stella? I could have. But then the Wall of Time would have been breached, and I would have swallowed them all.

I did what I could. I called a meeting of the three factions in the

174

House of the Gods. The temple-dwellers, of course, would not come. They were too busy worshipping me – begging me to do them favours, trying to compel me with magic spells recited from their holy book – to attend. Both of the other two factions sent a representative. A man and a woman. I fashioned three seats and we sat together, man, woman and giant, considering the world and debating what might be done.

Should I have told them what to do, Stella? I could have. But then the Wall of Time would have been breached, and I would have swallowed them all.

After years of debate, the man and the woman agreed to a truce. They left my house and returned to their own people. However, they discovered that their time in the House of the Gods had changed them. Having spent such a long time outside the Wall of Time, they were no longer mortal children. They dwelled on both sides of the wall. Their factions sent them back to the House, one fearful of what Keppia had become, the other hopeful that Umu could use her power to demand concessions.

Should I have stripped them of their power without their assent, Stella? I could have. But then the Wall of Time would have been breached, and I would have swallowed them all.

How I loved them! But when I asked them to surrender their powers, they refused. 'It is one or the other,' I told them. 'You would be best to return to your people. You will not enjoy life beyond the wall.' 'Nevertheless, we will not relinquish being gods,' they replied.

So they chose to live in the House of the Gods as my Son and my Daughter, yet soon they began to miss the freedom they once enjoyed. Beyond the wall, Stella, life is different. You do not face uncertain choices. I knew they were discontented, yet I was bound not to interfere, save offering advice.

What was I to do with Keppia and Umu? They were not content to pass their time in the House of the Gods. So I sent them to whisper to their people, to offer them guidance, to assist the weak and the downtrodden. Of course I knew they would likely interfere, but I had no choice. To prevent them interfering was to interfere myself.

They interfered. My beloved children raised vast armies and laid siege to the House of the Gods, demanding my surrender. Their solution to

Russell Kirkpatrick

the problem of the Wall of Time was to drive me beyond it, and to take my place themselves.

I need not have fled. I could have remained. But then there would have been slaughter, and my supporters, innocent of any crime, would have been wiped out. I had been left with an impossible choice. Remain and witness the death of those who followed me, or leave and so forsake the Amaqi, the children of the earth. So I left, and travelled north to Faltha to provide my followers with a new home.

My leaving, however, cracked the Wall of Time. Keppia and Umu saw this weakness and, desirous of a full return to the world with their god-like powers, have been trying ever since to exploit it. I attempted to raise a champion among the First Men to oppose their interference, but I failed. Kannwar was the result of a thousand years of careful instruction and breeding, yet he exercised his freedom and opposed me. Ever have the children of the earth had such refusal in their power.

And I cannot say he was wrong, Stella. I had such hopes, and my heart was filled with love. I thought he would embrace my plan. I allowed my love, my trust and my desperation to cloud my judgement, yet I would do it again. I must trust my children; otherwise, if I limit them—

I know, Stella said. *You will breach the Wall of Time, and creation will end.*

Kannwar turned against me. He decided to reveal my offer to his fellow First Men by partaking of the Water of Life, the water I had planned for him to take gradually over many years, just as Keppia and Umu did. But, as you know only too well, your bodies are not able to bear such a dosage of the Water of Life. Kannwar wished the First Men to become gods, but despite my warnings he partook of the Fountain.

Then you interfered, didn't you? Stella said. *You punished him, and all the First Men.*

Yes. I had made the mistake of introducing a command into the lives of my children. Something they could disobey. When they disobeyed, I was forced to act. And in acting I further weakened the Wall of Time. I reached through to Dona Mihst and cracked the earth, causing a great earthquake and flood.

176

Since that time I have been very careful, only exercising my power when invited, and then only through the will and bodies of others.

Like Hal, said Stella. *And Leith.*

And yourself, the Most High added. *Among others.*

Kannwar, said Stella.

Yes. After running from me for two thousand years, he is very unhappy about it.

Do you think he will remain true to you?

This was not the question she most wanted to ask. Under her superficial thought lurked the question: *Will he remain true to me?*

The Most High gave her an answer. *I do not know. It is his choice. He will betray us. He has a history of deception.*

Yet he surrendered himself to me, allowing me to use him to drive Keppia from the House of the Gods and the body he inhabited. He could have betrayed us then, but he did not.

What sort of god are you? Stella asked angrily. *You choose not to see the future, you refuse to interfere, you withhold miracles. Are you any use at all?*

I am a reluctant god, he said.

Conal awoke from darkness as thick as tar. His remaining eye was stabbed by daggers of light, forcing him to blink rapidly. Dirt ground itself into his eyeball, but he could not raise his hands to remove the irritation.

Someone had buried him.

But I'm not dead! Why would someone bury me alive?

Panic rippled through his body, but still he could move nothing but his eye. The last thing he could remember was Duon's foolish attempt to free them from Husk's clutches. It had obviously not worked. Conal could have told the stupid southerner and the fat girl it would not work, the voice was too clever for them. He could feel the voice even now, nestled in the back of his head, ready to inflict further suffering on him and everyone else.

Conal willed his muscles to move, but there was no response. His head was clear of rocks and dirt, but the rest of him had been covered. *Why, why, why?* Had he been caught in a landslide?

A slurry of mud trickled into his good eye. He tried desperately to blink it away, but it filled the gap between his lower eyelid and his eyeball. Needles of pain burned into his eye, reducing his vision to blurred shapes.

Something moved above him.

'They buried you deep,' it said. 'They must have wanted you to stay dead.'

A hand scraped the mud from his face, one of the fingernails casually scoring his eyeball. He yelped, and his mouth filled with dirt.

'Won't be long and we'll have you free,' said the voice. 'Then we'll see what shape you're in. Not good, I expect.'

While Conal attempted to spit out the dirt, the figure busied itself clearing mud and rocks from the priest's torso and limbs, humming all the while. It seemed to take forever.

'Who are you?' Conal forced the words out.

The figure bent over him and the face drew close.

Conal screamed.

The storm had blown itself out. All that remained was a thin, cold rain spattering from low, formless cloud. Lenares insisted the hole in the world had gone and that Umu was nowhere near, so Kannwar had let the barrier above them dissolve.

Strength had been slow to return to Robal's limbs. Even now, hours later, he leaned against the cracked base of the former column at the edge of Corata Pit, his shaky legs barely able to bear his weight. The Destroyer apologised to him for such an abrupt and deep drain of his energy, but stopped short of acknowledging it as theft. Instead, it seemed he wished for praise, repeatedly emphasising how Stella had survived and the barrier had held.

'Had you not been willing to give of yourself, many more people would have died,' the man said in an oily voice. Robal seethed at the patronising words. 'Though the depth of your strength was a surprise. You kept pouring yourself at me long after I'd taken what I thought you could bear.'

What on earth was the loathsome man talking about?

178

His wittering continued. 'Have you ever been tested for magical potential?'

'We don't do that in Faltha,' Robal responded. He didn't care how rude he sounded; this man could not be borne.

'I have returned the favour,' said the Destroyer. 'You should be feeling better. I infused you with some of my own strength.' When Robal didn't respond, the man frowned and said: 'You should be honoured. In Andratan my servants compete to be the ones I drain to perform my magic.'

'This isn't Andratan. I gave nothing to you willingly, thief. You took it. You ripped it out of us.'

'Your queen lay dying on the ground, man! What did you want me to do? Hold a meeting perhaps? The Daughter could have struck at any time. Lenares' brave actions gave me the time to repair the canopy, and then everyone's strength kept Stella alive. How can you find fault with that?'

'There is no fault,' Stella said.

Her voice had an odd timbre, as it had since she had awoken; something damaged in her throat perhaps. Whatever the cause, it made Robal's flesh creep.

'No fault,' she repeated. 'Everyone did what they could. Now we need to move on.'

Robal flushed at the rebuke. How could the woman be so ignorant of the Destroyer's manipulation? Or was the priest right after all? Was she in his thrall? He settled for casting a single glare at the Destroyer.

'Move on from blame, or move on from this pit?' said Anomer.

'Both,' she replied, 'but particularly the former.' Absently she scratched at her face and a piece of skin flaked off.

Something is wrong. Stella is conscious of her appearance. She ought to have noted that. A dark suspicion entered his mind, but he dismissed it. *Surely not.*

'I'm more concerned with the latter,' Anomer said. 'The locals have gone to search for their loved ones, and I intend to follow them. My father and sister are out there somewhere, alive but exhausted, easy prey should the gods return. Does anyone object to my plan?'

'Do you want company?' Mustar asked.

'Of course,' replied Anomer. 'As many as wish to come.'

But the words sounded less than sincere to Robal. *He is wary of the boy around his sister*, he thought. *Jealousy is such a petty thing when displayed in such an obvious fashion*.

'People are weary,' Moralye said. 'Should we not wait for the others to rejoin us?'

Anomer shook his head. 'I'm no longer in communication with them. In Raceme mind-contact led the gods to us. I don't want Umu or Keppia to sense them out there on their own.'

'We do have to work out what to do next,' Robal said, trying to impose himself. 'We need to capture or destroy the gods, but every time they come close we can do nothing but flee or take shelter. Shouldn't we think of a way to trap them?'

Every head turned to the cosmographer.

Her tongue flicked over her lips and she fiddled with her hair. Everyone knew the story of how she'd captured Umu. Robal could see just how much of their hope was fixed on her.

'I . . . I do have some ideas,' she said.

'Then share them with us all!' a voice boomed across the pit. Striding towards them, a wide grin on his face, came Conal the priest.

Dryman – or the thing now inhabiting his body – had dug him out of his burial pit, then hauled him to his feet. Its mouth drew close to Conal's face, the breath like the stink of a latrine. The priest tried to break the monster's grip, but could barely move. Some sort of paralysis then, and not the weight of the soil, had prevented him moving.

'Good to see you again, Umu,' it said.

Conal had always considered himself smart. As a child he'd been vastly more intelligent than his peers, so obviously so that they'd reacted in the traditional manner by beating him at every opportunity. Not that this stopped him demonstrating his superiority at every opportunity. His career in the Koinobia had been characterized by rapid promotion and jealous gossip. Despite appearances he had always been a keen student of behaviour. Even so, it took him a few moments to realize what Dryman's words meant.

'I'm not Umu,' he meant to say, but there was no connection between his thoughts and his mouth. Instead, the presence in the back of his head leapt forward and took control of his speech.

'You look like a mummer,' said his mouth.

Oh, Most High, he wailed, shut up and silent in his own body. *Please, not this, not again!*

'And you look a great deal plumper than I remember,' Dryman's mouth said, breathing foetid fumes into his face.

Conal's mouth laughed. 'The fool inside this body thinks I've gained temporary possession of it.'

'As does mine, though the Emperor of Elamaq is beginning to taste the first flowering of despair.' A grin split the horrid face opposite Conal's. 'You died, priest. You are forever severed from your body. Since you were not using it, my sister has taken it for her own. You may still see, hear and feel, but you are merely a spectator. She can banish you into the void at any time.'

I died?

'He does not yet understand, brother.'

'Your essenza has already gone to the void beyond the wall,' Dryman said, 'as has that of the man who once occupied this body. However, memories are slow to fade. We have prevented them fading completely so we can use these bodies with a degree of subtlety.'

This is not a spike? You are not controlling me from somewhere else?

A laugh echoed in his mind. *I need a body, and here yours lay cooling.*

How did I die? Real fear began to grow, though it was a strange fear, not affecting his glands or his muscles.

I do not know, and I do not care. From your injuries it appears you were beaten perhaps, or you fell. Given the cliff above us, I'd guess the latter.

Injuries?

Oh dear, I've picked a clever one. Of course injuries. Your legs are

181

shattered, your back is broken, your skull shattered and your heart has failed.

But I'm standing now and I don't feel any pain.

You'll never feel anything again, Umu said. *I'm doing the feeling for you.*

It has been many centuries since I enjoyed physical sensations, and while this is not pleasant, it is better than the void. You see, your body is not alive. I am merely animating it with magic. It will not do to allow anyone too close, but there are advantages. I can, for example, walk with fractured legs.

He – she – took a few steps, and he could hear the crunching of bones and gristle. His fear crested – *this is real, it is not a dream –* and he thought he would go mad.

Please, let me go!

If I let you go you will find yourself in the void. Surely an unsurpassed intimate view of my triumph is better than that?

Why did Keppia dig me out? I thought you and your brother hated each other!

Oh, we do. Once we have killed or enslaved your friends and broken asunder the Wall of Time, we will fight again. But until then we will cooperate.

'Does he understand yet?' Dryman's body asked.

'He's beginning to,' Conal's body replied. No, not Conal's body. Umu's body. 'Perhaps he'll appreciate his position a little better on the way back to Stella and her friends.'

What are you going to do with me?

With you? Nothing. I am going to take this body and use it to bring mayhem to those you ought to have trusted.

She began rummaging through his memories, pushing and prodding his body from the inside, matching her movements to his gait, her expressions to his.

You were rather an unpleasant person, she said to him. *I'm sure no one liked you. They are certain to hate you after I've finished with you.*

Despite her boast that she could propel his injured body, it was so badly damaged she had to take the time to exercise some rough

182

healing. Bones fused together, skin healed, and something akin to blood flowed through his veins. She had walked him backwards and forwards, perfecting his slightly waddling gait, laughing and taunting him all the while.

Now he stood at the lip of a giant hole in the ground. His friends – he truly thought of them as friends now, in contrast to the enemy that had hold of him – looked up at his greeting. He could not fight it. He was a puppet with the strings cut.

'Conal!' Stella cried, a smile on her face.

Inside his tiny prison Conal shrieked. Far, far better to be dead and gone than to watch this.

'Where are the others?' asked Noetos's brat. 'Where are my father and sister? Have you seen them?'

A memory stirred: a whirl of arms and legs, falling. A pact he'd tried to pull out of. Arathé explaining how one of them needed to die in order to break Husk's hold on them all. His memories, lying open to Umu.

'I have seen Arathé,' she said through his mouth. 'She and Duon are well.'

'Where are they?' pressed Anomer.

Not a question Umu could answer. 'They will be here soon,' she temporised. 'In the meantime, what are our plans?'

The cosmographer girl stared at her, at him. Conal tried to prevent Umu from accessing his memories, but she rifled through them. *Bah, I know all that, she said. With her strange powers she will see through me very soon. Therefore she must be our first target.*

'What has happened to you, Conal?' Lenares said as he drew closer, walking carefully around the rim of the hole.

Umu's thoughts flashed across his mind like fireflies. 'I was badly hurt,' he said, pulling a pitiful face. 'About to die. But I used some residual magic from my captivity by Husk to heal myself. It is no wonder I appear different.'

Curse Umu's cleverness.

'That could be it,' Lenares said doubtfully. 'But who is Husk?'

'Sit down, everyone, and I will tell you,' said his mouth.

When they had done so, Umu began his sorry tale, tapping

183

his memories. She kept largely to the facts, surprising Conal. The key difference was, of course, his death: Umu told her listeners that the combined effects of three falls were enough to break Husk's hold over them. 'He is now no longer a factor in this conflict,' she concluded, 'likely licking his wounds in Andratan.'

'Andratan?' said half a dozen voices.

Umu quailed inside Conal's body. She'd made a mistake of some kind perhaps. The priest rejoiced.

Kannwar stood, towering above him, his shadow falling across Conal's face. 'This voice controlling you called himself Husk and dwells in Andratan?'

Conal's head nodded.

The tall man, possessor of so much power it unnerved even Umu, turned to Stella, his face clouded with anger. 'I know who this man is. You and I, we have made a huge mistake.'

'Doesn't anyone want to hear my plan?' Lenares said, but the others were no longer paying her any attention.

'I do, tell me,' said Conal's mouth.

But even Lenares turned away, wandering over to where Stella and Kannwar sat, heads together.

Umu ground Conal's teeth in frustration.

CHAPTER 8

SHIPWRECK

'I'VE NEVER SEEN ANYTHING LIKE it,' Kilfor said.

Sauxa stepped carefully over another body. ''Course you haven't. We're from the plains, boy; we don't get storms like that one, ulcers to its black soul. 'Cept, of course, the whirlwinds of 990. Now there were storms set to blow your teeth out your—'

'Enough of your foolish stories,' Kilfor said, not ungently. 'This was not a normal storm.'

'Oh? You're an expert on Bhrudwan weather then?'

Kilfor pushed aside a splintered and broken pile of timbers. 'No, of course not.'

'Well then.' The old man folded his arms, his smug expression indicating he thought he'd won the argument.

'But the people who lived in this village would have been experts,' Kilfor said. 'If storms like this one were commonplace, they would not have been slaughtered like this.'

'Huh,' Sauxa said grudgingly, unfolding his arms.

The two men arrived at the end of the street. At least, it was the end of the street now: the paved road ended in a newly formed cliff twenty feet high. Between them and the sea, a hundred paces distant, lay a pile of mangled wreckage. The upturned hulls of fishing boats, timber from houses, large tree trunks, boulders and bodies – everywhere, bodies – were covered in a thin layer of sand. Seagulls and other winged scavengers fought over any morsel they could find, whether fish or human flesh. Beyond the wreckage,

185

which stretched as far as Kilfor could see in either direction, the sea lapped gently.

The stench was unbearable.

'Huge waves smashed the village to a pulp,' Kilfor said. 'The wind would have been bad enough: we've seen what it did to the farmhouses and barns inland. Like I said. No normal storm.'

Kilfor and Sauxa had made their way east and then south through the fringes of Patina Padouk, beginning their long walk home to Chardzou. They had seen the clouds forming out to sea, their plainsman's weather sense warning them to hurry southwards. Even so, they had been forced to take shelter in a shallow limestone cave, while all around them the violent wind ripped trees up by the roots. They had sheltered for a day, venturing out only when the storm had ended, to find the great forest decimated. A few trees remained standing, stripped of leaves and branches, while the majority of the forest lay broken on the ground, bare trunks pointing to the northeast like accusatory fingers.

The two men had looked at each other for a few minutes; then, without a word being said, turned and made their way north, back from where they had come.

'Can't leave Robal and his friends to deal with this,' Sauxa said eventually.

'They might need help,' Kilfor agreed.

'Even that magician might not have been able to protect them,' Sauxa added.

They had emerged from Patina Padouk – or what was left of its northern marches – on a bluff overlooking the remnants of a fishing village. There had been a pier, Kilfor thought, judging by the few bent piles some distance out to sea. There had been fishing vessels. They had passed two of them an hour or so back, wedged high up in trees. The men had wondered what else there had been, and what might be left.

Now they knew. What was left were flies, millions of them, and a liberal coating of debris.

'How many people do you think lived here?' Kilfor asked his father.

'A thousand perhaps. I don't know. I'm not skilled at estimating the size of places like this.'

'Why not? You spent enough time inside their taverns and dosshouses.'

'Inside being the operative word,' the old man said.

There was no heart in their sparring, it was a reflexive action. 'No one alive.'

'I don't know about that.' Sauxa leaned forward, better to look to his right along the beach, to where the coast curved around to a headland. 'Look there.' He pointed. 'Tell me what your young eyes see.'

Kilfor squinted. 'There's wreckage, lots of it. It looks like a boat – no, a ship. A large ship.'

'I could see that,' said his father. 'What else?'

'Movement,' Kilfor concluded after a long look. 'Can't tell what.'

'People clambering over the wreckage?'

'More like birds, I think, after whatever food the ship was carrying.'

'We had better see if there are any survivors who need our help,' Sauxa said.

Kilfor laughed. 'Better see if any treasure needs our help is what you mean.'

'If we can't help the people, we'll help ourselves,' said the old man, chuckling. 'Come on.'

The day was about done by the time the two plainsmen reached the wreck. As the fiery sun set behind them, it lit up the cracked and broken timbers of the ship's hull with a golden glow. Spars and masts littered the beach around the shipwreck. Apart from the groaning of overstretched timber, the scene was silent.

'Where are the people you saw?' Sauxa asked.

'Hola!' cried Kilfor. 'Anyone there?'

A flock of brightly coloured birds leapt into the air at his shout, arrowing away towards the headland to his left.

'No one. Come, boy, let us examine the ship more closely. It might be to our advantage.'

Kilfor felt uneasy about this. 'Father, I have no objection to taking whatever valuables we might find. But Robal might be lying under a tree somewhere. I think we ought first to assure ourselves our friends are well before spending time searching for treasure.'

'Fine sentiments,' Sauxa said, smiling. 'At first light tomorrow we head back to the place we left him. But we can't travel anywhere now, can we? Look, the sun is about to set. Do you fancy walking through this land at night, with the bodies of the dead everywhere and debris ready to ensnare you? We're here now; what harm in having a look?'

Kilfor had to laugh. The old man was clever still.

The travellers sat in a wide semicircle, Kannwar and Stella at its centre. Ten hard faces, all wearing accusatory expressions, sitting in judgement on them. Stella wanted to weep.

They had every right to be judgemental. The story Kannwar had told was an evil one, with few redeeming features, and even Stella had not known it all. The bare facts seemed to confirm everything Falthans believed about the Destroyer and his consort. She knew that after the telling had ended they would be fortunate to keep any of their companions.

Deorc of Jasweyah was a very ambitious man, Kannwar had said. The mountainous land of Jasweyah was an amalgam of various kingdoms, always warring, requiring much intervention on the part of Andratan – until Deorc rose to power and changed everything. From being a drain on the Undying Man's resources, Jasweyah under Deorc was transformed into a net exporter of men and produce. Kannwar rewarded Deorc for this by promoting him to Lord of Andratan Keep, second in the Bhrudwan Empire only to the Undying Man himself.

Deorc had not wanted the promotion, apparently being content to rule in Jasweyah, yet he could not resist the Undying Man's summons. In truth, Kannwar told them, he promoted the young magician to keep him under close surveillance, fearing he would lead another rebellion. Deorc was clever enough to know this, yet not strong enough to refuse.

So began years of planning for the invasion of Faltha. Deorc lobbied to be granted the leadership of the Undying Man's mighty army, but was refused. That honour would not be given to anyone but the Destroyer himself. Instead, Deorc was given the task of infiltrating Faltha and using his magical power to corrupt the Falthan leadership.

Instruere, Stella explained, was Faltha's largest city, a city independent of the sixteen kingdoms that made up the land of the First Men. Here the sixteen Arkhoi – each an ambassador, the representative of their king – met to coordinate the government of the land. So it was to Instruere that Deorc took himself, and in Instruere he settled, beginning his task of deception and betrayal. He seduced members of the Council of Faltha, offering Arkhos after Arkhos whatever they desired, until he held a majority in the Council. Instruere's defences were neglected under his dominion, and plans were laid to open the gates to the Undying Man's army when, in the fullness of time, his master chose to invade.

But resistance had arisen in the form of a group of northerners, led by Leith and Hal Mahnumsen. Their parents had been taken captive by four Lords of Fear, a response to Mahnum having discovered the timing of the coming invasion. Leith and Hal, along with other villagers, pursued the Lords of Fear and rescued their parents, ending up in Instruere. Stella explained that she had been one of those villagers.

While in Instruere, she told them, she had fallen in love with a mysterious stranger called Tanghin. What she did not know was this man's real identity. When her friends advised her against the liaison, she ran into Tanghin's arms, only to discover him in magical communion with the Destroyer. Tanghin was Deorc.

Kannwar continued the tale. He told them how he had commanded Deorc to capture Stella, seeing something magical in her. Deorc complied, but his bitterness grew as he wanted Stella for himself. Stella seized on this and lied to Kannwar, claiming Deorc had taken her for his own. Enraged, Kannwar had engulfed them both with his blue fire, pulling them from Instruere across the world to where his army was encamped, waiting for the signal to invade.

'I tortured Deorc,' Kannwar admitted. 'I had to know the depth of his treachery. I forced Stella to watch. Yes, I am ashamed of these things, but it was a time of extremity, and I had long ago abandoned the restraint with which ordinary people hedge themselves about. It soon became clear to me that Stella had tricked me. Deorc had not touched her. Yet he had acted traitorously. It was Deorc who had sent the four Bhrudwan Lords of Fear west to take Leith and Hal's parents captive, because he wished to learn my secrets. Do you see? Had he not betrayed me, Faltha would have had no warning of my invasion. No resistance would have been raised and I would now be ruling throughout the northern world. To their betterment, though I accept Queen Stella sees this differently.

'I was angered beyond reason. I encased the wretch in filaments of magic, binding him in a place of near-death forever. He was entrapped in the seconds before death, eternally reliving the pain of his torture. This I judged sufficient to balance the great harm he had done.'

'You did it to frighten me,' Stella said, her eyes dark.

He nodded. 'You were even more dangerous than he. If once you discovered the reservoir of magic the Most High had deposited within you, I might not have contained you. So I kept you frightened, unsure, always on edge.' He lifted his face to them all. 'Of anyone alive, Stella Pellwen has seen the worst of me.'

'And this is the man who calls himself Husk?' Conal said, his voice high and sweet. 'This man eternally on the cusp of death, his magic bound?'

'I have underestimated him,' Kannwar said. 'Seventy years ago I bound him, and seldom have I looked in on him since. You see, with the loss of my other hand and my subsequent defeat, I was forced to re-evaluate my goals. My long years of planning for revenge against the Most High seemed a waste to me. In fact, as Stella can testify, I walked in the borderlands of madness for a long time.

'In my weakness I drew on all the magic I had, some of which I had invested in the bonds imprisoning Deorc. In my long path to healing I may have disrupted this magic, allowing him to free himself from his prison. It is the most likely explanation for what is a clear fact: Deorc of Jasweyah is now Husk and has become a formidable magician. I will tell you this, though it chills me to the bone. As Stella can attest, the way to make a great magician from a good one is to immerse them in suffering. Such has happened to Stella, though she is yet to test her limits. And such, I believe, has happened to Deorc. I have an enemy, and he is housed in my own citadel.'

'And he is your own problem, surely,' said Moralye. 'Pheman-derac ended up trusting you, though he was old and perhaps easier to sway. And I do not deny the things I have seen: how you have rendered aid to the Most High. Yet I cannot help thinking, along with Hauthius, that "the enemy of my enemy is my friend."'

She turned to the others. 'Why ought we be concerned about this Husk? Ought we not to seek this magician out and see what aid he can give us in defeating the gods? Might he not be a better choice to rule Bhrudwo than the man who, with his rebellion, broke apart Dona Mihst, the man who became by choice the greatest enemy of the First Men?'

'Aye,' Robal said. 'We're assuming that the man standing before us is a reformed character. But I say he is not. I say he is still the man whose army killed thousands of Falthan sons, orphaning a generation of children. If we trust him now, we will end up as amusements in his dungeon. For myself, I would see him dead, or at the least bound in the manner he bound Deorc.'

This is not going well, Stella said.

No, replied the Most High. *Despite Kannwar's masterful applica-tion of the Wordweave, there are still six of your companions who do not trust him, and one I cannot read.*

The latter comment took a moment to penetrate Stella's consciousness. But before she could question her guest, someone else had asked for clarification.

'How could we consider Husk a potential ally given what he made Arathé do?' asked Mustar, the young Bhrudwan fisherman. 'I saw her tearing the Padouki apart with her hands and her teeth. What sort of monster would make an innocent girl do that?'

Sautea growled his agreement.

Robal snorted. 'If he can do that much with hands and teeth, what could he do against the Destroyer with his magic?'

'We don't want to bring one tyrant down only to replace him with another,' Moralye said. 'We need to learn more about Husk before we decide anything.'

Kannwar is behaving with remarkable patience, Stella thought. *The Destroyer I knew would have ground every nay-sayer into the dust.*

'Are you proposing an expedition to Andratan?' Robal asked Moralye.

'No one enters Andratan without my blessing,' Kannwar growled, but only Stella heard him.

'No need,' said Conal brightly. 'Wouldn't it be easier simply to ask one who has suffered at his hands?'

The travellers agreed to listen to Conal's tale. Only Lenares objected, wishing instead to regale them with her ideas of what they should do. But no one was in the mood to listen to the cosmographer, no matter how bravely she had behaved. More pressing mysteries had presented themselves.

'Husk ensnared three minds during his time in Andratan,' Conal said. 'Mine, that of Arathé of Fossa, and of Duon, the explorer of Elamaq. With these three minds he planned to have his revenge on the Undying Man by using them to draw three groups of travellers from the three corners of the world. I ensured Stella came east, while Arathé drew her family, and others, north. Captain Duon influenced the decision of the Emperor of Elamaq to send an expedition, from which we have our cosmographer and her, er, paramour.'

Stella stood up. 'This was all his plan? How long have you known this?'

'He told us only in the last few days,' Conal said. 'Before that we did not even know his name.'

'He tells the truth,' Lenares said. 'But something does not add up.'

'Much does not add up,' Conal agreed. 'I am a man of few

192

powers, so what did Husk think to achieve by bringing me here? Or was I just the instrument by which Stella was brought?'

'I cannot see why he wants me,' Stella said.

'I can,' said Kannwar. 'Revenge. You were the one who betrayed him to me, and that on false pretences. You tricked him and he suffered for it. I should have made an end of him.'

'Who knows what his insane plans were?' Moralye said. 'What matters is how you were treated.'

'We were treated very well,' Conal said.

At this Lenares hissed.

'Very well, all things considered,' the priest amended. 'Most of the time he was only a voice in the back of our heads. Without his intervention, Stella would be dead and one of the Lords of Fear would be immortal. Hard to see that as a good thing. Yes, in the last weeks he has been a harsh taskmaster and I wished with all my heart to be free, but I am alive still.'

'And you say you are now free of his control?' Stella asked him.

'Yes. He cannot touch me now.'

There was a deathly certitude in the words that tickled some warning thoughts in Stella's mind, but in reviewing what he'd said she could make nothing of it.

'Very well,' Moralye said. 'I suggest we think on this tonight and resolve the issue in the morning. As Lenares would no doubt remind us, our ultimate task is to remove the threat posed by the gods. But I will not be party to this if the price is the reinstatement of a tyrant in Bhrudwo. Any tyrant.' She looked around the semicircle, ensuring everyone understood her meaning.

'Rest well,' she added.

The others echoed her words, and made preparations for sleep.

In her present state Stella required no sleep. She had grown weary of conversing with the Most High, who seemed to have little to say, and had been left with her own thoughts. What few there were soon suffered an interruption by Lenares.

'Don't listen to the priest,' Lenares said, even as she shook Stella by the shoulder, assuming she was sleeping. 'Don't listen to him.'

Stella levered an elbow under herself and raised her head, the most she could achieve without the intervention of the Most High. Amused at the woman's intensity, she smiled. 'I've already listened to him. How should I now remove the words from my ears?'

'You make fun of me, but you know what I mean. Don't consider his words in your plans. He is wrong.' She sucked at her lip, frustrated at her inability to communicate her meaning. 'I don't mean his ideas are wrong, though they are. I mean there is something wrong about him.'

Now she had Stella's attention. Stella called for the Most High to listen, but there was no answer. Was he listening regardless or was he elsewhere? Could he not be in a place? One of a hundred questions Stella had not asked him.

The crack of a trodden-on twig made them both spin their heads. Conal stepped out of the darkness, a cudgel in his hand and something dangerous in his eye.

Stella cried out and thrust Lenares behind her. At least, she attempted to: the arm she lifted was the one ending at the elbow, and her push achieved little apart from her own pain.

'Not you I want,' Conal said. 'Not yet. Get out of the way.'

'I'll burn you with my magic,' Stella said.

'You wouldn't hurt your devoted priest, would you?' the figure snarled. 'Of course you wouldn't, because you can't. Your magic is locked up.'

Lenares looked on with wide eyes. 'Just like Dryman,' she whispered, and began to back away.

'Enough.'

The figure stepped over Stella, raised his cudgel and struck Lenares a fearsome blow to her shoulder. Bones shattered like thin sticks. She collapsed to the ground with a scream.

'Conal!' someone cried. 'What's happening? What are you doing?'

Conal turned his eye on a wide-eyed Stella. 'Shut your mouth, bitch, or I'll break your face,' he rasped.

He turned away and called to the others. 'Some sort of wild

animal. A rat. I'll have it dead in a moment.' He raised the club a second time.

'No!' Stella cried, and threw herself at Conal.

The club descended, its tip scraping her forehead above her right eye. She backed away, slithering on her back, one hand raised, shielding herself and Lenares from the death facing them.

Please don't kill them, Conal whined.

Too late for that, said Umu. *It's amazing how much strength one can transfer to such a weak arm as yours – what is that?*

A roar came from the far side of the camp and Kannwar stood, his burning eyes staring in their direction.

He has a link to Stella, Conal said quietly. *He knows something is wrong.*

You should have told me! Umu raged.

You didn't ask, Conal said, his voice freighted with spite; then squealed as she took his fragment of consciousness and squeezed it.

The Undying Man started towards them.

'Is that Conal?' cried another voice. 'But he's dead! We buried him!'

Umu glanced to Kannwar's left, to where Noetos strode into the camp, followed by Duon and Arathé. For a moment she was paralysed, knowing trouble came for her but not realising why. Then she remembered Husk's two other spikes.

They know you died, she said, and dropped the cudgel in dismay. A moment later she sent Conal's arms scrabbling for it.

'It's Conal's body, right enough,' Duon said. 'But who is that inside?'

Conal moaned in an extremity of pain and self-loathing. His arm had just struck down his queen, was about to slay the only woman he'd ever loved.

Don't be so sure, Umu said. *Stella has immortal blood. People have thought her dead before.*

She hissed to herself, the element of surprise lost. She spun his body around and set off into the darkness at a shambling run.

A commotion broke out behind them. Shouts echoed across the rim of the pit, voices yelling at each other in anger.

Perhaps I will have to come back and kill her again and again. You'll enjoy that, won't you, Conal?

He ignored her taunts.

Something rippled across his damaged consciousness, a light-headed uneasiness akin to a short dizzy spell. Conal wondered, now he no longer had access to his glands, how he could feel anything.

'Not you I want,' his mouth said to Stella, who stood defiantly in front of a frightened Lenares. 'Not yet. Get out of the way.'

This is odd, Conal thought. Stella ought to be lying on the ground, but there she stood, along with Lenares, who had definitely been badly hurt.

'I'll hurt you with my magic,' Stella said. She raised a hand to her head, as though checking it was unhurt.

She remembers being struck.

'You won't hurt your devoted priest,' the figure snarled. 'Your magic is locked up. You need the assistance of the Undying Man to make use of it.'

Lenares' eyes were as wide as saucers. 'Just like Dryman,' she said, backing away.

What has Umu done to my memory? He paused a moment. *No, not just my memory. Lenares and Stella know something is wrong. Umu doesn't realise though.*

'Enough.'

Conal's body stepped over Stella and raised his cudgel. Lenares, clearly knowing what was coming, turned her shoulder away from the blow, but it fell anyway, striking her savagely on the head. She collapsed like a falling tree.

Come on, he begged them all. *Do something to change this!*

'Conal!' came the voice, right on cue. 'What's happening? What are you doing?'

Umu turned Conal's head to face a wide-eyed Stella. 'Shut your mouth, bitch, or I'll break your face as well,' rasped his voice.

She doesn't know; she's blind to the – what did the Padouki warrior call it? This double-time. How can we use this?

'Some sort of wild animal,' his mouth called back. 'A rat. I'll have it dead in a moment.' His arm raised the club again, exactly as he'd known he would.

'No!' Stella cried, and threw herself at Conal.

The club descended, this time taking her above her right eye, and she fell to the ground like a discarded toy.

Conal watched all this in impotent horror from somewhere far behind his own eye. The time-doubling had hurt two of his friends. As he screamed at Umu, the dizziness intensified, then vanished.

'This is our chance,' Kannwar insisted.

'Our chance?' Robal shouted, his face red with rage. 'Stella's hurt! Heal her with your magic!'

'It is likely one of the gods is trapped inside the priest's body. If we take that body and imprison it, we eliminate one of our enemies.'

Robal turned Stella's limp body onto its back. Though he despised himself for it, he couldn't help the frisson that burned its way up his arms. He had not touched her since their first meeting, when he'd mistakenly thought she was offering herself. How could he think this way when Stella might well be dead?

All such thoughts vanished when he saw her blood-spattered face. The blow had caved in her cheek, the whole right side of her face unbearable to look upon. He turned his head away.

'She is alive,' Kannwar said, his words clipped. 'She cannot be killed. She cannot be healed by anything you or I might do. Her blood will restore her. The best thing we can do is pursue her assailant, which is what I intend to do, accompanied or not.'

'We ought to stay together,' said Sautea, the older of the two Fossan fishermen. 'If we separate, the gods can pick us off.'

'Like fish in a shoal, friend?' Noetos stooped to stare at the injured women. 'Less chance of being eaten when the shark comes calling?'

'Unfair, Noetos.' Mustar clapped a hand on Sautea's shoulder. 'We're as brave as you, fisherman, and far more sensible.'

'If you're sensible, you'll come with Heredrew and me. We need to find the priest.'

'Heredrew?' Robal said, his temper flaring. 'Heredrew's a fraud. Hasn't anyone told you?'

'Please! I need assistance! Can anyone help me?'

The voice cut across their debate. Torve the Omeran stood at the edge of their circle, his face white.

'Lenares, she is hurt. I think she is dying.'

The others turned to where the dark-skinned man beckoned them. A figure lay prone right on the edge of the pit, and a number of the travellers rushed to her side. Robal stayed where he was, his hand on Stella's wounded forehead.

'Oh, Stella, my queen,' he whispered. 'I am no guard to have allowed such things to happen to you. But I would be your lover, not your guard; your husband, not some impotent watcher. I could guard your heart and keep you safe.'

Her flesh warmed under his hand; she stirred and began to pant. Her eyes sprang open.

'I wish I were dead,' she said, her words slurred by the damage to her face. Blood dribbled from the corner of her mouth. 'How . . . how is Lenares?'

'Think of yourself for a moment, my dear,' Robal said. 'She is well.' He had no idea, of course. 'But you are not. I cannot stand to see you so badly hurt so often, Stella. I wish you would leave the fighting to others and find somewhere to stay safe with one who can look after you, providing your every need.'

His heart began to pour out with his words; he could not have stopped it even if he'd wished.

'Again and again you have put yourself at risk,' he said, 'suffering captivity and injury in the service of people who do nothing but despise you and question your loyalty.' He ran a finger tenderly down her left cheek. 'You deserve so much better, yet you continue to close yourself off from those who care about you the most.'

'Oh, Robal, this is not the time for ourselves. Of course I wish I could rest. You know better than anyone how tired I am of this existence. I cannot face my friends and had to flee from my subjects. I am a thief, stealing life from some storehouse to which no one else has access. Yet I have this gift, this curse, this magical blood, and I cannot hide it away. If we keep to ourselves, how will we be able to defeat the immortal gods?'

'I don't care about the gods,' Robal said, hissing the last word. 'I don't care about him either. I only care about you and me.'

He'd said it. Something within him, some knotted emotion, came free and a supernatural calm descended upon him. *She knows. Up to her what she does with the knowledge.*

'I'm just a soldier,' he said. 'Not a very smart one either. I listened to you talking with Phemanderac and understood one word in ten. I don't share the abilities and memories linking you to the Destroyer. But, Stella, I can give you love.'

As he watched her face, the blood dried and the dreadful mess began to fade away, as though painted out by an artist. *Truly, nothing can hurt her*, he thought, then remembered her arm. His own sword had taken it off below the elbow.

'Love is not enough,' she said, her voice firm. She glanced at her missing hand, as if she had read his thoughts. 'Love can sometimes be the very worst thing a friend can give you, especially if it cannot be returned. It is fierce when it needs to be gentle, selfish when it needs to look beyond itself. Robal, I know you will misunderstand these words, but now is the time to keep your love to yourself.'

'You are wrong,' he said. 'Wrong. It is exactly what we need to make sense of everything. It will cause us to fight on instead of giving up, as you seem to wish. Love drives me, Stella. What drives you?'

She sighed and closed her eyes. 'You don't want to know.'

'I do, my dear; I do.'

Apart from some bruising, her face had restored itself. What magical stuff her blood was, and how deeply he wished she would share it with him! To watch the centuries pass, the rise and fall of kingdoms, the ages of man succeeding each other; to travel the length and width of the earth, walking unknown paths, standing on cold mountain peaks and in the midst of the harshest deserts. To engage with history or to remain aloof from it, entirely as they chose. To explore the depths of their love, kept together by the accumulation of tender moments, of shared experience. To develop their own language of intimacy.

'I cannot make you see,' she said. 'I cannot subject you to my suffering. And I will not watch you grow old and die. Robal, there is no future for us.'

'There is,' he said, daring all, willing her not to misunderstand. 'All you have to do is share your blood with me.'

Stella said nothing for three, four, five beats of the heart.

'Is that what this is all about?' she said. 'Do you crave immortality that much? Is it me you love, or unending life?'

The words he wanted never to hear had finally been uttered, and with them, it seemed, went any hope he had of winning her.

'You rightly explained that for there to be the one, there must be the other,' Robal said, the words coming out too fast. 'Be rid of the curse, or share it with me; either way I get what I want, which is you. I tell you the truth: I would rather have you and a normal life than live forever without you.'

But he had no doubt she could hear the uncertainty in his voice. *How much of my love for her is my desire for immortality?* He could not say, he could not say; and the guilt finally stopped his mouth.

She lay there, the Most High burning in every vessel and sinew, his presence pulsing with a pain she could not have borne had he not dampened it. Her blood bubbled and sparked with power too fierce for mortal flesh to contain, every mote bringing healing to her broken and exhausted body.

But it could not heal her heart.

Kannwar loved her, a love born of need, of desperation. From the time she delivered him from the retribution of the Falthan army at the end of the Falthan War, he had been in her debt. And his act of infusing her with his immortal blood ensured that, of all the people of the world, she was the only one like him.

Robal loved her, but his love was a ravenous hunger, as much self-preservation, it seemed, as passion for her. Both loves were more than she was entitled to but less than she needed. Only Leith had loved her selflessly, and now Leith was dead, setting in motion this most unhappy period of her life.

I am leaving you now, said the Most High. *The rest of your healing you must accomplish alone.*

Suitably enigmatic, she responded, but he had gone. What healing? Her body or her emotions?

The only true healing, she realised, *will come when I die.*

His body was already becoming a stranger to him. Umu pushed it beyond mortal endurance, crashing through copses, rebounding from trees, stumbling over fallen trunks, thumping its feet in an endless procession of leaden steps, while Conal sat as an unwilling passenger, locked in a corner of what was once his own mind. He could not feel the pain these abuses undoubtedly caused, and this, more than anything, forced a final separation between what remained of him and what was once his own flesh.

So pain gives us ownership of our flesh, he considered. *Keeps us grounded in a world of actions and consequences.* Becoming a philosopher was no comfort to him, but there was nothing else he could do except think.

You may well be right, Umu said. *I am certainly experiencing unpleasant stimulation from these nerve endings.*

Let me feel them, Conal begged.

And gift you life? She laughed. *Keppia is a fool. He refuses to feel the Emperor's pain, unloading it all onto his captive. I, on the other hand, may well have discovered the way to make my presence permanent on this side of the wall.*

Do you really want to become me?

Better that than what the Father relegated me to, she said. *But no, I'll leave you well before I'm imprisoned in your poor flesh-sac.*

And I'll have it back, he said fiercely.

You still refuse to understand. Your connection to this body has been severed. If I cease sustaining it, you will leach into the void. It's cold there.

Ahead, the night was giving way to dawn, a soft, pearly light revealing the devastation wrought by the storm. The body picked its way across a waterlogged field, passing carcasses piled at the western end against a low bluff. Cresting a hill, the vista was one of unrelieved destruction. Vegetation stripped of foliage, the ground churned as though trampled by a thousand oxen.

Down a gentle slope jogged the body, slowing to pick its careful way through a village.

I did a thorough job, Umu said, pride colouring her thoughts. *My storm harvested thousands of untimely deaths. I am now stronger than my brother. Soon I will have no rival in all of heaven and earth.*

Then why are you running?

Her answer was a mental squeeze that smeared his memories, giving him something akin to pain, coming near to snuffing him out. *Careful,* she said. *You remain here only on sufferance.*

Conal doubted that, doubted it very much. He could not imagine Umu, or her brother, suffering anything unnecessarily. His presence, he concluded, was somehow necessary to her possession of his body.

Worse comes to worst, he told himself, *I'll find a way to leave her here, trapped.*

The body staggered and fell. It had been struck a blow to the head, one neither Conal nor Umu had seen coming. Umu's thoughts faded for a moment, then snapped back into sharpness. She pushed the body back to its feet.

Sweat mingled with blood obscured his – her – one eye. A figure crouched before her, then, curiously, bowed to her. Conal watched as she raised the cudgel and took a lurching swipe at it. The figure seemed to dance backwards just far enough for the stick to flash over its shoulder.

He recognised the figure. Knew why he stood there. And definitely did not want Umu to know.

The first catechism of the Koinobia, he recited, *is to serve the Most High with all one's heart and soul. The second is to serve the First Men under the guidance of one's superiors.* With a furious concentration he began to run through the rest of the list.

The dark figure, clothed only in a light, knee-length jerkin, took a step forward and dealt three blows to Conal's body. Two slaps to the face, followed by a kick that seemed to start from somewhere under the ground and finished in the sky, collecting his head along the way. Umu yelped as the body's feet left the ground.

Conal kept reciting.

Who is this? she cried as she staggered backwards, trying to keep out of the range of the figure's swift fists and feet.

The fifth is to spread knowledge of Hal's redemptive sacrifice at every opportunity, he chanted, like he had ten thousand times before. A well-worn path: before every meal and again before retiring, the Twelve Catechisms needed to be repeated twelve times each. *Empty the mind, narrow the focus, think of nothing else. Do not think of the name of the person assailing Umu.*

The pressure increased on his tiny spark of life and memory, but he was gone into the catechisms now. Pain would not recall him. He'd abandoned the recitals during his journey with Stella, but now immersed himself in them as though they were the fluid of his mother's womb.

'Lenares told me what you are,' the figure said to Umu. 'Your blow did not kill her, though her wits are addled.'

A series of spins, twenty at least, fists flashing randomly to strike hard blows in the body's ribs and sternum. Conal heard a rib crack, though the sound was distant, happening to someone else.

'Who are you?' said Conal's mouth.

'You may have damaged Lenares' mind,' the figure carried on relentlessly. 'If so, I curse you for it. I defy you and your plans. With these blows I declare my enmity and that of all my kind.'

The figure struck from behind, the crack of hard-edged feet bruising, then breaking the body's spine. It collapsed like a discarded rag doll.

Umu screamed in pain.

Conal continued his recital, ignoring her. *The tenth is to seek knowledge of everything concerning the Most High and his plan for the First Men.*

Magical power roiled within the body as Umu sought to repair the damage. The spine knitted itself back together, the discs fusing into one stiff rod. At the same time the attacker stomped on the body's legs, breaking both with audible cracks, drawing further shrieks from the mouth.

'You have something of mine,' the figure said, scarcely breathing with effort. 'I want it back.'

Conal's body scrambled away, spidering backwards on its palms, dragging its useless legs behind it. Healing power poured into the broken bones and ruptured ligaments.

'I want back what is mine.'

The figure darted forward, curly hair matted in sweat, and slammed bare feet down on the newly healed legs, breaking them anew. It whirled, stabbing a kick that connected with Conal's chin. The priest imagined he could feel the sickening snap of his body's neck.

Umu's scream was a constant thing, a high-pitched wail that broke through Conal's recitation. Flames burned throughout the body and in places the skin caught alight. Umu spent every scrap of energy she could harvest on healing the damage.

Look how limited you are, locked in this prison of flesh and bone, Conal mocked. *You can be defeated by a mere mortal.*

Who is this? Umu cried, seizing on Conal's return.

No harm in telling her now, or at least hinting at it. *You took something of his as a trophy. You made him angry. You ought to give it back.*

With an effort of pure will she made the battered body stand, then back away from her fierce assailant. She forced the mouth open: blood sprayed from it, and she spat out a chunk of tongue.

'You are Lenares' plaything, the Omeran?' she made the mouth say, though Conal doubted if Torve understood. 'You are a very brave man. Nevertheless, I think I will keep my trophy.'

The body turned and sprinted away, heedless of the damage it did itself.

The figure bowed his head and did not follow.

Exhausted, Moralye struggled to lift a fallen palm from their path. Noetos and his children, young and fit, had gone on some distance ahead, their anxiety overriding their concern for her. She took no offence; in her fifty years of life it had always been so.

Besides, she really ought to be paying the price for keeping her real age from her companions. A woman in her twenties, they all thought, not knowing how long-lived Dhaurians were. Despite Phemanderac's near-century of life, despite the Domaz Skreud and its revelation of the preserving power of the Fountain, these outsiders assumed she was young and fit.

Neither young nor fit. Thirty years of service in the Hall of Scrolls had done nothing for her fitness, not that she was the sort of person to walk the steep tracks above the city, those favoured by lovers seeking privacy. No, Moralye was married to her scrolls. Everyone knew that.

Oh, she was pretty enough. One of the beauties of her clan, in fact, but her father and uncles had not been required to beat the boys away from her door. The outsiders, these friends of Phemanderac, thought all Dhaurians were bookish. But books and scholarship had long fallen from favour with Dhauria's young people, and her interest in the past, imperfectly concealed, had made Moralye an object of derision. Her large, luminous eyes attracted particular ridicule. Hamapha, the boy she'd set those eyes on, had taken delight in telling her friends how suitable she was for work underground in the scholars' cave. Soon they were all calling her 'The Mole.' Moralye the Mole. Oh, it was all in fun, and she laughed along with them, but those eyes cried many bitter tears in private.

Her left hand slipped on the palm's smooth trunk. She caught a splinter in the heel of her palm, then squealed as the trunk struck her foot, forcing a word out of her lips that her mother would have rebuked her for. The palm tree finished exactly where it had been before she'd begun struggling with it.

A rustle in the undergrowth caught her attention. She had just begun to look up when a shape leapt over the tree trunk and landed beside her. A meaty hand slammed into her chest, thumping her to the ground and driving the wind out of her.

She was still wheezing when Noetos stepped over the palm tree.

'Did he hurt you?' he asked, then, without waiting for a response, continued, 'Where did he go?'

'I didn't see,' she said, then added with a trace of asperity: 'And I am fine, thank you.'

The big man reached down a hand and hauled her up. 'Follow me. We need to catch that thing.'

Moralye nodded. Though always a little uncomfortable around the big red-haired Bhrudwan, fearing his unpredictability, she recognised the sense in his words. If she remained here she would soon be lost. Gritting her teeth, she forced herself after Noetos.

Within a few minutes they emerged on a low cliff a few metres above the coast. The man Lenares had said wasn't Conal – although it was certainly Conal's body – was nowhere in sight, evoking a series of salty curses from the fisherman. A noise behind them caused Noetos to set his hand to his sword, but the figures to emerge from the wreck of the coastal forest were those of his son and daughter, along with the southerner, Duon.

'Seen him?'

Arathé began signing and at the same time Duon spoke. 'No, Fath – Noetos, no sign of him.'

Anomer came and stood beside his father, nodding to Moralye. 'What is that?' he asked, pointing along the coast to his right.

Moralye felt the fisherman stiffen, his body turning rigid. 'Alkuon,' he breathed. 'Oh, Alkuon.'

With an inarticulate cry he hurled himself from the cliff, his body falling a frighteningly long way before landing, rolling and tumbling on the sand.

'Is it?' Anomer shouted down. 'Is it the *Conch*?'

The words meant nothing to Moralye, but she recognised the urgency in them.

'Come on,' she said to Arathé. 'I saw a less dangerous way down back in the village.'

The impromptu path was far more difficult than Moralye had thought, and she and Arathé arrived at the shipwreck some time after the others. The ship lay on its side, its back broken, the deck perpendicular to the beach. Waves lapped against the broken timbers, chasing each other through gaping holes into dark spaces. The whole wreck groaned as though teetering on some balance point.

A closer look at the surf revealed bodies bobbing up and down. Moralye loathed the sight: limbs floating at unnatural angles, mouths open, hair spread out like fans, eyes staring vacantly into the sky. Empty vessels, their owners gone. Death in Dhauria was a far more civilised affair, with violence almost unknown and virtually no natural hazards to upset the normal functioning of the city. Deaths happened – her own mother had died not two years previously – but they were confined to special hospices, associated with drawn curtains, perfumed rooms and whispering staff.

A roaring sound came from within the ship, the sound of someone enraged or in pain. Arathé and Anomer flung themselves forward into the surf, splashing their way towards the closest of the holes in the ship's hull. Moralye followed, trying not to look at the corpses.

The hulk moved slightly, swaying with the waves, groaning as it did so. The morning sun vanished as she waded into the hole, ducking to avoid splintered timbers.

'Give me a hand!' Noetos called, his voice echoing in the cavernous spaces rendered by the storm.

Arathé and Moralye assisted each other across the interior wall of the hull, then one by one reached up to Duon's proffered hand, who pulled them up to find their balance on an interior partition.

Smashed wreckage littered the hull: shattered timbers; cargo, both intact and broken open; the grotesque bodies of sailors. A piquant spicy scent helped mask what Moralye imagined would be a powerful stench, as many of the bodies appeared to be putrefying. The sailors would have endured a fearful death, she thought, down in the hull, trusting to their captain to deliver them.

Partition by partition the three of them climbed to the other side high above them – port or starboard; Moralye knew the terms but had no idea which it was – where Anomer awaited. The lightless void stretched away either side, broken occasionally by a faint ray of light where the sun penetrated through a damaged spot in the deck to their right. Eventually they reached the left side of the hull – the port side, she thought – and rested a moment. A hatch opened to the exterior, and Moralye gasped at the height they had attained. The beach was much too far below them for her comfort.

This is madness, she admitted. *I should have remained behind to give Lenares the help I could.* But Kannwar – she could never, not ever, even think that name with any degree of ease – had told her he would be sufficient. It had taken no more persuasion for her to leave the opening to Corata Pit and the Destroyer's side. Yet she would be of little assistance here.

Ahead of her, Duon stood on the rail, balanced himself, and stepped carefully forward, making his way towards the platform upon which Noetos stood. Anomer followed close behind. Moralye was unsure of the architecture of such a large ship, having only been on small inshore boats, but she guessed the structure under Noetos's feet was a cabin, and he stood on a wall. Duon offered Arathé his hand and the pair of them stood, clearly struggling for balance.

I've come far enough, Moralye decided. She perched on the rail, the beach below visible between the slats, and hoped it had not been weakened by the storm. Up here the ship's gentle rocking motion was translated into an unsettling sway. The Dhaurian scholar found herself gripping tightly with both hands. Had her feet had fingers instead of toes, she would have thrown off her shoes and used them as well.

Noetos edged his way to the near end of the wall, lowered himself to his stomach and reached over. With a series of sharp raps he knocked on a door.

'Come out, Kidson,' he said. 'I have an army here. It will go badly for you if we have to storm the cabin.'

A muffled voice shouted something Moralye couldn't catch in response.

'No guarantees, no bargains,' Noetos replied. 'Just the point of a sword if you try to hold us out.'

More indistinct shouting.

'I'll behave better than you did. That boy died on the dock at Long Pike Mouth from the blow your man gave him. Come on, now; there are more important things on the wing than you and your stubbornness.'

This time Moralye heard the words, 'I have a hostage.'

This gave Noetos pause.

In the silence, Moralye called out to the others: 'Why won't the man in the cabin come out?'

'We sailed on this ship not long ago,' said Anomer. 'Captain Kidson treated us poorly, and dealt roughly with one of our party, who died. But my father's chief complaint is that . . . er . . .' He turned to his sister for support.

She signalled to him.

'Yes, my father fell in love with one of the crew and Kidson would not let her go.'

'You allow ships to have female crew?' Moralye said. 'I am surprised. I have not seen many examples of such free-thinking in this land.'

'Not crew, exactly, no,' said Anomer, his face colouring.

'Quiet,' Noetos said.

Such directness always bemused Moralye, familiar with more sophisticated ways of phrasing such a request. The bluntness here in Bhrudwo was difficult not to take personally.

Noetos leaned closer to the door. 'Who is your hostage?'

'You know who,' Kidson said. 'You make a move to take me, she dies.'

'Let me speak to her.'

'Hard for her to speak with my sword in her mouth,' came the voice, faintly amused. 'It's all she can do to keep still. Don't rock the ship overmuch as you leave, that's my advice to you.'

Noetos cursed. 'Just when magic would be most useful, our magicians are not here. Arathé, could you bind Kidson for me, or aid me in some way?'

'She could,' Duon said, 'but the effect would not be instantaneous. It is likely Cylene would die.'

Moralye wondered at that. She did not know who this Cylene was, nor why she was so important to Noetos and his family; and Duon speaking for Arathé seemed rather odd, especially since he gave the interpretation before she made the signals. But she thought of something else just then that took her mind away from signals and strange captives. Barely visible in the darkness just below the deck she had seen some serious damage to the timbers. She compared her memory to where she now stood, and hope rose. There might be another way into the cabin.

She eased herself backwards along the railing, away from Noetos's frustrated mutterings, and down through the hatch. Yes, it was there, she hadn't been imagining it: a darker patch among the shadowy recesses of what looked like accommodation of some sort. Other holes let in light through the deck; this hole must therefore issue into a place where the sun could not penetrate. The only such place she had seen on the deck was the cabin.

She ought to return to Noetos and report. He was the fighter, he had the sword; she was the one with common sense. A scholar, eyes suited to see things in dark places, not fit for boldness or battle. As she began to struggle upwards through the hatch, she could hear Hamapha's genial, oh-so-reasonable laughter. She said another word her mother would never have approved of, shrugged her shoulders and let herself down into the darkness.

The hole lay some distance along the rightmost wall – what would, in the normal course of events, have been the room's ceiling. Bunks, attached to the floor, now hung from the wall to her left. Bedding and clothes lay strewn on the floor – wall – below her. There seemed to be no way for her to reach the hole.

There was a lamp-holder though. At least, she assumed that was the function of the hook set in the ceiling – wall – just within arm's reach. Without thinking about it she launched herself towards it, snatching at it with one hand. For a wild moment she thought she'd missed, and imagined herself thumping to the floor – wall – amid the sheets and blankets, but she made contact and her grip held. She swung forward, then back – *this time, it has to be now* – forward again and, extending her other arm, reached for the hole.

Missed. Swung back, kicking back with her legs to generate speed. Reached again, getting a handful of splinters. Her breath whistling from burning lungs, she swung a third time, her right side rubbing along the wall, and this time her fingers found a firm grasp.

For a stupid moment she hung there, stretched between two precarious handholds, trying to remember what she needed to do next. *Let go*, she told herself, and forced her right hand to release the lamp-holder. She fetched up against the hole with a rustle and thump.

Just another noise from the shipwreck, she willed those above decks to think.

Blood dripped between the fingers of her left hand where the splinters had dug deep. Ignoring the pain, Moralye pulled herself into the hole.

She encountered unexpected resistance. Some kind of material had been slung across the hole: did Captain Kidson know of the gap? Had he patched it with a tapestry? She forced herself to think. *I am coming up through the floor: this is likely to be a carpet of some sort*. It certainly smelled of dust and something sour, the sort of state a floor covering was likely to get into out at sea. Once a floor, now a wall. Nailed down then. No real idea where she would emerge, but likely into the captain's eye line. Not a risk she wished to take; better to return to Noetos and tell him of her discovery.

A hand seized her hair.

Moralye had no idea she had such self-possession. Though she imagined Kidson's hand dragging her into the cabin, sword raised in his other hand, she managed not to scream. The soft skin of a woman's fingers, not the calloused hand of a seaman, touched her face, found her lips and placed a finger firmly across them. She breathed out gently.

Abruptly a voice sounded in the cabin, shockingly loud. 'You have nothing I want. Go away and gnaw on the bones of Old Roudhos.'

Kidson's voice, at least a few paces away. Now a faint voice came in reply. He would be facing the one he conversed with, even though the adversaries could not see each other: thus it was even in the darkness of the Hall of Scrolls. Safe, then, to risk a glance.

The edge of the carpet lay close to the hole. It was something of a wriggle to force her head past the edge, but within moments she found herself looking into the dim cabin and into the face of . . . of Lenares the cosmographer.

No, not Lenares. This face was harder, more lined, hollower. The eyes were the same though. Exactly the same. She had seen that unnerving stare, so knowing, nowhere else.

'There's a hole,' Moralye whispered into the girl's ear, rather unnecessarily.

'Can I fit through?'

Voice a little deeper than Lenares', but otherwise so similar she wondered if the gods were playing a trick on her, on them all. She nodded.

More indistinct shouting, then Kidson laughed. She could see his back: wide-shouldered, muscular and intimidating, yet his jerkin had been shredded and his skin was covered in what looked like dried blood.

'Wounded,' the girl whispered. 'Weak. Desperate. Has a sword though.'

'Come with me,' Moralye said.

'It will take a while. Have to free this carpet.'

It took perhaps five minutes of quiet struggle before the girl worked the edge of the carpet free of its nail. During this time Kidson never turned, his ramrod-straight body focused on the voice coming from beyond the door.

'Now,' Moralye breathed.

Her heart in her mouth, she withdrew from the hole and waited while the girl eased her way out of the cabin. She imagined the captain turning, seeing legs protruding from the carpet, crying out in anger, lifting his sword . . .

She hadn't thought this through, she realised. She could not maintain a grip on the edge of the hole and at the same time allow the girl to pass through. Taking a deep breath, she allowed herself to fall.

She knew the floor was close, but it seemed so far away – and she thumped into the bedding with far more force than she'd imagined. Her knees smacked into her chin, clacking her teeth together. The sound, though muffled, was surely loud enough to draw attention.

A moment later the girl landed beside her.

'Come on,' she said, 'we are not out of danger yet.'

As she drew Moralye to her feet, she whispered 'Thank you.' Just once, but the sincerity made the risk worthwhile.

Hamapha wasn't laughing now.

Moralye and the girl, who had introduced herself as Cylene, were approaching the hatch when Kidson let out a blood-chilling roar.

'He knows then,' Moralye said, and smiled.

'Aye, he knows. He knows his life isn't worth much now I'm not there to guarantee his safety. Tell me, Moralye, that was Noetos I heard, wasn't it?'

The girl's smile at Moralye's nod was a sight to behold, transforming an already pretty face into something of remarkable beauty. *Lenares never smiles like that, to her detriment. Too serious by half. Though she does have a great deal to be serious about, as do we all.*

'And you are his friend? One of the party from Faltha perhaps, or from Elamaq? What he told me, it is all true?'

'I don't know what he said, so I can't confirm it as truth,' Moralye said, always the scholar. 'But yes, I am from Faltha – or near enough anyway.'

She emerged from the hatch and pulled Cylene through after her. The noise drew attention from all four on the deck. Their eyes widened when Cylene came into view.

Noetos called her name, joy transforming his face, banishing the hard lines.

She smiled again, dazzling them all.

INTERLUDE

IT IS DARK, IT IS COLD, IT IS SILENT.

Thick fog rolls in from the ocean, a damp blanket tumbling across the grass of the treeless hills, smothering the stone of Andratan's keep, causing the walls to weep. The faint sound of dripping water is muffled almost to inaudibility, but the drops find his raw skin, each one a cold sting. It is night, so no other sounds reach this high up in the keep, so near the top of the Tower of Farsight. The servants have gone to their sleeping cells, leaving him alone to haunt the corridors and stairs of the Undying Man's fortress. No one to hear his frantic breathing, his grunts of effort, his cries of pain. Until tomorrow, when they come to hunt for him.

Husk hurts, Husk is confused, Husk is frightened.

He is no longer sure where he is. Once he knew this castle better than he knew the workings of his own body. He knew every dungeon, every corridor, every door, every room. None had been barred to him, not even the Undying Man's own throne room. But now he is lost.

He is lost because of the terrifying thing that has happened to him. Before the terrifying thing, his connection to the void beyond the Wall of Time had given him strength, had enabled him to repair the damage inflicted by all those decades of pain and torture. It had held out the promise of improving him, of making him more than human. Of turning him into a god. More than a god.

217

But then he was deceived. His three spikes tricked him, working together somehow to fool him, drawing him in, then seeking – ah, such a shock! – to kill themselves. Oh, how clever they had been!

How could Husk have guessed? All three of them leaping at once from a high place, somehow coordinating themselves without their thoughts giving them away. His power was stretched – overstretched – as he instinctively tried to save them. Such a fool! His pride would not let him release them, would not let him admit they had outsmarted him, so he held on, trying to slow their fall, strengthen their skin and bones, cushion their landing, remove the rocks towards which they plummeted; so many things all at once that even the beautiful conduit to his god-power was stretched to its limit and beyond. It did not break, for that he is thankful, but he had to let one of his spikes go. The priest. The other two, the more valuable, he believed he could save and still keep his conduit safe.

Conal had hit the rocks with such a crushing impact it had knocked the wind out of Husk. He had staggered, fallen to his knees, and the glamour keeping him invisible had vanished, gone like a startled bird. Those sharing the corridor with him had cried out in fear at the man-monster appearing from nowhere. He paid them no attention.

The next few moments had been the very worst of a pain-drenched life. Realising what Conal's death might do, he tried to sever his contact to the priest's spike – *but something kept the connection wide open*. Such a dreadful surprise! It could have been one of only two things: one or both of the remaining two spikes; or one of the two gods. No one else could exploit his magic like that. The priest had died in an instant, his back broken, his brain pierced by bone fragments, his heart shocked into failure, and the man's death had flowed back along the connection like a black tide. One fearful breath, that was all Husk had time for, and the tide slammed into him.

It stabbed, it tore, it crushed.

For a moment he'd thought he could limit the damage. Perhaps, he thought, if he severed the two remaining spikes and ceased his magical interference in the running of the keep, he might only lose his most recent gains. He did this, losing his spikes forever, but those gains were nevertheless sluiced away in the first instant of the black tide, and within moments he was reduced to the slug-like animal he had been before. His beautiful new limbs burned away. His lips melted. His skin excoriated, bubbling in the magical heat. He screamed, a piteous sound, and people ran.

But the tide of death continued to crash over him. He thought he would die, he thought everything had been lost. Godhood gone, humanity destroyed, even the pitiful, tortured existence he had led in the dungeon leached away. The black tide reached its peak, then slowly drained away, taking most of him with it.

He was blind, he was burned, he was broken.

Calling on everything available to him through his conduit – which had mercifully remained intact, oh render praise! – Husk summoned enough power to enable him to slither along the corridor, leaving bits and pieces of himself behind, force open a door and slip into the nearest room. The girl there had screamed at the sight of him, his whole body a weeping sore, but he had silenced her. In the extremity of his need he had drawn her to him, compelling her with the magic remaining to him, then absorbed her body into his. This had kept him alive barely long enough for more power to arrive from his connection to the void. Had the room been untenanted he would have died.

He was forced to shut himself down; he could do nothing else. He placed a spell on the door, then let every bodily function remaining to him slowly trickle to a halt. Blood cooled, lungs deflated, skin dried. The magical conduit alone sustained him.

Husk relives the memories, neck-deep in a pool of horror. He wishes to stop them playing and replaying in his mind, but cannot. He is wretched.

He is alive. That is enough for now.

But it will not suffice, not in the long run. What so nearly killed him is no more than a setback, albeit severe, despite how painful it seems. He has endured pain before; the point of such endurance is to have his revenge. If he must endure more, how more fulfilling will his ultimate revenge be! At present, however, he must restore himself to full functionality, so his survival, while pleasing, does not satisfy him. He is not grateful.

He is angry.

He is angry that he has been outwitted. The death of one of the conspirators is nowhere near enough to assuage his mortification; the other two must die. But that will have to wait, because he is angry for a far more important reason: he now has no way of ensuring the Undying Man and his evil consort come to Andratan. Has no way even of knowing where they are and what they are doing. His possession of the three spikes has drawn everything he needs so close, but now the group is in danger of breaking up again, distracted by their need to destroy the gods.

Don't worry about the gods, he wants to tell them. *I will deal with the gods. Just worry about coming to Andratan. See how I will reward you then.*

Hubris, that is what those thoughts are. He can do nothing about the gods now. He is vulnerable to them, which is why he is frightened. His conduit may well be visible to anyone who cares to inspect the hole in the world; and, once discovered, he is sure it will be severed. He must walk small for a time, while rebuilding his strength. Now he no longer has eyes watching Stella and Kannwar, he must hope they journey to Andratan soon. He must rely on the fisherman's desire for vengeance, and hope his children do not tell him that the object of his anger sleeps nearby every night. He must rely on Stella's lust, her desire to find someone to share herself with. He must rely on Kannwar himself and whatever scheme he is currently running. And, despite all this, it may still not be enough. He must formulate plans of his own while he is recuperating. Husk hates relying on anyone.

He wonders if the gods might be of some use to him. He wonders if they can be persuaded to help him recover. Failing that, he wonders if he can draw them to Andratan. Does he have anything the gods want? Or, more likely, can he fool them into thinking he does? Such a risk, contacting the gods, but they have already interfered on his behalf at least once that he is aware of. Do they view him as a potential ally, or with tolerant amusement? Just how much more powerful are they than he is – or was? What might they do to him if he offends them? He doubts they are capable of destroying him, as Andratan is hedged about with powerful spells. Husk himself cannot leave, and strong magic cannot in turn penetrate. The black tide of Conal's death – he rages again as he remembers it – was effective only because it bypassed the magical barriers, the spike having been set in place when the priest was in Andratan itself.

So, perhaps he is safe here, yes indeed. And if he is safe, he just needs to find a lure large enough to make the gods snap at it. Then he can befriend them if they are powerful or enslave them if they are not. Either way, they in turn could draw or drive his enemies, the objects of his dark desires, north to Andratan.

As he thinks of this, Husk finds he needs to breathe, needs to pant. The hoarse sound fills the room, rattles the few wet bones lying on the bed, slaps off the dripping walls.

His day of revenge may be postponed, but it is not cancelled. It cannot come soon enough.

FISHERMAN

CHAPTER 9

CYLENE

NOETOS GLANCED UP WHEN HE heard someone emerge from the hatch – the woman Moralye. He returned his attention to the cabin. Kidson had shouted something a moment earlier; the fisherman half-suspected it was a prelude to some foolish dash for freedom and eased his sword an inch or so from its scabbard. Cyclamere took a step towards the cabin, his blade in his hand. But a flash of sunlight on honey-blonde hair caught the corner of Noetos's eye and his head snapped back even before his brain made sense of what he'd seen.

'Cylene!' he cried, and she smiled.

Her hair was bedraggled, her skin pale, cheeks hollow and eyes ringed with weariness, but none of that mattered to Noetos. He saw only the golden halo surrounding her caring features and the bright intensity of her smile. A moment later she was in his arms, repeating his name as he did hers, her tears beginning to flow. There were other noises, sudden movement around them, but he was robbed of the capacity to notice them. His heart had returned to him.

'I didn't realise I'd given myself to you when I told you my story,' she said to him. 'But I have.'

He held her fiercely. 'And I you,' he replied. 'I have missed you.'

'I can see,' she said, amusement in her voice. 'Thank you for coming back for me.'

'Was it terrible, the storm?' he asked. At her nod, he continued: 'It was beyond description on the land. I can only imagine how frightening it must have been on the sea. It was a god-storm, you know.'

She kissed him on his cheek. 'I was a stone in a basket. Apparently we lost a mast at the beginning of the storm, and many of the crew were dragged overboard in the rigging, but I never saw it. Kidson locked me in his cabin, said I was the only cargo on the vessel worth saving.'

'The man got something right.'

'What, locking me in his cabin? How could that be right?'

For a moment he thought she was serious, that he'd offended her; but her merriment played around her eyes and on her lips.

'No, you foolish girl,' he growled, assuming a mock-ferocious grimace. 'Saying you were the only cargo worth saving.'

He was rewarded with a smile, which changed into a frown.

'Kidson left the passengers to fend for themselves,' she said. 'Those who stayed below decks were battered, many to death. Others ventured topside during a lull in the storm, only to be swept away when the wind returned. Eventually even Kidson gave up trying to sail the ship and joined me in his cabin.'

'Did he—'

She put a finger on his lips. 'I am his property,' she said, an answer of sorts. 'But his thought was to get as drunk as he could so he would not be aware of his own passing. He barely spoke to me.'

'How did you survive?'

'Noetos, I will tell you all of my story, but not now. We are not safe here. Perhaps you could introduce me to your friends and we could exchange stories later? That is, if you aren't just going to leave me on this beach?'

'Leave you? Of course not!'

Something thudded into his back. Cylene gasped.

'After him!' someone cried.

Noetos turned his head. Anomer had dropped onto the cabin wall and he and Cyclamere were leaning over and staring down at a broken section of the lower rail. Noetos could not make any sense of what had just happened.

Arathé was trying to say something, but she had forgotten to signal, so urgent were her words. She came towards Noetos as quickly as she could.

'You have been hit,' Duon said, his eyes wide.

It took a moment for Noetos to realise the man was talking to him. He let go of Cylene. 'Hit? What with?'

The coldness spreading across his lower back answered his question; he knew what he would find even before his hand touched the knife handle.

'Sit down,' Duon said, his voice firm; but Noetos was already on his knees, breathing shallowly as the pain began. It was far more intense than anything he'd received in his youth on the practice ground. His thoughts started to flutter, his mind fogging.

'Do we take it out?'

'He'll bleed to death!'

'It is the captain's poison-tipped knife.' Cylene's voice, edged with panic, fading into the mist.

More words, all incomprehensible.

'Noetos, can you hear me?'

The last speaker was Opuntia, apparently. She stood over him, her blonde hair obscuring her features but not the dreadful wound in her stomach. It dripped blood onto his chest. What was this? Noetos didn't want to dream, not now when Cylene had returned to him. He tried to wake up.

'You can hear me; stop pretending otherwise. I'm barely cold in my grave and already you've found someone else to distract you. You needn't think I'll let you forget how you treated me, fisherman. Do you think for a moment a new love will remove all the bitter self-destructiveness at the heart of you?'

'No, 'puntia,' he croaked.

His dead wife bent over him, her hair touching his face, stinging his eyes.

'You imprisoned me in that fishing village,' she said. 'I was destined to be the queen of Neherius and you were to be my king.

But for a little courage, we could have ruled them. Our every desire indulged! Fortune and fame! Knowledge, travel, consorting with the best people! But you lied, you kept the truth from me; instead of a crown, you gave me the stink of fish and their sandpapery scales in your clothes. When I desired your caresses, you gave me callouses on my hands and bruises on my face. You gave me talk of the sea, of currents and shoals, when I wanted to hear of heroic deeds and faraway places. You drove me to Bregor and Merle, yes, you did; it was your fault I slept with them. At least they did more than grunt! And you killed me with your foolish rescue. You meant to kill me. You were more interested in revenge than in rescue. It suited you that I died! Don't deny it – I can read your thoughts, such as they are. And now I live beyond the veil, in this emptiness, where you drove me!'

She spat in his face. It stung like acid.

'I hope you die,' she said, and he could see her face now, her beautiful features distorted by hatred: her mouth twisted, her eyes bloodshot and staring, her cheeks flushed, her breath hot on his face.

'I hope the poison takes you. I am pouring my power into the poison to increase its potency. I want you here in the void with me, where I can punish you forever for what you did to me.'

'No, my love, you do not understand,' he said, or thought he said. 'I could not tell you of my family. The Neherians were searching for us. Had they found us, they would have taken you and . . . and done to you what they did to my family. You would have died screaming, as their men or their dogs; if you can see my thoughts, you know this. You know this! Ruling in Neherius was just a fantasy. Old Roudhos is no more than a dream, Opuntia!'

He might as well have not spoken for all his argument swayed her. 'You were pleased I died,' she said.

'Yes,' he admitted. 'Yes. Relieved rather than pleased, but your death did take a great weight from my mind. I'm sorry for what I did to you, but I didn't make you into the mean-spirited seagull you became, picking over the bones of others' lives rather than finding food of your own. It is not where you live that makes you big or small, Opuntia. Mean people can live in castles and great souls in fishing villages. What of the widow Nellas? She lost two husbands, yet remained as generous with her heart as ever. She was greater than any of the Neherian nobility.'

'The widow Nellas? That ignorant fishwife? She was generous with far more than her heart, so all the talk went. I suppose you desired even her, didn't you?' Opuntia's voice shrilled in his ear.

'No, dear; I just no longer desired you. Your beautiful body and your sword-edged tongue held no attraction for me. I couldn't bear to touch you. If I had not loved you so deeply I could have closed my ears and used your body, but it was precisely because I once loved you dearly that I was so hurt by your constant tearing down of everything I did.'

He blinked a couple of times, but her face seemed oddly out of focus, as though turning to smoke.

'You had been dead for years,' he said to her. 'You were a hook in our mouths, serving no purpose other than to irritate us at best and leave us flopping in the boat at worst. When I saw you dying in Bregor's arms I felt saddened for you, but glad that your bitter spirit was about to find rest.'

'Rest?' Her voice was a mixture of outrage and terror. 'What do you know about life after death? Rest is something I'll never have, thanks to you, not here in the void. And as repayment for a life of bitterness I will ensure you never have any peace. Turn and turn about! Fisherman, I promise I will haunt you for the remainder of eternity. Do you hear me, Noetos? The remainder of eternity!'

'Noetos?' another voice said, insistent. 'Stay with us.'

'On the count of three,' said another. 'One, two, three!'

'They'll not save you,' Opuntia insisted, her face growing even harder. 'You're coming with me!'

Something like fishhooks tore at his back, pulling him out of his body. He hovered above the broken ship, gazing with interest on his companions – his former companions, he supposed, now he was dead – as they bent over him. There was Cylene, her face above his, tears in her eyes; alongside her stood Arathé and Anomer, hand in hand, eyes closed.

'Put it back, put it back,' a voice wailed. 'He's bleeding to death!'

'It's not lack of blood we need to worry about,' Anomer said. 'It's the poison working towards his heart.'

'He's gone,' Arathé signalled, though Noetos heard her voice in his head, that pure voice she'd possessed before Andratan had started them all on this bitter path. It warmed his cold heart.

'No, he's still close. Hold onto him!' Anomer's lips turned pale with effort.

'Let him go!' Opuntia shrieked.

All three faces turned towards the place where Noetos hung in the air.

'Hold him, hold him!' Anomer commanded, and the hooks bit deeper into the fisherman's skin. In moments his vision faded and his world was reduced to those bright points of pain, the fishhooks tearing at his soul. He groaned, then gave in and let go.

'His eyes are twitching,' Cylene said, her voice excited despite being laced with obvious weariness.

Anomer turned from his sewing and scrambled across the beach to his father's side. 'How are you?' he asked, placing a hand on his father's battered face.

'Is he going to be all right?' Cylene's hand joined Anomer's on Noetos's forehead.

Noetos's eyes sprang open and fixed on Cylene. 'Get her away from me,' he whispered. 'Why do you permit her to be here?'

'What?' Anomer supposed he must have misheard. He glanced at Cylene; her hand remained on Noetos's brow, but her eyes had opened wide in surprise.

'Get her away from me! Make her leave!' his father shouted. 'She wants to kill me!' He took a feeble swipe at her, still enough to connect with her shoulder and knock her to the ground.

'What are you doing?' Anomer cried. 'This is Cylene! She helped save you from the poison. She does not want to kill you!'

Cylene had begun to shake, her lip quivering, her face suddenly bloodless, in the grip of shock.

'She does wish to kill me,' said Noetos, speaking with a disconcerting reasonableness. 'She poisoned me. She intended for me to die. I will not have her anywhere near me.' His hand felt around his belt. 'Where is my sword? I'll deal with her.'

The girl started sobbing. Arathé took her by the hand, pulled her to her feet and led her away.

'She's gone now, Father,' Anomer said. 'Lie still; you are gravely wounded. Arathé and I drew the poison out with our water magic and attempted to heal the wound, but neither of us is trained and we may not have been entirely successful. Had it not been for Cylene, we would have lost you. She has real strength, Father, and she never gave up hope. You should be proud of her.'

He was babbling, he knew, but he could not understand what was happening. Why had his father turned on Cylene? Was it some strange side effect of the poison, or was something else at play here?

Certainly the girl had done more for his father than he had done himself. He'd had a chance to let his father die, and for a moment the anger within him had overruled his feelings and he'd been willing to let Noetos go. *Just like he let go of Mother.* But Arathé had connected to him, exhorting him to lend her his magical strength, and he could not refuse her. Together they had immersed themselves into a battle for their father's life, and all the while Anomer had wrestled with his rising guilt, knowing he would not have intervened without his sister's prompting, and knowing she knew this. After a few moments Cylene had joined them, along with Captain Duon, and together the four of them had prised Noetos away from the force dragging him into darkness. It was more complicated than that, of course, but Arathé had handled the complexity; Anomer had merely supplied his strength. Boorish, so much like the man they had struggled to save.

Anomer would give anything not to turn out like his father, yet it seemed that exactly this fate lay in store for him.

Arathé signalled to him.

'I don't know what is the matter with him,' he replied, 'save being rescued from death. But something is definitely wrong. Even Noetos would not behave like this.'

There is nothing wrong with me. On the contrary, it seemed, he saw perfectly, perhaps for the first time. It had been Opuntia hovering over him, ready to strike him dead, and he wondered why the others had not seen this. Perhaps it took an experience like the one he'd just endured, a close encounter with death, to remove the scales from his eyes.

The fisherman eased himself onto one elbow, stared angrily at the woman who had tried to kill him – and saw Cylene. Saw the hurt expression on her face, saw his children staring at him in puzzlement and anger. He blinked once, twice, but nothing changed.

I have been deceived.

'What have I done?' he croaked.

He knew well what he had done. And what had been done to him.

'You struck Cylene,' Anomer said, speaking slowly as though to an imbecile. 'You knocked her down.'

'Cylene, I'm sorry,' Noetos said, and licked his lips nervously. He had to say something or he would lose her for ever. She deserved nothing less than the truth, but the truth might prove difficult to speak, especially with his children present.

She nodded. 'You were befuddled by the poison from Kidson's knife,' she said. 'You did not know it was me.' *But you still struck me*, her face said.

Her recent past would have involved much physical abuse, he reminded himself, including violence from patrons unhappy with her performance.

'It is worse than that,' he said, and took a deep breath. 'Opuntia, my dead wife and the mother of my children, visited me in a fever-dream.'

He went on to tell as much as he could remember of his discussion with the dead woman. To their credit, none of his audience doubted him. Noetos supposed it was as much a sign of their present lives as anything: given what had happened to them over the last weeks and months, any story, no matter how far-fetched, might well be true. They heard him out without interruption.

'You suffer from guilt,' Anomer said, shaking his head. 'Your mind has manufactured our mother and turned her into a monster because you have been reunited with Cylene. Until you deal with your guilt, you will never be free to love again.'

Arathé shook her head violently. 'No,' she signalled. 'Opuntia may well have really been there as Father lay dying. Because of the hole in the world, the boundary between life and death is breaking down: hence the Emperor coming back to life, and more recently Conal. Remember, Lenares believes she can communicate with her dead foster mother. So Mother may well have discovered the breach in the Wall of Time and found a way to trouble Father. She's certainly determined enough to do so.'

'She said she will haunt me for ever,' Noetos said, sickened.

Cylene stood and came over to where he lay. Her steps were tentative, the cautious approach of a wounded animal who must nevertheless trust its torturer. He nodded, and placed his arms carefully by his sides.

'How old was your wife when you married her?' she asked.

'Just a little older than you,' Noetos said, and for a moment her features blurred and were replaced by Opuntia's older, thinner face. His breath caught in his throat.

'Did you love her with all your heart?'

'Yes,' he whispered. It had been the truth, but love hadn't been enough to conquer the dark cliffs of Fossa.

'And did you really treat her as well as you intend to treat me?'

He swallowed. Truth, now. 'No,' he said. 'I tried, I really tried, Cylene. I intended to give her the world, but I was afraid. Had we left Fossa in pursuit of the life she desired, the Neherians, in all likelihood, would have found me. I didn't want her to be hurt.'

Cylene's face softened. 'You tried to protect her, to keep her

233

from being hurt, and in doing so hurt her nonetheless. Noetos, do you intend to protect me?'

'No,' he whispered, not knowing what she wanted to hear, afraid that every word he spoke might be the word that drove her away. 'I cannot. You have already faced many things I am unable to protect you from, and we are all threatened by forces beyond my power.'

'Even if you could keep me safe, you ought not,' she said. 'Otherwise you will smother me as you smothered her.'

So different: gentle where Opuntia was abrasive; calm where Opuntia was excitable. Brave where she was fearful. Yet every time Noetos looked at Cylene's face he saw Opuntia's features.

This is what she meant when she said she'd haunt me, he realised with dread. His punishment was he would always see Opuntia in any woman he desired. The future stretched before him and it appeared bleak. With one stroke his dead wife had stolen everything.

An hour or so later Cyclamere returned, his rough clothes slathered with mud and grass stains, frustration in his eyes. Noetos managed to struggle from a lying to a seated position, though the effort cost him. One look at Cyclamere's angered visage ensured he did not have to ask his former tutor whether he'd been able to catch Kidson, which was fortunate, as he had insufficient breath. He gulped a few deep lungfuls, the last of which set him coughing.

'Listen to the old man,' Cylene said, leaning into Arathé, who was sitting next to her. She raised her voice. 'You're not going to peg out on us, are you?'

The two girls laughed, genuine mirth mixed with a deal of relief.

Noetos couldn't help himself: he felt a surge of emotion for Cylene. He had never met anyone like her. Though she was the same age as his daughter, the cheerful girl seemed a full generation older. Attributable to the life she had led, of course: the appalling childhood, having been used by her father, suffering guilt over the loss of her twin sister and the deception that followed; and more recently the prostitution she'd acceded to as a way of escaping her family. Noetos could barely credit her survival, let alone the shining beauty of her personality.

He felt ludicrously happy that Cylene seemed to be making friends with Arathé. Anomer acted a little more standoffish, though that was understandable. The boy continued in his unreasonable anger at his father, still blaming Noetos for his mother's death. Noetos was prepared to acknowledge there had been a degree of reconciliation, but Anomer still harboured a serious grudge. The boy would not sanction anything that made his father happy, and of course refused to acknowledge Cylene as any sort of replacement for Opuntia. Noetos wondered how long his patience with his son would last.

'No, I'll draw breath for a while yet,' he answered, and waved his hand in their direction. 'I can see a number of reasons to keep breathing.'

Cylene smiled, but did not gush, and Noetos silently thanked her. He had seen old men fall for young women and had been of the repeated public opinion that there was no more pathetic sight. Janne Lockleg, who ran the largest stall at Fossa market, had made a fool of himself mooning after the long-limbed daughter of his business partner. Enela had exploited the man's obsession, leading him on, the inevitable result being a brawl on Lamplight Street and the subsequent acrimonious termination of the business partnership. The girl had been sent away somewhere west. Noetos sighed. She was probably still alive – unlike Lockleg and Petros, who were probably both dead, killed by the Neherians.

The only survivors are those who left Fossa, Noetos realised. *A message in that perhaps: I should never have stayed. Opuntia*, he admitted, *was right. In fact, had Arathé not left for Andratan and later returned, drawing me out of that cursed village, I would likely have died there.*

Cyclamere nodded to him, having waited patiently for the exchange to end. 'I pursued the sailor for some time,' he said, 'but I lost track of him in the rubble of Long Pike Mouth.'

Noetos groaned as he adjusted his position. 'The town is destroyed?'

His old tutor nodded.

'They were good to us when Dagla died,' Noetos said sadly. It had only been . . . what, a week ago? A little more? He'd lost track of the days. 'They gave us food and treated the injuries Kidson and his men inflicted on us. They did not deserve such a fate.'

'No one deserves to be taken before their time by a storm like that one.'

'Did you see any supplies?'

'Aye, my friend; though much is broken and scattered across the town, the forest and the beach, there were plenty of supplies. A town's worth. Certainly there are no people left alive to consume them.' He frowned.

'You're worried about the Padouki.'

Cyclamere nodded approvingly. 'Something your grandfather might have noticed. Yes, I wonder how they fare in the wake of the great storm. But my mind tells me that if anyone could survive, they could.'

'But the Canopy?' Noetos could imagine the devastation such a severe storm would bring to the treetop city.

'Would have been abandoned at the first sign of high winds. There are caves in the sacred heart, at the base of the great plateau you call the House of the Gods. I have little doubt the Padouki sought them out.'

'Would they have taken shelter in the House of the Gods?'

'Never, not even if it had been their only hope of survival. The place is sacred to the gods, and for the Padouki to travel there would mean the loss of Keppia's gift.'

'Will you remain with us?' Anomer asked.

'Aye,' Cyclamere said, an odd note in his voice, and nodded to the boy.

Ah, Noetos thought. *The fourth generation. Cyclamere may well become Anomer's protector, not mine. Perhaps a glimpse of my son's swordplay will encourage the swordmaster. It might be best for everyone if the old warrior does attach himself to Anomer.* He wondered how he might promote such a liaison.

'We need to eat,' Cylene commented. 'Should we try to move Noetos to the village, or will some of us go to the village and bring food back here?'

'I am well,' Noetos said, 'just a little weak. My son and daughter healed me.' He could not keep the pride out of his voice.

'As to that, I'm a little puzzled,' Anomer said. 'I thought we'd need to rid you of the huanu stone in order to effect our healing. We searched your belt and then your clothing, but—'

'But you couldn't find it,' Noetos finished. 'Have you forgotten that Captain Kidson relieved us of our possessions before tossing us off the *Conch*? The stone is my pack, somewhere on that wreck over there – assuming he didn't just throw our effects overboard.' *He wouldn't have, surely; the Sword of Boudhos alone would be of immense value to him.*

'What are you talking about?' Cylene asked. 'What stone?'

Noetos jerked his head towards her; not only did her face once again carry Opuntia's severe features, her voice was that of his dead wife. He turned away, struggling to keep his composure.

Staring fixedly at the wreck a hundred paces or so to his left, he told Cylene of the huanu stone. He explained how he'd found the stone and had paid a sculptor those precious gold coins to shape it in Arathé's likeness. Omiy the alchemist had explained its worth and something of its power, or, strictly speaking, lack of power – its ability to absorb magic. As Noetos told the tale, weaving it into the story she already knew, he wondered whether, if he turned, he'd see an avaricious light in her eyes, as he had in the eyes of others who had learned of the stone. Or whether he'd see his late wife's face.

He did not turn.

'Show me the stone,' Opuntia's voice said.

Noetos shuddered: the voice scraped along his nerves like a shoal on the keel of a boat. The voice couldn't be audible though, or his children would have commented on it. Opuntia was doing something inside his head, in the place between his senses and his brain.

'Show me the stone,' she said, her voice peremptory, but Noetos had to believe it was Cylene's soft voice asking him, not Opuntia's voice commanding him.

'Let me see if I can get to my feet,' he replied.

'Send one of our children.'

*She said one of our children. No, I heard that, but she said "the,"
I'm sure of it.*

'I cannot. Both of my children are magical. Should they handle the stone directly, it would drain them of their power.'

Cylene would know something was wrong, would be wondering why he did not face her, but as yet she'd not mentioned it.

'I'll go then. Where exactly is the stone?'

The huanu stone was something he would never have allowed Opuntia to handle. Not because it would do her any harm – she was as magic as . . . well, as a stone – but because she would have seen it as a prize, something to be used to further her ambition. *She's in my head, not in Cylene*, Noetos told himself, but it was so hard not to believe his wife had taken possession of his . . . his what? His girl? There were few terms not demeaning both to him and to her.

Perhaps he *was* making a fool of himself.

So be it.

'When you enter the wreck through the large hole in the hull,' he said, 'look up and to your right. You should see a hatch leading to the steerage class accommodation. That's the place I last saw my pack. Of course, it might well be in Kidson's cabin, but start in the bunkroom. And make sure you don't touch the stone! I would hate to see you discover some hidden magical reservoir only when it was being burned out of you.'

He turned then and looked full in her face and forced himself to smile. He was a poor actor, he knew; he hoped she could see the sincerity behind the act.

'Look after him,' Cylene said to Arathé. 'He's still in pain.'

It was only as she approached the wreck that Noetos considered the danger of entering the wreck alone.

That there was something wrong with her father was beyond dispute; he'd been stabbed, after all, by a desperate man, and had suffered a forced healing by two amateur magicians. A wonder, Arathé acknowledged, he'd survived at all. But she'd noticed something adhering to his face, like a second layer of skin, and had pointed it out to Anomer as they effected his healing. The nearest she could come to a description of it was a caul of fog, a cloying layer of magic obscuring his face, interfering with his senses. There was a faint cord attached to it, stretching away into a nothingness that was less a matter of distance and more of 'away-ness.' Arathé did not know what to make of it. The nearest she could come to a solution to the puzzle was the idea that perhaps the Most High had left this odd thing behind as a result of his use of Noetos's body. But the explanation did not convince her.

Anomer had not noticed the strange phenomenon, and could not see it even after Arathé endeavoured to show it to him. It was not easily discerned: whenever one focused directly on it, the caul seemed to vanish. But she was certain it was not a construct of her imagination. That Anomer had not been able to detect it was not surprising: he had ever been the more powerful one, but with far less finesse.

No, Arathé considered as she watched Cylene walk across the beach, Anomer was not a real concern. Though tardy, he had been a willing participant, his ongoing anger at Noetos held in check as he gave her his strength. The most disturbing thing about her father's healing had not been Anomer's belated acquiescence, but the fact that the foggy caul seemed *familiar*.

Moralye sat down where Cylene had been, interrupting Arathé's thoughts. Arathé liked the scholar. She was a pretty young woman, her beauty barely marred by successive burnings from the sun and the inevitable cuts and abrasions incurred on such a journey, especially by someone unused to travel. She had never complained, even when it had been clear she wished to spend more time than could be afforded at Phemanderac's impromptu graveside. Endlessly dependable, she had revealed something more than mere stolidity in her brave rescue of Cylene from Captain Kidson's cabin. Arathé had wondered why Moralye had been drawn from her faraway home to be with the travellers – her encounter with the Most

High had brought her around to the belief that forces were at work beyond those of Husk and his spikes — but the woman had fully justified her presence. Actually, Arathé had begun to warm to her reserved manner and hoped in time to make her a friend.

If they ever had time for such things. So much had happened in the last few days that all normal life had simply evaporated. They ate rapidly whenever they halted; it had been a week, at least, since they had taken the time to partake of a proper meal together. Conversation lagged behind events, so much so that Arathé had yet to explain in detail the nature of their escape from Husk. She particularly wanted to speak with Lenares, as aspects of their dealings with the voice in their heads might, she felt, be pertinent to how they could deal with the gods. Lenares herself had been a hero, apparently, drawing the Daughter's fire during the great storm — another story still untold except in summary.

Some way along the beach, Cylene disappeared into the wreck of the *Conch*.

'I don't think—' Noetos began.

He was interrupted by a strange howling in the air around them, as though something huge was cutting through the fabric of the sky. Accompanying the noise, which grew louder as it raced towards them from somewhere in the distance, was a series of crackling booms, the sound of someone flicking a giant bullwhip.

'Cylene!' he shouted.

The howling noise roared overhead, accompanied by a wind that tore at their hair, the few remaining trees and the debris around them, then dived, screaming, and detonated on the wrecked ship. With a crash the *Conch* shook, then dropped, settling far lower in the water on the near side. The hole through which Cylene had entered simply vanished. Large pieces of timber splashed into the sea and smaller splinters pattered on the sand.

The howling ceased, but the crackling, hissing noise continued all around them for some moments, gradually falling into silence.

Even as the noise faded Arathé had put a hand under her father's armpit and, with Anomer, began dragging him towards the wreck.

'Let me go,' he said. 'Just lend me your strength.'

Anomer opened his mouth, but Arathé shot her brother a glance. *Don't bother arguing with him.*

The connection was still there. Arathé doubted how much strength they could supply him, given she had lost the spike in her head. She'd not thought she would ever lament the loss of Husk! She gathered Anomer's grudging contribution and fed it hurriedly through the connection to her father.

There was so little. What they had, they'd expended on Noetos's healing. As a result her father could barely stand up unaided. Nevertheless, he staggered across the sand towards the incoming tide and the settling wreck.

Take mine, Duon said.

We have no right to ask, Arathé replied.

Take it anyway. Take as much as you can. Whatever the outcome, he needs to believe in you both.

Yes, she said, acknowledging his point, and drew deeply from the southerner.

As Duon crumpled to the ground, Noetos roared and sprinted forward into the surf.

No time to think, no room in his head for coherent thought. He'd suck the world dry to keep her safe, drain anyone and everyone to ensure she lived. He'd call on the Father, any of the gods, trap them somehow, make them help, get them involved, force them to take his side. Anything, anything.

She hadn't wanted him to protect her. Fine words, with the best of intentions, but he could have prevented this simply by not telling her about the stone. Just like he'd kept Opuntia safe by not telling her about Neherius.

The wreck loomed in front of him. It had dropped a considerable amount, collapsing on itself having given way at the weak point, right where Cylene had entered the hull. There was no longer a hole, no longer a way in. Noetos kept sprinting, didn't slow down, would not, and smashed into the thick planks of the hull at full speed.

And broke through.

241

Russell Kirkpatrick

His body had become a missile, a rock thrown from a catapult, a force unable to be resisted. Behind him, wood, caulking and tar splashed into the water. With considerable effort he pulled up, ankle-deep in water, and peered around in the relative darkness. The strength in his body faded.

'Cylene!'

No reply, of course there was no reply; if she had been in a position to reply she would surely have noticed his arrival. Injured then. Unconscious. He couldn't penetrate the gloom, despite his frantic searching, and found her only because he stood on her outstretched arm.

He took a backward step, horrified.

She was pinned by the hull wall. At first sight it appeared to have cut her in half. Her upper body lay almost fully submerged in the water, face down, her hair spread out like pale coral around her head. His splashing made her body rock gently.

Dead, undoubtedly dead.

A moment passed and she did not move. Another moment. He refused to believe it. Hauled her up by the hair until her face emerged from the water, her unmarked face, its warmth already fleeing.

The sight of her was unbearable.

He drew a deep breath and, as he did so, pulled in every ounce of magic he could through the connection between himself and his children. A part of him knew it was dangerous, that he might empty them of magic – more, might drain them of life – but he literally could not stop himself. Couldn't make himself care. He could sense power coming from places only distantly connected to his son and daughter; in particular, one remote, reluctant participant fought to keep from being tapped, but Noetos drew from him with fierce glee. He hoped it was the evil voice that had enslaved his daughter.

He let his breath out with a roar.

The noise he made was indescribable, something far greater than any beast of the field or forest, shriller than an animal in pain, more powerful than the collapse of a hill. Under the assault the hull shattered into uncountable pieces, the largest chunks flung away, the remainder little more than a cloud of splinters and dust. The sudden sun made him blink. There she was, still floating in the water, but now at least free of the hull. Not cut in half, but still crushed. Still drowned. Still dead.

Noetos took her broken body in his arms and carried her through the waves, up and along the beach, in the sunshine, to the silent group awaiting him.

Laid her on the sand, her face so beautiful and so empty.

Waited in hope for the time-doubling effect to occur, unable to believe that her death was real, was final. Grasping at any chance, however unlikely.

Waited.

Waited until her body stiffened. Watched as the blood drained from her lovely face, leaving her features pinched and mean. It was clear no doubling of time would occur.

Walked away into the ravaged forest and screamed every ounce of feeling at the uncaring trees.

No one followed.

CHAPTER 10

SHAKY GROUND

NOETOS STAYED AWAY FOR HOURS.

'We must find the stone,' Anomer said.

'I don't care about the stone. Let it be lost forever. It cost us Cylene. No stone is worth that. Forget about it and think instead about what must be done. We must bury Cylene before the ants find her.'

Anomer frowned at his sister. With one hand she signalled her replies, too distressed to mind-speak, while with the other she mopped Duon's pallid face. The man was still unconscious from the morning's terrible events, having been drained almost to the point of death first by Arathé and then by Noetos. His sister seemed to be developing some feeling for the southerner, not surprising given they seemed to share minds. Anomer wasn't sure what he felt about that, but he certainly wasn't comfortable with it. Arathé had been his special playmate and they had shared their lives; now someone else threatened to take his place.

'It's not a matter of what the stone is worth or what it did,' he said, snapping at her. 'We might need it. It might well be instrumental in our defeat of the gods. Do you want to be the one to tell Lenares you left it lying on a beach?'

Arathé waved her hand lazily, clearly weighed down by exhaustion. 'It's Father's stone. If he wants it, he can go and get it. Neither you nor I can touch it, and I suspect even Duon would be hurt by it, given the degree to which he and I are linked.'

'I could go and look for it,' Moralye said softly.

She of all of them – barring Noetos, of course – had been most affected by Cylene's death. She'd known the girl for an hour, no more. Anomer supposed it was a reaction to knowing her bravery had been wasted; that perhaps in conducting her rescue she had set their cause back rather than advancing it, despite her good intentions. Such things were unknowable, he thought. If a god refused to foretell the future, claiming it was as yet unformed, what chance did any of them have to make sensible decisions?

'I don't think Noetos would object,' the scholar added.

Anomer grunted. 'Who knows what he'd care about? He's out of his mind with grief. Anyway, he's never been the most predictable of men even at his best. That's what I hated most about our childhood. You never knew what he'd be like: one night he'd come home with presents, little wooden carvings for me or earrings for Arathé; the next he'd arrive half-drunk and haul us out of our beds to inspect our fingernails or the shine of our shoes, and he'd keep looking until he found something he could punish us for. It got so I could hear his footsteps coming up the rough Old Fossa Road long before anyone else, and I'd tidy up all my possessions so I might better please him. He was capricious, that's the term for it.'

Silence greeted his words.

'I'm sorry, I don't know where that came from,' he said.

'I never knew you felt like that,' Arathé signalled.

'Didn't he frighten you?'

She shook her head. 'I was older. He was gruff to me at times, but I never felt frightened, little brother. Not like you just described. I wish you had said something to me.'

'I spoke to Mother,' he said. 'She said there was nothing we could do, he was like that with everybody. She told me she hated it too, and that she must have done something bad to make him angry.'

'Did she really?' Arathé signalled, her stiff movements betraying her feelings. 'Did she really say that? I think it's nonsense. She knew exactly why he was angry with her. The more I hear, the more I suspect our mother was trying to enlist us in her private war against Father.'

'Excuse me,' Moralye said, her command of the Bhrudwan common tongue perfect as always. 'As I do not wish to offend your father, I won't retrieve the stone unless one of you gives me your blessing. It ought to be retrieved, don't you think?'

The late afternoon air remained warm, the stench of corruption from the nearby town had lessened, and birds had begun their tentative return to the coastal forest. The bay described a lazy arc from north to south; they were, Anomer judged, very near the southern end. Behind the wreckage of the *Conch* rose a line of low hills, jutting into the sea and forming a headland, no doubt protecting the bay from bad weather. Though not, of course, from the fury of a god-storm. In better times, Anomer supposed, this coast might be considered an idyllic place to visit. Certainly it would have provided a generous livelihood for those fishing here. Not now, though. Detritus from the storm formed a barrier between the golden sands of the beach and the eggshell blue of the sea. Branches, bodies, fixtures from the village, planks from the jetty, all rose and fell with the gentle waves of the incoming tide. As Moralye and Anomer walked towards the remains of the *Conch*, it became clear that it would be a long time before anyone enjoyed the vista from Long Pike Mouth.

Little of the *Conch* remained. Hard to believe this scattered wreckage had transported them north such a short time ago. Anomer wondered what had happened to the passengers, what their last moments had been like. The woman who had been sailing north to visit her sick mother, had she been battered to death below decks in her first-class compartment? Did the Fallows family, whose youngest daughter had caught a fever and died on the voyage, end up being washed off the deck by a huge wave? Did they die in each other's arms, or alone amidst towering waves? From what Cylene had said, there was none alive bar she and Kidson by the time the wreck fetched up on the coast. It would have been a terrifying last few hours, he had no doubt.

He joined the scholar in picking through the wreckage, searching for Noetos's pack and their other possessions. Noetos had reduced the vessel to pieces the size of his forearm or smaller, the result of a detonation of magic so strong it had knocked Anomer to the ground where he stood at the far end of the beach. A few larger beams lay together further up the beach, towards the forest, and the two searchers focused their efforts there.

There were a few heartening finds. Anomer's own sword and some of his clothes lay under a pile of decking, along with a couple of Mustar's shirts. As the searchers sifted through the wreckage a raft made of clothes and sailcloth floated in on the waves. And Morayle let out a whoop, holding up the Sword of Roudhos. After that, their returns diminished.

As the sun touched the treetops, Arathé hailed his mind.

Brother, it strikes me there's a better way of searching, she said. *The huanu stone is anti-magical, right? And we were taught in Andratan that everything has its own magical quotient, its essenza.* He nodded mentally to her. *So if you search using magic, you should be able to sense the absence of magic in a specific place.*

Like using torchlight to find something lost in the dark? He imagined having a magical sense that could sweep over the beach, and instantly found he could see magic.

It was breathtaking.

The nearest he could come to describing what he could see was a lattice of thin golden threads matting the landscape, connecting everything with everything. No, not everything: the threads were thickest between the individual pieces of the shipwreck; because, Anomer supposed, they had until recently been parts of one thing. Threads ran through the air, though there were not nearly so many and they appeared much thinner. Something about the thickness was important, though he had no idea what. He doubted it mattered to the task at hand. Larger objects, those composed of many things, were lumps of magical gold, node-like junctions of thousands of threaded pathways.

Beside him, Moralye stooped, lifted and peered, oblivious to his amazement.

This may be what Lenares sees, Arathé remarked, her strength trickling in union with his. *If so, I can understand why she is so different from the rest of us.*

I don't see any obvious gap, Anomer said, trying to focus on the mundanity of their search. *The threads seem to be evenly spread across the beach.*

Have you looked in the water?

No; I never thought it might have been thrown into the sea.

He turned to gaze out on the placid bay, and immediately saw what he was looking for: an absence, a place where the threads melted into nothingness.

'Are there toothwhales?' Moralye's voice intruded upon his inward vision of splendour.

'Toothwhales? I've not heard of such things. What are they?'

'Good.' She nodded in obvious relief and waded in the direction he pointed.

She worked through a tightly packed zone of debris, taking a wide berth around a knot of bobbing bodies. Anomer wondered if they were from the *Conch*, if they had made it through the storm only to die as the ship cast itself onto the beach. Would he recognise them if he looked closely at their cold faces? This led to thoughts of Cylene and he tried to think of something else.

'Keep going forward,' he called to her as the water reached her waist. 'Forward; about ten paces more. Left a little, to your left. About there.'

She seemed to stand still for some time, the waves surging around her chest. Anomer guessed she was feeling the sandy floor with her feet.

'I have something!' she cried.

'Did you mean sharks?' he asked her.

'What?'

'Sharks. Big fish with very sharp teeth. Is that what you meant by toothwhales?'

Moralye froze in the act of reaching down into the water. 'Yes,' she said. 'Do you have any of those?'

'Not around here,' he said, hoping he sounded convincing. 'We see them out beyond The Rhoos sometimes, shadowing the

Neherian fleet, but they don't often come inshore. Water's not deep enough for them.'

She clearly didn't find this at all comforting. 'They are so large that this depth of water cannot sustain them?'

Anomer noted the quaver in her voice. He didn't answer her.

You are such a stupid brother, Arathé said to him. He shot back a mental agreement.

'See if you can pick up the pack,' he called to Moralye.

She grimaced at him, then leaned over until her head practically touched the water. Clearly, she still could not reach the pack.

The next wave approached her.

'Moralye, watch out,' he called.

She jerked up straight, eyes wide, her head turning left and right.

'Just a wave,' Anomer said. 'Look, I'm coming out to help you.'

Such a clever boy, Arathé said. *Frighten her when she's feeling vulnerable, then emphasise her weakness by offering to help. Such wonderfully sensitive creatures, males.*

Aye, and females show such good sense by distracting people from the task at hand. He started into the surf, which was surprisingly warm.

Moralye bent over again, resignation on her face, and was struck by the next wave. With a squeal she disappeared.

'Damn,' Anomer breathed, and began to run towards her.

A moment later she emerged, one arm held high. 'I have it!' she called, then coughed and spat seawater from her mouth.

He joined her in the surf and together they stared at the green-stone carving of his sister. Arathé looked too, using his eyes. *It must have burst free of Father's pack,* he said to her.

Not very prepossessing, is it, she said. *Not for something that has caused so much trouble.*

Something rippled across the magical lattice.

Things don't have to be prepossessing to cause trouble, he answered her grimly.

Did you see that? she sent, interrupting him.

What? he replied, just as a larger ripple sped across their golden vision.

That. What is it?

He stared in the direction from which the ripples had come. There, in the sky, far out to sea, was another absence of magic: a vast circular maw where threads ended as though severed by knives. Faint stars were visible within the hole in the sky, a window to another place.

Moralye tugged his arm. 'Are we going to go back to shore, or shall we wait for the toothwhales?'

'We're going back,' Anomer said hastily. 'We need to hurry.'

Another ripple began to form below the hole in the sky. Anomer knew they were in danger, but the sheer size of it kept his eyes fixed to the spot. Arathé shrieked a warning.

'I see it, sister,' he said aloud. 'Come on,' he added, turning to Moralye. 'Run!'

The huge ripple struck just as they were leaving the water. The magical lattice billowed up into a mountain, then surged over them. A moment later the earth shook, knocking them both to the ground. Beside him Moralye screamed. Somewhere nearby his sister emitted a high-pitched whine. He himself bellowed in fear. The shaking intensified, pulling him left and right, throwing him into the air and dashing his head into the surprisingly hard sand, once, twice and again.

He tried to stand, but the earth kept throwing him back down. He caught a glimpse of Moralye kneeling in the shallow water some distance away, though she had been beside him a moment ago.

The sand collapsed beneath him.

For a moment he visualised himself falling into a bottomless pit, but he found himself in a hole a foot deep, the sand below him hot to the touch. He scrambled out of the depression and clung to the ground as the tremor continued.

Another ripple surged past.

The ground heaved. Sand billowed into the air. Anomer found himself lifted off the ground as though bucked from a horse. His landing knocked the wind from his chest.

The earth groaned like a wounded animal: the sound was

deafening. A deep grinding noise came from somewhere beneath him and he levered himself to his feet in fear. Then his eye caught something that disoriented him further. The trees in the coastal forest were moving southwards relative to the beach.

With a violent jerk the further part of the forest relocated itself a dozen paces to his right and some indeterminate distance further away. The motion was accompanied by a noise that seemed to exploit every pitch his ears were capable of hearing, from a deep growl to a shrill scream.

Booms, rattles, crashes and bangs surrounded him.

Beside him the sand began to move. He rolled away in a panic, then stood to see the sand fountaining up as though it was water forced through a pipe. All over the beach the same thing was happening. The booming and banging continued; the remaining upright trees began to crash to the ground. Another shake knocked the legs out from under him.

Above the beach, the hole in the world stared down at him like a giant dark eye.

The shaking began to slacken.

Arathé? Sister?

Here, Anomer, she said, and stood up from the place in the forest where she'd been thrown.

Are you hurt?

Bruised, she said. *Duon is awake.*

I'm not surprised.

Another tremor rippled across the beach and he fell to his hands and knees.

A moment later Moralye had an arm around him. 'Anomer, are you all right?' she asked.

He nodded, and the two of them struggled across the sand towards his sister, who had Duon in tow.

The four of them clung to each other.

'When will this end?' Moralye whimpered.

'When we end it,' Anomer said.

Duon probed a bloody scrape on his cheek. 'The gods are too powerful.'

'Not powerful enough to have killed us yet,' Arathé signalled.

'No, but powerful enough that in time they will break the world,' Moralye said.

Anomer looked at their crazed surroundings: fountains still heaving sand into the air, the coastal forest flattened, the bay choppy with waves heading in every direction.

'Where is Cylene's body?' he asked.

Noetos had no memory of anything since he'd laid Cylene on the beach. He supposed he'd been walking about the forest. Nothing else would explain the scratches and bruises on his arms and legs, no doubt from repeated encounters with fallen trees. He'd lain face down on the pine needles for some time after the last fall, heedless of anything around him, which was where the corpse of Dryman found him.

Thick fingers curled around his shoulder and jerked him to his feet. At any other time, shock would have claimed him at a confrontation with a dead man; however, the fisherman was so drained he could stare into Dryman's face with equanimity.

Dryman's face, yes, but it was not Dryman who stared out of those dark eyes. The eyes crinkled a little and the head tilted to one side, as though the body's occupant was somewhat puzzled by what he saw.

'You are the fisherman?' asked the mouth in a well-modulated voice. Dryman's voice, but not his inflections. Someone else used the mercenary's apparatus.

'You've done the voice well,' Noetos replied. His heart burned with an icy fire; all he wanted to do was to goad the god standing before him. He cared nothing for the consequences. 'I'm not so convinced by the way you wear the body.' He screwed his face up theatrically. 'It looks a little . . . *large* for you.'

At these words, the tiny muscles normally continually mobile in a face froze for a moment. 'Answer my question,' the thing said, in a voice designed to command.

It moved Noetos not an inch. 'You'll need to work on your presence,' he said, and sneered at the god-monster. 'What is it like to spend eternity on the far side of the Wall of Time? Plenty of things to do there? Interesting people to talk to?'

At this moment he did not fear any outcome. Finally, a game he could not possibly lose.

'I will not ask again,' the voice said.

'That is fortunate, for I am already bored with you. Go about your business.'

The thing's mouth twisted cruelly. 'Did you enjoy watching the hire-girl's death, fisherman? Did you take as much pleasure from it as I did in killing her? Oh, it was so touching, seeing you and her reunited; what else could I do but await my chance to slay her the moment you let her out of your sight?' The blue lips barked a laugh.

No conscious thought. Duon's sword was out of its scabbard and in his hand, the first cut underway, even before Noetos realised he was angry. He took the corpse's left arm off at the shoulder, surprised to meet no resistance, but did not stop his attack.

'Pain anchors me to this world,' the thing said, as clotting blood dribbled from the wound. 'Kill this body and you may well—'

Noetos had no will to listen. Everything was bent on chopping the unnatural life out of the thing that had killed his Cylene. His third cut took the corpse in the mouth, effectively silencing it.

The body took some time to die.

Noetos stood over it, breathing heavily, and watched the life ebb from its eyes.

'I am enjoying this,' he whispered to it.

The body settled on the ground with a sigh like escaping marsh gas. Just after the moment of death, the few birds in the forest rose up from their perches and flew off in a flurry of wings.

A moment later the ground heaved.

The sand had ceased its strange fountaining, leaving miniature volcanos dotted across the beach, each one collapsing a little more with every aftershock. The forest around them was silent save for the rustle of leaves whenever the earth shook.

Could you have used magic to protect us from the quake? Duon asked her.

Those were the words his question translated to, but within the question was laced a genuine interest, not a fearful demand that she protect him. She could see it was neither thoughtless nor malicious.

I did not think to use magic, she replied. *A trained magician's first instinct would be to employ a shield. I don't think anyone would be capable of actually defusing the earthquake itself.*

To have been a trained magician would have meant learning how to exploit others. This you did not want to do. I approve.

Yet I do it all the time. It seems there is a new crisis every hour of every day. I took from you what I would not take from those poor prisoners in Andratan.

You took nothing, he sent. *I gave it.*

Such intensity, she thought, and held the idea deep in her mind, not allowing it to leak into her surface thoughts. *I thought he was such a weak man, dry and passionless, when first I met him. Yet he accompanied my father and aided him in his defeat of the Neherians, and confronted his Emperor even though he knew the man had become a god.*

I could have killed you without meaning to, she sent. *Could have drained you dry.*

No one was thinking clearly at the time. All we wanted to do was to protect Cylene. We failed. Arathé, if we cannot even protect ourselves, how can we overcome the gods?

She mind-smiled at him. *Husk has given me some ideas,* she said, but did not elaborate.

You're worried about your father. I know you want to go searching for him, but if you do, he may resent it. I'm sure he's safe. You still have a connection to him, so you would know if he was in serious trouble.

Only if he asks for help.

You're right; we should try to find him.

Despite this thought, she could see he still wasn't sure.

Cyclamere's most likely with him, he sent.

She had forgotten that. *Oh yes, the man who trained him. He'll be a levelling influence, for certain.*

Perhaps the Padouki removed Cylene's body from the beach.

During an earthquake?

Duon had a wonderful heart, but sometimes she wondered about his common sense. Actually, she supposed, the fact that they were here was compelling evidence that none of them had any common sense.

Then who took it?

Duon, I was thrown clear into the forest. Cylene may have ended in the sea, or further in the trees. She might have been buried by one of those sand fountains. Of all our troubles, her missing body is low on the list.

She sensed the fright in his mind before he expressed his thought. In a very odd moment, she shared his vision: he was looking out over the bay as he spoke, and she saw it through his eyes while facing towards the forest. The ocean was emptying of water. The crazy phenomenon was accompanied by a loud sucking noise.

Where is it going?

At that moment, in a reversal of the previous sensation, she felt Duon look through her eyes to see her father stagger into view.

Noetos lumbered forward like a bear, blood streaming from a cut to his scalp. Eyes wide and unfocused, he didn't seem to notice his children rushing towards him.

'Where is she?' he growled. 'Where is she?'

'Father, we don't know,' Anomer said, and waited for the explosion.

'I am here,' said another voice.

Unbelievably, Cylene herself emerged from the forest.

'How are you alive?' Noetos asked, his voice filled with wonder.

It was the question Anomer wanted an answer to. Alarms began to sound in his head as Cylene started her explanation. *This is not right. People don't come back to life just because their deaths are tragic.* Dozens of unlikely things had happened since the gods had begun to break the world, but happy endings had not been a part of any of them. Through his connection with his sister he could sense she too was uneasy.

'I died,' Cylene said, her voice husky with pain. 'There was a noise, then the ship smashed down on top of me. It broke my back and forced my face into the water.' She took a strained breath. 'I tried to breathe, but all I could take in was water.'

'You drowned,' Noetos said.

He hovered over Cylene like a mother hen, kneeling beside her as she sat against a fallen trunk. He obviously wanted to embrace her, but just as clearly was concerned that she might still be injured.

She gazed up at the fisherman and Anomer's breath caught in his throat. Had her eyes always been this dark? Was this an effect of the drowning?

'Yes,' she said. 'I drowned. I struggled, but everything faded away and I floated in blackness, surrounded by a million pinpoints of light. Some of the lights whispered things to me, but I can't remember what they said. Everything about the black place scared me; it wasn't anything like the heaven my parents taught us about when we were children. I heard you roar, and your magic pulled me back towards my body. But I could not make the leap and I hovered at the edge of the hole in the world, waiting to see what happened.'

'So what happened?' Noetos asked.

'I watched my body start to disintegrate,' she said. 'It was awful. My skin became dry and hard and I could see it turning a dreadful green colour around my mouth and eyes. There were things crawling under my skin and strange eructations throughout my body.'

This still did not ring true. Had Cylene been so absorbed in her appearance while alive that it would become her primary concern when dead? To be fair, Anomer had never been dead, so perhaps he was misreading her – or maybe his love for his mother continued to prejudice him against the young woman. He chastised himself. Ought he not to be rejoicing with his father at this turn of fortune?

Arathé's thought came through. *Eructations? What sort of a word is that for a provincial girl?*

Ah, so his sister was suspicious. Even better.

Noetos nodded, encouraging Cylene to continue.

'Then a great power began to pour in through the hole in the world, drawing magic from the void. One of the gods enacted some sort of violence against the earth; you tell me there was an earthquake, so that must have been the result of the power. The flow pulled my essenza out of the void and through the hole with it. I couldn't have avoided being reunited with my body even had I wished to stay dead.'

'Hah! Defeated by their own schemes!' Noetos cried, and hugged her.

Anomer saw the girl stiffen for a mere fraction of a second, then relax into his embrace.

Just like Father to accept this at face value.

And just like you to reject it, came Arathé's thought.

Do you believe it? Is this Cylene returned from the dead?

Her answer was equivocal. *Many strange things have happened since this adventure began. Wait and we will see.*

Oddly, the sea had not yet returned to the empty bay. Anomer had no idea what had made the sea vanish, though he could imagine it draining into a great chasm caused by the shaking. Perhaps the water had gone for good, turning the bay into a wide plain.

'We're so pleased to have you back,' Noetos said, tears in his eyes, and widened his embrace to include his children, beckoning them closer with his hands.

Arathé put her arms around her father and Cylene, but Anomer pretended he hadn't noticed.

'Noetos!' cried a voice in the distance. 'Are you there? Are you alive?'

It came from somewhere in the forest. Anomer began sprinting in the direction of the sound even before the others had disengaged themselves.

'Be careful!' came the voice, closer now, as Anomer struggled over the strewn vegetation. 'There's a hole . . .'

And there was. An enormous gash slashed across the forest floor like a wound in flesh, perhaps twenty paces wide and – he leaned forward to check – unguessably deep. A blood-red glow rose from the depths. *They have wounded the earth!*

On the far side stood his father's Padouki friend, Cyclamere.

'Is there any way across?' Anomer asked him.

'I do not think so. I have travelled much of its length and have found no easy crossing point. This chasm describes a great circle, a mirror of the hole hovering above us. You are marooned on a fortress surrounded by a moat.'

Anomer pointed down into the chasm. 'Is that where the water has gone?'

The Padouki shook his head. 'I think not. Were water to drain into this unnatural fissure open to the hidden fires below, the steam would rise into the heavens, obscuring even the sun. The sea must have found some other inlet to the subterranean depths.'

Noetos and the others lined up beside Anomer, their mouths open at the sight of the cleft in the forest. Cyclamere repeated his observations.

'Anywhere narrow enough to cross?' Noetos asked.

'Two places I thought might be worth the risk,' his mentor replied. 'It is at its narrowest right here, but still much too broad for a leap. Far easier to place a few of these fallen trees across the gap.'

'Ah,' said Noetos, clearly embarrassed he'd not thought of the obvious.

Anomer reflected on the meaning of this. *We're always looking for the magical solution. Our good sense has been usurped by the commonplace occurrence of the supernatural.*

'It would still be safer for Heredrew to perform his levitation trick,' Duon commented.

'Where are Heredrew and the others?' Noetos asked Cyclamere. 'Have you seen them?'

'They may still be at Corata Pit,' the Padouki said. 'Wondering where we are. Or perhaps the earthquake has provided them with problems of their own.'

A faint rumbling shook the ground. Everyone froze, waiting to see if it built into another quake. The hole still hovered overhead, an eye alive with mischief, and Anomer wondered just how strong the gods had become. Would the next shake be even greater? The gentle rumble failed to build in intensity, but neither did it die away.

Cyclamere hissed through bared teeth. The urgency of the sound drew Anomer's attention: the warrior's suddenly concerned gaze was fixed on something behind them. As Anomer began to turn, the skin on the back of his neck prickled. He knew his history and the aftermath of the Great Aneheri Quake came swiftly into his mind.

There it was, a dark smudge far out in the bay.

None of the others reacted with anything like the fear rising in his chest. Likely they knew nothing of what sometimes came after an earthquake at sea. Cyclamere knew, of course: he had been Father's tutor, after all. Father clearly had not listened to his lessons.

'You need to run,' Anomer said to Cyclamere. 'Get as far inland as you can.'

'How can I leave when my lord is in danger?'

'Danger? What danger?' Noetos said, head swivelling between his son and his old teacher. 'What are you talking about?'

'What are you going to do?' Anomer continued. 'Fend it off with your sword?'

'I cannot run away. Better to face it here.'

The vibrations had become, if anything, a little stronger.

Noetos grabbed at his son's arm. 'What are you talking about?'

Anomer shook him off. 'If nothing else, friend, you must warn the others.'

Cyclamere nodded once, sense penetrating his stubborn loyalty. 'Aye.'

Only now did Anomer address his father and the others. 'A wave is coming. When the earth shakes under the sea, it sometimes creates ripples in the ocean. They become waves when they arrive at the coast.'

'A wave? Ripples? What are you talking about, lad? We have waves all the time.'

'Not like this,' said Cyclamere. 'This one will be as high as a tree and will break upon us with the full weight of the ocean behind it. The shaking you feel is the wave coming.'

'Very well,' said Noetos, clearly disbelieving. 'What can we do about it?'

'Nothing, Father; just as the gods planned, we are trapped. Separated from the magicians, exhausted from overuse of our power, surrounded by this chasm. Please, order your servant away. Let someone at least be saved.'

'It's just a little wave,' Moralye put in, shielding her eyes from the sun with her hand as she stared out to sea. 'What damage can it do?'

'A great deal,' said Cylene dreamily. 'What is coming is neither little nor a wave. It is a surge of the sea, a sudden raising of its height, and it keeps coming long after you think it must stop, battering everything in its path. Then, after it ends, the surge withdraws from the land, pulling that which it has destroyed back out to sea with it. It is irresistible.'

Could no one else hear the relish with which she spoke?

'How do you know this?' Moralye asked her.

'My father told me stories,' she said. 'Stories of the sea and the great surges that came after the earth shook. I thought they were just stories, but it seems today we are fated to discover they are far more.'

Cyclamere extended his hand across the unbridgeable gulf. 'If I hurry I can bring branches,' he said. 'Search on your side for timber. I do not want to see you swept away.'

For a moment Anomer considered wrestling with the fallen trunks around them, felled by storm and quake, but the wave was much closer now. Far too close. Even had they begun dragging a log the moment they had seen the danger, they would not have made it in time.

The broad expanse of white foam surged up the beach towards them.

Cyclamere turned and ran, shouting his frustration.

The wave drew closer.

'Gather around me,' Duon said, his voice barely audible above the roar of the water.

There was a thump like the collision of stars and the wave

fountained up into the air. *It has found the seaward side of our moat,* Anomer realised; *perhaps the wave will vanish into the earth.* But the hope lasted only a second. The water leaped across the chasm, the power of the ocean far too strong for a mere crack in its bed.

'Open yourselves to Arathé!' Duon shouted.

Anomer heard the southerner's urgent voice in his mind more than with his ears. He opened his connection to his sister and instantly sensed her searching for power.

The water surged towards them.

Birds fell from the sky, insects stopped crawling, things smaller than insects died as Arathé drew essenza from every living thing around them. She reached further, and further still, into the silent and dark world of inanimate objects. Every object contributed something; Anomer felt his sister pull power even from the approaching wall of water.

The wave struck.

It surged around the small group cowering together without touching them, slipping past and over them as though unable to penetrate a barrier. And barrier it was: Arathé had hastily erected a wall of pure gold essenza between them and the wave.

Anomer turned in time to see the wave strike the chasm behind them. The fissure swallowed the water, but was not large enough to take it all and within moments the wave surged up the other side and out into the forest. The ground rumbled and shook and steam swirled around them.

Still not safe, Arathé sent, though her thoughts were triumphant rather than worried. The ground continued to shake, and suddenly began to rise. Another quake. Anomer threw himself to the ground.

Relax, brother, this is part of my plan.

The whole of the fortress – the land surrounded by the circular fissure – rose a pace, two paces, five paces, and the water battering at them drained away. Within moments they found themselves on a large island in the midst of a roaring, foam-cloaked sea.

I thought I might be able to do this, Arathé sent, exulting. *Our teachers at Andratan talked about the new magical discoveries being made, and told us that sorcerers didn't have to draw power from within themselves to work their magic. But they wrongly assumed that power would have to be stolen from others. That's why I refused to cooperate with them: I hated the idea of taking power from others. So they took me and made me a source of power for others. But they were wrong! Everything has power.*

So the more powerful the weapon the gods throw at us, the more we can draw our protection from it?

Yes, she sent. *Yes. That is exactly what it means.*

Then we're safe.

Yes.

Anomer had not realised how heavily his constant fear had been weighing upon him until it lifted.

The wave roared in the distance as it crashed through the forest, tossing fallen trees around like kindling wood. The steam from the deep fissure condensed above them and began to fall as a light drizzle.

How long will we have to wait here? Anomer heard Duon ask Arathé.

The sea will drain away soon, Taleth. We will wait a while to see if any further waves come, then return to the others at Corata Pit.

That sounds sensible. Thank you, Arathé.

The jealousy Anomer felt at this exchange was foolish – it wasn't Duon's fault he now had an intimate link to Arathé – but his sister had called the southerner by his first name. Anomer hadn't even known he had one. Moreover, the mind-tone she had used had been friendly, to say the least of it – as had his.

Foolish to feel it, he knew, but feel it he did.

The group waited through the night for the water to recede. Five enormous waves came past their circular island during the hours of darkness, the second and third larger than the first, the fourth and fifth tapering away.

The waxing moon rose some time in the small hours, and Anomer bumped into Cylene while returning from relieving himself over the side of Arathé's magical island. The unguarded look of rage on the girl's face frightened him, though within moments it was replaced by her usual friendly, slightly licentious grin. He almost asked her what she was so angry about, but then remembered his suspicions and said nothing.

At least Father isn't sleeping with her yet. But how much longer could Noetos resist her charms? She had draped herself around his neck like a scarf while they partook of their scanty meal of fresh fish, but he'd not said much to her – or to anybody.

Indeed, few of the group had felt like talking. Cylene tried to make conversation, but no one offered her more than perfunctory replies. Moralye and Arathé spoke in low tones for a few minutes, then settled down to sleep.

The silence, Anomer considered, was fitting, given how the hole in the world still hovered above them, marked at night by an absence of glittering stars, perfectly mirroring the island on which they stood.

COSMOGRAPHER

CHAPTER 11

MENSAYA

LENARES HATED UNCERTAINTY.

There was no telling how Torve would react to the questions she intended to ask him. Perhaps he would become angry and tell her he wanted nothing more to do with her, and that would make her sad. Just when she had found someone she was comfortable with, whom she talked to with ease, she feared she could lose him. Of course, he might show sensitivity and understanding. He might even promise to remain with her, though she doubted this. The doubt made her miserable.

A frightening thing, not being able to control someone else. Lenares' world depended on being certain of those close to her. Mahudia had always responded swiftly to her needs, and over the years Lenares had devised ways of getting what she wanted from her foster mother. But Torve owed her nothing. No duty, no responsibility, leaving no way Lenares could make him do what she wanted. Worse, she had come to realise that even if she could manipulate him, such behaviour would work against her happiness in the long run.

If only she knew more! On the afternoon they had left Corata Pit and made their way north she had spent an hour or so talking with the Undying Man, Kannwar. She had asked him to tell her whatever he knew about the effects on a man of having his worm cut off as well as his balls. At first he'd refused, claiming that he didn't want to distress her, but he was lying, behaving 'diplomatically.' Eventually, though, she pestered him into telling her. Lenares usually got what she wanted.

In some respects Kannwar knew entirely too much. The procedure was called castration, he told her, and had been a not-uncommon practice all across northern Bhrudwo until about five hundred years ago. Apparently begun as a punishment for enemies defeated in battle, its practitioners believed it allowed them to possess the sexual energy and prowess of their victims in addition to their own. Lenares had frowned at this, barely believing that people would be so foolish, but his words had the ring of truth about them. Castration also resulted in a more practical outcome, Kannwar had added, in that it justified the conquerors' taking of the enemy's women. What use were they, after all, if their emasculated men could no longer service them?

Such talk angered Lenares. It made women seem like child manufactories. Kannwar himself didn't believe this, he'd said when she'd snapped at him, but her anger did not lessen. It was so unfair that men did things and women had things done to them. If women had the outies and men had the innies, things would have been different, Lenares was sure.

Kannwar had laughed at her outrage. Sexual politics, he had called it, and advised her to abandon her concerns. 'Women are what we make them,' he had said, his long face carrying a faintly distasteful look, not caring or even noticing Stella's frown as she walked beside them; she a woman once queen of an empire the equivalent of his, answerable to no man bar her husband, and, according to what Stella had said, seldom even then.

Did this mean, then, that Torve would no longer be considered a man? Of a certainty, Kannwar had replied to her anxious question. Eunuchs had formed a third class of people, not as low as women but lower than men, considered ideal for bureaucratic work because of their serene emotional state. Lenares had questioned this. She would have been anything but serene had she lost a part of herself like that, but Kannwar assured her that the removal of the penis and testicles – the first time she'd heard a man's thingy given such names – removed the strength and passion that made a man a man, sinking him into a life directed by the mind rather than the glands.

Lenares thought this would be rather an improvement for most of the men she had known, but was careful not to say so.

'Can a castrated man still love?' she had asked, trying and failing to keep the hope out of her voice.

Stella had looked on with pity in her lovely eyes as Kannwar had all but mocked her with his reply. He'd ridiculed the idea of a eunuch being capable of love. 'What, dear girl, could he love a woman with? Why would such a man want to become involved with a woman when they have nothing to offer each other? No, love takes passion, and passion has been sliced away from the eunuch.'

What, then, of the eunuch's future?

Magnanimously, Kannwar offered to take Torve into his employ. 'He seems a bright enough fellow,' the Undying Man had said, seemingly unaware of, or perhaps impervious to, the distress his comments were causing. Ignoring the disaster that had been Torve's life serving the previous tyrant.

He's wrong, Lenares had thought then, and thought now. *The Undying Man is wrong. Torve is still a man, is still capable of emotion, of passion, of love.* His years with the cruel Emperor of Elamaq had crippled him far more severely than the loss of a flappy bit of skin, yet he had revealed passion hidden in the depths of a scarred character. Surely he would still love her.

But what worried her was the possibility that Torve might believe of himself what Kannwar had said. That he might simply give up loving her and leave her alone.

The nine remaining travellers were accompanied by perhaps a hundred of those they had rescued from Corata Pit, straggling in a long line behind them. Most of the survivors had departed in various directions to seek out family and friends or to recover what they could from their towns and villages; these hundred who remained were, in the main, too frightened to leave the shelter of the powerful magicians in case the god-storm – or something worse – returned.

They surmounted a low ridge and came to an involuntary halt

as the spectacle of the Malayu Basin spread out before them. Directly ahead the land fell away to a vast level plain, a chequerboard of fields and forests fading into the distance, dotted with animals, everything painted golden in the soft morning light. But many of the animals were motionless, heaped together in the middle of green fields, others lying alone where they had fallen. And the trees of the forests were strewn about as though harvested by a scythe wielded by a blind and careless giant. To their right, in the west, the sea glimmered, the wide curve of Malayu Bay looking like a rough bite out of the land. Closer to hand a village lay athwart the path they trod, some distance down the slope, but even at a distance they could see that not one roof remained intact and many of the houses had been blown or shaken to pieces.

The travellers were drawn to the village like flies to a carcass, and as they picked their way along the narrow path between piles of debris, they looked in vain for someone alive. Bodies they saw aplenty, but no movement.

'Just how fierce was this storm and earthquake?' Mustar asked, shaking his head in sorrow.

Lenares knew. Fierce enough to extinguish thousands of lives. The hole in the world had grown rapidly, and was perhaps now already wide enough to admit the gods on a permanent basis. The void beyond the wall was leaking into the world, meaning that time itself had begun to lose its grip. Everywhere she looked Lenares could see severed threads, vanished nodes.

The world was unravelling.

'They have killed my subjects,' said the Undying Man, and Lenares flinched at the tone of his voice. The Emperor of Elamaq had frightened her, but not as much as this man did.

'They have killed my subjects,' he repeated, 'and destroyed my land. They are fools and tyrants, and I will destroy them.'

Stella put a hand on his elbow. 'We, Kannwar. We will rid the world of them. The Most High has called us all together for this purpose, remember? This is not just your fight.'

'Oh?' he said, and as he turned to her, his face, limbs and body began to elongate as he struggled to retain control of his illusion.

His voice emerged from his lips like a ghost from a grave. 'Whose land is this, Queen Stella? Are you able to look me in the eye and tell me that were this happening in fair Faltha, and were you to look down from Fealty on the devastation of the Central Plains and the ruins of Instruere, you would not feel as I feel? That you would not vow as I have vowed? Can you? Can you tell me that?'

'No,' she said. 'I would react the same way you have.' She licked her lips. 'But I would be wrong.'

'Your caution is why an unruly gaggle of priests rules your land in your stead.'

Her eyes flashed. 'And your folly is why Husk likely sits in your throne room while you lament the loss of your citizens.'

'Ah, Stella, could you ever doubt why I love you?' Kannwar said, his lips curling into a smile. 'I fell in love with your tongue before any other part of you.'

'You did nothing of the sort,' she snapped, really angry now. 'You were intrigued by the aroma of the Most High set in me, and held me against my will while you plotted to harness it. Don't play the lovable cad with me. I remember what you were, and what you did. I heard what you said to Lenares this afternoon. You were an evil man seventy years ago, and I fail to see any evidence you have changed since.'

She took a series of swift strides away from him and disappeared down a side street. After a few moments Robal followed her, just as Lenares knew he would. Kannwar stared after her, expressionless.

'What is the name of this town?' she asked the Lord of Bhrudwo, as much to fill the awkward silence as anything. As she asked, she realised this was a very human thing to do. She was becoming like them.

'Mensaya,' he replied gruffly. 'Though, as there is no one left alive, it is a town no more. I doubt its name will be remembered in future by anyone but me.'

There seemed a deep sadness in his voice, and Lenares wondered about the man. *How can a man so steeped in evil display such compassion?*

The travellers spent an hour or so gathering food in the village. It was risky work and they had to choose with care the buildings they entered. More than one house groaned and settled lower while one or another of the group fossicked around inside, but no one suffered injury apart from Tumar, who ended up with a nail in his foot. Lenares saw many dead people, most with fear etched permanently on their faces. *They didn't have to die*, she told herself. *I must be able to do something about this*.

Perhaps you can, a familiar voice whispered. *But first you must talk to the Omeran. He is the key*.

'Mahudia?' But the voice had withdrawn, all hint of her presence erased, and within moments it seemed a product of her wandering mind. *Hah*, she thought. *Rouza always told me I had no imagination*.

Yet the voice – or her imagination – was right. She and Torve needed to have words.

Stoneheart. Stoneheart. Torve repeated the word in his mind as though pounding a rock into his own temple. *Torve Stoneheart.* His stone heart clenched a little at the repetition, but only a little.

With one stroke the Emperor had cut him away from the world of men, a world of companionship and respect to which he had only just been allowed entry. Once again he had been rendered something other, a mere animal, even less than an animal. Lenares had little to do with him these days, a clear sign she was unable to face what he had become.

Yet there was still a great deal to be thankful for, foremost amongst the list being the death of the Emperor. The horrors of his obscene research were finally over. Torve thought of the last time he had walked through a devastated town: Raceme had been severely damaged by whirlwinds and the Emperor had taken advantage of the confusion by seeking out victims trapped in the wreckage and torturing them to death in his insane quest for immortality. Torve had been forced by his inbred obedience to do dreadful things and he would never be rid of the feel of flesh under his fingers, nor the memory of the indignity of the human body involuntarily revealed. So many things burned in his mind: the fear and the pleading of his victims, the implacability of his master, the light going out in the eyes of the newly dead.

And yet . . . his only friend was dead, the man he had hated and loved, and Torve's grief threatened to obliterate every other feeling in his confused heart. How could he grieve for such a butcher? But how could he fail to lament the loss of his other half, his only childhood friend? And whom could he talk to? Now his companions knew something of his master – though by no means all of it – they would not understand his feelings.

Torve was not sure he understood them himself.

Preoccupied with his thoughts, he found himself at the lower end of the village, where the last houses – or what until yesterday had been houses – gave way to pasture. The stink of dead animals wafted across from the fields. He'd always been sensitive to smell and doubted the others would be too troubled by it.

'Whaddaya doing here, mister?' piped a small voice.

A lifetime of control over his body prevented the Omeran from jumping with fright. Slowly, carefully, he turned to face what might be a deadly adversary.

It was a little girl. She stood in the doorway of the last house on the street, her pink dress ragged and torn, smeared with blood and dirt. The house behind her had partially collapsed, but it had survived the storm and earthquake with at least two rooms intact.

'Ma says everybody's asleep,' said the girl, scowling at him. 'Why aren't you asleep?'

'Because I'm hungry and looking for food,' Torve said to her, squatting on his haunches the better to look her in the face. She had a nasty bruise above one eye, and one of her arms hung awkwardly at her side. Sprained at the least. 'Do you have any food?'

'We already ate all the food. Some of it smelled funny. Pa was sick all night.'

'How many of you are there?'

The girl blinked a couple of times as she looked into his eyes, clearly unable to give him a number. *That many?*

'Can I come in and meet your ma and pa?' Torve asked.

'No, they're asleep,' said the girl, and turned away.

'Asleep? Do you mean sleeping, or dead?' Torve couldn't think of any tactful way of asking the question.

The girl gave him no answer, having been swallowed by the shadows. Torve followed her inside, once again thankful that his master was gone. He could not bear to think what the Emperor might have done to the little girl if she was indeed on her own.

The air was warm and close in the dark interior. The girl stood in one corner, tugging on the shirt of a figure lying prone on the floor. 'Pa, Pa, wake up,' she said.

'Leave him be, Py,' came a woman's weary voice from deep in the shadows. 'He needs his sleep.'

'But there's a man. A black man. He smells like poo.'

'I'm afraid she's right,' Torve said, peering into the darkness. 'I'm sorry to come unannounced into your house, but I'm looking for food.'

'We have none,' said the woman. 'But we have swords and knives. Go away before we use them.'

A series of small noises issued from all around the room. The people probably thought they were being quiet, but Torve could identify eight of them by their movement.

'As you wish,' he said, backing away. 'I didn't mean to trouble anyone from this village.'

'We're not from this village,' said the little girl. 'We're from a boat. Our boat crashed.'

'Away with you, stranger,' a man said. 'Go try your luck somewhere else.'

'Very well.' Torve repeated his acquiescence. 'Please do not be concerned. I am leaving.'

'No need for that,' said another voice, a voice he recognised. 'Come in and sit down, Torve.'

'You know him?' said two or three from the shadows.

It took the Omeran a few moments to place the voice. 'Kilfor?' he asked, trying to see the speaker.

'Aye, and his father,' growled another familiar voice. 'Sit on this bench, lad. Shove over, Kilfor.'

'You shove over, old man. Your backside's wide enough to make space for three people.'

Sauxa grunted, but moved over enough for Torve to perch on the end of the bench.

'I thought you'd left us,' Torve began, unsure of the reception his words would win him. 'You objected to assisting Heredrew in his intention of bringing down the gods.'

'Call him by his real name, boy,' Sauxa said. 'Call him Kannwar, ulcers to his soul, and name the devil. Call him the Undying Man, the great enemy of Faltha. Let us have no soft talk, no hidden identities and agendas. He's the Destroyer, and that's that.'

'Is it true?' a woman asked. 'Is Lord Sauxa telling the truth? Are you really travelling with the Undying Man?'

'Yes, ma damme, we are.' *Lord Sauxa?*

'What will he do to put all this to rights?' she asked him. 'We survived a great storm at sea and were helped from our ship by these two men, only to be assailed by an earthquake and a great wave from the sea. This is not right! This is not natural! Everyone knows this! Something magical is happening. Someone is assaulting our fair country, and we wish to offer our great Lord of Bhrudwo any support he requires.'

Torve turned to the man sitting beside him. 'You saved these people from a shipwreck?'

'Not really,' Kilfor said. 'They were trapped in their cabin, and when we came across them they may have been in some danger from rising water, but I don't think they would have died.'

''Course they would have,' his father exclaimed. 'Even if the tide hadn't got 'em, the great waves would have. We broke in through the hull and let 'em out. Heroes, that's us.' The man's eyebrows waggled in self-congratulation.

'You're a fool, old man,' Kilfor said genially. 'Or should I say, you're a fool, Lord Sauxa. All we did was let them out.'

Torve smiled, then turned to the woman. 'The Lord of Bhrudwo is already searching for those responsible, ma damme. He is in this village as we speak.'

'Here?' a couple of the men exclaimed. 'He is here now?'

Torve could not see their faces in the gloom, but they did not sound entirely happy.

'Ah . . . perhaps the Lord of Bhrudwo does not need our help if he has such great men as Lord Sauxa and his son to aid him,' the voluble woman said after a noticeable pause. 'We'll just remain here, out of his way. Perhaps we could tidy up the village after he leaves. Do you think he would object if we settled here for a time?'

'I cannot answer for him,' Torve began.

'But I can,' said Heredrew as he stepped through the door and stood in the middle of the room, bringing his own light with him. Everyone gasped, and the Bhrudwans cowered on the floor.

'The great enemy of Faltha?' Heredrew said, his voice gentle.

'You might be old, but your hearing's good,' Sauxa said, unabashed.

'I won't be ridiculed in front of my subjects,' Heredrew said, not so gently. The magical light pulsed around him.

'Then stop being ridiculous,' Sauxa snapped. 'These people have asked you a question. If you heard my insults, you heard the question. So, great lord, what's your answer?'

The shipwreck victims looked from the bright figure to the belligerent old man facing him down, and Torve could see them reassessing their view of 'Lord' Sauxa. Perhaps they now saw him as a great magician, a trusted companion, maybe even a rival to the Undying Man.

'You are right, my friend,' Heredrew said, clapping the surprised Sauxa on the shoulder, then addressing the others. 'I owe my loyal and sorely tried subjects an answer. It would ease my mind greatly if you would make your home here, temporarily at least, until you feel able to travel back to your true homes. Only two things would I ask of you: to render assistance to anyone left alive, and to bury the dead with all ceremony. Is this acceptable to you?'

Self-conscious shuffles and awed mumblings of assent were offered in answer.

'Easy to lord it over such a spineless bunch,' Sauxa muttered to his son. Heredrew flared even brighter in response, but held his temper.

276

Beyond the Wall of Time

'Very well then,' said the Lord of Bhrudwo. 'I will leave an imprint of my seal in the town. Should anyone challenge my agreement with you, show them the seal. In the meantime, Torve, Lenares is looking for you. Are you coming with us?'

'Beg pardon, great lord,' said one of the men in the shadows. 'There is someone in this room hiding from you. He threatened to kill anyone who betrayed him.'

Heredrew spread his light even further, illuminating the whole room. 'Really? Who is this person?'

'Him, lord,' said a woman, pushing at the shoulder of an older man who sat hunched over, head buried in his arms. 'He's the captain of our ship. He ran it aground, and he didn't behave like a sea captain ought.'

'Carry on,' said the Lord of Bhrudwo.

'Locked us in our cabin, he did,' said another man. 'Told us he didn't care if we lived or died. Then, when the ship beached, he refused to come to our aid though we pounded on the door and begged him for help, while all around us the ship creaked and groaned fit to bust. 'Twas only these gentlemen saved us from the death he'd left us to suffer.'

'Does this captain have a name?'

The hunched man did not reply, and refused to raise his head.

'His name is Kidson, great lord. Captain Kidson. Though he's no captain now.'

'Indeed not. And how much longer he remains alive depends on how much truth he's prepared to tell. But not right now; we have many other things to do. You, Kidson, will come with us.'

The Undying Man closed his fist and drew it toward himself. Kidson cried out, then stood up jerkily as though he'd lost control of his limbs. A wet patch on his breeches showed he'd definitely lost control of his bladder.

'I . . . locked them in . . . for their . . . safety,' Kidson wheezed.

'I did not invite you to speak,' Heredrew said equably. 'I'll hear from you at my convenience, not yours.' Kidson began to make choking sounds. 'Until I determine your innocence or guilt, you will be silent.'

Continued gurgling followed this statement; the men and women who had accused Kidson looked on, horror in their faces.

'Don't hurt him, bad man,' said the small girl.

'If this man tells the truth he has nothing to fear,' Heredrew said, his voice shaded with anger.

'You're frightening us,' the little girl continued. 'Go away.'

A man and a woman clutched at the girl. 'Forgive her, great lord,' the man said, his eyes averted, as if that would protect him should the Undying Man take exception to his plea.

Torve sensed that Heredrew would ordinarily have made an example of Kidson and this man both – Torve's master, the Emperor of Elamaq, certainly would have – but was forbearing because of Stella.

Kidson continued to choke; his face began to turn blue.

'Can't my subjects remain silent for even a moment?' Heredrew said. 'Can they not be quiet and reflect upon their lord's goodness and his gift to them? Can they not be grateful that he will deal justly with this would-be murderer?'

The frightened folk nodded at each question.

'Then they can also keep out of sight in this building until I and my companions have left. Does anyone question this?'

The folk demonstrated they had learned their lesson.

Torve followed Heredrew and his prisoner out into the sunlight. They were followed by Sauxa and Kilfor.

'I thought I told you to keep out of sight.' The Undying Man's voice was ice-cold.

'You don't get to tell us what to do,' Sauxa said tartly. Kilfor winced.

'I have no idea why the Most High tolerates you Falthans. From your queen down to the most insignificant peasant, you are unfailingly insolent and defiant. You do not seem to understand that you are living as a guest in my country. I make the rules. If you do not wish to abide by them, I can enforce the penalties due to disobedience. They are very severe.'

'Aye, we are guests here,' Sauxa said. 'But we are not your guests. If I understand right, we are all the guests of the Most High, who

278

is using us as weapons against the rebellious gods. And as he has given me no instructions as to how I should speak to you, I believe I have broken no rules and am behaving exactly as he would have me. If he didn't want a hard-headed, contrary plainsman as part of his plan, why did he invite me?'

Heredrew's shoulders shook at this, whether from anger or amusement Torve could not immediately discern. The tall man sat down on a wreckage-covered porch, behind which the house had gone, and turned to the old Falthan. Torve was relieved, and somewhat surprised, to see a smile on Heredrew's face.

'So, old man' – the irony laid on the word "old" was unmistakable – 'you have decided to stay with us after all?'

'You heard that, did you?' Sauxa smirked toothlessly at the Lord of Bhrudwo. 'Perhaps you are as smart as they say.'

Heredrew returned the smile: a little sardonic, but genuine nonetheless.

'I thought we were leaving,' Kilfor exclaimed, surprised.

'You, on the other hand, are even more foolish than I had thought. You make me ashamed to have brought you into the world.'

Torve winced, but a moment later saw the grin splitting Kilfor's face and recalled the way the two men spoke to each other.

'Hah, a compliment,' the younger man crowed. 'To be thought foolish by a fool is to be intelligent in truth!'

Kannwar addressed Kidson. 'You will keep to the back of the group. This is not a choice, it is information. If you try approaching any of your former passengers you will be struck down. I do not want unnecessary confrontations.' The white-faced captain nodded shortly.

'Kannwar!' a voice called; and Torve turned to see Stella leading the other travellers down the debris-strewn street towards them. Striding next to her, at her right shoulder, was Lenares, her face set in that familiar look of concentration. She never failed to excite interest in him. *Is that why she fascinates me so? Because, just like my childhood friend, the Emperor of Elamaq, everything she does is done with all of her being?*

It didn't matter. In the end, the last thing his childhood friend had ever done to him had rendered the question moot.

This totally destroyed place was the first town of any size Lenares had been in since Sayonae, the town in which she had met the woman who turned out to be her real mother. Unsurprisingly, it was to Martje that her mind turned now. She was glad that her mother was alive, and gladder still that she suffered. The Bhrudwan lord had told her what he had done to the evil woman, fully expecting Lenares to be shocked and upset at the news, but she had been happy to hear it. Very happy. The woman had raised a family in order to satisfy her monstrous husband's perverted desires, and had shown no remorse for what he had done to them. Moreover, in her effort to recapture the person she'd thought was her wayward daughter Cylene, she had been willing to expend her sons, seemingly unconcerned that the Undying Man had hurt them. And from what Conal had confessed, Lenares knew she'd not held back from using one of her daughters as part of a magic spell to bind Kannwar. Martje had actively encouraged her daughter to have sex with the unpleasant priest as part of her plan. Still using her family as tools.

There had been a moment when Lenares had allowed herself to rejoice at discovering her true family. That moment had been all too brief. She had quickly realised that, of all her siblings, she had been the fortunate one. To preserve his secret, her father had sold her as a slave to someone who took her south to Elamaq. Lenares remembered none of it, but it must have happened that way. In the exchange she'd lost a family, but had gained a life.

This, Lenares was certain, would be the last time she thought of Martje and her natural family. For all their fractiousness, poor Rouza and Palain and the other cosmographers had been her true family. As much as they had irritated Lenares, they had lived with her and worked together with her, and some of them had even loved her. Mahudia had been her real mother, and Lenares would never forget her.

But she was alone now. All the cosmographers were dead. She had lost every member of both families. Fated, perhaps, to be on

her own – though Mahudia's unquiet shade seemed still within her reach, on the other side of the Wall of Time. She glanced in Torve's direction, and saw him look away. She'd lost him too, she knew, through no fault of her own. The losses made her bitterly sad, but she still had work to do. Recapturing Umu would make her happy.

In the gloaming of the day, the hundred-strong band reached the base of the long slope leading to the Malayu Basin. Ahead of them the land steamed in the half-light, radiating its heat to the purpling sky as dusk gathered like a cloak of secrecy. A few of the children cried, a hungry ache beneath their ribs, as no one had found enough to eat in the village behind them. Their parents and the others in the party walked in a tired shuffle, heads down, their lips pressed closed in a determined effort not to complain.

So it was they did not see the small group waiting at the place where the road levelled out. The first Lenares knew of it was a shout from someone at the head of their party, a hail returned by a distant voice.

'Is it Noetos and his family?' Stella asked.

'Can't tell,' Robal replied. 'Doesn't look like it.'

'Where's Noetos!' someone called, but the voice came from well in front of them. Not more refugees from the storm and earth-quake then.

'He's not here,' Kannwar replied. 'Who are you?'

A few garbled introductions later, the two groups had met and mingled and had found seats on a series of felled tree trunks. The leaders of the dozen or so new arrivals were a man and a woman: he, small with a largish belly; she, middle-aged, standing on the balls of her feet like a Three-Spire dancer from lost Talamaq. Bregor he called himself, the Factor of Raceme, and his new-wed wife, she of the elegant poise, he named Consina. She smiled politely at this, her self-possession and reserve an odd contrast to the sweaty effusiveness of her husband.

Lenares looked at them with her numbers, then realised with a sudden shock that it was the first time she'd used her unique gift at all that day. *What has happened to me?* She felt like a castle of sand slowly eroding away, a special-shaped fortress absorbed into the ordinariness of the beach. Mahudia would know. Lenares longed to talk to her, but didn't want to draw the attention of the gods to her mother.

Bregor and Consina knelt before Kannwar – the Emperor here, Lenares reminded herself – and began speaking to him in low tones. Lenares moved closer. They wanted to keep their conversation secret, but why shouldn't the world's last cosmographer know what was being said!

'I was told of events in Raceme by the Noetos you seek,' Kannwar was saying.

The tubby man sweated freely, even though the air had grown cold. His wife passed him a kerchief, with which he swatted at the moisture glistening on his temples. 'Did he tell you of the devastation wreaked by the gods, great lord?'

'He did, Factor, but he did not mention you. What is your relationship with him?'

'Great lord, I was his village Hegeoman until the calamity that overtook us.'

'Do you mean the Neherian invasion? Speak plainly, man; we're not players in a bard's tale.'

'Yes, lord,' the man said, mopping perspiration from his brow. 'I mean, yes, it was the Neherians.'

Lenares noted how adroitly Kannwar had taken over the conversation.

'Ah, I place you now,' said the Undying Man. 'You're the man who slept with Noetos's wife.'

Bregor gave a strangled squeak, and the woman kneeling next to him started, then turned an angry face towards her husband. Lenares laughed, not unkindly. Consina had not known of Bregor's complex relationship with Noetos.

'Has he – how much has Noetos told you, great lord?' Bregor said, his voice low.

'Do you mean, has Noetos told me how you betrayed your village to the Neherians? Of course not; he's far too loyal a man to say such things.'

282

The distraught man swallowed hard. 'How do you know?'

'Why don't we sit down, you and I, the Hegeoman of an obscure village and the Lord of all Bhrudwo, so I can share with you the secrets of my rule?'

Consina hissed. 'You toy with us,' she said, 'while our town is being overrun by Neherians bent on revenge. Punish Bregor if you must, but please first listen to his words.'

'*Your* town? Raceme is not Makyra Bay, Hegeoma Consina; it is not your town. I know Bregor was elected as interim Factor following the death of the last governor, and the loss of Makyra Bay to the Neherians sent you and your few surviving villagers north to join forces with him. In more ways than one, clearly. But it is the Undying Man's prerogative to appoint Factors; they are never elected.'

'We know, great lord, but—'

'Yes, I know, conditions were such that you couldn't allow Raceme to descend into lawlessness, so you reluctantly took up power. I heard your acceptance speech given in the ballroom of the Summer Palace, so recently the site of slaughter.'

'You heard the speech?' Stella leaned across, eyeing the Undying Man in a way only the truly unafraid could do.

'Of course I heard it. I have a few informants in Raceme, as I do in every city of interest to me, which, incidentally, is all of them. Naturally they sought to inform me of these developments.'

'How?'

Kannwar laughed. 'Ah, Stella, do you really want me to reveal my secrets to all and sundry?'

He didn't for a moment think she'd reply in the affirmative, but Lenares could see it coming.

'Yes,' Stella said.

The cosmographer studied the emotions that sped across the man's illusory face. Frustration, anger, resignation. No one else would have been able to read them, but with her ability to perceive his life in numerical terms, she could predict his response to the pressure Stella insisted on placing him under.

Betrayal.

Of course, he was not bound to do that which Lenares could foresee: she was fairly certain her ability was guesswork, albeit well informed, rather than knowledge. How could it be knowledge, given the future, unlike the past, was not fixed in place? Certainly she didn't like the idea that someone else with her gift – if anyone else like her existed – could accurately predict her own actions. But betrayal was written all over his numbers.

'He's going to play you false, ma damme Stella,' Lenares said in a quiet voice.

'Of course he is,' the woman replied. 'I know that. Why else do you think I want him close by?'

Because you like playing with fire, Lenares thought of saying to the Falthan woman, but held her tongue. She would have sworn such talk would provoke the Bhrudwan lord's anger, but as always he managed to surprise everyone.

'When you two have finished talking about this disreputable man, he'd like to answer your challenge.'

Stella retained her equanimity. 'Go on then.'

'Actually, I'm not sure why you hadn't worked it out, since you've experienced it yourself.'

'Ah,' Stella said. 'The blue fire. You contact your informers regularly.'

'Where else did you think I was going all those nights?'

'Off to betray us all, I expect.' She accompanied her words with a wry smile.

Consina leaned forward. 'Great lord, have you heard from your informers in Raceme these last three weeks?'

'No, Factor Consina, I have not,' said the man, his voice gentle, enquiring.

'Then, my lord, you will not know what has happened. Your informers are likely dead, along with many if not most of the survivors of Neherius's original invasion. Three weeks ago a huge fleet materialised off our harbour and swept into the defenceless city. They had come to avenge the deaths of their leaders, slain, they said, by a renegade Neherian with a personal vendetta, though we knew better. We' – here she glanced at Bregor, who immediately rearranged his scowl into a neutral expression – 'regard Noetos as the hero of Makyra Bay, and many of the survivors of the Neherian invasion of Raceme see him as a champion of that city too.'

'Get to the point, woman.' Not so gentle this time.

'They went through Raceme without mercy, my lord. I must report that they slew every male of fighting age they could find and piled the corpses on the Summer Flame before setting them alight.' Her voice suddenly changed. 'They were at pains to say that this killing, and their campaign against the towns and villages of the Fisher Coast, was all done in the name of the Undying Man, Lord of Bhrudwo.'

'Was it?' Bregor snapped, and suddenly there was a knife in his hand.

This has been planned all along.

'Yes,' Kannwar said.

Stella gasped, a sound like the final breath leaving a body.

Bregor drove forward with his knife and buried it to the hilt in the Undying Man's chest.

'Don't!' Stella cried, but far, far too late.

Bregor slumped backwards, his jerkin stained red. Kannwar took a step forward and stood over the man, his stern face set in stone.

Why didn't I see this before it happened? Lenares asked herself, frantic. *Have I lost the ability?*

No, the ability to see her numbers remained. Truth was, she admitted to herself, she was coming to rely on other ways of interacting with others, more human ways.

Losing herself.

Consina stood frozen, seemingly unable to believe what she had seen.

'Heal him,' Stella demanded.

The Undying Man turned his adamant face on her, and Lenares could see his anger crawling across his features like maggots on a carcass. 'Never. He committed suicide. He knew any attack on me, successful or not, would lead to his death. This is the outcome he expected.'

'But you lied to him,' Lenares said. She drew on all her powers of analysis.

'Ah,' said the Undying Man, and the full power of his eyes bored into hers. 'I had forgotten about you.'

'Lied? How?' Stella grabbed at Lenares, as though she could force the cosmographer's answer to come more quickly.

'The killing was done in his name, but not with his full knowledge. The attacks were planned by the Undying Man, but he asked for them to be postponed after I showed him the hole in the world. The Neherians ignored him. I don't know why, because Kannwar doesn't know why.'

'How do you know this?' Consina breathed.

'I am a cosmographer,' Lenares said. 'The best cosmographer ever to have lived. I can read truth because I can see the links between things more clearly than other people can.'

'Your explanation doesn't make it sound as though he lied,' Consina continued.

'He did, by not explaining himself. He wanted to make Bregor strike at him.'

'Then how can Bregor be blamed for his actions?' Stella faced the Undying Man. 'Heal him.'

'He's already too far gone.'

'Your fault. Heal him.'

No one else could see the struggle going on in the Undying Man's mind. His authority depended on such ruthless behaviour, which the man genuinely believed was fair. And it was: Bregor had acted knowing the price for his action. Yet he valued Stella's regard highly. No, he was deeply in love with her, a love inextricably bound up with dark cords of self-loathing. If he didn't do as she asked, he would lose her. Yet if he did, he risked losing his authority and his empire.

This is who I am, Lenares exulted. *Not an ordinary human, having to guess what people intend to do, but a cosmographer, one who sees.*

Kannwar grunted, then placed an illusory hand on the wounded man's chest. An audible sizzling was accompanied by a sudden weakness in all those around him, judging by the slumping of their

286

shoulders. Lenares felt as though she'd just woken up after a poor night's sleep, and found herself falling to her knees.

'He will wake in a moment,' Kannwar said wearily. 'But there are consequences to follow from this healing. First, this man will likely strike at me again. The next time he does will be his death. Second, I have drawn power from everyone in the area, making us vulnerable to the gods. We must move from here, and move quickly: I expect Umu or Keppia to launch an attack against us almost immediately. Third, I am publicly announcing my estrangement from the Falthan queen. This is my land, these are my subjects, and I will not be told how to deal with them.'

He took a deep breath, turned and regarded the shocked woman. 'You and I are finished.'

A wave of dizziness passed through Lenares, a weakness not associated with these events, but an external event. Something was happening . . .

Her eyes blurred. When she regained focus, Consina and Bregor stood before Kannwar and Consina was talking.

'They went through Raceme without mercy, my lord,' she said, genuine sorrow in her voice, underlain with artifice. 'I must report that they slew every male of fighting age and piled the corpses on the Summer Flame before setting them alight.'

Truth, Lenares realised, but also deception. *They are trying to trap Kannwar into a confession because they wish to kill him.*

As always, Lenares revelled in her unique abilities. *This is who I am. Not an ordinary human, having to guess what people intend to do, but a cosmographer, one who sees.*

And yet . . . something was wrong. What . . . time was folding back on itself. Folding and folding again. She tried to say something, to warn the others, to somehow break the spell, but it was as difficult as grabbing her ankles and lifting herself into the air.

The woman continued. 'They were at pains to say that this killing, and their campaign against the towns and villages of the Fisher Coast, was all done in the name of the Undying Man, Lord of Bhrudwo.'

'He has a knife,' Lenares gasped, and the pressure around her lessened.

'I know,' said the Undying Man.

'Was it done in your name?' Bregor asked, and went to draw his knife – but it was gone.

Of all of them, Stella had acted the swiftest. She had taken two steps, then snatched the knife from the man's belt.

'The terrible thing is,' she gasped, 'I can remember everything you were going to say and do.'

Bregor's face went white and he put a hand to his chest; clearly he also had retained some memory of events – events that had never happened.

'I remember you saying that you and I were finished,' Stella said to Kannwar.

'I did. And yet I never said it.'

'You ordered the destruction of the Fisher Coast,' Bregor said.

'I did,' said the Undying Man, raising his voice to be audible to everyone listening. Unafraid of their opinions. 'But I counter-manded that order when I learned there was an external threat to the empire from the gods, and that the grandson of the Duke of Roudhos lived still.'

'Noetos? You mean Noetos? Why is he important?'

'The Fisher Coast is not a viable political unit,' said the Undying Man with exaggerated patience. 'Within a few years it would have been consumed from within by a series of small rebellions, by infighting and guerrilla wars. These wars would have cost thousands of lives and laid waste to valuable land. It seemed better to encourage the assimilation of the Fisher Coast into a Greater Neherius. That is, until I learned of Noetos's existence. If the grandson was even a shadow of his grandsire, I believed he might forge a strong and prosperous vassal state akin to Old Roudhos.'

'And is he that shadow?'

'No.'

Bregor bridled. 'No? Not even a shadow? I'd like to see the man who could have done what Noetos has done!'

The Undying Man smiled. 'You misunderstand me. He is no mere shadow. Noetos is the equal of the Red Duke, my old friend, murdered at my command. And that even with the impediments shackled around him. I decided to reunite Roudhos under his banner and so gave the command for Neherius to cease its invasion.'

'But they went ahead anyway,' Consina said bitterly.

'Yes. As a result they will pay a heavy price.'

Bregor breathed a weary sigh. 'When did you first learn about Noetos?'

'From a young woman held captive in my dungeon,' Heredrew said.

'Arathé?'

'Indeed. It was too late to save her tongue, but I prevented her exposure to the worst of what my dungeon-master calls "punishment."'

'But you didn't retrieve her. You didn't reveal your knowledge and ask her to take you to her father. You didn't heal her.' Unspoken, but still loud in their absence, were the words *yet you healed me*.

'I intended to, and my failure to do so is perhaps my largest mistake in this whole affair. I was drawn away by the Most High, who tried to enlist me in his plan to defeat the gods.' Kannwar outlined his discussions with the Most High, and the looks of wonderment on his listeners' faces deepened as he spoke. 'When I returned, months later, the girl had left the keep in the company of four Recruiters. I could not supervise a search as my presence was required in Dhauria on . . . other matters.'

'Your largest mistake?' boomed a voice from somewhere behind Lenares, a voice filled with a febrile hunger. 'No, your largest mistake was keeping me ignorant of your true identity. Now stand aside, everyone. I have some questions to ask the Lord of Bhrudwo.'

A small group of familiar people strode down the street towards them, Noetos at their head, sword in his hand, his face crimson with rage.

But Lenares only had eyes for the girl walking beside him. It was herself, Lenares herself somehow, as though space had been folded; and over her and in her was entwined the presence of a god.

CHAPTER 12

THE SNARE

AFTER IT WAS ALL OVER, Lenares had the luxury of time to sort out all of what had happened that afternoon. She was able to consider at leisure Noetos's heroic but futile assault on the Undying Man, and reflect on the surprise they had all experienced at the identities of those who came to defend him. A surprise, yes, but far easier to deal with than the fate of the girl Cylene who accompanied the fisherman. Just when Lenares thought she'd evaded the world's snare it had reached out a final hand and trapped her, condemning her to life as a human. Or so it seemed to her as she sat weeping amidst the ruins of Mensaya and contemplating all she had lost.

As events unfolded, however, there had not been the time for much coherent thought. Noetos had come storming towards the gathered assembly, murder in his eyes. Most there had stepped back, reacting involuntarily to the enormous power of his rage. It took a strong spirit to withstand the fisherman in those moments.

Lenares had remained where she was. She could see he would ask his questions before he used his sword. Besides, her attention had been taken by the girl beside him.

'You are my sister,' Lenares said; and it was no surprise that the girl said the same words at the same time. They both grinned.

The girl then continued: 'Not only your sister, but your twin. My name is Cylene.'

No folding of space and time then. But, as Lenares looked more closely, supernatural interference nonetheless.

Her attention was dragged away by the coming together of the fisherman and the Lord of Bhrudwo.

'Do not judge me for keeping my identity a secret, Roudhos,' the Undying Man called.

So clever, the use of that name, Lenares noted.

Noetos clearly knew how clever the Lord of Bhrudwo had been. 'Don't call me that,' he growled. 'I hid in Fossa to protect my family. You hid in our midst in order to more effectively bend others to your will.'

'You are embarrassed because everyone else knew my identity but you.'

'That I am.' The fisherman drew up to where Kannwar stood. 'But it is a minor concern compared to the anger I feel towards a liege lord who serves no one but himself. I stood at the edge of the crowd and listened to you condemn yourself out of your own mouth. You admit you knew my daughter languished in your dungeon through no fault of her own, a loyal subject still, yet you did nothing to save her.'

'As you say.'

'Why did you not act?'

Lenares desired to hear every word, drawn by the incipient violence that hovered like storm-clouds, but the bright face gazing into hers commanded her attention. Not the least because, this close, it was comprised of a combination of black and white threads, writhing with loathing as they touched each other.

'Which one are you?' Lenares asked.

'Which one? I told you, sister, my name is Cylene. What are you called now, Merla of Sayonae?'

'You seek to distract me with emotion, you thing. But I see you. You are possessed by a god. Which one are you: Keppia or Umu?'

A short pause, and the writhing ceased for a moment. 'We continue to underestimate you, Lenares,' Cylene said in a voice subtly changed, comprised of the black threads rather than the white. A man's voice.

Horrified gasps rose from many around her. Not from Noetos though, Lenares noted with interest, even though he'd swung his head in her direction. He'd known.

'Keppia then,' Lenares said calmly. 'Go away, Keppia. I wish to talk to Cylene.'

'Cylene is not here,' said the voice, moving Cylene's lips, and giggled.

An inarticulate moan came from somewhere nearby. The tongue-less girl, Arathé.

'Did you know about this?' Lenares heard Anomer ask his father.

'From the moment she returned from the forest,' Noetos replied, his voice made of stone. 'She is dead, and her shell is inhabited by a monster. Yet because the monster thought I knew nothing of its possession, it has followed us here in the mistaken belief that it is safe.'

'I am safe,' the monstrosity said. 'None of you has the power to dismiss me. You are all too late. The breach in the Wall of Time is sufficiently wide now. Drive me out of this body and you will break my last connection with the void. I will be returned to this world for ever.'

'Then the answer is simple, fool,' Sauxa said, sneering as he spoke. 'We'll leave you to moulder in that body you're wearing.'

'Ah, but you won't,' it said; and, as Lenares watched, the black threads wriggled back under the surface, allowing the white to emerge.

Cylene shrieked.

It was a sound to chill the marrow. Deeper than the mere agony of pain, more forlorn than one who has lost her only love, her scream tugged on those around her like the cry of a baby for its mother.

'Alkuon,' Noetos breathed. 'She's still alive.'

'If you want to save the girl,' said the monster, the black threads squirming back to the surface, 'you'll need to drive me out, out, out into the world. Otherwise she'll remain trapped in here forever, with a very angry and inventive god for close company.'

The silence following this statement was broken only when Noetos's sword clattered to the ground, dropped from frozen fingers.

Now was Lenares' time. She could feel it coming upon her.

She looked the black threads in the face and saw past them to the frightened, tortured girl entombed there.

'Keppia has made a very bad mistake,' Lenares said, willing sincerity into her voice. 'Just do as I tell you, Cylene, and all will be well.'

'Do as you say?' the black voice mocked. 'She is powerless and in terrible pain. She cannot even scream unless I give her leave, and I do not give her leave. Don't you understand? If you do not rescue your sister, Lenares, if you do not save your lover, Noetos, neither of you will ever be able to live with yourselves again. Courage, Noetos. Now is the time for action, not flight. Or will you once again turn away from the rape and murder of a defenceless loved one? And, Lenares, what else is the gift of numbers for if not to drive me out? If you do nothing, your gift will surely not survive.'

'Both Lenares and Noetos know you are lying to them,' said the Undying Man. 'They know that love has limits. Neither would sacrifice the whole world to reclaim even their dearest loved one.'

Noetos snatched up his sword and turned on the man. 'You are not the appropriate person to speak of love and sacrifice,' he said in a cold voice. 'My reckoning with you is merely delayed, not denied. By Alkuon, if you say another word, I will cut out your tongue.'

Astonishingly, the Undying Man merely nodded, then took a step back, conceding the point.

'Why should I try to drive you out when you are imprisoned?' Lenares said to the monster. 'If we do nothing, you are trapped in Cylene's body until you give up and go away, your connection with the void unsevered.'

'Why?' cried Keppia. 'Because she suffers!' And the mouth opened wide, impossibly wide, and Cylene's voice came out: 'Please! Please! Help me!' and tailed off into a scream.

'Impressive,' Lenares said, and turned her back on her sister and her suffering.

Duon turned his head from one scene to the other, knowing that the cusp of their adventure had come. Knowing also that he had nothing to contribute, would be nothing more than a witness. He had hoped that his involvement in the events that would change the world in one way or another would prove to be a chance at redemption, a chance to put right his failure in the Valley of the Damned; but he was once again irrelevant. The knowledge left him both bitter and relieved.

Lenares continued to walk away from her sister, abandoning any attempt to rescue her. The reason for this was impossible for Duon to discern. Had she called Keppia's bluff? Unlikely in the extreme: Lenares was not such a sophisticated person. She could not tell lies even by omission. She used her gift as a hammer to bludgeon sophistication into truth and falsehood. More likely, given her detachment from normal human emotion, was the simple explanation that she'd decided to abandon her sister. After all, she'd shown little love for her real family when she encountered them in Sayonae. Why should she show compassion to the one who was favoured by her parents?

No, she's more complex than you think, said Arathé in his mind. *She has a plan, I'm sure of it.*

I hope you are right. I can't abide the idea of that girl locked away in her body forever.

Cylene continued to shout and scream, the voice alternating between the warnings and gloatings of the god and the girl's agonised pleas. The shocked crowd began to follow Lenares along the road, out of the village, away from the unbearable sounds.

This feels dreadful, Duon said to Arathé. *Walking away from someone's suffering. There must be something we can do!*

As they reached the open road, a space suddenly cleared around Noetos and the Bhrudwan lord. Further words had clearly been exchanged, a conversation Duon had not overheard but could guess at. 'You heard my explanation. I would have prevented any further unnecessary suffering had I not been drawn away from Andratan to a meeting with the Most High.'

Noetos leaned forward, the courtesy and restraint in his words not matched by the strain on his face. At least the man had sheathed his sword.

'What,' he asked, 'could have been more important than, as you rightly say, the unnecessary suffering of an innocent girl?'

'Innocent? I doubt that. But even given her so-called innocence, am I to take it you are objectively arguing that the alleviation of your daughter's suffering – remember, her suffering was not going to end in death, because of my intercession – was more important than hearing what a god had to say?'

'Yes, of course,' Noetos said, and turned in surprise when he realised his words had been echoed by another voice. That of Stella, the Falthan queen.

'The fact she's your daughter has nothing to do with it?'

'It has everything to do with it, you fool,' Noetos said, courtesy and restraint cast aside. 'Had it been someone else's daughter, I would not have known of it. Given that I know what happened to Arathé, I am led to wonder how many other faithful sons and daughters of Bhrudwo have suffered similarly.'

'He doesn't understand your question,' Stella said, as the crowd continued to walk along the road out of Mensaya. 'To the Lord of Bhrudwo, good government is the cold-hearted weighing of numbers. This action will save a hundred souls, while that action will save two hundred. Therefore the second action is favoured over the first, irrespective of how repugnant that action might be. If imprisoning and repeatedly draining young girls achieves an incrementally positive outcome for his empire, he will do it.'

'Yes,' the Undying Man said fiercely, almost proudly. 'See how well my queen understands me?'

'Do not call me that,' Stella grated.

'My apologies. But Stella is right. Actions that for you, with your limited knowledge, would be immoral are for me not only moral but necessary. Do you not see it? For you to lay waste to a town would be a crime. But if I see that such an action would prevent civil war and ultimately save thousands of lives, would it not be immoral to refrain from destroying the town?'

'Now we are at the heart,' Stella said. Noetos looked on, his bemusement at this hijacking of his question plain to see. 'You employ spies and researchers to gather information and statisticians to analyse it all. You then apply the solution that brings the least pain to your people. Yet you continue to be ignorant of what you are really doing.'

'And what is that?'

'First, you have no proof that your solutions are the most appropriate, only the word of your statisticians. Unless you are somehow able to fold back time and try multiple resolutions to your empire's problems, you cannot prove that your actions are, in fact, in the best interests of your subjects.'

'You discount my two thousand years' worth of experience.'

'I do not. I just do not believe it is infallible. Second, your statisticians calculate a less-than-complete set of outcomes. While a particular action may conclude with fewer lives lost, the fear and hatred spread thereby adds to everyone's burden. Millions of lives are subtly altered for the worse.'

'Ah, yes, Stella, I have considered that. Show me but one way of measuring such harm and I will factor it into my calculations.'

'Fool! Empiricism is not a sufficiently flexible philosophy to assess such things! Third, you increase the blot on your own soul with every action. You make yourself more susceptible to the most outrageous cruelty. And fourth, you load intolerable burdens on those without your scope of vision and experience. What of your statisticians? How do they deal with the fact that their calculations condemn innocent people to death? Do they enjoy long working lives, or do they beg to be retired after only a few years of service? How many of them commit suicide, I wonder?

'And what of those chosen to live? I remember you putting a village to the sword in an attempt to cow me. Did your calculations consider the damage that did to your soul – or to mine? You may be able to live with the guilt, but I still wake imagining myself smothered in bloodied silks, having been forced to watch the impalement of men, the rape of women and the dismemberment of children for no more useful purpose than to make me your tool. Such an action has led inevitably to this moment, the moment where I reject you. Do you understand, Kannwar? Those people died in vain! Had they lived, I might well now be your willing queen! As it is, Kannwar, I wish to have nothing more to do with you. You have miscalculated. I care nothing for your fate.'

She stood for a moment, breathing heavily, then strode swiftly down the road, her smirking guardsman at her heel.

'Are you answered?' the Bhrudwan lord asked Noetos.

'Yes,' said the fisherman. 'But I judge the answer insufficient.'

Arathé cried out then, her voice inarticulate in its desperation, and even Duon had trouble deciphering the spear of fear and panic that pierced his mind. She knew her father, and knew what he was going to do.

Out came the man's sword, drawn as swiftly as thought, and the first cut flashed at the Undying Man's throat before anyone had a chance to act. Kannwar jerked his head back and the tip of the sword nicked his larynx. Within moments the blood of an immortal began to trickle from the wound.

Another man came and stood beside Noetos. Cyclamere the Padouki, a mysterious ally of the fisherman's through some prior relationship Duon had not quite understood, drew his own sword and began to strike against the seemingly defenceless man.

Who proved not to be defenceless at all. He drew no famous weapon, nor did he create some counterattack from the air or another of the elemental forces of the world. He took a blow to the arm and another to the shoulder, both cutting him to the bone, before two men stepped forward to defend him.

Bregor the Hegeoman, the man Kannwar had but recently struck down and healed in a time that no longer existed save in the memory. And Torve the Omeran, although Duon could think of no reason why he would defend a tyrant so similar to the Emperor of Elamaq.

In the distance Stella turned to watch, a look of despair on her face. She had lied. She cared.

Bregor faced Noetos with nothing more than a walking stick, while Torve had not even that: barefoot and unarmed – and unmanned – he took a strange stance in front of Cyclamere, forcing Kannwar backwards.

'Why do you oppose me?' Noetos asked Bregor. 'You know my cause is just. Or has he bought you? Are you still in Neherian employ?'

'He could have let me die, but he didn't,' Bregor said, his face white with fear. 'Noetos, do not strike at this man. Any blow you land could end up killing yourself. You saw what happened to me.'

'I saw,' Noetos said as he drew his sword back for a powerful blow. 'Yet his tyranny must be answered. I am sure I will fail, but my actions may inspire others to try. One day he will fall.'

His blow fell, and Bregor barely managed to divert its power away from his own arms. His stick splintered, and the end was sheared off and fell some distance away.

Torve exploded in a flurry of movement, not fast exactly, but fluid, as though dancing between Cyclamere's strokes. He rained blows at the swordmaster from every direction. Cyclamere withdrew a pace, baffled and more than a little bruised.

'Was this part of your calculations?' Noetos called out to Kannwar.

'Not at all,' the immortal replied.

'Order them to move aside then. I do not want innocent blood shed.'

'I follow no one's orders,' Torve said. Was that anger shading his voice? Duon had never heard it before, had not believed it possible of an Omeran. 'This man healed me. He saved my life. I do not love him, nor do I agree with him, but how can I do less for him in turn?'

'This is perfectly ridiculous,' said Noetos, frustration spilling over into his voice. 'You are being defended, coward, by people who are behaving morally and yet making exactly the opposite calculation that you would make in their place. They do not consider the thousands of lives forever safe from your possible future depredations should you be slain here today. Instead, they think only of their debt to you. Do your statisticians have a column for loyalty, coward? Or if they do, does it record only how such loyalty can be exploited?'

'He can order me to move until he runs out of breath, Noetos,' Bregor said. 'I will defend him in this. But there must come an accounting even for the Lord of Bhrudwo. Moral men and women must be given access to the calculations of his statisticians. Others must weigh the morality of his actions. You, Noetos, are not one of them. Step aside, lay down your weapon, see this adventure through to its conclusion and then observe Bhrudwans put this empire to rights. At the end we may still have an immortal lord, or we may not.'

This brave but foolish speech was barely out of Bregor's mouth before the Lord of Bhrudwo drew himself up. 'You mortals think you can decide my future and the future of this land? I have suffered far more grievous challenges than yours and withstood them all! Where were you when the sorcerers of the Had Hills banded together in a thousand-strong cabal against me? I did not see you lining the parapets of newly built Andratan to help me throw back the grease-smeared hordes from Kanabar, who had laid the whole of the Malayu Basin to waste. Were you one of those who stood with me when I faced down the Most High himself in golden Dona Mihst? I have restrained myself amongst you short-lived maggots, but now the carcass upon which you feed bestirs himself. I am not dead. I have suffered you until now at the behest of the Most High. But no longer.'

The Lord of Bhrudwo strode forward, his hands thrusting aside Bregor and Torve as though they were mere leaves, and began to swell. Larger and larger he grew, until he stood ten paces tall.

'Larger target to hit,' Noetos commented to Cyclamere, and hefted his sword.

Lenares never wondered where she found the courage. In fact, she did not consider her motivation for what she did 'courage' at all. If pressed, she would perhaps have admitted to annoyance, even anger, but not bravery.

Foolish, wasted words. These men wanted to strike at each other and in so doing ease their pain. All the words did was to make it easier for them to strike.

Seeing this, she ceased her conversation with Mahudia and stepped forward, faster than light, and in an eye-blink stood between them.

So this is magic.

Yes, girl, said her true mother. *But because it is magic, it comes at a price; a price which falls to me to pay. Please use it sparingly.*

Squeals, exclamations of shock, fear and wonder on their faces. Lenares tried to keep herself from enjoying the reactions of her friends. To them it would have seemed she simply materialised among the combatants.

'Put your swords down,' she said, 'and listen to me.'

'Not until I've dealt with the Undying Man,' Noetos said.

Lenares raised her gaze to rest on the bear-man. 'Look at you, stupid man, choosing hate over love. Which is the better answer to the death and destruction of your family: to kill everyone around you, or to help someone you love regain life?'

'Get out of my way, girl.'

'No. Answer my question out loud for everyone to hear. Would you rather have the Undying Man dead or Cylene alive?'

'But we cannot do anything for Cylene!' the bear growled.

'We can, but I need you all to put down your swords. What is your answer?'

'I'd rather have both.'

One of the man's friends called out to him, an older man with a round belly. 'Come, fisherman, show us your heart. Which well do you draw from when you need strength – love or hate?'

'What do you think, Sautea?' Noetos snapped. 'You saw enough of me.'

'I would have said "love" without a doubt in the days you and I worked The Rhoos,' the older man answered. 'But now, after what happened to Opuntia, I'm not so sure.'

The big red-haired man sighed. 'I meant to make this man's death – or, more likely, my death – a gift to my daughter, to show her justice still exists in the world.'

Arathé waved her arms around and mouthed noises. 'I don't want your gift.'

'I never thought you would, child. But someone needs to show you that those that hurt without cause will have to give account of it.'

Duon spoke. 'Arathé reminds you all that there is one among us who has hurt thousands of people in the last few days without cause. He is busy hurting another as we speak.'

'All right, all right!' growled the fisherman. 'Lenares, show us what we can do to help reclaim Cylene from the Son. But I do not withdraw my interest in this man. He still has questions to answer and I reserve the right to press for those answers.'

Lenares breathed a deep sigh, part relief, part apprehension. Time to begin. She turned back towards the village, now some distance behind them, and began to trudge up the road.

'Everyone follow me,' she said.

She had always enjoyed being the centre of attention. She well remembered the day she had demonstrated she wasn't just a half-wit, that she could reason better than any of the other trainee cosmographers, better even than her teachers. Smarter than them all. She still brought that memory to mind whenever she felt sad or neglected. Mahudia's look of surprise, followed by a deep pleasure, bathed her mind again now.

But never had she been the focus of such illustrious people's gazes. The most powerful magicians in the world had been gathered here, and Lenares Half-wit was the key. Without her, they could throw magic at Keppia and all he had to do was to hide deep in Cylene's body, letting the poor girl absorb the blows until her body died – and then he'd be free. But she had a plan, she knew how to trap Keppia beyond the Wall of Time and, in so doing, free Cylene.

She had a plan, but it was Mahudia's plan. Mahudia had come to her, tug, tug, tugging on the invisible connection between them, the link between this world and the void. Even as the stupid fisherman and the stupider Undying Man had made ready to slash

301

at each other – as if that was remotely important – Mahudia had whispered her plan to Lenares. Lenares wished it were her own plan, but she would never claim it as her own, no matter that no one else could hear Mahudia, no matter that her foster mother would not begrudge Lenares her moment of glory.

'When I captured Umu,' she explained to her friends, 'I thought I was being clever. I thought I had caught her by dividing the zero of the hole in the world into smaller and smaller pieces, until Umu was trapped and I could bind her. But what really happened was someone else from the void helped me. That someone says she is Mahudia, the Chief Cosmographer, who was killed by Umu.'

Nearer to the village they drew, nearer to the ranting, wailing figure of Cylene. Behind Lenares came less than half the crowd. The remainder were obviously too frightened to venture any closer.

'We are going to drive him out,' Lenares said, more quietly now, as they continued their slow march back towards Mensaya. 'But not out into the world where he can do more mischief. Instead, we will drive him back along the conduit he uses to draw power from the void.'

'How will we do this?' Kannwar asked. 'And what conduit is this? I can see no conduit, not even with the eyes of magic.'

'I can,' Anomer said. 'My sister taught me to see the essenza in everything, the lattice that connects all things in the world, from which comes all energy and all magic. Cylene is a mixture of two essenzas, one white, one black; and there is a black cord stretching behind her, going up, up into the hole in the world and out of sight.'

'There's no "up" or "down" in magic,' Kannwar said scornfully.

'Doesn't matter whether we're seeing a truth or a metaphor,' Anomer answered him, colour in his cheeks. 'What Lenares says she sees is what I see. Are we both imagining it, Lord of Bhrudwo?'

The man pursed his lips and did not offer an answer.

'So,' Keppia said, as the remaining travellers, magicians to the fore, surrounded him. 'You have come to save your friend. Go on then. I won't put up a fight.'

Mahudia, Lenares sent, her whisper travelling instantaneously along the tenuous connection to her mother. *Now.*

Beyond the Wall of Time

The great storm had killed many thousands of people north of Patina Padouk; the huge earthquake and accompanying waves had ended the lives of many more. Mahudia had explained that the void pulsed with a myriad new stars, all once nodes in the wall of the world, now torn untimely from the pattern of life and cast into the ever-widening maw of the hole in the world. *Many are still nearby*, Mahudia had said to Lenares. *They are frightened and they are angry. They have agreed to help us.*

Lenares waited, but saw nothing for some time. She ignored the threats coming from the monster's mouth, watching for any change – and finally saw it: a pulse in the broad connection between Cylene and the quarter-sky hole in the world hovering above them.

'What are you doing?' Keppia said, an edge to his voice.

'Nothing,' Lenares answered him. 'None of us is doing anything.'

'Then what . . . is that you, Umu?'

The pulse arrived at Cylene's body and the thing's mouth opened in a bellow. But it was Keppia's voice, not Cylene's, that came out.

It is working, Mother, Lenares sent.

Good, said Mahudia, her voice faint. *Few here want the gods to break through into the world. They think of their loved ones still alive, and, apart from a few selfish ones, do not want them to die. And there are those who simply want revenge.*

Lenares glanced upwards and saw a multitude of stars glittering beyond the hole in the world.

She returned her attention to the animated corpse before her and watched as the black began slowly to leach out of it.

'Stop this! I will kill the girl, I swear I will!'

'She is dead already,' Lenares said to him. 'And we cannot stop what we did not start.'

The monster began chuffing heavy breaths, undoubtedly summoning all his power. The conduit expanded still further as he drew on the void. The blackness began to return to Cylene's body.

'All you magicians!' Lenares commanded gleefully. Truly, she was the centre of the world at this moment. 'Use your magic to see the dark essenza in this body before you. Pick at it, grasp it, and push it away from Cylene, towards the cord. Draw from those around you who are not magicians. Now!'

At her command a dozen bright blue filaments snapped into existence, arcing towards the monster. Keppia threw back his head and howled.

'He will flee,' Kannwar said. 'We will have saved Cylene, but lost Keppia.'

'He will not flee,' Lenares said. 'This will weaken him so much that Umu could destroy him should he abandon Cylene's body. This is his only chance. He will try to hold on.'

Blue fire assailed the monster from all sides, and the hungry conduit continued to suck at him. Around them people began to collapse.

'Lenares! They're dying!' someone cried.

Oh, I never thought of that. 'Stop drawing on them!'

'It's not us. Keppia is draining them dry,' said Kannwar.

'Then some of you must protect them!'

Instantly six of the blue arcs vanished and the bystanders were surrounded by a faint azure glow. Keppia roared and began to reclaim Cylene's body.

'Umu! Help your brother!' the monster shouted, his attention fixed on a row of denuded trees lining the side of the road. His sister, if she was anywhere within earshot, gave no answer.

The very ground around them began to shrivel and crack as the warring magicians drained essenza from every source. Plants withered, grass collapsed into a grey mat, insects were fried where they crawled or flew.

'I have never . . . been this deep . . . into magic!' the Undying Man said.

'This is my world!' Keppia screamed as the black began once again to fade. 'I belong here! I was tricked into leaving! You cannot *dooooo* this to me!'

Lenares saw the moment Keppia gave up trying to remain in Cylene's body and attempted to flee. All the black collected at the entrance to the cord – which was now as wide as Cylene was tall – and made to run, taking the cord with him.

There came a faint cry from her own conduit, and at the same moment Keppia's cord suddenly stiffened, locking more firmly into Cylene's body. Keppia shrieked, then was jerked bodily into the cord, from where he fell upwards, twisting and jerking, towards the distant hole in the world.

'Push!' Lenares cried.

All the magicians united in one final effort, their blue fire pushing through Cylene and along the conduit. Screaming and cursing, Keppia vanished from sight.

Amid the exhausted cheering, Lenares heard Mahudia speak. 'Goodbye, child,' she said.

'Goodbye?' A cold premonition bit at the cosmographer and she suddenly found it difficult to stand. 'Why goodbye?'

'If your sister is to live, Lenares, the conduit must remain open. Keppia no longer animates her body, after all. But if we leave the conduit open at this end, Keppia may return at any time to possess her anew. We can't guard the conduit forever: the newly dead want to pass on. So I will wrap our conduit around Cylene's, ever tighter, tighter' – the thin cord vibrated as she spoke – 'until the merest trickle of magic flows down to Cylene.'

'Will you still be able to speak to me?'

But the question was wasted. She knew the answer already, knew she had but moments left with her mother.

'I am the conduit,' Mahudia said, her voice growing fainter. 'You must let me go, beloved daughter, so I can make Cylene safe. Don't weep, girl; you still have memories of me, and soon you will have your sister. She is special, Lenares, just like someone else I know.'

Don't weep, she says. Lenares could do nothing but weep as she took the end of the tether linking her to Mahudia and held it loosely in her shaking hand. Lose a mother, gain a sister, overcome a god. The latter a great victory, and yet it felt so much like a defeat.

She opened her hand.

CHAPTER 13

THE LIMITS OF LOVE

NO ONE HAD THE ENERGY to take to the road the next day, or the one following. Smoky, haze-filled days, the weather humid, the air heavy, tiredness draped over their shoulders like a damp cloak. The travellers spent their time foraging for food, sleeping off their magic-induced weariness and trying to understand what had happened.

Lenares received more praise than she ought for the banishment of Keppia, but less sympathy than she deserved for the loss of Mahudia. None here, save Torve, had ever met the Chief Cosmographer, and most seemed to regard Lenares' explanation of Mahudia's role in Cylene's rescue as some sort of made-up story, an attempt to avoid the limelight. Their behaviour made Lenares angry: her mother deserved unending praise for her brave sacrifice, but no one seemed to care.

They cared far more about reports that Umu knew what had happened to her brother. Lenares remembered the moment when Keppia had cried out for his sister's help and had looked imploringly at the trees at the roadside. A few of those people who had remained on the open road, too frightened to follow Lenares back to the village and her confrontation with Keppia, reported seeing a small, rotund man limping through the trees. Their descriptions matched that of Conal, the Falthan priest.

So close, some said. We could have defeated them both in one day.

306

But the people who said this were not magicians, nor were they friends or relatives of the eight people who had died that afternoon, drained of their essenza by Keppia in his quest to free himself. They had no appreciation of the cost the battle had incurred, nor did they realise, according to Kannwar, just how lucky they were, how lucky they all were, that Umu had fled rather than attack.

'She did not accurately assess our condition,' the Undying Man had said. 'Had she done so, she could have destroyed us all.'

'If she saw Keppia's failure,' Moralye asked, her brows knotted in thought, 'is she likely to try to force us into liberating her in similar fashion?'

'I think not,' the Undying Man had replied, as if conversation between himself and a Dhaurian scholar, his fiercest of enemies, was the most natural thing in the world. 'She is likely to find another way. We need to recover our strength and confront her before she grows too strong.'

'What will she do in the meantime?'

'You know the answer to that, scholar. She will slaughter as many people as possible in an attempt to widen the hole in the world even further.'

'Such an action will yield unpredictable results,' Moralye commented. 'Phemanderac taught us about the Wall of Time, and his thesis was that the Fountain of Life weakened it in and around Dona Mihst, meaning exposure to the eternal void lengthened the lives of those dwelling there. He argued there may not have been a simple correlation between exposure to the Water of Life and the age to which men lived.'

'And what do you think of his thesis?' The Lord of Bhrudwo's voice was devoid of inflexion.

'I . . . ah, perhaps I would defer to one who actually lived in those days,' she said, proving she was not only knowledgeable and brave, but wise.

'No matter her tactic, we all know her ultimate goal. With Lenares' cleverness and our strength we have rid the world of Keppia, but he was the less intelligent of the siblings. I fear we have a far greater task ahead of us.'

Lenares agreed with the Undying Man's assessment. Umu was very clever. She had tricked Lenares into letting her go just when she might have done the most good. She was much sneakier and less direct than her brother had been. And she was bent on revenge against Lenares for having ensnared her.

Lenares had been thinking about Umu on that first night in Mensaya when someone approached her.

'Sister, might we not speak?'

Fear prickled anxiously in her stomach as she swept her lank hair aside, looked up and met Cylene's troubled gaze. 'I don't really want to,' she said.

'I know you don't,' Cylene said, nodding slightly. 'No one understands that while everyone else has gained something today, you have lost.'

'Do you see this?' Lenares said, on the verge of tears. *Don't cry. You must never cry in front of others. They will tease you and call you names.*

'Of course I see it. But I haven't come to offer you counsel. Sister, we have both lost mothers today. I have only just learned the fate of my . . . *our* family. I know she deserved it, but . . .'

The tears came, and soon neither girl could tell where one's sorrow ended and the other's began.

'I don't like you,' said Lenares, sniffing. 'They kept you and got rid of me. What made you so special?'

'You were the special one, Merla,' Cylene said, seemingly unoffended. 'You stood up to what Daddy did to us. You were always getting beaten. It hurt us to see it, and made us frightened to disobey him in case we were treated like you.'

'I'm Lenares, not Merla. Merla is dead. She fell from a cliff nearly ten years ago. I don't want to hear her name any more.'

'And you don't remember . . . ?'

'I remember nothing.'

'It's as though you lost something essential in your mind and you became a new person.'

Lenares scowled. 'Or maybe I gained something extra that no one else has,' she countered.

Cylene nodded. 'I'm sorry, Lenares. Forgive me for my rudeness. I, too, have gained something, thanks to you. I now have a small capacity for magic.'

'Can you hear Mahudia? Does she speak to you?'

Cylene shook her head sorrowfully. 'No, sister. Our mothers are gone. You and I will have to do for each other.'

Lenares grunted an ungracious reply, but had not really expected to drive her sister away. Nor wanted to when it came to it. Cylene was her sister, after all.

Sister. She wished to deny it, but the word brought a warm glow to her chest. Though her sorrow at the loss of Mahudia was almost unbearable, she knew she could not have resisted her foster mother's last request. Some people might feel they were betraying the newly departed by talking to the one responsible for that loss, but Lenares prided herself on always seeing the truth. This wasn't Cylene's fault.

'What's it like to be dead?' she asked her sister.

Cylene's face fell. 'Noetos asked me that and I couldn't give him a satisfactory answer,' she said.

'Is he your . . . is he special to you?' *He's so old. As old as our father would have been.* The thought made Lenares uneasy.

'Noetos and I are very good friends,' Cylene said, smiling. 'We don't yet know what we might become.'

'Do you love him?'

'He asked me that too. I'm not sure I gave him a satisfactory answer to that question either.'

'Do you remember Keppia?'

Cylene sighed. 'I wish I could forget. I'm not sure where I went after the ship crashed down on me, but it was a place of wide-open spaces and twinkling lights, filled with countless voices, some laughing, others weeping, arguing or speaking quietly. I was drawn back into my body, and he was there, filling it up. I can't describe to you what it feels like to be inside your body but not filling it. To me it seemed as though my whole body was a blister I needed to slough off, or perhaps an unnecessary layer of clothing.

'Then he started to hurt me. It was horrible.' The colour faded from her face. 'Lenares, do you mind if I don't talk about it?'

'I wanted to know,' Lenares said, unabashed.

'You're a very direct person,' Cylene said, a small frown marring her features. 'Noetos told me about you. I think I understand your gift. Sister, can you tell me more about it? What was it like growing up in a foreign land?'

Lenares and Cylene shared stories with each other well into that night. The more they talked, the more intoxicating the talk became; small intimacies led to larger ones, and long after everyone else had found sleep under the stars, the sisters whispered the secrets of their hearts to each other. As the fire died down and the stars came out, they became aware of the great gift Mahudia had given them.

It was one of the best days Lenares could remember.

The next day was not so memorable.

It began with hunger. Despite the many talented hunters among their number, it was impossible to find enough food to keep the whole party satisfied. Arguments started, and twice that morning angry men left the group, taking dozens of people with them. Kannwar did not try to prevent their departure, suggesting it was for the best.

'How will they survive?' Mustar wondered aloud.

'The same way we all will – or will not. No village will have food to spare, no grocer will be willing to part with any surplus he has.'

'Couldn't you command them?' Stella asked.

'I could,' Kannwar said, 'if I thought it would not further inflame those who look for any cause to take issue against me. Objectively speaking, we are the most important people in the world and our survival is more important than any village we might raid. But weighed against that is the division such a raid might cause. For better or worse, the Most High has chosen us. I do not want to lose anyone he thinks should be part of this endeavour.'

Lenares was unconcerned about the lack of food. In Tal-amaq

the cosmographers had learned out of necessity to make do with very little: the Emperor had systematically reduced their funding, making Mahudia's position very difficult. It had been whispered among them that the only reason the cosmographers survived was because Mahudia used her own personal fortune to subsidise them.

She got up, stretched and made her ablutions in a cool stream some distance from the village. The sight of so much water flowing freely still confounded her senses, and as she bathed she felt like an emperor herself.

As she reached for her clothes, she realised someone was watching her.

'Torve,' she said, and made no move to cover her breasts. Such ought to have been the behaviour of a proper lady – though a proper lady would never have bathed naked in a stream – but Lenares cared nothing for such behaviour. She beckoned him closer.

He had obviously never been taught the male equivalent of proper decorum. Why should he have been? Torve was an animal, after all, according to Amaqi traditions. Such teaching wasn't wasted on animals. He came closer, edging down the slope to the stream, and crouched on the bank within touching distance.

Lenares couldn't help it: her thoughts returned to the moment the Emperor had taken his worm. Her mind told her it changed everything, but her mind seemed to have very little influence on her heart. The pink feeling began to spread up and down her body. She wanted him, but she could never have him.

He looked at her with eyes filled with longing.

'Can I touch you?' he said.

Why? Lenares wanted to ask him. *Kannwar told me you would no longer feel those desires.* But as much as she wanted to know the answer, she was reluctant to ask. She did not want to hurt his feelings.

'Yes,' she said.

He reached out and took her right breast in his gentle fingers. She gasped at his touch, and a delicious heat spread across her skin. His eyes filled with tears.

'I can't feel anything,' he said.

311

'I can,' said Lenares, biting her lip.

'There is no future for us,' Torve said, and the despair in his voice stole her pink feelings away.

After washing and drying her clothes, she dressed. Torve waited patiently for her, then walked with her back to Mensaya. They talked as they walked, the discussion a pessimistic one.

Once there, Lenares and Torve walked boldly into the town square, where the others had gathered. Various conversations were proceeding, accompanied by arm-waving and even diagrams drawn in the sand. Lenares wished she could have taken part in them – her thirst for knowledge seemed to be increasing with every day of this adventure – but she needed their help. How should she do this? The old Lenares would simply have stood in the centre of the square, held up her arms and called for everyone's attention. But Torve was a private person, painfully private. She could not make a public spectacle of him.

She flicked a glance over the crowd and saw her sister. Cylene sat beside Noetos, their hands entwined, flanked by his children. Lenares had heard murmurs about the age difference between her sister and the fisherman and once again wondered if her sister knew why she was attracted to the older man.

They are in love. I will start with them.

As Lenares approached, Noetos looked up, shielding his face from the sun. 'What has happened?' he asked her. 'Is it the Daughter? Is another disaster on the way? Are we in danger?'

She gazed at these people, strangers to her, yet people she hoped to make her friends. They were here because they trusted her, because she had saved them, because they saw her as their hope against Umu and the hole in the world. At the least, she was their warning should Umu attack them. They respected her and would help her.

'I need your advice,' she said.

They waited patiently.

'I am gifted,' she told them, 'in many ways. I am the last cosmographer in the world, and the best for many centuries. Perhaps of all time. I am not like you: I do not lie, and I see many things more clearly than others. But because I am immersed in my gift, I am not familiar with a number of the things you take for granted.'

A couple of sniggers followed this comment. Others in the square had ceased their discussions and were listening to her. She sighed. Ignorant people could be found everywhere.

'This is private,' she said loudly. 'Mind your own affairs and leave me to mine.'

Their faces turned away.

'Torve and I are considered animals back in our homeland,' Lenares said, more quietly. 'He is Omeran, and I was called a half-wit. Neither of us were instructed in matters of love. We want to know—'

'You wanna know 'bout fuckin'?' someone called out.

They were still listening!

'Is that all there is to love?' Lenares responded angrily.

'All that matters,' called another male voice.

The words were followed by a sharp comment from a woman and a ringing slap, an indignant cry, then hearty laughter from somewhere to her left.

'You want to talk about love?' Anomer sounded puzzled.

'Such questions should surely wait until we have done what the Most High has called us to do,' Kannwar said.

Lenares almost leapt into the air, so startled was she by his voice. He stood only a few paces behind her.

'You should stop telling us what to do,' she said, turning to point a finger at the Undying Man. 'I rescued Cylene yesterday. I drove Keppia away. If people want to help me in return, you don't get to stop them.'

'He's only opposed to it because he has nothing to contribute to the topic.' Robal stood near the edge of the square, arms folded, a bitter smile on his face.

'Very well,' Kannwar said. 'Continue your most important discussion. I, however, have other matters to attend to.'

People poured out of the square like water through a colander. The sight angered Lenares almost to the point of incoherence.

These were the people she had risked everything to save! The people Mahudia – no, she couldn't think about it. She knew her anger was irrational; she had told them not to listen to her, so why should she be unhappy if they chose to leave?

Perhaps twenty people remained in the town square when the water finished draining away. At least her sister, the fisherman and his children had not left. Moralye smiled up at Lenares, and behind the scholar sat Robal, Kilfor and Sauxa, the three Falthans surprisingly interested in the proceedings.

Stella sat to one side, alone.

The rest were people Lenares had not properly met: interested locals, those perhaps too weary or heartsick to join those who had left the square. A couple wore trouble on their leering faces.

'You want to know about love, girl?' Sauxa asked, his perpetual scowl fixed on his face.

Lenares liked this man, so she nodded enthusiastically. He wore his frown like a mask, but he was a man who feared nothing and valued the truth, even though he played strange games with it. She was pleased Sauxa had asked her the question.

'Yes, I do. You all know what happened to Torve,' she said. Torve stood beside her, saying nothing, obviously uncomfortable with the exposure but willing to trust her. 'We want to know if we can still love each other. We want to know what to expect.'

'Alkuon, woman, he's lost his manhood.' Noetos spoke kindly, but his words still hurt. 'You keep asking the question and the answer remains the same. What you can expect is nothing.'

Cylene frowned at him.

'If by nothing you mean no . . . ah,' Lenares stumbled over the word, 'no fucking, no children, then we understand that. But can't we love without it? I was in love with Torve before he . . . before the Emperor made him a eunuch. We hadn't made love, but we loved each other.'

'Fair point,' Robal said.

'Maybe,' said Noetos, 'but you were looking forward to the day when you could consummate your love.' Lenares didn't need to see the faint blush spreading across her sister's face to know that,

314

for her, that day had arrived. 'Without such promise, love has no meaning.'

'Aye,' said one of the locals, an older woman. 'I'm sorry for your friend, lass, but nature and the gods made us this way. We long for love. Only when we're in love can we approach the exalted state of the gods. It's the highest, most noble feeling in the world.' A single tear leaked from the corner of the woman's right eye.

'Exactly, madam,' Robal said, clearly warming to the argument. 'We're born male or female, and even the most ignorant can look at the equipment we're born with and tell that we are all one of two pieces of a puzzle waiting to be put back together. Anyone who withholds their piece of the puzzle, whether because they're unable or unwilling, can't say they're truly human.'

He was so blatantly trying not to look in Stella's direction as he spoke that Lenares' attention was irresistibly drawn to the woman sitting alone. Her stony expression did not waver.

Sauxa sucked loudly at his teeth. 'So you're arguing that love implies fucking, and that fucking is what makes people human?' he said, his coarse voice edged with something like menace.

'Not quite. I think it marks the dividing line between child and adult. Those who remain on the child side of the line can never enter fully into adulthood.'

Murmurs of agreement from around the gathering suggested that Robal had neatly summarised the majority's view.

'I think you're wrong,' said the old man. 'You've got it all backwards. I'm the oldest here and an expert on the subject, so—'

'An expert on loving hundreds of women and breaking their hearts, you old goat,' Kilfor said, his whisper intentionally loud.

'None of 'em objected at the time,' Sauxa said. 'And you're assuming that because I left 'em they were heartbroken. Most of 'em were glad to see the back of me.'

'Well, there is that,' his son conceded.

'Please,' said Lenares to Sauxa. 'Tell us what you think.'

'You got all these people tellin' you you're not normal if you don't love someone, marry 'em and have children,' he said. 'They think this is their idea. But they're sheep, the lot of 'em. Sheep.

315

Every village, every town, every city, every country wants children. To protect and provide for their parents in their old age, defend them in time of war, all that. Of course they want their sons and daughters to breed. So they perpetuate the old "true love" myth. How else will they persuade otherwise sensible youngsters to lose their freedom and independence and throw away their lives on someone who might be totally unsuitable?'

Moralye cleared her throat. 'Hauthius once advanced a similar argument,' she said. 'Society raises the ideals of love, monogamy and commitment in order to coerce young people into contracting permanent relationships, thus making them easier to control. The result is less migration, a more settled population, guaranteed replacement, all leading to the reproduction of society.'

'I'm not sure about all the long words, young lady,' Sauxa said. 'What I mean is—'

'What rot,' Robal said. 'Who is this "society"? Anyone seen this list of instructions "society" wants us to follow? Love is very simple. We're led to fall in love with someone because we want to have a family with them. What's so difficult about that?'

'Plenty of women can't have children,' said one of the local men. 'Is their love wrong?'

'Not wrong, but ultimately futile,' said Robal.

'You are a singularly ignorant man, even for a soldier,' said Kannwar from the far side of the square.

'Thought you weren't interested in this nonsense,' Robal replied.

'It is hard to ignore such blatant stupidity,' said the Undying Man. 'You talk as though marriage is a choice. For most people it is no choice at all. They marry for duty, or for business, or survival, or because they are forced to by avaricious parents. Love comes later, if it comes at all. "Falling in love" is not the normal state of affairs. It is an ideal beloved of troubadours and old women.'

'Exactly,' said Sauxa. 'Romantic love is a nasty joke. You lose control of your sanity and make decisions you later regret. It never lasts. One day you wake up amid the snoring and the smells and realise it's all a confidence trick.'

'You think that because you're a selfish old man,' Robal shouted.

'While the feeling has you, you act unselfishly, in the best interests of your beloved. Then when it wears off you revert to your cranky old ways and get the inevitable heave-ho. No point in arguing, you know I'm right.'

'So it doesn't matter that I rid the world of Keppia,' Lenares said. 'People here won't accept Torve and me as real people because of the cruel thing the Emperor did to him.'

'What does it matter, girl?' said Robal. 'After all this is over, take your friend and find some place where no one knows you and make your home there. They don't have to know what happens in your own house.'

'You want us to hide?' Torve said, his voice rasping.

'Well, you haven't done anything deserving of such treatment, but there will be those who will not accept you because of what you are,' said the guardsman.

Sauxa hissed. 'Stupid boy! Those who oppose these two are the sort of people who've listened to you and your blather. Ulcers to your soul, you are an ignorant man! Tell me, can you describe this feeling you talk about? What does it mean to fall in love?'

Robal took a step forward, again looking anywhere but towards Stella.

'Love is the realisation you have feelings for someone so wonderful, so far above you, that you do not deserve their favour. It makes you forget about your own desires and focus entirely on the one you love. Then, as you and your beloved form a relationship, sex follows naturally. That's what "making love" means. The act of sex makes love.'

'There are so many things wrong with that foolish notion, I don't know where to start. This "falling in love" is the most selfish of desires. It's just an exaggerated form of the excitement you felt when you were young, when a certain fond uncle promised to carve you a serpent for your birthday. Something you desired was finally within your grasp. You barely ate or slept until I'd finished it. Then a week later I found it outside in the rain, cast aside, the thrill gone. Perfectly natural, that, but don't dignify it by calling it "love" or the highest feeling.'

Robal went to reply, but a hand on his arm stopped him.

'Let me tell you a story,' Stella said, pushing her way past the guardsman, her dark eyes fixed on Lenares' own. Now this was a woman almost impossible to read.

'I was loved by a great man, one of the most decent and least selfish men I've ever met. When we were both young I was aware of his devotion to me, but spurned it as being of no worth. Instead I reached out for the promise of darker, more exotic desires and was ensnared by Deorc of Jasweyah, the lieutenant of the Undying Man of Bhrudwo.'

Lenares saw Arathé twitch and a connection suddenly came into focus. She wanted to ask the question, but decided to listen to what the Falthan queen had to say.

'This man delivered me to the Undying Man himself, who tried to woo me with pain and suffering. He forced me to serve him and I became known throughout Faltha as the Destroyer's Consort, a byword for collaboration with the enemy. Yet after I escaped the Destroyer's clutches, King Leith protected me, even to the point of taking me as his wife.'

'Did he love you still?' Lenares had no need to ask the question, as the answer was obvious from Stella's numbers, but the others could not see.

'He did. His youthful passion had gone, killed by my betrayal, but he chose to honour me regardless. Something special grew between us, something strong and precious, if bittersweet.'

'You never loved him.'

'No, Lenares, I never did. Not with the sort of love Robal talks about. But through the years we found something better, Leith and I, a friendship built on a shared vision for Faltha. He named me his queen, despite the protestations of everyone of the Sixteen Kingdoms, and we set about restoring Faltha, along with Phemanderac, who devoted his life to assisting us.'

'So you've never been in love, my queen?' Robal asked.

'I never said that,' she replied. 'I fell beak over tail in love with a most handsome councilman from Firanes, and in my latter years I was charmed by an importer of dyed wool from the Wodranian

Highlands. But I chose true love over this "falling in love" the stories tell us of and stayed with Leith. I never regretted it.'

'Yet you never slept with him.' The Undying Man's voice rang out around the square.

'And that is no one's business but mine and my friends'. A man with any understanding of how a woman feels would have kept those words to himself.'

'I am a man who knows you value the integrity of your argument higher than your own feelings,' Kannwar said. 'You yourself would acknowledge your story is not complete without that salient fact.'

'A fact that was mine to reveal when and how I chose!' Stella snapped.

Sauxa, the rebellious Central Plains itinerant, stood. 'Queen Stella,' he said, 'you make my argument far more convincingly than I can. No one could describe you as less than complete.' He bowed to her and sat down.

Torve stood as still as a post, allowing none of his emotional turmoil to show. *Stella understands me*, he realised as the Falthan woman told her story, then went on to explain why she had never consummated her marriage to the King of Faltha. It seemed to Torve that she tailored her story specifically for him as she spoke frankly of her love and her frustration. *Her poison blood makes her as crippled as I am, yet she found something approaching true happiness in her partnership.*

Robal, her star-crossed guardsman, was having none of it. He had no conception of how much the fool he was painting himself with his churlish words, his ridiculous assertions that Stella was somehow lacking. Others in the square had become noticeably angry with the man, having been swayed by Stella's eloquence and sincerity.

'Love is essential,' he argued. 'It should not be resisted, no matter the cost.'

Heredrew stared at the man as though he was a cockroach found in a lord's parlour. 'You're saying the Falthan queen ought to have

319

cuckolded her king by fornicating with this highland woolman? How long do you think she would have remained in power after such a dalliance became known?'

'Who cares? At least she would have pursued her heart. At least she would have been alive.'

'What utter nonsense,' Moralye said. 'You speak as though the heart must always overrule the head.'

'In matters of love, yes!'

A younger woman with short, curly hair spoke up in a soft, shy voice. 'I think the idea's romantic. Imagine givin' everythin' up for love!'

'Yes,' Sauxa growled. 'Just imagine it. The good opinion of your friends, the love of your family, the respect of your comrades, all thrown away in pursuit of something that doesn't exist.'

'Doesn't exist?' said the young woman. 'Of course it exists.'

'Describe it to me then, girl,' demanded Sauxa.

'Well, it's a . . . ah, it's a feelin',' she said, stumbling over her words. 'A glorious feelin'.'

'What sort of feeling?'

'Makes me feel ill,' said a young man not much older than a boy. 'I can't eat, I can't sleep, I spend all my time thinking about her.'

'Who?' asked the curly haired woman.

'Not saying,' said the young man. 'You wouldn't know her. Down in one of the northern villages. She might not even be alive.'

'So that's love?' Sauxa said. 'And here's me thinking that was what we on the Central Plains call obsession. You know, that selfish feeling we get when we want something we can't have.'

'That's a completely different thing.'

'Is it? Is it really? We train our women to search for this impossible thing, a thing they can't even describe, this notion of romantic love, because it provides us the most effective way of controlling them. Of making them want to settle down and waste their lives with us. Look at you, boy. There isn't a woman in the world who'd consider your stupidity attractive even for a moment were it not for the lies we've told each other for generation upon generation.

As a result, we enslave women – no, women enslave themselves – and they end up spending their lives on us. In a world made up of cruel jokes, romantic love is the cruellest of all.'

'Look, old man,' growled Robal, taking Sauxa's arm in a meaty hand, 'you can mash our words together and make them mean whatever you want, but love is what makes the world work. There's nothing I wouldn't dare for the sake of love, and in so daring I would enlarge my soul. The lack of love is why you've turned into a wizened-hearted old goat. It's why your wife left you, why all those women turfed you out after a single night. Your soul is too small, Sauxa.'

The plainsman let out a long, hissing breath. 'Son,' he said, his voice hoarse, 'if you really knew anything about love, you wouldn't have said what you just said.' With a twist of his forearm he freed himself of Robal's grip, heaved himself to his feet and strode out of the square.

'He always hated being wrong,' Robal said to no one in particular.

'You are such a fool,' said Kilfor. 'Always have been, always will be. You come in with your big hoofs and trample all over everything worthwhile. Ulcers to your soul, Robal, you have some fences to mend before you and I next share a drink.' He followed his father away from the small gathering.

'So what is my pink feeling?' Lenares asked, breaking the silence that followed Kilfor's departure. 'Is it love?'

Duon frowned. 'What do you mean, "pink feeling"?'

'When Torve is close to me I feel pink. My arms and legs tingle, and my face and, ah, other places heat up. It is a very strong feeling. It makes me want to ignore the good advice my mind gives me. Is that love?'

'Yes,' said Robal, at exactly the time Stella said, 'No.'

'No?'

'No. What you experience is desire. Your body wants his body. It is a wonderful feeling, but it is not love.'

'Oh, yes it is,' Robal said, the intensity of his gaze boring into his queen's dark eyes.

321

Torve had heard enough. Though every instinct commanded him to restrain himself, to exercise his Defiance in private, he put those instincts behind him, despising them for the chains they were.

'This is ridiculous,' he said, stepping forward. 'Everyone speaks as though love is the most important thing in the world, yet no one can agree on what it is, or who is entitled to enjoy it. Having listened to you all, I can only draw the conclusion that love can be anything you make it.

'You people seem to think we'll not be regarded as truly human because I am unmanned. Lenares and I are familiar with such regard. I doubt it will bother us. If she is willing, I am prepared to find out whether it is possible for people like us, people less than human, to love each other. We thank you for your time and your well-meant words.'

He bowed to the small crowd, exactly as though his Defiance was over. As it was, he supposed; though this Defiance had been expressed with words rather than dance.

Later, when most people had left the square and he and Lenares were left alone to take the first tentative steps towards each other, Stella came over to them.

'I am sorry,' she said, 'sorry for our intolerance and ignorance. If I were to offer you anything, children, it would be every encouragement to explore your relationship unfettered by any sort of expectations. Find out what you have rather than worrying about what you might not have. And if what you have is not enough, don't be frightened to let go.'

'I don't want to let go,' Lenares said, and Torve felt his throat tighten.

'Neither do I,' he said, and squeezed her hand.

'Good,' said the Falthan queen. 'I hope you find happiness.'

'When Umu is dead and the hole in the world is repaired, then I will be happy,' said Lenares.

Torve nodded. Lenares would always be reaching for knowledge and understanding, always trying to fix whatever she saw as being wrong; she would never be satisfied with the mere love of one man. He couldn't help feeling a surge of relief course through him at the thought.

Queen Stella turned away and began to leave the square. There, on the edge of the open space, stood Robal, his beefy arms folded, a broad smile on his face, waiting for her. Torve did not hear their brief discussion, but as Stella spoke, the guardsman's smile contracted and vanished, replaced by a frown. His interjections were short, and overridden by her increasingly irritated replies. After a few minutes of this, she drew back her hand and slapped him across the cheek, then strode off into the shattered village.

A short while later Robal left the square, his shoulders slumped. Torve did not need Lenares' gift to work out what had passed between the two.

That night, the travellers determined to go on the next day. They sat around a small fire set in the road on the northern outskirts of Mensaya, talking in subdued voices while beyond the flickering circle drones buzzed and cicadas chirped.

'We need to find somewhere isolated,' Kannwar argued. 'We do not know where Umu is, or even if she "is" anywhere. Therefore we need to draw her to us. I do not wish to meet her in a populated area as our attack would necessarily be constrained by the presence of innocent Bhrudwan citizens.'

'Never imagined there was any such thing as an innocent Bhrudwan,' Sauxa whispered to his son in a voice just loud enough to be heard.

Kannwar ignored the old man. Lenares could see the extent of his self-control. This was a man who wished to be treated as an emperor, who was used to instant obedience and unquestioning respect, but who received none of these things from the Falthans. Moralye had explained the antipathy to her. Two bitter invasions, one within living memory, had earned Kannwar the epithet 'Destroyer.' The Falthans seemed to be having trouble accepting Umu as a greater enemy than the man who led them.

Not as much trouble, though, as Noetos. His anger at the

Undying Man's presence among them constantly threatened to boil to the surface. During that afternoon he had engaged in a shouting match with his own children, accusing them of betrayal for not telling him of Kannwar's true identity. After that he'd sat alone brooding, no doubt trying to think of a way to revenge himself on the Bhrudwan lord. *Don't waste your time*, Lenares wanted to tell the red-haired man. *He's far too powerful to be wounded by your sword arm.* There was only one person sitting around the fire who was capable of wounding the man, and she sat alone, as she had done earlier that day, head bowed, her black hair hanging over her face.

So much sorrow.

Seemingly heedless of Stella's dark mood, Kannwar went on to explain they ought to strike out for the coast. The inland plains were densely populated, he said, and had likely been sheltered in part from the storm and the quake. The sheer numbers of people living in the Malayu Basin ensured there would still be many alive. There were, by contrast, only a few fishing villages along the coast.

'Oh yes,' said the small, rotund man, Bregor. 'Fishing villages are expendable.'

Kannwar sighed. 'I have done nothing to deserve your ire,' he said testily. 'The villages are likely devastated by the storm and the great waves that followed the earthquake. Short of turning south and inflicting more damage on areas already devastated by this conflict, I see no other option.'

'You'll be wantin' us to leave then, great lord?' said one of the locals.

A few villagers had returned to the wreckage of their houses from whatever place they had holed up in during the storm and quake; most had borne injuries of some sort. Heredrew had not offered to heal them. Saving his energy for the final conflict, no doubt. Lenares approved of the man's practicality.

'Yes, you ought to get as far away from here as you can. Go south and west.'

'Cravin' your pardon, great lord, but there's nothin' but jungle and savages south and west. We'd be safer under your wing, so

324

t' speak.' The woman who spoke was the same curly haired woman who had been in favour of romantic love earlier in the day.

'When the battle comes, none of us will have anything to spare to protect you,' said Kannwar. 'You'll be crushed like insects, and no one will notice your passing. Certainly a few more lives lost in the context of what has happened means very little, though perhaps it might do to you. Come with us if you wish,' he concluded, and gave the woman a lopsided smile.

'Ah, no, great lord, you have commanded us to leave. Leave we shall, at sunrise.'

'Can we be certain that Keppia has been dealt with permanently?' asked Seren. 'My apologies, all, but I'm only a simple miner, a digger in dark places. I know nothing of gods and magic.'

'You know a great deal more now than you did,' said Noetos, who was, through circumstances Lenares had not yet enquired about, the miners' master. 'And more than most other people do, or would want to.'

'Aye,' Seren said. 'Doesn't stop me wondering, though. Or lying awake when I ought to be sleeping. So is he gone?'

'Lenares said so, and I believe her,' Kannwar said.

His words brought a rosy glow to her chest.

'I saw him, you know,' Noetos said. 'Just before the earthquake. He tried to get me to set him free.' The big man described his encounter with Dryman's corpse in the beachfront forest. 'All the while I thought I was outsmarting him, he was tricking me into releasing him. But the hole in the world was at that point not sufficiently large to admit him fully into the world. I hacked at Dryman's body until it could no longer sustain the presence of the god, but Keppia did not achieve freedom. The earthquake followed within minutes. Provoked, no doubt, by an angry and frustrated god.'

'We have been fortunate,' Moralye remarked. 'We came far closer to disaster than we knew.'

'We must be much more careful,' Kannwar warned. 'To that end, I believe we should appoint Lenares the leader of this expedition. More than anyone else, she has the sensitivity to see

Umu's attacks before they arrive. She has held the god captive before, and still has a link to the void. We need to follow her.'

There were words spoken after this, many words, but Lenares could later remember none of them. All she could remember were those Kannwar had spoken, placing her right at the centre of the world.

Finally, for the last time, her counting could stop. She had no need to orient herself with regard to some fixed point. She was herself the very centre of everything. Wherever she chose to go, the centre would move with her.

Yes, she said to herself. *Yes. This is who I was born to be.*

QUEEN

CHAPTER 14

DEATH OF A CAPTAIN

STELLA KEPT HER FEET MOVING, her arms swinging and her face expressionless as she and Robal slowly drifted further behind the other travellers. It did not matter what he said or how he said it, she would not reveal how deeply torn she was.

She had known this agony before, of course. The Arkhos of Firanes had been a man she could have given herself to, heart and soul, had she not ignored her heart and remained loyal to Leith. And even her relationship with Leith himself had not been simple: far from it. Phemanderac had loved the Falthan king with far more passion than she had ever been capable of generating, much as she'd grown to love him. Moreover, she and Phemanderac had grown closer over the years, until the regard she held him in was similar in every respect to that in which she held Leith. A perfectly triangular relationship, unrequited but energised, enabling them to achieve great things together. Faltha had never enjoyed such a golden period in its history.

Yes, she had known the bittersweet agony of loving more than one man. And, given the never-ending future stretching away from her, she would know it again.

Knew it again now.

She worried that all she had done was to replace Leith and Phemanderac with Robal and Kannwar respectively. Robal's passion, energy and naivety for Leith's, and Kannwar's wisdom and experience for that of Phemanderac. But whether or not this was what she had done was irrelevant really. She had been about to give her heart to Robal, until it had been taken by Kannwar.

Both men were manifestly unsuitable. Robal was insufferably arrogant, ridiculously overprotective towards her and foolishly outspoken. Kannwar was far worse with his genocidal morals and his constant dissembling. Yet she loved them both, fool that she was. In this, and only this, aspect of his discourse on love was Robal correct: the heart could seldom help where it gave its affections. But what she had learned, what she knew more completely than anyone else alive, was how the heart could be overridden. How, in fact, it must be overridden if anything beyond momentary pleasure was to be achieved.

So as Robal walked beside her, his hand on her arm, cool fingers whispering secrets that ran along her nerves and straight to her brain, she fought to reveal none of her feelings to him.

'Are you going to give me any hope at all?' Robal asked her. He had remained silent all morning, at the risk, it seemed to him, of one or more of his internal organs bursting, but her closeness and her silence could no longer be borne.

She turned to him and, as always, he found himself overwhelmed. She was beautiful, of course, none would dispute that, but beautiful women were common, more common than men realised. Certainly in his career as a soldier he had romanced his share of beautiful women. No, what captivated him about her was the sheer intensity of her gaze. It was as though she made every second count, as though time itself mattered more in her presence. He wasn't entirely sure he understood what he meant, but he knew it was as a result of the life she had lived, a long and painful one, filled with suffering and discipline. It made her all the more precious, a singular jewel, unique; and should such a jewel shine only for him, ah! He would be envied by all men.

'I have said all I wish to say, Robal, back in Mensaya town square. You spoke plainly, expressing your hopes of me, and I replied as clearly as possible. I cannot prevent you taking hope from my words, but I intended you to have no such hope.'

Robal glanced down the road: the travellers had turned a corner and were hidden from view by a row of poplars, their upper branches sheared off by the storm.

'Fair enough. You said your piece, Stella, and I don't need to hear it again. No one for you, not now, and not in the immediate future, which for you could mean years. I don't agree with you, I think you're in denial, but I must respect your choice. For now, Stella, it seems we must travel separate paths.'

This got the reaction he intended. He would have said anything to break down the wall she'd erected to keep him out. She loved him, he knew it. Knew it. The despair on her face at his words confirmed it. It was all he could do not to smile.

'You will no longer guard me?'

'You need no guard. I would guard your body with my own, but your immortal flesh needs no guard. The only person to do you harm since this adventure began was me, your guardsman. I would guard your heart, but it seems I am, in fact, the chief enemy of your heart. I plot to capture it. But you have placed a guard on it so strong, so impenetrable, that it is proof against all would-be conquerors. Body and soul both safe. So what need do you have of me?'

Something in her face broke at his words. 'Robal, Robal, don't force me to make a choice.' Her voice had grown small and carried a note of desperation. 'Remain with me, dear one, or leave me, but do not make it my decision.'

'You're the queen, Stella. I am merely your guardsman. You are responsible for me. You must send me away. If I leave you of my own volition, I could be tried as a deserter.'

Cruel, what he was doing, but love sometimes had to be cruel.

'That is fiction. You deserted your post to protect me in the first place.'

'Nevertheless, I am now in your service. Do you dismiss me?'

Robal watched her face as they walked together, booted feet crunching on the gravel road. She didn't cry, but her cheeks reddened and her eyes grew moist. Her throat worked away as she swallowed again and again, keeping her emotions under control. Woman of iron.

Robal's life hung suspended as he waited.

'Yes,' she said, after many minutes of silence. And again: 'Yes. I dismiss you.'

Stella may have guarded her heart, but Robal had constructed no such defence. Her single word laid him open from throat to groin, as deeply and effectively as a mortal sword blow. He had gambled, he had lost, he was dismissed. She would turn to him, the dark temptation, of that Robal was now certain. She would give herself to the Destroyer.

He turned and walked swiftly away.

'Robal. Robal!'

He refused to halt, to turn, to acknowledge her in any way. It was the only counterthrust he could make, the only wound he could inflict.

No, he thought, his own darkness drawing closer. *Not the only wound.*

He could have tolerated her rejection. After all, she wouldn't be the first girl who'd turned him down, and not all of them had continued to resist him. He could be patient if he had to be.

What he could not tolerate was Kannwar's continued interest in her. The man's every glance sullied her. She had little choice in the matter, he realised that now: the Most High himself had appointed the Destroyer as the leader of this expedition, and Stella had decided this time round to be obedient to her calling, no matter the cost. He certainly didn't want to see her suffer like she'd suffered the first time.

But it was clear that Kannwar was not to be the source of their salvation. That task, it seemed, had been given to the strange southern woman, Lenares. The Destroyer himself had anointed her as their leader.

What further use then for Kannwar?

This interesting thought occupied him as he walked on.

A night passed, and a day, and a second night. Robal barely noticed the passage of time. Did not stop for food and only reluctantly for water. Spoke to no one, ignored the increasing numbers of people he encountered on the path to Corata Pit. Refused to answer their welcoming hails, their requests for news, their desperate enquiries about loved ones.

What further use for Kannwar?

'He left without another word?'

'I tried to call him back,' Stella said bitterly. 'I have no idea whether he even heard me.'

'You cannot blame yourself.'

'Perhaps not, but I believe you are right. We have all been drawn together by the design of the Most High. Every person we lose makes it harder, if not impossible, to do what he wishes us to do.'

'That is my fear,' Kannwar said.

Noetos, who had not strayed far from the Undying Man since learning his true identity, leaned towards them. 'Send someone to fetch him back,' he said.

Another man of action, Stella thought, *another man who speaks to find out what he thinks.*

'Are you volunteering?' Kannwar said.

'You'll not be rid of me that easily. Delayed, I remind you, not denied.'

'Indeed,' the Undying Man said, inclining his head. 'And when the time comes I will gladly be held to account – by your daughter.'

'By Alkuon, you will not! You have done her more than enough harm already. I will not stand to one side and watch you destroy her again!'

'No, you will not,' said the Undying Man, and Stella heard the Wordweave in his voice. *Obey me*, it said. 'I will converse with your daughter in private. What I have to say to her is for her ears, not yours.'

To his credit, Noetos shook off the Wordweave. 'We Dukes of Roudhos have made a habit of disobedience,' he said.

'Ah, now. You are making formal claim to the title?'

And so the trap opens wide, ready to swallow this man.

Noetos stepped into Kannwar's path, forcing him to halt.

'I make claim to nothing. The Duke of Roudhos is what I am. If some day I want the title as well as the reality it will be because I believe it to be in the best interests of those who live in Roudhos, understand? Those who live in Roudhos, not those who see it as a buffer state between Neherius and Jasweyah.'

His face hovered a hand's span from that of Kannwar, and if the fisherman was at a slight disadvantage in that he had to lift his head to stare into his lord's eyes, the stare did not show it.

Stella nodded. *The trap is sprung, the mouse avoids it, and may well yet get the cheese.* She was getting to know Kannwar and this was the sort of backbone he approved of. Could work with. Was, in fact, she reminded herself, exactly how she had behaved during her captivity and what had drawn him to her.

Ahead of them the rest of the travellers continued on, Lenares at their head, bless her, taking her role seriously. Not even a backwards glance.

Stella caught a glimpse of a white-faced Cylene peering out from behind Noetos. This was a courageous girl, yet she could only believe she was about to witness the destruction of her beloved. After all, he was confronting the man who had destroyed her family.

'The dukedom is mine, fisherman, mine to distribute as I see fit. As a reward for service, as a bribe, as a plaything, as anything I want. Be assured of this: it will be given to the one whom I believe will serve the best interests of Bhrudwo. I applaud your speech, but am wondering if your years in that tiny village might have left you more parochial than ought to be the case in the duke of such a large duchy.'

'What do you know of Fossa?'

Kannwar turned to Stella. 'You see?' he said, his hands spread wide in an exaggerated gesture of helplessness. 'Mortals simply do not understand the time at our disposal and therefore the breadth of our accumulated experience. I spent some time in Fossa a few hundred years ago. You were lately the Fisher there?'

Noetos nodded warily.

'Then you live in a house that I helped construct.' His eyes narrowed. 'If you want to escape my influence, better go and live on some other continent.'

Another trap, one that Stella, for all her statecraft, hadn't seen, closed around the fisherman. She could almost pity him. If you remain in Bhrudwo, Kannwar was saying, you will forever be dependent on me.

'Hope it wasn't you who did the mortaring,' Noetos said, his look indicating that he understood perfectly what was being said. 'Poor job, that. We've got leaks all along the cliff side of the house. Could do with a real builder.'

Clever man. Trap avoided, message sent.

Kannwar laughed, just as Stella knew he would. Say what you like about the Destroyer, he had a breadth of soul greater than anyone else she had ever met.

'It may have been me who did the mortaring, at that,' he admitted with a smile. 'One man can't be good at everything.'

A breathtaking invitation.

Turned down.

'No, but there are some things he must be good at. Nations need mortaring together. What I see is Neherius allowed its head, to the destruction of Saros and Palestra.'

'Old Roudhos is a building that must be torn down, and Neherius is undertaking the demolition. I am sure you will not appreciate this, but I intend something greater to be built from the rubble.'

Bregor scuffed a foot on the path. 'Forgive me, great lord, but I don't see why Old Roudhos needed to be reduced to rubble. Couldn't the blocks have been taken apart carefully and reassembled without hurting anyone?'

Consina put a hand on Bregor's shoulder. 'He is about to tell us that Neherius is not a sophisticated instrument, but that their armies were all he had. That his sincerest wish is that this could have been achieved without bloodshed, but that had it not been attempted, the loss would have been far greater.'

Kannwar gave the woman a strange look. 'How did you escape the eye of the provincial administrators in Tochar?'

'You said yourself that someone has drawn us together for a

purpose,' the Hegeoma of Makyra Bay said. 'Perhaps our part in all this is to achieve a better resolution for Old Roudhos.'

'Or to show people how to rebuild after the devastation wrought by the gods,' Stella said, certain she was right. Certain in a way only someone fire-touched could be.

'Then why, Stella, are you here?' Kannwar asked.

Robal climbed over the rubble and made his way down into Corata Pit. So fixed was he on his goal he barely noticed the devastation wrought by the storm and the earthquake. The granite finger had come down right across the path into the pit; that it had been more than a simple collapse was clear from the limbs, belonging to at least two people, protruding from under the fallen rock. Other huge boulders had been strewn about the pit, and across the far side of the vast space a large slab of the wall had collapsed, taking hundreds of tons of rock with it. The sheer force required to do such things was beyond comprehension, even for one who had been caught up in it, and for a moment this gave him pause.

But only for a moment. So what if the Destroyer had magic enough to hold off a storm? He would not be able to hold off the storm that Robal was preparing for him.

It would not be fair to Robal to suggest he suffered no qualms of conscience about what he intended to do. Far from it. The single most difficult aspect of this entire affair was the fact that Kannwar was not the thoroughly evil being he had expected the man to be. In fact, he was distressingly human. Whether the Destroyer was called Kannwar or Heredrew, he behaved no worse than any other ruler Robal had known, making difficult decisions with alacrity. Robal knew King Leith and Queen Stella had made similar decisions: one such had led to an army crushing the nascent rebellion of the Central Plains. Robal had come to believe King Leith had acted correctly, and even his friend Kilfor admitted as much, though only in private and not within earshot of his father. There had been deaths, including those of good patriots, and Sauxa had named some of them as friends.

Why couldn't Kannwar have been a monster? Someone other-worldly, supernaturally, insanely evil, as the Son and the Daughter had proven to be? Why was he not mercilessly destroying anyone who got in his way? Why was he so rational, so reasonable, so human?

Moreover, he actually compared well to the behaviour of others. The woman at the Sayonae steading, the cosmographer girl's real mother, had acted callously by giving her daughter to the ugly little priest in an attempt to bind the Undying Man. Dryman, the Emperor of Elamaq, had cut off Torve's private parts for no more reason than the lad was enjoying himself. It was almost as though they were conspiring to make Kannwar appear wholesome.

Why did the Destroyer not behave like the tyrant everyone knew him to be?

There could be only one answer to that question, and it was this answer that kept his feet striding further into Corata Pit, towards the small clutch of buildings at its base and what he knew would be housed there. The duplicitous man was hiding his true personality in an attempt to win Stella's trust. And once he had her in his thrall he would take her, would take her and Faltha both, and rape them until they were dead.

Let the magicians deal with the gods. He would deal with the real threat. He would destroy the Destroyer.

The gear he needed cost him a great deal of money, far more than he'd been able to steal from Stella's purse. The three miners, their faces covered in grey cloths, had not been swayed by his pleadings nor moved by his threats. They reduced their price not one iota when he reminded them how he and his friends had kept Corata Pit safe during the great storm. In the end he'd had to barter away the shard of huanu stone he'd stolen from Lenares. They had been eager when, in desperation, he'd revealed the shard, so eager that he had almost expected fights to break out even before he handed it over. Another betrayal of trust, another stain on his conscience; it seemed ironic that in order to defeat his enemy Robal had to become as double-dealing as Kannwar himself.

By the time the sun set on his third day away from the other travellers, he was well on his way north from Corata Pit, coaxing along his two placid donkeys from the uncomfortable wooden seat of his newly purchased wagon. And behind him, stacked carefully in neat piles, lay the materials that would rid the world of its most duplicitous inhabitant.

Why am I here?

There were a dozen answers to the question, all of them partial, none satisfactory to Stella.

Because the Most High required a presence here perhaps; though Kannwar himself had served just as well when the time had come for the Father to reveal himself. Even Noetos, a Bhrudwan, had – if she'd apprehended his story correctly – served briefly as an avatar of the Most High.

To represent Faltha? More likely, that, as there seemed to be a symmetry amongst the travellers. Clearly someone thought people from all three continents ought to be involved in the attempt to hold back the gods. But this still didn't explain why she had specifically been chosen. And when considering the symmetry, it would not do to forget Husk, the invisible puppet-master who until recently had controlled Conal, Arathé and Duon. Stella thought it likely that their role had been to shepherd others towards Andratan. Duon was to draw the Emperor north; Arathé, her father – and his huanu stone; and Conal – well, Stella herself. For what purpose, no one knew, though if the magician was trapped in Kannwar's dungeon, the motive had to be either escape or revenge. Likely both.

There was, of course, another answer. An answer that had been growing within her for seventy years as her immortality weighed more and more heavily on her spirit and she realised just how unfit for human company she was becoming. An answer she refused to examine.

A death ended their second day north of Mensaya.

Lenares had been acting strangely most of the afternoon, walking beside Torve for a while, then ducking back among the crowd of refugees who still trailed them. The girl was normally fidgety, but this behaviour was excessive even for her, and odd for a leader. Clearly she was experiencing some difficulty. The third time she did this, Stella followed.

She passed by refugees walking with their heads bowed and shoulders slumped. A few of the women had babies on their hips. Older children trailed after them, faces blank with weariness. Some of the men seemed to have enough energy to talk, but most were silent, drained. Thus they paid the price for being in the vicinity of the battle with Keppia.

Lenares strode to the rear of the group, then took a legs-wide stance, her arms folded, chin forward. A scruffy man with a week-old beard stumbled into her.

'Sorry, sorry,' he said, his head down.

'I remember you,' Lenares said to him, her eyes narrowing.

Lifting his head, the man blanched and ducked away.

Her eyes bored at him. 'You captained a ship. A slave ship. I sailed in it.'

'You're mistaken, young lady,' said the man, as men and women trudged past them. 'Mistaken. I ain't never captained no boat.'

Stella was no expert on Bhrudwan dialects, but the man's coarse accent sounded phoney. And if there was one thing Lenares never was, it was mistaken.

'I see truth,' she said. 'It's my gift. You were a sea captain, and you still are.'

'What is your line of work?' Stella asked the man.

'I'm a farmer,' the man answered, still reluctant to raise his head.

'What crops?'

The hesitation was just a moment too long. 'Sheep, lady. I farm sheep.'

'A hard life,' Stella said equably, raising an eyebrow to Lenares. The girl took the hint and bit back the question she was about to ask. 'How many in your herd?'

Again the hesitation. 'Twenty.'

'Really? That many? How many workers do you employ to deal with that number?'

'Four – no, five.' Eyes flicking nervously in search of rescue; the man knew he was under suspicion. 'You a farmer or somethin'?'

'My husband was responsible for a number of sheep farms,' she said. 'But he never sailed on anything bigger than an outrigger. Nor would he have needed any assistance to care for twenty sheep. He certainly couldn't have afforded help on the money he'd make from them.'

Time to end this, before the man became violent. 'Go fetch Noetos,' she said to the nearest listener, thinking to place a stout sword between herself and this impostor.

The man cried out, raising his head to show a face made pale by her words. 'No, lady,' he said. 'I will leave. Let me leave.'

Stella caught the eye of two men who had halted to watch the entertainment. 'Hold this man,' she said. She'd meant to ask rather than command, but her queenly habits intruded at the most inopportune moments. Fortunately the men nodded, each taking one of the ruffian's arms.

'Why do you wish to leave?' she asked the frightened impostor. 'What have you to fear from Noetos?' *How do you even know him?*

'Perhaps I might bring some light to bear on that,' said the fisherman himself.

He nodded thanks to the woman who had fetched him, then, as she was bowing herself away, re-thought and took her arm. 'Hold. Fetch Cylene for me, goodwife, please.'

'No need, Noetos,' came the girl's voice.

It seemed the travellers had noticed the halt in the march and had come to see what the trouble was.

'Ah, yes,' Kannwar said a moment later. 'I had forgotten about this man. I am surprised he hasn't tried to run before now.'

'What is this?' Stella asked, faintly annoyed. The remaining colour had drained from the man's face and he looked about to vomit with fear. 'How many of you know this man?'

'Everyone who sailed on the *Conch*,' Cylene replied. 'This is Captain Kidson.'

'Ah.'

Noetos had told the story of their sea voyage by the fire yesterday evening. Having listened carefully to the tale, and heard Moralye and Cylene describe the latter's escape from the wreck, she was inclined to echo Kannwar's question: why had the man not fled before now?

'All the confirmation I need,' Kannwar said, a mask dropping over his urbane features. Despite herself, Stella froze with fear; she, more than anyone here, knew what would happen once that mask appeared.

'This has nothing to do with you,' Noctos snarled at the Undying Man. Truly, the fisherman had far more courage – or much less wisdom – than anyone Stella had met. *Or perhaps he remains very angry.*

'Oh?' The mildest of responses. 'Are you suggesting that this man' – he nodded in the direction of the ship's captain struggling in the grip of the two locals – 'is not one of my subjects?'

'Of course I'm not. As a lord you are free to dispense justice as you see fit. But I presume you do not spend your life – your long life – travelling from town to town, holding court and executing justice upon every offender in the land? You leave justice to those affected by the crime, as my grandfather did before he lost his lordship.'

Stella had wondered when that little historical fact might be raised. She had seen the fisherman's grandfather die, writhing on a stake as the flames consumed him, refusing to the last to concede a point of principle to the Undying Man. The wholesale burning of the Red Duke and his followers had been at least partly a display to frighten Stella as she languished in captivity. She hoped the Red Duke's grandson knew nothing of this last detail.

'Ah, your grandfather,' Kannwar said, and Stella held her breath. 'You deserve an accounting for that, I think, but not right now. Instead, let us devote ourselves to making an end of this thief and murderer.'

'And slaver,' Lenares added.

'Slaver? He used his ships to transport slaves?' Cylene's eyes had widened in shock.

'He was the captain of the ship that took me south to Elamaq.'

341

'I thought you didn't remember much of – yes, sorry, sister.'

Time and again Lenares had proven her accuracy in such matters; Cylene would soon learn not to question it.

'So, Kidson,' said Noetos. 'Slaver, smuggler, murderer, thief. Are we all agreed?'

The man's face worked for a moment before he could force the words from his lips. 'Aye, I was a smuggler. Confiscate my ship if you must. But I know nothing of the other crimes.'

'You're not a very good liar,' said Lenares, that fearsome look of concentration making every bit as commanding a mask of her face as that of the Undying Man. 'The ship I sailed on was the MF *Periwinkle*. I remember the name on the front of the ship as they led me on board and told us what was going to happen to us.'

'You told me you had a ship with such a name,' Noetos said flatly.

'I have sailed on her,' Cylene breathed.

'The girl could have heard that name anywhere!' Kidson cried. 'Miss Sai, did you ever see any slaves on board my ships?'

'No,' the girl admitted.

'I have met you before,' said Kannwar unexpectedly. 'Six years ago you came to Andratan to apply for a recently vacated licence to carry goods to and from Andratan. What was the name of the ship? Ah yes, the *Nautilus*. As I recall, those whom you paid to refit her reported some interesting discoveries in her lower holds.'

'Everyone had to run at least one slaver!' the man shouted. 'A fleet is an expensive business!'

'You were told when you received the licence what happened to the previous licensee, and why.'

Kannwar did not elaborate, but Kidson clearly knew what was meant.

'So, a smuggler and a slaver.' Noetos put his hand on his sword hilt.

'And a murderer,' said Kilfor.

'I've murdered no one!'

'Tell that to young Dagla,' Noetos growled, and Stella recoiled at the depth of the man's fury. Noetos seemed to have raised anger to something almost supernatural. 'The boy your first mate struck down. He died on the docks at Long Pike Mouth. Your fault.'

'And tell it to those you refused to rescue from the wreckage of your ship,' Kilfor added.

With suitable interjections from his father, the plainsman told the story of their discovery of the wreck and how they had rescued those trapped in the holds.

'He shut them in before the ship foundered,' Sauxa summarised. 'Then he ignored their pleas and left them to rot.'

Anger coursed through the crowd at these words.

'Enough,' said Noetos, and at his command everyone fell silent.

The man certainly has a presence about him, Stella thought.

'Time for judgement. Cyclamere, give the man your blade.'

'I'm no swordsman,' Kidson said, his hands shaking. He had the look of death in his eye.

Stella had seen such a look many times before, as criminals tottered their way to the gallows. Stories were told of the bravery of condemned men, such heroes even sparing time to shower the watching crowd with witticisms, but in her experience hangings were all about naked fear, blood and piss and the crack of the neck as a man's life ended. As necessary as such events were, she detested executions.

More than anything, they remind me of my immortality, she admitted to herself; but though a final rest would be welcome, the accompanying terror was not something she wished to embrace.

Noetos drew his sword. 'Defend yourself or do not: I am about to strike you down for your crimes.'

The crowd stepped back half a dozen paces.

The Padouki warrior's blade landed in the grass beside the frightened captain.

'You don't have to kill me! I have ships, three other ships! I can sign papers, give them to you. My office in Malayu has the deeds!'

'They are forfeit,' Kannwar intoned.

Stella watched it as though it was some mummers' show, with

an equal air of predictability. The man offered a few more bribes, then begged, such appeals doing nothing but making his end all the more bitter – for his judges as much as for himself. She predicted almost to the second the moment when the man finally acknowledged his fate, and was not surprised by his desperate lunge for the sword lying on the grass.

'Stand back,' Noetos said, 'lest he take anyone hostage.'

'If I defeat you, I am free?' Kidson asked.

'This is not some children's tale,' Noetos answered. 'If you strike me down, another of your accusers will take my place. Make no mistake, Kidson, this is your execution, not some trial by combat.'

One last plea. 'These accusations are very convenient for you,' the man said, the blade wavering in his hand. 'At one stroke you get my ships, revenge for your friend's unfortunate death and possession of my slattern.' His eye swept the crowd. 'Does anyone think that is fair?'

'He is pretending to be frightened,' Lenares said. 'He is good with a sword.'

'Oh, I know,' said Noetos. 'No one carries a sword like the one he wore on his ship unless he knows how to use it.'

It was undoubtedly supposed to be a surprise attack, but even Stella could see it coming. Kidson roared as he slashed at Noetos. He wielded the blade with vigour, but treated it as though it was an axe, taking huge swipes, each designed to cleave Noetos in half. The fisherman had no trouble blocking each swing, leaning forward and not giving any ground. Clearly Noetos was not to be fooled into striking too soon.

Seeing his tactic would fail, the captain changed his grip, then began to fence with it. Much better, thought Stella dispassionately, though she did not want to see Noetos harmed. There seemed little chance of that: even though Kidson worked hard, running through a series of underhand and overhand forms, Noetos parried with ease.

Stella was by no means an expert with a sword, but in her seventy years of rulership she had been subjected to many lectures on the subject and had been taken on countless interminable tours of fighting schools and training grounds. *The captain still does not put forth all his skill*, she realised. *It looks as though he is trying to deaden the big man's arms*. Indeed, blow after blow rang heavily on Noetos's blade.

'Stop!' Noetos cried, lowering his sword.

Kidson took one more swing, which the fisherman parried, then froze in place. *Magic*.

'I'm not having this,' Noetos said, fury writ even larger on his face. 'Someone is supplying me with strength. Who is it?'

No one answered, but Stella saw his children turn their heads away. The fisherman clearly noted their reluctance to face him, for he said: 'Must my every attempt to put things right be interfered with?'

'Blame them if you will,' Kannwar said, 'but it was I who gave you strength.'

'You?' Noetos spun round to face the Undying Man. 'I'm not sure I believe you. But whether then or now, you are interfering. Can you not simply let things play out? Must you always shape events to your purpose?'

'You are too important to me to be thrown away in some foolish, misplaced bout of anger. Everyone standing here knows what you're about, Roudhos, even though you do not. You cannot strike at me, so you relieve your feelings of frustration by striking at someone else. Once you have disposed of Kidson you would go on to vent your anger at your children, I have no doubt, or at anyone else you imagine disagrees with you. Noetos, you have it in you to become the greatest Duke of Roudhos in a thousand years, but this will happen only if you learn to harness your anger.'

The fisherman's eyes bulged. He turned away from the Undying Man and lifted his sword, making ready to swing at the motionless Kidson.

'You're too late,' Kannwar added. 'He's already dead.'

'What?' The word came out flat.

'Dead. Strangled. I've put an end to this risky nonsense. Can no one else sense the urgency of our position?'

Noetos strode up to the figure held upright by the Undying

345

Man's magic. The lips were blue, the tongue lolling, eyes bulging but empty of life.

The fisherman turned to confront Kannwar, but the Undying Man spoke first.

'Is this a game to you all? Some sort of puzzle to be solved? To me it is the future of Bhrudwo. Am I the only one here who grieves for the thousands of people already slain by the gods because you and I, god-selected, have not been smart or brave enough to do what we've been called here to do? How many more thousands of people must die before we defeat Umu and heal the hole in the world?'

Stella could not contain herself. 'But you killed him with no warning. He could not even defend himself!'

'A deed I should have done when I met him days ago in Mensaya. I knew him guilty then, through the testimony of a family I met there who had been on his ship. But I held off, Stella, because I am being taught by a fellow ruler to exercise caution. Do you see what the outcome of such caution must inevitably be? What would you say to me now if the future Duke of Roudhos lay dead, cut down by a lucky blow from a should-have-been-dead man? Would you congratulate me on my judgement? Ah!' He barked his disgust. 'The best of you has been alive for less than a hundred years, and in my foolishness I thought to at least try to regard your ideas as wisdom. You have made me soft, you people, with your ideas of individual justice and personal rights. You are wrong, and you always will be wrong. Until you have lived two thousand years, do not dare teach me how I ought to run my empire.'

'You've been considering what we said?' Stella stared at Kannwar, trying to read something, anything, in the illusory face.

'Why else would I have behaved with such stupidity? Of course I have been thinking. What, did you think I have survived this long by believing I have nothing to learn?'

The unnaturally erect corpse collapsed to the grass, occasioning a gasp from the onlookers, some of whom were obviously struggling to keep abreast of developments.

Beyond the Wall of Time

'The Most High drags you all to Bhrudwo in order to assist me in defeating the gods,' Kannwar continued. 'This battle could have been fought anywhere, you realise. The hole in the world is a metaphor for something spiritual. It is not real, and it is not here.' He flung an arm towards the sky, where, some distance behind them, the unnatural circle let starlight – void-light – into the world. 'Well, it is here as much as it is anywhere. We see it in one place, but the hole represents a weakening of the magical bonds that god-fuse the world into a functioning whole rather than a collection of disparate things. In order to return to the world, the gods need to break those magical bonds to the point that the threads tying them to their own allocated place – beyond the Wall of Time – dissolve. That point has been reached. It has been reached everywhere. The fact that we are here and not in Faltha or Elamaq ought to tell you that I, the one whom the Most High called from childhood to defeat the gods, am the nexus of his plan. You'll think me arrogant, but you already think me cruel. I maintain that I am merely experienced and thus I see what you do not.'

'The hole is everywhere,' Lenares said. 'So why are we going to an empty place to confront Umu?' She paused a moment, then exclaimed: 'Oh.'

'Yes. Think it through.'

'Because we are anchored to the world. We have a place. Each of us is in one place at one time. Therefore any interaction between the gods and ourselves must happen in one place, even though it also happens everywhere.' She smiled a greedy smile, enjoying the new knowledge as though it was a sweet treat. 'Mahudia would have called that a paradox. It makes so much clear to me.'

'Good.' Kannwar spread his arms, encompassing them all. 'Only by exercising your unique gifts can you eventually arrive at the plane of understanding from which I start. You – we all – would do better to question less and follow more closely.'

'So why are we here then?' Stella enquired, as levelly as she could in the face of this conceit. 'Why has the Most High not simply left this task to you alone?'

347

'I don't know,' Kannwar said, frowning, not hearing her sarcasm. 'Clearly you have some part to play. I thought I knew what it was, Stella, but I may have been wrong.'

Lenares spoke. 'How long has the Most High lived?' she asked.

'What?' The Undying Man seemed bemused by the question.

'How long has he lived? Longer than you?'

'Of course he has.'

'And you claim a better view of his plan than we have,' she continued.

'Yes, but – ah.'

'Yes, ah,' she said, a manic grin plastered across her face. 'Think it through.'

'You're reminding me that he began planning this two thousand years ago? But that would mean he intended me to . . . it was his *plan* that I rebel and drink of the Fountain?'

'He says he doesn't have a plan,' Noetos said.

'You've spoken to him?'

'I've been possessed by him.'

'And you haven't told anyone? Am I surrounded by fools?'

'The Father might not have a plan,' Lenares said, 'but that doesn't stop him making it up as he goes along. How can he have one single plan if we have freedom to do what we want? He must have hundreds, thousands of plans, changing from one to another every time one of us decides to do something he doesn't want us to do.'

'So he had a plan for me to defeat the gods two thousand years ago, a full thousand years after they drove him out of Elamaq north to Faltha. I was probably not his first plan then.'

'Nor his last,' Lenares said, her voice shaking with suppressed emotion. She was actually bouncing up and down on her toes as she spoke. 'You refused your calling, then rebelled and broke his law by drinking the magical water. So he changed his plan. Your rebellion held things back two thousand years.'

Silence as everyone took this in. A few of the refugees had drifted away, but most stood listening.

'Look around you,' Noetos said eventually. 'Those thousands of corpses you're so angry about? They are the stinking fruit of your rebellion. Well the Falthans named you Destroyer.'

'The Most High put too much pressure on him,' Stella said, the words tumbling from her lips. 'Who here would have coped well with his calling at such a young age?'

'A thousand years of careful breeding,' said Moralye. 'The Most High knew what he was doing. Kannwar was the reason for the First Men's existence, and their confinement in the Vale. A vast breeding program designed to generate one man. So Hauthius always taught, though he never said why he believed this.'

'You know who Hauthius was, don't you?' Kannwar asked softly.

Moralye's face crumpled in horror. 'No, no,' she breathed.

'Oh, yes,' said the Undying Man. Revelation upon revelation: Stella could hardly bear the way her mind was being enlarged. 'Yes. How else was I to keep a close eye on my enemies?'

'How else was the Most High to prepare you all for this eventual partnership?' Lenares said, and again everyone stilled.

'You asked who else would have coped with Kannwar's calling,' Noetos said. 'According to him, none of us are like him. He ought to have coped.'

'Like you, the scion of a noble grandfather, coped with the deaths of your family?' Kannwar shot back. 'For all my faults, I never turned my back on my responsibility!'

Noetos's angry reply was lost in a general uproar. Shouting, arguing, hands clinging to arms in an attempt to restrain them, or waving in a threatening manner, yet no use of magic or steel.

We are drawn together by the will of the Most High, Stella acknowledged, *but we are not yet one instrument of his will.*

The travellers ate a nervous meal, eyeing each other balefully over the last of the stale bread. Before they moved on there was one last debate over the fate of Kidson's body. Cylene asked for it to be buried, but Sauxa argued against this.

'Let him rot,' he said. 'He deserves not a moment more of our time. He will not be dignified by a burial. Better men than he are rotting in crushed houses and open fields as we speak. Let him join them.'

The flaw in Robal's plan became apparent when he returned to Mensaya and the Malayu Basin. Of course he'd anticipated his quarry would have moved on by this time – there had, after all, been talk of finding a relatively unpopulated area near the coast – but the further coastward he travelled, the less he heard of his former companions. Those few people he came in contact with were far too busy rebuilding their lives to answer his hail; it took nearly two full days' steady travel east of Mensaya to meet someone who could state unequivocally that the travellers had not taken the coastal road.

Early in the evening of a furious day later, he found himself drawing up to Mensaya Square, donkeys lathered, wagon still overloaded and a desperate ache in his heart. For a few mad moments he considered striking out in a random direction, or even ditching the wagon, somehow finding his companions on foot, then returning for his cargo. Muttering under his breath, he cursed the gods who seemed to have granted everyone else supernatural visitations or gifts while leaving him solidly normal.

A young lad tugged on his jerkin. 'Hey, mister, weren't you with the magicians?'

'I was,' he said. 'I have urgent supplies for them. Do you know where they are?'

Perhaps the gods were smiling on him after all.

'Dunno,' said the boy, scratching at his nose. Robal's heart sank. 'We came back here with my father. He didn't want to go inland with the magicians.'

'They're going inland?'

The boy didn't answer, preferring to talk about his father. Perhaps Robal had been too eager and had spooked the lad. He cursed under his breath.

'Where is your father?' he interrupted in exasperation. 'I need to speak to him.'

'What's in your wagon?'

'Please!' Too sharp; the boy turned away. Robal grabbed the lad's arm. 'I must speak with your father!'

The boy stuck out his bottom lip, clearly unimpressed with Robal's manners. 'You'll have to wait, mister,' he said. 'He's out in the fields. Said he'd be back before dusk.'

Robal glanced up to see the sun nearly touching low hills behind the town. He let the boy go, then set his mind to wait.

Kannwar led the travellers inland, having decided that the safest place for a potentially devastating final confrontation with Umu was in the perpetually mist-shrouded hills of the sparsely inhabited Zizhua province. Many days they were on the road, and every turn they made seemed to lead them into rougher country and along narrower, less kempt paths. Rutted earth replaced gravel, fading in turn into overgrown, barely discernible tracks winding between steep-sided hills. True to the province's fame, the mist descended every evening and did not lift until after noon each day – if it lifted at all.

After two weeks all their accompanying refugees had drifted away. Perhaps they had been encouraged to put aside their fear by the absence of god-activity, or maybe the Undying Man's warning that they would be defenceless should the gods strike had finally made an impression on them, but on the day the travellers emerged from a narrow gorge into a wide valley, they were reduced to the groups from the three continents. Kannwar, Noetos and his children, Cyclamere, his former fishermen Mustar and Sautea, Cylene, the two miners, and Bregor and Consina from Bhrudwo; Lenares, Torve and Duon from Elamaq; and Stella, Moralye, Kilfor and Sauxa from Faltha. Called from their homes to serve the Most High, pursued by a god bent on making the world her personal possession.

Stella had travelled most of her life, having left her childhood home of Loulea far, far to the west at the age of sixteen to travel across the face of the world. Since then she had been to every one of Faltha's Sixteen Kingdoms and many of the independent nations, as well as latterly to Dhauria itself, and to Bhrudwo. Yet she had never seen anything to compare with the sheer heart-lifting beauty she was confronted with as she gazed into the Zizhua Valley.

A broad, languid river lay quietly in its bed just below them. Fields of yellow grass lay to the left and right of the river, waving gently in a slight breeze. The golden glow of the fields was interrupted irregularly by tall, broad trees with spreading limbs more like feather dusters than the vegetation Stella was familiar with. In the middle distance rose a series of steep-sided hills, each a few hundred paces high; the closer hills green, the further hills purpling into the misty distance.

There was no sign of human habitation.

'It's beautiful,' Moralye said.

'That it is,' Kannwar responded. 'A thousand years ago I determined that this valley was the cradle of human civilisation, the site of the oldest remains yet found. We came from here, as far as I can tell. I placed a ban on new dwellings, and many of the valley's residents drifted away. Some still remain, but they live in such a secluded place they are unlikely to be vulnerable to the Daughter's machinations. '

'It would be a terrible thing to see this land devastated,' Stella said, entranced by the fields of gold and the hills of green and blue.

'Yes. But in a thousand years from now any harm done by a god will have been undone by nature and the passage of time. Yet anyone killed by the god in her quest for control of the world – or by us as we resist her – will still be dead.'

They wound down a barely discernible track into the valley, and were bathed by warm, sweet breezes as they walked. Though her heart ached for Robal, and for Conal, for Kannwar and especially for herself, Stella felt those breezes as a balm to her spirit.

'No matter what happens,' she whispered to Kannwar as they crossed the first of the golden fields, 'I'm glad I came here.'

He smiled in response, and she believed it to be genuine.

CHAPTER 15

THE WAGON

THE JOURNEY NORTH WAS, FOR Robal, an unpleasant one. He gradually came to realise that in deciding to pursue his desperate plan, he had exchanged a world of light for a dark tunnel. When he had allied himself to Stella, assisting her escape from Instruere, his life had taken on new meaning, expanding from the humdrum of soldierly service in a city that had not seen war in a generation, to a world-encompassing quest to defeat gods he'd never even known existed. He had traversed the Great Desert, visited fabled Dhauria, been drawn through the blue fire and walked the paths of Bhrudwo. He'd consorted with sorcerers, argued with emperors, witnessed miracles, stood in the House of the Gods – and fallen helplessly in love with an immortal queen. Enough to fill many pages in the history books.

He ought, therefore, to consider himself a lucky man. His fellows in the Instruian Guard would certainly regard him so. But with such an irresistible, deep love as his came jealousy, and it had eaten at him like a worm in an apple. First the absurd Conal had tried to claim his beloved, an action more ridiculous than threatening. But latterly his greatest fear had been realised: the Destroyer had exercised his fascination and hooked his queen. As a result, Stella was about to betray them all by joining herself with Kannwar's unquestioned corruption. This could not be allowed to happen.

That thought consumed him. Everything else about his daily

life since the moment Stella had called his bluff was mere mechanics: food, sleep, directions, all taken as required, all pleasure suspended, nothing more satisfying than dust and ashes. The world around him disappeared. He rode northwards through this dark tunnel, noticing nothing, his thoughts reduced to a few repetitive phrases that solidified his fears and grievances into something resembling truth.

This cannot be allowed to happen. She must be stopped.

He met people he recognised from the days after Corata Pit, people journeying southwards towards home, having abandoned their dangerous alliance with Robal's former companions. They told him of the Bhrudwan lord's change of plans, confirming what the young boy's father had explained the night he left Mensaya and set out slowly on the north road. 'Bound for Zizhua,' they said. 'A place of ill repute. A place of ghosts. A place too strange for people to live.' And some whispered: 'Stay away.'

Robal's resolve hardened as he heard these words. Wherever the Destroyer was taking his friends, it was clearly a place of secrecy and danger. A place, he feared, of betrayal.

Despite his inattention to the world around him, he was careful to exercise all the care over his cargo he had been warned about. The many precautions seemed foolish to him, especially after those hurried first few days when anxiety had overcome prudence, all cautions ignored, and the stuff might have failed at any moment. Not that he would have cared overmuch. Keep it covered by the sawdust, the miners of Corata Pit had told him. Make-sure it is kept out of direct sunlight and rain. Of course, they said to him, you must never park your wagon anywhere near a bonfire or other flame. A single spark . . . well, do we have to paint you a picture? Do not expose it to rough handling – preferably, one had said, holding up a handless arm as evidence, don't handle it at all. If you must handle it, wear the gloves we have provided you. Don't get any on your eyes, nose, lips or even on your skin, as your body will drink it in and it will fix inside you, causing terrible headaches and ague, possibly unto death.

A hundred fears, each one ready to claim the unwary.

The two dejected, ill-used donkeys recovered slowly over the long, slow days of the journey, and Robal was largely successful in keeping them in feed – when he remembered to feed them. The miners had sold him food as part of his cargo, and he shared it with his beasts: bran mash, groats, rotting vegetables and hard biscuits. No meat. It didn't matter. He ate a little of everything and tasted nothing. Their diet he supplemented with grass and other plants from the side of the road and adjacent fields, letting them eat whatever they chose.

He came back to something approximating life on the day a middle-aged, dwarfishly short farmer told him that a party of a dozen or more were only a few hours ahead: he'd sold them food that morning, apparently. Robal asked if there was another road to Zizhua from here, and was told there was not. But, the farmer added, for a fee he would show the barbarian a little-known stock route into the Zizhua Valley. He used it himself to graze his sheep there in the winter, where they did far better than on his own land. The farmer was breaking some law or other; Robal didn't listen to the man's blather. After the promise of coin the guardsman did not have, the farmer hoisted himself aboard the wagon and pointed across his fields.

Progress was painfully slow. 'It's a direct route,' the farmer insisted, or at least that was what Robal understood by the man's words: his accent was strange even for a Bhrudwan, and Robal, relatively new to the language, struggled to make sense of it.

'What you got in the wagon?' the man asked him.

'No questions about that,' Robal growled.

The farmer nodded wisely, no doubt assuming some sort of contraband.

'If you try to find out, I will cut off your hands,' Robal added, easing his sword a little way out of its scabbard.

The man nodded again, wide-eyed.

Unless the cargo takes your hands first, Robal added, but did not say it aloud. He could not afford any knowledge of the contents of the wagon to be noised about. For all he knew, any person he met – that fat woman kneeling by the river washing her clothes,

or this old man chivvying a flock of sheep along the dirt road –
could be one of the Destroyer's spies.

The farmer was a talkative man. He told Robal about his dutiful
wife and three lovely daughters, and about the collapse of his house
in the dreadful earthquake. He had buried his wife and two of his
daughters; the third had married a year ago and now lived far to
the north, where, the man hoped with oft-repeated fervour, she
had escaped the quake.

'I was to go north anyway,' he said. 'When I leave you, I will
take to the Malayu Road. I must tell her what happened to her
mother and sisters. The farm can look after itself until I return.'

The farmer didn't look particularly sorrowful at his loss, but
Robal couldn't really tell whether the man's constant smile was
a cultural thing or relief at finally being alone. Possibly the latter.
*Serves the fellow right if he settled for a less consuming love than
mine.*

On a crisp autumn morning they broached a high saddle and
looked across a wide valley. Fog hugged the ground, and at irregular
intervals steep, isolated hills poked through the pale shroud.

'Zizhua,' the farmer announced unnecessarily.

'Do you think we have arrived before my friends?'

'Oh yes,' the man said, smiling rather slyly. 'Your friends will
come soon, but not today. Time for you to make ready your surprise.
Bang bang bang!'

'What do you know about my intentions?' Robal asked sharply.
Not sharply enough.

'You have explosives in your wagon,' the man said, carrying on
blithely. 'I can smell them. When I am a boy I make fire-candles
for the great celebrations of Malayu. They make a distinctive smell.
Oh, do not worry,' he added, belatedly noting the anger on Robal's
face, 'I keep your secret to myself. Your plans are safe with me.'

'Indeed they are,' Robal said bitterly. 'Or, at least, they soon
will be.'

What was to prevent the man making his way straight to the
Destroyer and selling him Robal's secret? Perhaps the man would
demand more money from Robal to keep his secret. Whichever,

the man had to be silenced. This was too important to be left to chance.

Time slowed down as Robal watched himself draw his sword. He willed the blade to come out more swiftly, hoping he could do this before he had a chance to think, but his thoughts raced far ahead of his will. *Murderer*, they shrieked at him. *You should never have walked away from those keeping you on the straight path.*

One death to save thousands of lives, he told his traitorous thoughts. His sword came clear of its scabbard and he lifted it into the air.

'Please . . . my daughter . . .'

One death to protect yourself, his conscience corrected him, reminding him of another man who had made a similarly venal argument only a little while ago. A man who regularly played god with his empire, killing the few to save the many.

The tip of the blade parted the farmer's outstretched hands and slid easily through his quaking chest, grazing a rib but finding his heart.

Robal's fellow guardsmen would have applauded him. A pragmatic man of action, they would have said.

As the light went out in the farmer's eyes, eyes that would never now see his one remaining daughter, Robal's conscience disagreed with the guardsmen. *You have become a man who would take an innocent life out of expediency.*

The body slid off his blade and slumped sideways on the wooden seat. As it came to rest, time resumed its normal pace and Robal drew a huge, sobbing breath.

Some time later a man with a pale, sweaty face, a thin line for lips and eyes reddened with suppressed weeping, drove a large wagon down into the Zizhua Valley. The man barely noticed when the body at his side toppled from the wagon and landed softly in the grass.

That night the travellers rested in a grove of the strange feathery trees. Their branches quivered gently in the breeze, creating a susurration oddly pleasant to the ear.

'It appears the storm did not penetrate this far inland,' Kannwar remarked as they laid out their makeshift bedrolls. 'I am pleased they have survived: the lauren tree grows nowhere else but the Zizhua Valley.'

'Is the tree responsible for that aroma?' Stella asked him. The whole valley had smelled faintly of cinnamon, but the scent was much stronger here amidst the strange foliage.

'Oh, yes,' Kannwar said. 'Look!' He gestured to the base of the nearest tree.

There Stella saw a strange arrangement: a smaller tree, little more than a bush, had been cut back near to its roots perhaps a season or two ago, and the tender shoots had grown to an arm-span or more in length.

'Harvesters will strip these shoots of their bark,' explained Kannwar, 'then dry out the bark and roll it into strips. All the cinnamon in the world comes from this valley.'

'I often had cinnamon on my morning bran,' Stella said in wonder. 'I had no idea it came from this far away.'

'There are severe restrictions on how much can be harvested. I can remember receiving a delegation of Zizhua natives a few centuries ago, come to make an argument for increasing the volume of production. They wanted easier lives, they told me. I replied that if it was ease they wanted, they ought to leave the valley.'

Stella frowned. 'I suppose you had them put to death to impress on others the foolishness of questioning their lot.'

'Not at all,' Kannwar said. 'I acceded to their request, but asked that one young person a year be sent to Andratan for training. They saw that as a fair trade.'

'That's something, at least.'

'No, it isn't. None of the youngsters ever adapted to life outside the valley. They all missed their lauren trees, they claimed, and I was unable to command their loyalty. At that point there were a few deaths. The natives never learned of the true circumstances surrounding those deaths, so I would thank you not to mention them.'

She snorted. 'To travel around the world trying to make right

all the wrong you have done truly would be a task for an immortal.'
A thought struck her. 'We are to meet these natives?'

'Indeed. None but those born in Zizhua are allowed in the valley.
According to their gift, negotiated with me many years ago, the
inhabitants will seek to enforce this rule by slaying us. We should
expect a visit tomorrow morning, if not sooner.'

'Oh? Would you have told us this had I not asked?'

'I intend to sit up tonight and take every watch. There is, therefore,' he added complacently, 'no need to worry.'

'Every word from you serves to amplify my worries still further.'

'You?' Kannwar said. 'What do you have to worry about?'

She sighed, the weariness of nearly ninety years weighing
heavily. 'I left Instruere with one companion and another man
trailing me. That man is now a corpse animated by an inimical
god, wandering Bhrudwo to serve some dreadful purpose. My
guardsman has left me and I have no idea where he is or what
he intends. I'm frightened that they will meet and it will go well
for neither.'

She lifted her face to his. 'And I am currently enduring what
must be the strangest, most diffident courtship of all time. My
paramour seems to think that displaying himself at his worst is
somehow attractive to me. I suspect he hopes to impress me with
the small gleams of humanity he allows to shine through his deliberately brutal façade. I am not impressed.'

'Is there any point in his continuing then?'

'None. He knows full well that he horrifies me, yet if I wish to
risk becoming close to anyone without condemning myself to watch
that person wither and die, he is the only choice. He knows this
too. What he doesn't fully appreciate is that I am unsure whether
I would rather be his companion or be dead.'

'He would be flattered to hear that.'

'And yet I see occasional glimpses of Kannwar, the boy born
two thousand years ago, the hope of his generation, and he never
fails to thrill me.'

'Because you have already shared a life with the hope of another
generation and you cannot now settle for anything less. Poor Robal!

359

A worthy man driven mad by his intended's impossibly high standard.'

She nodded, acknowledging the point. Truly, she'd never thought of it in quite those terms. Leith had been the chosen tool of the Most High, just as this man had once nearly been, and now was. *I always was ambitious*, she thought, remembering her desire to leave Loulea and its limited supply of small-minded boys all those years ago. *Ambitious – and foolish.*

'So, you see, I feel responsible for the fates of Conal and Robal,' she continued. 'This adventure is bringing out the worst in good men, using them up. Can you not see that this piles guilt on my shoulders?'

'You ask me that? Guilt and I are close companions.'

'Yes, I imagine you are. The deaths you bring about in the present are real ones, while those you hope to save in the future are notional at best. It is no wonder you suffer.'

'Stella, Kannwar!' someone called. 'The food is ready!'

'Ah, joy,' said the Undying Man. 'More gruel.'

The Falthan queen drifted away, her false hand clasped tightly in the Destroyer's illusive palm. From behind the lauren tree Robal watched them go, then melted silently into the night.

The Zizhua came before dawn, brandishing knives and clubs. The party numbered no more than ten, at least to Stella's bleary eyes as she rose, stretched over-tired muscles and walked guardedly towards them. Kannwar had spun some kind of magical web around the camp in which the attackers had become ensnared like so many giant flies.

'I am the Oldest Man, Lord of Bhrudwo,' he said to them without preamble. 'I signed your gift many years ago. I have come to see how you are using it.'

'We still obey the terms, as you can see,' said one of the young men struggling in the web. Like the rest of the Zizhua he was curiously dressed, wearing a woollen waistcoat and skirt made of grass rather than the ubiquitous Bhrudwan jerkin and trousers. His face had been pierced with a number of decorations made from what appeared to be bone, lending him an altogether wild appearance, but he spoke the common Bhrudwan tongue well enough.

'Yes, I can see you still attempt to preserve the integrity of this land,' Kannwar said. 'Do you continue to produce cinnamon and osmanthus?'

'Release us from your snare and we will show you,' the young man replied.

Within the hour the travellers had broken camp and were striding through the grasslands, struggling to keep pace with the Zizhua. The waist-high grass glowed in the morning sun, giving off a piquant fragrance when crushed underfoot. *Sights and smells to enchant the senses*, Stella thought as they approached one of the steep-sided hills.

'Limestone,' Noetos said, pointing at the forest-cloaked hill before them. 'Such hills will be riddled with caves. I suppose that's why we see no habitations.'

The nearest Zizhua grunted, the closest these perfunctory people seemed to come to unnecessary conversation.

Kannwar nodded. 'A perfect place for civilisation to begin,' he said. 'A valley rich in soil and livestock, with an equable climate and ready-made shelter. I trust you can see why I insist that visitors are kept from this place, even at the cost of a few incautious lives.'

'And you have brought us here,' Stella said carefully, not wishing to alarm their hosts, 'because of the protection such a valley offers its inhabitants. '

Kannwar nodded again.

'It's so old,' said Lenares. 'Nowhere in the north have I found a place as old as Talamaq, but this valley feels far older.'

The party reached the base of the hill and was guided to a narrow, dark cleft in the rock. 'Welcome to our city,' the Zizhua spokesman said, clearly feeling the need for some small ceremony. 'Follow us closely. I do not want our people alarmed.'

Inside, the air was close but not unpleasant, bearing a faint perfume of cinnamon intermingled with wood smoke and some unidentifiable fragrance. *Perhaps this osmanthus Kannwar mentioned.*

The Zizhua lit torches and the darkness gave way to white walls, intricately fluted. The path was narrow and winding, leading downwards, reminding her of Bandit's Cave and the Hermit of Firanes who dwelled there. She had thought of neither for many years. A man, she remembered, who had turned from his calling. Was such rebellion a Falthan characteristic? Were the more regimented societies of Bhrudwo and Elamaq more likely to be obedient to their gods?

The sounds around them changed and the scent became stronger. A moment later they rounded a corner and stood on a shelf high above the city of Zizhua. The astonishing sight sent four of Stella's fingers into her mouth, a habit she thought she'd freed herself from decades ago.

Far below them hundreds of lamps made patterns on the floor of the vast cave. Streets and houses were illuminated by a yellow glow uncannily similar to that of the fields outside. Other lights, whiter and brighter, bobbed between the yellow lamps. There was enough light to illuminate the walls and roof of the cave, much further from them than Stella would have guessed given the size of the hill. These surfaces were adorned with riotous patterns, clearly carved by no human hand but by indescribably patient natural forces.

'Glorious,' she breathed, aware that the others had halted too, held in place as involuntarily as she was by the awe-inducing sight.

'Like something from a fairy tale,' Sauxa said.

'And where do you think fairy tales come from, if not from our earliest civilisation?' Kannwar asked them.

'It is difficult to imagine my ancestors living in this valley, perhaps in this very city,' Anomer said. 'Truly, I am sorry they ever left.'

'I am not,' said Cylene. 'I'd far rather be outside. The view is pretty, but these walls seem as though they are about to collapse on top of me.'

The Zizhua spokesman grunted again. 'Make your visit short,' he told her. 'Outsiders often find our cities uncomfortable places.'

'You do entertain visitors then,' Kannwar said, an edge on his voice.

'A few get this far, yes. They are either killed or forcibly escorted out of the valley, depending on who discovers them. And of course we must entertain your officials when they make their irregular visits to check our production, according to the terms of the gift. None is allowed to stay.'

'Good,' Kannwar said.

The journey down to the floor of the cave was not unlike that into Corata Pit, excepting of course the canopy of rock overhead and the never-ending variation of tortured limestone on the wall to their left. The whispers and smells of the city intensified as they descended.

'Can the god find us here?' Stella asked Kannwar.

'I hope not. I would not be pleased if this place was destroyed.'

'Nor its people,' she prompted.

'Nor its people, of course,' he added.

Its people proved hospitable enough, though they appeared to be acting under duress. They had clearly not forgotten the terms of their agreement with the Lord of Bhrudwo, and knew he could end their isolationism at any time by flooding the valley with eager immigrants. So the adults were civil without ever quite approaching pleasantness, and it was only the children who gawked in open horror at the strangers.

The travellers were met in front of a large building by the city Factor, a tall, cadaverous man without a single hair in evidence anywhere: not on his head, arms, legs – what Stella could see below his ceremonial robes, anyway – ears or nose. He uttered a few words of greeting, indifferently phrased and completely insincere, then beckoned them into the interior of the building.

'Huh,' Seren said, his eyes as round as saucers. 'These buildings were not built.'

'What d'you mean?' Mustar asked him. 'How else did they get here? They didn't grow them from seeds!'

'No,' said the miner. 'They carved out the roads and spaces between the houses, then the spaces within each house. This city is carven.' He ran his hands over the nearest wall. 'The craftsmanship is perfect.'

'Are you a worker of stone?' asked the Factor, the question seemingly torn out of him.

'I am a miner,' Seren said, 'as is my friend here. We work in a vast open-air quarry, have done all our adult lives. Nothing compared to this though; nothing at all.' He stood transfixed. 'I can feel the stone here in a way I've never felt stone before. Is that foolish? I'm not a religious man, but such work makes me wish I was.'

As though this praise was only to be expected, the Factor nodded, but Stella could see the corners of his eyes crinkling in hastily stifled approval. Of course, the dolt Noetos nearly undid all the goodwill generated by his liegeman.

'It's just stone, for Alkuon's sake,' he said. 'What are you talking about?'

The Factor scowled. One of the men who had come for them cleared his throat, and the Factor nodded to him. The man spoke, addressing his words to Noetos.

'True builders know the difference between stone cut from the ground and stone still part of the earth. Your companion senses it without understanding it. You will never know what we mean. This city is the unceasing work of many generations, stretching back thousands of years. Rather than building something human on the earth, we have cut away what we do not need, revealing the hidden strength and power of the rock. Thus we have made caves within the cave. This is not cut and dressed stone. It is the bedrock of the earth.'

Clearly the words impressed Seren and his fellow miner, but they meant little to Stella. *So every man feels about his long-lived-in home: parochialism turns mere quirkiness into something sacred, unique, more to be prized than that found in other places.*

Servants brought food and served it on a long stone table carved out of the floor. Or, better to say the rock had been hollowed out, leaving a table, immovable chairs and an intricately decorated surface under their feet. The seats were cool but comfortable, their surfaces polished into comfortableness by the posteriors of thousands of previous feasters, no doubt. The Factor headed the table, and

Kannwar was given the honoured place at his right. To the Factor's left sat his family: wife, three daughters of marriageable age and a younger son. The boy looked sufficiently different from the girls, and was at least fifteen years younger; the Factor's wife seemed little older than the eldest daughter. A second marriage then. The rest of the places were taken by the travellers and three of the guards.

The young boy gave the blessing. In a high, sweet voice, and under the proud eye of his father, he thanked the god for keeping them another day intact, for providing sustenance and – here he hesitated, before extemporising – for bringing their exalted visitors to share their table. 'In the name of El Kuhon,' he finished.

Out of the corner of her eye Stella saw Noetos start violently, while beside him his children raised their heads, as did the others from the Fisher Coast. She had no idea what had caused this reaction, and as no one passed comment, she let it be.

The food tasted heavenly. Partly, Stella surmised, because of the monotony of the simple fare they had been forced to subsist on for many weeks; but beyond this explanation there seemed such a delicacy in the blend of spices, now cooling, now firing her palate, far greater than she had experienced even in the high feasts of Instruere. Oddly, there were no plates: they were expected to serve themselves, placing the food directly on the table in front of them. Stella supposed it would be sluiced down once the meal was finished, a most practical idea. The seemingly flat table had slight hollows in its surface and the juices from the food contained themselves close to each person's meal.

'Nice grub,' Sauxa said, ladling more food from a delicate stone bowl. His son grunted agreement.

A gentle lassitude began to creep over Stella. So many months in motion, day after day walking until her feet blistered or, occasionally, bled. Burned by the sun, soaked by the rain, subjected to storms natural and unnatural, witness to violence and death. It felt good to be somewhere safe, a place where some of the good things of life could be enjoyed. She sighed, wishing she could stay in this city for a while, not caring for the moment whether she met with the approval of the locals, able to forget for a time the hole in the world that surely lurked outside.

She desired to throw herself into selfish reflection and ease, but her damnable conscience would not let her. Once, seventy years ago, she had left her Company because of what she believed was true love, only to be betrayed. Robal had, it seemed, done a similar thing though in his case he ran from it rather than to pursue it. How could she not wish his return? How could she think of ease when he no doubt suffered confusion and loss, alone in a strange land? It seemed she was more selfish—

Shouting outside, the raised voices carrying an uncomfortable booming quality in such a confined space. The noise drew closer and two men burst in on them.

'Factor,' one said, 'there's a man on a wagon. A stranger. Chen brought him in. Says he wants to speak to the Undying Man.'

'Conal,' said Stella, her mouth going dry. Two other voices – Kannwar and Noetos – said the same name. The travellers looked at each other, horrified.

Stella stared at Kannwar. 'I thought we were safe here.'

'As did I.'

The Factor stood. 'Who is this man who calls for you, lord, and why does he frighten you so?'

'Not who, but what. He is a dead man, a corpse, made into a host for the Daughter of the Most High, our enemy. Tell your people to take shelter where they may. I do not know what is about to happen.'

The man hissed. 'Had we known you were pursued, we would not have invited you into our secret heart.'

'You had no choice,' Kannwar said tersely. 'Send runners. Get your people off the streets. Do it now. I do not wish to be responsible for their deaths.'

White-faced, the guards vanished in several directions, their swift passage disturbing the yellow glow-globes set into the walls. Shadows flickered all around the room, giving an ominous cast to every face, then settled again.

In the silence Stella could hear a man crying: 'Kannwar! Undying Man! Destroyer! Come outside!'

'She is desperate,' Noetos said, 'to risk all in this way.'

'That's not Umu,' Lenares said.

'Who else could it be?' Kannwar said. 'I'm going out there. Stay inside, everyone, until I call for you.'

He rose, easing his long limbs from underneath the table, and strode to the door. As soon as he had gone from sight, everyone of the travellers stood, united in disobedience, and followed him.

Things had not gone well for Robal since he'd taken the farmer's life. His sour luck was a punishment of sorts, he supposed; had he kept the man alive, the farmer might have helped him understand this strange, accursed valley. No roads, no visible tracks, no houses, just seemingly pristine emptiness. Having spent years on the Central Plains of Faltha, themselves grasslands – though vaster by far than these – the guardsman could not imagine such a valuable resource as this valley lying fallow. *There must be some explanation*, he told himself, and again wished he'd not yielded to the frightened impulse to shut the farmer up.

His self-control deserted him entirely when, some time after dark, he stumbled across the travellers' campsite. He had not been able to resist approaching the camp during the night, listening to their conversations and trying to discern their plans, but later wished he had not. He'd heard intimacies to sicken his stomach, belittling words from his own beloved queen's mouth. *Fool, fool, fool*. Everything had gone wrong since he'd left Stella's side, unable to bear any more of her consorting with the Destroyer.

Worse, the delay meant he found himself exposed in the middle of the tall grass plains as the sun rose, easy for the natives to spot. And spot him they had: one moment he sat on the wagon, chivvying his donkeys to make progress towards the nearest of the impressive green hills; the next he was surrounded by club-wielding men who had simply appeared from nowhere. He might perhaps have killed one or two of them before they beat him to the ground had he struck immediately, but had he done so his

367

plans would have ended in failure and the farmer would have died in vain.

He couldn't stop thinking about the moment his blade had entered the farmer's chest. It was as though the man's frightened soul had poured out of the wound, flowed along the blade and entered his own body. He could feel it now: a dark weight dragging him down, making it hard for him to think. Not a religious man, no . . . but his mother's teachings crowded into his already cluttered mind, setting his knees shaking.

He sincerely hoped her stories were not true. And that if they were, he would never find out.

Two of the natives climbed onto the wagon, taking a seat either side of him. 'Ride on, stranger,' said one, holding a knife to his ribs, while the other relieved him of his sword.

'What do you want from me?' Anger rather than fear animated his voice. To have come so close only to be thwarted now!

'We have sent men to surround your friends. We will leave none of them alive, as is our gift from the Lord of Bhrudwo. You we will spare for a time. You will appear before our Factor to explain your purpose in entering Zizhua Valley.'

Robal laughed. 'You think you are going to ambush my companions?' he said with as much scorn as he could manage. 'You won't harm a hair on any of their heads. They are a group of powerful magicians and soldiers, led by the Undying Man himself. You had better look to your men!'

At that the two men fell to jabbering in their own language for a few moments, then turned back to him.

'Ride on,' directed the man with the knife. 'You will still make your explanation to the Factor.'

'Very well,' said Robal. *Be patient and wait for the opportunity. If there is any justice in the world, it will present itself.*

They had led him on a long circuit around the hill, halting before the wide entrance to a cave hidden in the shadows. There they exchanged information with other strangely clad men that Robal took for scouts, dressed in colours to blend into the landscape. The donkeys had not wanted to go inside, but the men struck them with large feather-like sticks and into the darkness they went. It was like entering a children's tale. A city under the earth! His sleep-ridden eyes could make little sense of the vision blurring in front of him. Yellow lights, white lights, pale stone walls, massive carvings, a multitude of people calling out to him, some obviously not friendly.

'We have brought your friends here,' said the knife-man, and Robal felt his luck turning for what he hoped was the final time.

'They're here? Can I meet them? No . . . not yet.'

'You are in no position to ask any favours. Do you not understand? You will be asked questions, after which we will have no further use for you.'

Robal smiled at the man. 'Do you think I am a fool? Your men were supposed to kill my companions, yet brought them here to your secret city instead. That tells me they discovered the truth of what I said to you.' He'd seen the knife-man talking to another fellow as they descended to the city, no doubt being told of what had happened when the natives had confronted the Undying Man. Robal didn't know exactly what had transpired, of course, but he could guess. 'The Lord of Bhrudwo goes exactly where he wants. I am his trusted companion, with my own abilities as yet unrevealed.' There, let them consider that half-truth. 'I wish to speak with my master immediately,' he finished.

More jabbering. 'Very well,' the man said finally. 'Your wagon is blocking the street. We will find you a place to store it, and inspect the cargo as our gift requires us to. Then we will alert your master to your presence.'

Robal nodded, determination replacing doubt in his mind. 'Don't take too long,' he warned them.

They found him a largely empty building the size of an Instruian warehouse, and he urged the two nervous animals through the wide door and into the vast space. Oddly, he felt more uncomfortable in here than he had 'out in the open,' as he'd already begun thinking of the cave itself. Two men remained, tasked with inventory.

'Be careful with my cargo,' Robal warned them. 'It is special material commissioned at great expense by the Lord of Bhrudwo himself. He is most anxious that not a single stick is damaged.'

'Oh,' said the younger of the men, clearly impressed. 'Sticks? What do they do?'

'They are tools designed to help carve the rock more efficiently,' Robal extemporised. 'Small explosions, cracking the rock and making work easier.' He waved his hands around vaguely.

Both men broke into smiles. 'We have heard of such material!' the older man breathed. 'I am surprised the Factor and his elders have allowed it in. The more progressive among us have long argued to be allowed to acquire some, even if only on a trial basis. I am pleased the Lord of Bhrudwo has seen fit to respond to our petition.'

Robal grinned at them. Luck, luck, his luck had finally come good. But what was keeping the Undying Man?

'Wait here,' he said to the two men, 'and don't touch anything.'

Once Robal had found out where the travellers had been housed, he'd called out the Destroyer. Of course, the man hadn't realised he'd been called out, not in the sense of a one-on-one duel; he had, Robal guessed, suspected nothing. He strode out of the building willingly enough, nothing more than his usual wariness on his face.

The guardsman had considered a hundred different scenarios for this moment, each more elaborate – and unlikely – than the last. A master of deception, his intended victim would see through anything complicated with ease; so Robal had decided to use the simplest of subterfuges.

'Need your help with something,' he said. He tilted his head as though glancing behind the Destroyer to look worriedly at Stella and the others. 'Not for the women to see,' he added, rubbing his hands down the front of his jerkin, as though wiping blood from them.

'What have you found?' the man asked, clearly curious. He turned and held up a hand. 'I'll be but a moment,' he called to his companions. 'Wait for me.'

The two men entered the warehouse. The wagon was twenty paces away.

'Good to see you again, Robal,' said the Destroyer affably. 'Stella misses you.'

'Does she now.' The guardsman winced at the degree of bitterness revealed in those three words. *Mustn't do anything to make him suspicious . . .*

As part of the purchase paid for by the sliver of huanu stone, the miners had given him a slip of valuable sulphur paper – and had coached him carefully on how it ought to be used. Robal had made his own modification to the paper, an addition, no doubt, of which the miners would not have approved. He drew the lead-weighted paper from the inside pocket of his jerkin, then swiftly peeled the gum-stuck papers apart.

Five.

'Show my lord the contents of the wagon,' Robal said to the two Zizhua men.

Four.

The Destroyer frowned, no doubt sensing that something wasn't quite right.

Three.

But he shrugged and strode over to the wagon.

Two.

One of the men stripped the oilskin covering away from Robal's cargo.

One.

A young boy's voice broke the silence. 'Donkeys! Donkeys!'

Every head swung in the direction of the doorway.

Far too late to stop now.

Robal lobbed the paper into the back of the wagon, heaved himself backwards towards the nearest pillar and took what shelter he could. He knew he might live, he knew he might not . . .

CHAPTER 16

LIFE WITHOUT END

EAGER TO SPEAK TO ROBAL, hopefully to clear the air between them, Stella had taken one step onto the marble road when a sharp cry jerked her head up.

The world exploded.

She glimpsed an instant of blurring. The pale building opposite her shivered, then dissolved, bursting upwards and outwards. An indivisible moment later – moving far too swiftly for her mind to acknowledge, let alone her body to react – something solid struck her squarely in her belly, hurling her backwards into the wall behind her. Bones shattered, blood spurted; but, though consciousness faded, it did not vanish completely. For an intolerably long moment, Stella had nothing but dread of what she was about to feel.

Immortality did not mitigate pain. If anything, it indirectly amplified her senses. Seventy years of suffering had not succeeded in inuring her to agony. Instead, it had taught her that she was not to be afforded the blessed relief of unconsciousness granted to others, to mortals. She waited for the pain to arrive.

It arrived.

Curse it, it did. Such pain. A hundred messages shrieking in her brain all at once as crushed limbs reported their various agonies. For a time she was drawn into a silent scream.

Only when the initial wave of pain had rolled over her did she receive the report she really wanted. Her eyes sprang open – to a pale smear. Her ears remained unhearing. She waited, enduring the unendurable because she had no choice, but the smear failed to resolve into anything that made sense. The world continued to blur, shake, fall apart. Dust filled the air. Rocks crashed to the ground in uncanny silence, bouncing or shattering, eerily like snowfall. She waited, waited for the world to settle, to regain its meaning, but the blurring and shaking increased.

A face intruded on this panorama of uncertainty. Kilfor. Saying something to her, inaudible. The horrified look on his face as he cast an eye over her confirmed the messages her body continued to send to her, telling her everything she needed – and feared – to know.

'The others?' she asked him. Or tried to ask: she had no idea if the words came out of her mouth. If she still had a mouth.

Dare she try to stand? Even move? Success seemed laughably unlikely.

Before she could make the attempt, something white landed on the street in front of them, exploding into a blizzard of knife-sharp shards. She felt a few of them hit her, sink into her, dull thuds adding mere increments to her pain. One took her in the left eye: vision was replaced by yellow whorls.

Kilfor took the brunt of the stone rain, falling to the ground in a red haze.

She couldn't move to help him. She didn't need to. There was no point. Even through one eye it was obvious that the man was dead.

He did live, apparently, but by the god-cursed torture in and around his waist – and the numbness below – Robal immediately wished he had not.

A price worth paying if the trap had worked.

The pillar had collapsed on top of him, pinning him. He lay staring into a cloud of dust, covered in something warm, sticky and metallic. Blood.

Whose?

His enemy lay beside him, torn asunder beyond any hope of

repair, his blood pulsing from multiple wounds in already-decreasing fountains.

Oh, oh, *oh*.

Robal lay there, pinned, unable to move, irretrievably broken, undoubtedly dying – and covered in the Destroyer's immortal blood.

He licked his lips. Stretched his tongue as far as it would go. *Not enough. The Lord of Fear drained a chalice full of Stella's blood. I need more.*

In utter desperation he forced one of his hands to move, then his arm. Placed it under the Destroyer's neck, ripped open in a gaping red grin. Waited as the blood oozed into his palm. Then brought it carefully, carefully to his lips. Swallowed it down without gagging.

More, more. More! Hurry!

His arm snaked back to the wound, shaking now with the effort, spilling half the red harvest. Three more times his hand made the journey, until the man's throat ceased its bleeding, denying him any more of the world's most precious liquid.

His mind whirled in an agony of fear and hope. Had he done enough? Would the miracle blossom within him? Would it be enough to give Stella another choice? Certainly something, some new thing, had begun to take shape in his veins . . . burning . . .

The vast cavern shook as though suffering its own agonies. High above them millennia-old rock formations, formed with infinite patience one small grain at a time, were shaken loose and plunged to the cave floor, crashing into streets, houses and people who had run into the open to escape collapsing buildings. Each formation smashed into a thousand deadly pieces, shredding anyone unfortunate enough to be close by.

As the groans subsided and the shaking diminished, the natives of Zizhua City began to venture from their homes. Many of those unlucky enough to live within a hundred paces of the warehouse had died, or were in the process of dying, whilst a random selection of those living further away had been killed by falling debris, the collapse of their homes due to unseen fractures in their walls or roof, or had been choked to death by the unrelenting dust. None within five hundred paces had heard anything after the initial blast, and therefore did not breathe a relieved sigh as the sounds of tortured stone gradually faded. Nor did they start with fear when enormous spears of rock continued to crash to the ground among them.

Those more than a thousand paces away from the explosion heard as well as saw the dust settle with something akin to a sigh, as though content with what had happened. The best – or worst – view of all was afforded those travelling down into the cavern from one of the entrances, though more than one of them was knocked from the path by the bucking rock to add his screaming form to the rain of projectiles plummeting into the city.

A deep crater had replaced the warehouse. Only one wall and a few pillars remained. In a wide circle around the centre of the blast lay the ruins of homes and other buildings. Small figures began to scurry from one ruin to the next, bending over unmoving shapes, then in most cases abandoning them.

After a full minute's silence, as eerie a thing as anyone there had ever heard, the wailing began.

Stella awoke to her old friend, suffering. She knew this pain though, this old friend, this old enemy, for what it was: the pain of healing. Already her limbs had regained some of their movement. Her left eye seemed open again, seeing as through a broken window, but seeing nonetheless. Beside her was a bloodied stone chip, lying where it had fallen from her face. Her immortal curse, it seemed, was determined to repair her.

But what of Kannwar? He had been in the warehouse when it had exploded. It had been his cry she'd heard. Whose doing had the explosion been? No magic had been involved, she was willing to swear it before any tribunal in the land – and, depending on their hosts, it might come to that. Had it been some kind of ghastly accident? Was this some trick of Umu's? Had something Kannwar had been attempting gone wrong? What had Robal wanted with him? Had the two men survived?

She doubted that last. She doubted it very much.

The sound of sobbing came to her ears. She turned her neck slowly, slowly, to see Sauxa kneeling by the sodden form of his son, weeping.

'Why you?' he was whispering, or at least that seemed to be the phrase playing on his lips. 'Why not me?'

Stella.

She shook her mind clear of the imagined voice and placed a shaking hand on Sauxa's shoulder. He hissed in fright, jerked his head towards her, nodded once and turned away. His face was a rictus of grief.

'He saved me, Sauxa,' Stella tried to say. 'He absorbed all the shrapnel that had been heading towards me.'

But perhaps she still hadn't made any noise, or maybe he, like her, had been deafened by the blast. He made no indication he had heard her words. *The true act of kindness would have been to let the rock shards slice me to pieces.* Though maybe even then she would not have been able to die.

Enough people have died. Enough misery. Enough heartbreak. Enough! She screwed her eyes tightly shut against the dreadful sights to the right and left of her.

Stella. Not an imagined voice at all. *Send someone to retrieve me. One of our companions. Noetos. He's the only one I really trust.*

His flat, pain-riddled voice raised a thousand questions, and his request raised a thousand more. *Alive at least.* She'd think about the rest of it later.

She reached up a red hand and pulled Sauxa down to whisper in his ear, relaying Kannwar's message. He nodded and left, a broken man.

Gentle hands eventually lifted her to her feet and through the silence she heard muffled words: 'Lucky, this one. The blast must have missed her. Or poor Kilfor took the blow.' They would never think of the restorative powers of immortal blood. Never realise she should be dead. At rest.

'Kannwar,' she said, naming her secret fear. They could not lose him; *she* could not lose him. 'Kannwar. Is he all right?'

'I am here,' he said, right at her elbow. It was his strong arm under hers, supporting her as she hobbled down the street, her rapid recovery continuing but not yet complete.

Her heart warmed.

'Robal?'

'You know no mortal could have survived that blast,' came Kannwar's sonorous voice.

Oddly phrased, that. As though avoiding a question he wanted left unasked. She was far too tired to pursue the matter. She would grieve for her recalcitrant guardsman later. So much would come later.

'The others?'

'Seren the miner is badly injured. He's lost an arm and his leg may well go the same way. He and the two fishermen, Mustar and Sautea, were standing under a roof that gave way. The other two have less serious injuries.'

'Can you heal them?'

'My lady, I barely have the strength to heal myself. But if you wish it, I will try.'

'I do wish it.'

'Very well.' He bowed his head, as though reaching inwards to gather strength.

'Any deaths?'

'I'm coming to that. Kilfor is dead, as is Tumar. The girl Moralye is near death and is not expected to survive. Both Arathé and Anomer have suffered internal injuries of some kind. The rest of us sustained cuts and bruises.'

'Heal the most badly wounded,' Stella said. 'The Most High surely hasn't brought them this far to be killed by some stratagem of the Daughter.'

'It wasn't . . . The children of Noetos believe they can heal themselves. They are drawing on some substantial power; I can feel it, they acknowledge it, but will not explain from where it comes. They will offer succour to as many as they can.'

377

'And you, Kannwar? How did you survive?'

'Just as you did, my dear. Courtesy of our shared curse.'

They exchanged grimaces, those two cheaters of death, and understood each other completely.

'My wife died,' said the Factor of Zizhua, his voice muffled by the intervening wall. Robal had to strain his ears to make out the words. 'She survived the explosion but was struck down by a falling rock-spear.'

'We are sorry,' one of the travellers responded.

Anomer, Robal thought it might have been. One of the young men, certainly. The guardsman wished he could call out, somehow attract their attention, but even though his friends were in the next room he could not make himself heard. Not with this gag bound tightly over his mouth. Not with the restraints fastening him securely to the stone bench, a bench now fractured and covered in stone fragments that gouged into his back whenever he struggled.

And struggle he did, for all he was worth, wriggling his arms and legs partly in an attempt to loosen his restraints, partly involuntarily in response to the incredible burning power pouring through his veins. Something had happened to him, there could be no doubt. The immortal blood had worked. Why else was he still alive? How else could he now feel his legs? Though he strongly wished he could not.

'My son and heir also died in the blast,' the Factor added, as though it was of little consequence.

Robal knew better, could hear the anguish in the words. He himself had seen the boy, his bright little face happy at the sight of the two donkeys, stumbling in his eagerness as he rushed into the warehouse just as Robal's sulphur paper ignited.

'We also have lost people dear to us,' the young man continued. Anomer, most certainly. Why was he the spokesman? How many of Robal's friends had died? How could he have miscalculated the extent of the blast damage so severely? Had there been some enclosure effect, the confined space forcing the explosion into something more violent than the Corata miners had warned him to expect?

'Only three,' the Factor said, and the bitterness and deep anger in his voice could not be missed. 'You lost only three. And your magicians healed your injured. We have suffered far greater loss.'

No doubt from the tone of voice that the Factor wished the toll amongst the travellers had been much higher.

'You are certain Robal brought the explosives with him in the wagon?'

'Oh, yes. Such items have been banned from this province on pain of torture and death. The use of such material is tantamount to the abrogation of everything the Zizhua have achieved. So argue the stalwarts among us. Some of our younger members desire explosives to make their task easier, but I have no doubt their ardour has been somewhat reduced by these events.'

Dry, reserved, almost uncaring, that voice. But Robal was not fooled. An uncaring man would not have had men fetch Robal from under the pillar, would not have had him confined to a bedchamber. Bound and gagged. Prepared.

'Your friend Robal died in the blast,' the Factor said. 'We are sorry we cannot provide you with a body: it was . . . ah . . . deconstituted. As was that of my son.' The steely self-control slipped a little at that last word.

Robal renewed his struggles, trying to cry for help, but could make no headway against his restraints. Supernatural life did not confer supernatural strength, it seemed, only supernatural pain.

'Kilfor died also,' said a voice Robal knew only too well.

Kilfor? Ah, my friend! What have I done? I didn't intend . . . But he no longer had the stomach for fooling himself. Of course he would have exchanged Kilfor's life for the Destroyer's. No one was above sacrificing in order to see the Destroyer dead. He ceased his struggling as much as he was able to, not wanting his friend's father – and for many years more of a father to Robal than his real father had been – to know he was alive. He had no doubt what the old man would say, how his lips would curl, just what form the well-earned curses would take. Sauxa would never understand. *Oh, Kilfor.*

'How does your city fare?'

Stella. Robal's heart contracted in his breast at her voice. He knew with absolute certainty how she would regard him now, and the thought burned him more deeply than the tainted blood in his veins.

'Hundreds have died. A large section of the cavern roof collapsed, obliterating an entire suburb. None there survived.'

'I was nearby,' a woman said, her voice husky with emotion perhaps, or the astringent dust. 'We heard the explosion, the ground shook and we all fell over, and then directly above us the roof detached and began to fall towards us. We ran, my lord, we ran screaming. I could see I was safe, but others behind me, they . . .' she faltered, 'they stopped running and put their arms around each other. I . . . they . . . I didn't see anything else.'

She'd seen it all, Robal had no doubt. He could see it now, in his mind's eye: the vast slab of rock falling, the people running, stumbling, hurling themselves forward, and at the last, as the inevitability of their deaths became clear, raising their arms in futile defence.

The conversation droned on for a while, then the travellers' voices drifted away. Or perhaps Robal himself drifted away, lost in a labyrinth of pain and regret. Whichever, he came to full alert when a voice spoke beside his ear.

'I am still alive. You failed. In every possible sense, you failed.'

Eyes widening in shock, the guardsman tried to turn his head, an instinctive and unnecessary action. He knew whose voice had spoken the words.

'You intended to set off the explosive charge.' Not a question. 'It was no accident. You sought to destroy me. Instead you destroyed yourself.'

Robal issued a muffled denial. The Destroyer sighed and removed the cloth from his mouth.

'No, I . . . I . . .' No use denying it. 'Yes. I wanted you dead.'

'You wanted me dead from the moment you realised Stella was seeking me out,' said the Destroyer, his face coming into view as he walked around the bench on which Robal lay. His perfect face, his unmarked face, below which there was no sign of the gaping wound from which Robal had drunk his blood. 'You were never content to be her servant. Having already been raised above your ability by your appointment to the Instruian Guard, you then thought to elevate yourself further by applying yourself to your queen. And you accuse me of arrogance.'

'I love her!' Robal shouted. 'I sought to protect Faltha from more of your lies!'

'Ah, a hero, are you? Problem is, in order to be a hero you have to succeed, and you did not.'

'I have your blood. I'm immortal now. You can't kill me!'

'Yes, I'd assumed you'd helped yourself. Fool. You really haven't thought this through, Robal. Stella can't kill herself, true, because to do a thorough job of it she needs assistance. Assistance I would provide without blinking should she ask me for it. On the other hand, there are many willing assistants waiting eagerly for the chance to aid in achieving your death.'

'How? How can I die? How can you kill an immortal?'

'There are so many ways. You tried one that came distressingly close to succeeding. The best way of killing an immortal is to separate his or her body into non-viable parts so small as to render reconstitution impossible. Blow you up. Cut you up into little pieces. Burn you. Dissolve you in acid. Even something as crude as decapitation will do it. Or at least I assume it will, unless you have the capacity to grow a new head. You see, the blood you have stolen from me has within it the Water of Life, which has the power to preserve life and the power to *transform* life. The power to preserve begins immediately: it comes from the Water of Life, the power you can feel burning you from the inside out. You have to do nothing except endure, and avoid accidents, to live for ever. The more important power, however, is the power to transform. This the ancients called the Fire of Life. It sets something of the essence of the Most High within you. My study suggests it provides a variety of benefits. However, these benefits mature only with time and training. One of the crucial benefits is to prevent those accidents that might shorten your life.

'Do you see your problem? You have the capacity to live for ever, but, as yet, you cannot harness your latent power to avoid death. Something of a conundrum for a man chained as you are, helpless in the house of your enemies.'

The Destroyer smiled, and Robal knew he had not misjudged the man after all. He was implacably evil. As what was about to happen to him sank into his mind, Robal's bowels turned to water.

'You have heard the man's confession,' said the Destroyer. 'You may now read the charges against him.'

Six Zizhua natives clad in long black robes – mourning robes, Robal supposed – strode into the room.

'You tricked me!' Robal cried. 'That was no trial!'

'You tricked yourself,' came the Destroyer's answer. 'You are a distressingly simple person whose stupidity and short-sightedness has caused a great deal of pain. Be assured that this pain will be redeemed in full upon your person.'

As the Factor led his fellow Zizhua to stand in a line facing him, Robal felt himself drift into a waking nightmare. His vision seemed to triple: as well as the Zizhua, he could see the past, the foolish past, where he plotted the fall of an immortal for what now appeared to be all the wrong reasons; and he could see the future and all the ways the Zizhua might revenge themselves on him. Tears of sheer terror began to roll down his cheeks.

The Factor spoke. 'You, stranger, have confessed to the crime of regicide, the attempted assassination of our lord. That in itself is a capital offence, the punishment for which we naturally cede to the Undying Man to be carried out at a time and place of his choosing.'

The Undying Man nodded sombrely. 'In turn, Factor, I cede my rights back to you, judging you the more wronged.'

'Where's Stella? She wouldn't stand for this!' Robal shouted. 'Stella! Stella!'

'Cut out the prisoner's tongue,' said the Factor calmly.

'No! I'll be quiet!'

'Do you promise to remain quiet during the rest of the proceedings?'

'Yes! Yes!' Robal panted his relief.

'Excellent.' The Factor nodded contentedly, then fastened bleak eyes on him. 'Cut it out anyway.'

Robal's pleading made no difference. They loosened his bonds a fraction, rolled him onto his side and forced his jaws apart. His pleading ended as efficient hands captured and held his tongue, stretching it out so the fellow with the sword could reach it more easily.

The moment of pain in itself was but a small addition to that coursing within him, but the loss of his tongue was, Robal knew as he leaned over to spit out the blood, the loss of his last weapon of consequence.

'Never mind, Robal,' said the Destroyer. 'As you mature into your immortal gift you might learn enough about the Fire of Life to grow a new one. It's a shame, however; you're unlikely to live that long.'

The Factor resumed his summation of Robal's deeds as though he'd not been interrupted. 'Further, stranger, you stand accused of causing the deaths of many hundreds of Zizhua, effected as a consequence of the ignition of explosives as part of your assassination attempt. Because these deaths were accidental, you will avoid, in theory, the ultimate punishment. However, because they were the side effects of an assassination attempt, each death is treated in law as though it was itself an assassination. Therefore you are sentenced to as many deaths as there were deaths among us.'

Ridiculous, Robal thought as he spat blood from his maimed mouth. *I can only die once.* Except a dark suspicion had already begun to form in the back of his mind. *No. Pray Most High they haven't thought . . . they won't . . . of course they won't.*

'The first death,' the Factor went on, 'was that of my son and heir, Shan, whom we nicknamed Sunrise, the light of my eyes. In his eight years of life he pleased everyone he came in contact with. He was unfailingly polite, always respected his elders and worked most diligently at home and at his studies. In time he would have made an exceptional administrator, unencumbered by the suspicious mind and hard heart most administrators are necessarily cursed with. Sadly, his heart was too trusting and he blundered into the middle of your plot without ever realising he'd encompassed his own death.'

'I saw him,' said the Destroyer. 'His face beamed with happiness as he ran towards the donkeys. You saw him too, Robal, but you did not stay your hand. You touched off the explosion, turning the boy into a red mist.' The gathered Zizhua groaned in unison at the words. 'You judged his life as worth less than my death.'

You do that all the time! Robal wanted to cry out, but even thinking of speech hurt his mouth.

'You slew my son,' said the Factor of Zizhua. 'In doing so you ripped my heart out. Therefore I slay you.'

He took up the guardsman's own sword, only slightly bent despite the power of the explosion, and walked over to where Robal lay.

'This first death will be a simple one,' the man continued, and thrust the blade through Robal's ribs and into his heart.

Tired, sore and sick to her stomach, Stella stumbled through the outer suburbs of the city, her fellow travellers striding along briskly some way ahead of her. She had begun to shake some time back, some sort of delayed reaction to what might very well have been her death, she supposed, or to the memory, constantly replayed, of Kilfor dissolving in front of her. The sights and sounds of the city added their contribution to her miasma.

Robal's dead, she thought. *That charming, funny, brave, perpetually indignant blockhead is dead.* Funny, she had not realised how final, how irrevocable, death was until this moment. Leith's death had set this deadly adventure in motion, but subsequent events had occupied her mind. She'd grieved for him, yes, but had not dwelled on his absence. Robal, though, nestled like sorrow and failure in her chest.

That was the difference, she realised. She had been responsible for Robal, had miscalculated the strength of his feeling for her, and had lost him. More than that: if she was interpreting the signs correctly, she might have inadvertently cost many innocent people their lives.

But I couldn't have given him what he wanted. Could I?

Knowing the cost as she now did, of course she could have. Would have, to prevent this awful tragedy, without demur. But it was too late now – and she knew, better than anyone else alive perhaps, save the Undying Man himself, how futile were self-recriminations. *If Robal brought those explosives into the city with the intention of killing Kannwar, he was the cause of all this. Not me. Not my spurning of his heart.*

She would have appreciated the time to examine the scene of his death more closely, if only to pay her respects to him, to Kilfor, Tumar and to the many Zizhua people killed. But the Factor had ordered them out of the city forthwith – oh, it had been phrased most politely, but she had been a ruler and knew a command when she heard one – and they had not been allowed even to inter Kilfor's poor remains in the catacombs that served the city as a cemetery.

Sauxa placed a shaking hand on her shoulder. 'My lady? Are you well?'

'Oh, Sauxa, no, I am not well,' she said, her voice a raw wound. 'We've lost him, lost them both. I'm so sorry.'

'Aye.' The man blinked twice, as near to tears as he'd ever likely get. 'Reckon you had a small part to play in that, if my eyes still see. I know you're thinking about it, my lady, as am I. But these deaths, they're not about us, not yet. Let's wait until we've put some distance between us and the dead, and then perhaps we can decide what our responsibilities are, and what we ought to do about it. In the meantime, content yourself that they made their choices: Robal to taste the sour fruit of anger; Kilfor to give his life in saving yours. Kind of balances out, wouldn't you say?'

Stella said nothing to correct his impression of his son's last moments. *If it helps the old fellow to think of Kilfor as a hero, let him so think. And perhaps he was.*

'Anyway, they sent me back here to fetch you. The Zizhua guards are tellin' us to hurry. Eager to get back to the city, if you ask me.'

Stella nodded, and willed her leaden legs forward. She lifted her gaze to the winding path before them, leading to the entrance and the real world – and glimpsed something.

'Sauxa, can you see that light?'

'No, my lady,' the man said.

'Look, sight along my arm. Some way up the cavern wall.'

'Ah, no – oh. Yes. What is that?'

Perhaps twenty paces up from the floor, the wall ahead of them had cracked and rock had fallen to the bottom of the cavern. Caused by the explosion, no doubt, given how fresh and unadorned the rock around the crack appeared in contrast to the sculptured wall to either side. But what had drawn Stella's attention was the glow coming from the crack, as though liquid gold burned within the rock and had only now found a way out.

She took a pace backwards and the light failed – or, more likely, she was at the wrong angle to see it. A similar result when she stepped two paces forward. On, off, as though someone was alternately covering and uncovering a lamp with a blanket.

'Wait here, my lady. Someone needs to take a look at this. It don't look natural to me.'

Sauxa lumbered off, struggling to catch the others, leaving Stella alone with the glow in the cliff and a rising disquiet.

Kilfor, Kilfor, he thought he called out as the dream ended and reality began, slamming into him like a stone wall. *Kilfor!* But Kilfor was dead, dead by his hand, and Robal was alive, the possessor of life without end. Most High help him.

He had come back to life.

Please, please, have mercy, he wanted to plead, but his burbling communicated nothing but his terror. His body had quickened, obedient to the immortal blood, but his tongue had not grown back.

'—will make sure he never leaves this room, my lord. When the debt is paid, we will burn him.'

'Make sure you do. I cannot afford – ah, he has returned. Farewell, Factor. For this service I will allow you to name your reward.'

'I will think on it,' said the Factor.

'Let me have a moment with the prisoner.'

The request was followed by the clatter of booted feet leaving the chamber.

'Your body is about to be tortured beyond anything I've managed to accomplish, and I have tried very hard,' said the Destroyer, his mouth close to Robal's ear. 'It is only fair, then, that we extend this torture to your mind.'

How could anything be worse than this?

'I am returning to Stella's side. I shall woo her and win her, and while you are dying, again and again, I shall possess her. Again and again. Then, as you guessed, I shall betray her. Her powers I will press into my service. I will use her up and discard her, broken and forgotten, to rot. And you, my friend, will not be there to protect her.' The creature smiled. 'The knowledge of how much you are about to suffer eases my own pain,' he added. 'I will not say "'fare well,'" for you will fare very poorly, I predict.'

With that the monster turned and walked from the chamber.

Stella, oh, Stella!

The Zizhua returned to the chamber.

'Your second death,' the Factor began, 'will pay for the loss of my wife.'

'It is an opening of some kind,' the senior Zizhua guard opined.

'To the outside?' Stella didn't think so: the light had a different quality about it. Otherworldly.

'Unlikely. This is the long axis of the hill. The crack would have to extend many thousands of paces into the rock to let in light from the outside world.'

'Some unusual seam?' Seren asked. Kannwar had healed his horrific injuries. Though there remained some unsightly remnants, he required minimal assistance to walk, and was likely to recover completely.

'Never have we seen rock that glowed,' the younger guard answered. 'I would wish to examine this more closely.'

'We are commanded to return to aid in the search for further survivors,' the other guard reminded him. 'We have already lingered too long.' He glanced meaningfully at the travellers.

Lenares peered at the crack. 'There is power coming from it,' she said. 'It reminds me of . . . I'm not certain. We must climb up the wall. I must know what this is.'

'You're not certain?' Stella repeated. 'But you think you might know?'

'Faah. I want to be sure before I say anything. But that light reminds me of the light in the House of the Gods. I am wondering if the earthquake loosened this rock and the explosion brought it down, exposing . . . somewhere else.'

'The House of the Gods buried in a mountain?' Torve said.

'The entrances have to be somewhere,' the cosmographer replied reasonably enough. 'The gods wouldn't put them where everyone would come crawling all over them. Perhaps there is an outside entrance, and we're looking in through the back door, so to speak.'

Stella turned her head at the sound of crunching feet on the road behind them. It was Kannwar, seemingly completely recovered from his near-death – or full-death – experience. She wondered about that for a moment, remembering how long it had taken them both to heal after Conal pushed them over a cliff back in Dhauria. She herself was nowhere near recovered, yet he had been far closer to the blast. And he had given of himself to help heal the injured.

The man appeared almost ridiculously cheerful, humming under his breath.

'What are you looking at?' he asked as he drew up to them. 'The Zizhua want us to leave as soon – oh. Now that is interesting.'

'We think it might be—' began Lenares.

'Yes, one of the Houses of the Gods. Or, more correctly, another entrance to the one and only House. Another mystery solved; seems like our day for them.'

'What mystery?' Stella asked. All this cheerfulness made her skin prickle.

'I came across a scroll once, in the scriptorium at Dhauria, claiming to be a comprehensive list of the locations of the Houses of the Gods, although it didn't call them – it – that. Named it the Crèche. The list can't have been comprehensive though, as there was no record of the entrance Lenares and Torve say they found in Elamaq.'

'And on the list was an entrance in the Zizhua Valley,' Lenares interrupted, not to be outdone.

'Indeed,' said Kannwar agreeably, showing no resentment at the interruption. 'So, something good comes from an act of darkness. We should be able to use this against Umu. We have likely been followed into the valley by the Daughter's avatar; at least, we have no reason to suspect otherwise, given the gods have identified us as the only impediment to their plan and have therefore followed us since this began. And you all saw the hole in the world following us, as though we dragged it along.'

He paused, clearly seeking acknowledgement. Various of the travellers nodded.

'Umu must know where the House is. What better place to confront us?' Noetos growled. Kannwar nodded encouragingly. 'Therefore,' the fisherman concluded, 'we should stay well away.'

'You were correct until that last, friend Noetos,' Kannwar said, still insanely cheerful. 'What better place for us to confront her? No one else but us to get hurt.' He nodded to Stella. 'It is a place that focuses power, and that will magnify any advantage we have over her. And she will not be able to resist the place, even though she must suspect it is a trap.'

Stella smiled at him, then frowned. 'You said "another mystery solved." What other mystery?'

The man grinned even more broadly, and for a moment Stella could see the real Kannwar, the boy-man raised in the service of the Most High two thousand years ago. His glamour was entirely natural and utterly irresistible.

'Nothing you should concern yourself about,' he said. 'Just an interesting way one might prolong the punishment of a criminal for a truly horrific crime.'

'You have a terrifying way of thinking. One moment human, the next something entirely other.'

'Wait until you've lived two thousand years, then see how many people understand you,' he said.

Stella could think of nothing, not a single thing, she'd like less.

—please, please, let it end—

Robal's return to consciousness was as meat through a grinder. Someone was talking, but it took him a while to recognise the words.

'—struck by a roof-spear while trying to help her neighbour who was pinned by the wall of her home. She was my beloved daughter.' Sobs, wailing.

Limbs twitching, thoughts firing uncontrollably, a cascade of images, all of them grey, red-edged. Entering a land between life and death. Entering the realm of insanity.

'We have the right to choose the punishment.' The words came slowly, amid weeping. 'I want him flayed.'

His last clear thought before the agony began – the agony that finally drove him into madness – was a desperate wish that the doubling of time they had experienced might send him back to the moment before he threw the sulphur paper. The moment before the madness began.

Another chance! he screamed. *A chance to undo what I have done!*

Silence. And then pain.

CHAPTER 17

GODHOUSE

ONLY TWENTY PACES SEPARATED THEM from their goal. But those twenty paces were vertical. The first three were relatively easy, scrambling up a mound of newly fallen rock, but the rest appeared impossible to Stella.

'Can you do anything?' she asked Kannwar, who stood beside her watching Noetos and his son lead the first attempt to scale the wall.

'Yes,' he said. 'I could fashion a stair out of the air itself that we could ascend to the entrance.'

'Then do it,' she urged him. 'Umu may already be within, planning our deaths.'

He inclined his head towards her. 'Do you remember my escape from Instruere, Stella?'

Did she remember it? Of course she did. At the climax of the Falthan War, Kannwar had arrived in Instruere a conquering king leading a victorious army, having defeated the Falthan champion and accepted their surrender. Stella had been his handmaiden, already cursed with the immortal blood, in thrall to him.

He strode into the Great Hall of Instruere to sign the surrender documents, which were to be sealed magically with a truthspell. Stella herself had been compelled to deliver the documents into his hand; the walk up to and across the makeshift stage had been the single most humiliating moment of her life, watched by a thousand of Instruere's citizens who clearly saw her betrayal, not knowing how hard she struggled to break his iron will. As Kannwar raised the pen, his hand was struck off by an unseen assailant in a bizarre parody of his encounter with the Most High two thousand years previously. Leith claimed to have seen what happened: his story, ever unchanging, was that the carving of the Most High in the Great Hall loosed an arrow at the Destroyer, taking off his hand at the wrist. Well, everyone saw the arrow flaming as it stood stuck fast in the signing desk, quivering. Everyone heard the Destroyer's cry of anguish as his hand was severed from his arm. And, much later, everyone saw that the face of the Most High on that carving had turned into the face of Leith's brother, Hal. And so the Halites were born.

Even thinking about it now raised beads of sweat on Stella's skin.

Kannwar had made his escape in the confusion of the moment, forcing Stella to lend him her strength. They had fled across Instruere, his handless arms resting on her shoulders, she bearing most of his weight as his magic leached out of him. He would never have escaped had it not been for her assistance – and the sacrifice of the pride of Bhrudwo, Kannwar's Lords of Fear.

They had come at his call, had found him in distress and had sacrificed themselves, one after another, allowing him to drain them to form a walkway down from the city wall and across the Aleinus River. What a long mile that had been! For every twenty paces, another Lord of Fear had fallen, eviscerated, nothing more than a shell of skin and bone. With such horrendous cost Kannwar had escaped, and had limped back to Bhrudwo to rebuild his strength.

'I remember it,' she said.

'How many of your companions should I use up to make the stair?' he asked her. 'You are asking me to perform perhaps the most difficult magic of all, and I am barely recovered from my injuries. Don't you think we ought to save something in order to oppose Umu?'

'You are right,' Stella admitted.

'It will not do the men any harm to achieve this by ordinary mortal strength,' Kannwar added.

'If anyone should fall, can you at least cushion their landing?'

'Yes, I can do that. But so could you, if you were willing to explore the limits of your power. Stella, you have had the fire of the Most High within you for seventy years and never once have you even fanned the embers of its flame. What would it take for you to embrace the gift you have been given?'

'To see it as a gift and not as a curse,' she snapped. 'All very well for you. You snatched the so-called gift from the Most High in open rebellion. You may not have received exactly what you expected, but at least it was your hand reaching out. What did I do but defy you one too many times and suffer the consequences?'

Seven decades, it seemed, had not dimmed her outrage after all.

'I struck you down, Stella. But I saved you from death by sharing my blood with you.'

'And I have felt polluted from that moment to this!' she hissed.

He turned away from her. Had she finally daunted him? Broken through his complacent self-confidence? He muttered something she did not quite catch. She asked him to repeat it.

'Anomer has reached the opening,' he said.

Stella bit her lip to stop from screaming.

It took an hour for all the travellers to climb, assisted or unassisted, to the glowing crack in the wall. The younger members of the party made a good fist of the climb: Arathé, Lenares and Torve, Mustar, Cylene and Moralye all scampered quickly up the rockface as though they were spiders. Cyclamere took his time, moving more cautiously but just as sure-footedly, with Noetos making the climb immediately following his son and remaining just below the opening to lift anyone who required it over the last few paces of smoother rock. Consina and Bregor proceeded slowly, but arrived without mishap. Sauxa was a problem, slow and proud, refusing assistance. Twice he lost his grip, but both times Kannwar supported him with a light touch of magic, keeping him anchored against the wall. Seren came next, his difficulties caused not by fear or ineptitude but by his incomplete healing, and he muttered angrily to himself during his ascent. Duon made the climb as easily as the youngsters. Sautea proved the most difficult to coax up the wall, reluctant to take any risks. In the end Noetos clambered halfway down and hauled his friend up by main force. The old man spluttered indignantly all the way and thanked Noetos profusely when he reached the opening.

Stella's limbs felt as though all the life had been leached out of them – a side effect, she supposed, of forced healing. Shaking with weariness, she approached the rocks, her eyes fixed on anything but the task in front of her.

The next thing she knew she was sitting on the cold limestone floor, weeping.

'I c-c-can't,' she sobbed, shuddering at the touch of a hand on her shoulder.

'Please don't give up now, Stella. We're so close.'

'You d-don't n-need me. I'm j-just in the way.'

'We do need you,' Kannwar coaxed.

She took a racking breath. 'I'm so tired.' She dragged the word out into an embarrassing whine. 'Let me s-s-sleep.'

A voice filtered down from above. 'Are you all right down there?'

Kannwar didn't bother replying.

'So, girl, what happens now?'

'I'm s-sorry.'

Too much, she'd been through far too much. Walking for months on end with no clear destination in sight. Watching others fight, watching others die. Leith. Phemanderac. Robal. Each one worth a lifetime's sorrow. Dying twice herself. Struggling with the deepest of emotions: love, hate, attraction, revulsion, confusion.

'You're worn out.'

'I've b-been worn out for years. Walking around as though I'm alive but d-dead inside.' She tried to seal her mouth closed, but the traitorous words kept coming out. Small, selfish, complaining words. 'No use to anyone. A figure of hatred.'

'It's not like you, Stella, to feel sorry for yourself.'

'It's not like anyone else to feel s-sorry for me.'

She wanted very badly to apologise to Kannwar for her weakness. Knowing how much he despised any sign of it, imagining the look of disdain that even now must be forming on his face, she dared not look up at him. But part of her knew how much trouble she had caused for herself – for everyone around her – by trying to be strong, by refusing help, by going her own way.

'Other people know nothing,' Kannwar said harshly. 'They assume we are the most fortunate of people, blessed with life everlasting. They envy our positions of power. Tell me, Stella, do you feel fortunate?'

'You know the answer to that,' she said. 'For a long time I was able to ignore the stares, the gossip behind the hand' – *cowardly gossip, hurting Leith more than it hurt me* – 'because I had an empire to care for. The Halites were free to create their religion with me as its evil witch, as long as it kept them happy. All I cared about was paying back the debt I owed Falthans for the way I betrayed them.' *The way I was forced to betray them.* 'More and more, as Leith slipped into his long decline, the real work of administration fell to me, with assistance from Phemanderac whenever he was around, despite the increasingly strident opposition from my powerful enemies. Then Leith died.' She hiccoughed a sob. 'Everything changed. It was as though in that moment, everything meaningful about my life was stripped away, like the blankets torn from a familiar bed, leaving me naked. Without Leith I suddenly felt like I had no identity. I certainly had no protection from those who wished me harm. I fled for my life, and with Robal's help barely avoided the Halite Archpriest of the Koinobia and his minions. Do you understand, Kannwar?' It was so important he understood. 'I lost virtually everything when Leith died. My entire kingdom shrank to an uncouth guardsman and a Halite priest, and now they've gone. What you see sitting here is a hollow shell. I have nothing to keep me going save duty and memory, and neither is strong enough to serve. My flesh endures, but my spirit has left me.'

She buried her head in her folded arms, too weary even to cry. Above them Noetos asked some question or other. Stella let Kannwar deal with it.

Stella. Kannwar's voice swam into her mind as smooth as honey, as warm as a winter cloak. *You and I are linked by more than circumstances. We are bound together by the immortal blood we share. Let me help you.*

No! she retorted. *I don't trust you! Leave me alone! Get out of my mind!*

I'm speaking in your mind to save your embarrassment. You trusted me enough to accept my help when the hole in the world first came for you, back in the Maremma marshes. What is so difficult about allowing me to lend you the strength to climb a little wall?

Because I am empty now, she said simply. *And if I allow you access, you will take me, fill me and never let me go.* Her secret fear, her secret desire.

No, Stella. Elation, disappointment. *I give you my word.*

She laughed mockingly. *Your word?*

A glimmer of anger came through the blood-borne connection. *My word is all you have, my queen. At any point in the last seventy years I could have overwhelmed you just as I did during the Falthan War. Any time, Stella, but I forbore.*

The Most High broke your power over me, Stella sent, trying to hide her uncertainty, her growing terror.

Really? Then how do you explain this?

He seized her, his fist wrapped around her heart, taking her body and mind. Breath stopped, throat closed, eyes bulging, she stood – he forced her to stand – and walked two paces, placed her hands against the wall, as though about to climb. Then he let her go.

She collapsed onto the pile of rocks, gasping like a landed fish. 'You, you,' she said, searching in vain for a swearword sufficiently dire.

'Come, Stella. We have shared so much on this quest. This is the Most High's business. Would he have put us together and left you defenceless?'

'Apparently,' she breathed.

'I am your defence. I will protect you.'

'It is you I need protecting from! Ah, this is meaningless. All we do is go around in circles. Leave me. I'll climb your wall.'

Halfway up she turned and snarled at him. 'Don't think I can't tell what you're doing. You're sending me strength, curse you.'

Hugging the wall just below her, he offered no comment apart from a bland smile.

I could never give myself to you, she thought. *Not when I have no idea what is going on behind those black eyes.*

The opening led to a narrow corridor, barely wide enough to squeeze through. Stella barked the skin on both knees trying to ease her way past one sharp, stony obstruction.

'All this is new,' Noetos said, indicating the tunnel they were navigating. 'The rock is clean. No growth, no patina.'

'Get on, rock expert,' his son said to him, a smile on his open face.

Now there's one I could have fallen for seventy years ago, Stella admitted to herself.

'It's the Children's Room!' Lenares said, her voice drifting back down the corridor to where Stella laboured.

'So we've found the House of the Gods?' Kannwar called out.

'Oh yes,' came the reply, from Duon this time.

'Huh,' said the Undying Man under his breath. 'I didn't think it was possible.'

'What wasn't possible?' Stella asked him.

'To get into one of the Houses apart from using the proper entrances.'

'If you were so doubtful, why did you suggest we all climb up here and risk breaking our necks?'

He smiled crookedly. 'I was curious.'

After assembling in what Lenares had called the Children's Room, the travellers stood and stared at what lay around them. Even those who had been here – wherever it was – before found themselves astonished anew at the room; and those who had not – Cylene, Cyclamere, Bregor and Consina – wandered around the space with their mouths open. Of them all, Cyclamere looked the most troubled. Keppia had forbidden this place to the Padouki. It would no doubt take him time to overcome his unease.

'The child who grew up here must have been enormous,' Bregor said, one hand resting on a bulbous object twice his own height that might have been some sort of baby rattle.

'Children, I think,' Kannwar said. 'My suspicion is that the House of the Gods was built by the Most High as a place to raise his two children, the Son and the Daughter.'

'That doesn't make any sense,' Lenares protested. 'The Son and the Daughter were selected as adults from the world of men. How could they have become children?'

'Things were likely much more . . . fluid back then. Just because Keppia and Umu were adults doesn't mean they didn't have to become child-gods. And I'm not entirely sure, Lenares, that either Keppia or Umu were ever what we'd call human.'

He crossed the room to a pile of rocks. 'Counting devices, if my guess is correct. Stones from an abacus.'

Bregor grunted what sounded like suspicion, if not outright disbelief, but he did not follow it up with a question. Still in awe of his lord, no doubt. With reason.

The feature of the room that bemused Stella was the open sky above. She knew they ought to have been deep beneath the limestone hill in Zizhua Valley, but that didn't seem to make any difference to the House of the Gods. It seemed as though whenever someone crossed the threshold of the Godhouse they were transported somewhere else.

Lenares came and stood next to her as Stella stared into the cloudless night pierced with stars. 'Is it even night in the Zizhua Valley?' the cosmographer wondered aloud, echoing Stella's own thoughts. 'Where exactly are we?'

Stella smiled tiredly at the woman. 'What surprises me is that there might be more than one entrance to the House of the Gods in each continent. Seduced by the symmetry, I suppose. Three continents, three entrances, I thought. The place you told me about in Elamaq, by the river . . .' A glance at the cosmographer, an unspoken encouragement to supply the name.

'Marasmos,' Lenares said. 'But you're forgetting Nomansland. There was an entrance there too.'

'Hmm. Two in Elamaq then, and two in Bhrudwo: Patina Padouk and Zizhua. I wonder where in Faltha the entrances are, if there are any at all. I would surely have heard of them.'

Kannwar spoke from just behind them. 'My guess is that the entrances themselves are fluid. The Patina Padouk entrance is fairly recent, I'm certain of that. It was negotiated with the Padouki in return for . . . a favour. I suspect neither of the younger gods has been back to Faltha since the Most High brought the First Men north with him after their eviction from Elamaq. No gods, no entrances necessary. '

'So they just wither away from lack of use?'

Kannwar shrugged. 'Perhaps we ought to search the House for any unwelcome guests,' he said, raising his eyebrows in Lenares' direction.

She heads the group in name, but he is the real leader. Stella frowned. *Has there ever been a time when Kannwar didn't get his own way? Aside from the climax of the Falthan War, of course. And in his choice of consort.* That was entirely within her own control. She hoped.

'We must find Umu,' Noetos said. 'Shall we split up to search for her?'

'No need for that,' Lenares said smugly. 'As soon as we entered the House of the Gods I could tell she was here.'

'So what do we do then?' Seren asked on behalf of them all. On Stella's behalf, at least.

'Everything depends on the huanu stone,' said Lenares.

Mustar grunted. 'But we defeated Keppia without the stone. Why not do the same to Umu?'

'Because we received help from Mahudia and all the newly dead.' Lenares frowned. 'Mahudia has sacrificed herself by becoming a living tourniquet, holding Keppia on the other side of the Wall of Time. We might be able to muster enough strength to drive Umu out of the world, but it would only be temporary. What we need is something to heal the breach in the wall. Since the breach is magical, and the huanu stone can undo magic, it seems we have a weapon that can win us this battle.'

Stella cleared her throat. 'Umu saw what happened to her brother.

Do you not think she has thought long and carefully about how to avoid a similar fate?'

'So we will exercise caution,' Kannwar said to her. To them all. 'But we are here now, and have an opportunity without parallel. We must strike.'

'But we need a plan,' Stella tried to argue.

'No plan long survives a change in circumstance,' Noetos said, glancing across the room at his old tutor, the Padouki Cyclamere. 'What is most important is that we remain flexible.'

'I still want to know how the huanu stone can be used to heal the hole in the world. And if it can, why we haven't used it before.'

Stella thought her questions were perfectly legitimate, even pressing, but the others had already moved on.

'Follow me,' Lenares commanded, waving her hand at them.

Oh my, Stella thought worriedly. *The last time we found ourselves in the House of the Gods we needed the intervention of the Most High himself to survive – and we did not survive intact.* Had everyone forgotten Torve? There he was now, walking awkwardly after Lenares. What might happen this time?

The first serious check came as the travellers passed through a narrow corridor between the Orange Pool Room, in which mist rose from a small pool and allowed itself to be sculpted into ever-changing shapes by a slight breeze, and the Room of Nine Ponds, where each pond was overlooked by a shady palm tree. Lenares had led most of her charges over the threshold when they felt a sudden shift. Looking behind her, Stella realised the rooms had changed position relative to each other. The Rainbow Room had taken the place of the Orange Pool Room. Who had been following her? Noetos, Cylene, Anomer, Arathé, Cyclamere and Duon, who had no doubt gone . . . somewhere with the Orange Pool Room.

'Damn,' Kannwar said as Stella explained what had happened.

'Indeed,' said Consina. Others nodded their agreement. 'Noetos's huanu stone is crucial. Now it is lost to us.'

'For the moment only, surely,' Lenares responded. 'The rooms do all connect up. We just have to be patient.'

'My fear,' Kannwar said slowly, thinking it through, 'is that Umu has control of the mechanism for changing the position of the rooms. She has isolated Noetos, and now she can play with the controls, dividing us into smaller and smaller groups.'

'I hadn't thought of that,' Lenares said, her face turning pale. Then she brightened. 'I bet the mechanism is in the Throne Room. I bet that's where she is. That's where we need to go.'

'Perhaps,' said Kannwar. 'But we must be cautious.'

Caution, as Stella anticipated, turned out to be Kannwar assuming the leadership from Lenares and instructing them to run between rooms. She doubted the cosmographer was aware of the subtle change, but everyone now addressed their concerns to the Bhrudwan lord.

They had no defence, however, against a repeat of the shifting rooms. They lost Sauxa, Seren and Moralye between the Standing Wave Room and the Sculpture Room, and then the remaining group was divided neatly in half as they tried to hurry into the Rainbow Room from the Rotten-Egg Room: directly in front of Stella the corridor went blank and was replaced by the Children's Room, taking Mustar, Sautea, Bregor and Consina with it.

'This is deliberate,' Lenares said, clearly distressed. 'Umu is separating us out.'

'But you told us the House of the Gods was different in Patina Padouk than in Marasmos,' Kannwar said. 'Surely—'

'It didn't change this quickly. Umu has been too clever for us. We should never have come here.'

'All that matters now is to find Noetos,' Stella reminded them, 'and then the Throne Room. The others will find us eventually.'

'If they are still free,' Torve said.

Lenares grunted agreement. 'If they are still alive.'

'What do we do now?' Seren asked.

'Find the others,' replied Sauxa.

'Stay put until the others find us,' Moralye responded at the same moment.

The three of them stood panting in the middle of the Standing

Wave Room, looking at each other with wide and troubled eyes. The room loomed over them; it had been given its name by Lenares because of the walls, which bent inwards in uncannily realistic replications of breaking waves, complete with foam and even drops of water that seemed to hover in the air.

'We have no magic between us,' Moralye reminded them. 'Every time we cross into a new room there is a chance we might encounter the Daughter. I do not want to face her without the protection of our fellow travellers.'

'We may have to take the risk,' Seren said.

'Oh, Most High,' Sauxa breathed, his eyes widening further.

The scholar and the miner turned to the plainsman, then followed his gaze up, up to where the standing waves shimmered, transforming from stone to water, and came crashing down on them with a thunderous roar.

A moment later the water pulled back, draining towards the walls, and the standing waves were restored, leaving an empty room.

'The only way we can beat Umu is to split up,' Anomer argued, as they prepared to leave the Sculpture Room. 'We need to make this more difficult for her. The more variables we introduce, the more complex her problem.' Cyclamere nodded his agreement with this plan.

'She's a god,' Duon said, but the thought was Arathé's. 'We won't confuse her.'

Cylene glanced around the Sculpture Room, her face anxious. 'I don't want to be separated from the rest of you. I don't want . . . I don't want the Daughter to find me.'

'I can understand that,' said Noetos.

Arathé screamed.

She had brushed past one of the sculptures – an evil-looking thing, a tortured melange of human figures – and now was held firm by the merest contact. Sand began to flow upwards from the floor, coating her legs.

Duon cried out, grabbed at her and shouted again, this time

in horror. Within moments he too was falling victim to the sand.

From the corridor between the rooms Noetos bellowed his rage, slapped a hand to his belt and pulled out the huanu stone. Took a step forward, then vanished along with Cylene as the rooms rearranged themselves.

His mouth open in shock, Anomer watched, impotent to interfere, as the sand crawled its way up his sister, the Padouki warrior and the captain, swarming like a plague of insects. Covering? Absorbing? Knee, waist, chest, neck, mouth, eyes. Within minutes Arathé, Cyclamere and Duon had vanished, their increasingly desperate cries for help choked off, replaced by two new sculptures.

Anomer srood miserably in the centre of the room, alone save for the remains of people unfortunate enough to have been ensnared by the sculptures. These he cringed away from as he settled to wait for help. A hissing sound drew his gaze downwards. Sand had begun to climb his legs.

Torve had been taken by the orange pool. He'd stepped in it and the contact had started a whirlpool that had torn him from his feet, then pulled him around and around until he'd disappeared. Lenares had caught only the end of it as her Torve had not cried out, unwilling, it seemed, to see her caught in the same snare that had taken him. She'd shrieked in rage, but that had not stopped the water pulling him under.

The pool had instantly returned to its calm state, but Lenares had not dared the water. Forces far beyond her understanding were at work here.

She bit her lower lip, fighting panic. One hand went to her hair, twirling it in an automatic comforting motion. 'Clever Umu,' she said. 'We will have to go on without him.'

She expected an answer like, *How can you be so callous?* and was fully prepared to argue that he had merely been taken by the water, which did not necessarily mean he'd been killed. There had been no change in the nodes and threads she could see, which implied he was still alive. She hoped.

But there was no answer.

She glanced up: Kannwar and Stella had already gone on to the next room.

Oh dear.

There seemed little doubt as to what would happen next. The House of the Gods – or someone manipulating it – had divided them and was now picking them off one by one. She was on her own now. When she walked through the corridor to the next room, she had no doubt she would still be on her own.

'Fascinating,' Kannwar said.

'Fascinating?' Stella replied. They had seen Torve pulled to his doom in the whirlpool, but the House of the Gods had whisked them away to somewhere else – a room bordered by glittering walls – rendering them powerless to help. 'You call the likely deaths of everyone in our party but us – and that only a matter of time – *fascinating?*'

'Indeed. I'd wondered how she would do it. This method is particularly ingenious.'

'But . . . Kannwar, what do you mean?'

He sighed. His illusory right hand took hold of her arm and at the same time his consciousness penetrated hers, possessing her. *Why the Most High persists with such material as yourself is beyond my comprehension. Such blind trust! Capturing Umu will have to wait, my queen. We must go. We have a more dangerous opponent to dethrone.*

A hundred contradictory questions roared in her head, striking her temporarily mute. Though, no doubt, he'd taken her power of speech anyway. *Oh, Most High, Robal warned me . . .*

You thought you were behaving in such a sophisticated fashion, didn't you, my queen? Extending your trust to one who appeared to have reformed himself? Surely the Most High would reward such trust? Ah, Stella, you are his tool. He uses his tools hard, my queen, I should know. Uses and then discards them. Welcome to the discards pile.

What are you going to do? With me? she added in the back of her mind.

He didn't answer her, instead yanking her forward, past the innocent-seeming lake that spread across the floor of this room and to the base of a broad stone stair that disappeared into a huge mound of sand.

Up there is one of the House's entrances, he remarked, then waved a hand at it. A shock spread out from his hand – she could see it, ripples in the air – and crashed into the shining walls, shaking the room. Parts of both walls came down, falling into the narrow gap at the top of the stair, above the mound of sand.

An entrance no longer, he said, his voice a smirk in her mind. *One entrance closed, three more to go.*

He beckoned her forward, and her feet were already dancing in obedience before she'd even thought of resisting him.

Lenares stumbled into the Throne Room at precisely the moment she least wished it. Alone, weary, defenceless.

There Umu sat, atop one of the three rebuilt chairs, looking small and rather ridiculous in Conal's body, but Lenares knew better than to tell her that. The Daughter lifted an arm in sardonic greeting.

'Welcome, cosmographer,' said the priest's voice, overlaid with Umu's thick cadences. 'I have spent some time thinking how I would repay you for my days in captivity. I believe I have come up with a satisfactory plan.'

She raised her – Conal's – fist and opened it.

Lenares turned and ran, but the rooms beyond the entrance changed faster than thought. Flicker, flicker, flicker. No escape save into some nowhere void.

'Aren't you going to look at what I have?'

'No need,' Lenares said, keeping her voice even. 'I know what it is.'

'And if you'd let me alone, you could have known it, and its former owner, a great deal better. But as it is, it is a powerful talisman in my skilled hand. Observe.'

She – it – breathed on the dreadful thing and Torve materialised at the base of the chair. Lenares ran towards him.

'Ah, ah,' Umu said, wagging an admonitory finger. 'Stay where you are, please.'

Lenares ignored her. A pale bubble appeared, encasing the pale-faced figure of her beloved – his face has the look of the drowned, she realised – and began to expand. She didn't bother to test the strength of the magical barrier.

'You should have taken better care of your huanu fragment,' Umu said, clearly delighting in every word. 'You thwarted me with it at Corata Pit, and never thought of it again. I see your hand darting to your pocket. How many days ago did you last think to check on it? Robal had it from you, claiming it as part of his own dark plans, some time ago now. Just imagine, girl. With it you could have marched right through my barrier and called your Omeran toy back from the cold lake in which he currently lies. Too bad, Lenares. Too bad you are only half a person. A shame you are so narrowly obsessed with yourself that you do not ever think of the wider picture. And you wanted to be a god! You! You'd make a splendid anti-god. People would flee from you in case you offered to help them!'

Lenares gasped at the cruelty in the words, and at their truth. *Look what has happened since you began to lead the others*, she acknowledged.

'You see it, don't you?' the Daughter said, baiting her.

It's only truth, the cosmographer told herself. *Why should it frighten me?*

But Umu clearly thought such words would damage her, even destroy her. The notion puzzled Lenares. *What will happen if I play along?* She lowered her head to her chest and began to shake her shoulders, as though sobbing.

The sound that came from the throne above her was as much a purr as a laugh.

Stella could do nothing but watch as Kannwar gambled and won, moving from room to room without encountering Umu or indeed any of their fellow travellers. She wondered if he had some control over the House of the Gods, or if Umu and he were in collusion.

As he strode ahead and she stumbled unwillingly behind, he continued to expand on his theme of his own brilliance and her incompetence. She judged this not as some gloating lord at the moment of his triumph, but more an attempt to keep her off balance to prevent her mounting a defence or even a counterattack.

It follows, therefore, that he believes me capable of such a counterattack. The thought sharpened her mind.

'I had to do little to incite Robal to madness,' he was saying. 'The man was more than somewhat mad already, the possessor of what he believed was a great love. All I had to do was drive him to jealousy. He was cleverer than I thought, however. I never imagined he'd try to use explosives. It was I who suggested he take the stone from Lenares – though he thought the instructions I gave him were but a dream – and I expected him to try to use it on me directly, as he did at Martje's house in Sayonae. He'd learned his lesson though. I admired him for that. Others never learn.

'I had a few scant seconds to save myself. Ah, Stella, even you would have to admire my genius. Not only did I protect myself from the worst of the explosion by diverting it outwards and upwards, I artfully laid my supposedly dying body beside Robal and practically invited him to partake of his own doom. So eager he was, cupping my blood and drinking death to himself.'

Stella shuddered. It broke her to learn that Robal had succumbed at the last.

'He's still alive, of course,' Kannwar remarked. 'After a fashion, at least. The angle of the blast killed many more Zizhua than he – or even I – expected. But they have him and will exact their revenge, killing him again and again until the number of his deaths equals the number of theirs. I suspect he will live many months, if not years.'

Stella leaned forward and vomited on the stone floor of the Children's Room.

'I was always going to betray you, of course. But when Umu started playing with her house, I moved my timetable forward somewhat.'

You are frightened of him, she said into his mind.

'Indeed I am. From what Arathé and Duon have said, I have very good reason. He grows stronger every day and is ready to claim my fortress for his own. That, Stella, I will not tolerate. Umu can wait: I am going after Husk.'

He waved a hand and the new-forged link between the House of the Gods and Zizhua City vanished under a pile of rubble.

'There,' he said, rubbing his hands together. 'No escape now, except for us.'

How can you do this? These are people you lived with for months. You shared danger with them, ate with them, laughed with them.

'And I'm relieved to be rid of them. Fools and half-wits, without exception. If I were you, Stella, I would keep silent in my presence regarding these people. It would be just as easy for me to slay them all, thus ensuring their silence.'

But they'll die anyway, trapped in the House of the Gods.

So much death, and she again at the Destroyer's side, an unwilling observer. A dupe. To be remembered in histories as betraying her friends. Again.

'At least they'll have time to prepare themselves for death. Something you must envy them if all your talk of the curse of immortality is more than mere posturing.'

Did you ever love me? The question sounded plaintive even to her own ears.

'Of course, my queen,' he said, bowing slightly. 'But in my own way.'

By Alkuon, the huanu stone had to be worth something. It negated magic, so dead Omiy had said; then let it negate the surely magical effect of changing rooms in the House of the Gods. Let it undo the magical snares his companions – his children – had fallen foul of. Let it be of some use. Or, by every god of the sea, he would throw it away.

In these moments of terror, separated from his family and surrounded by walls so terrifyingly reminiscent of Fossa, Cylene was his rock. Noetos wanted to stand in the middle of the room and howl his rage; Cylene took him by the arm, steadied him, and led him onward.

'Come on, love,' she whispered in his ear. 'Our enemy may have disadvantaged us, but the battle is not over. Not yet.'

Snare after snare had been activated as they walked through the rooms. In the Children's Room, the giant toys had begun hurling themselves randomly around the enclosure, as though propelled by some petulant hand. Probably re-enacting some earlier time, Cylene speculated. They managed to avoid most of the objects, though the huanu stone in Noetos's hand may have diverted a few of the swifter shapes. The floor of the Blood Room turned to . . . well, blood, Noetos guessed, but not under his feet. Again, the protection came from the huanu stone. The Sculpture Room ensnared Cylene momentarily as she touched one of the outstretched limbs, but Noetos broke her free by holding the stone at the place where her arm had fused to the statue.

I suppose it is of some use, after all, he admitted.

Finally, through the corridor, he spied the room he was looking for: where Torve had been castrated weeks before, and where Keppia had been driven out of Dryman, at least for a time. At least, he assumed it was the Throne Room: the thrones seemed to have been rebuilt. He approached the entrance, Cylene by his side.

A figure sitting atop one of the thrones peered in his direction. The room began to fade.

'Oh no, you don't,' Noetos breathed, and held the huanu stone in front of him as he strode through the entrance. The room froze, half-dematerialised. Entering it was like breaking through a thick spider's web.

The figure on the throne was Conal the priest. No, not Conal – Umu. The Daughter wearing a body of rotting meat. At the base of her throne cowered another figure. Cylene's twin, Lenares.

'Ah. The man with his stone – and Lenares' sister. Perfect. Welcome, welcome.'

The dead priest beckoned them forward as though he – she – had been expecting them. Could this have been part of Umu's plan?

Had she allowed for the likelihood of his making it to the Throne Room?

'What have you done with my children?' Noetos asked, his voice as hard as he could make it, disguising the quaking inside him.

'Of course, your children. A more sensible man than you would have written them off, realising that my defeat was worth more than their lives. But you are not a sensible man, are you? You are a child, able to focus on nothing more than the next innocent receptacle of your wrath. And thereby you can be held hostage.'

She drew something out of Conal's bloodstained pocket. 'For this to work I needed something from each of you. I took hair from your son and your daughter; be thankful I didn't take anything less easy to replace.'

'When did you take it?' Cylene asked, her head tilted to one side, birdlike. She took small steps towards her sister, who sat, head bowed, as though she'd not noticed their arrival.

'Does it matter?'

'You are sorely reduced for a god,' Cylene continued. 'Look at you, wearing a body decaying all around you. How can you stand it? Walking around in it, following us northwards, stopping and going through our cast-offs, picking over our food, our combings, our sleeping places, looking for hair or shit or skin. How demeaning.'

Cylene had clearly guessed right. Noetos supposed the god would have flushed had there been blood left in Conal's body. Certainly it drew itself up and regarded Cylene stiffly.

'What do you know of godhood?' the voice said. 'Are you like your sister then, lusting after power and knowledge without being prepared to pay the price?'

'I am nothing like my sister. The things I desire, Umu, you can never have.'

The god laughed. 'You imagine yourself to be unsettling me,' she said, 'when in fact you do little more than supply me with a moment's amusement. A moment that is now over.'

Cylene smiled then, and Noetos backed away in fright, the hair on his head prickling in awe. For in her smile was power from beyond the Wall of Time.

Umu saw it too. Her – his – mouth snapped shut. Lenares raised her head. The cosmographer's mouth described an 'O.'

'You watched Keppia as he was driven out of the world and sealed beyond the Worldwall,' Cylene said. 'You were surprised I lived afterwards, but you thought no more of it, suiting your plans to those you considered dangerous. Kannwar, Lord of Bhrudwo. Noetos and his huanu stone. Stella, who bears the fire of the Most High. Lenares the cosmographer, who had snared you once before. But you forgot me.'

'Who are you?' asked the god, fear in her voice.

'You ate me once,' Cylene said.

As she spoke, she reached down and touched Lenares on her shoulder. The girl burst into tears.

Noetos shook his head. He had not the faintest idea what Cylene meant. At this point, however, he no longer cared: anything that put fear into the Daughter was fine in his opinion. Even if it was pure bluff.

'Want to talk again about my children?' he asked Umu.

The Lord of Bhrudwo made Stella dump the sticks he'd forced her to scavenge from around the room, then coaxed fire from them with a flint from his belt.

'You know this fire, I think,' he said to her.

She knew this fire. She had travelled in it twice, borne from Faltha to Bhrudwo both times. Once at the beginning of the Falthan War, as an unintended side effect of the Destroyer's wrath. And a second time as a means to escape from Dhauria. Both times the journey had been painful and disorienting.

He drew a pouch from his belt, took from it some blue powder and cast it on the flames, muttering an incantation as he did so.

Stella readied herself for the pain. What else could she do?

'You seek to bargain with me?'

'Is that so strange?' Noetos said. 'Wasn't that how you ended up a god in the first place, Umu? A bargain with the Father?'

'Don't speak his name in this place,' the god hissed.

'As you wish,' Noetos replied blandly. 'A bargain. You return our companions to us, we leave you here to live in the House of the Gods. Better than being cast back into the void, surely?'

Cylene shook her head. Noetos ignored her.

'I have enlarged the hole in the world sufficiently to live exactly where I choose,' Umu said.

'Right,' Noetos said, nodding. 'Mmm. Which is why you're here, wrapped in some poor man's putrid skin, fear in your voice, trying to find a way out of the snare you've made for yourself. See, I think you need a body to live in, an anchor to this world. Or a succession of them probably. You've engineered things here so you have not one but two bodies to choose from. Twins, no less. Once the first one wears out, you'll have another one to be going on with. After that, who knows?'

He took two paces towards Umu's throne. 'Live where you choose? You don't fool me. Now return our companions to us and we'll talk about bodies.'

Cylene glanced at Noetos, fear on her face. 'What do you mean?'

'Sorry, Miss Sai,' he said to her. 'But this was always my plan. From the moment I realised you were Lenares' twin, I have worked tirelessly to bring you before Umu and make my bargain. Take these two, Daughter, and give me my own son and daughter back.'

'But you didn't know—'

Cylene intercepted a pleading look from him. *Trust me, beloved.* She'd known him mere weeks: would she understand? Everything depended on her now.

'You *bastard*,' she breathed, putting everything she had into the word. 'You'd sell me out? You don't know what it is like, being dead and possessed by a god. Please, Noetos, please. Don't condemn me to a prison of pain in my own body.'

He turned away from her.

'Do what you like with these two,' he said to Umu. 'After we've gone I can't stop you leaving the House of the Gods anyway. Do we have a bargain?'

Umu dipped dead hands into pockets in Conal's tunic, pulled out a variety of personal effects and blew on them. Either side of

Torve's phantasm others appeared: Arathé and Anomer, and the other travellers, all wearing the frozen expressions they had worn when they had been captured.

'Thaw them, or do whatever it is you need to do,' demanded Noetos.

'Please, Noetos. Don't do this. I'd die if it would rescue your family. But I can't face this living death.'

'Shut up, slattern!'

Something about his voice gave him away, or perhaps Umu simply thought things through. Her hand closed around the travellers' possessions.

'Mahudia!' Lenares shouted.

Cylene rippled. For a moment it was as though Noetos saw her through a sheet of flame. Then her body resumed its normal aspect – on the outside, at least.

Mahudia? Oh – the woman Lenares claims fostered her, who died and was instrumental in keeping the Son from returning through the hole in the world. Comprehension grew within Noetos like the rising of the sun. Wasn't this risky? If Mahudia lent Cylene her strength, wouldn't Keppia get loose?

No chance to ask, as several things happened at once.

Cylene extended a hand and Umu screamed. Lenares began to climb up the throne. And Noetos heard a whisper in his mind: his daughter's voice. *We're very well, Father. Place the huanu stone on the ground and be ready.*

Lenares clambered up onto the seat of the giant chair. Conal's body lunged at her, fetching her a blow across the chest. She staggered sideways, barely keeping herself from falling.

Cylene's face screwed up with effort. Noetos could see nothing of what she was doing: he had no magical vision. As soon as the thought entered his mind, his vision seemed to fade out, to be replaced by another's eyes. His daughter's.

Golden wires ran from place to place in a huge chaotic web. A thick golden cable ran from Cylene's back up into the pale blue sky above the Throne Room. Other wires radiated out from the young woman, up towards the throne, pulsating with energy and light.

413

Oddly – disconcertingly – he could see himself standing near Cylene, surrounded by golden wires of his own, none as thick as those touching Cylene. The largest, he realised, connected him to his children; another linked his body with Cylene's.

He took a few steps back, but his vision didn't change. Well, of course not. Arathé took the hint and stepped backwards, her body distressingly pale and see-through at the edges. Still not returned to this world from wherever Umu had put it.

Better. Noetos could now see atop the throne. Lenares and Conal struggled, each hammering the other with blows that would be unlikely to do any permanent damage.

Conal could remember being human. The memories were faint and growing fainter with every passing moment, though time itself had faded also, until a minute and an hour seemed indistinguishable. All that he could now distinguish were shades of pain. Umu transferred every unpleasant feeling to him. Or what was left of him. He barely noticed them, so faded had he become.

He was dead. Deserved to be dead, if what he remembered was true. He'd done some bad things, had let his friends down, and it had ended up like this. He didn't feel guilt exactly; the churning ache in the centre of what he supposed was his soul would better be described as sorrow. Deep, deep sorrow. Not for himself; he was over that now. Dead was dead. He'd pass into the void when this was all over and face whatever judgement his deeds had earned him. But he felt sorrow for the living, his friends for whom the never-ending sequence of events meant something.

He didn't even feel angry at Umu. How could he? She'd appropriated his body, but it wasn't as though he'd been using it. The only uncomfortable result of her actions had been this delay in going where he was supposed to go. That would be over soon. After a few minutes or hours or somethings. Whatever. They were all the same.

His fading soul hid in the back of his non-functioning brain, a helpless observer of the events unfolding around him. Or perhaps not so helpless.

*　　*　　*

414

Noetos saw the first signs that something had gone wrong with Umu. Her lunges at Lenares were clumsier, and she began to totter a few steps after every swing. As if she was drunk. He supposed Cylene's – Mahudia's – magic was having an effect, but Arathé's eyes told him different: the golden outpouring from his beloved still stopped short of the god, countered by a reciprocal ray of magic from Conal's body. For a moment Noetos could not discern what was happening.

Umu cried out in anger, then fell on her bottom with a slap. Lenares kicked at her once, twice . . . and on the third kick, Conal's body fell from the chair, thumping into the sand.

Immediately the ethereal figures of their companions resolved into their normal forms and were set free from whatever stasis they had been held in.

'Draw from the room itself!' Anomer cried.

Instantly half a dozen shafts of magic pierced Conal's prone body and the Daughter cried in pain.

Where was the Undying Man? At this moment of crisis, the fulfilment of his god-appointed quest, where had he gone? Noetos suspected something underhand. But without both his and Stella's magical power, it seemed unlikely they could drive Umu out. Nevertheless, they were hurting her: her magical flame began to retreat.

'Something's happening,' Anomer said, then he doubled over. His hands went to his head, as did Arathé's. Duon screamed and fell to the ground. Noetos found his own vision returned to him, all golden threads gone. He snatched up the huanu stone and ran to his son's side. Something in Noetos's head seemed to have caught fire.

'Umu . . . she . . . she is forcing her way . . . she has found the connection between we three spikes and Husk,' Duon panted. 'She has Conal's mind wide open. We . . . I . . . aaah! . . . can feel her widening the . . . the channel . . . ah, she's going to burn out our minds!'

'Stop trying to drive her out!' Noetos cried to Cylene, who was again rippling with the effort of channelling the power of a dead cosmographer.

Another voice erupted from three throats. 'No!' it cried, a deep male voice, the words audible from the mouths of Duon and Conal, a wordless cry from his daughter's tongueless mouth. 'No! Stay away! Do not . . . I will . . . AAAAAAH!'

The three bodies convulsed and lay still.

'She's gone,' Anomer said in a small voice as he bent over his sister.

'Gone where?' Noetos whispered.

He'd felt it too, through the connection he shared with his children. Something had forced its way into and through Arathé's mind, some evil beast scouring a path along a previously formed channel.

Anomer breathed out heavily. 'Gone to possess the voice that drove the spike into her brain, and into that of Duon and Conal. Gone to claim Husk's body for her own.'

'We've driven her out then?'

'Oh yes. But it appears that we may have made things much worse.'

INTERLUDE

HUSK IS TORN. ON THE one hand, he wishes his foes overthrown, given that he is still weakened and not yet sure of victory against them. On the other, he does not want either the Undying Man or his consort damaged in any way. They must be unharmed when finally he encounters them. So it is with profound relief, countered by a sudden apprehension, that he notices their disappearance.

He can still see through the eyes of his two remaining spikes: even though they have broken his control over them, the connection remains open. They are fools, of course. Were it him in their situation, he'd ensure he found some way to close it. But of course he cannot see what his spikes cannot see, and once Stella and Kannwar are swallowed by the shuffling rooms of the House of the Gods, he has no further knowledge of them.

He hopes they are safe.

Husk breathes heavily, having arrived at the top of the final staircase. Such a long time he has been creeping through this fortress, along corridors, up and down stairs, hiding in long-forgotten rooms, avoiding contact with the hundreds of denizens required to keep such a place functioning. He has travelled – oozed, he supposes the correct term would be as applied to his early journey – from the deepest dungeon in Andratan to the highest tower, by what may be the most circuitous route possible. And, of course, despite his caution, he has been discovered many times; each time he has dealt ruthlessly with his discoverer and anyone else necessary to cover his presence. And, ah, now he is here. The Tower of Farsight.

The tower is empty, as it has been since the Undying Man last left his fortress. Empty and gathering dust, and now gathering a deadly enemy. He eases himself onto his knees, then his feet, pushes with his handless arms – the buds that will eventually become hands are still formless – and the door swings open.

He breathes in the stale air as though it is the sweetest scent he has ever inhaled. And it is, oh yes. He drops back to all fours and crawls across the flagstones to the seat by the window, the place from which the Undying Man rules Bhrudwo.

Husk has paid a great price to come this far. In savouring this moment, he takes the time to consider all he has suffered. He thinks particularly of how his spikes damaged him; how, after all his cleverness and hard work, he almost lost everything when Conal sacrificed himself, his death tearing the spikes loose from Husk's grasp. He had been tempted by despair then, coming closer to giving up than at any other time. In the end he had gone on. Easier to go forward, he'd thought, than to retrace his path back to that dungeon.

Slowly his strength has returned. By no means is he back to the almost godlike position he occupied before Conal's trick, but he is strong enough, he judges. His body is not the superhuman thing he had planned for, but he has husbanded his strength. He is ready.

He levers himself to his feet and sits on the seat.

He is the new Lord of Bhrudwo. Deorc, Lord of Bhrudwo.

He'll wait until they come into the room before he binds them. He sees where they will stand, unable to move. Stella there, the Undying Man there, shock on their faces. Not fear, not until they realise they cannot defeat his binding. He will drag Stella forward, screaming, until she lies before him, her eyes filled with terror. Then he will ease himself down from his seat and take her, savagely and without ceremony, with the member he has sculpted specially with her in mind. The screams will continue for a long time.

There is a flash outside the window, down amidst the gnarled bushes just above the high-water mark. He strains his eyes, but cannot see clearly. But, but . . . he can *feel*.

Someone has arrived.

So soon!

Yet not soon at all. Seventy years of suffering is about to culminate in an orgy of glory. Husk exults as the Undying Man emerges from the bushes with his consort in train. The man will know exactly where Husk sits. The knowledge will do him no good.

This is Husk's time.

There is a buzzing at the back of his head. He takes it for part of the excitement: his body is still relatively new and he does not know exactly how it will react to the stress it is about to be subjected to.

The buzzing grows and his scalp becomes warm. Some sort of attack from the Undying Man perhaps. Still he does not panic. He draws from his conduit to the void and prepares his defences. Chief among them is a strong shield to keep out any magical assault; so much power is at his disposal that he cannot conceive of anyone penetrating it.

The shield snaps closed around him, yet the buzzing does not cease. Instead, it grows; and now he can hear voices.

No.

Something's happening, says a voice.

No, oh no. He has no defence against this.

Another voice whispers in his mind. *She has found the connection between we three spikes and Husk. She has Conal's mind wide open. I . . . can feel her widening the channel – ah, she's going to burn out our minds!*

The artery he made to link himself to his spikes, the connection he'd strengthened until it was impossible to break, begins to burn, to blister. Something begins to move along it, towards him.

Frantic with terror, Husk tries to cut the link.

His magical power has no effect.

He tries to assemble a barrier between the channel and his own body.

The intruder bursts through it with ease.

It is coming, it is coming – it is here.

'No!' he cries, the word ripping out his throat. 'No! Stay away!'

It reaches for him, fastens onto him.

'Do not . . . I will . . . AAAAAAH!'

It slides into his mind and fills it, evicting him with no effort.

It is the Daughter, Umu, and she is unimaginably strong. She tears his mind open, laughing as she does so, leafing through his thoughts of revenge, whispering mocking things at what she finds. She throws carefully nurtured concepts away as though they were so much rubbish. Husk sits at the back of his own head, a tiny ball of misery, beyond terror.

'Ah,' says Umu, settling into his mind as though it was a rented room. No, a room repossessed by a moneylender. 'I will be comfortable here.'

Husk screams, but no one can hear him.

THE BROKEN MAN

CHAPTER 18

THE BRONZE MAP

THE FLAMES WRAPPED THEMSELVES AROUND Stella like a former lover renewing an unwanted embrace, licking, caressing, burning. She could not move, whether because of Kannwar's power or the strength of the blue fire, she could not tell. She remembered panicking the first time she had travelled this way, and how it had so nearly destroyed her. Would that it had. But she could not struggle, could not fight, and so the flames overwhelmed her, burned her to ashes, and bore them away.

The first thing she felt as she came to herself was a cool wind whipping at her hair. *Alive then*, she sighed. A moment later, the second realisation. *Still under Kannwar's spell*.

'Come, my queen,' growled the loved, hated voice from beside her. 'We have business to attend to.'

She opened her eyes reluctantly and scrambled to her feet. The bitter wind whipped at the stunted bushes around them, the thin branches clacking together, creating an unpleasant sound.

'Cold wind and thorny bushes,' she said. He'd returned her voice, at least. 'Why doesn't that surprise me, Destroyer?'

'Ah, Stella,' Kannwar purred. 'Delight of my heart. Unquenchable spirit.'

Hatred for the man boiled up within her, underlain by something darker. She wanted to hate him, wanted to . . . She *couldn't* want *that*. What was wrong with her?

They reached the end of the bushy grove and emerged into

425

the open. To Stella's left the land dropped away to the dull grey sea, whose great surges boomed and sucked at the coast. Above them the louring sky darkened towards twilight; towering clouds, pale at their tops, dark and forbidding at the base, blurred where rain swept across the water. Ahead lay the island itself: a table-top of rolling grass interspersed by gnarled trees. Her gaze followed the lie of the land forward, and snagged on the fortress.

Andratan stood there, towers, battlements, keeps and walls all purpling in the last of the day's light. Like a champion before battle it seemed to adopt a confident stance, immovable, certain of its own strength.

'Home,' said Kannwar. 'You'll like it here.'

'Only if you find somewhere else to live.'

The Destroyer smiled at this weak sally. Then his face changed.

'You dare sit on that seat?' he breathed.

Stella quailed at the anger in his words, then realised they were not meant for her. He snatched at her hand and began to drag her forward.

The sodden ground kept trying to snare her feet. After the second time she'd fallen, he hauled her mud-soaked figure to its feet and sighed.

'Come on, Stella,' he grated. 'We have an uninvited guest to be rid of. And I had so hoped our nuptials and their consummation would be a more select affair.'

Again his words stirred something within her as thick as tar, as black as pitch. She was frightened of him, petrified in fact, but what seemed to be building inside her scared her far more . . .

'The Sea Door,' he said. 'He will be expecting us to use the main entrance. Always direct, our Deorc. We shall just have to confuse him.'

'You are enjoying this,' Stella said in wonder. 'A man who betrayed you seventy years ago has escaped from the most appalling torture and now controls your castle, and you are enjoying your-self!'

The Destroyer turned to her and not for the first time she saw the delight of a young boy shining out from his dark eyes. 'How else does one know one is alive?' he said, grinning widely.

He led her down a slope to their left, to the top of a stone stair that led all the way down to the sea. They were much closer to the fortress now, but the largest tower stood well to their right. Across a small inlet, in which three ships lay uneasily at anchor, stood an adjunct tower at the base of which Stella could barely make out a small door.

'Mind your step,' said the Destroyer.

The steps were wet with spray and hard to see in the gloom. Stella rolled her ankle on the third step and fell in a heap.

'Are you doing this deliberately, my queen? Do I need to possess you in order to carry you over my threshold?' He lifted her chin in one illusory hand. 'Do you ever want to exercise free will or must I compel every aspect of your life from now on?'

'No,' she said, attempting to stop the tears that had begun to fall. 'I'm trying. Please, help me to my feet.'

He raised a finger to her face and traced one of her tears as it rolled down her cheek. 'This will not do,' he said, his voice gentle. 'We cannot enter my house like this. We are not beggars come to request a favour from some great lord that we should creep and weep.'

He waved a hand and his guise changed. Gone was Heredrew, that elongated man. In his place was a shorter, more compact figure, long blond locks framing a handsome face with an aquiline nose and deep blue eyes. The hair tumbled down to the high collar of a formal brown jacket, embroidered in green and gold; his leggings were similarly adorned. He wore white gloves and long black boots, and the overall effect was unsettling. The syrup deep within Stella stirred. She had no doubt she was seeing Kannwar as he had been when he had rebelled against the Most High, before the Water of Life had twisted his body. A figure altogether fair, the best of his generation, the culmination of a thousand years of patient planning by the Most High. The true First Man.

Almost unbearable to look upon.

His hand waved again. Her bedraggled, soaked attire vanished, to be replaced by a flowing red dress. Ankle-length, gold-threaded silk, hugging the curves of her body, the high collar tickling her chin. Crystal slippers on her feet and a tiara in her hair. She raised a hand to explore how her hair had been styled.

He smiled. Her hand dropped back to her side.

'That's how I see you, my queen,' he said. 'That's how I've always seen you. Come, now. Let us enter our house with dignity.'

This is some kind of glamour, she thought. *I am helpless in the hands of the Destroyer. My friends are trapped in the House of the Gods. Umu is loose and the world is still endangered. And ahead of us waits another madman, someone who believes I betrayed him seventy years ago. And all I care about is how beautiful my captor looks?*

Something within her urged her to forget everything and surrender to the moment.

As they reached the base of the stair, a huge figure stepped out from an embayment in the cliff to their right. 'Halt!' it cried. 'Give your name and – oh.' It lowered the enormous sword it had drawn, laid it on the stone step and bowed. 'My lord,' it said, in a voice like gravel.

'Prepare the boat,' the Destroyer commanded the figure.

As the man rose, Stella was forcibly reminded of Noetos; certainly this fellow was of the same stock, if somewhat larger even than the fisherman. His red hair was cut short, his hairy arms exposed by the short-sleeved jerkin he wore. Stella had never seen a man so muscled.

The man disappeared around a bend in the path, then came back a moment later and beckoned them forward. A boat slopped in the water. The Destroyer gestured her towards it. 'You first, my queen.'

She thought of pitching herself in the water. Saw herself carried out by the sea, then pitched back against the rocks by the first wave. Imagined the crack and shatter of her bones, felt the water filling her chest. Sighed deeply as she envisioned herself coming back to life, and plunked herself in the boat.

The bay was perhaps two hundred paces across, an effective barrier preventing an easy approach to the tower. The red-headed giant rowed them across in twenty powerful strokes of his oars, leaped out of the boat and made it fast in one swift motion.

The Destroyer pursed his lips. 'Come with us,' he instructed the man. 'Draw your sword.'

The man nodded, content to leave his lord's command unquestioned. Or frightened perhaps, though he did not look frightened. His expression was remarkably blank. A dullard? Stella thought of her brother, her poor dead brother, killed seventy years ago by drink, and the uncomprehending look on his face when the bottle had taken him.

The Destroyer led them up the ten steps to the door of the tower. The remains of the day were leaching away, but Stella could still see the disturbing architecture of the tower above her. Surmounting the door was a carving of some battle scene in which a man with a flashing blade held off a horde of wild-looking soldiers. The artist had injected the scene with a manic quality and the snarl on the face of the defender was little less sinister than those on the attackers'.

'That happened,' said the Destroyer, noting the direction of her gaze. 'The hordes of Kanabar overcame my armies and drove me back to Andratan. Actually, we were never in any serious danger of being overrun but feigned defeat, thus stretching the foolish barbarians' supply lines to breaking point.' He laughed. 'It did my legend no harm to have fought their elite troops single-handed at the door to the Sea Tower.'

'How long ago?' Stella croaked.

'Over seventeen hundred years ago,' he replied. 'Seems like yesterday.'

As he spoke the words, something thickened in the air around them. A trap?

'Ah, now that I did not expect,' the Destroyer said. 'No matter how clever my plans are, some dupe always blunders in and upsets them. Conal Greatheart, Leith Mahnumsen, lucky fools.'

'What has happened?'

The Destroyer pursed his lips. 'Umu has been extremely clever,' he said. 'Ironic, really, in light of where we stand. She has pretended to flee from the hordes intent on her destruction and has now found a far safer place from which to wage her war. Not that Deorc will think so.'

Stella shook her head, not understanding a word of it. The Destroyer leaned on the door and swung it open, and she followed him inside.

And so this ends, one way or another, for everyone else, she thought. *But for me, it begins.*

Conal's body lay empty and stiff at the base of the throne.

'Has she gone? Is she still hiding in there?'

The travellers gathered around, staring at the body, most of them unclear as to what had just happened.

'Umu has gone,' Duon confirmed.

Cheers accompanied this statement, dying out as it became clear that the principals did not share their joy.

'She's not been driven beyond the hole in the world then?' Bregor hazarded.

'No,' Noetos said. 'You're all aware that my daughter, the Elamaq captain and' – he kicked the corpse with his boot – 'that thing were all linked to the magician's voice. You know that we discovered his identity and location, being one Husk of Andratan, who had opportunistically spiked these three when they visited the fortress. You also know they broke free of his control by exploiting the death of Conal.'

Everyone nodded. As much had been explained to them during their journey north to Zizhua Valley.

'But what you didn't know – and what we did know, but discounted – was that the magical channels formed between Husk and his three spikes remained open, even though Husk himself could no longer exploit them. That's right, isn't it?' he finished, turning to his daughter.

She nodded, and extended a hand to Duon, gesturing for him to speak.

'We might have been able to close them,' the southern captain admitted, 'but we never tried. It seemed to us that we might be able to utilise the link to draw power from Husk, in the same way he had once used us. Turn and turn about, in a way. In fact that's just what we did when we rallied together to drive Keppia out of Cylene's body.'

'But Umu found the link, didn't she?' Lenares said, her eyes sparkling as she solved the puzzle. 'She discarded Conal's dead body and leapt into Husk's live one.' She giggled. 'How surprising for Husk!'

'Yes, but what I want to know,' said Noetos, concern on his face, 'is how easily she might return.' Everyone stared at the body at their feet. 'Not Conal's body, but down one of the other links, to Duon or Arathé – and through them to others.'

Duon saw the worry on the man's face. *He's concerned for his daughter, and also for himself. As am I.*

As are we all, Arathé whispered, her voice a caress even in its anxiety.

'Then the two of you need to work together on some form of defence,' said Anomer, clutching his sister's hand.

'Aye,' Mustar agreed. The fisherman's eyes flicked over Arathé. *That one fancies you,* Duon said.

He does. He's quite the handsome young man, don't you think?

Indeed, if you like them vacuous.

She laughed in his mind. *Jealous, Captain?*

Anomer cleared his throat; clearly they were spilling over into his mind's ear. 'Perhaps,' he said, 'you ought not to use your mental connection for now, in order not to draw the Daughter's attention?'

Ah, Arathé and Duon said at the same moment, and damped their minds down.

In the silence, the group heard an exhalation from the corpse's body. *How undignified we all are in death,* Duon reflected; though a moment later he began to wonder. *This corpse is weeks dead. How could it still be manufacturing gases?*

'It's trying to say something,' he said, and bent down to the rotted face.

'Careful!' Mustar cried. 'It might be Umu!'

'Whoever it is, we ought to hear it,' Duon replied.

The breaths, exhalations, came rhythmically, as though something mechanical was expelling breath from the lungs. He winced at the dire smell contained in the vapour.

'He's saying sorry,' Lenares said.

'Priest?' Sauxa said, bending over the body. 'Is that you?'

'Yesss.'

Duon leaped backwards. Sauxa stayed where he was.

'Speak,' said the plainsman.

'Ssss-Stella?'

'She's not here,' the plainsman said shortly.

'Sss-sorry,' said the body. 'I let everyone down. Too weak. Wanted to . . . to pleassssse.'

The breathing stopped, and for a moment Duon thought the priest's spirit had finally fled.

'Ssselfish. Paid for it now. But I fought the monssster, made her sssluggish. S-ss-sent her away. Saved you all.'

'That you did, priest,' Duon said, choosing not to elaborate on the problems this act might have caused. 'Your sins have been absolved.'

'Sssss,' said the body. 'Sss-say goodbye to Ssstella for me. I go now to sssee what judgement has in ssstore for me.' The mouth clicked in what could only be macabre laughter. 'I don't hope for much.'

'Aye,' Sauxa said, his face troubled. 'Nor should any of us.'

The body seemed to deflate, as though the breath had gone from it – which, Duon presumed, was likely exactly what had happened.

'Fare well, priest,' Sauxa said, his face stony. Wishing, no doubt, he'd had the luxury of last words with his own son.

Noetos sighed, and eased himself to his feet with a groan. 'What next?' he asked the group.

'We must find Kannwar and Stella,' Lenares said firmly. 'Then we can decide what to do next.'

'Whatever we decide, it will necessarily involve Andratan,' said Consina. 'If that's where Umu has gone, it is where we must follow.'

'Aye,' Sauxa said. 'Why not? Travel with the Destroyer and

invade his fortress. I'm sure I'm asleep in my tent, the *Journeys of the First Men* lying across my lap. Someone wake me up at the end of this dream.' He licked his lips and corrected himself. 'This nightmare.'

They buried the body with no ceremony. Everyone felt ambivalent about the little priest, Noetos judged. Brave at the end, though. The burial was easy, given the soft, sandy floor of the Throne Room.

'So,' he said, as Seren and Mustar hand-shovelled the last of the sand over the shallow grave. 'Our quarry is hundreds of leagues away. By the time we travel to Andratan any conflict will long since have been resolved.'

'We still have to go there,' Lenares said stubbornly.

Such a strange girl, so like and so unlike her sister. Both stubborn, fortunately for him. He took Cylene's hand in his own; she smiled in response.

Cylene had said nothing about Conal's demise, but he knew it had affected her deeply. How else would it have taken her, given how close she had come to a similar fate? Of them all, she knew best what the priest had endured at the end. Her face had been pale as they had buried Conal.

Noetos tried not to think of the dead woman keeping his beloved Cylene alive. Madness, the whole story seemed; something to have been dismissed without comment in the days before this crazy adventure had begun. A dead soul sustaining Cylene, allowing an infinitesimal amount of magic down the conduit once belonging to Keppia himself? He'd not known what to think when she'd come to him that first night after her . . . well, her resurrection, for want of a more accurate term. Offering herself without a trace of embarrassment. He'd not known whether she was still the same woman he'd fallen in love with, and had been reluctant in his own secret heart. Partly, he admitted, because of his upbringing. He was supposed to bring his intended home for the family to inspect: *Look, Father, I've found a chaste woman mad enough to spend the rest of her life with me!* Except Cylene was anything but chaste, and she'd make no such promise. *Nor do I need her to,* Noetos had realised. *Keeping such a woman will mean wooing her anew every day.*

He'd looked her in the eye, there on the road north of Mensaya, and had quashed his fear. *You don't need someone frightened of you,* he told her in his mind, knowing she couldn't hear him and glad of it, glad she couldn't see his confusion. *You need someone to comfort you, to reassure yourself you are human.*

He had reached out his hand and taken hers, then led her to a sheltered place far enough away from where the others slept, and there had loved her with his body, exercising restraint and tenderness. She had cried in his arms, not needing to explain her tears, knowing he understood. Healing.

She squeezed his hand now. Perhaps she too had been thinking of that first night.

'The swiftest way north is by ship,' she told her sister.

'No, there is a quicker way,' Sauxa said. 'If we can find the Undying Man, he can take us there in but a moment.'

'How?' This from Sautea, the stocky fisherman.

'His blue fire.' Sauxa reminded them of the Falthans' journey to Bhrudwo and their arrival at Lake Woe. 'It's not a comfortable voyage, but if it's speed you want, I can't think of anything comparable.'

'Can we trust him?' Noetos asked.

Anomer turned to face him, his eyebrows raised. 'Father, haven't you had enough evidence that the Undying Man is on our side? Didn't you hear his words? He's not like us: his morals are necessarily more rarefied than ours. Arathé has accepted his explanation, as have I. Can't you accept it too, and move on?'

A fair question, deserving a fair answer.

'No,' he said.

Anomer snorted in disgust and turned away.

'Nevertheless, Sauxa is right,' Noetos continued. 'We need to find our two missing companions, whether or not they can provide us with a shortcut to Andratan.'

'Can we trust the House of the Gods to let us alone?' Cyclamere asked, his face a mask. Noetos wondered how painful had been his capture.

'We should go in pairs then,' he said. 'Enter each new room side by side, so you are not separated. Gather here when you have investigated as much as you are able.'

'And let us not be too long about it,' Seren said. 'I, for one, am in need of sleep.'

Noetos glanced up at the sky, now full night, with piercing stars scattered across the heavens. They all needed sleep. How long had it been? Since the night before Robal had blown up Zizhua City – how long ago had that been? He rubbed his beard.

'In pairs,' he said, and began to lead Cylene towards the corridor.

'Cylene!' Lenares called. 'The search doesn't need us all. Someone needs to work out how Umu controlled the House of the Gods. I'm staying here. Could you stay with me?'

'No, Noetos,' Cylene said, tugging against him. 'I'm going to stay here.'

My beloved, he thought to insist, then remembered. *You'll never be held against your will, not again. See to your sister.*

'A good idea,' he agreed, the words coming reluctantly from his tongue. 'I'll go with Sautea.'

'Ah . . . yes, Noetos,' Sautea said, and came dutifully to his side, leaving Mustar on his own.

'Problem, old friend?' Noetos asked him.

'No,' came the abrupt answer.

It was Sautea, in fact, who discovered Stella and Kannwar – or evidence of their passage. But that discovery came after a number of far more unpleasant discoveries.

'The entrance to the Rainbow Room is blocked,' Torve reported when the travellers had all gathered back in the Throne Room. 'A recent rock fall. An unfortunate accident, if accident it was.'

Duon frowned. 'The same thing has happened to the route back to Zizhua City,' he said. 'This cannot be a coincidence.'

'It seems not,' Sautea said. 'Noetos and I found the embers of a fire in the Children's Room. Did anyone else see it?'

No, came the replies. They'd all been in the room at some point over the last few hours of searching, but none had seen the embers. Looking for people, they were, not embers, a few said defensively.

'What do you make of it?' Mustar asked.

'He's telling us that Kannwar and Stella have already escaped this place,' Lenares said, 'using the blue fire Sauxa told us about. Leaving us behind.'

'Aye,' said Sauxa, sucking his teeth. 'Betrayal, that's what it is.'

'Why now?' Bregor asked aloud.

'Why not sooner?' Noetos countered.

He did not look at his children for fear of angering them with the look of triumph no doubt plastered on his face.

'So, they have abandoned us and blocked our paths out of this place,' Duon said. 'Is that it then? Quest over?'

'Hard to believe,' Sauxa said.

'What, that our journey is at an end?'

'No, Mister Explorer. Hard to believe that Stella would betray us. I suspect she is not acting under her own volition.'

'It doesn't really matter at this point,' Noetos said impatiently. 'Though we will be sure to ask her when next we see her. In the meantime, we need to find a way out of here. I do not feel like adding my corpse to that of the priest.'

'As to that,' Lenares said, 'I have some thoughts.'

Everyone turned to her, and Noetos watched her swell at the attention. He wondered how much she would lie and exaggerate to keep their attention fixed on her. *No*, he chastised himself. *She adores our consideration, but would not lie to obtain it. Our constant failing has been in not listening to her often or closely enough.*

'Gather around,' she said, 'and listen.'

Something dark lurked within her, Stella admitted to herself. Something attracted to dark men, to men who dealt in falsehood, trickery, bullying and death. Something repelled by decency, by ordinariness. How else could she explain her willingness to be seduced time and again by power and its concomitants? Her long rejection of everything good encapsulated in Leith Mahnumsen? Her avid pursuit of Tanghin, who proved to be Deorc of Jasweyah in disguise? And her secret – well, not so secret – desire for the Destroyer himself?

The door to the Sea Tower closed behind them and soldiers came forward with weapons presented and questions at the ready. Their voices changed from belligerent to respectful as they saw who had come through the door. Stella cared nothing for their conversations, totally absorbed in this belated moment of self-awareness.

Even after he wounded me near to death and tortured me back to health, I lusted after him, she admitted to herself. *I hate him, but want him.* She thought of her parents. Ineffectual Pell, her father, his meekness at home and on the village council; kept meek by her mother Herza's constant criticism. Both powerless to help her older brother with his drunkenness. Neither pleading nor nagging helped. Not an ounce of real strength between them.

A village boy, Druin, had lusted after her. He'd wanted her body, had said so whenever he'd been able to catch her alone – and sometimes, embarrassingly, in front of her friends or his. Yet something had stirred in her at his words, something wicked, something urging her to dive right in, to immerse herself in this futureless passion, so far removed from the petty nagging and calculation she'd been brought up to believe was virtue.

By contrast, Leith's attempts to woo her had been pitiful. An assignation under the village oak, probably for nothing more than awkward conversation; dreadfully shy, he'd never have ventured as far as a quick fumble. It had been too easy to agree with Druin's cruel assessment of Leith's intentions. She'd stayed away, leaving him to waste the afternoon under the oak.

Events had unfolded as they had and she'd fled the village, delighted that her deepest wish was to be granted: a passage out of this dead-end place, new vistas opening up before her. The darkness within her had jumped at the chance.

Then Wira had come into her life. Poor Wira. Virtuous and handsome but somehow flawed; she'd been able to tell that right from the beginning. Such a contrast to his older brother, Farr, a man with a stick up his backside if ever she'd met one. Of course Wira attracted her. It was because of his flaw she'd been drawn to him, not in spite of it. The darker the man, the stronger the attraction . . . Wira had been a drunkard, and had died trying to save her from the Lords of Fear. The darkness within her had lamented his death while simultaneously rejoicing in it: such a bright soul dying to save her! How evil she had become, even then.

A question stirred itself in her mind. 'What happened to your Lords of Fear?'

'A failed experiment, my queen,' said the Destroyer, his voice just behind her in the darkened corridor. The red-haired servant's torch bobbed some distance ahead. 'One that will not be repeated. I ended their lives myself on my return to Andratan.'

'You didn't track them all down,' she said. He gave no answer to this.

They climbed another stair, this one circular, inscribed into the barrel of the Sea Tower. No one save the servant and his torch shared the stair with them. *Perhaps the servants go home in the evening,* Stella thought, then considered the island. *No, this fortress is their home. What a bleak place to live.*

She returned to her thoughts. Between herself and her parents, they had succeeded in birthing and nurturing something dark within her. Something that had lusted after Tanghin without considering the consequences; another man who had appeared to be pure – a member of the Ecclesia, high in their confidences – while hiding a dark secret. Darker by far than she'd suspected. Tanghin had been Deorc, sent by the Destroyer to Instruere as a vanguard of invasion, a spy to infiltrate and control the Council of Faltha. A far deeper kind of evil than even her inner darkness had believed possible, let alone contemplated joining with. This was well beyond the delicious excitement of the forbidden and into the terror of the truly depraved. Torturer, executioner, killer. Stella had betrayed him to his master, who turned out to excel in the vices in which Deorc was merely competent.

Was this dark companion an indivisible part of her, or could she put it aside?

Seventy years, Stella, and finally you ask the right question.

She stopped, arrested by the shock of the voice speaking into her mind. The Destroyer bumped into her.

'Something the matter, my queen?'

'Apart from being force-marched through the rancid home of the man I hate most in the world, you mean?' she replied sweetly.

The Destroyer tilted back his head and roared with laughter, each bark echoing – resonating – with the dark tar inside her.

Can I, Leith? Can I put it aside?

No, said the most patient and loving man she'd ever known. *No, these desires are a part of you, a part of all of us.*

Not of you, surely, she said to him.

Stella, we all suffer from such things. Take them out – even if it were possible – and you leave behind something less than a human.

She resumed walking, following the Destroyer now. The link between her and the man in front of her felt more like a string, less like a chain. She wondered at the change and what it might mean.

There was nothing wrong with wanting more than a small village could offer you, Leith said. *Nor in desiring dark and dangerous experiences. What trapped you and led you here was the day you made it the core of who you are. From that day on you sought out abusive relationships and gloried in the pain they brought you.*

Why didn't you tell me?

I didn't understand. Only when I passed through the veil and into the void beyond did I see clearly.

You were given insight into my problems? she said ruefully.

He laughed. *Only incidentally, dear one. What I saw most clearly were my own problems, and the choices I'd made affixing them to me.*

Too late then, she said. *What's the point of realising where you went wrong when your life is over?*

Over? Leith said, and the question hung between them like the promise of eternity.

Ahead of her the Destroyer unlocked a door and stepped out into the night air. She followed, to find herself on a roofed walkway high above one of the fortress's keeps. People and animals moved about far below.

And besides, your life here has not yet ended, Leith added.

She acknowledged the corollary. *I, therefore, can benefit from the knowledge.*

Indeed, he said.

She smiled at his voice. *Stay with me a while?*

As long as I can, he said.

Lenares pushed her mind as far as it would go, thinking furiously. She paced around the Throne Room, climbed first one then another of the three great chairs arranged around the great bronze map set into the ground, and stared at the map, searching for inspiration. Occasionally one of the others tried to speak with her, but she waved them away. *Well meaning but ignorant, of no help here.*

The bronze map held immense fascination for Lenares. She remembered the power she'd felt when, on her second visit to the Godhouse, she'd climbed into one of the seats and first understood the map. It was a wonder of the world without a doubt, representing a way of thinking beyond even her imagination. Distance wasn't measured in leagues on this map; instead the scale was logarithmic, and the size of things was large in the centre and shrank towards the edges. The Elamaq Diminiq, the most southern of Elamaq's peninsulas and a vast ice-locked land, took barely more space on the periphery of the bronze map than the House of the Gods had in the map's centre, despite being many thousands of times larger. *Scale,* she reminded herself, *is far less important than distance and bearing.* There had to be a reason for this, but she could not work it out.

Umu had used this room to control the House of the Gods. She had been able to come and go from the House without using the entrances. What was her secret? Was it something stemming from her godhood, or something intrinsic to the Throne Room? It had to be the latter, it had to be: why else would she have come to this room if any of the other rooms might have served equally well?

Despite Lenares' repeated signals intended to tell Cylene she wished to be left alone, her sister joined her on her search. She wanted to tell Cylene to go away, but could you say things like that to a sister? It had been so long she couldn't remember . . . she supposed not. And she didn't want Cylene to go away, not really, not now, leaving her alone with no cosmographers, no Mahudia, no family.

The sisters walked slowly around the perimeter of the room, asking their companions to move despite many of them having settled down to sleep. A few grumbled, but moved when Lenares reminded them of their predicament.

'You love Torve, don't you?' Cylene asked her as they walked.

Lenares turned away from her sister, highly embarrassed for some reason. Certainly not a logical reason: love was nothing to be ashamed of, and she'd had no difficulty in talking about her feelings for Torve to a square full of strangers. This was her sister! Of course, that might be the problem.

She took a deep breath and forced herself to smile as she nodded to Cylene. 'Yes,' she said. 'He makes me go pink.'

Her sister raised her eyebrows at this. 'Hmm. How many others have you loved before?'

'You mean love between girl and boy?'

'Well, unless you're more broad-minded than I suspect, yes, love between a girl and a boy.'

It took Lenares a moment to figure out what Cylene meant by this. 'Why do you steer every conversation away into irrelevant places?' she complained.

Cylene frowned. 'Humour, sister. We're trapped in a frightening place. Even I can feel the strangeness here and I have no magic at all. I don't know if we'll ever get out. So I try to make you feel better, to take your mind off the seriousness of our situation, by making you laugh.'

'But I don't want to laugh. And I certainly don't want my mind taken off finding a way out of here.'

Her sister nodded politely, but Lenares could tell she was angered by the rebuff. They continued for a while in silence, running their hands over the rocks within their reach, looking for some clue to understand how the room functioned.

'What do you mean, Torve makes you go pink?'

Lenares clicked her tongue. How could she concentrate with such interference?

You're angry because you're embarrassed, she told herself. *That's not reason enough.*

'Torve is the first man who makes me . . . makes me want to lie with him,' she admitted.

'You mean you've never lain with a man?'

The surprised look on her sister's face compounded Lenares' embarrassment. 'Why would I? I haven't loved any man before.'

'Why? Because it feels so wonderful, that's why.'

'You're lying with Noetos.'

'Of course!' Cylene smiled. 'He's a wonderful man. I think I'm falling in love with him.'

'He's a grumpy old man with a bad temper and he's mean to his children,' Lenares said without thinking. At Cylene's stricken look, she put her hand to her mouth. 'Oh. Sorry . . .'

Cylene shrugged. 'He appears that way, doesn't he? But he's been through a great deal. I can understand why he's protective of his children: after all, he has lost an entire family, and saw his wife cut down only a few months ago. But he's a sensitive fellow under all that grumpiness. And he's not old, not really, not compared to . . .' She faltered.

'Compared to what?' Lenares didn't like it when people left things unsaid.

Cylene squared her shoulders. 'Compared to many other men I've slept with.'

'You've been in love with men even older than Noetos?'

'Not in love, no. Lenares, for a clever person, you really don't know much about how the world works, do you?'

Why was her sister insulting her? *It's been nice talking to you,* she wanted to say, *but go away now and let me search on my own.* But she couldn't say that: the first part was a lie, and the second part was too truthful. Learning to live, really live, with other people on their terms was very difficult. She sighed. Why couldn't they all behave sensibly, like her?

'I slept with many men I didn't love, didn't have any pink feelings towards, and some who revolted me, so I could escape Sayonae and my family. Do you think I would have been better to stay on the steading?'

'They paid you money to sleep with them?'

'Yes,' Cylene said.

'Oh. That I can understand. It sounds like a sensible arrangement, actually. If you need food and clothing, and they have . . . urges, it makes a good trade. Better than staying with Martje and those dreadful boys.'

Cylene regarded Lenares, wide-eyed. 'Sister, you are a constant surprise to me. I love you.' And she wrapped Lenares in a hug.

Don't touch . . . The words died on her lips.

They completed their third circuit of the room, then moved back to the centre where the chairs stood. Lenares wished she knew what she was looking for; her numbers helped to a certain extent, but the purpose of the three chairs and the bronze map remained tantalisingly hidden from her.

'Was our father like Noetos?' she blurted to her sister.

'What? Of course not! No similarity at all, apart from the age. Don't you remember Father?'

'No. I know he must have existed, and I've been told the bad things he did to me – to us – but there is no picture of him in my mind.'

'Why do you ask?'

'Because if I were you,' Lenares said carefully, 'I would be worried that I was loving Noetos only because he was like Father.'

'A substitute, you mean? Lenares, how horrid!'

'But isn't it possible, sister? We had a bad father, so now you've fallen in love with someone you think is a good father?'

'Oh, I thought you meant . . . Well, yes, that is probably part of it, though there have been many other older men – Captain Kidson, for example – and I never wanted . . . Ah, Lenares, you ask the most awkward questions.'

'You started it.'

'Indeed I did. And what I realise now is that while we are sisters

– twins – we couldn't be more different. You've slept with no one, I've slept with everyone. You think logically, I think emotionally. You're clever, I'm . . . well, slow.'

'Noetos says he loves how you are able to cut through words and get to the heart of a person,' Lenares said.

'He told you that?'

'No, I heard him talking to his son. But I think you and I are alike, sister. We've walked very different paths, but we are still twins.'

'I'm looking forward to getting to know you better,' Cylene said, and her smile warmed Lenares' heart.

'Wait here a moment,' she said. 'I want to keep talking, but I need to go to relieve myself.'

Not that it really mattered where in the room she went; there was no privacy here. She left Cylene leaning against one of the chairs and walked towards the wall in the deepest shadow. As she strode past another of the chairs she reached out and slapped a stone leg in frustration.

Beside her the bronze map flickered.

'I am a fool,' Lenares breathed to herself. *Such a colossal fool.* Where had her wits gone? Of course, her attention had been distracted by Cylene's well-meaning conversation. But it was more than that. Lenares had been making an effort to fit in, to be like the others. She had to learn more about how to be human or how could she lead them? This journey had changed her, she could see that. No longer did she count every step. Once, she would have had a total for the number of rocks in this room she'd touched, the number of words she'd spoken in a day; even on a bad day the number of stars visible in the night sky. She'd stayed indoors at night for that reason.

Was it wrong to want to be like others? To be thought of as human and not as some kind of animal?

Yes. If it meant losing her gift, yes. Yes, if it meant becoming someone different. Yes, if it meant she was condemning her friends to a slow death in this many-roomed trap.

But there was no danger of that, not now. The key had fallen into her hand. So simple. She sighed. Time to be Lenares as hard as she could.

She woke them, ignoring their complaints – they were just ordinary people, after all, ruled by their bodies – and made them stand in a circle around the bronze map.

'I have a question for Torve and Captain Duon,' she said. 'Why did Umu return the bronze map to this room?'

'What do you mean?' Duon answered her, but even as the question slipped out of his mouth, comprehension dawned on his face.

Lenares willed him on, wanting him to work out what it implied. The four southern survivors of the Valley of the Damned – Lenares, Torve, Duon and Dryman – had been corralled into Nomansland, where they were trapped in the House of the Gods. There, in the Throne Room, they were snatched up by a god, chair, bronze map and all, and deposited in Raceme. The huge, circular bronze image had landed on top of Lenares, knocking the breath from her.

Torve saw it more quickly even than the explorer. 'The map was ripped away from this room when we were taken up by the god and dropped in Raceme. Yet here it is now. Umu must have gone to a great deal of effort to bring it back.'

Lenares smiled. 'Umu has rebuilt the chairs and retrieved the bronze map. There can be only one reason. They are the components of the secret mechanism.'

She scrambled up onto the chair she associated with the Father. 'Cylene!' she called excitedly. 'Get up in the chair nearest you!'

Dear sister, she did what she was asked without question. Who else should Lenares ask but Torve?

'Torve! Please, Torve, could you climb the remaining chair?'

Yes! she exulted as Cylene reached the seat and sat herself down in it. Immediately her rear made contact with the stone, the numbers embedded in the bronze map changed . . . amplified . . . began to make sense. There were just as many lines and names on the map as before, but some of them thickened and changed colour, making the whole map easier to read. Now, if only there was a legend.

445

Torve sat on the third chair. For the first time in who knew how long, all three chairs were occupied. Not by gods, but did that matter?

Everyone in the circle gasped as the map began to glow as though backlit with sunlight. The room filled with light, and the travellers cast huge shadows on the walls behind them.

Yes, yes, yes!

The legend appeared. Not that it was really needed now: Lenares could read the map as though it was a part of her own mind.

Oh, of course. The centre of the map wasn't in the same place as she remembered from Marasmos, because they were much further north now. The bronze map was centred in the Bhrudwan continent, and Elamaq and Faltha were small and stretched around the periphery of the map. Bhrudwo was much larger, and many places were marked. One colour for towns, another for roads – all named, if she looked closely enough – a third for rivers. And so it went. Forests, bays, oceans, mountains.

But the legend had far more on it than mere physical features. It was the oddest legend Lenares had ever seen on a map, and she had seen – and drawn – plenty of them as part of her training. She focused on the heading 'Fear' and the map changed. Muttering from below indicated the others saw the change too. The names were still there, but they had turned grey and become smaller. Instead, the map was covered by shades of red. A pinprick of bright red pulsed in the room at the centre of the map – the room they were in. She desired to see this more closely, and the map obliged. She found she was looking down on the back of her own head, and in the centre of the bronze map was . . . a bronze map, which, if she looked more closely – no. She stopped, worried that she might be starting down a never-ending path.

Could she enlarge other areas of the map? Anywhere else wouldn't entail the sick-making effect she'd just experienced.

Talamaq, her mind said. Immediately she was drawn down into the map – or the map swelled, she couldn't tell which – and the red-coloured city spread out before her, just as it appeared on the maps she had studied in the city's scholarium. *Oh.* Thinking the name

446

sent her down, so that she hovered just above the scholarium itself, an annexe to the Talamaq Palace. The view readjusted.

Something odd was happening. She could actually see the heads of people running to and fro across the map – although not a map: at this scale, she was seeing the physical world as it actually was, watching events as they happened. Everything was covered in a deep red wash. The scholarium's glass roof was broken and smoke spiralled up towards her, borne away to her left on a sea breeze. Part of the palace was in flames, and as she looked more closely she saw that the people were fighting with each other. Some lay prone on the ground. She almost found herself shouting down to the figures, warning them of soldiers approaching from around a corner. She doubted they would hear her – and, of course, she had no idea what side she should take, if any.

Voices were calling out to her, but she ignored them: not from the map. Fear? Was this a map of fear? Well, there was certainly enough fear in this room to show up as a red patch on the map. In fact, it had grown since she'd first changed the legend. *Hah.* Just like her, her companions had been frightened when she'd swooped in for a closer look. Where else did fear lie? Another scarlet blob lay on – she zoomed closer – an island off the coast of Malayu. *Ah, Andratan.* That made sense. Other places she knew glowed red: Aneheri, Raceme. And Talamaq, of course. She greatly wished she could return there.

Back to the legend. 'Wealth' said one heading. 'Love.' 'Weather.' 'Wars.' *Oh my.* She so wanted to explore, but there wasn't time, she knew that. Her body shook with excitement, the glory of revelation almost overwhelming her. *Oh, if I could only sit here forever.*

One more thing to try. She reached into the map with her mind and touched one of the rooms of the Godhouse. Immediately it was outlined in gold. She tugged it to her left, and all the rooms changed places. She tore her gaze away from the map in time to see the corridor out of the room blur.

So that's how she did it.

Lenares could not resist the sweet feeling of power pulsing through her body. *So this is what it is like to be a god.*

In her exalted state she almost missed the last heading. 'Travel' it said, in small letters.

Containing her excitement, she mentally indicated the heading and the map reverted to its initial appearance – but now threads snaked out of the map, connected to every feature, and up into the night sky. She needed no explanation as to what this was.

'Duon!' she said, her voice not much more than a croak. 'Take hold of that thread there! No, the one to the right, the one marked "Andratan."'

'Wait, everyone,' Noetos said. 'Think about this. I know what this looks like, but we have no way of knowing what will happen if one of us does as Lenares asks.'

'But it says "Travel"!' Lenares said, agitated.

'And I'm sure that's what it allows us to do,' the fisherman said reasonably. 'But why not take a moment to test it? The room next to this has an orange thread. I'll take hold of that thread and see what happens. If it works as we think it will, I'll be back amongst you in a moment. If not, well.' He stepped forward and leaned over the map.

'Someone else,' Cylene said. Lenares didn't think her sister had intended to say the words aloud.

Sauxa snatched the thread in his beefy hand and nodded to the fisherman. 'More expendable, me.'

'Aye,' said Noetos, and nodded back.

What should Lenares say? Was intent enough, or was there some magic word? Examining the legend was no help: the word 'Travel' was now lit in the same orange as the thread the plainsman held in his hand.

The answer, she supposed, was the obvious one.

'Travel,' she said.

Sauxa vanished.

A thin orange line appeared in the next room, spearing up into the sky. *Or*, Lenares corrected, *spearing down into the room*.

A few moments later Sauxa came walking back into the Throne Room. 'That was . . . odd,' he said.

'Can we go now?' Cylene called from her seat.

'Not just yet,' Noetos said. 'Sauxa, we need to repeat the experiment.'

'Why?' the plainsman asked. But Lenares knew.

'We need to know if we can make a return journey,' said the fisherman.

It was disconcerting to see Sauxa vanish, but even more so to see him return. One moment gone, the next moment there.

'I can return myself,' he reported. 'Just by keeping hold of the thread and saying the word "Travel."'

'A third time, my friend,' Noetos said.

This time even the old man understood. 'You want to see what happens if I release the thread.'

A few moments later he returned to report success. 'It just hung there in the darkness.'

Noetos leaned across the map and grabbed a strand, then vanished.

'Such an impulsive man,' Sautea said. 'I know exactly where he's gone.'

An odd comment, Lenares thought, as his destination, Fossa, was marked clearly on the map. But the older fisherman wasn't looking at the map, staring instead into the night sky as though expecting to see his friend returning, sliding down the thread as though it was a rope.

Noetos reappeared about ten minutes later. 'We have a problem,' he said.

'Oh?' Bregor said. 'What's happened to Fossa?'

'Nothing beyond what we already knew,' the fisherman replied, wiping at his eyes. 'Houses burned, no sign of anyone from what I could see, no lights, boats lying around in the harbour or beached on the rocks. Deserted, destroyed, desolate. That's not what I meant.'

Bregor gave a huge sigh. 'What then?'

'I didn't end up in Fossa,' he said. 'The beam of light deposited me at the top of the Cliff of Memory, about half an hour's walking distance from the centre of town. It took me a few minutes to work out where I was, actually.'

449

'The map is inaccurate?' Moralye said, alarmed.

'A little, I think,' Noetos acknowledged. 'Enough to be of concern.'

'Only a few minutes' walk,' Consina said. 'Better than walking from here!'

'I've worked with maps and charts before, and inaccurate charts are dangerous things,' said the fisherman. 'Unmarked shoals, hidden reefs, islands marked on the map but not really there. Hegeoma, what would have happened had I arrived, say, ten minutes' walk out to sea?'

'Oh,' the woman said, and nodded acknowledgment to him.

'Well, we may not be able to get to Andratan,' Seren said, 'but at least we can come close. The sooner we start, the more time we have to walk the extra distance required.'

'Or swim,' Mustar said quietly.

'We can do better than that,' Lenares said, her mind whirling. 'I suspect the map was damaged when it fell into Raceme. Bent, perhaps, out of its perfect shape. So all we have to do is send people to various parts of the world and measure the extent to which the map is inaccurate. I can then calculate the degree of error for travel to Andratan.'

'We'd be trusting to your figuring?' Noetos said.

'Unless you think you can do better,' she snapped back at him.

The next hour was likely the strangest in their lives, Lenares considered. Certainly of their journeys so far. One by one she sent people to their chosen destinations: Moralye to Dhauria, Sauxa to Instruere, Seren to Eisarn Pit, Sautea and Mustar to Fossa, as they could not be persuaded otherwise, Bregor to Raceme, Cyclamere to the canopy at Patina Padouk, Consina to Makyra Bay. Everyone but Sauxa and Bregor wanted to go to their own towns; if it were her, Lenares considered, she'd go somewhere storied and exotic, like Crynon or Lake Pouna. Or Ilixa Island, which until this moment had been considered a legend. She ached to take one of those threads in her hand and travel there, but she dared not move from her seat. The travellers might be able to leave their threads and return, but the cosmographer doubted she could climb down from the seat without dire consequences. She imagined the threads winking out, her companions left on their own with no hope of resuming their adventure.

She wondered how many of them would return. Would any of them opt to resume their lives at home, leaving the contention with Umu to others?

Sauxa reappeared first. 'Nothing wrong with the map,' he said. 'I appeared in the middle of the Great Hall of Instruere, exactly as I intended. Gave a few fellows putting out chairs quite a fright.' He laughed shortly, then frowned. 'Things aren't going so well there, it seems. The Koinobia have taken over the city, according to one fellow I spoke to. Guardsmen replaced by priests, citizens forced into Hal worship, public houses closed or converted into places of worship. Violence in the streets, so the lad said.'

'Didn't he wonder about the beam of coloured light?' Torve asked.

'Didn't see it,' the plainsman said. 'Said he didn't anyway, and he had no reason to lie. Queen Stella needs to go back there and straighten that Koinobia out. Put this Halite thing down.'

Moralye and Seren returned within moments of each other. The scholar echoed Sauxa's comments about the accuracy of the map, explaining how she had appeared within ten paces of the door to the scriptorium. 'I walked in and that blind oaf Palanget greeted me as if I hadn't been away. Didn't anyone notice I'd gone?'

'But you returned,' Lenares prompted.

'I couldn't get out of there quickly enough,' Moralye said, her face sour. 'I'd rather be a part of making history than stuck in the darkness reading about it.'

Seren shook his head at Lenares' enquiry. 'I walked for a thousand paces or more,' he said, 'before I came across the Altima Road. Even then I was perhaps another hour's journey on foot from the pit, not a journey I'd undertake at night on my own.'

'In what direction would you have had to travel from the beam of light to go directly to the pit?' *Bearing and distance*, she wanted to demand of them. *Give me bearing and distance!* But these were ordinary people and didn't calculate such things as a matter of course.

'Seven thousand paces, give or take, in a sou'souwest direction.'

Hopefully not much give or take. Sou'souwest? She converted it into proper directions – just to the daughterwards of fatherback – and considered the result. A greater distortion than that Noetos had experienced and in a different direction. Maximum distortion, then, to be expected between the two.

Confirmed by Consina when she returned from Makyra Bay – or, at least, from as close to it as she could come. Out of breath, she explained how she'd run hard along the North Road and finally found the top of the cliff, and had spent no more than a regretful moment staring down at the darkness where her town used to be.

Bregor's return added further confirmation. 'Racème is on fire,' he said, puffing out the words. 'All is confusion. I could hear the shouting and the crackling of the flames from atop the hills beyond the Shambles. Wanted to go closer but I would probably just have met my death.'

When the last of the travellers had returned, Lenares smiled at them as confidently as she could. 'The map is dented, not badly distorted. I have calculated the error for the region of Andratan and have chosen a feature from the map to travel to. If you please, I want to make one final test: I do not want to end up swimming for my life in Malayu Bay.'

'What test?' Noetos asked, impatience in his voice.

'Send someone to Malayu itself,' she said. 'It's near enough to Andratan that the amount of error is almost exactly the same. If I select a feature the error-distance away, the traveller should be transported into the heart of Malayu.'

'Lenares,' Noetos said, his arms wide, 'we would have been literally lost without you. None of us could have worked this out for ourselves. You are a marvel. But there just isn't the time to check everything. We must trust you. Let us leave.'

'Really?' she asked, her eyes shining.

A dozen nods.

'If we all go,' she added, 'the thread will most likely disappear and we will not be able to return.'

'The alternative is that we leave you, Torve and Cylene behind. You are coming with us.' The fisherman was adamant.

'How do we reach the thread?' Cylene asked.

'The others should grasp it,' Lenares said. 'You, Torve and I only have to visualise it. Everyone ready?'

Cries of assent. Unlike her, they had spent long enough in this weird place.

'Travel,' she said.

CHAPTER 19

ANDRATAN

'MY FRONT DOOR,' SAID THE destroyer, nodding to his right. 'From the inside.' Beyond a broad hallway stood wide wooden doors, barred and reinforced with iron. They looked every day of their nearly two thousand years of age. 'Using these doors would have given us an easier approach, but I couldn't risk the possibility that my guards had been suborned. Deorc is clever enough on his own; allied with Umu, there is no end to the tricks they might have devised.'

The first of those tricks claimed the red-haired servant soon after. At the top of a wide stair located at the far end of the hallway, the man paused and drew a flint from his pocket. The corridor ahead was unlit, so he struck a spark and ignited the nearest torch. The thing exploded in his face, showering him with flame. With a scream he threw himself to the floor and began to roll in an attempt to douse the flames.

The Destroyer stood and watched the man die, his arms folded.

'Damn you!' Stella shrieked, and threw herself towards the man.

She ran into a solid wall of air and fell to the ground, bruised. The thing on the other side of the invisible wall screamed for a long time, then fell silent. His body twitched a few more times and went limp.

A pair of boots moved into Stella's blurred field of vision. 'Imagine you are a god sitting somewhere in this fortress, waiting

454

like a spider for the fly to fall into her trap. Your first snare is triggered. It's a simple snare, one unlikely to trouble your opponent. So you build another feature into the snare: should anyone attempt to douse the flames, the corridor itself bursts into flame.'

'How . . . how did you know?'

'I don't. I had to stand there and watch my hand-picked servant burn to death, not knowing whether this was a simple trap designed to be an irritant, or something more elaborate.'

'With a mind like yours,' she said evenly, 'you can invent an excuse to justify any action you choose. Even a cowardly one.'

His expression froze. 'Cowardly? You stand in the Square of Rainbows and face down the Most High in his anger, then talk to me about cowardly.'

'I didn't call you a coward,' she said, 'but to let your servant burn to death was an act of cowardice. Or, more correctly, a cowardly inaction.'

'You're a prisoner in my fortress and you choose to bandy words with me?'

'I'm not sixteen any more, you beast. You can't intimidate me with words.' She smiled at him. 'You might be two thousand years old, but you've never before dealt with anyone of my experience. It is you, not I, who is at a disadvantage.'

He frowned, pulled his collar forward and stepped over her. With a flick of his hand he banished the wall of air; a further gesture pulled her to her feet.

The Destroyer said little after this, and their journey through the largely deserted fortress grew noticeably slower. Stella had a reasonably good memory, but after the third unexpected change of direction she realised she had no chance of finding her way back to the front door. They passed many distinctive features: a bright wall-hanging eerily similar to the carving in the Great Hall of Instruere, a suit of armour built for someone at least ten feet tall, a mosaic running the entire length of a hallway, a sequence of arched windows high up in a wall, letting in moonlight – all combining to impart a less gloomy impression than she would have expected.

There were further booby traps, but these seemed designed to irritate rather than destroy.

'There is a limit to how much magic one can leave in a place unsustained by one's continued presence,' the Destroyer explained as he held her steady over a sudden-appearing gap in the floor. 'These traps were, I think, intended to stretch me thinner, making me protect any companions I might have with me, rendering me vulnerable. Umu wasn't to know I would choose to leave our companions behind.'

'You sealed them in the House of the Gods.'

'For their own good!' He set her down on the nearest solid floor. 'What happened to my servant could have happened to Noetos, or Sauxa, or Moralye. How many of them would you have wanted to see die before your eyes?'

Until today I would have believed you, she fumed silently at him. *But they had no way of travelling here in time, whether or not you blocked the exits to the House of the Gods. How stupid do you think I am?*

She chose not to vocalise her thought, just in case he chose to answer.

At the base of perhaps the sixth set of stairs since the Sea Door, the Destroyer halted in his tracks, one hand going to his temple.

Stella cast an eye left and right, searching for the trap.

'Huh,' he said, after a long pause. 'I am constantly amazed by that woman.'

'Who? What woman?'

'I've said enough. Prepare yourself, my queen: we have visitors.'

Having no idea what he meant, Stella simply nodded and followed her captor as he retraced their steps all the way to the front door.

Duon found it difficult, no, impossible, to understand what happened after Lenares uttered the magic word. The beam of light suddenly came alive in his hand, jerking him upwards so fast he thought his neck would break. He could see other hands above and below his own, but not their owners; beyond a few finger-widths from the beam all was dark. Well, perhaps not: in the distance, far below him, lay the bronze map. It had become far larger, world-sized; or he had become far smaller.

A moment later he began to descend towards the map-world, faster and faster, heading towards an ocean – no, an island – the ocean – the island, with a castle in one corner – the coast. They were about to be smeared on a dark coast.

He slammed to a stop, against all reason on his feet. He looked down: there were no dents in the soft ground where his feet had landed. Around him the others stood and stared at their surroundings, faintly visible in the darkness.

'Better than the blue fire,' Sauxa said.

'I need help,' Noetos called, his voice strained.

Duon spun around: the voice had been close behind him. In doing so he almost walked off into nothingness. Lenares, it seemed, had hit her target – barely. Noetos lay prone on the ground, his head hanging over a cliff, the sea far below. He must have fallen, perhaps hurt himself. Duon rushed to his side.

The fisherman was unhurt. At the end of his arm, however, dangled Cylene. *Ah, not quite on target after all.* Duon threw himself to the ground and fastened his hand onto the woman's wrist, just above the fisherman's huge fist. Her wide eyes stared up at him, not quite in focus, as though she didn't know where she was.

'Thank Alkuon, my friend. I was losing her.'

Together they hauled Cylene up to the top of the bank, where she lay on the grass and was immediately sick.

'Everyone else here?' Duon called, seized by a sudden anxiety.

Fifteen pairs of eyes searched the immediate area. To their backs lay a cliff perhaps fifty paces high, below which the sea battered against needle-sharp rocks. Under their feet, wet ankle-high grass stretched into the darkness in front of them. In the distance a single light gleamed.

'Stay still!' Noetos cried out, looking up from where he bent over Cylene. 'You might walk off the cliff.'

Everyone froze at that.

'I am sorry,' Lenares said into the silence.

Cylene raised herself onto her elbows. 'You have nothing to be sorry about.'

'I nearly killed you.'

'That you did,' came the answer, swift as thought. 'But in the process you saved me. Saved us all. We owe our lives to you, Lenares.'

There, Duon thought, nodding his head. *It could hardly be expressed more clearly than that.*

Fourteen people thought on Cylene's words for a moment.

'Where are we, does anyone know?' asked Sautea. 'Don't mean to sound ungrateful and all that, but I can't see a castle.'

'You mean you can't see in the dark?' Noetos chaffed his offsider. 'There could be a whole mountain range in front of us and we wouldn't know. Though I'll give you some assistance, old man. See that lone star there, just above the horizon?'

'Aye, young fellow, I see it.' The exaggerated patience in Sautea's voice indicated how familiar he was with this sort of by-play.

'Don't tell the others,' Noetos whispered loudly. 'It's not a star.'

Sautea smiled good-naturedly, recognising, as Duon himself did, the fisherman's attempts to lighten their peril, landed as they were on the most ill-named island in the world. Andratan was not a place for the faint of heart; even on his previous visit, while entertained as befitting a representative from a foreign power, Duon had sensed the despair in the place, ingrained in the very stones. He'd visited the legendary dungeons below Talamaq Palace a time or two, and they were almost pleasant compared to the dark and brutal caves he'd been shown on his guided tour of Andratan. The tour during which he'd likely been infected by Husk's spike.

They set out in the direction of the single light. If that was the light at the top of the Tower of Farsight, which, the castellan had claimed, was always kept burning, the fortress was either not as large as he remembered, or much further away.

The latter, it seemed initially, until they surmounted a ridge visible only by being slightly greyer than the dark vale in front of them and saw the fortress in its fullness, no longer partially hidden by the hills of the island. Duon shook his head. His memory had sold Andratan short.

Outlined against the starry horizon was a dark city, or so it seemed. To the far left, abutting into the ocean, was the Sea Tower, taller than any of the three towers of Talamaq Palace. High in its flank a walkway connected it to the Tower of the East, named, Duon recalled, because it was the place where the Undying Man met his guests from Bhrudwo. City Factors, mostly, though once it had housed the *Maghdi Dasht.* Now there was a name of ill repute.

The third and shortest of the five great towers, the Tower of Voices, was the most feared of all, his guide had told him proudly. It squatted over the deepest dungeons and the Hall of Voices where, it was said, the Undying Man peeled apart the minds of his prisoners and took from them everything they had, including their sanity. The guide had laughed at that, in an attempt to take the menace from the words, but Duon had not doubted them. He had not been shown the Hall of Voices itself, for which he'd been thankful.

Odd, that when Heredrew had been revealed as the Undying Man, how little menace he had communicated, unlike his counterpart Dryman, unmasked as the Emperor of Elamaq – and the god Keppia. Perhaps it was a matter of degree: nothing Heredrew could do would match the vicious insanity demonstrated by Duon's own ruler. In fact, the ruler of Bhrudwo had been urbane. Gracious, even. Which did nothing to explain why he had fled the House of the Gods with Stella.

The fourth tower was the newest, having been capped less than fifty years ago. Called the Spindle, it was more of a spire than a tower. His guide had not explained its purpose, despite Duon's questioning.

Inevitably and finally, his eye was drawn to the Tower of Farsight, a thousand steps from its base to the light set atop it. Symbolic, of course: even at that dizzy height one could not see the mainland, let alone the rest of Bhrudwo. It contained the Undying Man's vast collection of books and scrolls, and it and the Sea Tower housed most of the fortress's servants and soldiers.

The five towers surmounted a vast complex of halls, vaults, keeps and courtyards, all surrounded by a tall crenellated wall. The visual and emotional impact as they drew close to it was overwhelming, enough to induce a pain at the back of his head.

'Big place,' Sauxa said.

Noetos had taken himself away to speak to his children. Arathé was suffering from a headache, she said, and Anomer was worried. Lenares spied Cylene walking through the darkness alone and decided to join her.

'I am very grateful for what you said about me,' Lenares told her. 'Most of the time my specialness goes unnoticed.'

'Not by me,' Cylene said. 'I'm so happy to have a sister at last.'

'But you had sisters. I spoke to Sena.'

'My mother's creatures,' Cylene said. 'Sena barely had any self-will left in her. I never shared anything special with her. Never spoke to her, actually.'

'And you want to share special things with me?' Lenares could not think of anything she wanted more. To be special in a sister's eyes! To have secret confidences whispered in her ear!

As if echoing her thoughts, Cylene drew closer to Lenares and spoke quietly. 'You know, there are things you and Torve could do together that don't need his . . . ah, equipment to accomplish.'

It took Lenares a moment to work out what her sister meant. 'What?'

Cylene licked her lips, as though about to attempt something difficult. 'You've seen animals mate. I know you have: I can remember watching the horses with you. We thought they were fighting.'

A memory of sound and movement presented itself to Lenares' mind. 'Vaguely,' she said.

'The stallion mounts the mare with no concern for how she feels. Sometimes her body is not ready and she is damaged as a result.' Her face folded inwards for a moment. 'But you, sister, are lucky. Your stallion has no urgent need to be relieved. He will not mount you unprepared. He will not damage you. So you can take your time and teach each other that which gives you pleasure.'

'Oh, Cylene,' Lenares said, and tears began to run down her cheeks. This was what she needed to hear, had wanted explained to her in the town square at Mensaya. More than explanations, she just wanted to hear someone say it was allowable for her to find joy with Torve. 'What gives a man pleasure?'

Her sister giggled and enfolded Lenares in a hug. 'It's one thing to give a man pleasure, and I know all about that, but it's another to love him with your body. So I am on my own voyage of discovery. Be sure I will share my findings with you, if you promise to put them into practice.'

'I will,' Lenares said. 'If we pass through this fortress alive.'

Cylene shuddered in her arms.

And so we come to the sharp end of the adventure, Noetos told himself grimly as the travellers approached the fortress of Andratan.

The fortress hunkered on the landscape like an immense animal, asleep for the moment. High above them the single light winked like a half-lidded eye ready to spring open at the slightest sign of disturbance. *There'll be more than a slight sign*, Noetos thought, fighting down waves of uneasiness.

Arathé clung to his left arm, muttering wordlessly to herself. A headache, she'd claimed, only a headache. But they had been on this journey long enough to mistrust purely natural events. *She has a conduit to Husk, who may well now be in the possession of a god. What will happen if that possession is challenged? Where might the god seek to go next?*

Noetos desperately wanted to run. Run down the path leading away from the door looming over them, run to the shore, commandeer a boat, any sort of boat, and put out to sea. He'd hated the sea his whole life, but now it seemed his family's only place of safety.

Irrational, he told himself. It didn't matter where his daughter hid, she could be reached through the magical connection to Husk. On the ocean, in the favelas of Malayu, or under her blankets in

Fisher House at home in Fossa, it was all the same – she could be found anywhere. As could Anomer, through his sister. Duon, who shared a similar connection. And, through his daughter, Noetos himself.

His children knew this, yet they were determined to go on. How could he do any less? Yet these thoughts did nothing to dampen his incipient terror.

A hundred paces from the door Noetos turned and held his arms up, palms forward, then motioned the travellers behind the last piece of cover: a few low, wind-battered bushes.

'We should have a strategy for this,' he said in a voice that sounded disappointingly weak to his ears. Fearful. 'Otherwise we are doomed to react to the plans of others.'

He took a deep breath. With this moment in mind he had wooed and won Cyclamere to his cause. The blunt Padouki, his former tutor, stepped forward at the fisherman's signal. His face was marble, showing none of the uncertainty Noetos himself felt.

'I yield to the Swordmaster of Roudhos,' Noetos said.

'The Duke of Roudhos and I have discussed our approach many times in recent days,' said Cyclamere in clipped tones. 'And, as you know, I have spent time with each of you, discussing your strengths in preparation for the inevitable confrontation in this fortress.'

He discussed their weaknesses too, at some length, Noetos added mentally. *But he does not mention them now.* Not a word, not a hint of the negative immediately before a battle: his tutor had repeated the lesson enough times to make it a mantra.

'We have two powerful magicians at our disposal,' the old warrior continued. 'The children of Noetos have ably demonstrated their ability to protect us, as Captain Duon of Elamaq and the Duke of Roudhos himself will attest to, after vanquishing the Neherians in the Summer Palace at Raceme.'

Good, remind them of past glories. Not that Raceme was in any way glorious.

'They contained the attack of the gods at Lake Woe, and at

Corata Pit fought off Umu herself. Anomer and Arathé have demonstrated the ability to draw power from everything around them, which I have been told is the mark of a superior magician.'

Told by the Undying Man, who is no longer with us, Noetos thought; *who may, in fact, be one of our adversaries. Certainly mine.*

'In addition, they have pioneered the technique of distributing physical injury amongst their allies to prevent a serious or fatal blow afflicting any one person.'

Here it is, the moment at which the travellers might baulk.

'Each of us was called on this journey. All of us have already proved our worth, each necessary at various stages. We cannot tell what else we might be called on to do, but we must take comfort in the fact that the Father has not finished with us yet. We must all assume we are, each one, about to see action. None of us is here as a mere spectator. At the very least, that action will entail giving of our essenza' – his eyes flicked to Anomer, as if reassuring himself that he had the unfamiliar word right – 'and being prepared to receive wounds on behalf of others. I will not ask whether there are any here afraid of this: we all are. But I will also not ask if anyone here wishes to resile. You had that opportunity in the House of the Gods when you travelled magically to a place of your own choosing. You returned, knowing what awaited you. Therefore you elected to continue to the end.'

Assorted nods from grim faces.

'We also have a number of gifted swordsmen in our midst. In my prime I was accounted the best in Roudhos with a blade, and I am still in my prime.' He smiled bleakly. 'I know tricks that short-lived swordsmen, no matter how gifted and trained, do not, and I have used them in battle. The Duke of Roudhos was – is – one of my pupils and has acquitted himself well during this adventure, as young Mustar can testify.'

The young son of Halieutes nodded his head enthusiastically. *So Cyclamere had that story from the boy,* Noetos thought, not entirely displeased.

'Captain Duon is a trained soldier, modest in his claims regarding his ability, but I have seen him work the forms and would be honoured to have him guard my lord's back and those of my lord's children.'

Clever: the captain's grim face cleared for a moment.

'Anomer is good with a blade,' Seren put in, unaware of the soldier's discipline requiring silence as a battle plan unfolded. Not that the miner would have cared much for the rule had he known it.

'Aye, he is not forgotten,' Cyclamere said. 'Nor is his sister. Arathé will need to wait until we liberate a blade from inside the fortress, but if circumstances require it, she can also fight. It was part of the reason she was selected to come here as a servant of the Undying Man in the first place, after all.'

Setting off this whole venture, Noetos finished morosely.

'Others among you can wield a weapon at a pinch, but I would encourage you not to arm yourselves unless in protection of your own life – and even then, think twice.' Noetos smiled, pre-empting the aphorism to follow. 'A weapon in the hands of the untutored has no handle but blades at both ends. You will likely do more damage to friend than to foe.

'The rest of you will enter Andratan without weapon or magic. But you are not defenceless. You are quick of mind, adaptable, able to think on your feet. You are leaders, but also able to obey commands without question.'

Was that a slight glance in Noetos's own direction?

'I speak as a veteran of many battles: had I been in possession of soldiers with your talent, I would never have lost a single one.'

It was hard to tell in the darkness, but Noetos imagined he could see a brightening of countenance in some of those around him.

'And now, our two main weapons, those we must protect at all costs. I refer to the huanu stone carried by the Duke of Roudhos and the special abilities of Lenares the cosmographer.'

Darkness or no, Noetos could see the girl's grin from five paces away. Could almost feel the heat of her pleasure radiating outwards. *Truly, Lenares does not care if she lives or dies, as long as she is praised.*

'That is the list of our assets. Now, our strategy. We have two weapons: a stone to abrogate magic and the vision to guide it. Both are essential. Therefore we will become two teams, each tasked with the protection of one of the weapons. Arathé will hedge her father about with magic, and will be accompanied by my own sword. Bregor, Consina, Seren and Cylene complete the team, commanded by the Duke of Roudhos. Lenares will be protected by Anomer's magic and his sword, and will have at her back the blade of Captain Duon. Torve, Sauxa, Moralye, Sautea and Mustar will go with her. Captain Duon is charged with leading this second team. Duon and Arathé, as former spikes of the devil-magician Husk, can speak together mind to mind. They will therefore keep the teams in close contact, even if they should be separated.'

Moralye cleared her throat. 'What if we find Stella or Kannwar here? Either one, or both together? Do we invite them to be part of our team? How could we stop them?'

'You'll need to make that judgement in the context of the situation,' Cyclamere responded. 'Remember, your brain is your weapon. A good decision may undo all the stratagems of the enemy.'

'But what do we do when we get in there?' Consina asked, unable to keep the anxiety from her voice.

Cyclamere frowned momentarily. Noetos could see the word *patience* forming on his lips.

'We cannot devise a comprehensive set of tactics,' he said. 'Too much is unknown about the situation within the fortress. Who is in control? Husk? Umu? The Undying Man? What are their desires, that we might thwart them?'

He began to pace. *A bad sign*, Noetos thought. *My war leader is unable to keep his unease under control.*

'The ultimate task set us is to drive the Daughter back through the hole in the world and seal it behind her. If this task was beyond us, the Father would not have so painstakingly assembled us and brought us here. I deem we have one other necessary task to perform: the rebinding or death of Husk.'

Murmurs of agreement from his listeners.

'We may have a third task, one forced upon us by recent events. Until a few hours ago the Undying Man was our ally and perhaps our most important weapon. We appear to have lost him now. It cannot be helped. Indeed, I never factored him into our plans: such a one is above any plan we might have conceived. But Stella is a grievous loss. Immortal, magician in her own right: if she is in this fortress, we should consider rescuing her and putting her abilities to use in our cause.'

'Consider it?' Sauxa said, indignant. 'Consider? Surely her safety ought to be our first concern?'

'Alas, no,' said the swordmaster. 'We must not jeopardise the achievement of our ultimate goal. Indeed, Stella or anyone else in this fortress tonight must be sacrificed without hesitation if it brings us closer to defeating Umu.' Cyclamere lowered his voice. 'You are supremely gifted men and women. You have pride, and are familiar with command. You make your own decisions and expect others to follow you. But know this: I am in charge here tonight. I will have your obedience, or you will wait for us outside the walls of the fortress.'

He waited until fourteen voices had given their assent.

'Very well,' he said, and broke cover, setting out for Andratan with long strides.

At the huge wooden gate, Cyclamere nodded to Noetos. 'In the name of the Duke of Roudhos, open the gates!' cried the sword-master, and rapped on the wood with the hilt of his sword.

A beat; then the gates swung silently inwards, opening on darkness and two small figures.

'It would have been far more sensible to sneak in somewhere,' Consina breathed to Bregor.

Noetos groaned. In the silence there was no hope of the words remaining unheard.

'Sautea, Mustar, you are transferred to Noetos's team,' Cyclamere barked. 'Consina and Bregor will stand down.'

'Stand down? What do you mean?'

'I mean you will wait outside the gate. You will not enter Andratan. We must work together as a team.'

'But—' Bregor began.

'Enough,' Noetos said. 'Must I fight you to enforce discipline?'

'You were just waiting for an excuse!' Bregor shouted. 'Revenge for your wife!'

The fisherman released his anger. It surged down his arm and into his closed fist at precisely the moment it met the Hegeoman's jaw. Consina squeaked as Bregor crumpled to the ground.

You are right, my friend, Noetos acknowledged to the unconscious man. *I was waiting for an excuse and you were stupid enough to give it to me.*

Noetos glanced up to see the two small figures advancing through the gate. *Damn you, Bregor, for the distraction.* It wasn't until one of the figures spoke that he knew who they were, and even then he wasn't entirely sure.

'Welcome, my friends, to my home. Come in, won't you?'

Kannwar's front doors swung back into the wide hallway. The wind outside stirred the two small torches offering the only light, and one of them sputtered and went out. Stella squinted into the darkness; it only needed a simple head count to work out who stood there.

'You couldn't keep them away,' she whispered. 'Is there anything you can control?'

He snorted, then held up his hand for silence. 'I'm having more success than the fisherman,' he said after a moment.

'Than a hot-tempered hick from a fishing village? You ought to be,' Stella said blandly.

He ignored her and strode forward. 'Welcome, my friends, to my home!' he called to his former companions. 'Come in, won't you?'

'I wonder how they escaped your trap,' Stella said, looking for any needle she could find. 'Maybe you should have killed them all.'

'And maybe I should kill you,' he retorted. He waved his hand and her throat seized up.

Strangling me? she wondered, strangely unconcerned. *He can't kill me by depriving me of air, can he?* Her immortal blood would keep her alive somehow. Curse it. No, she could still breathe. But she could not talk, she discovered, when she tried to ask her captor what he had done to her.

'Why should we surrender ourselves to your hospitality, Kannwar?' Noetos called out. 'We don't trust you.'

Stella applauded the man's courage, if not his wisdom. *You have to find a way of allying yourself to the Destroyer,* she wanted to tell him. *You'll never get close enough to Umu to make an end of her if you don't.*

'I told you to come in,' the Destroyer said. 'If that sounded like you had a choice, I apologise.'

He closed his fist and at least half those standing outside the gates were jerked forward as though on the end of strings. Walking like marionettes, they made their obviously reluctant way inside the gate.

A bell rang behind Stella. She couldn't talk, but she could turn her head, and saw a boy hammering at a bell with all the energy he had.

'I don't need reinforcements, if that's what you're thinking,' Kannwar said. 'I've called all my servants and soldiers to defend the keep from imminent attack.'

You want chaos, she guessed. *You don't care who survives, as long as you can creep up unseen on whoever sits atop this fortress.*

After struggling to hold back their fellows, the rest of the travellers followed them through the gates and into the hallway.

'That's better. I'm disappointed you seem to have turned against me, especially since I am the world's best hope of getting rid of our remaining gods. You do know why I left you in the Godhouse, don't you?'

'I'm sure you can supply us with any number of plausible reasons,' Noetos said, striding up to the Destroyer. 'Just as you can take on any disguise you like. What's this one: foppish Malayu courtier?' He looked the Lord of Bhrudwo up and down. 'Doubt it'll catch on. Who in their right mind cares for fashions worn by two-thousand-year-old cadavers? Now step out of the way, yesterday's man, and let us do what you will not.'

468

Stella's blood sang as, beside her, the Destroyer's blood boiled – almost literally, so hot did it grow at these words. But by some superhuman degree of self-control he battened his temper down and waved them ahead.

'Go on then,' he said absently.

'Stella,' the fisherman said, 'are you coming?'

No, said Leith's voice. *You have unfinished business here.*

'She's not talking to you, my friend. She has more interesting people to talk to. Be on your way and mind you don't damage my house.'

Wisely Noetos said nothing in reply to the Destroyer's words. He bent his head close to Captain Duon's.

'Which way?' Stella heard the fisherman whisper.

The Destroyer groaned. 'And with this the Most High hopes to redeem his mistakes. The fool is more out of touch than ever. The god you're looking for sits atop the Tower of Farsight. Take any passage: they'll all get you there in the end.'

He flicked his hand lazily and released those in thrall to him.

Noetos could stand no more of the fatuous baiting from the man. With a curt signal he chose the stairway at the far end of the hall.

'I don't know what that bell means,' he said to Duon, 'but it must be some sort of summons. Soon the corridors will be filled with soldiers. Swords out.'

'Should we split into our two teams?' Duon asked him.

'Not yet,' Cyclamere said. 'But we must hurry. Get as far as we can towards the Tower of Farsight before we encounter opposition and have to start spending lives.'

They didn't run, but they still moved quickly up the stairs and down the first wide hallway to the right. Noetos looked twice at an odd suit of armour standing in an embayment, obviously decorative rather than functional given its enormous height and girth.

'Why did he leave us alive?' Duon asked him.

'At a guess, I'd say he wants as much fighting as possible while he deals with Umu in his own way.'

'So why not stand back and let him?'

A good question. 'In case of what might happen if he fails. Or succeeds.'

'I don't understand.'

'We don't have to understand,' Noetos said. 'We're soldiers. We've been given our orders. Let's seek to carry them out.'

The hallway ended in a locked and barred door. Barred from their side, fortunately, but the lock defeated their attempts to fiddle it open.

'Break it down,' Noetos said, pointing to Duon and Cyclamere. 'We'll charge it together.'

The swordmaster pursed his lips but did not offer a comment. The three men took ten steps back into the corridor.

A shout rang from behind them. Soldiers.

Cylene put her hand on a door in the left wall. 'I'll just look in here, shall I?' she asked.

'Now!' Noetos called. The three men crashed into the door, shoulders forward, and ended in a heap on the floor. The door had rattled in its frame but no more.

'No time for another try,' Duon said, picking himself up. Ten grey-liveried men were almost upon them.

'Follow Cylene!' Noetos ordered the others, as the swordsmen readied themselves.

The grey-clothed men halted just beyond reach. 'Surrender,' the oldest of them barked.

'Certainly,' Noetos growled, and the man nodded. 'We accept your parole.'

'No, you southern fool, I meant for *you* to surrender.'

'Ah,' said Noetos, delighted the old trick had worked to unsettle the man. 'Sorry. I'm not used to northerners with the power of speech.' He made ready to charge.

'Noetos!' came a cry from behind him.

Damn you, Cylene! the fisherman thought, then smiled as he felt a breeze on his back. 'Again, my apologies,' he said to the soldiers. 'We'll talk more about surrender later.' He spun on his heel and dashed for the open door.

470

With it slammed and locked behind him, Duon and Cyclamere, he leaned on the wood and allowed himself a moment to recover. They stood in a small courtyard open to the stars – or what stars there were: a light mist had rolled in, obscuring most of the familiar constellations. To his right was an arched window, slats broken and thrown wide.

'Thank you, Cylene,' he said.

She dimpled at him. 'Would have been for nothing if the key hadn't still been in the lock.'

'Onward,' Duon said, without his usual diffidence. 'The men behind us will figure it out. Eventually.'

It's time for something to be explained to you, Leith said to her.

I am listening. She rubbed her throat as she trudged after the Destroyer. *It's not as if I can do anything else.*

Do you remember the Hall of Fealty? he asked her.

Of course. We sat there not ten years ago, rain beating on the roof, listening to the petitions of the hill men of the Veridian Borders. One of the most boring afternoons I've ever spent.

Indeed. The voice seemed amused. *Do you recall the first time we were there?*

Oh yes, she did. Leith had taken her there the year after the Falthan War had ended, to honour her before the Knights of Fealty. She'd endured as mixed a reception there as anywhere else and Leith had been distraught. 'They don't honour you,' he'd said as they lay together that night, 'and yet you were the true hero of the war.'

'They can't honour me,' she had replied. 'I upset their simple notion of a black-and-white world. Someone who served evil yet achieved the purposes of the Most High.'

She'd believed that, back then. It had taken long decades of gritted-teeth endurance for that belief to be eroded away. She'd served no one's purposes but her own, and failed miserably at that. Leith had risked his life to save her. She'd been nothing but trouble.

Kannwar planted Deorc in our camp as a spy, to confound our plans. The Most High planted a spy in Kannwar's camp. Do you know who she was?

'Keep up, my queen, or I will bind you,' said the Destroyer.

A troop of soldiers ran past them, saluting as they went.

'Or perhaps detail others to carry you,' he added.

Stella picked up her pace.

I see, she said. I am about to die, my unlooked-for blessing coming after all these years. You've been sent here to ease my passing, to tell me things to lighten my heart.

I'm lying then? His voice sounded hurt.

N-no, not lying, she stammered out.

You were the Most High's thorn in his enemy's side. As you are again. It was your virtue as much as your vice that saw you enslaved. Yes, you desired darkness. But darkness could not have ensnared you unless you decided to trust it, to treat it as though it was light.

Oh. Her head hurt with this convoluted thinking. *Everybody has an explanation for my behaviour. I don't know who to believe.*

Consider, the voice said as they strode along a hallway with a series of tall arched windows high in the right-hand wall. *She'd been along here before this evening, or a corridor like it. In the Hall of Fealty I told Leith he was but one of many I'd called to my service. Not the bravest or the best, just the first to arrive. It is the same with you, dear Stella. That was the lesson of the Hall of Fealty.*

You're not Leith?

No – and yes. It is not a simple thing, this issue of identity. I have told you I am a reluctant participant in these affairs. I created this . . . problem when, in attempting to help, I took away too much choice. Were I to continue to interfere, I would be solving one problem while creating another.

Not sure I care, Stella said, now aware whom she was speaking to. *At least our problem will have been solved. Interfere all you like.*

Fine for a mortal not to care for the next generation. But you're no mortal, Stella. Of anyone alive, you ought to care most deeply about how this present crisis is resolved.

Ahead, the Destroyer came to a halt in the middle of a large hall set up for a banquet. He put his finger to his lips. Stella shrugged: she couldn't speak anyway.

You are not the best, Stella, but you are here while better women and men turned aside from my calling. Are you willing to let me kindle what has been set within you?

That didn't take much thought. *It's yours, after all,* she said, and nodded.

Across the courtyard, down a passageway and through a truly enormous banqueting hall. Moralye caught her shin on a chair and sent it flying into a table; crystal goblets and porcelain plates crashed to the flagstone floor. After that they moved more slowly for a while, Mustar supporting Moralye under one arm. *He's sweet on her,* Noetos realised. *And I thought he was after my daughter.*

'Are we heading in the right direction?' he asked Duon.

'Yes, though in a roundabout way. That there,' he pointed out a window to his left, where a slender tower rose into the mist, 'is the Spindle. The Tower of Farsight is beyond it.'

'Good,' Noetos said, even though it wasn't. Something had begun scratching at his mind, as though an insect had been trapped in his head and was attempting to burrow its way out. Beside him, Arathé groaned, putting her hand to her head at regular intervals. Duon had turned pale and licked his lips when he thought no one was watching.

When the attack came, Noetos realised, it was unlikely to require a swordsman to respond.

The Fire of Life blazed within her, an oxygen-starved flame opened to the air. It burned through the string-like binding between herself and the Destroyer, but left the ends trailing. It burned higher and higher, searing the pain of her cursed blood. Removing it.

Free of pain after seventy years.

You . . . you . . . She shook with anger. *All this time you could do this for me and you never spoke of it? Where are you? I'll kill you with my bare hands!*

Never spoke to you? I spoke to you every day of your life. You never believed me.

I could have . . . Leith and I could . . . Her words dissolved into an inarticulate groan born of the deepest recesses of her self.

I am sorry. But to have done this uninvited would have broken your sovereign will.

As opposed to breaking my heart? You are cruel, cruel; and I thought Kannwar cruel for his calculations and his fatal mercies. You are far worse.

The Father spread his hands: she felt them pass over her. *I acknowledge the point. Kannwar is right, you know. Hal once told Leith it is better to break the lamb's leg to keep it still than to let it alone and watch it wilfully run off the edge of the cliff. Small hurts to bring great good.*

And that's not a violation of the lamb's sovereign will?

Ah, the Most High said. *You have me there. I am reluctant for a reason. It is time for me to turn my work over to someone more passionate, less disinterested, with better judgement.*

You don't care about us?

Just the opposite, Stella. I care far too much. I care so much it breaks me into a million points of light whenever you hurt. I need . . . I need someone with whom to share the burden.

Not me!

No, not you. Be thankful it is not you.

What of Keppia and Umu? Could they not share it?

They did, for a time. They became my son and daughter in truth, but they chose their fates under duress, as a sacrifice. No, I need someone who would embrace godhood as his or her deepest desire.

What am I to do? she asked him.

Of that, Stella, I am not yet sure. But I know this: you will have to be brave.

Across the grassed courtyard stood the Tower of Farsight, an enormous structure, looming over them. Sustained by magic, so the stories went.

It didn't matter what it was sustained with, thought Duon. It was unreachable. They would never cut through the hundreds of soldiers massed in front of the tower's entrance.

'Another way in?' he asked Noctos.

'Cyclamere has already sent Seren and Moralye to scout.'

Duon pursed his lips. 'When I was last here, the guide told us this was the only way into the tower.'

'Notorious for their truthfulness, the denizens of Andratan?'

'Not in my experience,' Duon acknowledged, nodding. 'But he had no reason to lie.'

'Duon,' Anomer said, 'Arathé has an idea.'

Oh. I'm sorry, Arathé. I didn't mean to shut you out.

He noticed the frown on Noetos's brow. *Perhaps you ought to include your father in the conversation?*

I'm afraid to, she said. *I would rather not remind Umu of all the options available to her.*

He raised his eyebrows. *And I spoke to you unthinking.*

She shrugged, or as near to it as she could achieve mentally. *She already knows about us, Duon.*

He smiled into her mind. *One day, I hope, they will all know about us.*

The smile she returned was warm enough to compensate for all the nights she had lain with her family, beyond his reach.

'This is Arathé's idea,' he began, then nodded to Noetos. 'She apologises for not speaking to you, our leader, but doesn't want to draw Umu's attention to you. She hopes she has done the right thing.'

Her father nodded, one corner of his mouth crooking up. *You have a talent for making people feel better about themselves,* he told her.

'She has been thinking about her ability to unite people's essenzas to spread the affliction suffered by one amongst all, and wondering if it might work as an offensive weapon.'

'What do you mean?' her father began, but beside him Cyclamere exclaimed out loud.

'We must try it,' he said.

Wait, dear Stella. You will only be able to surprise him once.

She trailed along behind the Destroyer, dragging her feet as though at the end of her strength, hoping the deception would hold. The blood-binding between them was in tatters, severed by the reignited Fire of Life that had been given to her – and others of the Company – at the beginning of the War of Faltha. Yet the Destroyer had not noticed anything amiss. She would do well to ensure he did not notice.

A small door led to a tunnel within the wall encircling the fortress.

'None but myself knows of this route to my tower,' he said to her. 'I've read of other rulers putting out the eyes of their architects and builders so such secret passages can be kept secret. Such matters are much easier – and far more pleasant – when one is immortal. One just has to wait until they are all dead.'

Somehow she doubted he had waited.

He led her to a grille in the floor of the tunnel, which was, it seemed, set in the ceiling of a library. A flick of his hand removed the grille, setting it aside.

'You first,' he said.

The floor was made of stone, at least twice her height below where they crouched either side of the manhole. She would break both legs, at least, if she attempted the jump, but could not speak to argue with him, and did not want to cause him to try speaking in her mind. With the blood-bond broken, that might not be possible. Without comment she eased herself as far through the hole as possible, and jumped.

She wafted to the ground like an autumn leaf, her red dress flaring out. *I am a parachute bug,* she told herself, almost laughing. A moment later, the Destroyer stood beside her. She'd landed softly, but had no idea whether by his power or by that of the fire within her. Her captor said nothing, though that was no real indication: he was perfectly capable of pretending not to know about her pretence.

'Come along,' he said.

Without warning all the books in the library burst into flame.

The Destroyer swore.

Stella couldn't remember him ever swearing before. He must be deeply discomposed.

'Damn her eyes,' he finished, having spat out enough invective to set fire to another library. 'Anything but this. If I could have avoided this room, I would have.'

He grunted at her lack of response and waved his hand.

She had to guess. He'd likely freed her voice – what else could the gesture mean? It hadn't, for example, dampened the ever more exuberant flames that were claiming his library.

'At least it's a cool evening,' she said.

Essenza, Arathé discovered, was an elusive thing, and hard to grasp if not offered you. Some soldiers were locked down so tight by fear or selfishness that she had nothing on which to pull. Others, however, unwittingly gave her a handhold: from there it was like unwinding a knitted garment. Or it would be, if she required more than the little needed to tie their essenzas together.

'Hurry,' Duon whispered. 'There are more coming.'

Find somewhere to hide, she told him.

'I'm not leaving you out here undefended!'

I am not undefended, she said, smiling crookedly. *Enough. I am ready.*

Noetos led a young soldier forward. The unlucky fellow had been snatched by the simple expedient of reaching through a window and pulling him into the corridor as he leaned against the frame. He'd made no noise, not with Noetos's meaty paw fastened over his mouth, and with a sword at his back had decided to remain quiet.

Now, she told herself. *Hope you haven't smothered your essenza – ah, no, good.* She tied him to the lines she'd teased out from the soldiers and waited until she was sure they were properly bound. Then she nodded to her father.

To his credit, he'd objected when her plan was explained to him. He'd been held in the Summer Palace and tortured for the entertainment of the Neherian nobility, who had not realised that Arathé, linked to her father, had distributed his wounds amongst five thousand refugees. 'They were volunteers,' he said. 'These boys are not.'

477

'Would you rather we took swords to them all?' Duon had asked, reasonably enough.

Noetos had grumbled some more, but had relented in the end. Relented, and insisted his would be the hand that would wield the blade.

The boy's face went white as Duon stretched out his shaking arm. Noetos raised his sword and struck it off. Or tried to. The blade skittered across the boy's arm as though the flesh was made of tempered steel. At the same moment, a cry came from several hundred throats.

It works, said Arathé to Duon, peering through the crack in the door.

'Again,' said Duon.

The boy shrieked, holding his arm as though it had been injured. 'Not fast enough. Hack him to death.'

Four swords fell upon the boy, who cowered under the assault. The look of terror on the lad's face told Arathé he thought he was about to die – the look, and the sudden stain at the front of his breeches. But the repeated blows, though driving him to the floor, left no mark upon him.

Outside, it was a different tale. Hundreds of soldiers lay on the ground, wounds bleeding freely. A few were still. Screams echoed everywhere, the sound as much one of confusion as of pain.

Not good enough, Arathé thought. *Don't you have a leader?* Of course, their leader might already have been cut down. No. Commands were barked and the soldiers who were able assembled in lines ten deep. Behind her the swordplay continued.

'Company, dear heart,' Duon said, breathing heavily.

A small squad of soldiers emerged into the corridor. Arathé snatched at their essenzas, grabbing all but one at the first attempt, and wove them into the knot. A moment and they too writhed on the floor, save one of their number who stared at his fellows in utmost confusion. With a cry of horror he flung his sword aside and ran.

Arathé glanced out into the courtyard. The soldiers able to walk, most of them unbound, were double-timing across the open

478

space towards a door in the distance, held open by their frantic commander. The rest lay twitching or still.

Time to go, she said to Duon.

A minute later the travellers had sprinted across the courtyard and were working at the latch to the Tower of Farsight. Arathé and her father helped Mustar carry Moralye, who still favoured her ankle.

'She's a lot older than you,' Arathé signalled to Mustar. She smiled to take the sting from her words.

'Pretty, though,' Mustar replied incorrigibly.

'And intelligent,' added the woman herself. 'Not that my intelligence appears to have saved me from the clutches of Fisher-boy.'

Arathé laughed at this, and her father snorted.

'The latch is hot,' Cyclamere said, uncertainty in his voice.

'Hot?' Noetos repeated, puzzled. Then his face clouded over. 'For Alkuon's sake, don't open—'

His advice came too late. The door swung open onto an incandescent scene from the netherworld. The fire inside the tower swelled hungrily, reached out fevered tendrils and dragged them in.

CHAPTER 20

THE BROKEN MAN

HUSK IS DEAD. AT LEAST it seems that way to him. Umu holds his essence tightly in one taloned hand. His beautiful, precious essence, the heart of who he is, carefully sculpted by years of risk, judicious choices and self-sacrifice. Not only Deorc paid the price in becoming what he is; many others died during his quest for lordship. How can such a tragedy be borne? As much as he hates it, Deorc can accept pain, for all pain does is stimulate the nerves of his body. Imprisonment reduces opportunity, but does not restrict the mature mind. This, however, is theft of his soul.

He is violated beyond imagining.

She has evicted Deorc from his own body, hollowed out his mind and made a place for herself there among the bleeding ruins. Even if he were somehow to defeat her and reclaim himself, he is destroyed far more completely than he had been by the Undying Man all those years ago. Memories trashed. Skills shredded. Ways of thinking lost. Enormous holes in his magical powers.

Dead. Might as well be. But he still feels pain.

Not physical pain. He is so tightly locked away by his possessor he cannot reach his nerve endings. Some pain would be welcome, actually, a sign that he still owns something of his body. He envies Umu her access to the world of sensation, and is embarrassed by his previous prayers, repeated during his long imprisonment, for his pain to end.

No, the pain he feels is emotional.

His revenge has been stolen from him!

Truly, he would exchange his entire future for the simple con-summation of his revenge on Stella and the Undying Man. Dreams of their humiliation have sustained him all those years, and now those dreams are spoiling like meat left in the sun.

'You're not much of a human, are you?' Umu says in his voice, using his mouth.

How an essence without the aid of glands can feel anger is beyond Deorc's understanding, but he is angry. Furious. *Leave my voice alone!*

'Pathetic,' she carries on. 'A minor manipulator of the weak-minded. You may have done something of note a century ago, but nothing since. Yes, you've been imprisoned for a little while, as a direct result of your self-indulgent foolishness: what of it? Keppia and I were imprisoned on the far side of the Wall of Time for thou-sands of years, but unlike you we wasted no time organising things to suit ourselves. Shifted the stars, rearranged the constellations, reshaped the void to our will.'

Boastful, this thief. Deorc has heard her like on many occasions, and in each and every case he discovered exaggeration or outright falsehood. *Let your deeds talk for themselves*, his father had said. *Only the failure needs to advertise his success.* Has heard talk like this, but never in his voice.

'I don't think much of this body you've tried to make,' she says. 'I'm looking for a permanent home and I must have something better than this.'

Then get out, Deorc wills.

She cannot hear him, he realises. But at least she stops speaking. He has tired of the sound of his own voice.

In its quest for air the roaring fire pulled the door right off its hinges, barely noticing the small figures it dragged screaming into its heart. It had all but consumed the library, drinking the dry parchment and preservative fluids as though they were the elixir of life itself, but there was still a great deal of flammable material

481

for the flames to consider. As Arathé cracked her elbow on the door frame, inadvertently knocking loose her father's desperate grip, she saw the fire creeping across the wooden floor. Her likely landing place was already aflame.

She had one single moment in which to act. No time to consider the morality of what she intended to do, no time to ask for advice. This was something more than self-preservation: after all, she could protect herself with her magic. She knew in that moment she could not extend that protection to cover all her friends. Not enough time, not enough strength.

She snatched the loose ends of her companions' essenza and fastened it to the soldiers' snarl she had already made.

A moment later the travellers fell into the flames.

Her father tried to draw on her magic, but the huanu stone prevented him. However, his stone dampened the effect of the flames somewhat, indicating they were of magical origin.

Anomer did better. His shield flashed out, enfolding Arathé and Noetos in a soft, water-like substance.

The others expected to die. She could see it on their faces, which bore exactly the same shocked, pleading look the soldier boy had worn a few minutes earlier. Some rolled into foetal balls, awaiting the pain; others tried to beat the flames away.

But no pain came.

One by one they scrambled to their feet, unharmed, confusion and relief mixed on their faces. No bruises from the fall, no horrific burns from the flames groping impotently at them.

Every face turned to the door, beyond which lay the courtyard. No sound could be heard above the roar of the fire, but Arathé had no doubt what was happening out there.

The staircase at the far end of the library had a wooden banister, already beginning to flame. She beckoned the others on. They could not afford to remain paralysed by shock: once the soldiers were spent, the magic would no longer work.

Up the stairs they ran. Arathé saw that Moralye, who climbed just ahead of her, was favouring her ankle. Did she have the strength and finesse to heal her friend? As she watched, the bruise faded and the swelling vanished. *Oh. Every hurt?*

She imagined each soldier losing a tiny amount of his tongue, and hers growing to balance their loss, growing until it filled her mouth in the way she barely remembered. But it seemed there was a limit to this magic of distribution after all.

Arathé tried not to begrudge Moralye her ankle.

The stair took them up to a second library, the floor of which was already beginning to steam. The next level appeared to be some sort of dormitory accommodation, though empty at present. Unwillingly, Arathé's eyes were drawn to the window at the far end of the room.

Noetos walked across to it and leaned out, then jerked his head back inside. Duon made to join him, but the fisherman shook his head.

'No,' he gasped, his face pale. 'Horrible.' He shook his head again. 'The smell. Don't ask.'

'We are alive because of them,' Torve said solemnly. 'Let us make sure we accomplish what we came to do.'

They nodded to each other and set their feet to the next level of the stair.

'No one will be coming up that stair now,' the Destroyer said with some satisfaction. 'Your friends will fight it out with my soldiers. I'm not sure who will win.'

'But whatever the outcome, they lose.' Stella was disappointed but unwilling to show it.

He grunted, clearly dismissing them from his mind. 'A thousand steps four times a day over two thousand years. Allowing for the time I've spent out of the keep, that is about two and a half thousand million steps. No wonder so many of them have needed to be replaced.'

What on earth was the man wittering on about? Could it be . . . was he nervous? There seemed no other explanation for the irrelevant chatter, so unlike him.

'Lenares would know the exact number,' she said. 'For a man so enamoured of statistics, you're rather approximate.'

'Maybe so,' he said, his grin twisted into something resembling a snarl. 'But today, when it matters, I'll be right on time. And your friends will be . . . late.'

A final stair, spiralling around the inside of the narrowing circular tower, led them to a small space in front of a plain grey wooden door. It stood slightly ajar.

'You will wait outside,' he said to her, and waved his arm. The magic slid over her but did not catch; he seemed not to notice. 'You would be destroyed by the forces about to be unleashed. I will call for you when you are required.'

He stood perfectly still for a brief time, then nodded once to himself, strode to the door and pulled it open. A moment later he had vanished inside, closing the door behind him.

Stella counted to a hundred, then followed.

'Hot air rises,' Noetos said, ripping off his tunic. 'With the inferno below, the whole tower is like a sweat-cave.'

'A what?' Moralye asked, panting from the climb. 'Never mind. Not difficult to work out the meaning.'

'Will . . . will the tower burn down?' Cylene asked.

'Mmm,' Noetos said. 'I don't know.'

'I haven't seen any structural timber holding the walls together,' Sautea said. 'As long as the stones themselves don't crack with the heat, I don't see why it shouldn't remain standing.'

'Held together by magic,' Duon reminded them.

Even the supremely fit explorer was out of breath. Noetos dropped his hands to his knees and tried to catch his own breath, difficult in this heat.

His daughter put a hand to her head. In the last little while her hand had seldom been anywhere else. 'I can feel something,' she signalled.

Noetos could feel it too. Power had begun to build far above them and, in response, pressure had begun to build in his head. Could heads explode? He remembered the Padouki woman's head exploding as she battled Kannwar in the canopy.

Duon fell to his knees, both hands pressed to his temples. Anomer grabbed the back of his head.

'Umu puts forth her strength,' Noetos said with gritted teeth.

Through his cloud of abject misery, Deorc sees the one thing he's kept himself alive for, the one thing he does not want to see. Not now, when he is impotent to act!

The Undying Man steps through the door, closes it gently behind him and stands there, hands clasped behind his back. Seemingly relaxed, unconcerned, but harvesting magic furiously from everywhere around him.

Will they exchange witticisms, the immortal and the god? Will they use their voices to gain some advantage in the trial of strength to come?

No. Suddenly Umu *expands*, filling Deorc's poor mind with an unbearable weight. There is a conduit open to the void beyond the world and she draws from it flagrantly. In the distance, visible to the broken man's inner eye, stars begin to go out.

Deorc has sampled the Undying Man's strength, knows and appreciates the man's limits. Worked with him for a decade and more leading up to the Falthan War, then suffered under his powerful hand. At the time there was not another man alive to match him. Since then, however, the Undying Man has been broken by the arrow of the Most High, wreaking severe damage on his magical abilities. It has taken him many years to recover. Surely now, at best, he can only be as strong as he was at the commencement of the Falthan War. And if that is the measure of the Undying Man's strength, it will not be enough. Not nearly enough. Deorc is appalled by the reservoir of pure power Umu has assembled. She may be able to be tricked, as Lenares did once, and subsequently bound, but there is no chance of overwhelming her by using main strength.

The Undying Man has miscalculated. Badly. Fatally. It may not be by his hand, but Deorc will see his long enemy die. And if the Daughter has spent her godhood wisely, accumulating interesting practical knowledge, that death promises to be both protracted and inventive.

This may be satisfying, after all.

She sends her magic forth, not as a bolt of lightning but as a roiling, smothering blanket of world-eating darkness.

The Undying Man snarls, extends his hands and shapes a shield. Wrong move.

The darkness eats at his shield like acid.

As the shield melts, an unnatural wind begins to blow. Pressure difference in the air. The Undying Man has vanished the air around Umu, around Husk's poor body sitting on the chair by the window. *Clever, that.* The darkness flows back towards Umu. Deorc cringes, despite knowing she will bear the pain. He does not want to see his hard-won body corroded.

She puffs out her cheeks – his cheeks – and the miasma is blown through the window, dissolving chunks of rock from the lintel as it expands into the open air outside the tower.

Kannwar is sweating heavily. His face is lined with worry. He begins to apprehend the trouble he is in.

Umu laughs out loud. A weakness, this displaying of emotion. It smacks of anticipating a victory as yet unearned, however inevitable.

Deorc begins to wonder if his victory might be achieved regardless of who wins this battle.

Should Umu win, she is likely to discard this husk of a body as worthless. She could take the Undying Man's own body perhaps, with its immortal blood. Were gods immortal already, or would her conquest of Kannwar give her something extra? Either way, she would certainly abandon Deorc. Perhaps she might not kill him first.

In the unlikely event of the Undying Man's triumph, Deorc might well be in the position he has wished for, after all. Depending, of course, on the nature of the victory. Somehow Deorc will need to persuade the Undying Man to spare his body.

Desperate chances, and nothing he can do to affect the outcome either way.

Umu spits something out of her – his – mouth: things she has fashioned from trace elements stolen from his body.

At that moment, everything changes. Stella walks through the door.

The phrase 'nothing to lose' had been a popular one in Leith's court. Introduced by Phemanderac, it bespoke a certain degree of risk-taking, an innovative approach to difficult political problems. Leith had adopted the term with glee: as he matured, he had abandoned the nervous, introspective disposition that had characterised him as a young man and had become quite adventurous. Sometimes too adventurous. The affair with the Central Plainsmen came to mind as an example of an outrageous but ultimately successfully negotiated solution to what had been thought an intractable problem.

'Nothing to lose' summed up Stella's thoughts exactly as she closed the door behind her. If she died, she achieved an unexpected but welcome release. If she lived, it would be because one or the other of the colossi in the room had lost everything. So as the door clicked gently into its frame – a sound drawing the attention of both parties – she stood there with absolutely no fear.

She expected surprise to rise into the face of the Undying Man. Instead, she saw relief.

He turned from her to face the oncoming peril. A thousand tiny spikes sped through the air towards him, each one rotating vigorously, impelled by dark magic. Stella knew she could not have stopped a single one of them. The Undying Man stopped almost all of them.

The fact that a dozen or so slipped through his defences implied deliberate intent on the part of the Undying Man's opponent. Carefully calculated to overwhelm without utterly destroying him. Stella watched in fascinated horror as the spikes dug into his skin, vanishing in a cloud of blood and flesh.

Hooks, they were, made fast in his flesh. Magical ropes extended from them to the body sprawled on the chair. An appendage – not a hand, more a flipper – held the ropes and jerked at them. The Undying Man skidded across the room. To finish up in a heap at the feet of a . . . a monstrosity.

Stella clapped her hand to her mouth, burying four fingers in her long-ago childhood gesture, at what Deorc of Jasweyah had become. He was the shape and texture of a slug. Body covered in slime, skin glistening, solid only in patches, abraded in others. Covered in deep red gouges, as though hacked at by swords. Riddled with suppurating sores. Leaking fluids onto the chair and floor. Something that had once been a man, his former identity visible only in the general form and the vestigial appendages. Not in the face; there was no face. No real head. Just the top of the slug-like torso, from which twin stalks jutted, each ending in a single large eye able to swivel to view the whole room at once. Now focused on the form at his feet.

No wonder he'd called himself Husk.

Horrified at the sight, Stella found herself on the point of regretting what she'd done all those years ago.

A fifth appendage in the centre of the ghastly shape drew her eye. What . . . was that? Length and thickness of a forearm, sharp edges protruding, leathery, some sort of weapon perhaps. Pus dribbled from its end in a slow stream.

No. Nausea grabbed at her stomach as she realised what it was, what it had been designed for. Who it had been designed for.

Conal had been spiked in order to draw her here. To where Deorc could exact the cruellest revenge he could imagine – and he'd had seventy years to imagine it.

'Nothing to lose' suddenly became a mockery. Deorc of Jasweyah must not, must *not* win this fight. If she had been wearing a sword, she had no doubt she'd be hacking at him.

She breathed out, and let her anger go. As though this was a signal, the presence of the Most High unfolded within her.

She'd once thought the Firefall a rare and sacred experience. Certainly that was how the Halites understood it, though they denied she'd shared in it. Denied, in fact, the evidence of holy Hal's own brother. But if it had been so rare, why had it been repeated by the Son and the Daughter in their possession of Dryman, Conal and Cylene? And now, she guessed, Deorc. Noetos had reported a brief encounter with the Most High. And, of course,

Stella and the Undying Man himself, in the guise of Heredrew, had allowed the Father access to their bodies. Possession by a god, it seemed, was far more common than the Archpriest and the Koinobia thought.

The Most High possessed her, but she still had control. In that respect, she supposed, as she accessed his power to slice through the threads binding the Undying Man, this possession was different from that to which the others had been subjected. Less intrusive. Somehow she was more herself despite the overwhelming, crowding presence of the god. Expanded, not constrained.

She took the Undying Man by the hands and dragged him away from the monster on the seat.

He looked up at her through a glaze of pain. 'I knew you would come,' he said.

'What?' Stella asked. 'You brought me here.'

'The Most High. He'd not miss such an important nexus. Claims to be disinterested, but he's always there, interfering. Thank him, by the way.'

'Huh,' Stella replied, unable to think of anything more sensible.

A glance at the suddenly quiescent figure on the chair gained her nothing. With its lack of discernible face, there was no way she could tell how the Daughter was reacting to the presence of the Most High.

'Your father asks you to give up this selfishness,' she told Umu. 'Take yourself back to the void, he begs. There is much work for you to do there.'

'You won't unmake me,' Umu said confidently. 'Not your own daughter.'

'No,' said Stella. 'He won't. He will not raise a hand against you.'

The stalks quivered, the nearest, Stella supposed, the body she inhabited could come to a smile.

'He will have his champion do it instead,' Stella added.

'What?' said the god, the voice strained.

Kannwar nodded to Stella and dragged himself to his feet. 'I will not fail you,' he said.

489

The Father spoke the words into her mind just before she said them; and oh, she so enjoyed saying them. She knew how badly they would hurt the one who had so hurt her. Her revenge.

'You are not his champion,' she said. 'I am.'

The door at the top of the last stair was barely visible in the smoke-filled haze. Everyone wheezed and whistled, trying to draw breath. Poor Arathé still whimpered from the after-effects of the magical activity in the room above them: she had stood and screamed when Umu had begun to draw on her power. Duon had gone milky-white, while Noetos and Anomer clung to each other, unable to move.

Something dreadful was being shaped in the Tower of Farsight.

Eventually the fisherman drew himself up, wiped his mouth and beckoned them up the stair. Hands supporting each other, under elbows, resting on shoulders, in the small of the back, the companions struggled to the landing. The sound of stone crashing onto a wooden floor came echoing up the tower from far below.

'I don't want to go in there,' Cylene said, coughing as she eyed the door.

'Aye.' Sauxa rubbed at his left cheek. 'Somethin' weighty in there. Best I can describe it.'

'We have to go in,' Anomer said, but Lenares could see his whole body leaning away from the door.

'No,' Cylene moaned, and Lenares knew her sister had come to the end of herself. Shaking uncontrollably, no colour in her face. 'I can't.'

Lenares reached out her hand, touching her on the arm, and Cylene shrieked. Her body was rigid with fear for a moment, then she pulled away from Lenares' touch, breathed a low 'sorry' and ran back down the stair, sobbing as she went.

'Cylene!' Noetos called after her. He made to follow.

Cyclamere grabbed his arm. 'Too much,' the swordsman said. 'We've asked too much of her. She knows what it is like to have an evil god inside her. Which of us would not flee had we her knowledge?'

'But she'll burn,' Noetos said desperately as the sound of feet on stone faded into silence.

'My lord,' Cyclamere said after too long a moment, 'we've come this far. We must go on.'

The numbers told Lenares the fisherman was about to fling the swordmaster's arm aside and run after Cylene. The numbers were never wrong, but as she watched, they changed.

'Aye,' he said, and turned to Lenares.

'You and I,' he said. 'We must face the gods.'

His face was as blank as a stone wall, but his numbers told her which sister he would prefer beside him. Lenares inclined her head, strode quickly to the door – *don't think about it* – set a hand to the latch and pushed.

The problem with the Most High, Deorc thinks, *is that because he holds himself aloof from the world, no one factors him into any conflict. So when he appears, all calculations are rendered moot.*

Umu, he can see, is terrified. The Father made her thousands of years ago in an unparalleled act of intervention in the affairs of the world, and he can unmake her the same way. Can thrust her back into the void. Can even make it so she no longer exists. Has never existed.

Her red-edged thoughts leak to him. Deorc realises he is beginning to lose his sense of self, beginning to be absorbed into her. He huddles there, not knowing exactly where *there* is, as her thoughts and memories wash over him, leach through him.

A single image flicks through her – through his – brain. She and Keppia, sullen and defeated both, stare at each other across a sandy space, while between them stands a figure of light. A throne behind him, barely discernible. The House of the Gods, Deorc realises; though, he supposes, at that time more appropriately called the House of the God. He is seeing the truce between the two armies of creation. Not only humankind: other creatures fought in each army, according to kinship and disposition. The cause of the conflict has long been forgotten. Ancient history – though Deorc suspects Umu knows exactly what lies behind it. The war was prosecuted for a thousand years and more, and the world bled because of it.

So the Most High had despaired of his creation. He presented Umu and Keppia with a stark future. He was, he told them, prepared to wipe the world clean of life. There were other worlds, he said, where sentients lived together cooperatively. He would start anew here, with two people, and rebuild. Keppia and Umu were the chosen people.

In Umu's memory, Keppia was the one to plead for mercy. It was Keppia's plan to anoint himself and Umu as gods, truce-keepers, forsaking earthly life for a role in the heavens. Umu went along with this reluctantly, keeping her reservations to herself. So she remembers.

It happened so long ago that she now completely believes her memory. But Deorc can see the stamp of self-deception all over it. It was Umu who pleaded for the lives of her family and friends, for all of creation. Begging, persuading, promising, until the Most High assented to the plan. *Thus*, he said, *I give you more power over your own futures*. He was well satisfied.

Deorc wonders if this hasn't been the god's plan all along.

The Most High raised up two large thrones, one either side of his, and vested great power in them. He seated Umu and Keppia on those thrones and, as he spoke to them of statecraft, the power began to work in them, beginning the long transformation from human to god.

Deorc tries to project a thought towards Umu, desperate to exploit this knowledge. To unsettle her at the least. *You are a fool*, he shouts at her. *You have been manipulated from the very start!*

She hears nothing more, perhaps, than a faint whisper. Perhaps she hears nothing at all. Whichever, it does nothing to interrupt her endeavours: she is fashioning a spear of light, drawn directly from the magic of the void. A spear imbued with a magical tip, spell-shaped to cut through anything in its path.

'If I am safe from your hands,' she says in Deorc's voice, addressing the Most High, 'then I shall make an end of these tools of yours. And then we shall agree to a new pact, in which I assume your role and power while you fade away. I see your mind. It is what you want, what every part of you cries out for. You want to rest from your labours. I can grant your wish.'

She hefts the spear, holding it in an invisible hand. The sort of hand Deorc desired for himself.

The door opens.

The door opened and in came her friends.

Noetos first, sword in one hand, huanu stone in the other. Lenares beside him, her head barely reaching his shoulder, her large eyes open in what looked like fascination. The remainder of Stella's former companions shuffled in with various degrees of reluctance, spreading to the left and right of the cosmographer and the fisherman, fighting the wish of their bodies to shelter behind those in front. For all the world like a choir of nervous children on the first night of Midwinter celebrations.

Stella almost laughed, and the god inside her chuckled at the image.

Kannwar stiffened. Ah, he'd obviously written her friends out of this drama. Set traps below, no doubt, which would explain the smoke billowing into the room through the half-open door. The traps had worked too, Stella observed: Bregor and Consina were missing, as was Cylene. *The fisherman will be devastated.* Yet there he stood, his eyes burning, obviously having elected to continue.

And now it comes, the Most High said, his voice sorrowful.

I have lived long enough, she muttered to him. *I have seen all my closest friends into the grave. I am prepared for an ending.*

I am sorry, Stella, but there is something else I must tell you. There is a chance that the manner of your death may rip you entirely from the world and the void between.

I will cease to exist? Her chest began to burn.

Silent assent.

Can you tell me . . . What can I . . . She gave up. To be told details of the future would be to shape it, to potentially change the desired outcome. *You needn't have told me,* she whispered. *I am having enough trouble being brave.*

493

So, said the voice, *am I*.

'Can't keep you away,' the Destroyer said, nodding to Noetos. 'Are you here for me or for Umu?'

'Both,' said the fisherman, and strode forward brandishing the huanu stone.

Umu can barely contain her delight. The spear remains unthrown, and as the god's thoughts cascade through his brain, Deorc can see why.

To become anchored in the world she needs a body. Deorc's will not do: it is sustained entirely by magic, and is unpleasant both to look upon and live within. Umu intends to move out as soon as she can.

When Stella entered the room, the Daughter rejoiced – she was perfect. Immortal, beautiful, powerful. Umu desired her with an intensity that made his own desire seem trivial, until the presence of the Most High burgeoned within the woman.

Now other bodies line the wall, each one a possible candidate for possession. Arathé would be the easiest to take, having an already-open channel to Deorc's mind. Moderately gifted, yet badly blemished. Unattractive. By no means a worthy vessel, but might do as a transitional place to gather strength for her next leap.

Duon is equally problematic. Umu desires a woman's body, and Duon is most emphatically a man and too old. She sets him aside in her thoughts.

With that dreadful thing in his hand, Noetos is untouchable. She moves on quickly with a shudder.

His son, though, is another matter. Young, handsome, talented, yet to come into his full strength. Rightful heir to a dukedom. She built her earthly power base all those years ago from far less.

Ah, but there stands Lenares. One of twins. Her sister is likely beyond Umu's grasp, unless she can be freed from Keppia's accursed conduit without it killing her anew. Lenares, though, is exquisite. Such a mind! God-touched. And the prospect of a very intimate revenge for those days of humiliating captivity cannot be discounted. A close second to Stella perhaps.

But at that moment the presence of the Most High that has been glowing hotly within Stella vanishes. Frightened of the huanu stone, no doubt. Umu thrusts her debate aside and pounces.

She takes an instant to flick through Deorc's dying brain and retrieve the memory she is looking for: how to fashion a spike. The making that had taken him days takes her seconds. She drops the spear, lifts the spike and slams it into Stella's mind.

The Falthan queen stumbles at the impact.

Umu sees Noetos coming at her and forces the channel between her and Stella wide open.

Deorc sees his doom approaching. Umu is going to let him back into his broken body and mind just in time to be struck by the huanu stone. He tries to ready himself for vigorous movement, tries to assemble some sort of defence, but knows he will be too late.

Umu cackles in triumph as she pours herself out of his mind and into that of the Falthan queen. Full possession.

Deorc of Jasweyah hauls himself back into the wreckage of his mind, pausing for the merest moment to grab the tattered outliers of his thoughts. He is too late. The stone is coming.

The Most High disappeared.

A pain like the bite of a scorpion took her in the back of her head. A moment later her mind exploded in fire as something black and hot forced its way through the channel and into her brain.

She retreated to the place he had prepared for her, sobbing in fear and regret – how could she not? – as the brutal Daughter took her mind in taloned fingers, tore it apart – gone for ever – and reshaped it, like a vulture invading a nest.

The impact was fearsome and irrevocable. Stella did not have to feign her stagger. Into the path of Noetos and his stone.

Stella seized control of her body back from Umu, the Most High's strength underlining her own. At the same time the Most High seared the channel back to Deorc, closing it. The goddess screamed, dimly aware she had been out-thought. Trapped by her own desires. Stella hooked a foot around Noetos's leg and brought him crashing down on top of her. Two bodies, four minds, falling to the floor.

Three deaths to come.

She took his arm firmly in her own and guided the huanu stone down onto her chest, between her breasts. The sudden pain was intolerable, worse than a sword through the heart. Welcome.

Someone, somewhere in the room, began screaming.

In full possession of her bleeding brain, Stella looked into the eyes of the frightened man atop her, the huanu stone wedged between them. He clearly believed he had failed. That he was killing the wrong person.

'Don't be alarmed,' she whispered as the magic began to drain out of her. White water-magic, black, corrupted throne-magic and gold creator-magic, vanishing into the void in three distinct but intertwined streams. 'This is right. This is what the stone is for.'

Lenares and Arathé had kept up a constant whisper in his ear, alerting him as to the build-up of power and the intentions of those in the room. Then Lenares had hissed on an indrawn breath. 'Umu is attacking Stella,' she said.

As he lunged for the grotesque body in which, against all reason, Lenares claimed Umu was housed, he realised that he was likely wasting his last chance at revenge. The huanu stone absorbed magic, but at a cost to itself: each use rendered part of the stone inert, the size of the blemish proportional to the power absorbed. Striking at Umu now would probably use the stone up, robbing him of any chance of retribution against the Undying Man. Nevertheless, he struck.

He was halfway across the room, hand raised high, when Stella stumbled into his path. Stumbled deliberately. He tried to avoid her, but she snared his leg and pulled him down to the floor with her. Trapping the huanu stone between them.

Knowing the thing would drain her magic, he grabbed at it, trying to pull it away. But her hand held his arm motionless. He was a strong man, his muscles developed from years of hauling boats and nets, but he could not move the slim woman's hand even by a fraction of a finger-width.

'Don't be alarmed,' she said. 'This is right. This is what the stone is for.' As she spoke, blood began to flow from her nose, her ears and her eyes.

In that moment Noetos knew no right or wrong, was shown no clear path, had no one to ask for help. Had no wisdom to fall back on. Knew only that he was hurting a woman he'd come to respect; was stripping her of her immortality, maybe even killing her.

He turned his head to his left, afraid to look any longer into the tortured face beneath his own. The Undying Man had made it to his feet and was launching himself at the figure on the seat by the window. With every fibre of his being Noetos wanted to leap up and chase the selfish bastard who had done for his daughter and who had brought this vulnerable woman to this place.

But he did not. He could do nothing but trust Stella. For her sake, because she asked him to, he held the huanu stone to her chest and prayed most fervently that she knew what she was doing.

Lenares had no power of her own. She could do nothing but watch as the trap was set and sprung. She had seen it develop and knew it for what it was, which made her smarter than Umu. She derived a great deal of satisfaction from that.

Even as their power faded, Stella and the Most High held fast to Umu, containing her increasingly frantic attempts to withdraw from Stella's body.

'Lenares!' Torve cried. 'What is happening?'

To the non-magical onlookers this climactic moment must appear odd, a simple skirmish on the floor not even involving any of their enemies. So it seemed.

'No time to explain,' Lenares said, as Stella started to convulse in Noetos's arms.

He tried to pull away then; she could see the effort he applied to lifting himself free of her embrace.

'It's all right,' she said lamely to the others. *Despite appearances.*

We will plug the hole ourselves, Stella, the Most High said to her. *After we allow Umu to pass through.*

497

Is there no other way? she asked wistfully.

Yes, he said, always scrupulous with the truth. *I could let you trickle back into your body. Sadly, your mind has been damaged beyond repair by Umu's intrusion. I hoped she would be more careful, but she has never known the meaning of restraint. You would live the rest of your life – ten years perhaps, or more – in a madhouse. They would feed you with a spoon and wipe you when you messed yourself. You would be much honoured, but you would never know it. In the mean-time, I would try to hold the gap alone, and most likely fail.*

But if I want, she said, *you'd let me back?*

I cannot stop you, he replied. *Nor would I want to. As always, this is your choice, freely made.*

I would have the last seventy years over again, she said.

He smiled. *What if I could offer you better?*

She formed a question in her mind, but he answered before she could ask it.

I have in mind a tutor's appointment for you. A couple of youngsters need training into a new position of responsibility.

I thought I was to be employed plugging a hole?

That will heal itself over in time, after which you can devote yourself to your pupils.

I don't mind what task you have for me, she said, *as long as I have something useful to do.*

He smiled. *I think this is a task you will enjoy.*

Together they continued to hold steady, sharing the searing pain with the stoicism of veterans as the increasingly attenuated spirit of the former Daughter spun away towards the void. After a time the stream of black throne-magic died away, along with the shrieks, curses and pleading, and silence descended upon them.

A peace such as Stella had never known, had never imagined could exist, stole over her. She sighed.

Don't get used to it, said the Most High. *It won't last long. Remember, I have new tasks for you soon.*

I wish I could bid my friends farewell, she said. *They have been so brave.*

You are blessed that they are all here, gathered around you, to give

498

you their goodbyes. You may linger a while longer, but already the majority of your strength I have woven into the Wall of Time. I, too, will remain for a moment.

Stella died in his arms.

The horror of her death, of his killing her, overwhelmed Noetos. He realised that now she was dead, he had no one to speak up for him. He knew how this must have looked to the observers and feared the anger about to descend upon him.

He eased himself off the corpse of the Falthan queen, picked up the now inert stone and looked around wearily. The only movement in the room was over by the window, where the Undying Man hacked at the body of Husk with a sword. Thud, thud, thud went the blade, spattering gore on the walls and floor.

The Lord of Bhrudwo looked up from his work, his face bleak. 'Is she dead?'

'Yes.'

Noetos prepared himself for an outburst. A bolt of magic perhaps, or a blow with the sword. He knew he had nothing with which to protect himself from the former, and doubted his ability to defend himself against a blade. Not with his limbs shaking so fiercely.

The Undying Man sighed, and said, 'There were other ways of doing this.'

Noetos could not answer him. His family, friends and travelling companions stared at him in shock.

Finally someone dared to break the silence.

'What in the Most High's name have you done, fisherman?' Sauxa bellowed. 'You've killed her! You killed my queen!'

'Yes,' he responded, hardly trusting himself to speak even that monosyllable. 'I killed her.'

'She'll come back to life again, won't she?' Moralye said, but Noetos could hear the hope against reason in the scholar's voice.

'No, the stone has burned the magic out of her,' he said in a monotone. 'And because her immortality was magical, she lost her life as well as her power.'

'Why, my friend?' Sauxa asked. 'Why kill her? What had she done to you?'

Sautea spread his arms. 'Isn't the immediate question still what we do to defeat the Daughter? Isn't she holed up in that . . . body?'

'You're diverting attention away from the fisherman because you are his friend!' Sauxa challenged, his voice a roar.

Lenares pushed her way to Noetos's shoulder. 'Please! Stop, everyone. Listen to me. Umu is gone, driven back beyond the hole in the world, which is being repaired as I speak. I will explain what you didn't see.'

Noetos nodded to her. Say what you wished about her, the girl had a presence that gained people's attention. He was safe at least until she finished her explanation.

'The Most High set a trap for Umu,' Lenares explained. 'He seemed to abandon Stella during the confrontation, and Umu decided to leave Husk and jump to Stella. She most likely thought the Most High's presence had moved to the Undying Man, so she set a spike in Stella's mind and made the leap. Stella and the Most High trapped her there.'

'We saw none of this,' Sauxa said mulishly. 'How do we know it is true?'

'You don't,' snapped Lenares. 'All you can do is judge the source. Do I often get it wrong? If not, you might want to consider believing what I say. Anyway, I told Noetos that Umu was about to attack Stella. He acted rather precipitately and sought to assault Umu in Husk's body with the huanu stone. I can tell from his numbers that he attacked Husk hoping to destroy Husk and Umu both. Noetos wanted to use the huanu stone on Husk because he was angry at how the magician had spiked and abused his daughter. But his primary target was the Undying Man. Am I right?'

She smiled at him, her head cocked, waiting for a reply.

Noetos nodded his head slowly.

'It wouldn't have worked,' she said cheerfully. 'Had you tried to drain Umu's magic, she would have fled to the nearest person she had a connection with – probably your son or daughter. Once there she could have used them as a hostage, demanding you lay down the huanu stone or throw it out of the window.'

Noetos's grim expression sobered further. He had not thought of the implications.

'Stella pulled me down on top of her,' he said, hoping his voice sounded more confident than he felt. 'She didn't say why, but she held the huanu stone to herself until it had . . .' – he choked – 'until it had burned out every bit of magic from within her.'

'And from the two other gods within her,' Lenares added.

'Two?' Sauxa said, clearly struggling to follow the explanation. 'But I thought Keppia had already been banished?'

'Not Keppia,' Lenares said, demonstrating uncharacteristic patience. 'The Most High.'

Noetos groaned. The ends of his fingers tingled with the shock. 'I killed the Most High?'

The Undying Man came and knelt by the dead woman, his hand resting on her cheek.

'Not the way I'd planned it,' he said to the room at large in a voice laden with despair. 'Not that my plans mattered in the end. I was the dupe all along, it seems. How long have you been planning this?'

And so, amid the turmoil and doubt, the gift of revenge came to Noetos late and completely unexpected, a drop of blessing amidst darkness. He had denied himself his revenge and would never get another chance. Had to take this one.

'Ever since we learned who you were,' said the fisherman. 'It was Stella's idea really, to pretend to be attracted to you.' He shook his head, hoping he wasn't overdoing it. 'She suffered dreadfully. Often cried about how horrifying she found it all.'

'Misdirection,' breathed the Undying Man in wonder. His frame seemed to shrink as he absorbed the news. 'I recently told her I'd seen through her ploy when she falsely accused Deorc those many years ago. And all the while . . .'

'. . . she was deceiving you,' Noetos finished.

Behind him, Lenares was about ready to explode, Noetos could feel it. The others might understand what he was doing, or at least

501

not interfere, but Lenares would demand the truth be spoken. *Keep quiet, girl*, he willed.

The door opened. Everyone's head swung in its direction. Cylene came in, her eyes wide. Immediately Lenares went to her. The fisherman breathed out in relief. This mattered. It mattered very much. He would comfort Cylene in a moment. For now, he had a revenge to complete.

'Most of us were in on it,' he continued, waggling the fingers of his right hand behind his back, indicating for the others to hold their peace. 'Save a few we couldn't trust to keep quiet,' he added. 'Our apologies, Sauxa. The Undying Man was to be our lightning rod, drawing the attention of the great powers.'

The Lord of Bhrudwo looked sick. 'You convinced the Most High to go along with this?'

Oh. Noetos had forgotten about the Most High. He searched desperately for further invention: he'd never been quick on his feet . . .

'I needed no persuasion,' came a voice from everywhere and nowhere, accompanied by an increase in the pressure in the room, as though the spaces between them were now overfilled. 'I called you, Kannwar, to serve me. Two thousand years ago you turned me down, as was your right. This time . . . I had a different role for you. A lesser role.'

'You're bitter?' the Undying Man said, incredulity written on his face. 'You used me as a dupe in some sort of revenge on me?' His face turned red.

'Not at all,' the voice said smoothly. 'But you assumed you were the centrepiece of my plan. I made no such assurance. A vital part, indisputably, but not at the heart. That place,' he said, his words freighted with emotion, 'went to my beloved Stella.'

At the mention of her name, everyone fell silent.

The Undying Man, a very much reduced figure, shed tears as he straightened the red dress he had given Stella to wear, reaffixed a button that had come undone, and wiped the blood from her face. Something inside him seemed to have broken, or at least was in the process of breaking; no one thought to correct his misapprehension or to shore him up.

One by one the travellers came and bowed over her hands, now clasped between her breasts, covering the spot where the huanu stone had burned her.

There were no words, so none were said.

The dying embers of Deorc's soul try and fail to reconnect with the burnt-out remnant of his mind. If he can find even one place to attach himself he can begin the long healing process all over again. Seventy years isn't a long time to wait. He'd wait double that time, more, to live again. Ten times as long to have another chance at revenge.

The Undying Man took to his body with a sword, but the attack was irrelevant, the action of a frustrated man, and the fool must have known it. Deorc's magic-infused body can't be killed that way. He severed the eye-stalks, though, and Deorc – better call himself Husk, given the circumstances – can see nothing. Has to try to read air vibrations through his skin, and given the condition of that skin, cut to shreds by the Undying Man's blade, he is unable to hear a great deal.

He hears the Most High, though, and begins to piece together what has happened. Umu has been trapped, subjected to the huanu stone – the stone he expended so much energy to bring here! – and is now beyond the Wall of Time. This pleases him, though he wishes he had been the agent of her destruction. And in the doing Stella has died. Sacrificed herself. So says the cosmographer girl. Rage at this burns in the fading core of his soul. He wants to lift up his accursed limbs and stamp on her body; stamp and stamp and stamp until she is nothing more than a stain on the floor. But her body is well beyond his reach. As is his own.

Ah, Deorc, says the Most High, reaching into his mind and scooping up his soul in his hands. *Are you interested in a chance to redeem yourself?*

As long as I get a chance to heal, he says in reply. And to himself he says, *Give away anything, patience, wait, wait. Bargain. Stay alive.*

Stella speaks to him, her words a burning in the heart of his guilty soul. *Come with us, Deorc, and be part of the repairs to the hole in the Wall of Time.*

No! How could he bear it? To share a place of healing with her. The eternal shame! He keeps all of this out of his reply. *How long until I could return here?*

Never, the Most High states. *You are near death. Even the old magics binding you together will not hold you much longer. Spend your death wisely, Deorc, in a way you never spent your life.*

I want nothing to do with your plans, Husk replies, and waits for the counterarguments.

So be it, comes Stella's reply with the finality of a closing door.

I . . .

Silence.

CHAPTER 21

SON AND DAUGHTER

CYLENE EMBRACED HER SISTER, HER hands gripping Lenares'
shoulders tightly, undoubtedly leaving bruises.

'I'm sorry, I'm so s-sorry,' she kept saying, not listening to what
Lenares wanted to tell her.

'Sh, sh,' Lenares said. 'Nobody thinks badly of you. None of us
would have gone through that door if we had once been possessed
by a god, knowing that the god's vengeful sister waited there.'

'I k-kept thinking of the way he hurt me,' Cylene sobbed.

Lenares shushed her some more. 'In the end you came through
the door, sister. That took bravery.'

Cylene grimaced. 'It wasn't bravery. It is too hot out there. I
could feel my skin beginning to crisp.'

'That, we need to tell the others,' said Lenares.

'What has happened here?'

Lenares sighed. The story would be told again and again, she
had no doubt, until it achieved the status of a legend, and was
disbelieved as often.

Best to get it right, to confirm all the facts with the chief par-
ticipants, before telling the story again.

'We've won,' she told her sister, her voice fierce with emotion.

'What's it like out there, Cylene?' Scren asked. 'Can we reach
the base of th' tower?'

The travellers turned to Cylene. Many of them had forgotten
about the fire burning below. Until now. Seren's words started

many of them thinking about life beyond the hole in the world.

'The fire has consumed the accommodation floor,' Cylene said. 'I could go no lower.'

'It must be running out of material to burn.'

'I would not be so hopeful, Noetos,' Moralye said. 'There is a great deal of flammable material in a library. If there is a scriptorium associated with the library downstairs, there will likely be chemicals that could feed a fire for days.'

'Then let us hope the Undying Man does not have a scriptorium.'

The man in question raised his head from his vigil beside Stella's body. 'A scriptorium and a storeroom for rare manuscripts,' he said. 'All gone.' He turned back to his deathwatch.

'Come then, Lord of Bhrudwo,' Noetos said. 'Help us down from this tower.'

The face turned again. 'I'm not sure I can. Holding people above the ground for any length of time is impossible for most magicians, and very difficult for me. I doubt even Umu could have done it.'

'So if it is merely difficult, why not try?'

'You are persistent,' said the Undying Man. 'Like your grandfather, you get what you want by pig-headedness. But not in this case. I could perhaps transport one person down through hundreds of paces of air to the ground. No more.'

'Do it then,' the fisherman said. 'Send someone off to seek help.'

'What help could this person find? That is, presuming they don't just run for their own lives?'

'You've maintained a poor view of us; in line, no doubt, with your view of yourself.'

That one stung the Bhrudwan lord. His numbers, Lenares noticed, had thinned out considerably.

'There is no need to send anyone,' Lenares said. 'All we need do is wait here until the fire burns itself out.'

Noetos scowled. 'If we have to wait for days, as Moralye indicated, we will die of thirst.'

Lenares frowned. 'Then Kannwar can send someone to bring water to the base of the tower. Surely he can lift up a few jars of water.'

'If he can lift water,' Mustar said, his voice hesitant in case, no doubt, he was about to embarrass himself in front of all these clever people, 'then why not lift up a rope?'

'Ah,' said Noetos. 'I knew I employed you for a reason. Someone who can think!'

The travellers clustered around the Undying Man, entreating him to exercise his magic and lower Mustar to the ground.

They received an abrupt answer. 'Let him climb down the outside of the tower. It is not far.'

Mustar leaned back from peering out of the window. Stepping carefully around the body of Husk, he returned to the others. 'There is much smoke coming from the windows below, and I thought I could see some movement in the stonework. It definitely appears as though the wall of the tower is bowed outwards.'

'We will try to lower you down,' Anomer said, indicating his sister.

The Undying Man sighed. 'Don't be such fools. You will get him so far, then the strain will be too much. One of two things will happen: either one or both of you will have the magic torn from you, or, more likely, you'll let him go. Even twenty paces is a long way to fall.'

He stood. 'I'll lower one person. After that, I will grant you no more favours.'

'Less of a favour and more of an obligation, I would have said,' Noetos growled.

This earned him a strangely nervous glance, but no rebuke.

'Very well,' Lenares said. 'Who is the least heavy among us?'

'I am surrounded by the weak of mind,' Kannwar complained. 'Small variations in weight account for little. It is the distance without support that matters. Here, Mustar. Prepare yourself.'

With no further warning the young fisherman rose into the air, then was ejected through the open window. Lenares bit back a scream. 'Perhaps the rest of you ought to find out if the stair will see you to the ground,' the Undying Man said. 'Whatever you do, get out of my tower. I wish to be alone.'

He turned back to Stella. 'And no more words,' he added.

Lenares leaned as far as she dared out of the window, but

could see nothing in the darkness except shreds of mist and the twinkling of stars high above.

'Our lord is right,' Sautea said. 'We should at least try the stair.'

The moment he opened the door Noetos realised they had made a mistake. The door swung out seemingly under its own power as the fire-driven wind sucked at it – and them. The travellers stumbled forward, some of them already choking on the thick air.

'We need not all go,' he said. 'If there is a clear way down, we will return and fetch the rest of you.'

'Who goes?' Anomer asked.

'You and I, of course,' said Noetos. 'And Cyclamere.' He glanced around the assembled travellers. 'The three of us ought to be enough.'

'And if you get to the bottom, only to find soldiers lined up against you?' Duon asked.

'Then we surrender. But not before we've secured help for you – and, coincidentally, for the Lord of Bhrudwo.'

'He's beyond help,' Duon remarked. 'Seems he wants to burn with his dead ladylove.'

From somewhere far below came a low rumble. A moment later the grey darkness flickered.

'Stay out on the landing as long as you can,' Noetos told Duon. 'But if it is a choice between the flames and the wrath of the Bhrudwan lord, dare the latter. You can't reason with flames.'

'More chance than with that man,' said Duon, but he nodded.

Cyclamere led the way down the stair. Within twenty paces they had lost sight of those waiting above; already Noetos's eyes had begun to sting.

'Smoke is bad enough,' he said, 'but there are foul chemicals in the air.'

'Talk as little as possible,' Cyclamere said. He might as well have told him to keep his mouth shut.

They descended a hundred steps in relative silence, their careful passage punctuated by the occasional rattle or crash from below. But before the second hundred steps had gone by they began to see a deep orange glow below them. Far too soon, Noetos thought.

'Touch the wall,' Anomer wheezed.

Noetos did so, and snatched his hand away. The stone was scalding hot.

The next hundred steps were a descent into a roasting night-mare. There was plenty of light by which to see the walls buck-ling outwards, almost melting as they watched. Noetos felt his skin drying, and wondered how soon before it began to burn.

'Not halfway yet,' Cyclamere said. 'How hot must it be below?'

Noetos did not want to give up, not when their only other possible means of escape from the tower depended on a man who might well have been driven mad. But there seemed little chance—

Ten steps above him the wall suddenly slumped outwards. The stair cracked, then gave way, the stone falling into the orange glow below. Frantic, Noetos glanced upwards: Anomer stood two steps above the failure.

They waited far longer for the crash than Noetos thought plaus-ible, but when it came it was little more than another hollow boom.

'Do you think,' Anomer said, his eyes white in a blackened face, 'that the other sounds were made by falling stones?'

Noetos nodded.

'We need to get back up to the top.'

He nodded again.

'You could jump,' said Anomer, eyeing the five-step gap.

'Take ten steps up the stair, Anomer,' said Noetos. 'Please.'

The wall hadn't finished moving. A section the height of a man was moving outwards, slowly folding on itself. The treads under his son's feet were beginning to crack.

'Please!'

Anomer did as he was told, walking backwards, not taking his eyes off his father.

With a snap three more steps broke away.

From further up the tower came a rumble, then a crack. A moment later a whole section of stair dropped past them, the trailing edge taking Cyclamere on the back of his leg. The man didn't even have a chance to cry out: he spun from the stair and plunged down into the smoke.

'Oh, Alkuon, no,' Noetos groaned. 'Not Cyclamere.'

'Father,' Anomer said, and the fisherman heard the strain in his son's voice. 'I have him. Let me link to you – I can't hold him on my own.'

He opened his mind to his son and was immediately flooded by sensation. Panic from Anomer, driven frantic by the sudden demand on his magical powers. An answering power from far above, also laced with fear – and not as strong as Noetos might have expected.

We have problems of our own, Father, Arathé said, her voice weary, even resigned. *The floor is settling lower – something below us has given way, we think. We fear it is about to collapse.*

Then get back in the room!

We cannot. The Undying Man has barred the door.

Let him go, Noetos said to his son. *Send your strength up to your sister. They need you now.*

But, Father, Cyclamere is in terrible pain. The fire, it is burning him. I can't let him go now!

Then pull him up, son.

Up came Cyclamere. Or what was left of him. The fire had burned the hair off his body and fused his clothing to his skin. Large sections of his torso had turned bright red, and both feet were black. Noetos struggled not to faint, so dreadfully did the man suffer.

'Let . . . me go,' Cyclamere rasped through blackened lips.

'Aye,' Noetos said, bowed once to his old tutor, and nodded to his son.

The far edge of the floor had begun to smoke, as though it was about to catch fire. Arathé could feel her hair scorching; how must it be for her father and brother far below? While Duon hammered at the door behind them, demanding admittance to the lookout room, Arathé fed all the strength she could spare to the two men fighting their way back up the stair.

She had tried to re-establish the ties she had made to the soldiers' essenza, in the hope of exploiting them a third time, but too few threads remained. Most of the soldiers, it seemed, had died because of what she had done. Were she to try distributing the effects of the fire among the handful still alive, she would succeed in killing them and the travellers both.

The Undying Man had not been exaggerating the magical requirement for forming solid matter from air. It required a gathering of the air itself, compressing it until it was strong enough to support a man's weight. Two men's weight. It made no sense – the air was an insubstantial nothing, surely? But she thought of the wind, and could understand that a breeze was the movement of something.

Hah, she said, as the work suddenly became easier. Part of the problem was in imagining it correctly. Now she saw air as just another substance, albeit a thin one, she got on much more effectively. Just as well, as she had to support her men over a gap of twenty steps.

'How much more?' Duon gasped.

Arathé had drained those around her rather deeply. She shrugged.

As much as you have to, Duon said. She smiled gratefully at him.

A short while later Noetos and Anomer emerged from the thickening smoke and Arathé hugged them both. The others leaned against the warm stone wall, as far from the edge of the floor as possible.

'He holds the door,' Duon said to Noetos.

'The door wants to open to the pull of the fire below,' the fisherman said, and drew his sword. He wedged it in a crack in the seal of the door, then nodded to his son and daughter. 'See if you can lift the latch even a fraction.'

'We don't have much magical power remaining,' Anomer said.

'Just a fraction,' his father repeated.

Duon drew his own blade and found another place to wedge it.

Both men leaned on their swords and Anomer saw the blades begin to bend. With a grunt he drew on everything around him.

The fire, Arathé. We can draw from the fire. It is alive, after a fashion.

Her eyes widened.

The door crashed open, broke free of its hinges and tumbled across the floor towards her.

'No!' came the cry from at least three throats.

She ducked, but it took her in the lower back, knocking her off her feet, along the floor and out into the vast open space of the tower.

Terror. She closed her eyes and waited to hit the ground.

Opened them again to find herself suspended in midair.

The Undying Man stood in the middle of the floor, one arm outstretched. The hand was missing, she noticed muzzily.

'You tried to fall to your death once before,' he said to her. 'You're persistent, at least. Family trait.'

She found herself floating pleasantly to the floor. When she tried to stand up, she fell back to the ground.

'I suppose you think this pays your debt,' Noetos said into the silence.

The man gave him an ironic smile. 'Yes, I do, as it happens.'

'We lost Cyclamere,' Noetos added.

'I felt him fall. He was too far away for me to help.'

The travellers reassembled in the room.

'Not long, I think,' Duon said, his hand resting lightly on the stone. 'The tower is close to collapse.'

'Then perhaps you might like to try this rope I've hauled up here,' said the Lord of Bhrudwo.

The problem of how to anchor the rope was solved by Anomer, who used magic to punch out two sections of the wall on the far side of the room. He then threaded the rope through both holes and made it fast.

'Sailor's hitch,' he said to his father, the ghost of a smile on his face.

'I'd better check it then,' Noetos replied.

'As always,' said Anomer.

But their banter was light of heart, and Arathé knew something new had grown between them – or, at least, something old had died.

*   *   *

The climb down the rope was forever blurred in Lenares' memory. Exhausted from lack of food and drink, chronic fatigue and sleeplessness, drained by the events of this night, she could do nothing but cling to the rope as it was let down. A dozen people paid out the rope and she was in no danger of falling as long as she retained her grip, but she could not shake her fear.

She filled her mind with a simple count of the rows of stones as they moved up past her. She debated for a while whether to count the three rows that had collapsed together, and noted with interest the scorch marks on her tunic from where she'd had to scramble outwards over the molten stonework.

Then it was over, with a suddenness that took her by such surprise she collapsed to the ground, close to fainting away.

A familiar face bent over her.

'Lenares, are you hurt?' Torve asked.

'Yes,' she said truthfully. 'My hands are sore from the rope and I have burns on my knees. But I will recover from these things.'

The Omeran laughed. Rather than picking her up, he snuggled down beside her and held her close.

'You are the bravest and cleverest person I have ever seen,' he said, his breath hot in her ear. 'And I have seen explorers, dukes and emperors.'

'Torve,' she said, easing herself onto an elbow so she could better look into his dark eyes. 'You love me.'

His lovely eyes widened a little. 'I do,' he said, a smile breaking out on his broad face. 'But it is traditional to let the man tell rather than be told.'

'I don't care about tradition,' she said. 'I only care about you.'

A short while later she unfastened her mouth from his. 'Cylene has given me some very interesting advice. Perhaps when we've recovered a little I will share it with you.'

Torve nodded happily. 'I will listen,' he said.

Lenares was woken by a hand on her shoulder. After a short while stretching her limbs, easing out the cricks and kinks, she fought her way to her feet and looked about her.

It was morning. Just before dawn, to be precise: the glow in the east made the oily sea look like it was on fire—

Lenares snapped her head around. She had been lying on a blanket placed on soft turf, perhaps a thousand paces away from Andratan. Five-towered Andratan still, but the Tower of Farsight was on a lean.

'You would not have forgiven me, love, had I not woken you to see this,' Torve said, coming to stand beside her.

'Did we all get down safely?'

'Every one of us,' Torve said. 'Though it was very difficult for the last three or four. They had to clamber down the rope rather than be lowered. Noetos was the last, and he tore the skin from both hands in trying to hold on.'

Torn skin seemed a small thing. 'Is he—'

'His daughter healed him.'

Smoke billowed out of every window in the tower, including the one at the very top. The lower windows glowed red.

'Where are the others?' she asked.

'Taking breakfast in the banqueting hall. Arranged by Bregor and Consina, apparently. They have convinced the castellan that we are allies of the Undying Man, and for now we are being treated as nobility.'

An audible groan came from the direction of the tower.

'Is the Undying Man himself not ordering things?'

'He is still in the tower.'

'Oh.' *He means to die there.*

'Noetos told us he begged the man to come down the rope, but he would not leave the dead queen's side. The fisherman thinks he has gone quite insane.'

'A characteristic of emperors,' Lenares said.

Another groan, followed by a loud crack. The tower settled visibly lower.

A thought crossed her mind and she turned to the west, where the last of the night still resisted the incursion of day. Yes, there it was. The hole in the world, now a circle of stars, a new constellation set in the sky, as though a new piece of fabric had been sewn in by a master tailor. And a gifted seamstress, if she read the numbers she could see correctly. For a moment a patch of mist drifted across the scene and she clicked her tongue in anger, but within minutes the sky cleared and she peered at the stars with nearly closed eyes.

'Torve,' she said, reaching out and taking his hand, 'the work is nearly finished.'

'What do you mean?'

'The last thread is being sewn into the repair even as we look. Can you see?' She pointed to the sky.

'No,' he said. 'But I can imagine it. Tell me what you see.'

She had begun to cry. 'I see two threads – no, three threads woven into the hole. One is golden, so beautiful. That would be the Father. The second is white, much more pliant than the golden thread, woven in a delicate but strong pattern. It binds the golden thread to the sky.'

'Stella,' Torve said. He too was weeping.

'Yes. And, Torve, there is a third thread. It is blue. There isn't much of it, and it is very thin, but it is the finest weave of all. Oh, oh, I recognise it.'

He shook his head. 'I cannot guess, love,' he said.

'She is . . . she is so beautiful. The weave is exactly in the pattern I wove when I trapped Umu. I can see her!'

'Your mother,' Torve said, and her heart loved him for it.

'Now the hole is sealed, she no longer has to thwart Keppia's return to Cylene. Oh, I hope Cylene is still alive.'

'I can't imagine Noetos allowing the Father to cut off the magic necessary to keep Cylene alive, can you?'

They both laughed amid their tears.

A loud rumble signalled the end of the Tower of Farsight. Their heads turned in time to see the tower topple, falling to the right, away from the fortress proper and towards the sea. Smoke climbed to the heavens as the structure fell. The stone spire struck the ground, and a moment later the *wumph!* arrived at the same time as the shaking of the earth. The roar seemed to grow in volume, dying away slowly.

Small figures emerged from the gates of the fortress, drawn by the sound. As they drew closer, Lenares recognised them.

The smoke and dust began to settle, revealing a long, low pile of rubble extending from the fortress right to the ocean's edge. The very tip of the tower had landed in the sea.

'Lenares,' Torve said, a strange edge to his voice. Awe, perhaps. 'Look at the sky!'

She turned back to the newly patched hole. In the centre, blossoming even as she watched, was a new star. For a moment it rivalled the sun in intensity, then it faded slowly, though still the brightest star in the sky. As they watched, awaiting the arrival of their friends, the sun began to chase the stars from the sky, one by one. But it could not quite remove the newest star of all.

'Goodbye, Stella,' Lenares said.

There is very little of Husk left. He has been gradually eroding away, as though he is a sandbank in spring. He has given up trying to reconnect to his mind. His body has already ceased all meaningful movement.

The fire has finally made it to the room. He can sense when the floor ignites: the flash of heat sears his already corroded flesh. He feels the floor move, beginning to buckle.

And still the Lord of Bhrudwo does not move.

The man's fate consumes Husk now. He has nothing else to fix on: he has no hope of personal survival. But he wills, with the little he possesses, the Undying Man to remain where he is.

Fall with your tower. Let your life collapse in ruins.

The body lying beside the man is dead, and has been dead for most of a night, yet has not begun to corrupt. There is still magic at work. Inaccessible to him.

There is a rumble from far below and the floor lurches, then settles back. And lurches again – and this time does not settle, continuing to fall.

Too late, fool, Husk says, his gloating the last act of his life.

He rises from the floor, his soul still trapped in a dead body, as the tower descends. He wills his own death, not wanting to end in pain—

There is movement in the room. The crash blots out all sensation. He loses all contact with his body. Awake in a tiny universe of darkness the size of his soul. He will never know whether his hated adversary chose to escape.

He begins to scream.

After the long walk back to the fortress, and the equally long walk along the corridors to the quarters assigned them, Lenares wanted to shout at everyone to go away. Everyone but Torve. They had told her to take a bath – a bath, with hot water! – and make herself ready for a banquet in their honour. Servants fussed over her, showing her this dress and that, wanting to do things to her hair, telling her how pretty she was. She told them not to touch her, but they didn't seem to have proper ears in this part of the world.

The problem was, she was awash with emotions. How could one body hold all these feelings? Her Torve had kissed her in front of all their friends, and Cylene had hugged her tight. Everyone but poor Cyclamere had survived the tower, she was told. That had been enough to be going on with, as Mahudia would have said, but there was much more. She had seen the hole in the world repaired, the Most High and Stella sacrificing themselves to keep it closed forever. She had wept as Stella's star shone brighter and brighter. And Mahudia had been honoured too. Lenares knew from the pattern of Mahudia's thread that this in part reflected her own bravery, and that in itself was as much glory as she could bear. Her deeds were known. She was not just some pig-girl from the alleyway.

All she wanted to do now was to lie down by herself in a darkened room and think about these things, working them through her mind, turning each one over and over as though they were precious stones. Carefully studying the patterns they made.

Well, perhaps not by herself.

But her sister came for her when she was only half-dressed, and helped her choose something she swore was beautiful on her.

Lenares didn't know if it was beautiful, nor did she care. But she did not want to offend her sister, so she went along with all the fuss.

The banquet room was filled with servants and soldiers, the latter standing to attention, the former hovering around the single table set at the room's heart. All her friends were there, already seated – was she so very late? She looked for him, for his curly black hair, found him and saw the empty chair beside him. Detaching herself from Cylene, she made her way across the wide wooden floor, remembering a similar walk at the Court of Talamaq.

She'd known nothing then. Of course, she acknowledged, she knew next to nothing now. Her thirst for knowledge would never be satisfied.

To her astonishment, every guest at the banqueting table stood and applauded as she drew near. She looked around to see if someone else had entered the room. Her friends, they were clapping her.

'Why?' she called out. 'I did nothing! At the end it was Stella who saved us all. Well, and Noetos helped. Stop clapping me!'

Nothing she said had any effect.

She hurried to her seat and sat down. The others sat as she did, and the applause finally ceased. Cylene took another of the empty seats, between Noetos and Arathé, facing Lenares, and grinned at her.

'What's so funny?' Lenares asked her in a voice perhaps a little louder than she intended.

One last person came to the table, dressed in servant's livery. Oddly, all the other servants bowed to him.

'What's so funny, cosmographer, is that you have absolutely no idea what is about to happen.'

Two surprises jerked her upright. The first was the identity of the speaker.

'I thought you died in the tower,' she said.

The Lord of Bhrudwo bowed to her, looking incongruous in servant's garb. 'I did, in a manner of speaking. But now is not the time for my tale. We are gathered here for yours.'

The second surprise was that she could not read his numbers. Or any of the numbers of those sitting at the table, her friends.

'What has happened?' she asked.

'Don't be alarmed,' Noetos said from across the wide, food-laden table. 'We are assured your – ahm, how did he put it? – your diminution of faculties, yes, that was it, is only temporary.'

The others laughed and smiled at her. But it wasn't the horrible laughing-at-her kind. It was something else. Lenares began to realise that love was a far broader word than she had ever considered.

'We know a secret,' Cylene said.

'Don't tease the girl,' Noetos said in a gruff voice, placing a hand on Cylene's arm. But he wasn't really angry at her, only playing.

How did she know this, if her numbers were gone?

She wasn't an animal after all. She lacked nothing. She just had different abilities. Lenares had known this in her mind, but now, for the first time, she felt it in her heart. She began to cry.

'Not yet, Lenares,' Cylene said. 'But soon.'

The cosmographer turned to Torve. 'Do you know what is going on?'

'I got here just before you,' he said, 'and they clapped me like they clapped you. I know nothing more than you do. Less, probably.'

The Undying Man stood behind Noetos and waited for silence.

'My story is brief, Lenares and Torve, and as everyone else here has heard it at least once, I will make the barest mention of it. As you know, I remained in the tower, heartsick over the death of Stella. I ought not to have been so troubled, I told myself, but she had become a nexus for me – for us all. I saw in her death my own failure, my overweening pride having led me to believe she had been called to be by my side. I never envisioned for a moment I might have been called to be by hers. Had I accepted the role the Most High had planned for me, Stella would be alive today.

'This I learned through the long night as I kept watch beside her body. I knew the Most High had not finished with me as her body did not begin to decay, and I could sense at least a part of them lingering nearby. So I waited. As much to protect her body from whatever spark of life remained in Husk.

'I received my message. It will remain forever secret between myself and the two messengers. I had a decision to make, and I made it at the last possible moment. I removed myself from the tower as it fell, and returned to the fortress.

'But I was given a message for two other people, and a choice for them to make, a choice much different from my own. Lenares and Torve, the Most High has something he wants to ask you.'

The words stilled her. She felt Torve's hand, grasping hers under the table, stiffen.

'Lenares of Sayonae and Torve of Queda, the Most High wishes to announce his retirement. His time, he says, is over: he has a surfeit of knowledge and wishes to find somewhere peaceful to think about what he has learned.'

'But I already feel that way!' Lenares blurted.

Those around the table laughed. Even this laughter, aimed at her, did not have a hard edge. They did not think her full of herself or conceited. She could feel her heart beginning to tear in two with joy.

'Further, the Most High wishes you to know that there are three empty thrones in the House of the Gods. He is confident that the world will make progress without him, but invites you both to fill two of the thrones, knowing that you will fulfil the potential he put within you when first he selected your ancestors.'

Her heart seemed to stop.

'Take a breath, sister,' Cylene said, her eyes dancing.

Three empty thrones. One for her, one for Torve. A chance to go to all the places on the bronze map, to learn all the secrets of the world, to bridge the void and maybe see Mahudia again. Even speak to her.

But . . .

'Will I be cut off from my friends?'

The Undying Man paused for a moment, as though listening to a voice only he could hear. 'No,' he said eventually. 'The Most High has made that mistake once already. He says to tell you that the secret of the thrones is that they will make you into your true self. Keppia and Umu, he says, wished to play the lord over the rest of the world and so separated themselves, only realising too late what they had done. Neither you nor Torve has any such desire. You know only too well what it is like to be lorded over.'

'The power is in the thrones then?' Torve said.

'It is,' said the Undying Man. 'Those who sit in those seats are for ever changed: the longer the sojourn, the greater the change.'

Cylene gave a little squeak. 'I don't want to be a god!'

Lenares thought a moment. 'You won't be,' she said, certain of her words even though she could see no numerical evidence to support her claim. 'Mahudia, the woman who guarded your connection to the void, has gone to be part of the weaving keeping the hole in the world closed. I suspect she was able to leave because once you sat on the throne, you no longer needed a magical conduit to keep you alive.'

'Oh,' Cylene said. 'Will I be immortal?'

'No,' said the Undying Man. 'That curse is for others to bear.'

Others? Plural? Lenares stored the question away in her head.

'That's a relief,' Cylene said, and smiled at the big man sitting next to her.

'All the Most High has done, Lenares and Torve, is shape the circumstances to bring you to this choice. What you do next is up to you.'

She turned and looked into Torve's eyes, to find a question there and, behind the question, desire. A vision of the open desert, of a people lost and abandoned, bred like cattle, a people who could benefit from having a god on their side.

Cylene broke into their shared thoughts. 'I was thinking,' she said, her face a prim mask. 'You might want to consider some of the . . . er . . . advantages of godhood. In the area of equipment, that is.'

It took a moment for Lenares to solve this puzzle; then she felt her neck redden. Torve's grip on her hand strengthened, telling its own story.

'Who will occupy the third throne?' she asked, staring at the Undying Man.

'Ah, well, the Most High wonders if you would, ah, consider taking on an apprentice. Someone who has much to unlearn, but who has promised to do his best to – eventually – fulfil his calling.'

'But, but you are evil,' Lenares cried. 'The Most High can't let you on one of the thrones!'

The Undying Man pulled at his collar. 'The Most High anticipated this objection,' he said. 'He wishes to remind you that the people he is inviting to occupy the other two thrones are good. And he will, he says, give all three keys to the House of the Gods into your hands, Lenares. His offer of the thrones is not conditional on you taking the apprentice. And even if you accept him, you may end his apprenticeship at any time.

'I ought to add that I am by no means a reformed character,' the Undying Man said. 'I do not go back on anything I have said or done. Or perhaps only a very little. This offer is the Most High's way of neutralising me. He thinks I don't know this, but he is wrong. But he believes that between the three of us we will provide exactly the balance that the House of the Gods requires.'

'How can we take on an apprentice?' Torve said. 'Especially one such as you? We need to serve an apprenticeship ourselves.'

'Ah. As to that, he has organised a tutor for you. Her identity is a secret, but he assures me she is someone with great experience in the art of leadership. She knows all about self-sacrifice in the service of others. There is no one more qualified, he says.'

Lenares had run out of questions.

'Can you make up your mind, please?' Sauxa drawled. 'The food's getting cold.'

General laughter followed.

Torve nodded to her, his eyes alight. *Your decision*, he seemed to be saying.

She smiled. 'Tell the Most High that Torve and I will make a home together in the House of the Gods,' she said.

EPILOGUE

THE BANNERS HAVE BEEN RAISED, the flags ripple and crack in the breeze and the Summer Flame has been lit. Revellers from the Fisher Coast and all of Old Roudhos pour out of the taverns and down the wide streets towards the Summer Palace, where the (hopefully brief) ceremony is to take place. Adults and children alike know that this is an event like no other in their city's proud history: the elevation of a new Duke of Roudhos is momentous enough on its own, but to coincide with the announcement of Raceme as the capital of the restored dukedom is unprecedented.

The largesse distributed far and wide from the cellars of the Summer Palace has helped considerably in ensuring the festive atmosphere. There are unfortunate incidents, to be sure: petty thieves are caught and spend the day locked up in temporary cells built for the expected extra numbers; others make away with their booty and the injured parties lose the will to celebrate. Arguments and fights do not cease just because of a public holiday. And there are those who must work irrespective of the day – some, indeed, for whom a holiday provides extra employment opportunities. Some of these latter people line the streets, calling their entreaties to the young lads making their way down towards the harbour, and the wares they display are in some cases very tempting indeed. But few are buying this afternoon.

Sautea of Fossa makes his way slowly through the Oligarchs District, so called because it was once the preserve of the city's elite.

Not now though; at the height of the Neherian War it was razed to the ground, the old timber buildings housing their expensive imported furniture and artwork ending up as ash in the wind, along with their owners. The district now houses the poorer citizens of Raceme, many of whom once lived in the Shambles.

'Must you grumble every time you stretch your legs?' Sautea's wife asks him.

The words are gruff but the mischievous gleam in her eye belies her voice. Sautea knows this, having been married to her for nearly twenty years.

'Legs like mine, who wouldn't grumble?' he says. 'At least I don't grumble in my sleep, Nellas.'

The old woman smiles at her husband. 'You think the youngster will make a good fist of things?'

'Aye, well,' Sautea says, scratching his whiskers. 'He's not been seen much around here. Can't do a worse job than his father.'

The two old people wait at Broad Way for a parade to pass by. Floats feature such exotic stories as the Sword of Cyclamere – someone has fashioned a passable likeness out of one of the local softwood trees – and the Tower of Farsight.

'Now that,' Sautea says to his wife, 'is nothing like the real thing.'

A few of those following the parade stare at the bent old man for a moment, then speak to each other behind their hands.

'D'you think many of your friends will show up?' Nellas asks Sautea.

'Some,' comes the reply after due consideration. 'The obvious ones, definitely. Mebbe one or two of the out-of-towners.'

'Would be nice to meet some of these people at last.'

'Aye, though there's a couple I'll make sure I keep away from you. I know what you're like when you see a pretty face. Won't have you wandering after some young thing.'

She laughs, and they stroll across the road, their boots clacking pleasantly on the cobbles. Summer Way leads directly to the palace, and they find themselves arriving too late for any of the prime viewing positions.

'Wish I was taller,' the old man sighs.

'So do I,' Nellas says. 'You, I mean.'

'Ah, you old hag, I'm tall enough to climb your steps whenever the door's open.'

They both laugh, and resign themselves to staring at the backs of the crowd in front.

'He wasn't that bad,' she says, after a companionable silence. In front of them the crowd is becoming restless.

'Some hold-up in the proceedings,' Sautea comments. 'Who wasn't that bad?'

'Duke Noctos. He wasn't that bad.'

'He did some foolish things. What about the extra tax on fishermen?'

'How can you complain at that? He handed over the best boats in the Neherian fleet for you to manage, and gave you your own ship outright. You can hardly protest if he raised taxes a little.'

'Aye, I can,' Sautea says, 'especially when that young brat gets away with breaking every dockside and customs rule in the book.'

Nellas has no need to ask who that young brat is. He comes to tea at Sautea's modest home in the Artisans District at least once a week. Charming, devastatingly handsome and irrevocably single, Mustar is the very definition of a lovable rogue.

Her husband hasn't finished on the subject. Won't finish for some time, most likely.

'Did you hear the latest? Noetos gave Mustar exclusive rights to rock lobster from Fossa north to Makyra Bay!'

Nellas turns to Sautea. 'Didn't you bid for that?'

'Young brat outbid me,' he says, then his craggy face splits in a grin. 'What he doesn't know is that stocks are well down. He's overbid, in my opinion.'

The crowd has quietened somewhat. 'Something's happening,' some of them say. Children are lifted on their fathers' shoulders. 'Guards in full livery, coming this way. Looking for someone.'

In front of the couple, the crowd suddenly melts away and they are confronted by six guards in ceremonial get-up, spears held to attention. *Wouldn't be no good in a real fight*, Sautea observes to himself, but thinks it prudent not to mention this.

'Sautea of Raceme?' one of the guards says, peering at him as though he's just crawled out from behind a barnacle.

'Paid my taxes,' Sautea replies, frowning.

The crowd has gathered closer, trying to make sense of the sudden entertainment.

'Nevertheless, you must come with us, order of the Duke himself. And you,' he adds, dipping his spear in Nellas's direction. 'If you're his wife, that is.'

'Who do you think I am, his paramour?' she retorts, raising a small cheer from the crowd.

'This had better be about getting us good seats,' Sautea grumbles. 'I'll not be best pleased if we have to spend a day in the cells.'

The ceremonial guards slice a very effective path through the crowd. Past the Summer Flame they march, Nellas and Sautea in their midst. 'Slow down!' Nellas begs them. 'We're your combined ages together!'

The guards moderate their speed, but only a little. Sautea is exhausted when they arrive at an open space, in the middle of which is set a low platform. He rubs his chest worriedly: it has been giving him a few twinges lately.

'Ah, no,' Nellas says. 'We told him we didn't want none of this!'

They are marched across the open space and, in front of the whole city, forced to climb the platform. There they are shown to velvet-clad chairs and asked to be seated. The guardsmen melt into the shadows.

'I tol' you, I wanted no fuss,' Sautea says to the man who comes over to greet him.

'Don't tell me your troubles,' the man replies. 'My neck's killing me. Do you know how many times they starch the collars of these uniforms?'

'Not enough, fisherman,' Sautea says, eyeing Noetos dubiously. 'This was you, wasn't it? You got us brung up here.'

'Anomer, actually. If it had been up to me, you old fool, you could have spent the day in the shadows while others received their due recognition. What's so wrong with a little ceremony?

The people enjoy it, and your friends wish to show you their appreciation.'

'What for? I did nothing, apart from traipse up and down endless roads and try to save us from the worst of your temper.'

Noetos laughs. 'Aye, by Alkuon, that you did. That you did.' He turns and brings his head closer to the old fisherman's face. 'You saved Arathé's life, Sautea, and I will never forget it. We're all in your debt.'

'Enough of a debt to lighten the taxes on his take?' Nellas asks.

'We shall talk of this later – ah, the music's about to start.' Noetos nips adroitly back to his seat.

The band plays a series of military numbers, all stirring if you like the thought of blood and death. Sautea saw enough of it in this city twenty years ago, and in parts further north during their adventure. Many of the memories have dimmed, but he isn't going to forget the charred bodies of soldiers in Andratan, or villages north of Patina Padouk ruined by wind and quake. A darkness falls over his eyes as he remembers, veiling the crowd that is spread over every vantage point along the waterfront.

The music continues and Sautea takes the opportunity to look around him. His friends are there, more of them than he expected. Bregor and Consina, of course, sitting on the other side of Noetos, right and fitting for the Factors of Raceme. It is largely to their credit that the city has recovered from the terrible devastation wrought by the Fingers of God and the subsequent Neherian retaliation, but recover it has. Thrice the population than at the height of its former glory, the propagandists claim, but they'd say anything to attract new immigrants. Certainly the place is far busier than Sautea finds comfortable these days.

Consina bore Bregor two boys, now sent to Makyra Bay where they work the boats in the traditional manner. *Must ask him how they're getting on*, Sautea thinks, then promptly forgets.

On Nellas's far side, sitting like a king on his throne, is that young brat himself. To think Sautea taught him everything he knows about fishing. Mustar grins at Nellas, and she smiles back, unable to help herself. Oh yes, this boy charms the girls into his

527

hands all right. Not a mark on him and nearly forty years of age. He pursued Moralye at the end of their adventure, pressing his suit on her all the long way south, and for a while she'd shown interest; but eventually she'd spurned him, to everyone's surprise. There were so many relationships in the aftermath of the events of twenty years ago, it is a puzzle that Mustar was left out.

Isn't left out much these days though, Sautea reflects ruefully. *Never a cold bed, that lad; a different girl every week*. The lad seems to enjoy it tolerably well, though there's nothing like a familiar face in Sautea's experience. He pats Nellas's hand fondly.

Moralye made her choice a few years later, after a visit to Dhauria by one of her former companions. Anomer had decided on a life of scholarship and made the long journey across the wilds of western Bhrudwo to seek out the greatest minds in three continents. Chief among them, he discovered, was Moralye, revered even by the eldest and wisest in Dhauria. They had elected her *dominie*, the first woman in five hundred years to be so raised. Anomer had fallen for her. He'd spent years in Dhauria wooing Moralye, seemingly without success; the *dominie* was, after all, almost twice his age, though to the long-lived Dhaurians she was a woman in full bloom. He had devoted himself to book-learning, but at the end of five lovelorn years had readied himself to return home. As Noetos told it – often and loud – she came to him the night before he was to leave and begged him to stay. The coin she used was left unmentioned.

They lived together in Dhauria another twelve years, raising a family of three girls and enduring the endless gossip of the narrow-minded and insular Dhaurians. The relationship was never officially sanctioned by marriage, apparently. Such liaisons were forbidden, but it seemed that a *dominie* was allowed a certain latitude.

And here she comes, as though Sautea's thoughts have called her into being, on the arm of her husband, walking down the steps from their residence in the Summer Palace, making a handsome couple, she in a white dress and he in a crimson coat and dark green leggings. They mount the platform to cheers from the crowd and seat themselves on the far side.

Following them is the Duchess of Roudhos. Cylene of Sayonae was pretty when she was younger, but has developed into a celebrated beauty. Her face is solemn, seldom laughing; it is said among the populace that she suffered some great sorrow during the northern affair all those years ago. Sautea knows different, of course; but the loss of her newly discovered sister indeed robbed her of much of her joy. For a time, anyway. She is not tall, but her carriage suggests so. Her face is not perfect, sun-kissed as it is, but such imperfections merely serve to emphasise her beauty. And she is utterly devoted to her great bear of a husband, more fool her. Sautea loves her for it.

Noetos rises from his seat and goes to her. Taking her hand, he leads her to the far side of the platform, among the many dignitaries events like this attract.

All is in readiness for the ceremony. The chief alderman stands and clears his throat.

Away to the right of the crowd a disturbance is taking place. A fight of some kind perhaps. The guards will deal severely with the perpetrators, Sautea knows. Raceme is a good place to live, her laws are in the main sensible and their application is relaxed, but this is an important occasion.

The disturbance intensifies. The crowd parts and a massive coach, drawn by four horses much larger than any horse has a right to be, comes into view. It is made of polished blackwood and edged in gold. *Gold paint, probably*, Sautea thinks as he squints. *No, that is real gold.*

The coach pulls up in front of the dais and the driver steps down from his seat. Sautea recoils in shock: he knows this man. He is very tall, though not as tall as he once was, and his hair is white now when once it had been jet black. He wears a nondescript outfit: boiled-leather jerkin and trousers. A flute hangs from one shoulder. He has not aged, of course. Apprentice gods do not age.

Lord of Bhrudwo no longer, the man has not been reduced by his new role. There is a grace to his carriage that he did not have before, a stillness that has replaced the restlessness that once characterised him. He is more, somehow, than he once was.

529

His empire has dissolved into large kingdoms and petty fiefdoms. By and large there have been few wars, but the peace enjoyed by Bhrudwo no longer exists, as people struggle to adapt to the change. The great fortress of Andratan lies empty now, apparently, abandoned shortly after the Tower of Farsight was declared a sacred place. When the last servant left, the gate was locked, the key thrown into the ocean and the whole island declared off limits. Stories are told now of Ghost Island and the fiery glow that occasionally lights up the sky, supposedly on the anniversary of the fall of the Tower of Farsight.

Noetos has often said how the ending of Kannwar's rule is a blessing, even though it does not appear that way. Roudhos, he says, will be smaller but better than Bhrudwo was. There is no need for the calculating decisions the Undying Man once made. No need for an immortal ruler. The fisherman has no regrets, he says, at passing on his own rulership to his son.

Kannwar bows to the stage, then opens the door of the coach. No one emerges. With a sigh he produces a wooden step and places it in front of the door, then steps back.

'Aren't you going to announce me, ulcers to your soul?' comes a querulous voice from within. A few members of the crowd laugh.

'My apologies, old friend. Sauxa of – where are you from these days?'

A wizened old man makes his way out of the coach, taking the step with care. 'I'll do it myself,' he snaps. 'Sauxa of anywhere in Faltha a woman will have me!' he cries, then blinks in the sun. 'Sauxa of Chardzou, actually,' he amends.

By this time Noetos has left his seat and is already off the platform. 'Sauxa!' he cries. 'A cheer, everyone, for one of the heroes of the War Against the Gods!'

The crowd cheers dutifully, by no means convinced that such an old man could be the hero of anything.

By the gods, Sautea thinks, *he's not weathered well. Probably holed up in that tent in the middle of the plains, beating off the storms every winter and gales every summer.* Last Sautea heard, the old man had retired from his role as Arkhos of Straux, left the Council of Faltha and Instruere, and taken himself back to the Central Plains in high dudgeon, complaining about the younger generation, by which he meant anyone who hadn't seen seventy summers.

It is wonderful to see the irascible old man. As Sauxa is led up the steps of the platform, Sautea nods to him and receives a cheerful wink in return.

The plainsman has never been told the full story of his countryman Robal's fate. That tale, perhaps the darkest of a dark time, emerged a decade or so after the events. Noetos has never explained where he heard the story, but there is seemingly no doubt it is true. Sautea sincerely hopes it never comes to the ears of the old man. It would break his heart anew.

He notices the driver of the coach has not moved. 'Merla Umerta of Sayonae and consort,' he announces, his deep voice carrying to every ear on the waterfront.

'I told you not to call me that,' says a sweet voice from the darkness inside.

Kannwar inclines his head and a small smile plays on his lips.

From the coach descends a stunning couple. The man is dark-skinned, his broad, shining face surmounted by curly black hair. He wears the most outrageous pink jacket and pantaloons, clothes that ought to be appalling. But they look magisterial on him. The woman at his side is simply the most glorious creature Sautea has ever seen. More beautiful by far than her celebrated sister, her face lit by an inner glow that begins to bewitch the whole crowd. She smiles, and it is a shy smile.

'Travelled with her the whole way,' Sauxa says, his reedy voice clearly audible in the sudden silence. 'For a god, she's got a god-awful voice. Never shuts up.'

He looks around, realises everyone is listening and snaps his mouth closed.

Sautea has seen neither of the two gods for twenty years, and his heart aches at the memory of their courage. As he begins to weep, Nellas takes his hand and squeezes it.

'The Son and the Daughter,' she says, her voice a whisper. 'Old man, you weren't exaggeratin' after all.'

'They are holding in the best part of their glamour,' he says. 'If you had been there, old girl, when they climbed up them stone thrones, you would have had your eyes near burned out, like mine were.'

The Son and the Daughter, trailed by their apprentice, walk up to the platform.

'We have come to honour the Dukes of Roudhos, both new and old,' she says.

'And to spend time with old friends,' he adds, and smiles.

'Please . . . please be welcome,' stammers the chief alderman.

Nobody needs to be told who these presences are. Though everyone here has heard the tale of the War Against the Gods, told by raconteurs in taverns or sung by bards in those interminable verses, most consider the gods a myth. But here they are, almost too bright to look upon, standing amongst the citizens of Raceme.

They nod to the alderman and accept seats hurriedly drawn up for them at the end of the row in which Noetos sits. Sautea is some distance from the present Duke of Roudhos but he hears the man's question. 'Any news of my daughter?'

Lenares nods to Noetos, an answer of sorts. It is a question Sautea wants answered too, though not as urgently as Arathé's father. She married Duon of Elamaq in a simple ceremony immediately on their return to Raceme after the northern events, and the explorer promptly took her south to his homeland. Eight years later they reappeared for one golden summer, accompanied by a tousle-headed boy of about six years of age. Arathé had recovered much, though not all, of her beauty; and the boy was the image of Anomer, who had been in Dhauria at the time and so had not met his nephew. At summer's end, the family had left again, in pursuit of further adventures.

Elamaq is, apparently, in turmoil. They have had the news from the occasional trader claiming to have dared Cape Despair and made it to Talamaq; and Duon and Arathé have confirmed it. The Omerans rose up against their former masters, seemingly having freed themselves of their inbred obedience, and the conflict has been a protracted one. Noetos received one letter, a somewhat cryptic account of Duon and Arathé's preparation for a voyage to Ilixa Isle in which they mentioned his troubles in Elamaq, and has heard nothing since.

Sautea loves Noetos's daughter as if she were his own child. With Mustar, he rescued her from the sack of Fossa and, in a fearsome, storm-assailed journey, delivered her to her father in Raceme. His great contribution to the War Against the Gods. She was close to him in the weeks and months after the war, and her absence is one of his life's chief sadnesses. So the nod from the Daughter bodes well.

The gods are seated and hood their glamour still further, though everyone is still conscious of them. The alderman rises, clears his throat a few more times and commences his speech. As far as speeches go, Sautea supposes this one is a good one. Excellent, in fact. But he doubts anyone hears it. Whispers travel back and forth through the crowd and hands point to the various people on the platform – including, he notices, some at himself. Huh. Some fools will waste time on any minor celebrity.

The alderman has just finished wiping his face for the third time – the day is warm, but summer is still weeks away – when a shout comes from the direction of the rebuilt Red Duke Wharf.

'Hoy! Can anyone direct me to the Duke of Roudhos?' calls a bold voice. 'We were told in Tochar that the ceremony was tomorrow, but we've lost a day somewhere.'

The crowd draws away from the man and the woman hurrying along Wharf Street, daunted perhaps by his drawn sword. He waves it from side to side absent-mindedly. He is tall, middle-aged, but brimming with energy. She is also tall – certainly taller than Sautea remembers – no, she is slimmer than when he last saw her. He is wearing light ceremonial armour, and she is in a flowing pink dress that rather needs someone to lift its train from the street.

The alderman is knocked to the ground in the rush to greet Duon and Arathé. Sautea's eyes blur. He should have realised they would make every effort to see the new Duke of Roudhos confirmed. There are hugs exchanged there in front of thousands of bemused witnesses: gods embracing humans and vice versa, exchanging greetings like old friends. Then Arathé, bless her, calls out: 'Where is Sautea?'

She leaps onto the platform, ignoring the stairs, makes straight for him, plants herself squarely on his lap and kisses his forehead. 'Oh, Uncle,' she says. 'I am glad to see you.'

'Where have you been?' he asks, barely able to get the words out past a tightness in his throat.

'Stuck on Ilixa for years. Oh, what a terrible place! We've had such adventures – but I will tell everyone later.'

He is about to ask her another question when his poor old brain catches up to his ears. 'Arathé,' he says carefully. 'Am I imagining things, or can I hear you talk?'

She nods, eyes sparkling. 'The reason we dared Ilixa,' she says, 'was partly to see if I could recover my voice. And it worked,' she adds unnecessarily, and pokes her tongue out at him.

'Hmm,' Nellas says. 'Careful with that old man, girl. Much more happiness and he'll have to lie down for a week.'

After the dramatic entrances, the rest of the ceremony goes off hitchless, though rather anti-climactically. Anomer, looking every bit the Duke, accepts the sceptre from his father, along with a curious stone in the shape of a woman's head set on a block of wood. He and Moralye are sworn in as the Duke and Duchess of Roudhos and make the necessary promises. The crowd cheers, but is clearly somewhat distracted by the personnel on the platform.

Sautea's heart burns in his chest.

Music is played, songs are sung, and there is dancing in the streets, but Sautea has retired his dancing feet and contents himself with tapping them on the wooden platform. When the music is over and the last speech is made, they repair to the Summer Palace and the meal and fellowship waiting for them.

And as dusk falls and a single star rises from the horizon, the gods' apprentice leads them to the balcony above the city. There he cries, in a loud voice: 'Let us take a moment to honour she who triumphed in the War Against the Gods. Rise with me and bow your heads to the one to whom we all owe our lives. Stella Pellwen.'

Kannwar bows his head, and Sautea observes that the gods can indeed weep.

ACKNOWLEDGEMENTS

I'm a very lucky man. I get to make my hobby into my occupation, I get to entertain people (or perhaps frustrate or anger them) and to work on projects I'm proud of.

These books bearing my name are by no means all my own work. I have received valuable assistance from readers, editors and artists. In particular I wish to thank Dorinda and Iain for reading early drafts, Phillip Berrie for eagle-eyed continuity work, and Nicola O'Shea for outstanding editorial assistance. Nicola gets what I'm trying to do, and she works to a level of detail that puts a real shine on the manuscript. The bits that don't work for you are probably the bits where I ignored her advice.

I've been fortunate to have superb cover art. You can judge these books by their covers, as they are faithful to the feel and detail of the story. My thanks to Greg Bridges and the design team. Less visible but no less important are the hundreds of enthusiastic booksellers who put these books in your hands.

I continue to owe a great debt to Stephanie Smith, my Harper-Collins editor. She is patient and perceptive, and ensures I produce my best work. Thanks to all at HarperCollins Voyager Australia and New Zealand for their professionalism.

extras

www.orbitbooks.net

about the author

Russell Kirkpatrick's love of literature and a chance encounter with fantasy novels as a teenager opened up a vast number of possibilities to him. The idea that he could marry storytelling and mapmaking (his other passion) into one project grabbed him and wouldn't let go.

Across the Face of the World, the first volume of the Fire of Heaven trilogy, was the result of fifteen years of careful world-building, and introduced the reader to the rich detail of Russell's world and its characters.

Russell lectures in Geography and manages a small mapmaking business. He lives in New Zealand with his wife and two children. You can visit his website at www.russellkirkpatrick.com

Find out more about Russell Kirkpatrick and other Orbit authors by registering for the free monthly newsletter at www.orbitbooks.net

if you enjoyed
BEYOND THE WALL OF TIME

look out for

A CAVERN OF ICE

book one of The Sword of the Shadows

by

J. V. Jones

PROLOGUE

A Birth, a Death, and a Binding

Tarissa whispered a hope out loud before looking up at the sky. 'Please make it lighter than before. *Please*.' As her lips came together she looked up past the wind-twisted pines and the ridge of frost-riven granite, up toward the position of the sun. Only the sun wasn't there. Stormheads rolled across the sky, cutting out the sunlight, massing, churning, driven by winds that snapped and circled like pack wolves around sheep. Tarissa made a small gesture with her hand. The storm wasn't passing overhead. It had come to the mountain to stay.

Dropping her gaze, she took a steadying breath. She couldn't afford to panic. The city lay a thousand feet below her, rising from the shadow of the mountain like a second, lesser peak. She could see the ring towers clearly now, four of them, two built hard against the wall, the tallest piercing the storm with its iron stake. It was a long way down. Hours of walk, even. And she had to be careful.

Resting her hand on her swollen stomach, she forced herself to smile. *Storms?* They were nothing.

She moved quickly. Loose scree, bird skeletons, and snags of wind-blasted wood tripped her feet. It was hard to walk, even harder to keep her balance on the ever sharpening slope. Steep draws and creases forced her sideways instead of down. The temperature was falling, and for the first time all day Tarissa noticed her breath came out white. Her left glove had been gone for days – lost somewhere on the far side of the mountain – and she stripped off her right glove, turned it inside out, and pulled it onto her left hand. The fingers there had started to grow numb.

Dead trees blocked her path. Some of their trunks were so smooth they looked polished. As she reached out to steady herself against one of the hard black limbs, she felt a sharp pain in her lower abdomen. Something shifted. Wetness spilled down her thighs. A soft sting sounded in her lower back, and a wave of sickness washed up her gullet, depositing the taste of sour milk in her mouth. Tarissa closed her eyes. This time she kept her hopes to herself.

Wet snow began to fall as she pushed herself off from the dead tree. Her glove was sticky with sap, and bits of pine needles were glued to the fingers. Underfoot the granite ledge was unstable; gravel spilled from deep gashes, and husks of failed saplings crumbled to nothing the instant they took her weight. Despite the cold, Tarissa started to sweat. The pain in her back chewed inward, and although she didn't want to admit it, didn't even want to acknowledge it, her lower abdomen began contracting in rhythmic waves.

No. No. NO. Her baby wasn't due yet. Two weeks more – it *had* to be. She needed to make it to the city, to find shelter. She'd even held back enough coins for a midwife and a room.

Finding a lead through the rocks, she picked up her pace. A lone raven, its plumage dark and oily as a scorched liver, watched her in silence from the distorted upper branch of a blackstone pine. Spying it, Tarissa was conscious of how ridiculous she must look: fat bellied, wild haired, scrambling down a mountainside in a race against a storm. Grimacing, she looked away from the bird. She didn't like how it made her feel.

Contractions were coming faster now, and Tarissa found that it helped if she kept on the move. Stopping made the suffering linger, gave her seconds to count and think.

Mist rose from crevices. Snow flew in Tarissa's face, and the wind lifted the cloak from her back. Overhead, the clouds mimicked her descent, following her down the mountain as if she were showing them the way. Tarissa walked with her gloved hand cradling her belly. The fluid between her legs had dried to a sticky film that sucked her thighs together as she moved. Heat pumped up through the arteries in her neck, flushing her cheeks and the bridge of her nose.

Faster. She had to move faster.

Spotting a clear run between boulders, Tarissa switched her path farther to her right. Thorns snagged her skirt, and she yanked on the fabric, losing patience. As she turned back to face the path, the raven took flight. Its black wings beat against the storm current, snapping and tearing like teeth.

The instant Tarissa stepped forward, gravel and rocks began running beneath her feet. She felt herself falling, and she flung out her arms to grab at something, *anything*, to hold her. The mist hid everything at ground level, and Tarissa's hands found only loose stones and twigs. Pain exploded in her shoulder as she was thrown against a rock. Pinecones and rocks bounced overhead as she tried desperately to break her fall. Her bare hand grasped at a tussock of wolfgrass, but her body kept sliding downward and the roots pulled free in her hand. Her hip bashed against a granite ridge, something sharp shaved skin from the back of her knee, and when she opened her mouth to scream, snow flew between her lips, freezing the cry on her tongue.

She came to. There was no pain, just a fog of ragged light lying between her and the outside world. Above her, as far as her eyes could see, stretched walls of hand-polished limestone, mason cut and smooth as bone. She'd finally made it to the city with the Iron Spire.

Dimly she was aware of something pushing far below her. Minutes passed before she realized that it was her body working to expel the child. She swallowed hard. Suddenly she missed all the people she had run from. Leaving home had been a mistake.

Kaaw!

Tarissa tried to shift her head toward the sound. A hot needle of pain jabbed at the vertebrae in the base of her neck. She blacked out. When she came to again she saw the raven sitting on a rock before her. Black-and-gold eyes pinned her with a look that was devoid of pity. Bobbing its head and raising its scaly yellow claws, it danced a little jig of damnation. When it was done it made a soft *cluck*ing noise that sounded just like a mother scolding a child and then flung itself to the mercy of the storm. Cold currents bore it swiftly away.

Pushing. Her body kept pushing.

Tarissa felt herself drifting . . . she was so tired . . . so very, very tired. If only she could find a way through the fog . . . if only her eyes could show her more.

As her eyelids closed for the last time and her ribs pressed an unused breath from her lungs, she saw a pair of booted feet walking toward her. The tar-blackened leather melted snowflakes on contact.

† † †

They applied the leeches to him in rings of six. His body was crusted with sweat and rock dust and dirt, and the first man scraped the skin clean with deer tallow and a cedarwood wedge, while the second worked in his shadow with metal pincers, a pitchpine bucket, and heavy buckskin gloves.

The man who no longer knew his name strained against his bindings, testing. Thick coils of rope pressed into his neck, upper arms, wrists, thighs, and ankles. He could shudder and breathe and blink. Nothing more.

He could barely feel the leeches. One settled in the fold between his inner thigh and groin, and he tensed for a moment. Pincer took a pinch of white powder from a pouch around his neck and applied it to the leech. Salt. The leech dropped away. A fresh leech was applied, higher this time so it couldn't attach itself to skin that wasn't fit.

That done, Pincer stripped off his gloves and spoke a word that sent Accomplice to the far side of the cell. A moment later Accomplice returned with a tray and a soapstone lamp. A single red flame burned within the lamp, heating the contents of the crucible above. When he saw the flame, the man with no name flinched so hard that the rope binding his wrists split his skin. Flames were all he had now. Memories of flames. He hated the flames and feared them, yet he needed them, too. Familiarity bred contempt, they said. But the man with no name knew that was only half of it. Familiarity bred dependence as well.

Thoughts lost in the dance of flames, he didn't see Pincer kneading an oakum wad in his fist. He was aware only of Accomplice's hands on his jaw, repositioning his head, brushing his hair to one side, and pushing his skull hard against the bench. The man with no name felt the frayed rope and beeswax wad thrust into his left ear. Ship's caulking. They were shoring him up like a storm-battered hull. A second wad was thrust into his right ear, and then Accomplice held the nameless man's jaws wide while Pincer thrust a third wad into the back of his throat. The desire to vomit was sudden and overpowering, but Pincer slapped one large hand on the nameless man's chest and another on his belly and pressed hard against the contracting muscles, forcing them flat. A minute later the urge had passed.

Still Accomplice held on to his jaw. Pincer paid attention to the tray, his hands casting claw shadows against the cell wall as he worked. Seconds later he turned about. A thread of animal sinew was stretched between his thumbs. Seeing it, Accomplice shifted his grip, opening the nameless man's jaws wider, pulling back lip tissue along with bone. The man with no name felt thick fingers in his mouth. He tasted urine and salt and leech water. His tongue was pressed to the base of his mouth, and then sinew was woven across his bottom teeth, binding his tongue in place.

Fear came alive in the nameless man's chest. Perhaps flames weren't the only things that could harm him.

'He's done,' said Pincer, drawing back.

'What about the wax?' breathed a third voice from the shadows near the door. It was the One Who Issued Orders. 'You are supposed to seal his eyes shut.'

'Wax is too hot. It could blind him if we use it now.'

'Use it.'

The flame in the soapstone lamp wavered as Accomplice drew the crucible away. The man with no name smelled smoke given off from the impurities in the wax. When the burning came it shocked him. After everything he had been through, all the suffering he had borne, he imagined he had outlived pain. He was wrong. And as the hours wore on and his bones were broken methodically by Pincer wielding a goosedown padded mallet, Accomplice following after to ensure the splintered ends were pulled apart, and his internal organs were manipulated with needles so long and fine that they could puncture specific chambers in his lungs and heart while leaving the surrounding tissue intact, he began to realize that pain – and the ability to feel it – was the last sense to go.

When the One Who Issued Orders stepped close and began breathing words of binding older than the city he currently stood in, the man with no name no longer cared. His mind had returned to the flames. There, at least, was a pain that he knew.

ONE

The Badlands

Raif Sevrance set his sights on the target and *called* the ice hare to him. A moment of disorientation followed, where the world dropped out of focus like a great dark stone sinking to the bottom of a lake; then, in the shortest space that a moment could be, he perceived the animal's heart. The light, sounds, and odors of the badlands slid away, leaving nothing but the weight of blood in the ice hare's chest and the hummingbird flutter of its heart. Slowly, deliberately, Raif angled his bow away from the target. The arrow cracked the freezing air like a word spoken out loud. As its iron blade shot past the hare, the creature's head came up and it sprang for cover in a cushion of black sedge.

'Take the shot again,' Drey said. 'You sent that wide on purpose.'

Raif lowered his bow and glanced over at his older brother. Drey's face was partially shaded by his fox hood, but the firm set of his mouth was clear. Raif paused, considered arguing, then shrugged and reset his footing on the tundra. It never felt good deceiving Drey.

Fingers smoothing down the backing of his horn-and-sinew bow, Raif looked over the windblown flats of the badlands. Panes of ice already lay thick over melt ponds. In the flattened colt grass beneath

Raif's feet hoarfrost grew as silently and insidiously as mold on second-day bread. The few trees that managed to survive in the gravelly floodplain were wind-crippled blackstone pines and prostrate hemlock. Directly ahead lay a shallow draw filled with loose rocks and scrubby bushes that looked as tough and bony as moose antlers. Raif dipped his gaze a fraction lower to the brown lichen mat surrounding a pile of wet rocks. Even on a morning as cold as this, the lick was still running.

As Raif watched, another ice hare popped up its head. Cheeks puffing, ears trembling, it held its position, listening for danger. It wanted the salt in the lick. Game animals came from leagues around to drink at the trickle of salt water that bled across the rocks in the draw. Tem said the lick welled up from an underground stream.

Raif raised his bow, slid an arrow from the quiver at his waist. In one smooth motion he nocked the iron arrowhead against the plate and drew the bowstring back to his chest. The hare swiveled its head. Its dark eyes looked straight at Raif. Too late. Raif already had the creature's heart in his sights. Kissing the string, Raif let the arrow fly. Fingers of ice mist parted, a faint hiss sounded, and the arrowhead shot straight into the hare's rib cage. If the creature made a sound, Raif didn't hear it. Carried back by the force of the blow, it collapsed into the lick.

'That's three to you. None to me.' Drey's voice sounded flat, resigned.

Raif pretended to check his bow for hairpin cracks.

'Come on. Let's shoot at targets. No more hares are going to show now you've sent a live one into the lick.' Drey reached out and touched Raif's bow. 'You could have used a smaller head on that arrow, you know. You're supposed to *kill* the hare, not disembowel it.'

Raif looked up. Drey was grinning, just a bit. Relieved, Raif grinned back at him. Drey was two years older than he, better at everything an older brother should be better at. Up until this winter he had been better at shooting, too. A lot better.

Abruptly Raif tucked his bow into his belt and ran for the draw. Tem never let them shoot anything purely for sport, and the hares had to be taken back to camp, skinned, and roasted. The pelts were Raif's. Another couple more and he'd have enough for a winter coat for Effie. Not that Effie had much use for a coat. She was the only eight-year-old in Clan Blackhail who didn't enjoy running around in the snow. Frowning, Raif twisted the arrows free from the twig-thin bones of the hare's rib cage, careful not to break the shafts. Timber straight enough for arrows was rare in the badlands.

As he sealed the carcass in his game pouch, Raif checked the position of the sun. Nearly noon now. A storm heading elsewhere blew eastward in the far north. Dark gray clouds rolled across the horizon like smoke from a distant fire. Raif shivered. The Great Want lay to the north. Tem said that if a storm didn't begin in the Want, then it sure as stone would end there.

'Hey! Rough Jaw! Get your bow over here and let's shred some wood.' Drey sent an expertly pitched stone skittering off rocks and hummocks, to land with a devilish skip precisely at Raif's feet. 'Or are you scared your lucky streak just ended?'

Almost against his will, Raif's hand rose to his chin. His skin felt as bristly as a frozen pinecone. He was Rough Jaw all right. No argument there. 'Paint the target, Sevrance Cur. Then I'll let you take a hand's worth of practice shots while I restring my bow for wood.'

Even a hundred paces in the distance, Raif saw Drey's jaw drop. *Restring my bow for wood* was exactly the sort of high-blown thing a master bowman would say. Raif could hardly keep from laughing out loud. Ignoring the insult and the boasting, Drey snorted loudly and began plucking fistfuls of grass from the tundra. By the time Raif caught up with him, Drey had smeared the grass over the trunk of a frost-killed pine, forming a roughly circular target, wet with snowmelt and grass sap.

Drey shot first. Stepping back one hundred and fifty paces, he held his bow at arm's length. Drey's bow was a recurve made of winter-cut yew, dried over two full years, and hand-tillered to reduce shock. Raif envied him for it. His own bow was a clan hand-down, used by anyone who had the string to brace it.

Drey took his time sighting his bow. He had a sure, unshakable grip and the strength to hold the string for as long as his ungloved fingers could bear. Just when Raif was set to call 'Shot due,' his brother released the string. The arrow landed with a dull *thunk*, dead center of the smeared-on target. Turning, Drey inclined his head at his younger brother. He did not smile.

Raif's bow was already in hand, his arrow already chosen. With Drey's arrow shaft still quivering in the target, Raif sighted his bow. The pine was long dead. Cold. When Raif tried to *call* it to him as he had with the ice hare, it wouldn't come. The wood stood its distance. Raif felt nothing: no quickening of his pulse, no dull pain behind his eyes, no metal tang in his mouth. Nothing. The target was just a target. Unsettled, Raif centered his bow and searched for the still line that would lead his arrow home. Seeing nothing but a faraway tree, Raif released his string. Straightaway he knew the shot was bad. He'd been gripping the handle too tightly, and his fingertips had grazed the string on release. The bow shot back with a *thwack*, and Raif's shoulder took a bad recoil. The arrow landed a good two hands lower than the target.

'Shoot again.' Drey's voice was cold.

Raif massaged his shoulder, then selected a second arrow. For luck, he brushed the fletchings against the raven lore he wore on a cord around his neck. The second shot was better, but it still hit a thumb's length short of dead center. Raif turned to look at his brother. It was his shot.

Drey made a small motion with his bow. 'Again.'

Raif shook his head. 'No. It's your turn.'

Drey shook his own head right back. 'You sent those two wide on purpose. Now shoot.'

'No, I didn't. It was a true shot. I—'

'No one heart-kills three hares on the run, then misses a target as big as a man's chest. No one.' Drey pushed back his fox hood. His eyes were dark. He spat out the wad of black curd he'd been chewing. 'I don't need mercy shots. Either shoot with me fair, or not at all.'

Looking at his brother, seeing his big hands pressing hard into the wood of his bow and the whiteness of his thumbs as he worked on an imagined imperfection, Raif knew words would get him nowhere. Drey Sevrance was eighteen years old, a yearman in the clan. This past summer he'd taken to braiding his hair with black leather strips and wearing a silver earring in his ear. Last night around the firepit, when Dagro Blackhail had burned the scum off an old malt and dropped his earring into the clear liquor remaining, Drey had done the same. All the sworn clansmen had. Metal next to the skin attracted frostbite. And everyone in the clan had seen the black nubs of unidentifiable flesh that the 'bite left behind. You could find many willing to tell the story of how Jon Marrow's member had frozen solid when he was jumped by Dhoonesmen while he was relieving himself in the brack. By the time he had seen the Dhoonesmen off and pulled himself up from the nail-hard tundra, his manhood was frozen like a cache of winter meat. By all accounts he hadn't felt a thing until he was brought into the warmth of the roundhouse and the stretched and shiny flesh began to thaw. His screams had kept the clan awake all night.

Raif ran his hand along his bowstring, warming the wax. If Drey needed to see him take a third shot to prove he wasn't shamming, then take another shot he would. He'd lost the desire to fight.

Again Raif tried to call the dead tree to him, searching for the still line that would guide his arrow to the heart. Although the blackstone pine had perished ten hunting seasons earlier, it had hardly withered at all. Only the needles were missing. The pitch in the trunk preserved the crown, and the cold dryness of the badlands hindered the growth of fungus beneath the bark. Tem said that in the Great Want trees took hundreds, sometimes thousands, of years to decay.

Seconds passed as Raif concentrated on the target. The longer he held his sights, the deader the tree seemed. Something was missing. Ice hares were real living things. Raif felt their warmth in the space between his eyes. He imagined the lode of hot pulsing blood in their hearts and saw the still line that linked those hearts to his arrowhead as clearly as a dog sees his leash. Slowly Raif was coming to realize that still line meant death.

Frustration finally got the better of him, and he stopped searching for the inner heart of the target and centered his sights on the *visual* heart instead. With the fletchings of Drey's arrow in his eyeline, Raif released the shot.

The moment his thumb lifted from the string, a raven *kaa*wed. High and shrill, the carrion feeder's cry seemed to split the very substance of time. Raif felt a finger of ice tap his spine. His vision blurred. Saliva jetted into his mouth, thick and hot and tasting of metal. Stumbling back, he lost his grip on the bow and it fell to the ground point first. A crack sounded as it landed. The arrow hit the tree with a dull thud, placing a knuckle short of Drey's own shot. Raif didn't care. Black points raced across his vision, scorching like soot belched from a fire.

'Raif! Raif!'

Raif felt Drey's huge, muscular arms clamp around his shoulders, smelled his brother's scent of neat's-foot oil, tanned leather, horses, and sweat. Glancing up, Raif saw Drey's brown eyes staring into his. He looked worried. His prized yewbow lay flat on the ground.

'Here, sit.' Not waiting for any compliance on Raif's part, Drey forced his younger brother onto the tundra floor. The frozen earth bit into Raif's buckskin pants. Turning away from his brother, Raif cleared his mouth of the metal-tasting saliva. His eyes stung. A sickening pain in his forehead made him retch. He clenched his jaw until bone clicked.

Seconds passed. Drey said nothing, just held his brother as tightly as he could. Part of Raif wanted to smile; the last time Drey had crushed him like this was after he fell twenty feet from a foxtail pine three springs back. The fall only broke an ankle. Drey's subsequent bear hug had succeeded in breaking two ribs.

Strangely, the memory had a calming effect on Raif, and the pain slowly subsided. Raif's vision blurred sharply and then reset itself. A feeling of badness grew in him. Swiveling around in his brother's grip, Raif looked in the direction of the camp. The stench of metal washed over him, as thick as grease smoke from the rendering pits.

Drey followed his gaze. 'What's the matter?' His voice was tight, strained.

'Don't you feel it?'

Drey shook his head.

The camp was five leagues to the south, hidden in the shelter of the flood basin. All Raif could see was the rapidly darkening sky and the low ridges and rocky flats of the badlands. Yet he felt something. Something unspeakable, as when nightmares jolted him awake in pitch darkness or when he thought back to the day Tem had shut him in the guidehouse with his mother's corpse. He had been eight at the time, old enough to pay due respect to the dead. The guidehouse was dark and filled with smoke. The hollowed-out basswood where his mother lay smelled of wet earth and rotten things. Sulfur had been rubbed into the carved inner trunk to keep insects and carrion feeders away from the body when it was laid upon the ground.

Raif smelled badness now. He smelled stinking metal and sulfur and death. Fighting against Drey's grip, he cried, 'We have to go back.'

Drey released his grip on Raif and pulled himself to his feet. He plucked his dogskin gloves from his belt and pulled them on with two violent movements. 'Why?'

Raif shook his head. The pain and nausea had gone, but something else had come in its place. A tight shivering fear. 'The camp.'

Drey nodded. He took a deep breath and looked set to speak, then abruptly stopped himself. Offering Raif his hand, he heaved his brother off the ground with a single tug. By the time Raif had brushed the frost from his buckskins, Drey had collected both bows and was pulling the arrow shafts from the dead tree. As he turned away from the blackstone pine, Raif noticed the fletchings in Drey's grip were shaking. This one small sign of his brother's fear worried Raif more than anything else. Drey was his older brother by two years. Drey was afraid of nothing.

They had left the camp before dawn, before even the embers on the firepit had burned cold. No one except Tem knew they had gone. It was their last chance to shoot game before they broke camp and returned to the roundhouse for winter. The previous night Tem had warned them about going off on their own in the badlands, though he knew well enough that nothing he said would stop them.

'Sons!' he had said, shaking his large, grizzled head. 'I might as well spend my days picking ticks from the dogs as tell you two what you should and shouldn't do. At least come sundown I'd have a deloused pup to show for my trouble.' Tem would glower as he spoke, and the skin above his eyebrows would bunch into knots, yet his eyes always gave him away.

Just this morning as Raif pulled back the hide fastening on the tent he shared with his father and brother, he noticed a small bundle set upon the warming stone. It was food. Hunters' food. Tem had packed two whole smoke-cured ptarmigan, a brace of hard-boiled eggs, and enough strips of hung mutton to mend an elk-size hole in a tent. All this for his sons to eat on a hunting trip he had expressly forbidden them to take.

Raif smiled. Tem Sevrance knew his sons well.

'Put on your gloves.' It was Drey, acting just like an older brother. 'And pull up your hood. Temperature's dropping fast.'

Raif did what he was told, struggling to put on gloves with hands that felt big and slow. Drey was right: It was getting colder. Another shiver worked its way up Raif's spine, making his shoulders jerk awkwardly. 'Let's go.' Drey's thoroughness was beginning to nettle him. They had to get back to the camp. Now. Something wasn't right.

Although Tem warned them constantly about the danger of using up all their energy by running in the cold, Raif couldn't stop himself. Despite spitting profusely, he couldn't remove the taste of metal from his mouth. The air smelled bad, and the clouds overhead seemed darker, lower, *closer*. To the south lay a line of bald, featureless hills, and west of them lay the Coastal Ranges. Tem said that the Ranges were the reason why the Want and the badlands were so dry. He said their peaks milked every last drop of moisture from passing storms.

The three hares Raif had shot earlier thumped up and down

in his pack as he ran. Raif hated their warmth against his thigh, was sickened by their fresh-kill smell. When the two brothers came upon Old Hoopers Lake, Raif tore the pack from his belt and threw it into the center of the dull black water. Old Hoopers wasn't frozen yet. River fed, it would take a full week of frost before its current-driven waters plated. Still, the lake had the greasy look of imminent ice about it. As Raif's pack sank to the bottom, swirls of vegetable oils and tufts of elk hair bobbed up and down on the surface.

Drey swore. Raif didn't catch what he said, but he imagined the words *waste of fine game* in their place.

As the brothers ran south, the landscape gradually changed. Trees grew straighter and taller, and there were more of them. Beds of lichen were replaced by long grasses, bushes, and sedge. Horse and game tracks formed paths through the frozen foliage, and fat grouse flew up from the undergrowth, all flying feathers and spitting beaks.

Raif barely noticed. Close to the camp perimeter now, they should have been able to see smoke, hear the sound of metal rasping against metal, raised voices, laughter. Dagro Blackhail's foster son, Mace, should be riding to greet them on his fat-necked cob.

Drey swore again. Quietly, to himself.

Raif resisted the urge to glance over at his brother's face. He was frightened of what he might see.

A powerful horseman, archer, and hammerman, Drey pulled ahead of Raif as he charged down the slope to the camp. Raif pushed himself harder, balling his fists and thrusting out his chin. He didn't want to lose sight of his brother, hated the thought of Drey arriving at the tent circle alone.

Fear stretched over Raif's body like a drying hide, pulling at his skin and gut. They had left thirteen men standing by at the camp: Dagro Blackhail and his son, Mace; Tem; Chad and Jorry Shank; Mallon Clayhorn and his son, Darri, whom everyone called Halfmast . . .

Raif shook his head softly. Thirteen men alone on the badlands plains suddenly seemed unbelievably easy prey. Dhoonesmen, Bluddsmen, and Maimed Men were out there. Raif's stomach clenched. And the Sull. The Sull were out there, too.

The dark, weather-stained tents came into view. All was quiet. There were no horses or dogs in sight. The firepit was a dark gaping hole in the center of the cleared space. Loose tent flaps ripped in the wind like banners at battle's end. Drey had broken ahead, but now he stopped and waited for Raif to join him. His breath came hard and fast, and spent air vented from his nose and mouth in great white streams. He did not look round as Raif approached.

'Draw your weapon,' he hissed.

Raif already had, but he scored the blade of his halfsword against its boiled-leather scabbard, mimicking the noise of drawing. Drey moved forward when he heard it.

They came upon Jorry Shank's body first. It was lying in a feed ditch close to the horse posts. Drey had to turn the body to find the deathwound. The portion of Jorry's face that had been lying against the earth had taken on the yellow bloom of frozen flesh. The wound was as big as a fist, heart deep, made with a greatsword, and for some reason there was hardly any blood.

'Maybe the blood froze as it left him,' Drey murmured, settling the body back in place. The words sounded like a prayer.

'He never got chance to draw his weapon. Look.' Raif was surprised at how calm his voice sounded.

Drey nodded. He patted Jorry's shoulder and then stood away.

'There's horse tracks. See.' Raif kicked the ground near the first post. He found it easier to concentrate on what he could see here, on the camp perimeter, than turn his sights toward the tent circle and the one shabby, oft repaired, hide-and-moose-felt tent that belonged to Tem Sevrance. 'Those shoemarks weren't made by Blackhail horses.'

'Bluddsmen use a grooved shoe.'

So did other clans and even some city men, yet Raif had no desire to contradict his brother. Clan Bludd's numbers were swelling, and border and cattle raids had become more frequent. Vaylo Bludd had seven sons, and it was rumored he wanted a separate clanhold for each of them. Mace Blackhail said that Vaylo Bludd killed and ate his own dogs, even when he had elk and bear meat turning on the spit above his fire. Raif didn't believe the story for a moment – to eat one's own dogs was considered a kind of cannibalism to a clansman, justifiable only in the event of ice-bound starvation and imminent death – but others, including Drey, did. Mace Blackhail was three years older than Drey: when he spoke, Drey took heed.

As Drey and Raif approached the tent circle, their pace slowed. Dead dogs lay in the dirt, saliva frozen around their blunted fangs, their coats shaggy with ice. Fixed yellow eyes stared from massive gray heads. Glacial winds had set rising hackles in place, giving the dogs' corpses the bunched-neck look of buffalo. As with Jorry Shank's body, there was little blood.

Raif smelled stinking, smelted metal everywhere. The air around the camp seemed different, yet he didn't have the words to describe it. It reminded him of the slowly congealing surface water on Old Hoopers Lake. Something had caused the very air to thicken and change. Something with the force of winter itself.

'Raif! Here!'

Drey had crossed into the tent circle and was kneeling close to the firepit. Raif saw the usual line of pots and drying hides suspended on spruce branches over the pit, and the load of timber waiting to be quartered for firewood. He even saw the partially butchered black bear carcass that Dagro Blackhail had brought down yesterday in the sedge meadow to the east. The bearskin, which he had been so proud of, had been set to dry on a nearby rack. Dagro had planned to present it as a gift to his wife, Raina, when the hunt party returned to the roundhouse.

But Dagro Blackhail, chief of Clan Blackhail, would never return home.

Drey knelt over his partially frozen corpse. Dagro had taken a massive broadsword stroke from behind. His hands were speckled with blood, and the thick-bladed cleaver he still held in his grip was similarly marked. The blood was neither his nor his attackers'. It came from the skinned and eviscerated bear carcass lying at his feet; Dagro must have been finishing the butchering when he was jumped from behind.

Raif took a quick unsteady breath and sank down by his brother's side. Something was blocking his throat. Dagro Blackhail's great bear of a face looked up at him. The clan chief did not look at peace. Fury was frozen in his eyes. Glaciated ice in his beard and mustache framed a mouth pressed hard in anger. Raif thanked the Stone Gods that his brother wasn't the kind of man to speak needlessly, and the two sat in silence, shoulders touching, as they paid due respect to the man who had led Clan Blackhail for twenty-nine years and was loved and honored by all in the clan.

'He's a fair man,' Tem had said once about the clan chief in a rare moment when he was inclined to speak about matters other than hunting and dogs. 'It may seem like small purchase, and you'll find others in the clan willing to heap all manner of praise upon Dagro Blackhail's head, but fairness is the hardest thing for a man to practice day to day. A chief can find himself having to speak up against his sworn brothers and his kin. And that's not easy for anyone to do.'

It was, Raif thought, one of the longest speeches he'd ever heard his father make.

'It's not right, Raif.' Drey said only that as he raised himself clear of Dagro Blackhail's body, but Raif knew what he meant. It *wasn't* right.

Mounted men had been here; broadswords and greatswords had been used; clan horses were gone, stolen. Dogs were slaughtered. The camp lay in open ground, Mace Blackhail was standing dogwatch: a raiding party should not have been able to approach unheeded. Mounted men made noise, especially here in the badlands, where the bone-hard tundra dealt harshly with anything traveling upon it. And then there was the lack of blood . . .

Raif pushed back his hood and ran a gloved hand through the tangle of his dark hair. Drey was making his way toward Tem's tent. Raif wanted to call him back, to tell him that they should check the other tents first, the rendering pits, the stream bank, the far perimeter, *anywhere* except that tent. Drey, as if sensing some small portion of his younger brother's thoughts, turned. He made a small beckoning gesture with his hand and then waited. Two bright points of pain prickled directly behind Raif's eyes. Drey always waited.

Together the sons of Tem Sevrance entered their father's tent. The body was just a few paces short of the entrance. Tem looked as if he had been on his way out when the broadsword cracked his sternum and clavicle, sending splinters of bone into his windpipe, lungs, and heart. He had fallen with his halfsword in his hand, but as with Jorry Shank, the weapon was unbloodied.

'Broadsword again,' Drey said, his voice high and then rough as he sought to control it. 'Bludd favors them.'

Raif didn't acknowledge the words. It took all he had just to stand and look upon his father's body. Suddenly there was too much hollow space in his chest. Tem didn't seem as stiff as the others, and Raif stripped off his right glove and bent to touch what was visible of his father's cheek. Cold, dead flesh. Not frozen, but utterly cold, absent.

Pulling back as if he had touched something scorching hot rather than just plain cold, Raif rubbed his hand on his buckskins, wiping off whatever he imagined to be upon it.

Tem was gone.

Gone.

Without waiting for Drey, Raif pushed aside the tent flap and struck out into the rapidly darkening camp. His heart was beating in wild, irregular beats, and taking action seemed the only way to stop it.

When Drey found him a quarter later, Raif's right arm was stripped to the shoulder and blood from three separate cuts was pouring along his forearm and down to his wrist. Drey understood immediately. Tearing at his own sleeve, he joined his brother as he went among the slain men. All had died without blood on their weapons. To a clansman there was no honor in dying with a clean blade, so Raif was taking up their weapons one by one, drawing their blades across his skin, and spilling his own blood as a substitute. It was the one thing the two brothers could give to their clan. When they returned home to the roundhouse and someone asked, as someone always did, if the men had died fighting, Raif and Drey could now reply, 'Their weapons ran with blood.'

To a clansman those words mattered dear.

So the two brothers moved around the camp, discovering bodies in and out of tents, some with pale icicles of urine frozen to their legs, others with hair set in spiky mats where they had been caught bathing, a few with frozen wads of black curds still in their mouths, and one man—Meth Ganlow—with his beefy arms fixed around his favorite dog, protecting the wolfling even in death. A single swordstroke had killed both man and beast.

It was only later, when moonlight formed silver pools in the hard earth, and Tem's body was lying beside the firepit, close to the others but set apart, that Raif suddenly stopped in his tracks. 'We never found Mace Blackhail,' he said.